Beautiful People

By Wendy Holden and available from Headline Review

Simply Divine
Bad Heir Day
Pastures Nouveaux
Fame Fatale
Azur Like It
The Wives of Bath
The School for Husbands
Filthy Rich
Beautiful People

Wendy Holden

Beautiful People

headline
review

First published in Great Britain in 2009
by HEADLINE REVIEW
An imprint of HEADLINE PUBLISHING GROUP

1

Cataloguing in Publication Data is available from the British Library

ISBN 978 0 7553 4254 9 (Hardback)
ISBN 978 0 7553 4296 9 (Trade paperback)

Typeset in Janson by Avon DataSet Ltd,
Bidford-on-Avon, Warwickshire

Printed and bound in Great Britain by Clays Ltd, St Ives plc

Headline's policy is to use papers that are natural, renewable and recyclable
products and made from wood grown in sustainable forests. The logging and
manufacturing processes are expected to conform to the environmental
regulations of the country of origin.

HEADLINE PUBLISHING GROUP
An Hachette UK Company
338 Euston Road
London NW1 3BH

www.headline.co.uk
www.hachettelivre.co.uk

To William, Marcel, Peter and Brian

Chapter 1

Sam Sherman, head of the Wild Modelling Agency, strode through Covent Garden. She was on her way to a lunch appointment with Jacques Flash, an arrogant but indisputably rising French photographer. She walked quickly. Flash was famously no fan of waiting. No photographer was. Unless it was of people waiting for them, which was of course a different matter.

Sam did not particularly look like a fashion person. As she saw it, that crazy, spiky, shiny, short stuff was best left to those younger and more in fashion's shop window than she was. The models. The designers. The stylists. The muses.

Sam's style was muted: middle of, rather than ahead of, the curve. She was curvy too, as well as small, which was why her own modelling career had literally been cut short. In addition, her face, with its round eyes, full cheeks and firm jaw was not one that the camera had unconditionally loved.

But Sam's genius was the modelling business, not the actual business of modelling. In this she was formidable and frequently ruthless. Her sure eye for a new face and her confidence and accuracy in predicting trends had made Wild one of the biggest and most successful model agencies in London.

Sam, who had been a teenager in the seventies, generally stuck to a uniform of white shirt teamed with black waistcoat and jeans. The look – classic rock and roll, which no one, even in this most critical of industries, could criticise – was highly practical for someone in her position. She had hundreds of waistcoats, shirts and denims which, when combined with several large amber bead necklaces, chunky silver rings and bracelets, conferred on her a maverick, creative air that perfectly reflected the maverick, creative light in which the fashion industry saw itself. Even if, as Sam knew, it was all about the bottom line. Bottoms certainly loomed large in modelling. Or, rather, small.

Sam's jeans were tucked into high wedge-heeled boots of sand-coloured suede, rendered vaguely Native American with the addition of coloured beads. Her beige woollen wrap, with its fringed edge, billowed about her as she walked, and the bracelets the length of each of her forearms rattled.

Sam walked everywhere. This was not because she was fond of exercise – she wasn't. And there was certainly nothing pleasurable about picking one's way along the uptilted pavements of Endell Street and wincing at the deafening noise of the various drilling gangs engaged in the refurbishments this part of London constantly underwent. Sam walked because it made good business sense. It was more difficult to spot talent from the back of a taxi, and more difficult to get out and run after it if one did.

And spot it she must. Modelling was a competitive business. The Wild Agency might be one of London's biggest and most successful, but new agencies were always snapping at her heels, competing for the best girls and boys. Wild needed a constant stream of new talent. As Sam walked, her round, hazel eyes, firmly ringed with kohl, swivelled from side to side between centre-parted curtains of russet-and-black-striped shoulder-length hair. As ever, she was on the lookout.

It was trickier than usual today. Her antennae felt blunted, compromised by last night's party in which the definitive book about sunglasses was launched alongside a definitive new hand-bag collection. On offer had been the latest cutting-edge cock-tail, served by a cutting-edge mixologist and featuring champagne, ginger vodka and real gold flakes. There had been no cutting-edge food served with them, however, and Sam had imbibed several on an empty stomach. But that was normal for fashion. Fashion was all about empty stomachs. She wondered about the gold flakes, though. She had a flight to New York this evening and hoped the metal would not set the airport alarms off.

It was a glorious early summer day, with a hint of chill in the air, but with her hangover, Sam walked whenever possible in the shadows cast by the various scaffoldings. The air was too bright to do what she usually did, which was to quickly scan the various roofing gangs for big-biceped talent, even though the magazines preferred skinny and pale men at the moment. But biceps would be back, and when they were, Sam would have all of hers flexed.

As she walked briskly past, Sam fretted for the opportunities she might be missing. She consoled herself with the fact that looking at builders was a dangerous business because it was usually (loudly and enthusiastically) construed by them as sexual invitation.

She passed café after café, feeling queasy as the scent of toasted cheese and five-spice powder, alternating with whiffs of garlic and cleaning fluid, swirled into her nostrils. The sun, blazing on the aluminium chairs and tables, bored painfully into her pupils. Sam fished in her Birkin tote for a pair of huge and very black sunglasses, which she shoved hastily on her face. That was better.

It was easier now to look about her and scour every face that passed. Sam crossed Long Acre and walked purposefully down Bow Street, past where the vast bulk of the Royal Opera House blazed white against the blue sky. In the narrow shadows of Floral Street, a skinny girl with a graceful carriage caught her attention – one of the ballerinas, Sam assumed. Well, she had a good figure, but oh, dear God, that nose . . . no, no, *no*.

She entered the road where the tube station was. But there was nothing promising among the crowds either outside it or drifting aimlessly across the cobbled marketplace between the face-painters, cartoonists, bracelet-weavers, jugglers, buskers, human statues, and all the other theatrically inclined losers who daily congregated here. Sam narrowly avoided stepping into one of the laughably bad renditions of St Paul's or Marilyn Monroe and earned herself a snarled rebuke from one of the pavement artists. She regarded him scornfully from beneath her blunt-cut hair. Who did he think he was – Damien Hirst? To add injury to insult, he was hideous to look at as well.

No, the beautiful people really weren't out this morning. Which was unusual. Covent Garden was one of London's magnets for wannabe models; Topshop on Oxford Street another. But Sam found herself positively wincing at the unsightliness and dinginess of the crowd she walked among. Everyone looked the same: spots, terrible hair, short, thick legs in stonewashed jeans, white trainers and nasty black anoraks. Tourists, without a doubt, many gathered in an awestruck, giggling and mobile-phone-snapping ring round a street entertainer. Sam paused to watch the Afro-Caribbean man limboing under a stick placed on top of two wine bottles. His physique was good but his features were all over the place.

Which in some cases could work. And some things could be fixed: teeth, hair colour, skin problems – weight, especially;

not that one was allowed to say that these days, with all the fuss over size zero. But behind the scenes it still went on as before. The drugs, the self-denial, the workouts, the worry. Nothing had changed. That could not be fixed. Any more than the young men out today having faces like baskets of fruit could be fixed.

And while there were plenty of pretty girls about this morning, Sam noted with an air of weary professionalism, they were all East European blondes and that look had flooded the market now. The magazine fashion people wanted something new to shoot. Just recently Sam had signed what she had decided would be her last Russian until they became hot again.

The early summer sunshine continued to beat cheerfully down but Sam, behind her sunglasses, hardly noticed the way it polished the cobbles, warmed the butterscotch stone of the eighteenth-century market buildings and made the great white pillars of the Royal Opera House gleam. That was not the sort of beauty she either noticed or cared about. What was the point; one could hardly give it a business card, ask it to come in for test shots and subsequently launch it as the face of the moment. One could not make money from it.

There were a few home-growns, Sam saw, lanky, blank-looking British girls swishing their hair and dawdling self-consciously along in tight low-waisted jeans and skimpy tops. But none of them looked like the next Lily Cole to her.

God. The lunch. Jacques Flash. Sam glanced at her special-edition Cartier Tank watch and saw that she needed to get a move on if she was going to reach the restaurant on time.

'Ow!' Sam's progress was now halted in the rudest and most uncomfortable of manners. A great physical blow to the front of her lower pelvis stopped her agonisingly in her tracks. Reeling with the suddenness, eyes watering with the pain, she realised she had walked straight into a bollard. She gripped it tightly with her silver-tipped fingers and breathed in hard.

'Are you, um, all right?'

Sam, red-faced and agonised, glanced crossly at the person who had materialised beside her. He was very tall, his face hidden beneath tangled dark blond hair.

'I'm fine, thanks,' she managed tersely. She had no desire to discuss the damage to her intimate regions with some unknown callow youth.

The untidy blond head nodded. He now pushed his hair back to expose his face and instead of the spotty and misshapen bunch of teenage features she had been expecting, Sam found herself looking at one of the handsomest boys she had ever seen.

A huge surge of excitement replaced her pain. Slowly, Sam removed her sunglasses. Her eyes jabbed incredulously about, collecting the details; full lips, great ridges of cheekbone, hair thick and striped with gold like a child's, a straight and delicate nose, long eyes of the most amazing green – bright, pale lichen green flecked with yellow – she had never seen colour like that before. And set beneath thick brows so straight they could have been done with a ruler. She darted a glance at his other important asset, but could see nothing but baggy jeans hanging off a narrow waist.

She tried to gather her scattered wits enough to remember proportions. There were strict rules in the model business for the classically beautiful face. Did this boy's fit the template of perfection? She stared hard at him. Eyes should have space for an eye in between. Yes. Check. A perfectly proportioned face divided into horizontal thirds, the lines of division passing through the centre of the eyes and mouth. His did. Check. The ends of the lips should line up with the mid-point of the irises. Check. The ends of the mouth should be the same width as the outer points of the nostrils. Check. The upper lip should occupy a third of the entire area between bottom of upper lip and bottom of nostril. Check. Relief and awe swept Sam. This boy really was gorgeous. And it wasn't just her. It was official.

He was clearly perfect, about eighteen, Sam reckoned, and with all that delicious boyhood-ripening-to-manhood quality: smoulderingly sexy with those narrow eyes, those huge lips, that big Adam's apple. And yet still innocent with that boyishly smooth skin, that touch of fresh pink on his cheekbones, that endearingly puzzled expression . . .

'Look, are you sure you're OK?' the boy asked, unnerved by the way she was staring at him.

Sam nodded. She was more than OK. She was revelling in this boy, feasting on his looks. There was a golden glow about him, of classical gods, of medieval angels, of youthful Monaco male royals with big pink lips and blond hair blowing in the Mediterranean breeze. And more than that, of Armani campaigns, Ralph Lauren, Chanel – oh, they'd love him. Who wouldn't? And that voice; it had that just-broken quality of being deep and squeaky at the same time. Better still, it was posh, which the French and Italian designers especially loved. They'd got into that whole English public schoolboy thing in the eighties and they'd never got out of it.

Her eyes scoured his body again: amazingly tall, broad-shouldered but slender. Long legs and arms; nice hands. Pale; a quick blast in the spray-tan would do him no harm at all, but otherwise he was perfect. Completely perfect.

He could, Sam realised, her breath coming in quick, excited pants, her brain whirring with possibilities, be the discovery of the century. Compared to what he could mean to the agency – *earn* for the agency – banging her fanny on a bollard was a small price to pay.

She could not stop looking at his wonderful face, riding, like a surfer, every plane and hollow with her eyes, scanning it mentally into her mind like a computer.

'I'm a scout,' she smiled at him.

The boy, in his turn, stared at Sam. He'd heard somewhere that scouting had got more trendy lately, that it was more snowboarding and surfing than dib-dib-dibbing and doing old ladies' gardens. But all the same, this strange woman, with her make-up, bangles and clumpy heels, looked about as far as he could imagine from the side-parted, shorts-wearing, knot-tying Akela figures he still associated with the movement. He couldn't easily see her squatted over a camp stove either.

'Not my sort of thing,' he muttered, shambling from foot to foot. 'I've never been any good at putting up tents.'

Sam gasped in annoyance. Her creased lids with their gilded eyeshadow narrowed over her eyes for a moment. Was he joking? His face was completely, perfectly blank, however. 'Not *that* sort of scouting. I own a model agency. Have you,' she asked the boy, 'ever thought of modelling?'

At these words, she knew, almost every other teenager currently drifting through Covent Garden would punch the air with delight, their ambitions realised; their careers, as they saw it, made. But this boy said nothing. He continued to look blank and seemed frozen to the spot, his beautiful, long green eyes dilated with shock.

Beaming, Sam tipped her head to one side. 'Yeah, I know,' she nodded. 'Your dream come true, eh?'

He did not reply, disappointingly. She would have liked to hear that public-school accent again.

Sam pressed her plump, plum-lipsticked lips understandingly together. He was obviously overwhelmed. It was, of course, a great moment in any young person's life. 'Well, look, I'll just give you a card, you think about it, talk to your mother about it. And then give me a ring.'

But of course, Sam was smugly aware, there was no thinking to be done. No one ever thought twice about signing up to Wild, and she didn't encourage her models to think anyway. She rummaged in her bag for a card.

She registered with injured surprise the complete lack of recognition in the boy's face as, silently, he took it. The agency's famous logo, the roaring panther, was something he had evidently never seen before. Most kids she showed this to lit up with excitement. Some even whooped.

Sam felt suddenly full of doubt. Not about his beauty, but about whether asking him to get in touch was the best idea. There was something clueless about him, which was all to the good in a model, but it might be advisable not to leave the ball in his court.

She really didn't want this boy to get away. He was extraordinary. And Wild was not the only agency who had scouts out all the time, all over London. The risk of him being snapped up by someone else was just too great. No, she'd take him back to the agency herself, but, *bugger, damn it*, she couldn't. She had this lunch with Jacques Flash.

Sam stared furiously into the convoluted depths of her Birkin. Then the answer hit her. She'd phone a colleague. Stacy, a Wild scout, would, at this very minute, be patrolling Oxford Street Topshop. It wouldn't take her long to get here and she could then take this boy back to the agency.

The downside of this plan, of course, was that she'd be late for Flash and he'd be furious. But, Sam decided, now feeling back in control, she'd promise him first dibs on the next face of the moment. The one now looking at her with alarm and confusion written all over it.

9

'I think you've got an amazing future in modelling,' Sam now told the boy. Unexpectedly, the huge trainered feet opposite herself suddenly moved. With incredible speed the boy ran off into the crowd and within seconds had disappeared from sight. But not before Sam, with the presence of mind that had got her where she was in life, grabbed her mobile from her bag and snapped with its camera what could be seen of his departing face.

Orlando Fitzmaurice shot through the middle of Covent Garden market. Through the rows of painted novelty cuckoo clocks and triangular candles, past the hippies sitting cross-legged on the steps eating pulses with plastic forks out of polystyrene cartons, past the woman who may or may not have been an opera singer but who was belting out *'Nessun dorma'* with an ear-splitting vibrato none the less. He ran as if wild animals were after him, or the Wild Modelling Agency, which seemed even more fearsome a prospect.

Orlando's brain rushed with fear, his heart was pumping, and from time to time he looked behind him. The hamster-faced woman had not followed him, however.

Now slowed down to a fast walk, Orlando found himself before the large church in the piazza. The huge neoclassical building, with its gilded clock and pillared portico, was in deep shadow; the shadow of the building itself stretched out across the cobbles in front. There seemed to Orlando to be something protective about it; he darted gratefully into the gloomy refuge between the church's blue door and the thick brown sandstone pillars in front of it. He sat down on one of the broad brown stone steps and waited for his heart rate to return to normal.

He wasn't alone for long. A gaggle of giggling girls appeared, passed from the light into the shadow of the church and walked by him rather too closely.

Orlando ignored them, and watched with relief as the girls passed out into the bright sunlight on the other side of the shadow. Then his heart sank as they stopped, hesitated and giggled before turning and, giggling again, re-entering the shadow and coming past once more. They were leggy, with lots of eye make-up and long blond hair, which they swished about while looking coyly at him through it. Exactly the type of girls, Orlando reflected, staring hard at the step, who would never have given him a moment's notice before.

Before . . .

Before his appearance had changed. He looked different now from how he had looked a year ago. A year ago, and many of the years before that, he had been average height and above-average chubby and spotty. Girls had not given him a second glance; he had never had a girlfriend, although he had got on well with the shyer, less swishy-haired, self-confident ones. And this had suited him just fine. He had been plump, spotty, unremarkable – and content.

But in the year since then, his appearance had radically changed. He had no idea why. Or how. He had not started working out. He had not changed his diet. He had not begun any special facial routine. Yet for some reason, over the last twelve months, he had grown taller, much taller, and so fast that his bones ached in the night. He had also slimmed down, become quite skinny, in fact.

His spots had disappeared of their own accord, his thinnish lips had suddenly become fuller and pinker, and his eyes seemed to have lengthened and receded under what were now heavy, brooding brows. A prominent Adam's apple appeared in his newly thickened throat and his dull, unremarkably mousy hair, which he had never cut much anyway, developed blond streaks all by itself and now swished in a golden curtain about his neck without him having to put anything on it or even brush it all that much.

And so, without particularly wanting to – without remotely wanting to, in fact – the eighteen-year-old Orlando, who had never been interested in women in any other way but friendship, now realised with dawning horror that he was of great interest to them. And it was a lot more than friendship that they wanted.

They stared at him all the time, wherever he went. Orlando found that he disliked being stared at because he was handsome. He hated being looked at, full stop. And so he protected himself as best he could. He narrowed his eyes beneath his great level cliffs of brow and hid under his curtain of hair. He pushed out his full lips in go-away defiance. He slouched, he brooded, he muttered, he maintained distance. But this just made matters worse. Women and girls stared at him even more.

And now one of them had asked him if he wanted to be a model. It was hard to think of anything he wanted to be less.

Chapter 2

'Give my love to the Queen,' Dad shouted from the other side of the train window, his voice faint through the thick glass.

'I will!' Emma laughed, not caring if the other people in the carriage stared. Let them stare.

As the train pulled out of Leeds and her parents' faces, half proud, half anxious, slid past, a mighty wave of excitement passed through her. She was going to London. To seek her fortune, like Dick Whittington in the books at nursery.

She was on her way at last.

She fought through the jumble of people and luggage at the end of the carriage. 'Is anyone sitting here?' she asked a grey-haired, grey-suited, grey-skinned man whose pink newspaper was not only the one colourful thing about him but occupied an entire four-seater table area. If he'd paid for all four seats so he could spread out his *Financial Times* to the max, then fine, Emma thought. But she doubted this. He didn't look the extravagant sort.

'No,' the grey man admitted through a pinched, annoyed, apparently lipless mouth, moving his papers huffily to reveal the table was set with cutlery, plates, bowls and glasses. From behind his glinting glasses he scanned Emma as she edged into the seat, feeling, despite herself, rather self-conscious. Of course, she didn't care a button what a stuffy, miserable old wrinkly like that thought about her looks, but even so, it would be wonderful to have the kind of whippet-skinny figure that allowed one to slide swiftly into confined areas. But her build required a little more room.

Of course she wasn't fat – far from it – but she wasn't thin either. She defied anyone not to be plump when they lived with her parents. Mum put out two different types of potato every Sunday teatime – roast *and* mash – and there was always pudding and custard to follow. And Emma had never known the biscuit tin to be empty, even in the most difficult times, and there'd been a few of those. In fact, the leanest times were when the biscuit tin tended to be at its fullest.

But it wasn't, Emma reminded herself, physical appearances that mattered so much anyway, not in the business she was in. It was how good you were at your job – and she was *very* good at hers. Too good now, with all the extra qualifications she'd spent the last two years getting at night school. Her job at Wee Cuties, the nursery in Heckmondwike where she'd worked since leaving school four years ago, didn't really use all the new educational theory she'd picked up; the staff were quite set in their ways and tended to get annoyed if she suggested too many changes.

So Emma, fond though she was of the children, some of whom she had known since babyhood, and grateful though she was to the nursery for employing her, albeit at a wage a self-denying gnat could hardly get by on, had decided that now was the time to move on. Money, at Wee Cuties, was not the entire point anyway. Experience was what she had wanted; experience in every aspect of caring for babies to fives, and that she had now got in spades. Living with her parents, moreover, had allowed her to save a tiny sum of her meagre wages and had made it much easier to go to night school. But she had learnt all that she could. It was time to move on.

And so it was, when first her eye had fallen on the ad in the *Yorkshire Post*, that a thrill of recognition had gone through Emma. It leapt out at her immediately. 'Nanny sought. Smart area of London. Well-behaved children. Excellent pay and holidays.' With shaking hands she copied down the details – Dad hated his paper being vandalised.

It sounded like everything she wanted. She knew already that the West Yorkshire conurbation would not offer what she sought; should she stay, she would probably remain at Wee Cuties for the rest of her life, as most of her colleagues seemed to be planning to – the ones, that was, who were not planning to defect to the soon-to-be-completed supermarket, which was rumoured to be offering better wages and longer holidays. And while Emma sought both, she sought also excitement, challenge and possibility, none of which, so far as she understood it, were normally associated with supermarkets.

London was her aim, and to be taken on as nanny to a family.

Her equilibrium completely restored, her neighbour opposite forgotten, Emma looked happily out of the train window. What would the capital have in store? There would certainly never be a better time to move there. She was young – twenty – and yet experienced in the highly employable area of childcare. She had nothing to leave behind, no house to sell, no romantic attachments.

The train was hot. So that it would not crease, Emma removed the pretty fawn jacket with its nipped-in waist, bought, along with the skirt, from Whistles especially for the interview. In the shop, the pale brown had perfectly complemented the chestnut shoulder-length hair that was, Emma felt, her best feature, with its flash of red threads in the sunshine. She crossed her feet, in their smart, low-heeled brown courts, at the ankles and tapped her fingers on the new matching handbag. Perhaps she looked too smart, but better to be too smart than too scruffy.

'Breakfast, madam? Fresh fruit? Cereal?' A dark-haired youth in a white shirt had pulled up a trolley beside her. Emma glanced at the cereals and fruit juice it bore, realising this was what the cutlery and glasses on the table were for. Breakfast – how very civilised. She hadn't had any yet.

'I'll have the fresh fruit,' the man opposite said in a bored voice without looking up from his paper.

'The same for me, please,' Emma smiled at the waiter. One should always smile at waiters, she felt.

He ladled some out on to the shallow white bowl in front of her. Emma took her spoon and began to eat. This really was very nice.

'Can I see your breakfast ticket?'

With a spoonful of melon and grapes halfway to her mouth, Emma glanced up to see a hard-faced blonde in the train livery staring down at her. She laid the spoon back in its dish. 'Breakfast ticket?'

'That's right. Breakfast ticket.'

Panic swept through Emma. No one had ever mentioned such a thing. She scrabbled in her bag and produced the orange and white ticket she had bought at Leeds.

'This is a second-class ticket,' the hard-faced woman announced at what seemed to Emma twice the decibel level she had used before, plus an obvious degree of malicious enjoyment.

'Yes,' said Emma. 'It is.'

'And this is the dining compartment of the first-class

carriage,' sneered the blonde, her voice louder than ever. 'You need a first-class dining ticket to eat breakfast here. You have a—'

'Second-class ticket, yes I know,' mumbled Emma, her face beetroot and her heart thumping. The situation was hideous. She had stumbled into this carriage without looking what class it was; not being a regular train traveller, it had not occurred to her to do so. That she was sitting here was a simple mistake, although it now appeared – and the blonde was doing her level best to make it appear – that she was here under false pretences, was trying to deceive, had taken something she had not paid for, even if it was only a few grapes and a sit of half an hour opposite a bored man glued to his paper.

Emma felt as if everyone was looking at her. As if they were all thinking, ah yes, I should have known, fat with a northern accent. First class, don't make me laugh.

'It was a mistake,' Emma said desperately to the sneery blonde.

'Yes, I'm sure,' replied the blonde, in a voice that said clearly she was sure of the exact opposite. She pointed down the carriage. 'Second class is that way,' she said with a sniff.

Emma stood up, feeling the seams on her new skirt straining as she reached for her coat and bag on the overhead rack. Her newspaper-reading companion flicked her a stony look over the pink rim of his pages. Emma avoided his gaze, stung with shame, humiliated. It felt like a bad start.

Reaching the carriage door, Emma felt the tears well. The urge to get off at the next stop and go back home flashed through her. But she pushed these feelings fiercely back. She was escaping to a better and more rewarding life. That was what she wanted.

*

By the time she had reached London, her natural optimism and spirit had returned. Unlike Dick Whittington, and thanks to various school trips through the years, Emma knew the streets of London were not paved with gold. But it was certainly a city of light. Stepping out of her carriage at the station, Emma's gaze swung automatically upwards to the great glass arc of roof flung above the station, through which poured sunlight from an optimistically blue sky.

London was as fast-moving and purposeful as a colony of ants. To the right and the left of her people swarmed off the train, darting towards the shining chrome barriers in a jostling, heaving mass, weighed down with rucksacks and briefcases.

All the rush and running made her feel she should run herself, and Emma found her pace quickening past the glossy shops in the terminal; no scruffy cafés these, but smart book-shops, glamorous French patisseries with aluminium chairs outside, and fashionable florists whose chic bouquets arranged tastefully round the door bore price tags that made Emma gasp. She lingered in front of the great glass window of Hamley's toy store, her eyes running greedily over the big, shiny, colourful, wonderful things on the other side of it. The idea of bringing a small present for her future charges – if the interview went well – came to her. But everything looked so expensive.

Emma ventured inside, amid the lights and pounding music. The place was alive with moving objects: toy planes whizzed overhead, toy cars shot round toy tracks. There seemed to be nothing within her budget.

Then she spotted a small box of tiny toys by the till; the sort people bought with loose change from their bigger purchases. Quickly, Emma picked a little stuffed pink cat for the girl – girls always liked cats – and a small rubber train for the boy. She had yet to meet a boy who didn't like trains.

*

Outside the front of the station, the traffic roared at her like some infernal beast. There was grit in the air, but beauty too, Emma thought, looking at the mighty, contrasting grandstand fronts of King's Cross and St Pancras. She knew nothing about architecture, but she noticed the difference between the sober classical façade of the first, and the wild, spired, red-brick Gothic fantastitude of the second. Now both merged into one mighty terminus, which flowed into Europe, she had gathered from the station posters as she passed through. The entire place seemed to roar and thump with the heavy power of transport and, through it, of possibility. Emma felt her sense of excitement, of expectation, increase.

Would something wonderful happen for her here, in this legendary, ancient, ever-changing city, as it had for Dick Whittington and so many others?

She stared longingly at the taxi rank, where the gleaming black cars with their friendly orange lights promised to take her in comfort and without effort to the address on the letter currently folded in her jacket pocket. But Emma knew enough about London to know that taxis were the most expensive option. She would have to get the tube, although the prospect made her nervous. Or perhaps the bus. That way she could see something of the city that was to be her new home.

The station Information Desk was helpful about routes and it was not long before Emma was installed at the front of a double-decker bound in the right direction. The vehicle pushed forward through the sunny late morning and Emma stared around, full of provincial wonder at place names, signs, squares, shops and streets that were famous throughout the world.

She gazed down at the endless movement on the pavements. What was it like to be the people emerging from the underground, standing at crossings, staring through the windows of cars and buses, emerging from the doorways of hotels? Some obviously led lives of a grimness she did not want to contemplate. Others, meanwhile, provoked curiosity and envy.

Having chugged along Oxford Street – so small and crowded compared to the spacious boulevard one imagined – past Hyde Park, where Princess Diana had once lived, and down Sloane Street, where Emma was disappointed not to spot a single footballer's wife, the bus reached Sloane Square. From here it found its way over a beautiful, fairy-like pastel-painted suspension bridge across the river. Emma gazed about her in rapture. What a city this was.

Emma looked just right, Vanessa thought gleefully as she opened the front door. Fat, in other words. Size twelve at least, to her own carefully preserved ten. Fourteen even, at a pinch, and there was certainly more than an inch to pinch there. Oh yes. Emma was not the long drink of water Jacintha, the last nanny, had been.

One should always employ fat girls. They were so grateful and had absolutely no self-confidence. This girl, with her brown hair – not a highlight to be seen – and almost make-upless face had low self-esteem written all over her.

'You're late,' Vanessa said challengingly. Best make it clear from the start who was in charge.

'I'm sorry,' Emma said immediately, even though she did not consider the fault to be hers entirely. It would have helped a great deal in finding the house if she had known it was in Peckham and not Camberwell, as for some reason had been put on the letter. She had been looking, as the original ad had said, for a smart part of London, and neither its surroundings nor the tall, white house itself struck her that way. The house especially, while it possibly had once been grand, certainly wasn't at the moment, with its peeling paint, cracks and long-dead brown bush hanging off a broken trellis next to the door.

'My last nanny's father was a peer of the realm,' Vanessa loftily informed Emma. 'She was excellent. So if you get this job, you'll have some very big shoes to fill.' She glanced at Emma's shoes and twitched her lips disapprovingly. They looked plain and brown and possibly from Office.

Emma's reaction was not what Vanessa had expected. Instead of looking cowed and terrified, this girl from the north turned her brown and direct gaze on Vanessa and asked her, in a quiet yet steady voice, why Jacintha had left, exactly.

Vanessa felt banjaxed. The impertinence! It was she who was asking the questions! The role of the girl was to looked awed and submissive. But as Emma did not look either, Vanessa realised she had to give an answer and the windmills of her mind whirred in panic. That Jacintha had left in order to go and work for the family of a famous writer had been a bitter blow. A *more* famous writer, Vanessa corrected herself; she herself had a newspaper column and was extremely well known. Well, quite well known. In media circles. Her lack of influence in more general circles had been unpleasantly illustrated by Jacintha's resignation.

Vanessa had comforted herself by reflecting it was all to be expected; Jacintha's defection was symptomatic of a society riddled with snobbery and the worship of celebrity. Jacintha was hopelessly aspirational, obsessed with fame and more to be pitied than deplored.

'Jacintha had been with us for some time,' Vanessa hedged. 'It was time to move on.'

'How long?' Emma asked steadily.

Vanessa pretended to think hard, and that the answer – six weeks – had somehow been lost in the midst of much more pressing concerns; concerns that even now she was occupied with and to which such footling queries represented an unwelcome intrusion. 'Three months,' she said eventually, with an imperious toss of her head that warned Emma that she proceeded any further down this track at her peril.

But even so, Vanessa noticed, Emma – ridiculous name, and what a come-down after Jacintha – looked slightly feistier than anyone so wide – in every sense – of size twelve had a right to. And there was definitely an awkward tilt to her head.

They were in the sitting room of Vanessa's house, which, to Emma's surprise, was on the first floor. And the kitchen seemed to be in the basement. Emma avidly took in the sitting-room detail: a gilt mirror – albeit somewhat smeared – over the fireplace, walls of white bookshelves, and huge windows, which were not very clean either. There was an upright piano whose closed lid was piled with newspapers.

The whole place seemed a bit of a mess, Emma thought, with DVDs open all over the place and crisps ground into the carpet. She had read about shabby chic in magazines. Was this it?

Vanessa was, Emma thought, rather cross and unhappy-looking. But what she had to be cross and unhappy about, the nanny could not imagine. Her house was big and roomy; much bigger than any Emma had ever been in. The room was messy, but it was full of books, which gave it an optimistic air. None of the big, colourful abstract paintings on the wall had glass in them; Emma suspected this meant they were real, originals.

And Vanessa herself was very attractive, slim in a close-fitting white T-shirt and long purple denim skirt, her pink-sequined flip-flops revealing tanned feet with red-painted nails. Her shining blond hair was brightly streaked, but so finely it looked natural, and much chopped about in that artful way that only really good hairdressers can pull off. She had big blue eyes, which were pretty, if bulgy. And good skin, even though her face was rather red. So what did she have to look so grumpy about?

Perhaps Vanessa was unhappily married, Emma pondered. Perhaps with an overbearing alpha male husband. Yes, that could be it.

'Sit down,' Vanessa said, sitting on the edge of the battered mock-Georgian sofa.

It seemed to Emma that beyond the obvious about driving licence (yes) and criminal record (no), Vanessa was soon struggling for questions to ask her. She subtly took over herself, conducting her own interrogation of her employer-to-be, and established – to her amazement – how very little Vanessa knew about her children. She had no idea what Hero and Cosmo – *Hero and Cosmo?* – liked to eat, what books they liked to read, what games they liked to play or whether they had special words or names for favourite people or things. She did not, Emma thought, seem interested in her children at all.

'To be honest with you,' Vanessa said breezily at one stage, 'I think children are rather boring.'

'Boring?' Emma repeated.

'Absolutely. Intelligent, driven women – women like me – have nervous breakdowns if they spend too much time with young children. It's a proven fact. Women like me need stimulation and challenge.'

And women like me don't, I suppose, thought Emma. Warning bells were ringing loudly in her mind. She had established, by dint of her questioning, that no fewer than five nannies had left the family in the last eight months. She did not believe, as Vanessa claimed, that, apart from Jacintha, all those who left had had ill fathers in Poland.

She found out, in between everything else, that the husband Vanessa may or may not have been unhappily married to worked for the Foreign Office and had been sent to Equatorial Guinea, wherever that was. He would be back in several weeks. 'So you see, I really need someone urgently. Now,' Vanessa emphasised, skewering Emma with those blue eyes.

Her urgent need, Emma thought, was not reflected in the salary offered, however. On the plus side, she would be living in London, which was what she had wanted. Admittedly, not in as comfortable circumstances even as at home; while the lower floors of Vanessa's home had a certain shabby opulence and were reasonably warm, the tall house seemed to get colder the further up you got. And very cold indeed in the tiny bedroom with the peeling wallpaper, collapsing curtain rail and light fitting that appeared to be masking-taped to the wall and ceiling respectively. What Dad, a DIY enthusiast, would have made of that, Emma could imagine. While Mum would have snorted to hear Vanessa describe the shabby little room as part of 'the nursery suite'. The rest of the suite apparently comprised the children's bedroom – 'the night nursery' – and the playroom. Both rooms adjoined Emma's on the top landing.

While she did the opposite of showing it, Vanessa was relieved that the room on the top floor had passed muster. It had been a bone of contention with all the other nannies, as well as with James, who resented constantly having to replace the curtain rail; the plaster in the wall being too damp to support it whenever he tried to put it back. He complained that it was the most difficult thing he had ever done and that running the Foreign Service was less than nothing in comparison. From what Vanessa had heard from James about the Foreign Service, she could well believe it.

The nanny before Jacintha, an Honourable called Lavinia, had actually resigned over the room in the end. 'What's wrong with it?' Vanessa had demanded, despite knowing that the Hon. Lavinia's ceiling rose had just fallen out of the roof, and the light fitting with it. The bang had been heard several floors below.

'I'm sorry, Mrs Bradstock,' the Hon. Lavinia had said. 'But I'm afraid the accommodation is simply not suitable as it is. It's cold, there's a huge damp patch, the light's fallen out of the ceiling, leaving several exposed cables, and the wallpaper . . . well, of course it's a matter of personal taste, but if it was attached to the wall it would look better.'

Vanessa had smiled with the utmost insouciance. 'There's a simple solution,' she'd trilled. 'Redecoration!' she announced, rolling her Rs.

The Hon. Lavinia nodded, evidently surprised. 'Redecoration, yes. That would be very acceptable.'

'You can nip down to B and Q and get some paint and paper tomorrow. I'm sure it won't take you long to have the place looking marvellous. You could do the rest of the nursery suite as well while you're at it. Choose whatever style you like,' Vanessa added generously.

The Hon. Lavinia, crisply, politely, and with minimum fuss, had resigned on the spot. Even after Vanessa had relented and said she could get her materials from John Lewis she had not reconsidered.

Fortunately, however, this girl from Yorkshire seemed to have no problem with the accommodation. It was probably luxurious, Vanessa thought scornfully, compared with whatever hovel she lived in up there.

That room was hideous. The woman was mad. Emma went back downstairs with Vanessa full of uncertainty. Should she not get out now? Go home? She could always write off for other jobs, after all.

'You can start immediately,' Vanessa offered. Or, possibly, instructed.

'But I haven't seen the children,' Emma pointed out quickly. There was a fair chance that they would be ghastly too. The missing piece of the jigsaw. The children would decide it, one way or the other.

And then the children came in. Hero, the solid three year old, had a solemn little face and hair so flaxen, so impossibly white, that it seemed lit from within, a silver flame. Cosmo, at four, had eyes that were deep, sunken and anxious, and his hair was a caramel pageboy, striped with lighter gold. They regarded Emma suspiciously, but that, she felt, was understandable enough, especially if five nannies had come and gone in the last eight months.

'Ask me if I'm a passenger train or a freight train,' Cosmo demanded suddenly in a low, growling voice.

Emma thought of the toy train in her handbag. She had been right, after all. Was there any little boy who didn't like locomotives?

Vanessa rolled her eyes. 'God. He's absolutely bloody *obsessed* with trains. Just *shut up*, will you, Cosmo? You've driven all the nannies potty with this. I'm sure that's why they've all left,' she added, not particularly convincingly, to Emma.

But Cosmo, ignoring his mother, was looking at Emma expectantly, his blue eyes round through his blond fringe. She sensed it was some sort of test. She smiled, stooping down to his level and looked into his uncertain little face. 'Are you a passenger train or a freight train?' she asked obediently.

Cosmo shuffled his little feet on the crisp-scattered carpet. His fingers were joined together and pointing forward and both arms were revolving by his sides, imitating the moving parts of a locomotive.

'I'm a passenger train,' he told her now, his face entirely serious.

'Can I get on you?' Emma asked.

'No,' said Cosmo, causing Emma's heart to sink rather. Her initiative had been rejected.

'You can't get on me,' Cosmo added earnestly, 'because I'm a special train. But you can look at me. Woo woo!' And with that, the little boy steamed out of the sitting room.

'See what I mean? He wants to be an engine driver – I *ask* you. Is that what I'll be paying millions in school fees for?' Vanessa demanded angrily of no one in particular.

Emma judged it best not to answer this. She was not sure what she would say anyway.

'And Hero's obsessed with cats,' Vanessa added, as if this too was a crime.

Emma looked at Hero. While her brother had been talking she had seated herself quietly on the carpet and begun to build a house from the DVD boxes. Emma recognised in her the ability to play very concentratedly at the same thing for a considerable length of time, a skill developed, she suspected, as a reaction to a mother who had no interest in playing with her at all.

The children were fine, Emma could see. In fact, if there was a spoilt and unreasonable brat in this room – and there was, certainly – it was neither Cosmo nor Hero. In whose blue eyes, moreover, she had spotted an unmistakable, hungry look that was nothing to do with food but everything to do with the need for affection and attention. It twisted Emma's heart.

'I'll take the job,' she said, reaching for her handbag. 'And, actually, I've got a couple of presents for them.'

Chapter 3

In an apartment in Los Angeles, a phone was ringing loudly beside a bed.

A snort, a curse and a groan from the bed's inmate preceded the appearance of a plump hand, its back covered with black hairs and a thick gold chain bumping against a Rolex on its wrist. It groped about on the bedside table. As his short, fat fingers made contact with the receiver, Mitch Masterson, actor's agent, squinted at the alarm clock beside his bed.

Who the hell was ringing him this early?

As if he couldn't guess.

Mitch groaned. Last night had been the annual get-together of the Association of Motion Picture Actors' Representatives, an annual red-letter day in the agenting industry that provided unmissable opportunities for networking. This was an umbrella term for general excess, and Mitch had done so much networking he'd been barely able to stand up at the end of the evening. He had no idea how he had got home, let alone how he had undressed himself and got into bed. Yet somehow he had. And now his throat burned, his eyes ached and his head felt as if someone had stuck a sword in it. The last thing he needed was a call from Belle Murphy.

His heart, which was racing anyway, now plummeted. The day had barely started and it was a nightmare already. If only he could send it back and get a refund. Or swap it for another one. But no, thick fingers of daylight were poking insistently between the wenge wood blinds that Mitch had been persuaded by his interior designer gave his apartment that breezy, Californian, young-stylish-single-guy-with-money-to-burn feel.

Californian as in originally from Cataract, Tennessee, that was. Young as in forty-four. Single in the divorced sense. The money could be better too – Talent Incorporated was a super-successful agency, sure, one of the biggest in Hollywood. But he was only one of its medium-ranking agents. As for the stylish, in his franker moments Mitch, who knew he looked, despite spasmodic gym visits and a wardrobe full of Calvin, like a hairy egg on legs, wondered why he believed his décor rather than his mirror. When people told him he looked like a film star they always followed it up by saying, 'Yeah – Danny DeVito.'

'Hey, Belle, baby!' Mitch struggled to sound as if no call could be more convenient or more delightful.

As usual, Belle didn't waste time on pleasantries. 'You heard from Spielberg yet?' she demanded, her shrill, high-pitched voice drilling the tender insides of Mitch's ear.

Oh, for fuck's sake, Mitch mouthed at the ceiling. Of course he hadn't heard from Spielberg. Nor was he likely to. The casting director was an old girlfriend and had allowed Belle to try out more to get her off Mitch's back than put her in the film. The leading role of what was a Dreamworks cartoon about a female worm with issues had gone to Scarlett Johansson. Which presented Mitch with another problem. Once Belle heard her most hated rival had got the part there was going to be an explosion bigger than a bomb in a fireworks factory.

'You haven't heard from Steven?' the drilling voice on the other end of the phone demanded. 'Well, come *on*. You're supposed to be my agent, right? Call him, can't you?'

'Sure, baby,' Mitch murmured. Anything to put the phone down and snatch another hour or so of sleep before, as was inevitable, Belle rang yet again. She rang, on average, eight times a day at the moment. He was thinking of getting a phone line devoted entirely to her. Well, that was one of the politer things he was thinking.

Mitch wondered what Belle would do if she knew about the Fame Board. In a meeting room in the offices of Talent Incorporated, a room in which no client ever set foot, was a league table of those the company represented. The Fame Board, as it was known among staff, covered an entire wall and was adjusted each day, like the FTSE and the Dow Jones, to reflect clients' comparative status. On this cruel if accurate measure of exactly where she stood in Tinseltown, Belle was currently near the bottom. And yet this time last year she had been at the top; Talent Incorporated's number one most important client.

Even the CEO of the agency had answered her calls then, and at great length. She'd been sent Christmas, birthday, Thanksgiving, Halloween and every other imaginable kind of present from the agency, including some 'just because we love you'. Or, to be more accurate, just because of the hit film *Marie*, in which Belle had played Mary, Queen of Scots.

Ah, *Marie*. Mitch allowed himself a transporting moment of remembered joy at this most purple of patches. Belle had carried all before her – literally; the costume department had certainly made the most of her assets. Her take on the doomed, impetuous monarch, all plunging cleavage and passionate four-poster scenes, had been a stupendous success. For several months, Belle had been one of the hottest actresses in Hollywood. Her smouldering red pout had sizzled from the cover of every magazine. But then had come *Bloody Mary* as a follow-up. It had been out two months and was widely considered to be the biggest turkey since *Gigli*.

Mitch, who felt his forehead bead with sweat at the mere thought of the disaster, still had no idea why Belle's studio had imagined a film about an uptight pyromanic religious nutcase was a suitable vehicle for her. No doubt he should have advised her against doing it, but the enormous amount of money the agency had trousered over the deal had clouded his judgement, as was often the case in Hollywood. The film had bombed, or gone up in smoke, to be more accurate, and now Belle was colder than yesterday's breakfast.

As the voice on the other end yakked accusingly on, Mitch rubbed his round, greasy face and slitted his sleep-swollen eyes against the bright California morning. He thought of the scene beyond, the sunshine blazing down the bright boulevards, shining on the concrete, on the cars, on the palm trees, on the highlights of the women, on the dyed hair of the men, on the brilliant white teeth of both sexes. Even thinking about it was too bright for his eyes to bear.

Another sunny day in Paradise. Another perfect morning in the city of dreams and angels. Bring it on, Mitch thought wearily. Bring it on.

'And what about Ridley Scott? Sam Mendes?' Belle was screeching now. 'Have they got back to you?'

'Not as such, baby, but you know they're both pretty busy. Mendes has, ah, um, you know. Kids and stuff . . .'

'Kids?!'

'Yeah. You know how busy kids keep people.' Mitch was improvising as best he could. 'Can't get to the phone or anything . . .'

'What?!'

Mitch wondered why he didn't simply put the phone down on her. Any other agent at Talent Incorporated would have done, recognising that Belle needed them far more than they needed her at the moment. What complicated things for Mitch was that he felt sorry for her.

He would never have admitted it to either his bosses or his colleagues. It was probably a sacking offence. It was certainly the last thing an agent should ever feel. And no doubt it was the reason he had never got any further than he had.

He simply wasn't ruthless enough. Mitch knew. He empathised. He winced at the way the Hollywood machine chewed people up and spat them out. And although what had happened to Belle was anything but unusual – he'd seen it many times before – it didn't make it pleasant.

Actresses who wanted to be huge stars were one thing, but those who had got huge and had then got small again found life unbearable. There was a poignancy about them, a desperation that had been captured most famously in the film *Sunset Boulevard*. But modern Hollywood, where people rose and fell with blink-of-an-eye swiftness, was more, Mitch thought, like *Alice in Wonderland*, where Alice grew suddenly huge and then shrank with equally dramatic speed. Although of course, for Belle, Hollywood was anything but Wonderland at the moment.

And what made it worse, Mitch thought, was that he felt personally involved. To blame, even. He felt guilty that he had not objected to *Bloody Mary* as soon as it was mooted. That he might have had a hand – a very big hand – in Belle's fall. Since *Bloody Mary*, Belle couldn't get arrested in LA. Mitch even feared her studio was about to drop her. He was determined to stop this, although he had no idea how.

Studios were laws unto themselves, and Belle's studio, NBS, with the workaholic puritan Arlington Shorthouse at the helm, was more of a law than most. It could afford to be – it had a box-office hit rate second to none in Hollywood and was reportedly planning its most audacious assault yet on the multiplexes of the world.

There had been nothing definite yet to confirm that a space saga, provisionally entitled *Galaxia*, about an imaginary universe of robots, spaceships and fabulous creatures with improbable names along the lines of the blockbuster, all-conquering *Star Wars*, was being planned by NBS. But the rumours were insistent enough for Mitch to wonder if there was anything in it. If there was, Mitch thought, it could hardly be better timing for Belle, whose career would be transformed if she could get a part. She needed something – and fast – to turn things round for her.

The fact she was dating Christian Harlow, an actor who had been unknown before he had hooked up with Belle and now widely tipped to be the new Brad Pitt, was certainly not that something. It was, Mitch thought, pretty obvious that Harlow would dump Belle just as soon as she'd outlived her usefulness. Which was probably pretty soon. Mitch had seen that before too, and heard some nasty rumours about Harlow into the bargain.

'Relax, baby,' he pleaded with Belle, although he knew there was as much chance of this as of the Californian sun going out. And not without good reason, frankly. 'I'll call Steven today. Yeah. And Sam too. *And* Ridley, sure, yeah, mustn't forget him. No. Yeah. No. Promise. OK, baby. Sure. See ya.' Thankfully, he shoved the receiver back in its cradle and dived back into the refuge of his hot, stewy and rumpled bed. But barely had his soft belly flopped down on the expanse of sheet at the other side than the phone shrilled again.

'*Fuck off,*' Mitch screamed, pulling the duvet over his head. Jesus. Not again. The phone kept ringing but eventually rang off. Silence fell and Mitch poked his head cautiously out from under his duvet.

Shock suddenly convulsed him. His heart leapt within his hairy, fleshy breast. What was that? A noise outside the bedroom!

Oh God. Someone was in his house!

Fear rose in Mitch's throat and pictures of gruesome Hollywood burglary-murders reeled through his swollen and aching brain. As the door to the bedroom pushed open he cowered beneath the duvet, shaking, half sobbing, heart hammering, trying to press himself to the mattress to make it look as if no one was there, but knowing, given his girth, that unless the burglar/murderer was extremely shortsighted, he was unlikely to be missed.

The door opened further.

'Mitch?'

Mitch, feeling he was about to burst with terror, now realised through surging ears that he recognised the voice. That accent. *Me-atch.* He lifted the duvet slightly and peered out of the dark, malodorous hotness – he had farted several times in fright.

He found himself staring at a willowy blonde, entirely naked, with enormous breasts and a Brazilian bikini line. For a moment he thought he finally had gone mad before recognising Candy Jo, a glamour model from Kansas who had been one of the hostesses at the previous night's dinner. The mystery of how he had got home and got undressed was now solved. As was the mystery of some bite and scatch marks in unexpected places that he had been subconsciously wondering about.

'Hi,' breathed Candy Jo in a little-girl voice that none the less held an undercurrent of menace. 'I was just taking a shower. Nice bathroom you got there,' she added appreciatively.

'Thanks,' said Mitch. He realised his hangover had disappeared. Candy Jo had scared it off. He looked at her fearfully; there seemed to be purpose in her huge blue eyes.

'I'm glad you like the bathroom,' he jabbered nervously. 'My interior designer was going for a rainforest kinda feel. You saw the waterproof plasma screen in the shower, right? And there are three power settings – Amazonian Falls, Highland Mist . . .' His voice trailed away. He had a feeling that Candy Jo was not here to talk about bathrooms. The finer points of vitreous enamel did not interest her. This feeling proved correct when Candy Jo raised a hand tipped with sugar-pink nails and made a swatting motion.

'Hey, big boy,' she beamed, approaching the bed. 'You said last night that if I came back with you you'd make me a star.'

Oh, no. Not another. Mitch grabbed the edges of the duvet. 'I meant I'd make you a sandwich,' he muttered, collapsing on the pillows like a felled log. He yelped as the back of his head smashed against the headboard. He had misjudged the distance. Along with everything else, as usual.

Chapter 4

Burdened by luggage, James Bradstock walked slowly down the leafy Peckham street leading to his home. He had not seen it for several weeks. Not since setting out on the fact-finding mission in Equatorial Guinea on which his employers in the Foreign Office had seen fit to send him, and from which he had just returned. Not necessarily with the requisite facts, James was aware; the brief had been vague, to say the least. The only things he felt entirely confident about coming back with, in fact, were the pair of pencils with little carved dolls on the top for Hero and Cosmo.

As he passed the row of red-brick Victorian terraces with pointed roofs and small front gardens, of which his was one, James felt a rising excitement. His heart burned with eagerness to see his children. He had thought of them constantly while he was away: Hero, with her serious gaze and determined character; impulsive and passionate Cosmo. He longed to feel their small but strong arms around his neck and their faces snuggling into his. He wondered whether they had grown – but of course they would have; there would be something wrong otherwise – and what new words Hero knew. There was sure to be a new interest as well – when he left it had been Thomas and trains still, as it had been for some time, but Cosmo may well have discovered something else since. Music, perhaps – he knew Vanessa was starting them on music appreciation classes at – of all places – the Royal Opera House. Not that this was a surprise – apart from, perhaps, the cost. Vanessa never did anything by halves.

He was also looking forward to seeing his wife. She scared him rather, but he loved her and was proud of her. Slim, blonde and always smartly turned out, Vanessa was better looking and better dressed than many Foreign Office wives, not that there was much competition in either respect. Most FO wives looked like their husbands, only rather more masculine. The fact that Vanessa had a career of her own – her newspaper column – made her even more exotic and special.

James had spoken to Vanessa from the airport and had learnt, rather to his disappointment, that she would be out for the early part of the evening he was arriving home. She had a charity ball committee meeting to attend at which some crucial issue such as the sandwiches was being decided. James had not argued; in the register of his wife's concerns he knew his place well enough, and it was considerably below anything involving her social interests. She would see him later.

'What about the children?' James had ventured, having to shout through the row of the airport around him.

'Nanny's looking after them,' Vanessa said shortly.

'Oh . . . right.' James did his best to hide his surprise.

He had of course known that Vanessa was taking on a new nanny while he was away. The fact she was still there was a good sign.

'She's . . . OK then, is she?' he ventured.

'Seems OK,' Vanessa replied in distant tones. 'Bit fat and northern, but otherwise, yes, not bad.'

Fat and northern, James mused after she had rung off. Well, that sounded good to him. The last nanny, Jacintha, had been all sharp elbows and painfully thin calves. She had been painfully pretentious too, full of references to her ancient and venerable family. His wife, James knew, loved the thought of someone who claimed to trace their ancestry back to the Conqueror wiping Hero's bottom. But Jacintha had always made him feel as if the whole family was rather beneath her.

Jacintha's father was an earl and she was in fact Lady Jacintha. Had she not been so ineffably superior, James thought, he might almost have felt sorry for her. She stuck out like a very sore thumb in Peckham. James had seen Lady Jacintha, in her pale uniform, flat black shoes and bowler hat with its polished silver badge, marching Cosmo and Hero along streets where people mugged and shot each other on a regular basis. The only ladies normally spotted in Peckham with flat black shoes and silver hat badges were from the Metropolitan Police, and they had guns and bulletproof vests. It was probably only a matter of time before Lady Jacintha demanded them too.

But Lady Jacintha had had other ideas. Vanessa had been furious when she announced she was leaving to work for a famous author in Hampstead. 'Bloody snob!' she had stormed to James. 'Celebrity tart!' Which was rich, James had secretly felt, given Vanessa's own keen interest in social elevation. But that his wife was full of contradictions, some amusing, some less so, was something he had grown used to over the years, and he did not love her any less for it. Vanessa *was* the mother of his children, even if she was avowedly too busy to look after them. But then, he could hardly talk on that score. It was the reason the whole nanny circus was necessary.

As, for the first time in weeks, James slipped the key into his front-door lock, he felt a quiver of trepidation about what awaited.

The first thing he noticed was that the house smelt much cleaner than usual. It smelt of nice baths, shampoo and talcum powder. It also looked tidier than he had expected; than he ever remembered seeing it, in fact. The great bulging bundle of children's cardigans, bags, coats and other paraphernalia, traditionally attached in a clump to the hall coathooks like some multicoloured wasps' nest, had disappeared. One or two coats in regular use hung demurely there instead. James's gaze dropped to a row of children's shoes, neatly ranged and beautifully clean, beneath the coats. His eyes widened. The children's shoes were usually in a muddy heap of wrong sizes and missing other halves. This had been the case throughout the reign of all previous nannies.

It was now that he noticed the delicious smell. James ventured into the kitchen, which, unusually, was pin-neat. On the shining draining board, whose metal surface he did not recall ever seeing before, so choked was it normally with clutter, were two small plates, two sets of spoons and forks, two cups and a baking dish, all washed. On the otherwise empty and spotless kitchen table, whose wooden top James had not looked on for what seemed many months, a delicious-looking macaroni cheese, browned on top, evidently home-made and the twin of the empty dish on the draining board, sat cooling. James's mouth rushed with saliva and his stomach erupted in a surge of hunger, which he tried to suppress. The macaroni cheese was evidently for the children; no doubt a spare one for a few days' time.

He saw with approval and surprise the two cloth napkins rolled up in their rings and placed tidily to the side. Most nannies instantly gave up trying to impress proper table manners on Hero and Cosmo: not this one, it seemed. His gaze took in a small bowl in which a few pieces of left-over broccoli had been placed. At the sight of the broccoli, James did a double take. This nanny not only could cook but had managed to get the children to eat *broccoli*.

Jacintha's idea of cooking for Hero and Cosmo had been to open tins of Heinz, while Lady Augusta, for all her training in child nutrition at her prestigious nanny school, had served the children a rarely varying diet of custard creams and Mars bars, with the odd foray into oven chips.

The house wasn't silent, James realised now. He could hear something upstairs. A voice, not one he recognised.

He ran quietly in stockinged feet up the threadbare sisal staircase. The sound seemed to be coming from the direction of the 'nursery suite', as Vanessa liked to call the large, rather shabby bedroom that Hero and Cosmo shared and the adjoining, even shabbier upstairs bathroom.

James paused outside the children's bedroom door. The voice seemed to be coming from here. Someone was speaking loudly and dramatically in a strange accent. A bit northern, Vanessa had said of the nanny. But this didn't sound northern. It sounded French.

James took his glasses off and rubbed his tired eyes, wondering. Although Vanessa occasionally decided that the children needed lessons in conversational French, he hadn't realised she had done anything about it. He glanced at his watch and felt even more puzzled. If French wasn't off the agenda and a teacher had been appointed, what were they doing here, at half-past seven at night? Without Vanessa being around? What was she thinking?

James grabbed the round wooden handle of the white-painted door and pushed it open.

The French accent stopped immediately. James peered into the room.

The next minute, he was bowled over by small bodies running at him full tilt. 'Daddy!'

James pulled them to him and hugged them hard. They had both grown, he saw from an initial glance; their faces seemed to have lengthened, especially Cosmo's. They had obviously had their baths, being dressed in their pyjamas with their hair neatly brushed. They smelt divine. He buried his nose in their warm hair and sniffed in bliss.

He had almost forgotten about the strange French voice but now he saw that, sitting on Cosmo's bed, was a girl of about twenty with a very pretty face and shoulder-length reddish-brown hair. She wore black trousers and a white polo shirt and looked very clean. She did not, for the record, look remotely fat, James noticed. She was a bit plump, and nicely so, and that was all.

The room was dim and restful, the only light the lamp on top of Cosmo's chest of drawers. It threw a soft glow on the new nanny's straight brown hair. A pair of large brown eyes shone in a kind-looking face quite unlike the sharp visage of Jacintha. Her skin was creamy, with reddish cheeks like apples. Yes, Vanessa had definitely undersold her.

James proceeded into the bedroom with his long stride, his hand held out. 'Emma, isn't it? I'm James, Cosmo and Hero's father.' He ruffled their neatly brushed heads. 'Actually, I hadn't realised you were French. My wife told me you were from the north of England.'

'I am from the north of England,' Emma replied, her flat vowels illustrating the point precisely.

James reeled. 'I'm awfully sorry,' he back-pedalled. 'I really didn't mean . . . I mean . . .' He rubbed his hair in flustered fashion. 'It's just that I thought I heard someone speaking in a French accent . . . I'm obviously going mad,' he finished, shaking his head ruefully.

'No, no, you weren't. That was me,' Emma smiled.

'You?' James was more perplexed than ever.

From her comfortable perch on the bed, the children warm against her sides, Emma regarded Vanessa's husband with interest. He was not what she had expected. Not the sleek alpha male she had pictured at all, but tall, thin, bespectacled, apologetic, his collar awry and his glasses wonky.

'"Chicken Licken",' she said.

James felt for the chest of drawers to support him. It had been a long day and a long flight and nothing was making much sense. 'Chicken . . . ?'

'"Licken",' Cosmo interrupted in his high little voice. 'You know, Daddy. That story about how the sky is falling.'

In the dim recesses of James's mind, something stirred. 'Oh, yes,' he said uncertainly. 'That chicken. It goes and tells everyone. It tells Cocky Locky. Is that right? Chicken, um, Licken meets, um, Cocky Locky?' He looked anxiously at Emma.

'Yes. Chicken Licken meets Cocky Locky,' the nanny confirmed to his relief. 'And Ducky Daddles—'

'And Turkey Lurkey,' Cosmo interrupted eagerly, his eyes shining beneath his smooth pageboy fringe. 'And Emma does everyone in the story with a different voice. It's really funny, Daddy. You should listen.' He then said something James could not understand in a voice he could understand still less.

Emma laughed. 'Cosmo's being Henny Penny,' she explained. 'What do you mean, the sky is falling down?' she addressed the little boy in a perfect Scottish accent. 'How do you know it's falling down, Chicken Licken?'

Understanding burst over James. He smiled at Emma in

43

admiration and relief. 'That's really impressive, if I may say so. You're very good at accents.'

'Thank you.' Emma, on the bed, saw the children's father was frowning slightly, his eyes moving about as if searching for something.

'What's the matter?'

'Oh. Um. I was just wondering. You don't seem to be using an, um, book,' James said eventually. 'For "Chicken Licken".'

'No, I'm doing it from memory.'

'That's impressive.'

'Not really. I've read it so often to children that there'd be something wrong if I didn't know it off by heart,' Emma asserted cheerfully.

'Gosh, well, I think that's pretty impressive,' James repeated warmly.

Emma smiled and slid off the bed. 'Time for you two to go to sleep,' she murmured to her charges.

James, suddenly loath to leave, watched as Hero slid a pair of tired white arms about Emma's neck and was carried to her small bed in the corner and laid down with the utmost care. He did not remember them being so tactile with Jacintha, nor Jacintha being so solicitous.

Emma was now doing the lullabies, singing 'Twinkle, Twinkle, Little Star' in a soft, loving voice to Hero. Watching his small daughter smile and close her eyes, evidently luxuriating in the moment, James felt a lump rising in his throat.

Composing himself, he glanced around the bedroom. Something about it had changed. A lot of things, now he looked closely. The furniture had been rearranged in a more sensible, harmonious way; the children's beds had been pushed further apart, stuffed toys had been arranged in one corner to look like a tea party. Up on the walls were the embroidered names in frames that his mother, a keen needlewoman, had done when the children were born, but which Vanessa had always declared too naff to display.

A comfortable-looking chair had appeared from somewhere; he thought he recognised it from the spare bedroom Emma would now be occupying. Various lamps had appeared; the harsh, overhead light that had been in operation seemed to have been retired. Emma had, James thought, performed miracles. She had achieved far more during her first three weeks in her job than he had in Equatorial Guinea, he reflected guiltily. But then, Emma obviously had a sound grasp of what she was supposed to be doing, which he hadn't; nor, for that matter, ever had had.

She was settling Cosmo into bed now. James watched, feeling a sudden swell of emotion as she kissed both upturned faces on their pillows.

'I'll leave you to say good night to them now,' Emma murmured as she slipped past him out of the door, a clean, scented soap smell trailing in her wake. 'But I'd leave the lamp on for a while. Hero's afraid of the dark, as you know.'

James blinked back at her, stifling the instinctively honest response that this was news to him. Jacintha had been obsessed to the point of hysteria with completely dark rooms being crucial for proper sleep. At her behest and great expense they had fitted black-lined curtains and blackout blinds in the children's bedroom, although Hero's sleep had not seemed to benefit and she had woken screaming almost every night. But here was Emma, saying the opposite, and with Hero looking more relaxed than he had ever seen her.

As she passed him, and he inhaled her clean scent, James found himself looking into a pair of big brown humorous eyes. 'By the way, if you're hungry,' Emma said, 'there's a spare macaroni cheese in the kitchen. I was going to freeze it, but I like to cook the children something fresh every day, so you're welcome to it if you want it.'

James could not speak. He was beginning to wonder whether this woman was real, or a happy vision. She seemed too good to be true.

As the door closed behind the nanny, he crossed to the beds in which the children lay calm and soothed. In any previous childcare regime they would now have been bouncing hysterically around on the mattresses, shrieking and upsetting things. But they only looked up at him from their pillows, eyes large, dark and solemn in the dim light.

'We like Emma, Daddy,' Cosmo said in his gruff voice as James bent to kiss him.

'Yeth,' Hero piped from her bed in the corner. 'You won't let her go away, will you, Daddy? Like the otherth?'

'But we didn't like the others,' put in Cosmo.

'No,' Hero agreed, nodding solemnly.

'We were glad when they went way,' Cosmo added.

'Yeth.'

'Course she won't leave,' James assured them, emphatically shaking his head. What sort of an idiot would let go someone as good as this?

Chapter 5

In an apartment more lavish than Mitch's, and in a better part of Los Angeles, a thin blonde woman slammed down the bedside phone angrily. Damn Mitch for not picking up. OK, so she'd spoken to him only five minutes ago, but he was supposed to be her agent, at her beck and call. Her call, certainly. Belle was not entirely sure what her beck was.

Still, there were compensations. If Mitch didn't want to pay her any attention, there were others who would. Beside her, across the rumpled expanse of oyster-coloured satin sheets covering the vast bed, a handsome young man stirred. As she watched, Belle's artificially shaped and filled chest, balancing like two melon halves on its thin ribcage, swelled further with pride.

He was like a young lion waking, she thought fancifully, admiring the muscled arms – smooth, tanned and lightly oiled – as they moved upwards, pulling the powerful chest and stomach, with its clearly defined six-pack, into a stretch. Everything below this was twisted up in the oyster satin, but Belle knew what lay beneath well enough: the powerful thighs, the tight buttocks . . . she felt a sudden hot rush in which the thrill of ownership combined with lust. If Christian Harlow wasn't the hottest man in Hollywood at that moment, she'd like to know who was. And he was all hers. Of all the women in Hollywood, he had chosen to be with her. She couldn't be all that washed up, could she?

Her smile widened as Christian lifted his head from where it was squashed into the oyster satin pillow, revealing that impossibly handsome, deeply tanned face with huge lips and black hair, so very black that it had navy lights in it, dropping into smouldering eyes of a different blue, an intense, swimming-pool blue. The face that had currently got all Hollywood excited, Belle knew; that was starting to appear on the front of the men's magazines. All thanks to her. She had given him the contacts he had needed to make his dreams of being a Hollywood star come true.

Christian looked at her and, as always, just as she had the first time she had met him, Belle felt a tightening in her groin, a rush in the mouth, a tingling in her nipples. He was a prime piece of beefcake. The best.

Their meeting had, she remembered fondly, been a classic lady and tramp situation. Or perhaps lady and cramp. It had been a film industry party and Christian had been a human sculpture, painted silver and striking a pose which, he explained afterwards, had given him chronic leg-ache.

He had soon recovered, however, and it was that same night Belle discovered Christian's ability to give her orgasms so intense they made her teeth rattle. Even after all the veneering, which seemed a double achievement.

Of course, Christian was younger, but that had been no problem. Her being in her twenties, he had discovered, was no bar to sexual appetite or experimentation. She in turn had discovered Christian had a highly developed shopping habit and an obsession with first-class travel. As a result Christian now had a wardrobe to rival her own, a far greater number of products in the bathroom and a familiarity with VIP lounges from Sydney to Saigon.

None of which she begrudged him, Belle always thought when any of this occurred to her. Christian gave her profound pleasure in so many ways. She watched admiringly as the blue eyes opened, looked straight into hers and, right on cue, creased in a smile.

'Hey, baby,' Christian breathed.

Belle's lavishly lipsticked mouth stretched in a beam. She had put her make-up on immediately after waking. The thought of Christian seeing her barefaced was, well, unthinkable.

Christian, meanwhile, had arranged his features into their usual smouldering, impenetrable pout into which undying devotion or cynical lack of interest could be read with equal ease. Belle always chose to read the devotion.

But what Christian's silent smoulder was actually saying was that she really should get some clothes on. Jesus, she was skinny. He liked slim – who didn't? – but making love to Belle was like screwing a set of steps. Talk about the Hollywood ladder, thought Christian.

Of course, the odd nip and tuck was fine by him, but there were more nips on Belle than a colony of goddamn crabs. Belle was all fake, from the cascade of white-blond hair tossing constantly about, the equally unremitting blaze of veneered teeth, the stretched skin of her face, the exposed and prominent rounded domes of her breasts with a gap between them you could park a motorbike in. Belle always denied she had had surgery, but Christian knew the signs. He didn't think she'd had a fanny tuck yet, but she'd definitely had lipo on her bottom, which might have gone to the filling in her lips. And so every time her mouth sought his, Christian wondered if he was quite literally kissing her ass.

'You look gorgeous,' he assured her.

'Oh, baby,' purred Belle, reaching for him with one of her thin arms.

There was a growl from beside the bed. Christian raised himself on his elbow and looked with dislike at a small brown dog with a very big diamond collar. Belle's pet Chihuahua, Sugar, was, as usual, staring at him with enormous and very prominent black eyes.

Christian's heavy brows pulled together. His lips puffed with loathing, even though he realised he should be grateful to the dog. It had been a useful distraction; Belle clearly wanted servicing, and he'd done quite enough of that last night.

But here she was, wanting more, except the dog had appeared. *Caninus interruptus.* And yet Christian could still not look at Sugar with anything other than hatred, and was aware that the animal returned his feelings in full measure.

How could anyone love a mutt like that, Christian wondered. He was not one to lavish his feelings – or what passed for them – on anything that could not give him instant and full return, and preferably a profit. Sugar was bad-tempered and vicious. Belle spoilt it rotten and it wasn't grateful in the least. She lavished it with love which it did not return one iota. She was a mug if she couldn't see that, Christian thought disdainfully.

That there were similarities between how he and the dog treated Belle never occurred to him. But not much outside his own immediate ambitions and what was needed to realise them ever occurred to Christian. What else was important, after all?

Belle swung her thin brown legs off the bed and scooped the dog against her naked breasts. 'Sugar!' Christian watched scornfully as she lavished the dog's bony skull with kisses. 'This morning,' Belle crooned, 'I'm taking you to the dog beautician for a manicure.'

'Baby, you spoil that mutt,' drawled Christian in his thick, low voice, dragging himself upright against the pillows, pulling up his powerful legs and letting them fall open with just a switch of oyster sheet covering his manhood. This was less for reasons of modesty than fear that sight of his organ – of which Christian was justifiably proud – might rouse the dog to some act of jealous and irreversible savagery.

Belle looked at him fondly. The broad expanse of Christian's chest, recently waxed, gleamed against the shining oyster satin pillows and the vast mirror that spread behind them in a massive ornate gilt frame. The mirror served as a bedhead and stretched up to the ceiling from which pink gauze billowed softly, as in some exotic tent, caught up in the centre with a vast and glittering glass chandelier of daring modern design, based on an idea of Belle's of which she was very proud. The candelabra, which looked like twisting glass snakes from a distance, were, up close, actually shaped like penises.

Belle's smile twisted to a suggestive pout. Her eyes dropped to the satin heaping between his legs; she crawled towards him across the sheet, white hair spilling over her breasts, hot with desire.

Sugar, from the floor, growled warningly. Belle paused in her slithering progress, regretfully accepting this was neither the time nor the place for sex. Doing it in front of the dog, currently standing rigid up to its knees in the deep-pile pink carpet before the bed, and glaring at Christian, might lead to terrible psychological damage.

A yap from Sugar confirmed her unspoken thoughts. Belle, assuming that Christian had been coursing with lust just as she had, hastened to smooth over the situation between the two beings she was fondest of in the world. 'We'd better not, baby,' she said to Christian in tones of breathy apology. 'It might upset Sugar.'

'Oh, for Chrissakes,' snarled Christian, impatient with the whole idea of the dog's importance, as well as the idea he wanted to have sex with this scrawny bint yet again. He'd performed for Belle for the final time last night, knowing that this morning he was going to dump her.

Belle had outlived her usefulness and it was time he moved on to someone who could get him through the final bit of the journey, right up to the top of the Hollywood ladder.

'Baby!' pouted Belle chidingly. 'You're being hostile to poor little Sugar. He's so sensitive, you know. He can really *sense* hostility in the atmosphere.'

Christian disbelievingly raised an eyebrow and tried to look less hostile. It could just be that the dog had sensed what he was about to say to its mistress.

Belle had clearly sensed nothing of the sort. She smiled suggestively. 'We can have some time together later,' she said softly, approaching him and winding one arm around his neck. Christian felt her silicon breasts squash unpleasantly against him. 'All afternoon if you like. After I've dropped Sugar off at the manicurist's.' She let her wet red lips remain suggestively open.

Christian looked away. He didn't do uncomfortable, just as he didn't do guilt, but he felt a vague twinge of something at the sight of Belle's eager face. This twinge quickly changed to resentment. It was her fault. She was making him do it. If she was less neurotic, less clingy, demanding and desperate, more successful, he wouldn't be in the position he was now. If she had made the right choices after her big hit movie . . .

Christian's eye, too deep-set to allow realisation of how small and sly it actually was, caught the row of acting awards, gold masks, wreaths, globes and lumps of engraved glass, which stood proudly on the two mirror-panelled nightstands either side of Belle's bed. He felt a twinge of envy. He'd have all that too one day. It was all in front of him, Christian thought, his blue gaze sweeping appreciatively down the front of his massive, oiled waxed pectorals to the thick stem of his manhood. Which from now on would be servicing someone else. Someone more useful.

Because it was all over with Belle. She had let her career hit the skids with a turkey film. And so he had to move on for the good of his own. How was that his fault? She had no one but herself to blame. He was only doing what anyone in his position would do at the moment.

As her fragile frame snuggled into him, Christian remained rigid. He saw no point in beating about the bush. 'It's over, baby,' he muttered into the brittle white hair that was massed against his lips. 'We're over.'

He felt her convulse with shock. 'Over?' Belle gasped disbelievingly, her head twisting and her face emerging, blurred behind the hair. Her expression was so different from the confident, even predatory one it had just worn that Christian would have been perturbed, had he been given to such extremes of emotion. As it was he felt vaguely surprised that the scenario was departing from what he had imagined. In as much as he, with his limited mental resources, was able to imagine anything.

'I've gotta move on,' he explained.

'Move on?' Belle gasped, her eyes with their terrible expression fixed on his. 'Move on from *me*? But *why*? I thought you loved me.' Her voice broke into a sob.

'*Loved* you?' It was Christian's turn to gasp now, and with the first genuine amazement he had ever felt. *Loved* her? Was she kidding? Who could possibly love Belle Murphy – neurotic, demanding, self-obsessed and, above all, *failed* diva that she was?

He didn't love *anybody*, anyway. Success, fame, money – sure. But no person. Never had, never would. And certainly not this one. Panicked, his only thought being to reverse this ludicrous, dangerous assumption, Christian lashed out at Belle in even more brutal a way than he had planned.

'Look, baby. It's business, yeah? Only business. No offence. Nothing personal.'

Belle's eyes were bigger and huger than he had ever seen them. He had not imagined, given the constraints of her facial surgery, that so much stretching was even possible. 'Business?' she managed to force out. 'Nothing . . . *personal*?'

'Baby, this is Hollywood,' Christian said, more easily. As well as uncomfortable, he was beginning to find this boring. 'So you *were* huge last year. But a year's a long time in showbiz. You're losing it, and now you've lost me.' He put his handsome, heavy head with its great ridges of cheekbone on one side and gave an apologetic grin. 'It's just the way things are, baby.'

'You can't mean it,' Belle cried, emotion catching stickily in her throat.

Christian shrugged his shoulders. 'Baby. It's not you. It's Hollywood.'

Belle was sobbing. She was working the vulnerable look hard, Christian thought pitilessly. It was almost convincing, the way she hunched her thin shoulders and let her mouth, with its smeared red lipstick, hang open in apparent shock. If she'd acted as well as this in *Bloody Mary* he wouldn't have had to leave her at all, he reminded himself. It was her fault.

'Don't leave me,' Belle wept, stretching out her thin arms to him in abject and heartfelt appeal. 'I love you,' she hiccuped. From beneath his calm and level brows, Christian regarded her red, wet and swollen eyes, her tangled hair, her air of unhinged hysteria. What a mess. God, women were so emotional. So hysterical. And for what? She obviously didn't mean any of this. No one loved anyone in Hollywood. They just had sex with them, that was all.

'Sorry, baby,' Christian said briskly, manoeuvring his body off the bed. Time to go. He had places to go, people to see. No time to lose.

The dog, who had remained in the shagpile during the whole of the former exchange, watched him closely as he slid off the slippery satin edge, clutching a small pink satin cushion, edged with lace and bearing the legend 'It's Hard to Be Humble When You're as Good as I Am' protectively over his manhood. As Belle flung herself on the bed in a frenzy of weeping, beating the sheets with her frail fists, Christian snatched up his clothes, padded backwards across the bedroom and ducked out of the door.

Chapter 6

It was rare that Sam would bother to go back and look for someone she had spotted, let alone someone who had rejected her advances. No one *had* rejected her advances before, not in the spotting sense anyway.

But the memory of the beautiful boy, with his amazing pale green eyes touched with yellow, not to mention all his other attributes, haunted the agency head like magnificent salmon do fishermen whose hooks they have slipped. The fact that she had managed to snap him on her mobile phone only increased the sense of him being the one who got away. She could see what she had missed, although the boy did not look his best in it, his face being somewhat distorted. The shot was blurred too; in general, it would mean little to anyone else. It was, for example, useless to give it to any other scouts from Wild, send them out on the streets of London and hope they could spot him with it.

Sam pored endlessly over the image. She had spent most of the week since it was taken at her associate agency in New York and was haunted in her absence by the fear that a rival agency might have snapped the boy up in the meantime. His looks were perfect, so *now*, that it seemed impossible that they hadn't.

At the first opportunity, which happened to be the Friday following that when the young man had escaped her, Sam rose from her desk at around the same time she had the week before. She grabbed her fringed beige cashmere throw from the Edwardian mahogany coatstand she intended to give a boho air to her otherwise strictly contemporary glass-walled office. Her logic was that the beautiful boy might cross the piazza again at the same time; that he had some regular reason for being there.

She was due at lunch with a magazine fashion editor recently appointed to an important glossy. Sam knew she needed to butter her up to keep the bookings for Wild models at this publication at their current high level. In the hope that the boy might be one of those models, and that she would see him again on her way, the lunch was to be at the same restaurant in Covent Garden in which Sam had met Jacques Flash last week. When the great photographer had finally deigned to turn up, that was.

Sam paused before her new PA, Nia, who sat just outside her door at a state-of-the-art kidney-shaped glass desk. Sam had specifically chosen the kidney shape to remind her of her own beleaguered organs, and not to drink so much. It didn't seem to work, however; the party last night, to launch some cutting-edge bras by a celebrity's girlfriend, and a line of barely-there knickers by a leading socialite, had featured custard-flavoured vodka cocktails scattered with flakes of pure platinum, an effect that had reminded Sam of fish food when you put it in the tank. But that had been the nearest she had got to food, with the result that, this morning, she had a banging hangover. Still, hopefully that was a good sign. She had had a banging hangover last week too, after all.

'I'll be back at two thirty,' Sam warned her personal helper. Nia, a thin-faced brunette with shining shoulder-length hair, and dressed in regulation Wild black polo-neck and black Capri pants, flashed her boss a slightly knowing smile. Nia knew, just as Sam did, that a return before three was highly unlikely. There was, Sam felt as she left, something rather insubordinate about Nia.

In Covent Garden, everything was much the same as it had been the week before. The drills in Endell Street screeched once again into the centre of Sam's hungover brain, it was too bright again to look at the builders and the cafés she passed still smelt of things that turned her stomach.

Sam had given herself a few extra minutes in order to dawdle in the piazza. All was much as it had been last week: the same human statues, the same hotdog sellers, the same flower stall and even the same limbo dancer were all present. Very possibly the same tourists were too – they certainly looked it; stumpy-legged in their stonewashed jeans and clumsy in their padded anoraks. Carefully, Sam stepped round the taped-down chalked renditions of Marilyn Monroe and St Paul's. She didn't want to risk another mouthful from the pavement artists, who clearly had artistic temperaments, if no other attribute in that respect.

Sam wandered about the piazza, then, finding the bright sun too much for her eyes even through huge black sunglasses, decided to retreat into the welcome shadows of the steps of the church. This, had Sam known it, was the exact same place Orlando had chosen the week before as a refuge from her own attentions.

'Visualising' success had always been one of Sam's buzzwords. She firmly believed that if you could imagine something to yourself, it would then happen. 'Just picture it,' she would urge her models, whether the 'it' was landing a huge new campaign or losing a huge amount of weight. She had visualised seeing Orlando again so many times that the possibility he might not, after all, appear was unthinkable. Nevertheless, as the gilt-faced clock on the pediment above her head boomed one, the lunch hour, Sam found herself having to think it.

There was always the possibility that the new fashion director would be late at the restaurant, thus giving her a few more minutes. But Sam knew that Genevieve, whom she had known for many years at other publications, was not the late type. In Sam's experience, fashion directors fell into two categories: those who looked like messy bedrooms and those who looked like research scientists. Genevieve was in the latter category. She was a stick-thin brunette with dark retro spectacles, severe hair and plainly cut clothes in shades of aubergine, charcoal and moss. She was also extremely organised.

Swinging her beige cashmere angrily over her shoulder, Sam moved crossly off. As she went down the stairs she mused uncharitably that the youth in Covent Garden this morning were even less attractive than they had been the week before. Her glance swept, uninterested, over a group of rickety schoolgirls with narrowed, much-eyelined eyes and miniskirts exposing long white skinny legs. They should be at school, Sam thought.

Her eye lingered on a girl of about twenty, walking purposefully along by herself, with reddish brown shoulder-length hair and a pale blue cardigan. There was something about *her*, Sam thought. But of course she wasn't tall enough and far too fat, looking even more so in jeans and short, fur-lined suede boots that made her calves look huge. Only skinny girls could wear Uggs, didn't she know that? Obviously not, Sam thought scornfully.

She kept looking at the girl anyway; taking in the details in her rapid, professional way. She was, Sam thought, remarkably pretty, with thick, shining hair, a sweet, open, heart-shaped face, clear, slightly flushed skin and what Sam could see across the short distance to be thickly lashed eyes and full pink lips.

Milkmaidy. Healthy. Fresh. She looked, Sam thought fancifully, like someone in a nursery rhyme who ate nothing but cream and lived in some beautiful garden. Her utter lack of self-consciousness was attractive too. Most people round here under thirty, and a great many over, were the opposite. They seemed to think the world was watching and admiring their every move.

This girl seemed unaware of anyone else as she hurried past the front of the church. She was humming as she went; a tune Sam almost thought she recognised, some nursery tune she had not heard for years. With a sudden and most uncharacteristic pang of wistfulness Sam watched the girl emerge from the deep shadow before the church to where the sunlight blazed on the cobbles, skirt the crowds around a busker and become lost to sight.

Emma hurried across the cobbled piazza towards the back of the Opera House and entered under the arcade. Cosmo and Hero had been at their Friday morning music appreciation class, an hour in duration and due to finish in ten minutes. While music appreciation classes were far from unknown among the children Emma had looked after before, this one was a little different, being at the Royal Opera House. But Vanessa, the children's mother, felt that nothing was too good for her children.

And so Cosmo and Hero, as of the last two weeks, had spent an hour each Friday morning in the red velvet stalls at Covent Garden while the Royal Opera House's resident conductor and the entire resident orchestra played for their edification. During the hour this took, Emma was free to look around the market and the shops, respectively full of tat she would not have wasted money on and clothes she could not fit into.

Now she hurried through various glass-walled and slate-floored passages until she reached the heavy glass doors of the opera house foyer, a grand, high-ceilinged space blazing with mirrors, heavy gilt decoration and rich red curtains and carpeting.

Emma slowed down as she approached. The other nannies were already there, standing around in a group on the carpet, but Emma felt no especial wish to join them.

While telling herself firmly she had absolutely no reason – she was probably better at her job than the rest of them put together – Emma could not help feeling rather intimidated by her professional peers. It wasn't just that she was the newest of the circle. The other nannies were so poised and polished: slim and groomed, their shiny swishy hair caught up with sunglasses, modelling-session make-up and impossibly skinny jeans. The most poised and polished of them all, a long-legged, heavily highlighted creature in tight white jeans, a sheer and clinging leopardskin blouse and the biggest sunglasses, was called Totty Ponsonby-Pratt. Emma knew this because she had come across Totty, as she had others of the group, at various children's parties. Totty looked after a gloomy-looking child called Hengist Westonbirt and the first time Emma had seen her, she had asked her, in a loud, slow, emphatic voice, what part of Eastern Europe she had come from.

'None. I'm from Yorkshire,' Emma had answered, looking Totty steadily in the eye.

'Oh God, sorry!' Totty had clapped a hand with long manicured nails to her lipsticked mouth and squealed with laughter. Emma, instinctively loathing every emaciated inch of this woman, also wondered how, given the exigencies of car seats, nappy-changing, fiddly buttons, bathtime and the rest of it, Totty managed to maintain such impressive talons. Perhaps she had an assistant.

Seeing from the other side of the foyer-door glass that the

children were now coming out of the auditorium, Emma pushed her way in. None of the children looked particularly delighted to see his or her nanny. They filed solemnly out with their brushed-down, parted and ribboned hair, pastel gingham checks and apricot knitwear, and the nannies received them with equal lack of enthusiasm; rolling their eyes at each other whilst cooing greetings full of artificial joy at their charges.

The exception to this rule were Cosmo and Hero, who hurled themselves at Emma in delight. Emma hugged them back almost as hard. They had regarded her suspiciously at first, but that had seemed to Emma perfectly reasonable given that five nannies had come and gone in the last eight months. But the children had almost immediately dropped their guard, and now Emma felt fonder of them than of any infants she had ever looked after before. But of course, she told herself, she always felt that way about her charges. One had to love them; the job was unimaginable otherwise.

'Woo woo!' chortled train-mad Cosmo, steaming across the carpet beneath the huge and brilliant chandeliers.

Laughing, Emma and Hero hurried after him. 'Did you enjoy the class, darling?' Emma asked as they reached the queue for the coats, scooping Hero's solid little frame up into her arms. Hero nodded seriously, her blue eyes, as big as but more oval than her brother's, gazing solemnly from her milk-white face. 'Yeth,' she lisped in her characteristically clear, composed voice. 'At de end dey played "Chitty Chitty Bang Bang".'

'"*Chitty Chitty Bang Bang*"!' exclaimed Emma delightedly.

There was a scornful noise from behind. Emma turned to find herself staring into the tiger-yellow, much-mascara'd eyes of Totty Ponsonby-Pratt. 'What *is* it about kids and *Chitty Chitty Bang Bang*?' Totty swung back her striped blond hair scornfully.

Emma saw Hero's blue eyes flick up in surprise and stare at Totty through her mop of twisted silver hair. Emma hugged her protectively and smiled. 'Well, I have to say it's one of my favourites too.'

Totty *tsked*. 'God. Give me Brad Pitt any day. Except without all those kids, obviously.' She snorted. '*Six!* Can you imagine? One's bad enough.' She shot a look of deep dislike at Hengist, shuffling unhappily alongside her. Emma did not reply. They were at the front of the queue now. She took Cosmo and Hero's coats, muttered goodbye and left.

Chapter 7

A week after the model agency approach, Orlando was in his bedroom with the curtains drawn. Outside it was a sunny day in early summer, but he remained in his large and messy room in the T-shirt and pyjama bottoms in which he had slept, watching Saturday morning children's TV.

A pair of chirpy northern presenters with gelled hair were sitting on a purple sofa and bantering with someone dressed in a bright yellow chicken suit. A recipe for pineapple-topped pizza followed.

There was a sharp knock, the door of his bedroom opened and the top of his mother's rather frazzled head appeared round it.

'Darling?' Georgie exclaimed.

Orlando grunted in reply and his mother came fully into the room. As usual, she was dressed in clothes several decades younger than she was. Georgie was small and thin, and proud of the fact she could get into Miss Sixty jeans like the slimmest of teenage girls. She was wearing them today with a flimsy purple blouse whose sequins caught what light had penetrated Orlando's drawn curtains. Her make-up, as always, was immaculate. Georgie's face was rather rabbity, with over-plucked eyebrows, but she made the most of what she had, as she believed everyone should.

'Sorry to interrupt . . . expect you're on Facebook,' Georgie smiled at her son, stumbling in her high-heeled sandals on the piles of trainers and hooded tops that lay scattered over Orlando's bedroom floor.

Facebook. Orlando groaned silently. Georgie was obsessed with the social networking site. She kept up with fashion and trends with an energy that amazed her son, who did neither, but Facebook was her special interest, with its opportunities for demonstrating social one-upmanship. His mother was a hopeless snob, Orlando knew, but hopeless in the positive sense that she was too kind-hearted, too spontaneous and too nervous to make a real success of snobbery, as well as utterly lacking the visceral instinct that made the flint-eyed parents of some of his school peers so terrifying, and in some cases the peers themselves.

Georgie had badgered him mercilessly to get his own Facebook page, sending him endless 'Georgie Fitzmaurice has invited you to join . . .' messages from her own account, and making her friends, also in their late forties but all keen Facebookers, to do the same.

Orlando secretly thought Facebook a boring waste of time, the acme of insincerity, a magnet for neurotics and the socially insecure. He held out as long as he could, but his email inbox had become so choked with invitations from mature ladies that the site crashed every time he launched it. He had had to give in.

After that, whenever curiosity got the better of him and he was actually on Facebook, Georgie seemed miraculously to know and would appear, as she had done now, lean over his shoulder and try to catch a glimpse of who his cyber-friends were. '*Orlo!*' she would exclaim. 'You've only got *ten* friends! And half of them are *mine*! Shouldn't you have *three hundred* or something? I hear that's the normal minimum. Tania Whyte-Oliphant was telling me yesterday that Ariadne – she's the part-time model, going to Cambridge – has over *six hundred* friends on Facebook! And Eliza Cocke-Roche gets poked over a thousand times a day!'

'*Mum!*' Orlando would groan. He absolutely didn't care about Facebook. But he did care about his mother, and to see her stooping to such levels was far more distressing than his cyber-unpopularity. He couldn't have cared less about that.

Facebook, however, had been the first indicator of his recently altered status. Some time before he grasped the extent to which his looks had changed, Orlando was puzzled to find that his inbox was suddenly full of people proposing themselves as cyber-acquaintances. None of them was a middle-aged woman, either.

From having five friends Orlando suddenly began to find he had twenty, then fifty, then a hundred, then hundreds and hundreds. And most of them were girls. Some he knew – girls from his own school, sisters of his school friends, girls in the sixth form – but many, many, that he didn't. He had scrolled through, dumbfounded. There was page after page after page of them, some extremely pretty, with long blond hair and big pink smiles. Others smouldered from behind black tresses. All seemed to be staring at him expectantly. Orlando was scared of all of them. What did they want?

As the numbers spiralled towards the thousand mark, Orlando stopped going online, terrified of his mother seeing the hugely increased figures. Her excitement would have been excruciating.

Georgie, having busied herself for a few minutes picking the mess up from the floor, had by now noticed that, far from cyber-networking, her son was lounging around in front of a remedial-looking children's show utterly devoid of aspirational content. Her habitually anxious expression deepened to annoyance as she scrutinised the screen. The pineapple pizza had given way to a group of children throwing foam pies at each other. The children were chubby, Georgie saw disapprovingly, which must mean they were common. Expending, as she did, great time and effort in maintaining her own sleek appearance, she had no sympathy with the overweight and slobby.

'Aren't you a bit old for this?' she asked her son accusingly.

'Yes,' Orlando agreed readily. He had no idea why he was watching it either. He had a vague inkling that the world of children appealed to him more and more as he got older and the pressures of adulthood revealed themselves. But he could not have said this to his mother, nor would she have wanted to hear it.

Neither had he said to his mother that a model agency had approached him. This was because he could easily picture her indignation – with him. So desperate was Georgie for him to be a success at something that she would have phoned Wild up on the spot and offered his services. And Orlando wasn't risking that, not for anything. He could think of few things he would enjoy doing less than prancing up and down on a catwalk, although he knew his mother would enjoy few things more. 'My son the supermodel . . .' He could hear her twittering about it now. The fact that she was proud of his newly handsome looks was, so far as Orlando was concerned, one of the few things that could be said in their favour.

As well as in his own. As Orlando reached his late teens, the fact that he was less and less the child his mother had hoped for was becoming more and more obvious. Of course, he loved her

– as he did his father – very much, and he knew that she loved him. But he also knew that she found him annoying. As she saw it, Orlando knew, he resolutely refused to make the most – or indeed, anything – of the opportunities she lavished on him. While Orlando, although he tried to feel grateful, was increasingly, bleakly aware that he had not wanted these opportunities in the first place.

His expensive private school, for which his parents had scrimped and saved, was the most glaring illustration of this. It maddened Georgie that the only determination Orlando had shown with regard to Heneage's was in relentlessly *not* trying to become friends with the sons and daughters of what his mother called 'the movers and shakers'.

'You never get asked to anyone's house for the weekend,' Georgie had wailed at one particularly frustrated moment.

Orlando felt a spasm of guilt. In fact, he often got asked these days, but he was careful to make sure his mother did not know he had refused. The frantic, competitive social fray revolving around whose smart house everyone else was staying at in the holidays, or which festival in the grounds of whose grandparents' castle everyone was heading to with their tents and Temperley party dresses, filled him with horror. However much he wanted to please his mother, he had felt utterly incapable of joining in.

He was even less outstanding in class. Orlando had never been academically gifted and was further hampered in success of this nature by what had been diagnosed as borderline dyslexia and more than borderline lack of interest in either the subjects or his teachers. So far as the latter were concerned, the lack of interest was mutual. Despite the staggering fees that his parents paid to make sure the most was being got out of him, most teachers wrote him off immediately and told Georgie and Richard that he simply was not trying.

These teachers seemed, Orlando had noticed, to make more effort with the equally unmotivated children of richer and more famous parents, but he had never mentioned this to his mother and father. It had suited him to be left more or less to his own devices at school.

Now, however, Orlando heartily wished he had made more effort. He had taken his A levels at the start of the summer and the results were due in the middle of August. They would be terrible, Orlando knew, and while he was unmoved on his own account, he cringed at the prospect of Georgie's disappointment. Her grief would be Shakespearean; or what he had gathered was Shakespearean from his scant exposure to the Bard.

It was largely to stave off thoughts of this future misery that Orlando currently spent as much time as was possible in his bedroom watching chubby twelve year olds throw pies at each other.

Downstairs, Orlando's father, Richard, had taken advantage of his wife's ascent to their son's bedroom in order to sneak into the kitchen to make a cup of tea. Georgie was in a more fractious mood than usual this morning and he felt it best to keep out of her way until it had passed.

He switched on the kettle and opened one of the cupboards, wondering if there were any biscuits. It was a remote possibility; Georgie was obsessive about her figure, and cheap sugary things of the type one might dunk into tea were rarely to be found in her immaculate cupboards. There was, Richard knew, a fair chance that Orlando might have a Mars bar or suchlike secreted amidst the mess in his bedroom. His son was never averse to sharing whatever sweets he had; a situation that had almost reached the status of conspiracy between the two men. But Georgie was up there.

Richard's thoughts returned to the matter he had just been

dealing with in his small cubbyhole of an office under the stairs. One of his constituents, a single mother with a violent and abusive former partner, had asked him for help and he was busily rounding up the various agencies and associations who could provide it.

As he waited for the kettle to boil, Richard's glassy, preoccupied stare fell on a paper print-out bearing a colour picture, which lay on the butcher's block. He shuffled over to pick it up, forgetting, as ever, about all Georgie's heavy copper-bottomed pans dangling from hooks along the sides of the block. One fell off and plunged to the tiled floor of the kitchen with a deafening crash.

Richard jumped at the shattering noise. He stared in confusion at his wife, who came in at that moment.

'Clumsy!' snapped Georgie. She looked intensely annoyed. Obviously whatever she had gone up to talk to Orlando about had not been a success. Flitting through Richard's thoughts came concern about his wife's jeans; slightly too tight, surely, for someone in their late forties. But Georgie prided herself on both her contemporary fashion sense and the slender figure she achieved and retained by virtue of many hours at the rowing machine installed in the bathroom. She was probably well up to Boat Race speed by now and had probably put in the strokes to have crossed the Atlantic countless times into the bargain, Richard would think from the bedroom as he heard the contraption next door creaking and slamming under Georgie's gasping exertions. It always made him feel uneasy for some reason.

Georgie herself often made him feel uneasy. While he loved her devotedly – she was his childhood sweetheart and wife of nearly thirty years – she had never been happy with his backbench status. However, reminding her of the reasons he had entered Parliament – to represent the interests of ordinary people and to try and improve their lives – usually fell on ground even harder than the kitchen floor she was clacking across at the moment in her high-heeled purple sandals.

Georgie had always nursed ambitions for him beyond anything he had wanted, but he had remained a backbencher and would, Richard suspected, continue to remain a back-bencher well into his senior moments. He had long since resigned himself to that fact, but he was aware that Georgie hadn't.

'Wonderful, isn't it?' Richard heard his wife suddenly ask him. Relieved at her friendlier tone, he realised she was talking about the piece of paper he still held in his hand, and at which he had not yet looked. He blinked at the picture, which was of a long, low house in golden stone with a red roof. It had a patio with big white sunshades on it and was surrounded by cypresses. There was a blue sky and a swimming pool in the foreground. Yes, it looked very nice, Richard thought. But what did it have to do with him?

Something, evidently. Georgie was looking at him with a rigid, expectant grin. He looked blankly back at her. 'What is it?' he asked, thereby admitting defeat.

'A farmhouse in Tuscany!' Georgie trilled. 'I've booked it. For the summer.'

'Booked it?' Richard repeated, looking back at the picture in horror. This place looked expensive.

Georgie's expression was defiant and defensive. 'I had to act fast. We haven't got anywhere else lined up. *Have* we?'

She spoke with a particular emphasis. The print-out being waved at him, Richard now understood, was a veiled criticism of their son, Orlando, who had failed to secure them a summer holiday in one of the villas or yachts owned by the wealthy parents of his friends from the school to which they had sent him at such great expense. It was also, Richard sensed, a veiled criticism of himself.

For all his twenty years as a Conservative Member of Parliament, he had failed just as spectacularly as his son to bond with anyone who might have a suitable holiday home. Not that he had tried; like Orlando, Richard had a built-in aversion to the types of people who swaggered about bragging about their wealth and influence. The fellow MPs Richard liked best were just like him: hardworking backbenchers struggling to maintain a place in London, as well as a constituency one.

Some MPs, of course, lived in their constituency and used cheap hotels when staying in London. Others used expensive hotels wherever they happened to be, as well as maintaining lavish London and constituency homes and several members of their family at the taxpayers' expense. But Richard's was not a hand-in-the-till temperament, and anyway, Georgie refused to live in the constituency, an unremarkable swathe of Hertfordshire. Which was why Richard was now struggling to maintain a large if battered Highgate terrace, plus a small constituency flat.

Richard had already, somewhat hesitantly, suggested to Georgie that they holiday in the Hertfordshire flat – it had been some time, after all, since those he represented had seen his wife – but she had laughed uproariously, even though the suggestion had been entirely serious. It might be on the High Street, and above a Chinese takeaway, but at least it was free.

Chapter 8

'Am I speaking with Mitch Masterson?'

'Yeah,' Mitch drawled, not bothering to conceal the fact that, contrary to his doctor's instructions concerning his increasing weight, he was chewing on a jelly doughnut as he spoke. A second jelly doughnut, as well. And he had just had lunch into the bargain.

But there seemed no reason to make any special effort. It was a hot Hollywood afternoon and the sun was shining strongly through the Venetian blinds of Mitch's office, highlighting mercilessly the mess on his desk and the dust on his computer screen. And this girl on the other end was yet another no-hoper, you could tell by her voice. Distant, formal, frosty. Christ only knew why the Talent Incorporated receptionist had put her through. Feeling heavy, sleepy and bored, Mitch flicked at some crumbs of greasy sugar and reached for his cardboard cup of coffee.

'I have Arlington Shorthouse on the line for you,' the female voice said.

Her words electrified Mitch. His hand jerked in shock and the coffee he was about to swig to wash down the last of his doughnut now landed on the front of his shirt. His eyes watered and he wanted to scream as the scalding liquid made contact with his nipples.

As well as the continuing pain, Mitch tried to master his panic. There was no reason for it. There were many reasons why NBS Studios, of which Arlington was head, could be calling him. At least fifty reasons: Mitch had upward of fifty clients, and they were all actors. But it was the fact that Arlington himself was calling that rang alarm bells.

Arlington, even though he was a well-known workaholic, and famously hands-on, only called agents directly for two reasons. One was because he wanted to launch a career. The other was because he wanted to end one. Remembering this, Mitch, for whom thoughts of Belle Murphy were never far away, had a sudden, sickening, guilty feeling that was nothing to do with jelly doughnuts.

'Good afternoon, Mr Shorthouse,' he said meekly, as if his own good behaviour could somehow mitigate for his client and earn her a reprieve. And yet it wasn't a surprise that the end had come.

Since being dumped by Christian Harlow, Belle had hit the ground running – literally and more than once after oblivion-seeking, champagne-fuelled benders in nightclubs that had been mercilessly covered by the press.

Day after day Mitch had opened the tabloids to find, to his despair, lurid photographs of his former star client struggling, blind drunk, in and out of limos in wisps of dresses with a glaring absence of underwear. She was, Mitch feared, about to be arrested at any minute. Yet his increasingly desperate attempts to prevent further such infringements of public decency met only with Belle's protestations of injured innocence, saying she couldn't remember doing any of the things he accused her of and that the person in the paper must be a body double.

While her inability to remember, given the amounts of alcohol involved, was all too believable, it wasn't, Mitch knew, a defence likely to impress the only person, apart from the state attorney, who mattered. This was the teetotal and puritanical head of her studio, who felt his stars should be paragons of American virtue at all times. Arlington Shorthouse, the man who was ringing now. Doubtless to knock Belle's career on the head.

Arlington's next words, however, knocked Mitch as flat as Mitch could be knocked, given that he was sitting up at his desk. 'We're making the *Galaxia* movie,' the studio head announced in the quiet, ominous voice that could, Mitch imagined, freeze vodka solid. 'We start shooting in the summer.'

Mitch blinked. Had he heard right? The series had got the green light after all? That was *sensational* news. Of course, many studios had tried and failed with space sagas since George Lucas had brought out *Star Wars*. But NBS's track record meant it had a very good chance – perhaps the best chance – of pulling it off. Mitch knew already that this would be massive.

Seized by excitement, he pushed his office chair – which was on wheels – back in a turbo-thrust. The movement was so abrupt that he went flying across the carpet and crashed loudly into the wall behind, which was cardboard thin and shook violently. The occupant of the next-door office, an ambitious young agent clearly determined to be CEO of Talent Incorporated in the next six months, if not sooner, poked his head through the door.

'Everything OK in here?' asked Greg Cucarachi, clearly hoping that it was not.

Mitch glared at him; this smooth, slim, handsome young man whose bulging eyes rolled everywhere and noticed everything. His reply to Arlington died on his lips. The news that *Galaxia* was going to be made would be round the agency in seconds. Long before he, Mitch, had any chance to disseminate the tidings in person. Knowledge was power and at the moment it was his knowledge.

'That's great news,' he said guardedly to Arlington as his next-door neighbour shrugged and left.

'Yes,' Arlington replied with his trademark caustic brevity.

Mitch's brain was moving fast. The film was a prospect almost as dazzling as the sunshine. He immediately resolved to do his utmost to get Belle a part. It was the least he could do, but more than the least he had done about *Bloody Mary*, which was nothing at all.

It occurred to Mitch now to wonder why Arlington was calling to tell him about the new film. The studio head, for all his well-known eccentricities, had not hitherto been in the habit of confiding in him. Indeed, it had always seemed to Mitch that Arlington disliked him – although admittedly he appeared to hate everyone. That Arlington wished to rescue Belle's career, especially after the recent headlines, seemed unlikely. But the news about the film was clearly connected to one of his actors, and Belle, for all her troubles, was the best-known actor on his books. Arlington could hardly be ringing about anyone else.

'You've got someone I want to offer one of the two main roles to,' Arlington confirmed now, in his cold, distant tones.

A main role? Holy crap. In the darkness below his striped shirt, beneath his flabby upper arms, Mitch felt a nuclear glow of moisture. Sweat gathered on his forehead. His heart rate rose still higher. The hope that it was Belle now bloomed into a certainty. Arlington was apparently quite religious; had he decided to view her exploits in the spirit of Christian mercy?

Mitch's mind zoomed joyfully away, into the golden distance where not only Belle's career was saved, but his own was too.

She'd be back at the top, the biggest movie actress of the day, probably even the best paid, which was the bit that interested Mitch, and which would interest the Talent Incorporated CEO when it came to doling out the promotions.

And not before time. Mitch had been passed over not once but many times too often recently, and there were other unpleasant reminders of the extent to which his status had slipped within the company. Talent Incorporated's thrusting, younger agents, who felt they were too important to handle anything other than superstars, were increasingly palming off their smaller or older clients on him. Thanks to people like Greg Cucarachi, who was one of the palmers-off in chief, Mitch's list was currently thick with duds, small-timers, old-timers and also-rans, and he had heard that some of the other agents sneeringly referred to him as 'the graveyard'.

The graveyard! Ha! He'd show them. With one of his clients a star in the new *Galaxia* film!

'Who is it?' Mitch asked, his voice smiling.

'Darcy Prince,' replied Arlington Shorthouse.

Mitch's mind instantly dissolved into a fog. He felt he was standing over a bath and watching the pictures that had formed of Belle and himself on the red-carpeted entrance to the Kodak Theatre, the Oscar-night paparazzi going crazy, disappearing down the plughole.

'Darcy Prince,' he repeated, with a calmness he did not feel. *Darcy Prince?* Who the hell was *that*?

Mitch groped about in the mist in his mind, panicking that Arlington had rung the wrong agency, that someone else was going to get this big chance, and wondering about the chances of finding this Darcy Prince and taking them on anyway, all in the next few seconds.

Then, with a great rush of relief, he realised that he did, in fact, represent Darcy Prince. He remembered the name vaguely; it had been one of the latest sheaf of hopeless cases dumped on him by Greg Cucarachi only the other day. Mitch had filed the slim sheet of details away without even reading them, never expecting he would ever have to. Now, with the receiver containing Arlington tucked unsteadily under his flabby, stubbly chin, Mitch shot again in his chair over to his filing cabinet, trying to open it silently and fish out the details with trembling, sweating hands.

'Darcy Prince!' he said in musing tones, whilst frantically shoving his stubby hands into overstuffed folders that cut his fingers. Is it a man or a woman? he wondered.

'Yes. I was in London and I caught Darcy in a play there,' Arlington remarked. 'What was it called?' he mused.

'Er . . .' gasped Mitch, screwing up his eyes as he tried to remember what was currently going down in the British capital. *Mamma Mia* was all that came to mind. Was that a play, strictly speaking? And if it was, was Darcy Prince in it? He should know, of course; have the information at his fingertips, being her agent.

'*A Doll's House*. That was it,' Arlington said, his thin voice faintly warmed with self-congratulation. 'She was impressive.'

A Doll's House? Was that some kind of Bratz musical, Mitch wondered. But at least he was now straight on one thing. She! She! Darcy was a woman. He had secured the crucial information on gender.

And now, miraculously, he had also found Darcy's details. He scanned them eagerly.

Name: Darcy Alethea Desdemona Prince
Nationality: English
Address: 43 Montague Mansions, Queen's Gate, London SW7
Age: 24

Education: St Paul's Girls' School, London; Girton College, Cambridge (BA Hons – first class – English); Royal Academy of Dramatic Art (RADA)

He could see why Greg had dumped her on him. There was nothing remotely Hollywood about this woman. She had never even made a film. No doubt whatever two-bit London agency represented her – it obviously wasn't a big one – had one of those deals with Talent Incorporated in which they paid the American agency to handle their clients' LA interests. 'Drawer deals', as they were known, because the dark inside of a filing cabinet into which they were immediately shoved, never to be extracted, was usually all these British clients saw of the famous bright lights of Hollywood. And at Talent Incorporated, most of these unfortunates were shoved in filing cabinets in Mitch's office.

Acting career: Ophelia in *Hamlet*, Cambridge Shakespeare Company, 2006; Viola in *Twelfth Night*, RSC, 2007; Nora in *A Doll's House*, Orange Tree Theatre, Richmond, 2008; Cordelia in *King Lear*, CSC, 2008.

Mitch blinked. This was all way off the usual Hollywood acting résumé. Most of the women he handled didn't mention either their education or early experience, not without good reason. He wondered what Darcy looked like. There was no photo attached to the résumé. She could be fat, thin, anything.

Fortunately, Arlington rode to his rescue. 'She's gonna be the next Keira Knightley,' he asserted.

Mitch felt his excitement peak. Keira Knightley. So Darcy looked like her? Wow. Keira Knightley was one hot babe. Thin, and maybe a bit flat chested. But definitely hot.

'I want her to play Princess Anatoo,' Arlington was saying in his cold voice. 'She's the young Grand Duchess of the Galaxy who must enlist the help of her dead father's supporters, the Kinkos, to overcome the evil that threatens her and her realm, the Kingdom of Anoo.' The synopsis, Mitch thought, sounded if anything even more improbable when delivered in Arlington's distant and austere tones. Not that he let this put him off. He would be a fool to.

'Darcy's your woman,' Mitch said confidently. 'If ever anyone has Grand Duchess potential, it is her.'

'Yeah, well, it's not cut and dried yet,' Arlington snapped. 'I think she'll be great, but she needs to meet with the director.'

'Oh, sure,' said Mitch warmly. This of course would be a technicality. If Arlington wanted the film to go ahead with Darcy in it, then go ahead with Darcy in it the film duly would. The director was hardly likely to make a difference. 'Who is the director?' he asked, as if it mattered.

'Jack Saint,' said Arlington.

'I thought he'd retired,' Mitch said, his spirits slumping slightly. It had been a loss to the studios, no doubt, when the celebrated Saint had bowed out last year with an unparalleled string of successes behind him. The agenting industry, however, had breathed a sigh of relief. Saint had been an extremely difficult person for their clients to work for. He had wanted them to act, for a start. He had begun each day's shoot with an improvisation session that had proved almost more than the average Talent Incorporated client could bear.

'He had,' Arlington returned. 'But I persuaded him out of it with enough money and the chance to out-Lucas George Lucas. He's always been pretty competitive with him.'

Mitch absorbed this dejectedly. This vehicle, this film, was his best chance of the past ten years. Probably ever. So why did its director have to be the reclusive, autocratic and all-controlling Saint? A man every studio head bowed to – even Arlington. Meaning, Mitch recognised, that Arlington's choice of Darcy would be only a recommendation to the director and the final decision really would be Saint's. Meaning, too, that this probably was not the time to bring Belle Murphy into it.

'Can you get her over here for next week?'

'Sure I can.' Mitch's confidence shot back. What choice did he have? He absolutely could, even if he had to go over there, to – he glanced at the résumé – 43 Montague Mansions, Queen's Gate, London SW7, and drag Darcy back by the scruff of the neck. Which of course, he would not have to. No one in their right mind was going to turn down a chance like this.

Chapter 9

It was, as always, gone midnight before Darcy Prince, her pale face scrubbed of make-up, her black hair drawn back into a roughly brushed ponytail, emerged from the stage door of the theatre. She felt, again as always, drained after yet another performance of *King Lear*, in which she played the troubled monarch's fatally honest and tragic youngest daughter, Cordelia.

The part was exhausting enough, but equally harrowing was the proximity, for more than three hours, of the naked septuagenarian actor playing Lear, giving it his all in every sense.

Fortunately, his playing Lear semi-naked was interpreted by both critics and audience as a metaphor for the exposed and vulnerable predicament of Shakespeare's tragic king, rather than the blatant exhibitionism Darcy suspected it really was. And of course this publicity was helpful; the production was by one of London's least famous, most experimental directors and in one of the city's smallest and least well-known theatres. Basically, it needed all the help it could get. Still, everyone in the play was passionate about their work, passionate about Shakespeare and the theatre, and this was all that mattered to Darcy.

As she wandered through the narrow back streets on her way

to Oxford Street and the night bus stop, Darcy's exhaustion increased. The experimental director had, only this afternoon, devised an additional experimental introductory scene in which all the actors had to swing from tightropes and jump over vaulting horses for reasons Darcy could not now quite remember, but which seemed to have made sense at the time.

She emerged from the dark, narrow, winding canyons of Soho, with their dustbins and extractor fans, into the bright thoroughfare of Oxford Street, where, despite the time, the shopfronts continued to blaze as though it was the middle of the day. Perhaps some megastar was in there having a private shopping session, Darcy thought. Flitting through her mind came the half-idea that that might be her one day, a film star, rich and famous beyond her wildest dreams, so mobbed by fans that shopping at night, with the whole store closed for her convenience, was the only way she could buy anything. But just as quickly came the scornful certainty that that was the last thing she wanted. She was serious about her acting. She was from generations of theatrical royalty and she was only prepared to do the good stuff. The serious stuff. The stuff which meant something. Which meant the theatre.

Leaning against the bus stop, watching taxi after taxi go by, all enticingly lit up in front with that glowing yellow rectangle, Darcy wondered whether she was being slightly hard on herself. With the allowance from her grandmother she could easily have afforded to take one of them. She dismissed this as a weak moment. Struggling actresses couldn't afford taxis across town at night-time rates and she was determined to live within the means of her earnings – the absolute Equity minimum – not what inherited money made possible.

She was equally determined to make her own success, not trade on the name of her family. Her paternal grandfather,

Sacheverell Prince, had been *the* Hamlet of his day, despite looking, in all the pictures Darcy had even seen of him acting, an irascible middle-aged man with a moustache. A far cry, she had always thought, from the volatile and indecisive teenage boy of Shakespeare's play.

Her own mother and father were among the most celebrated classical actors of their generation and extremely politically committed. As a child, Darcy was taken to far more demonstrations than she ever was birthday parties, and once suffered terrible fright at the sight of her father in handcuffs; by his own volition, it was quickly explained to her, and attached to the railings of a bank that had interests in the then-ostracised South Africa. At home, the kitchen seemed permanently full of people with impassioned eyes thumping the big wooden table, and throughout her childhood Darcy had rarely come home from school without wondering what ANC activist or Soviet defector would require her to give up her bedroom this time. Although some, admittedly, had seemed to prefer that she remained in it; an even less inviting prospect.

Darcy had detected from an early age the fact that neither her mother, Angharad, nor her father, Caractacus, held her grandmother in particularly high esteem. Anna de Blank, Angharad's mother, had been a very successful light film actress of the forties and fifties, starring in Ealing comedies and Disney films. It was she who had made the family fortune, although no one, it seemed to Darcy, was terribly grateful. Personally, she and the chain-smoking, purple-haired old lady who drank at least half a bottle of champagne a day had always got on tremendously well, although performing her grandmother's old song-and-dance routines at home was, Darcy had quickly discovered, frowned on. Theatre at Granny's may be fun and frivolous but at home it was terribly serious and important. Both her parents had impressed upon her the fact that they were political artists, and that she should be too. 'The theatre is the only thing,' Angharad would declare in her trademark dramatic husky voice, and Darcy would agree – as indeed she believed – that it was.

But there were times – such as now – when the weight of ancestral expectation pressed heavy on Darcy's slim shoulders. Playing Cordelia had meant seventy-hour weeks during the rehearsals, of which she had never missed one, and now that the show had started she worked six nights a week plus matinées on Friday and Saturday.

The night bus came and Darcy got on it, scanning her Oystercard beside the somnolent-seeming driver, and climbing up to the top deck with its red rails and purple seats eye-achingly bright under the lights. Before sitting down she checked, as she always did, that no one from the theatre had got on at an earlier stop and was up there already. But tonight, as usual, no one had. They tended not to go in her direction, towards Knightsbridge and Chelsea, but headed east and south.

Whenever her fellow actors asked her where she lived Darcy always said West London, as if it was Shepherd's Bush or Hammersmith, and not, as it actually was, a penthouse in Queen's Gate, a mere smoked-salmon-sandwich's toss from the gates of Hyde Park, and with a fine view of Kensington Palace and the Round Pond from the roof garden. Turn around, and you could almost shake the hands of the classic-figure reliefs circling the great dome of the Albert Hall.

Darcy got off the stop opposite the white mansions of Kensington Gore; the only one on the bus to do so. It had started raining and now taxis sped past, their tyres whooshing in the wet, their yellow For Hire signs glowing over their windscreens, their shiny black bodies streaked with the red and white and yellow lights of the night-time city. Perhaps she should have got one home, Darcy thought as she bent against the wet and felt it soaking into her uncovered hair; it would have been easier and quicker and drier.

She went up the stairs under the stout portico, one of whose thick white pillars had the house number painted on in black. Despite the traditional appearance of the entrance, you got in by using the electronic keypad beside the front door, or at least you did if you were Darcy and the occupiers of the two luxury flats below the penthouse. If you were Florrie, the nightclubbing German princess on the first floor, you forgot it almost every time and, irrespective of the invariably late hour, simply hammered on the door and shouted until someone – usually the long-suffering Brazilian plastic surgeon on the ground floor – got up and let you in.

Darcy punched the correct code into the keypad beside the great, black-painted front door, with its thick glass windows and enormous brass handle, and with a sigh of relief despite herself, entered the warm, deep-carpeted haven of luxury.

The palatial entrance hall boasted a suspended lantern of gold and bevelled glass, which shone brilliantly against the white walls. A sweeping, red-carpeted staircase with mahogany banisters rose up the entire six floors of the building, but Darcy took the old-fashioned cage-style lift at this time of night. Pressing the lift button and hearing the doors clang shut somewhere above, she allowed herself to luxuriate in the cosseting feeling of home.

But what made this impressive place home to her, what gave it its value, was not the fact that it was in a neighbourhood that was home to the greatest concentration of wealth anywhere in the world. It had nothing to do with the fact that flats here, flats like hers, were aggressively, even desperately sought after by the richest people on the planet. To Darcy, the apartment had for years simply meant her beloved grandmother. Anna de Blank had lived to the age of a hundred and five, and left the flat to her favourite – and for that matter only – granddaughter upon her death two years ago. Darcy missed her still.

The lift lurched to a halt, bounced up and down a couple of times and Darcy stepped out whilst trying not to trap her fingers in the cage. The door to the penthouse apartment was directly across the corridor.

Darcy let herself in. Automatically she glanced at the answerphone on the small Florentine table by the door. The green light winked steadily back. No one had called during the evening.

All was quiet and still and glowing, with lamps whose pink shades were fitted with pink bulbs. Anna had been a reluctantly ageing beauty who believed rosy light was the most flattering for the face.

Darcy smiled, as she always did, at the enormous portrait of her grandmother in the entrance hall, resplendent in lemon-yellow chiffon, smiling faintly and beautifully, and holding a plate of her favourite indulgences: macaroons.

From her earliest childhood, macaroons and her grandmother had been associated in Darcy's mind. There had always been a white card box of them in the refrigerator; be-ribboned and stamped with the address of a smart baker in flowing gold letters. Darcy had been entranced with the colours of these strange, exotic confections, half cake and half biscuit, that came in exquisite, old-fashioned colours.

But Anna, even as she sank her small white teeth into them and rolled her eyes in delight, would exclaim that even these, baked as they were by the best confectioners in London, were not to be compared with those she had tasted in France. 'But you know, my darling,' she would say, 'they are the hardest thing in the world to get exactly right, and no one makes them like they do in Paris.' Anna had travelled widely as an actress, and her stories of the great European cities, Paris and Rome especially, as they had been in the 1950s entranced her granddaughter, but not as much as the macaroons did, with their intense sweetness and intoxicating lightness. She could not imagine anyone making a better job of them.

She loved the fact that her grandmother had taken her passion for macaroons as the guiding inspiration for her apartment's decorative scheme. Each room was painted in a different pastel colour: lemon in the study, pink in the master bedroom, pistachio green in the dining room, lilac in the sitting room and pale orange in the hall. It was one of the gentle, whimsical and slightly camp jokes that Darcy felt were entirely typical of her grandmother.

Darcy had kept the décor exactly as Anna had left it. It was as ornate and feminine as she remembered it from her childhood, all florals, silks and delicate furniture with oval backs and slender gold legs. Small round tables still held Anna's collection of bibelots and small antiques. In the master bedroom, muslin and toile de Jouy curtains still swept up into a crowned half-tester above the big white flounced bed Darcy remembered bouncing on; on the white oval-mirrored dressing table, the rosy light made small decorative boxes and silver-backed brushes glitter just as Darcy, as a child, remembered them glittering.

There was still a big, old-fashioned roll-top bath in the ornate bathroom, which was entered through a pair of white double doors picked out in gilt. Here the bather could lie back and contemplate under a pink Murano glass chandelier, although, these days, without the glass of champagne that Anna had always enjoyed whilst abluting and to which she unhesitatingly attributed her longevity. Darcy felt her own life was quite indulgent enough and Niall, who scorned self-indulgence and any form of pretension, would have been dead against it too.

Darcy felt the whole place remained so redolent of her grandmother it was almost as if the old lady, with her impish smile, twinkling eyes and immaculate purple hair, might come tripping daintily in at any moment. But she was aware that Niall, who had never known Anna, felt rather differently about it. 'Camper than a Boy Scout jamboree' was how he had put it in his no-nonsense Scottish way.

When he had moved in, some months ago, Niall had not only suggested giving the entire place a coat of white paint, but had offered to do it. He had, he pointed out, trained as a builder, still had a part-time job on a construction site and therefore possessed all the requisite skills. But Darcy had been appalled at the idea. She had been yet more horrified at Niall's next suggestion that they sell the penthouse and move to more fashionably edgy Shoreditch. Accepting defeat, Niall had laughed good-naturedly, shrugged his broad shoulders and never mentioned it again.

There were mirrors all over the apartment, all large with ornate frames, mostly of carved and twisted gold. The exception was a vast and decadent Venetian mirror, age-spotted and splendid, and mounted opposite the portrait of Anna in the hall. In death as in life, she spent a lot of time looking at her own reflection, her granddaughter would think, amused.

'Bit of a narcissist, was she?' Niall had grinned, but Darcy had replied, trying not to sound too defensive, that no, she hadn't been really. A less self-obsessed woman than Anna had never lived. She was intensely interested in everyone and everything, including looking her best at all times. Being well presented was, Anna had taught Darcy, a way of showing politeness to others.

As she passed the mirror now, in the early hours of the morning, Darcy paused and wondered what her grandmother would think if she could see her. Her wide face was pale with exhaustion. Two large dark eyes with purple shadows, their full-lashed lids dipping downwards, squinted tiredly back from beneath thick, straight brows.

The full, raspberry mouth was drawn downwards with tiredness and her head lolled unsteadily on her slender neck. A few tendrils of long dark hair had escaped from the bunch into which she had hastily shoved it before leaving the theatre and snaked lankly over her shoulders. It needed a wash, Darcy realised. But not now. The only thing now was bed.

Darcy tiptoed through the sitting room. The lamps cast soft pink shadows on the lilac walls; Niall had left them on. The slither of newspapers on the lilac, cushion-scattered sofa and the various remotes for the television over the thick carpet, also lilac, gave the impression that her boyfriend had only just gone to bed. Rather regretting the fact he hadn't waited up for her, Darcy bent forward to inspect the papers on the sofa. As she had suspected, one was a book: a small, paperback copy of *Hamlet* left upside down with the famous 'To be or not to be' pressing against the petit point cushions. There was an empty tumbler on its side on the carpet. She picked it up and sniffed it: whisky.

But no doubt he needed it. Niall had an important audition tomorrow, for *Hamlet* at the National Theatre. He had been studying the part for weeks, as well as videos (Anna's old TV lacked a DVD setting) of classic performances of the role. Video boxes, their contents spilt, were piled before the television. Niall admired John Gielgud's the most, Darcy knew, and had not spared her with his opinion that he thought Sacheverell Prince's the worst. Darcy had not minded, however. Niall's unflinching honesty was one of the things she loved about him most.

She hoped desperately that everything would go well for the audition tomorrow. While Niall had been delighted for her to land the Cordelia role, had rehearsed her lines with her and been endlessly encouraging, she knew he felt keenly the fact that he had not yet landed a major role. If he got Hamlet, his career would be made, or, at the very least, off to a flying start. Niall, she knew, felt the pressure to succeed, as indeed did she, although his was a different kind of pressure from hers. Possibly because his was a completely different background.

Darcy, who sometimes felt that everything had been bought for her, from her privileged education to her career opportunities, deeply admired the fact that Niall was working-class Scottish and had created all his own opportunities. She loved and slightly feared the fact he had grown up on a council estate in Glasgow.

She found both admirable and intimidating that Niall had worked as a builder for several years before putting himself through drama school and therefore, despite being the same age as she, had had a real – not to say a hard – life before entering the rarified world of acting. Not like her, who had spent her early twenties in the cloistered and privileged surroundings of one of the world's most prestigious universities. Niall had an authenticity she secretly felt she lacked herself and was dimly aware that she was searching for through her work.

'She loved me for the dangers I had passed. And I loved her that she did pity them,' Niall would grin, quoting Othello's words about Desdemona. They had especially bonded over the importance of Shakespeare. He venerated her parents as great actors, and they in turn had been excited and enchanted by his council-estate provenance. 'A butcher!' Angharad had breathed in delight when he had told her about his father's business. 'A cleaner!' she had murmured ecstatically, when the subject of his mother came up. And she had positively purred when he had finished telling her how he had walked round Muswell Hill all night, unable to speak, after seeing her performance on DVD as Nora in a celebrated seventies production of *A Doll's House* transposed to an S&M Amsterdam brothel. 'It said everything about the condition of women,' he had told Angharad hotly, and she had pushed back her still beautiful but greying wild black hair from her still exquisite high-cheekboned face, and gazed at Niall with dark-eyed rapture.

Darcy now tiptoed into the bedroom where Niall lay sleeping. She smiled at how incongruously rugged and masculine he looked in Anna's enormous, rather princessy bed. Then the smile faded to something nearer to straightforward adoration. Niall looked so beautiful like this, his red hair rippling over the pillow, his handsome, fair-skinned face calm and noble, like a classical head in pure white marble.

Absorbedly, Darcy stretched out a hand over the thick, dark-red curls that, when he was standing, flowed almost to Niall's shoulders and lightly touched the reddish-brown brow, traced the jutting nose with its rounded end, brushed the red-gold stubble on the determined cleft chin. She half wanted him to wake, to open the big, pale blue eyes that she had, when they had first met, laughingly told him were the colour of boxes from Tiffany's. 'Are they?' he had replied in his Glaswegian growl. 'I wouldn't know.'

But Niall slept on, his left arm bent under his head, his hand only just visible beneath the hair. Darcy smiled as she saw the scrolled silver tops of the Celtic rings he wore on every finger of this hand like a Caledonian knuckleduster. The white-blond lashes, each one tipped with a fleck of brownish red, remained pressed against his white and freckled cheek. Even when she skimmed the flat of her hand over his pale, broad chest with its red-gold hair, he did not wake. Noticing the shiny purple hollows just south of his closed eyelids, she decided to leave him alone. Working on the building site was, she knew, exhausting and he had had *Hamlet* to learn on top of it.

He was sleeping in a particularly horrid and ancient T-shirt, she noticed indulgently; a dirty white one with a St Andrew's flag on it that she had nagged him many times to get rid of. But she loved the fact Niall utterly lacked vanity. Unlike some men she had known – and certainly unlike some of her current co-stars – he never blow-dried his hair, used fake tan or visited a salon for any reason other than to meet her there.

He had not the faintest idea what his T-zone was. He possessed neither tweezers nor eyebrow gel, and was the sort of man who could go an entire lifetime without ever stepping into Prada. He was real, Darcy thought with a wave of joy, wonderfully real, down to earth and humorous, and utterly lacking both the titanic ego and bottomless insecurity of most actors.

And he was a wonderful actor too, Darcy reminded herself, as serious about the profession as she was. More so, if anything. He was just taking some time to break through, that was all; his Scottish looks, coupled with the fact he actually was Scottish, meant that TV drama offers of Scottish policemen, Scottish drug-dealers, Scottish pimps, Scottish alcoholics, Scottish wife-beaters and, on one occasion, a Scottish corpse regularly came his way. But these were hardly the parts he was looking for and he was determined not to be pigeonholed. Or 'Macpigeon-holed', as he put it.

It was then that, in a corner of the bedroom, Anna's little white and gold telephone suddenly shrilled.

Darcy, yanked from her contemplation of Niall, glanced at the ornate carriage clock on the bedroom mantelpiece. Half-past one in the morning. Who on earth could this be?

Was it her mother? Her father? Panic seized Darcy's throat as she answered.

'We haven't spoken,' came the booming voice of Mitch Masterson, 'but I'm the agent representing you in Hollywood and I'm calling with some very good news.'

Darcy felt an uncharacteristic wave of annoyance. It was late and she was tired. If this was someone's idea of a joke it was not very funny. She had not even realised she was represented in Hollywood. Her London agents, a pair of exuberant, eccentric and much-powdered old ladies who had been her parents' and, towards the end of Anna's career, her grandmother's agents before that, seemed to have enough problems representing her in London. Darcy had stuck with them out of a sense of loyalty and history, but she had been sent to the wrong auditions too many times recently – the latest to be a singing grape in a wine commercial when she had expected to be testing for Miranda in *The Tempest*. The infuriating thing was that the woman who had been intended for the grape had landed the Miranda part and was now playing to great acclaim in Stratford.

'What good news?' Darcy said suspiciously, her voice low so as not to wake Niall.

At the LA end of the phone Mitch Masterson, the receiver under his chin, rubbed his hands gleefully and prepared to tell her.

Chapter 10

Mitch would never have believed it. Darcy Prince had actually turned the part down. He had almost choked on his jelly doughnut and had knocked his coffee all over his trousers. The scalding liquid soaked into his thighs, but he hardly noticed the pain this time.

'What do you mean, you're not sure you're interested?' he exploded, after listening to her speak in her rather high, prim, very English voice. 'It's one of the leading parts, for Chrissakes.'

It was late afternoon in LA and the Californian sun was beyond its zenith. But Mitch, squirming in coffee-stained horror in his leather-look office chair, was in a muck sweat. He'd expected almost any type of reaction from this unknown British actress. Screams of disbelieving joy. Sobs of passionate delight. Even a thud and a crash as she collapsed in an ecstatic dead faint to the floor. But never, not even in a million years, had he expected an outright refusal.

Not that he had any intention of accepting it. The woman was obviously insane – like most Brits, Mitch thought grimly – and clearly had no idea what she was saying. He was determined not to let her mess this chance up. Hers wasn't the only career on the line, after all. What sort of an agent would it make him look? What would Arlington Shorthouse think? Nor did he want to miss out on what that smug slimeball Greg Cucarachi would think when he realised he'd given Mitch a diamond amid all the dust. A side issue, admittedly, but potentially an extremely satisfying one.

'Do you realise what *Galaxia* is?' Mitch asked Darcy, in gentle tones as if he was talking down a dangerous lunatic bent on leaping off a high roof to her death. Which, in a manner of speaking, he was. If Darcy turned this down, she would be through in Hollywood. And so would he. He was, Mitch recognised, fighting for his professional life here.

'No,' Darcy said.

'It's gonna be the new *Star Wars*,' Mitch said tremendously. Surely if anything was going to make this dame focus, that would.

There was a sigh from the London end. 'Oh, right.'

As he waited for what she would say next, every hair inside Mitch's large, hot ears strained erect.

'I've never seen any of those, I'm afraid,' Darcy added, evidently unmoved.

Mitch's eyes were bulging. Never seen *Star Wars*? Was that possible? This chick was unreal. It wasn't that intellectual snobbery was unknown in Hollywood, of course, but the general rule was that you must make big commercial movies before you were powerful enough to look down on them. For someone completely unknown to sneer at them was outrageous. Mitch, for all his ambivalent feelings towards Tinseltown, wasn't prepared to overlook this lapse of etiquette.

'Hey, baby, they're modern classics,' he said. 'People fight to be in them. No one, but no one, turns the chance down. Don't you want to be famous?' It was a question he had never imagined asking anybody. As he heard it disappear down the line to

London part of him wondered if, in fact, it had ever been asked in Hollywood before.

Darcy had a stubborn streak and being rung at after one o'clock in the morning, by someone she had never met, telling her to fly halfway across the world and test for some kids' space film in which she had absolutely no interest, brought it out. No, she didn't want to be famous, not for some stupid-sounding film, anyway. She just wanted to get this man off the line and get to bed.

'I don't think that sort of movie is my sort of thing. I'm a proper actress,' Darcy stated primly. 'I do proper things. Theatre. Shakespeare. That sort of thing.'

Shakespeare! The blood rushed into Mitch's head so fast and furious he felt as if it might blow off. 'Theatre!' he roared, conclusively abandoning any effort at self-control. 'Shakespeare? Get real, darling. *Galaxia* is going to be massive. It'll make you *huge.*' He paused as he searched his mental dictionary for more words meaning 'huge'. 'Are you kidding?' he gasped, having failed to find any.

'No, I'm not kidding,' Darcy riposted. How *dare* this man say that – and in that tone of voice? What was wrong with wanting to do really good acting? In really proper things? Someone had to hold out. As Niall always said, there was so much rubbish around it was their duty to do only what was really worth doing. And her parents had never failed to impress on her the importance of the family art, and that they owed it to humanity to be serious about it. That they were among the keepers of the thespian flame.

Although, mercifully for him, Mitch had little idea of Darcy's thoughts, he had formed some conclusions of his own. Things could be going better, definitely. It was possible he was taking the wrong tack here.

He took a deep breath and thought as best he could, given that his mind was a hot churning mass of anger, frustration and disbelief. It was like moving a paddle through very thick, hot mud. But finally, in his darkest and most desperate moment, inspiration struck.

'Hey, don't write it off, baby,' he urged Darcy. 'Some of the greatest actors make these films. *Star Wars*, for example. Alec Guinness, you know, he was in it, and he was one of the most famous serious actors ever, right? English too,' Mitch added, striking home what he felt was his advantage.

He was right to feel this. Mention of the great name had made Darcy pause. Part of what had driven her initial refusal was the knowledge that Niall, even more of a purist than she was, would be in equal parts amused and appalled by the *Galaxia* prospect. She had not even wanted to speculate about what her parents would think; for them, she knew, Hollywood symbolised all that was worst and crassest about the American capitalist machine. But the fact that Alec Guinness had appeared in *Star Wars* films was something for both parties to consider.

Mitch sensed the tide had turned. Deftly, he increased the pressure. 'Look, baby, you make this film and you earn enough money to do whatever you like afterwards. It'll make you free. You can do all the Shakespeare there is.'

Another good argument, Darcy recognised. And she was too honest not to admit that, despite herself, she was curious about Hollywood. Who in the acting profession wasn't? Niall, of course, always strenuously denied he was, scornfully and ostentatiously never reading what celebrity magazines strayed into the flat. But to be interested in Hollywood didn't mean you bought the whole lifestyle, that you wanted to be Sharon Stone, Darcy told herself. You could be interested from the anthropological point of view, the human zoo aspect, see the funny side, observe from a distance, all of that.

'If you've ever been interested in seeing Hollywood – just for interest, y'know – this is the best possible way,' Mitch now breathed into her ear. To his own amazement, he seemed to have developed a psychic understanding of what was required. 'You'll breeze in as Tinseltown royalty, make a fortune, see everything and meet everyone and just breeze out again. None of that coming in by Greyhound bus and working in a burger joint for years while trying to land a part in a bitcom,' Mitch added, with what could have been a guilty glance in the direction of his filing cabinets.

'A bitcom?'

'A small sitcom. Kind of unsuccessful. As opposed to a hitcom,' Mitch supplied, helpfully.

She said nothing after this. He sensed that she was thinking. It wasn't a sense he often had. Most actresses he knew didn't think, they just shouted. Like Belle, whom he had to ring next. The dreadful thought made him all the more determined to close down Darcy's objections and make this offer a done deal.

'Darcy,' Mitch said, summoning his most serious, persuasive tones, 'the *Galaxia* series is gonna send your career into the stratosphere. Quite literally,' he added, snorting at his own joke.

'But I want to be known for quality,' Darcy objected, although she sounded less convinced than she had been. Almost as if, Mitch's ear detected, she wanted him to give her reasons to agree with him.

'And you can be,' Mitch reasoned. 'You'll be in such a good position after this film that you'll be able to choose whatever part you want. In any bloody theatre you like.'

Darcy darted an apprehensive look at the still-sleeping Niall. But a certain excitement was stealing over her as well. Mitch was offering a first-class flight to LA. When was that ever likely to happen again? Her grandmother had been a film actress, after all. It wasn't letting the side down altogether, following in Anna's tiny, high-heeled footsteps just for once, was it? Just out of curiosity?

'OK,' Darcy muttered. 'I'll come and meet the director.'

He might not like her, after all. It might lead to nothing, Darcy told herself. From what this agent – Mitch – had said, the director sounded very odd. He might take an irrational dislike to her, then that would be that.

'You've made the right decision, baby,' Mitch said as calmly as was possible while simultaneously pumping the air with exultation.

For five minutes after the phone call, he ran round his office, whooping in delight. The walls shook and Greg Cucarachi, whom Mitch had not realised was still in the building, suddenly poked his narrow, foxy face through the door.

'Good news?' he asked, his tone pleasant and interested but his eyes straining with competitive fear.

'Great,' said Mitch smugly, slowing to a halt and breathing heavily after all the exertion. He passed a plump hand over his sweating brow.

Expectantly, Greg raised one of the eyebrows which, to Mitch, had always looked suspiciously manicured. But after a few seconds had elapsed in which Mitch failed to take the opportunity to explain what had happened, a glint entered Greg's preternaturally shiny eyes. 'I see from the papers that Belle Murphy's had another great night out,' he said with a twist of his unpleasantly thick lips.

Mitch held his gaze steady but his hands shook and he felt his heart sink like lead into the soft mush of jelly doughnut in his stomach. He had not yet seen the papers, such had been his rush to get to the office and call Darcy Prince first thing. He had tried endlessly all day, but she seemed to have been out. He had left a lot of messages, but when he asked if she had heard any of them, Darcy didn't know what he was talking about. Mitch could not believe anyone could be so casual about the possibility their answerphone might not be working. In LA, people phoned their answerphones endlessly, terrified that they might have missed a call that could change their lives.

'Yeah,' Greg Cucarachi said. 'Major bender, by the looks of it. Lots of nice pictures of her.' Satisfied that his dart had found its target, he grinned wolfishly and withdrew.

Slowly, Mitch sat down. Cold coffee had collected at the points the material was gathered into the seat's cushion buttons and soaked into his trousers as his broad bottom made contact. His joy and relief at his triumph with Darcy Prince now evaporated, to be replaced by a sense of cold foreboding.

The telephone rang. He picked it up to find Arlington Shorthouse on the other line and his foreboding became immediately colder. 'I've made contact with Darcy,' Mitch blustered, in order to get the good news in first. 'She'll be here next week.'

'Sure she will,' Arlington snapped, as if any other scenario was unimaginable. 'I'm not calling about her. I need a meeting with you and Belle,' the studio head said, his chill voice a few degrees more frozen. 'She's becoming a problem,' he added ominously. 'A big problem. We need a meeting. Next Monday at seven a.m., OK?' Arlington rang off before Mitch could answer.

Mitch's heart plummeted. It wasn't just the timing that was brutal – everyone knew Arlington Shorthouse worked eighteen hours a day and slept for three. That it was now all over for Belle seemed inevitable. But she had no one but herself to blame. Apart from him, of course.

Chapter 11

'Was there something you wanted, Mum?' Orlando asked amenably. There had to be some reason why his mother had come up the five floors from the kitchen to his lair on the top floor. Not Facebook; he hadn't opened the site for weeks now and even Georgie seemed to have given up hope of catching him on it.

His eyes beneath his brows swept the Burberry miniskirt she was wearing and he cringed slightly. *Must you, Mum?* Unlike most people, Orlando didn't think his mother was in good shape for her age. He thought she was far too thin.

Georgie's plucked eyebrows drew frowningly together, as they always did when she smiled. It gave her every grin a touchingly uncertain look, Orlando thought. 'I came to remind you that the Faughs are coming for dinner this evening,' Georgie said. She wagged her finger playfully. 'So don't go out. Jago and Ivo will be dying to see you.'

Orlando felt he would almost rather die than see them. A burning, unpleasant sensation swirled through his stomach. He had never liked his parents' friends Hugh and Laura Faugh, and liked their sons less. He couldn't imagine why Georgie thought

Ivo and Jago were his age. She really should overcome her vanity about wearing spectacles.

Orlando watched his mother's expression melt to a dreamy smile. 'It's so nice that they're your own age,' Georgie added in her fluty voice. 'They're such a good influence.' A critical glint entered her eye as she looked around the untidy room in whose midst Orlando sprawled reading a comic and thinking vaguely about going out on his bike somewhere. 'Such nice, tidy boys. So well dressed,' she added, her gaze hooking on Orlando's oversized black T-shirt with its glow-in-the-dark printed-on skeleton ribcage.

He shrugged. So his clothes were tacky. He didn't care. He had bought this T-shirt weeks ago in a pound shop; it had appealed to his childish sense of humour.

The Faugh brothers, he knew, would never have worn such a thing, nor did they ever go in pound shops; facts that raised the appeal of his T-shirt even higher in his eyes. Ivo and Jago were two years his senior, and dressed a good deal older and squarer than that. The last time he had seen them – at a House of Commons garden party Georgie had dragged him determinedly along to – they had been wearing tight dark blue designer jeans with visible creases. Tucked into the jeans – and also into the underpants beneath, Orlando suspected – they wore merchant banker striped or checked shirts, open at the collar, with double cuffs and cufflinks. Tied around the twins' shoulders had been cashmere pullovers, jade for Ivo and ginger for Jago. Their hair had been flat, black and with ruler-straight partings, enlivened with Ray-Bans shoved casually on top.

'And of course, they're so clever,' Georgie reminded him now. 'Both at Oxford.'

Behind the curtains of his hair, Orlando grimaced. Oxford was a word that struck fear into him. He had been dragged to the town several times over the past year by his mother, positioned in front of various spiry college entrances and instructed to admire them. 'Wouldn't you just love to go there?' Georgie had demanded, eyes blazing with ambition. Orlando had taken one look at what seemed an endless stream of self-satisfied geeks coming out of the front entrance of Christ Church and thought that no, actually, he wouldn't. Even if, given his academic record, there was a hope in hell of him going to Oxford as anything other than one of the tourists that seemed to throng outside the innumerable teashops.

'You know, darling, I've just had a simply wonderful idea!' Georgie paused on the threshold of his room and looked back at him with frowning delight. 'Wouldn't it be lovely for you if we asked the Faughs to come with us on holiday? Hmm? To Italy?'

Orlando was so horrified at the suggestion that he sat straight up with shock, his mouth framed in a silent 'O' of objection. But his mother was already gone. He could hear her in her kitten heels clattering down the stairs excitedly, full of her new idea. Hope leapt within Orlando at the thought of his father; if Georgie mentioned her plan to Richard she was sure to be knocked back. His father, Orlando suspected, disliked the Faughs almost as much as he himself did, although he was too polite and generous to say so. Then Orlando groaned and sank back on his duvet with despair. His father had gone to Hertfordshire, visiting one of his constituents in trouble. What about his son who was in trouble, Orlando fumed to himself. Not to mention his family holiday.

Admittedly, he had been unenthusiastic about the holiday from the start. Being left alone in the house had been a much more inviting option, but Georgie had been hellbent on his coming to Italy, and resistance to the iron will of his mother was not an option. Once Orlando had thought about it he realised there could be an advantage so far as his A level results were concerned. The middle of the Tuscan countryside might be somewhere the long arm of the examinations board was unable to stretch. Might, but probably not, given his mother. She would have the date from the school; she would no doubt ring up on the day if he did not. And he had a feeling the results could be texted.

It was, Orlando thought despairingly, bad enough that the smug and pompous Faugh boys were coming to dinner. His A level results were going to be terrible and so was being with his parents when the dreaded fax arrived. The prospect of being on holiday with the twins then as well was almost beyond bearing.

As soon as he opened the front door, Richard sensed anticipation in the air. Proceeding to the kitchen, still in his coat and carrying the bags of papers from his constituency, he found Georgie rushing around the kitchen in a pale yellow apron, pulling plates out of cupboards and inspecting them frowningly, dragging glasses from shelves and holding them to the light to check for smears, darting to the oven and pulling out trays on which little white ramekins stood, filled with something brown and rising. Richard sniffed appreciatively. Georgie was a very good cook.

He picked his way over to her through the various obstacles in his way and slipped a hand around her waist. Georgie shook him off. 'Not now. I'm busy,' she muttered, as if, Richard thought to himself indignantly, he'd just suggested they go ahead and have full sex on the floor. He sighed slightly. Chance would be a fine thing.

She was looking at him accusingly, her gaze skewered on the plastic bag of papers that was digging into his coat sleeve. He dropped it hurriedly. Plastic bags were one of her pet hates, although not for environmental reasons. 'That's so scruffy,' she lamented.

'What's for dinner, darling?' Richard asked, to smooth things over. Georgie's pale green eyes, whose unusual shade Orlando had inherited, pulsed warningly; he had said the wrong thing, Richard realised.

'You haven't forgotten that the Faughs are coming?' his wife accused, one hand on her narrow waist, the other waving a kitchen knife in what struck Richard as a threatening manner. Mindful of this, he tried to look as if, indeed, he hadn't; few things annoyed Georgie more than her social arrangements slipping his mind. Although in this case it was more that Richard had been in denial that it was happening, from the moment it had first been mooted.

'You have forgotten!' Georgie wailed despairingly.

'I, um, well, no, absolutely, um . . .' Richard stammered helplessly. He was nothing if not truthful, which had never exactly been a boon to his career either.

'How could you?' Her green eyes, worried and angry in equal measure, bore into him. 'Hugh's one of your closest friends!'

'Um, well, actually, um . . .' Richard protested feebly, unable quite to express the horror he felt.

Hugh Faugh. Why on earth did Georgie persist in believing he was a close friend? They had never been close friends, even though their lives had, at one stage, run quite closely together; they had entered Parliament the same year; young Conservative MPs still wet behind the ears, or as wet as Hugh's ears ever got considering, or so Richard always suspected, he blow-dried his thick, black, shiny hair to give it that characteristic full, upward-sweeping look.

'Hair gets votes,' Hugh had once told him in that booming, confident, maddening way in which he said everything. He had swept an unimpressed look over Richard's even then thinning, greying scalp, his pale, dry, nondescript face with its monkish features, and raised one of the virile black eyebrows marking his own highly coloured, handsome if rather heavy face.

Had his underperforming follicles, Richard occasionally wondered since, stood in the way of Parliamentary favour? Would a more thickly populated pate have ensured election to the great offices of state?

But he knew in his heart that it wasn't killer hair he lacked. It was killer instinct. Certainly, soon after entering Parliament, his and Hugh's careers had dramatically diverged. Hugh, the more forceful and swashbuckling of the pair, had immediately disappeared into a cloud of glory with never a backward glance, gaining promotion after promotion, while Richard Fitzmaurice had contented himself with being a well-thought-of constituency MP, which was, as he reminded himself many times through the years, what he had been elected for. That this wasn't well thought of by Georgie was just one of those things.

Great friends with Hugh, Richard thought with uncharacteristic sourness. Oh, absolutely. Great friends to the extent that Hugh, recently promoted to the Cabinet, had taken to stalking past him in Westminster corridors without even acknowledging him. But Georgie had been beside herself in delight to find that her husband's former university friend was now so elevated, and this, Richard suspected, was one of the reasons she had invited him for dinner.

Of course, Hugh had accepted with alacrity. Not the least cause of Richard's disquiet was the fact that Hugh, or 'Freebie Faugh', as he was known in the corridors of power, was notorious for his interest in all things complimentary; famous in particular for the zest with which he proved there absolutely was such a thing as a free lunch, and a free dinner as well.

As Georgie, with a final roll of her eyes, rushed off saying she must get changed, Richard shuffled over to the kettle. After the testing day he had spent in Hertfordshire, tending to his crisis-stricken constituent, the Faughs were all he needed. Thank God it would be the summer recess soon, Richard thought. Time for a change of scene. Time for Italy.

Once he had got over the shocking price of the enterprise, Richard had decided that the farmhouse in Tuscany rented by his wife sounded just what they all needed. And given that their household outgoings were no longer as enormous as they had been, the expense was more bearable. There would, for example, be no more school fees for Orlando; he had taken his A levels this summer and they could afford a little financial leeway. This would be their first real treat holiday for fourteen years, since Orlando had started at prep school and his education had started to dominate the budget.

To what end, Richard was not sure. His only son had never been academic; a fact that had emerged early, and personally Richard had been all for him going to the local state primary, which had a good reputation. But Georgie had had other ideas. 'Contacts!' she would insist. 'He has to make contacts. Good contacts will get him through life.' But Richard's own best-known contact was the overbearingly self-confident Hugh Faugh and all he had ever got from him was tinnitus. As well as an abiding sense of resentment.

Of course, Richard mused, household expenses could easily go up again if Orlando went to university, as his mother was determined he should. Personally, Richard rather hoped that he wouldn't. Better the boy should leave and do something useful with his life, although goodness knew what. Not politics, obviously; too many family resources had been sacrificed to that already. Richard pushed the worrying matter of Orlando's future aside. There was quite enough to fret about at the moment. The Faughs were coming for dinner. Richard was a good trencherman, but if any thought could put him off his food, that could.

'Ta *da*!' Georgie suddenly appeared in the kitchen in a white kaftan. 'Like it?' she trilled. 'It's one of my new ones!' Her rather anxious eyes sought his. 'From the Countess of Minto's organic après-yoga collection.' She was twirling so hard that she caught her heel in its hem, lost balance and staggered, heels clattering, across the tiles.

Chapter 12

The twins looked even worse than Orlando remembered. The new jeans with a stiffly ironed crease in the front and the pressed City shirts with cufflinks were all present and correct as they exited the family Range Rover – parked illegally in a disabled spot, Orlando noticed – and tripped confidently after their parents up the front steps into the hall of the house. Orlando, in his usual unlaced trainers and baggy, unbelted jeans, looked in disbelief at the Faugh footwear. Ivo and Jago wore identical new brown deck shoes exposing a lot of chunky white foot.

'Good evening, Mrs Fitzmaurice,' the twins chirped smoothly, clicking their solid heels together and making a great display of kissing Georgie on both of her wan cheeks, which rose with delighted colour.

'So lovely to see you,' swooned Georgie. 'You look marvellous, as always.'

'Not as marvellous as you, Mrs Fitzmaurice!' she was immediately assured.

Orlando wanted to retch at the sycophancy.

He watched as the twins' father now moved in on his mother. '*Marvellous* kaftan, Georgie. You're just *so* fashion forward.'

How could anyone be so cheesy, Orlando wondered, seeing Hugh reverently take Georgie's tiny, fragile hand and raise it to his plump red lips, his eyes gazing fervently into hers all the while.

'As beautiful and gracious as ever!' Hugh declared. As his mother quivered and squealed with flattered delight, Orlando wondered how she could possibly fall for it. Yet fall for it she obviously had. Along with the majority of Hugh's constituents, presumably. It was, Orlando thought, incredible.

'How's it going? A level results due soon, are they?'

Orlando tore himself from contemplation of the father to find both the sons regarding him with amusement. His heart sank.

Richard, as he busied himself taking Laura Faugh's light cashmere wrap, was battling with many of the same feelings. He did not yet know of the Faughs' inclusion in the holiday plan; but only because Georgie thought she had already told him about it. In any case she had not anticipated any objection, or that the information, had Richard had it, would have precipitated him into a horrified panic. Passing down the hall in the direction of the cloakroom, his arms full of scented turquoise cashmere, Richard caught sight of the clock in the kitchen and estimated at least four hours would have to pass before he could retrieve the wrap and wave its wearer goodbye.

He had never liked Laura Faugh much, although, with his customary courteousness, had done his best to disguise this. In contrast to her booming husband, Laura had always seemed rather repressed, although not a mousy sort of repressed. On the contrary, she gave Richard the impression of being inordinately pleased with herself.

She was tall, pale and glacial, with a long neck, shoulder-length dark hair with a reddish sheen, and very straight shoulders. She had hooded eyes and lips that were always coloured in a dry-looking red lipstick and seemed always to twist slightly, with amusement or disdain. There was something a bit sly about her, Richard had always thought. As if she was laughing secretly at something. He had fancied an amused look in her eye as she had, with one glance, taken in the peeling paint of the hallway and the damp patch on the ceiling before handing her wrap to him with a rather grand air.

How he preferred Georgie's warmth, immediacy and excitability, even if she had her brittle and fragile moments and at times could seem rather unhinged. Unhinged, Richard knew, was how some of his colleagues saw her, and possibly this had been another brake on his progress. Laura, with her icy poise, had more of a power-wife air, although she had also managed to produce the two Faugh boys, which Richard felt he would not wish on anyone, even Hugh.

Richard liked children and young people. As an MP, he probably went to more schools and colleges to give talks than he should; the likes of Hugh, he knew, felt that this was a waste of time. But even Richard had difficulty seeing anything positive about Ivo and Jago Faugh. They were superior, boastful and, so far as he could see, entirely charmless. Quite an achievement, Richard considered, when one took into account how they had both gone to Eton and were now at Oxford.

A great many of his young constituents in the housing estates were the sort that only a mother could love, and the fact that no mother ever had only deepened the problem. That such boys and girls were hard to like was no surprise, and Richard, knowing something of their history, treated them with the sympathy all but the hardest cases deserved. But Ivo and Jago's history was one of unremitting privilege, exposed as they had been and were being to the finest teaching and most beautiful environments. None of it seemed to have rubbed off on them, however.

From outside, a tinkle of laughter (Georgie) followed by a cannon-like boom of mirth (Hugh) dragged Richard reluctantly back into the here and now. Georgie had ushered the guests out in the garden to enjoy the warm weather. She had spent some considerable time earlier arranging glasses, nuts, wine chiller and corkscrew at just the right angle on the white cast-iron garden table, the sort, along with the rest of the furniture, that either scraped the patio or put his back out whenever Richard tried to move it.

Richard, having spun out for as long as possible hanging Laura's wrap in the cloakroom, now had no further excuse not to join them. He descended the steps slowly, sensing this would be his last chance to relax or enjoy anything. It was a beautiful summer evening; the warm air was heavy with scent from Georgie's beloved wisteria, snaking along the wall dividing their garden from the neighbours' in a discreet mass of lilac flowers and pale green leaves. The unmown lawn – with a twinge Richard remembered this was supposed to have been his job – actually looked lush and lyrical in the lowering sunlight, whose yellow glow intensified the youthful green leaves of the old apple tree, which stood towards the back of it and cast such a useful shadow in the summer over anyone lounging there with the Sunday papers.

The mellow glow of the sinking sun, Richard noticed with gratitude, even managed to give the back of the house a romantically unkempt air rather than the mess of sills needing painting and bricks needing repointing that it really was. The difference between theirs and the rather more well-kept neighbours' houses was not as marked in this forgiving light, and Richard found he could admire without guilt the graceful back of the Georgian terrace, with its small brown bricks and generous white-painted window frames, stretching to the left and the right of him to each end of the street. Above, beyond the forest of chimney pots, aerials and satellite dishes, a few planes droned sluggishly across the blue sky.

At a booming laugh from Hugh, Richard's gaze dropped to the garden. He noted with dislike Faugh's big, tall form, clad, as indeed Richard himself was, in the usual summer uniform of pale blue shirt and light fawn trousers, albeit a more expensive version than his own. This big Faugh form, one hand thrust into a pocket, but not so deeply so as to obscure a wildly expensive-looking watch, was rocking back and forth in appreciation of one of its own jokes or observations.

'Ha ha!' boomed Hugh, nodding his head with its thick, shining, somehow horribly virile black hair. Next to him, Georgie, in her white kaftan, was evidently engaged in fanning his wonders to a blaze with which even he was satisfied. One of the twins was talking to them too.

As the dread word 'Oxford' drifted over, Richard winced inwardly. He could see from Georgie's face that the dream of her son in an Oxbridge graduate gown had roared back to life. He hoped the revival of the dream would not mean yet another trip back to his own old Oxford college, which had, far from reminding him of his golden youth, actually precipated an avalanche of long-buried regrets and remembered mishaps. And then there would be the revival of the idea of sending Orlando to a crammer. Once again he would be obliged to point out to an unconvinced Georgie that the only effective cramming would be of Fitzmaurice money into the crammer's bank account, and it would get Orlando precisely nowhere.

Richard glanced at his son. Under his hair, under the apple tree, skulked Orlando, arms folded in his ribcage T-shirt, hiding behind his hair and silently broadcasting the fact he wished he were anywhere but here. He wasn't being very polite to their guests, but Richard derived a vicarious pleasure from this.

As he got nearer, Richard realised the subject being discussed was the twins' university careers. His heart sank. No wonder Georgie was looking so excited. No wonder Orlando was hiding behind the double fringe of his hair and the apple branches. In the circumstances it was staggeringly polite of him to remain there at all.

As Ivo – or Jago, Richard could never be sure – boasted on about their cast of influential college friends, which apparently included the offspring of everyone from famous actors to American senators, Georgie turned to her husband. 'Contacts!' she mouthed excitedly.

Surging up within Richard came an urge he had not experienced for the last half-century at least. The almost overwhelming desire to spit.

'I'll just get some more wine; incredibly we seem to have run out again,' Georgie chirruped. Although there was nothing incredible about it, Orlando knew. Hugh and his sons had been pouring it down their throats almost non-stop, although Laura had eschewed the offered chilled Frascati and insisted on a special bottle of red being opened just for her. Now, arms folded, hand outstretched, she held the glass against her black sleeveless fitted dress at an angle to the setting sun; the rays as they shot through gave the red liquid the appearance of blood. Which was appropriate, Orlando thought; Laura had always reminded him of a vampire.

He watched with relief as his father now joined the group and changed the subject, describing the afternoon he had spent with his constituent. Observing with affection Richard's familiar, spare and stooping frame, his thoughtful, scholarly face with the thin nose on which his iron-rimmed glasses constantly slipped down, Orlando felt a swell of pride. His father was both conscientious and kind, and took his Parliamentary duties extremely seriously. Whereas, Orlando thought, you could tell that the only aspect of Parliament Hugh took seriously was how important it made him look. It was clear that Hugh thought the world owed him a living; was honoured by his being on the planet, even.

As it happened, these very same accusations, about himself, were made by Georgie in her very crossest moments. But Orlando had never thought the world owed him a living. He would love to earn his own living, although at what he had no idea. Nor any experience. The real reason he had never worked in his life was not because he had not wanted to, but because Georgie hadn't let him. During his entire time at school she had ruled out holiday jobs in supermarkets or on building sites on the grounds he could be using the time studying. In fact, he had used the time to watch television.

Behind the fresh green apple leaves, in the lovely early summer sunshine, Orlando felt heavy of heart. What career lay ahead? For all his mother's frequent enquiries, he had no idea what he was going to go into, apart from the dole office on a regular basis.

Richard, meanwhile, was finding that his attempt to turn the conversation into more altruistic channels had misfired. Hugh had listened with increasing – and possibly wine-fuelled – impatience to his host's account of trying to help his distressed single-mother constituent. Clearly able to bear no more, he had interrupted to set out his own political vision for Britain.

His absurdly confident voice, slightly slurring, echoed round the garden and those surrounding it. 'Family Values!' Hugh boomed. 'In the end of ends, it's what it all comes down to. Family Values!'

Richard nodded. 'I couldn't agree more. The thing is, what does it mean?' He turned to Hugh, his expression eager. 'How would your interpretation of family values be a solution to, say, the increasing problem of bad pupil behaviour in schools, particularly those in poor areas?'

Hugh swilled down half a glass of Frascati before answering. 'Well, it's obvious. We must look to the mothers and fathers to take responsibility. Discipline questions are not something the schools can be expected to solve all by themselves.'

'Yes, I'd agree with that,' Richard said, nodding seriously.

'We must go back to the parents.'

'Absolutely.'

'And sterilise them.'

Richard Fitzmaurice choked on his white wine. 'What?'

'Just think about it.' Hugh smiled calmly. 'If all women of social classes C, D and E were sterilised, they could screw whatever drug addicts and wastrels they fancied and the country and community wouldn't have to tolerate the resulting destructive, disruptive and invariably stupid offspring.' He grabbed a handful of nuts from the table and shoved them in his mouth. 'Not to mention pay for them,' he added. 'Do you realise it costs more to send someone through the state system than it does to send them to Eton?'

'So why not send them to Eton in the first place then?' Orlando piped up from the tree behind. He had listened to the debate with a growing disgust as well as an increasingly urgent sense that he absolutely had to say something.

Hugh guffawed and both Faugh boys dissolved in explosive nasal mirth.

But Richard looked approvingly at his only child. 'Good

question, Orlando. Simple and to the point. Don't you think, Hugh?'

Hugh, when he had recovered, looked witheringly at his host's son. 'I'm afraid I don't. That, Orlando, is a completely ridiculous and unfeasible idea. Social engineering of the crudest and most contrived variety. We'd be hammered for it.'

It was at this point that Georgie, who had been hovering in concern as the debate turned to argument, seized her chance and Richard's arm. 'Sausages!' she hissed, her eyeballs rigid with meaning.

Torn from the argument, still churning with indignation, he looked at her uncomprehendingly.

'Sausages!' Georgie squealed, her grip tightening painfully on his forearm. 'In the kitchen. *Nibbles.*'

'Oh. Right. Er . . . yes. OK.' Still coursing with most unhostlike feelings, Richard fled to the kitchen for the honey-glazed sausages. He found them on the butcher's block in a gold and white Meissen bowl that struck him as rather too grand for mere bangers. Seizing it none the less, he rushed out again to the garden; the familiar crash of a pan falling off a hook accompanying his flight.

'Here comes my honourable friend!' Hugh declared loudly. 'With the sausages, ha ha! I'm peckish.'

You would be, Richard thought as he approached with the gold and white bowl. Probably hours since your last free meal, Freebie Faugh.

Georgie turned. Her welcoming smile was only half formed before it disappeared into a worried frown. 'You've forgotten the dip!' she hissed. '*And* the napkins! The ones with the fleur-de-lis pattern.'

Richard fled back into the house, taking the bowl of sausages with him. 'Hey!' Hugh called after him in alarm. 'Leave the

123

bangers, old chap.' But Richard, pretending not to have heard, had entered the house by then, gaining a certain childish satisfaction from denying Hugh the sausages he obviously so longed to stuff into his overfed chops.

The sausage victory, he now discovered, was a Pyrrhic one. He lingered over the napkin hunt as long as he decently could, finally returning with dips and the requested fleur-de-lis finger-wipers to find Georgie waxing lyrical about the Tuscan farmhouse they had rented for the holidays. Richard instantly felt the tremor in his knees and feet that always meant danger, a feeling that increased as Hugh turned towards him, his large white teeth gaining a bloody red flash from the sunset.

'Jolly decent of your wife to ask us to Italy with you, old chap. We'd love to come with you – as your *guests*,' Hugh hastily added, with emphasis.

The sun chose this moment finally to sink behind the neighbours' wall and the evening suddenly felt dark and cold. Aghast, Richard hardly noticed, absorbing as he was the fact that Hugh had used the time he had spent looking for napkins in order to make further progress in his life's work of securing complimentaries. Far from demonstrating there was no such thing as a free lunch, Hugh had now abundantly illustrated the fact there was such a thing as a free holiday too.

Chapter 13

A frown creased Arlington Shorthouse's tanned, lean and somewhat elastic-looking face. Behind his thick lenses, with their distinctive heavy black frames, the small grey eyes narrowed with annoyance. He shifted his short body irritably in his chair. As well as cross, Arlington felt tired. It was only three in the afternoon but it had already been a long day.

It always was. Arlington Shorthouse was tied up, dawn to dusk. He had back-to-back meetings when he was lying on his front; on the massage table of the Bath & Racquets, usually, being pummelled by Svetlana. He made deals and phoned into conference calls even when having his neatly cropped, iron-grey hair made neater and more iron grey by Maurice at the Plaza.

Arlington was always open for business. He had been so, quite literally, on the operating table. He'd tried to take calls once when having his appendix removed, but the surgeon had snatched away his mobile. Arlington hadn't been back to that hospital since; the surgeon had obviously been in the pay of a rival studio.

Arlington worked twenty-four seven, three six five. How else did you run an outfit like NBS Studios? How else did you keep it, not just competitive but actually setting the pace in this most cut-throat of industries, hiring the best actors and making the biggest profits, with more top-grossing films than any other studio? Blockbusters, every one. Oscar winners. Box-office history-makers. An almost hundred per cent hit rate. And now they were planning to make the hit to out-punch everything else NBS had ever done; the first in a planned series of *Galaxia* movies. They would be so big, so fabulous, so full of big names, special effects and spectacular plots that they would give the previously all-powerful *Star Wars* a run for its money.

And in doing so completely obliterate from the collective consciousness the fact that NBS had ever made a bad film. Of course, NBS turned out fewer turkeys than any other studio. As Arlington liked to say at industry dinners, his studio had so few turkeys it was practically vegetarian. No Bloody Shit, that was what it stood for. Well, it actually stood for Niesewand, Bunsen and Scheckelburger, the three film directors who had founded it in the early 1930s. But No Bloody Shit was a hell of a lot easier to spell.

Turkeys *were* rare, but occasionally they happened. And boy, had they happened now. Arlington cleared his throat and drummed his fingers irritably on his desk. He hated turkeys; they felt like a personal failure. And the people who were in them made him feel the same way. They made him feel small, a sensation he particularly hated as Arlington *was* small. Very small. Short by name, short by nature. 'Pocket rocket', the fourth of his six wives had called him before finding herself in the middle of one of the most acrimonious divorces in showbusiness history.

Arlington had tried to conquer his small height the way climbers try to conquer Everest. He'd tried the lot: big hair, personality lifts in his shoes, even hats. Chairs, in the end, were the only satisfactory answer; while everyone else in his office had to sit on seats at a level normally associated with junior high schools, the throne-like construction behind Arlington's burr-walnut desk had special padded cushions to raise him to a comparatively towering height. As the effect was lost whenever he stood up, Arlington sat on this chair behind his desk for entire meetings. He was careful to drink little beforehand. Comfort breaks severely compromised his status.

From the summit of his chair, Arlington could look out across his meeting room like the commander of a tank. He did so now, and those present stiffened in response. There was about the room, with its grey carpet, grey smoked-glass walls and framed maps of the world showing the cities in which NBS's films had opened and what the box office takings were, an air of the war cabinet. And this was appropriate, as to all intents and purposes a war room was what it was. Arlington regarded himself as being in a permanent state of hostilities with all the other studio heads in the world and anyone else who dared to challenge him.

Mitch Masterson was among those present. He was at the boardroom table, crammed uncomfortably into one of the diminutive chrome chairs beneath the unusually low, black ash table. He was trying hard not to look how he felt, like a dad at a kindergarten parents' evening. Mitch didn't have kids, nor did he want them. His clients were his children, although not in the nice way that sounded. They were like children in the sense that they were unreasonable, endlessly demanding, spoilt, violent, prone to screaming and tantrums, and could not be trusted to behave. Just like Belle Murphy was not behaving now.

She had a meeting with the head of the studio, her ultimate boss, and was she on time? Was she even in the building? The hell she was. Great start, thought Mitch, trying to shove his trapped legs into a more comfortable position below the tiny table. He looked at the other men doubled up painfully on the miniature furniture for support, but they stared back at him coldly. Arlington Shorthouse's lieutenants to a man, they clearly knew, like everyone else, that if you wanted to make it big at NBS, you had to think small. Chairwise, at any rate.

Arlington, from his desk, scrutinised the conference table for signs of discontent. As a rule, he tried to hire the shortest people possible, but as these weren't always the best he had had to accept that a little height was occasionally necessary.

He pressed the intercom button. 'Where the hell is she?' he growled at his secretary and watched with satisfaction as, on the other side of the glass wall, Miss van der Bree, usually so steely and immaculate, fluffed up in her own low chair like an agitated hen and started pressing lots of buttons on various telephones.

'I'm so sorry, Mr Shorthouse,' Mitch assured him, the pain in his voice in every way reflecting the pain he felt physically. His awkward sitting position meant that cramp was now paralysing his leg. It had also totally creased and screwed up the new Armani suit he had bought for the meeting, inside whose lined interior he felt great patches of nervous sweat spreading from beneath his armpits. He'd put a Hollywood-power-meeting level of deodorant on as well, but it hadn't seemed to make the slightest difference.

As well as physically, he felt pained professionally. Belle was not only screwing up her own career with her rudeness, she was screwing his as well. Thank God Darcy Prince was due in town over the next few days for the Jack Saint meeting, although that could go either way. Or, knowing Saint, some other way altogether. Mitch sighed, locked his fingers and screwed his hands painfully together in order to distract himself from the pain in his legs.

Arlington Shorthouse, meanwhile, ground his veneered teeth and stared at his burr-walnut desk. He tried to still the panic that was rising within him at the thought of all the time he was losing; whole seconds, entire unfilled minutes that he would never get again, and which, no doubt, his rivals at other film companies were using to streak ahead.

The desk was no comfort, however. It was grand, with its green leather top and scrolled gilt handles, and was even historic, being the desk that all the presidents of the company had used before him. Legendary film stars had signed contracts here. Douglas Fairbanks had even scratched his name in the leather. Belle Murphy had signed here too, and a contract of historically huge proportions. Arlington felt sick at the memory.

He looked at his Breitling and scowled. She was fifteen minutes late now. No one was *ever* fifteen minutes late for Arlington Shorthouse. No one was ever *one* minute late for Arlington Shorthouse.

Belle Murphy, however, had been a diva from day one, stalking around the lot like she owned the place. Which, given her salary – at the thought of that contract, he winced again – she more or less did. Thinking of the NBS balance sheet after the mauling Belle and *Bloody Mary* had given it, he winced again. Someone was going to have to pay for this. And someone other than Arlington. He had, he decided, paid enough.

Of course it wouldn't be so bad if this were Belle's only crime. But to compound the problem, she'd recently been exhibiting out-of-control behaviour. Which would not itself have been so bad had it not been photographed. And then printed all over every tabloid in the US. She'd made Britney Spears look like Julie Andrews. Which was ironic really, as Julie Andrews – clean-living, upright, unimpeachable – was Arlington's ideal woman and the role model for all the actresses employed by his studios. Not to mention his wives.

Something had to be done about Belle Murphy. And would be, today, here in this room, by these people. Arlington, skimming over the wretched Mitch with his cold grey eye, appraised his henchmen.

Nearest to him, at the end of the black ash conference table, sat a dark, handsome man in a red striped shirt. Arlington's battleship-coloured gaze raked approvingly over Michael J. Seltzer, NBS's Head of Creative. Young, good looking, smart, determined, undoubtedly gifted and sitting ramrod straight in his chair, completely focused on the moment, there was a lot about the Head of Creative that reminded the company president of himself at a similar age.

Next to him sat Chase McGiven: young, restless looking and thin-faced, with burning eyes and fashionably cropped dark hair. As NBS's Head of PR, he'd come up with some interesting thinking about Belle Murphy. Very interesting thinking indeed.

Yes, thought Arlington. There was a lot about Chase as well that reminded him of himself at his age. Not wanting to waste a second, always some plan on the go, some scheme buzzing in his head.

The final member of the trio was Bob Ricardo, NBS's Head of Finance and the sharpest guy in the business. He looked sharp too, Arlington thought, with his pointy nose, bristly grey hair, surgical-looking rimmed glasses and sharply cut grey suit. He sat upwards, stiff and alert. In front of him was a large calculator with oversize keys next to a floppy white book open to display columns of figures. Yes, Arlington thought. Bob was ready. He had an eagerness about him that reminded the studio head of himself when younger, although that couldn't be right because Bob was more or less his age.

Arlington's eye rolled round back to Mitch, Belle's agent from Talent Incorporated, and his lip curled slightly. Sure, the guy had talked things up when he got here, about how his client was just down the block, in the lift, about to appear any minute. But as the minutes had gone by and Belle had failed to materialise, he had stopped pretending and was now staring miserably at the carpet. The guy was fat as well. Had he never heard of a low-carb diet, Arlington thought contemptuously.

A sudden movement behind the smoked-glass walls dividing the inner sanctum from the outer area caught Arlington's eye. It was Miss van der Bree's arms flying in the air as she tried to restrain something or someone. Someone now appearing at the doors of his office. Holy shit. Arlington's tanned hands flew to his chest to check that his bulletproof vest was in position. It was. His handgun was, as usual, in its holster under his arm. Physically as well as professionally, he was never less than prepared to withstand an attack from a rival studio.

The doors flew back, and, rather to everyone's amazement, in came Belle Murphy, her lavishly lipsticked mouth stretched in a dazzling smile the width of a watermelon.

'Hi, guys!' she trilled. The guys waited for a reference to her lateness, followed by an apology. They were disappointed on both counts.

Belle looked, Mitch thought, not only smaller than she appeared on screen – every star looked like that – but even smaller than when he had seen her last time. Clearly her relationship with food had got that bit more distant in the meantime. For all the movement and vitality of her presence – the shining hair, the flashing sunglasses, the exposed and prominent rounded domes of her breasts rearing beneath a necklace of very big diamonds – Belle's body, Mitch estimated, was about the width and thickness of a copy of *Vogue*. And not a new season issue either.

She looked pretty good, all the same. He noted with relief her clinging grey silk dress with plunging neckline, black high heels, enormous black sunglasses and the way her cascade of white-blond hair pushed back from her face and poured over her shoulders as far as her elbows. She was working the high-octane glamour look, as she should be. She was doing that bit right, at least. He shot a timid yet triumphant look at Arlington. Surely even Hollywood's chillest lizard, however angry, couldn't be immune to such a tasty piece of ass as this. He took heart when he saw Arlington was apparently staring at Belle's breasts.

Arlington was, however, looking at the bag Belle had under her arm. It was huge, heavy with gilt and buckles, and almost as big as she was. He recognised the type without enthusiasm. His fifth wife had had one in every colour. They cost a minimum of two thousand dollars a pop. What was even less appealing to Arlington was the presence in one corner of the bag of a small brown dog with a very big diamond collar. It was one of those trembly, skinny, yappy ones, Arlington saw with dislike. It looked restlessly about with enormous and very prominent black eyes. They held a ruthless expression, a look that clearly warned it might go for the throat at any minute. Arlington recognised the expression; it was one he often used himself in business meetings.

Mitch had by now noticed the dog and was appalled. What the hell . . . ? Why in God's name had she brought that?

Arlington's narrow, lizard eyes widened. Jesus, was that a *real* diamond collar that mutt was wearing? It looked like the one in Harry Winston he'd been about to buy for his sixth wife, when it suddenly went from the window. Hell. Belle Murphy really was too much. She cost too much, she spent too much, she got too much of the wrong sort of attention. And *Bloody Mary* hadn't made enough. Not nearly enough.

'Darling!' breathed Belle in her trademark little-girl voice. Holding out her arms, she staggered across the carpet in her high heels towards the burr-walnut desk. 'Arl! May I call you that, for short?'

The sound of four strangled, horrified coughs now filled the room. Four minds reverberated with one single thought. *She had called him Arl.* No one called Arlington anything for short. Short was not a word that was ever breathed in Arlington's presence, and she had done that too.

Mitch, who knew how the studio head also loathed unscheduled physical interaction, now watched in horror as Belle seized Arlington's neck with a white hand on which a huge diamond ring glittered. 'Mwah! Mwah!' Arlington gasped with pain as her razor cheekbones banged against his smooth and elastic cheeks.

It crossed the screeching, veering chaos of Mitch's mind that Belle might be drunk.

Belle, having smeared Arlington's tanned cheeks with red lipstick, now stood unsteadily erect in her five-inch stilettos. She held up the bag with the dog in. 'Gentlemen,' she pouted breathily, batting her wide green eyes behind her sunglasses, 'I'd like you all to meet Sugar. It's Sugar's fault we're a tiny weeny bit late. I had to take him to the dog beautician for a manicure.'

The men in the room stared dumbly. Each and every one of them was familiar with star behaviour. But this woman wasn't even a star any more. Mitch stared at the floor, wishing it would not only swallow him up but mash him to a pulp while it was at it. He felt he didn't want to live any more. And after this meeting it seemed unlikely that he would, professionally speaking anyway. The hopes he had invested in Darcy Prince floated away. The here and now was all, and it was awful.

'There you go, precious,' Belle crooned to the dog as she put him on the floor. 'You go runabout, sweetie.' Sugar immediately shot beneath Arlington's desk.

Mitch felt he could hardly bear to watch. That Arlington Shorthouse disliked dogs was common knowledge in Hollywood. NBS was the only studio that never put out movies with dogs in, which were the sort that more or less kept all the other studios afloat.

'I don't like dogs,' Arlington said ominously.

Belle's megawatt grin abruptly disappeared. Her mouth bunched disapprovingly and her darkened eyebrows snapped angrily together. It was, Mitch thought, like a sudden storm on a summer day.

'Why don't you like dogs?' Belle demanded.

Arlington did not answer. He was unaccustomed to giving his reasons. Mitch stared at his client pleadingly. How could Belle be unaware that she was not only digging her own grave but standing beside it and pointing the gun at her temple? He was the one here to do the talking, but, as Belle leapt in and ruined things before he could open his mouth, all he could do was sit and watch as she committed professional hara-kiri.

'Because Sugar can *so* tell when someone doesn't like him,' Belle warned. 'He reacts in self-defence, the darling. He's, like, so sensitive. So easily hurt, poor baby.' She bent under Arlington's desk and cooed some endearments. At least he gets to see her tits now, Mitch tried to comfort himself.

The platinum head shot up again. 'Sugar can, you know, really *sense* hostility in the atmosphere,' Belle said accusingly.

The ensuing absolute and not particularly friendly silence was ended by the sound of a clearing throat. 'Look, shall we get on with the business?' asked Bob Ricardo, looking at his boss and drumming his calculator with his fingers.

Looking at his Head of Finance, the studio boss felt the nearest he got to affection. Yes, Bob, with his razor brain, ability with figures and utter obsession with and devotion to business, in particular the business of making a fat profit, did indeed remind Arlington of himself when young.

Chapter 14

Belle was doing her best, Mitch could see. She had peeled off those vast sunglasses to reveal vulnerable green eyes, full of ready-to-spill tears. Mitch was almost convinced himself.

Arlington wasn't, however. As he spoke, he was flexing his stubby hands and staring at his neatly clipped nails. 'Look, baby. So you *were* huge last year. But a year's a long time in showbiz. You're losing it and there are plenty of other girls out there just dying to take your place.'

'You can't mean it,' the actress gasped, a catch in her throat.

Outside of a studio, Arlington thought, it was amazing how corny actors were. Although, given some of the screenplays, they weren't much better inside one either. That had been one of the problems with *Bloody Mary*. The dialogue had been much too contemporary. The dumb scriptwriters had had Mary Tudor, an uptight religious nut by all accounts, exclaiming 'Jesus H Christ!' and drawling 'Yeah, OK, right, whatever.' Even NBS's most on-side film critics – even the ones they *paid* – had had problems with that.

Belle was half sobbing. Dressed like that, with her tits

practically out, most of her thighs showing and crossing and recrossing her legs like Sharon Stone, she was probably trying to do a number on them, Arlington realised. Well, she could forget it. No chance. No one in this office had any time for sex. They were too busy making movies about it.

He yawned. This was already taking too long. 'You do your bit now, Bob,' he said shortly to his Head of Finance.

'Basically, the bottom line is this,' Bob Ricardo jumped in with his cutting, nasal voice. '*Bloody Mary* cost two hundred and fifty million dollars to make and so far it's grossed thirty.'

'Thirty million?' Belle beamed. 'Hey, it's only been out two months. Thirty million's not so bad?'

Bob shook his bony, crop-haired head. 'Not thirty million dollars. *Thirty* dollars. Three oh.'

Mitch gasped. He'd no idea it was this bad. This was historic.

'*Thirty?*' croaked Belle.

'Thirty,' confirmed Bob in his grating tones.

There was a silence that was almost respectful, as of mourners contemplating a body.

Belle was the first to recover. She had decided, Mitch realised in despair, that attack was the best form of defence. This was not a good decision. Attacking undergrown Hollywood moguls was not a form of defence. It was a form of madness. Why couldn't Belle see that hanging her head and taking the rap was her only hope of eating lunch in this town again? Or, as eating didn't come into it in Belle's case, of going to the restaurant and ordering it.

'Thirty dollars! But that's impossible!' Belle shouted. Her platinum hair glowed like white fire around her agitatedly shaking head. 'No one's ever made . . .' she screwed up her mouth to spit out the words, '*thirty freaking dollars* on a two-hundred-fifty-million-dollar picture! It's impossible, right?'

'Wrong,' Bob said with relish, his lean fingers gently tapping the white surface of his balance book. 'Sure, it's made a few million, but when you take away the taxes, the costs and so on, well . . .' He pulled a face. 'Thirty's what you're left with. Which means,' he frowned and tapped the large buttons of his calculator, 'a deficit of two hundred and forty-nine million, nine hundred and ninety-nine thousand, nine hundred and seventy dollars.'

Even though he had heard it before, the figure hit him just as hard as it had the first time, right slap-bang in the balls. Arlington closed his watering eyes and swallowed. Forget calling this a turkey. It was an outbreak of bird flu. An epidemic of H5N1 right through their balance sheet.

'I can't believe it.' Belle spoke through trembling lips. The eyes were welling again. Arlington felt impatience shoot through him. It was all so hackneyed. Like the worst sort of film. Like . . . oh, no. Had it really been that bad? The extent of the damage was still coming in. Moldovia had yet to report, and there was some confusion over whether *Bloody Mary* had been number six or number nine in Finland. 'It's the right number all right,' their contact there had reported. 'Right now we're just establishing what way up it is.'

'It can't be true,' Belle stormed. 'There's gotta be some kind of mistake.' Her nostrils were flaring, which, Arlington thought, probably took some doing when you'd had as much plastic surgery as Belle Murphy seemed to have had.

'You got your sums wrong!' Belle gasped, her breasts heaving up and down agitatedly. 'The critics said my acting was great,' she added desperately.

Arlington pursed his lips and surveyed her almost pityingly. 'It's box office that counts in this game. No one gives a gnat's snatch about the acting. Like I said before, you gotta stay big, or no one gives a gnat's snatch about you either.'

Belle's mouth started to tremble. The green eyes went filmy with tears. Oh God, thought Arlington. Here we go. 'Save that for the movies, baby,' he said unsympathetically.

Her eyes abruptly dried and the actress went into attack mode again. 'It's not my fault,' she snarled, addressing Bob. '*Bloody Mary* was a bad idea, right from the start.'

From under Arlington's desk, the dog growled.

'*I* always said we should make a sequel to *Marie*,' Belle declared passionately. 'But no one would listen to *me*.' She thumped a skinny fist heavy with diamonds so hard against the prominent bones of her upper chest that it seemed to Mitch that she might snap them.

'We couldn't do a sequel,' Michael J. Seltzer said shortly. Arlington looked approvingly at his Head of Creative.

'*Why* couldn't we do a sequel?' hissed Belle.

'Why didn't we do a sequel to *Marie*?' asked the Head of Creative, his voice a disbelieving drawl. 'She got her head chopped off in the last one.'

Belle glared indignantly at Seltzer. 'Yeah, and so what?' she blustered. 'You're the creative brains of this studio, aren't you? What *can't* be done with computer animation these days? Huh?'

Michael J. Seltzer snorted impatiently. 'Studios can't bring dead people back to life.'

'It was always a bad idea, *Bloody Mary*,' Belle repeated. 'We should have done Anne Boleyn instead. Or Elizabeth . . . whatever number she was. The one in the big dresses.'

'Elizabeth the First,' supplied Michael smoothly. 'Well, we would've. But she'd already been done recently. Cate Blanchett did her.'

'Well, OK, Henry the whatever, then. You know, that power-crazed psycho with the six wives.' Belle rolled her eyes. 'Six wives! How normal was *he*?'

'Erm,' Michael J. Seltzer interrupted, shooting a nervous glance at Arlington, who looked predictably thunderous. 'Well, Anne Boleyn's just been done as well. Bloody Mary was the only one available. The only one no one had done. Remember, guys,' he appealed to his colleagues, whilst carefully avoiding Arlington's eyes, 'we were pretty pleased to discover her at the time. A breakthrough, we said. We couldn't understand why no one else had done her.'

Arlington, behind the desk, groaned. The folly of it all pressed on him. He understood all too well why no one else had now. 'Burning desire' and all that. What the hell had the studio been thinking of to use that as the film's catchline?

Or, to be precise, Arlington thought, his nostrils narrowing and his eyes slitting as he looked at his Creative Head, what had *Michael* been thinking of? It had been his idea to make the film in the first place; make it, moreover, not straight and historical, but sex it up, make it like some sixteenth-century Catholic Playboy Mansion, with Philip of Spain running around pleasuring everyone from the lady's maids to the spit boy. He had even pushed for an alternative title, *Burn, Baby, Burn*, on the grounds that it was more commercial. Arlington stared hard at his Head of Creative. Bad move, Michael. A whole bunch of bad moves, in fact. And at his age, the studio head remembered, he never made bad moves.

Michael raised his well-groomed dark head. 'Well, I guess it wasn't a great decision to take out all the Protestant and Catholic stuff on the grounds it might offend people. It just meant that nothing made any sense and the executions looked a bit gratuitous.'

Arlington felt a flash of fury. The decision to do that had

141

been his, goddamn it. That was a careless remark on Michael's part. He was reminding Arlington less and less of himself at that age.

'But we live and learn, huh?' Michael added brightly, shooting a hopeful look at the studio head.

Ominously, Arlington did not reply.

Belle's sunglasses, which she had now replaced, flashed defiantly. '*Bloody Mary* did very well in the Ukraine.'

'Only because they thought it was about alcohol,' replied Bob wearily.

Arlington slid another look at his watch. Shit. He had another fifty meetings scheduled today. This was taking far too long.

Chase looked up and caught Arlington's eye. The studio head gave a barely perceptible nod. It was Chase's turn now.

Chase cleared his throat. He sat with one ankle raised to his knee, on which balanced a blue plastic folder he tapped restively with a fountain pen. 'Miss Murphy. We've been doing some, ahem, qualitative personality research,' he tapped the folder harder, 'which I have right here.'

The studio's Head of PR rubbed red and evidently exhausted eyes in which, Mitch noticed, the pupils looked suspiciously small.

'Qualitative personality research is qualitative research concerning a personality,' Chase informed Belle. 'See what they think of you, in other words,' he added, as she frowned incomprehendingly.

'Was this really necessary?' Mitch interjected, feeling he should say something, anything, to remind them all he was still here.

Chase ignored him. His red eyes were focused on Belle. 'According to our research, and of course this is confirmed by the figures from *Bloody Mary*, your popularity is, how can I put this?' He looked thoughtfully at a corner of the ceiling.

'Huge?' prompted Belle, with a titter. Her teeth glinted in the glow of the lowlighters round the glass walls. Arlington kept the lighting subdued for difficult meetings. It created a conspiratorial air he enjoyed.

'Slipping,' said Chase.

'Are you sure?' Mitch interjected desperately. 'Belle's got a lot of fans, remember.'

At least this time he got a reply, which had to count as a plus.

'Not any more,' Chase leant back in his chair and put his arms behind his head. 'Her popularity's at rock bottom.'

'Like the takings,' interjected Bob, with his usual relish.

The dog began to yap under Arlington's desk.

Chase sighed. 'C'mon, Belle. Your recent behaviour – falling out of nightclubs and all that – means that people are dropping you from projects left, right and centre. No film will touch you at the moment. You've lost your cosmetics contract, the perfume launch has been decommissioned and you're not even being considered for that Disney animation about a worm farm any more. The part's gone to Scarlett Johansson.'

Mitch's breakfast came shooting back up his windpipe in a sudden and unexpected manner. He pulled an apologetic face as Belle ripped off her sunglasses and whipped round to meet his eyes with the blazing balls of green fire that were her own.

'What?' she screamed. 'What the freaking hell . . . ?'

'I was gonna tell you, baby,' Mitch murmured unhappily.

Belle clenched her fists, bared her teeth and bellowed at the artificially lowered ceiling like a cow in pain. Under Arlington's desk, Sugar gave a long and rattling growl. The studio head, exasperated, aimed a sharp kick in his direction with one small foot in a tight, shiny tan brogue.

Chase ploughed on. 'Specifically, what our qualitative personality research tells us is that your recent behaviour has played badly with the fans.'

Belle pouted and affected to look as if she had not the faintest idea what he was talking about.

Chase went on, 'The point is that you've misread the Zeitgeist.'

'I've never read the *Zeitgeist*,' Belle riposted smartly. 'I can't read German and I never read newspapers.'

Except the cuttings about yourself the agency send, Mitch silently corrected. Although admittedly there were fewer of those than there once had been.

Chase stared at her with such a bewildered expression on his face that Mitch almost felt sorry for him. He had clearly underestimated the scale of the task before him, but then, who hadn't, Mitch thought.

'People don't want stars like that any more,' the studio PR explained in a voice that began faintly but then slowly built up to its former strength. 'Drunken, wild, dressed like hookers . . .'

'Hey,' interjected Belle indignantly.

'You gotta calm down,' Chase advised. 'Get some respect from somewhere. Get yourself some gravitas.'

Belle looked affronted. 'Hey, what's wrong with my ass?'

'Nothing, nothing,' Mitch put in hurriedly, wiping a paper napkin he had found in his pocket from this morning's purchase of jelly doughnuts over his perspiring brow. He felt a slight tightness form in the wake of the wipe: sugar crystals, he realised too late. He had frosted his own forehead. 'What Chase means is that you need people to take you more seriously.'

As Chase and the rest of the table nodded, Belle folded her arms tightly and glared at them from Botoxed brows she was struggling to pull into a frown.

'Yeah?' she demanded. 'More serious, huh? Whaddya want me to do, go play *Hamlet* at the Royal freaking Shakespeare Company? Huh?'

There was a silence. The men looked at each other. Chase's groomed, dark blond eyebrow raised consideringly in a forehead almost as unlined as Belle's. Did he have Botox too, Mitch wondered.

'*Hamlet*. It's a thought,' Chase admitted.

Belle gasped in angry disbelief. Fists clenched, eyes flashing, she seemed to Mitch to be hovering on the edge of a crevasse of fury, into which she might leap at any moment. But Chase interrupted her before she could.

'Fans these days,' he continued smoothly, 'want stars they can respect. Caring stars, loving stars. People who care about the big issues. Global poverty. Families. The environment.'

Belle stared at him disbelievingly. 'Goddamn it!' she burst out. 'I'm a celebrity. I'm not running for freaking President.'

Chase grinned wolfishly. 'Belle, let me tell you, you know what, you *are*. People expect their stars to have issues these days. Consciences. Just look around. There's Angelina and Brad there with their rainbow family, Madonna and that little African guy, Clooney and Darfur, Gwyneth Paltrow and, uh, her macrobiotic yoga . . .'

Belle's full red lips were twisted in a scornful sneer. 'So what are you saying?' she taunted Chase. 'That you want me to,' she snorted with disgust, 'adopt,' her eyes rolled incredulously and she tossed her white hair, 'an *African baby*?' She slapped her thin brown thigh and emitted a long and mirthless cackle.

No one else in the room smiled, however. There was a dead silence. Mitch tried to ease his legs from under the tiny boardroom table. His thighs tingled as the blood returned to them.

Arlington's eyes burned and his mouth rushed with water. His groin felt suddenly tight, as in moments of extreme sexual excitement. This was the answer. Or the nearest this meeting had got to one. 'That's *exactly* what we want you to do, Belle,' he said. 'And if you don't, you're dumped.'

Chapter 15

Darcy had never really given much thought to what happened when one turned left on a plane rather than right, but First Class turned out to be a revelation. The roomy cabin held, she calculated, a mere fourteen seats. Between each one stretched several feet of carpeted blue floor space in which three normal economy seats could easily have been fitted.

There were oil paintings and fresh flowers in the cabin, and a table with newspapers and magazines on, as if it was not a plane at all, but a smart club. The thick leather armrest of Darcy's seat harboured an entire personal entertainment centre. There were console pads, control buttons and power points for all manner of other things. One of the stewards, a man with gelled-up blond hair, spotting her investigations, swooped over to tell her that a selection of up to 40 DVDs was available to all First passengers, which you could request at any time and slip into the player in your seat.

She could imagine what Niall would make of it all. 'You're selling out, Darcy.' Selling out to the tune of what someone could easily take a year to earn too. The price of the return first-class flight, which she had spotted on the ticket, had rendered Darcy breathless for a moment.

She could imagine Angharad's distaste for so overt a display of conspicuous consumption. 'Elitism. Decadence. A slap in the face for the workers.' She could almost hear her mother saying it in her low, RADA-trained tones. Even though the workers in this plane – the two chic, chignoned women and the man with the gelled-up blond hair – seemed to be having a perfectly lovely time, gliding serenely about holding silver trays with glasses of champagne on them. Yes, as slaps in the face went, Darcy thought as she sipped her wine, there were harder and more painful ones than this.

There was a whoosh of expensive-smelling aftershave and the man with the gelled-up hair was at her side again. Startled, Darcy stared into his face, wondering about the burnished, almost metallic surface of it. 'I'm Sean,' he offered with a brilliant white smile. 'Your personally assigned steward for this flight. Canapés?' He proffered the square ceramic dish he held in his hand. 'Truffle-infused scrambled egg on a mini-blini,' he elucidated, letting a polished, manicured and scrupulously clean finger hover over the small yellow circle. 'Foie gras *en gelée*,' he added, gesturing at a perfect square of some orangey-pink substance with a shining clear-jelly top. 'And this,' he announced, his digit stopping at a tiny, shiny-brown profiterole filled with something dark red and white, 'is a miniature beef sandwich, filled with best Scottish beef and a dash of home-made horseradish sauce. Enjoy!' And with that, he sailed away.

Darcy, who was hungry, eagerly picked up the blini with the egg on. She had heard about truffle but never tasted it. Her eyes widened with delight as a powerful, musky sensation, almost more of a smell than a taste, burst on her tongue and spread simultaneously to her nostrils and her throat. She swallowed the last of it with regret. The foie gras, a rich, livery sliver, was devoured in an instant and Darcy lifted the Scottish beef sandwich last.

As she munched it, her thoughts went back to Niall. He'd made no bones – well, his father *was* a butcher – about his disapproval of her going to LA. 'You're an *artist*, Darcy,' he had stormed, his freckled Scottish face pinked up with anger, his brows drawn together in one long, disapproving, fox-coloured line. 'You're supposed to be serious about acting. And Hollywood isn't acting. It's crap. Money-spinning, commercial crap with no moral or artistic value whatsoever.'

A huge, hot wave of unease and embarrassment had almost overwhelmed Darcy as she tried to defend herself. Niall on the attack was a formidable opponent. She could imagine him, like the Highland ancestors he so often spoke about, like the one Hollywood film he did approve of, *Braveheart*, running, bellowing, down some glen-side, brandishing his sword, his ragged tartan billowing behind him.

Niall had drawn himself up to argue. He was stocky and powerfully built, but not tall. '*Galaxia*,' he growled. 'It sounds bloody awful. Simple-minded commercial space trash. How can you even consider it?'

Darcy twisted her fingers and shot him uncomfortable looks. What could she do? She had given her word to Mitch Masterson now. The pressure Niall was putting on her was at least equal to that her Hollywood agent, whose existence she had never previously suspected, had put on her. And she was still curious about Tinseltown. What was wrong with going to have a look?

'Because they'll suck you in,' Niall thundered, reminding Darcy of some handsome but terrifying Calvinist preacher shouting from a lofty pulpit in a grey-stone Edinburgh kirk. 'They'll corrupt your values. Twist your mind.'

Darcy felt half mortified, half exasperated. It was an audition she was going to, not the Moonies. He was overreacting, surely. Perhaps even overacting; the sense, with him, even with her parents, that she was participating in some scene from a play never quite went away. Of course, they were all four of them actors. But that impression of slight distance, of watching herself from the outside, had been with her for so long Darcy felt it was quite normal and that everyone experienced it.

'Look, I'm not planning to become a Scientologist,' she had told Niall doggedly. 'It's only an audition. It might not come to anything. They don't always,' she added, with meaningful emphasis. The fact that Niall's Hamlet at the National Theatre hadn't come off was a still-raw subject.

She regretted such below-the-belt tactics immediately. Niall's entire face changed. He looked at her, his – whatever he said about it – Tiffany-blue eyes large with childish bewilderment, appearing larger and more childish still because of his pale blond lashes. Her heart twisted; he looked like a five year old unable to understand why anyone would want to hurt him. Which she obviously had.

'Thanks,' Niall said bitterly, the bewilderment changing to a resentful stare. 'That's right. You swan off to Hollywood and I'll carry on trying to land a part as third spear carrier somewhere. But if I don't, there's always a part as a Scottish pisshead to fall back on.'

She had flung herself at him at that, full of the urge to comfort and reassure. 'You're a *great* actor,' she had soothed, stroking his turbulent dark-red curls. 'One of the very best. And people *will* realise it. They *will*. You'll get the recognition you deserve—'

'*When?*' he ground into her slender shoulder, gripping her to him hard.

'Soon.' She looked earnestly into his eyes, pushing back his russet hair with both hands to expose his face. 'It's got to happen,' she added, rather desperately. 'Probably before I even get back.'

He had broken into a grin at this, shaken his hair back over his broad shoulders and rolled his blue eyes ruefully. 'So you're definitely going, then?'

Darcy smiled back, trying to keep the mood light. 'Why not? It might be fun to have a look at the whole crazy place. See what we're not missing.'

'But you're a serious actress,' Niall repeated, although his expression remained indulgent and open, not bunched and thunderous as it had been before.

'Alec Guinness was in *Star Wars*,' Darcy reminded him, displaying her trump card.

'Yes, but he regretted it the rest of his life,' Angharad declared, when Darcy had got to this bit of her speech with her mother. 'Serious actors always do. I remember when dear Larry –' Olivier, Darcy knew – 'made a film with Neil Diamond in the eighties. He said he was more embarrassed about it than anything he'd ever done and it made him sick to think about it. Still, it's up to you, darling.' Angharad smiled brightly at her daughter, having launched this fusilade at the idea. 'You're at liberty to make your own decisions. Unlike so many people in the world, which reminds me, I've got a Free Tibet meeting at lunchtime. Must dash, darling.'

Darcy struggled out of this mire of uncomfortable thoughts by reminding herself she had no plans to get used to any of this. She was an observer, essentially. But it was certainly an interesting piece of research.

'More champagne?' Sean was back again, proffering a bottle whose gold neck protruded from swathes of white linen.

'Yes, please.' Darcy held out her glass, abandoning any effort not to enjoy herself. This was wonderful. Exciting. How could it be otherwise? Last week she had been grinding away in fringe Shakespeare to – at best – a half-empty theatre for a pittance. Now she was en route to meet one of Hollywood's most successful directors to audition for a major part in what, according to Mitch, would be the movie of the decade. How could anyone – Niall and Angharad notwithstanding – be expected not to enjoy that?

Before gliding off, Sean showed her the button on her seat that caused an opaque glass screen to rise and divide her from the next person for increased privacy. Darcy smiled and thanked him, but silently dismissed the possibility of using it. Only someone terribly rude or self-important would do that.

There was no need, anyway. The seat next to her was empty and, from where she sat, sipping, in the central aisle, she could hardly see her fellow travellers. A sort of shell surrounded each seat from which various crossed legs dressed in expensive-looking trousers and feet with shiny leather shoes protruded. The only disappointment was that, so far, she had failed to spot any celebrities. Mitch, ramping up the glamour and excitement for all he was worth, had claimed that the Heathrow–LAX First Class had, at any given time, almost more famous people on board than luggage.

But Darcy had arrived too late – thanks to the tube train she had taken as a sop to Niall and keeping it real, which had been horribly delayed, so much so that she had missed the opportunity – and who knew if it would ever come again – to enjoy the First Class lounge. Now, on board, the possibility that she was surrounded by stars was tantalising. But feet were all she could see; if some belonged to George Clooney it was impossible to tell.

Beautiful People

A commotion seemed to be going on at the other side of the cabin. With surprise, Darcy realised someone was shouting. The soothing music and calm ambience was respectively drowned and shattered by the sound of a very angry woman yelling in a strange accent somewhere between Cockney and American something about her bags.

Darcy leant forward further. Sean and his colleagues were standing round a seat in attitudes of concern. She could see the woman shouting now; a deeply tanned blonde in a shiny pink leather coat and silver boots. 'Don't you know who I am?' she was yelling. 'Alexandra Pigott, that's who.' Who was Alexandra Pigott? Was she famous? Darcy craned forward, fascinated. The cabin staff were crowded tightly about the irate blonde. Only a flash of gesticulating pink and silver could be seen.

'I've got my own reality show, yeah?' the blonde was thundering, in a manner that did not suggest to Darcy a firm grasp of life's more down to earth aspects. Amid the imploring, frantically conciliatory murmurs from the cabin staff, Alexandra Pigott went on to complain that one of her pieces of luggage had not been loaded on to the aircraft.

Darcy could see almost everyone in First Class now. They were all, like her, craning their necks, doing their best to circumvent the privacy-ensuring arrangements of their respective seats, eager to observe what was going on.

George Clooney was not among them, Darcy noticed, although this was less disappointing now she was witnessing a real-life celebrity tantrum – it was all rather exciting, even if she had never heard of the celebrity. She could see the point of First Class more and more.

Alexandra continued shouting; Sean and his colleagues continued in vain trying to placate her. Then, to add to the drama, two policemen arrived in the cabin, told the blonde she had the choice of staying on the flight and joining her bags at the other end, or disembarking. 'You'll be hearing from my lawyers,' screamed Alexandra Pigott.

'And you'll be hearing from ours,' murmured a stewardess passing Darcy as Alexandra rose, tossed her white-blond hair and stormed out of the cabin.

The drama over, everyone immediately disappeared back into their seats. The soothing music swelled again and, within minutes, calmness descended once more. Even Sean looked composed when, a minute later, he materialised, smiling, at her side, hardly a hair of his gelled head out of place.

'Madam?' He passed her a menu with 'FIRST' on the cover, along with the BA speedwing in silver. 'Order whatever you want, any time you want,' he urged as Darcy scanned the à la carte: filet mignon, rack of lamb . . . Delicious!

Her stomach rumbled almost as loudly as the aeroplane engines. Far louder than them, in fact, as the engines seemed to be at the other end of the plane.

'There's a full cheeseboard as well, madam. Better leave room for that!' Sean glided away.

The plane took off without further incident, without Alexandra Pigott and, presumably, without her bags. More champagne came round and Darcy, feeling rather light-headed by now, rose rather unsteadily to her feet and took the brightest and trashiest-looking of the magazines on the table.

It was partly an act of defiance. *HotStars America* was exactly the kind of magazine she would never have dared touch with Niall about; a celebrity publication of the most garish kind. Darcy flicked through with a guilty speed; then, as her eye hooked on the more sensational headlines, her perusal slowed.

CELEBRITY GRILL
We meet an A-lister for lunch

Actress Belle Murphy shot to fame last year in *Marie*, a bosomy biopic about Mary, Queen of Scots. Since then, she's rarely been out of the gossip columns. To celebrate the release of her latest film, *Bloody Mary*, we caught up with Belle and her inseparable companion, her Chihuahua dog, Sugar, in New York's hottest new restaurant, the pink-themed Rosie's . . .

There was a large, accompanying photograph of Belle Murphy sitting in a pink fluffy armchair wearing what looked like a black latex bikini.

HS: Belle, you're looking great. That's an incredible outfit you're wearing.
BM: Thanks. I like to keep my style original, but I always dress for myself.
HS: Belle, how do you keep so slim?
BM: I just can't put on weight. It's just so bizarre. I mean, I try. Last week I had four McDonald's in one sitting. And you should so see me on the set when the sandwiches come round, the biscuits come round, I'm so, like, whoa, hey, over here with that big old tuna melt!
HS: Talking of sets, how exactly is *Bloody Mary* doing at the box office, Belle? Is it true the figures are a little, how do we put this . . . ?
BM: No! It's doing great. I mean, I don't have the exact figures but it was the number five film in Serbia last week.

HS: Would it have helped if *Bloody Mary* had had more nude scenes, do you think? After all, these were a feature of *Marie*.

BM: I really believe that the nudity in *Marie* was integral to the character.

Darcy chuckled. She had seen *Marie*. Niall had lifted his usual Hollywood embargo on the grounds that it was a film about a former queen of Scotland. Although, in the end, Scotland had played the most minor of roles, far more minor than the two main ones played by Belle's bosoms. The way the nudity had struck Darcy wasn't just that it was integral to the character of Marie; it *was* the character of Marie. The film was, as Niall said afterwards, like lapdancing in period costume.

HS: On a different subject, we were sorry to hear about your break-up with Christian Harlow . . .

BM: Yeah. You know, it was fun with Christian while it lasted. But he wanted serious commitment and I don't want to be tied down. He's got over it now and we've both moved on. It's been very amicable. We're still great friends, call each other all the time.

HS: But now there's a new man in your life, we understand. A baby! Congratulations!

BM: Thanks. Yeah, motherhood's just, like, awesome. It was like all of a sudden I knew the secret, I became a member of this tribe of mothers and felt, like, really interwoven with everything, you know?

HS: You adopted him, right?

BM: Yeah. He's African. From an orphanage. You know, I feel a great empathy with African people. Particularly ones in orphanages. They have, like, *nothing*, but they always seem so happy with their lot. It's kind of humbling, you know?

HS: Are you looking after him yourself?

BM: Yeah. I've got this great British nanny. Called Jacintha; Lady Jacintha, in fact. She's from some top nanny college where they wear special hats and badges. Used to work for a famous author. She's very cool. Her ancestors go back to the Medieval Ages.

HS: So you're enjoying family life?

BM: It's beautiful, just the greatest. The moment I first held Morning I felt, you know, kinda so connected to the world. I didn't know I was capable of such love.

Darcy shoved the magazine in the plush seat pocket. The champagne suddenly seemed to be curdling with the truffles and foie gras in her stomach.

Unlike Niall, she was not a naturally cynical person. It was all too easy to imagine him condemning Belle Murphy as a monster of insincerity. But even so, Darcy found it hard to believe what she had just read. *I didn't know I was capable of such love.* Was there a celebrity, interviewed about their child, who didn't say that? Although one had to hope that they meant it, for the sake of the child. Particularly a little orphan child from Africa.

The feeling of pampered enjoyment and excited optimism gave way to a tight and anxious sensation. The interview she had just read was everything that her mother and Niall most despised. That she had once affected to despise too.

Now, it was different. She was on her way to Hollywood herself. Darcy felt her anxiety increasing, glancing around at the plush, wood-fitted cabin and Sean shimmering about with his linen-wrapped bottle of champagne. She remembered Alexandra Pigott's tantrum; suddenly, it did not seem so funny any more;

rather it seemed disrespectful and spoilt. Was that how people behaved in this new world she was entering? Perhaps, Darcy thought, she really was selling out, being sucked in, having her values twisted, after all. Perhaps she really was making the biggest mistake of her life.

'Another glass, madam?' Sean was beaming at her side. Darcy looked miserably up at him. 'Mmm?' He proffered the bottle.

The tightness inside her relaxed. She grinned and watched as the foaming pale gold liquid tumbled into her glass. On the other hand, all this might just be great fun.

Chapter 16

Naked apart from a million-dollar diamond necklace and matching bracelet and rings, a beautiful blonde was sunbathing on the top deck of a billionaire's yacht just off St Tropez.

It was her own yacht. They were her own diamonds. She was the billionaire; Belle Murphy, the stratospherically successful film star with a string of box-office mega-hits to her name.

She stretched complacently in the sunshine, noting the expensive flash of the diamonds as she moved and gazing with satisfaction down her long, slender, honey-brown body. Her nipples were pink and erect under the caressing heat, her pubic hair clipped into a neat landing strip, her legs, waxed by the best beauticians in London, stretched, parted and shone with sun-oil. Far away, her coral-painted toenails wiggled in sensual delight. She looked ready to receive a lover, but she had received many lately and just for the moment, at least, Belle had decided the caresses of the hot Riviera sunshine were delicious enough.

She raised herself slightly on slender, braceleted arms and pushed back some of her shining blond hair to view the sparkling blue waves stretching away all around the big white and silver boat. Life was so wonderful. Her every whim was catered for. She had only half formed the thought that a glass of champagne would be welcome when one of her white-uniformed, gold-braided crew appeared with a frost-beaded flute on a silver tray. And now, as she was sipping it and starting to think about lunch, here that came too. Belle glanced with casual satisfaction through her huge black designer sunglasses at the black dot in the sky, that full stop in the blue, that announced the helicopter coming from her favourite London seafood restaurant with the daily order of oysters and langoustines.

Belle waved at the chopper, a naughty pout augmenting her smile of seafood anticipation as she thought about its handsome pilot, Paul, whom she had hired as much for his looks as his expertise with the helicopter. Jacques had proved to be a very satisfactory lover, as had most of the crew of *Marie*, which Belle had named after her first big-hit film.

The only problem with Paul, Belle reflected, was that he had rather possessive tendencies. Of course, it was very flattering, he was ten years younger than she, but he seemed reluctant to accept the fact that she could not sleep with him every night, that Henri, the yacht's captain, and Sven, who ran the boat's toning studios and gave such wonderful massages, had things to offer her too. Very particular things. Belle closed her eyes and stretched luxuriously, recalling every delicious detail of last night with Sven. An athletic lover really was a revelation; Sven could make her teeth rattle in a way they hadn't since Christian Harlow.

Belle gasped. The thought, coming so suddenly, was painful, like a slap. The agony of Christian dumping her was still fresh. She opened her eyes wide to banish the miserable memories and stared through her sunglasses into a sky of uninterrupted Mediterranean blue.

Paul was approaching in his helicopter. The black nose of the chopper was near enough for her to see him, his handsome face set with concentration, his mouth firm, his thick and level brows drawn, his hands, that could produce such intense delight, gripping the controls. Belle waved, calling out amid the juddering noise that was so close and so loud he could not possibly hear her. She smiled, thinking how he would be enjoying the sight of her naked body, the body he was so complimentary about, always; the body he seemed to know exactly what to do with. Cupping her breasts loosely, her fingers trailing over her stiffened nipples, Belle pouted a kiss in the direction of the pilot and ran her tongue round her lips. She felt a sudden tightness in her groin, an urgent, burning buzz that demanded relief. Perhaps she would take him into her stateroom tonight, after all. Sooner, possibly. He could take her here, on the deck, before he even unpacked his oysters. That should assuage his jealousy, and a good deal else besides.

Paul really was getting very close, Belle thought. Admittedly, the place where she lay, now panting with desire, was on the top deck, which was where the helicopter pads were. But they were at the other end of the boat. Now she could not see the sun for this great clumsy black machine. The noise was getting louder and louder; she could see the blade rotivator now, whipping the long slashing pieces of metal round. What was Paul doing?

Only now did Belle realise that the man at the controls was not Paul after all. It was Christian. The ex-lover that had abandoned her so cruelly, not her him, with amicable results, the way she always said in interviews. Through the tinted black screen at the front of the helicopter Christian seemed to be laughing; what she could see of his eyes wore a strange, crazed, unfamiliar expression. She had seen him *in extremis*, in the throes of passion, of ecstasy, of profound physical fulfilment, but he had never looked like this. There was something terrifying

161

about his face now. Even more terrifying than that ghastly moment he had said he was leaving her.

Stunned momentarily by the pain of that betrayal, Belle tried to scramble up, but it was too late. The aircraft was so low she had to crouch, to flatten herself once again.

Hurriedly, she lay on her back on the burning plastic deck, her legs apart, her arms out, screaming into the screaming of the blades. Her fingers, thrashing in panic, caught the stem of the champagne glass, throwing its foaming contents all over her. She caught one final glimpse of Christian's face – his eyes blazing in triumph, his capped white teeth dazzling as the heavy-bellied black body of the helicopter lowered itself, juddering and bucking like some obscene parody of a lover, on to her very own landing strip . . .

With a terrified scream, Belle jerked out of her siesta, seeing with enormous relief that all that hovered above her was the ceiling of the London hotel penthouse. Christian, the helicopter, it had all been a dream. Her relief quickly gave way to a sense of disappointment.

Disappointment not because she was not suffering a hideous death in his helicopter blades, of course. Disappointment because she was in London.

London, Belle felt, had an oppressive atmosphere. Quite apart from the rain. June it might be but the gloomy, marbled-grey skies beyond the great penthouse windows gave, Belle thought, the impression that the whole city was on some great dimmer switch permanently turned down low. The trees in the park opposite were always bent under some windy blast. The pavements were always shiny with rain. How unlike the sunshine of California, as permanent and dazzling as everyone's grins.

London. The city where Mitch had sent her after she had adopted the African baby.

The adoption should, of course, have transformed her career. The studio had been convinced that it would – certainly, NBS had been the ones pulling all the strings with the embassies. While Belle hadn't followed events in detail – to do so would break the habit of a lifetime – she had gathered that an NBS deal to shoot a blockbuster in whatever country had come up with a kid fastest had been the carrot. International red tape had simply melted away in the promised glare of studio lighting.

Yeah, the adoption had been the easy bit. The actual baby had been less of a breeze. Those who said motherhood was hard were damn right, Belle thought. As she lacked a single maternal fibre in the whole of her emaciated body, pretending to be transported with delight whilst holding a child was one of the most difficult acting jobs Belle had ever had to do. Especially after it possetted on her Zac Posen.

But what was especially infuriating was that her Zac had been ruined in vain. The adoption had not achieved the expected result. While there had been coverage – an interview in *HotStars* and a couple of others – and even a few photoshoots with Morning, the general effect on the press had been far from electrifying. The consensus seemed to be that everyone had seen it all before. Celebrity African adoptions were nothing new. Madonna and Angelina Jolie had got there first. Damn them, thought Belle, with more venom even than when she usually damned them. Damn them *to hell*. Because now here she was, stuck with a baby she didn't want, who she wouldn't even be able to dump without a great deal of the wrong sort of press interest. It would be years before he could quietly be packed off to some boarding school somewhere and she need never set eyes on him again. The whole enterprise had been a disaster.

All that trouble. And for what? Her career was only slightly further out of the doldrums. Steven Spielberg wasn't exactly inundating her with calls, while the phone line once reserved exclusively for Harvey Weinstein hadn't rung in ages. Arlington Shorthouse, meanwhile, whose idea the whole fucking mess had been, had been conspicuous by his silence. NBS had not been in touch with new projects. And as for me, Belle fumed, I'm as washed up as driftwood on the beach.

Except she wasn't even on a beach. She was in London.

'Like, just what does a girl have to do to remake her image?' Belle had wailed at Mitch.

'I'm glad you asked me that,' he replied.

Morning, he tried to persuade her, had been Part One of her image remake and here was Part Two. Belle was in London as per her own – albeit ironic – suggestion in the meeting with Arlington, to land a part in a Shakespeare play and tread the stage in the great playwright's native land. He would arrange the auditions. He had contacts. He could make it happen.

The idea was that, having trodden the boards as Lady Macbeth or whatever in London for a couple of weeks, she would succumb to a sudden, convenient virus and go back to LA with prestigious serious-Shakespeare credentials, having got a few weeks of real stagework under her belt. And if that didn't silence her detractors and impress people, nothing would.

Belle was even beginning to wonder whether she cared any more. This morning's audition had been a particular nightmare. She couldn't even think about it without help. Belle pushed herself upward on the bed and lunged for the half-finished bottle of champagne, which stood on the marbled and gilded bedside table, next to the large, ornate lamp whose shade was, according to the hotel manager who had shown her fawningly around the penthouse on arrival, hand-painted and completely unique. He had looked, Belle thought, noticing his tinted foundation, much the same himself.

She put the neck of the bottle to her lips. The champagne was room temperature, but she did not care. She was in search of oblivion. Belle was so miserable that, for once, even Sugar yapping and scrabbling outside the door failed to stir her sympathies. Fortunately Morning was quiet, as indeed he was most of the time. As indeed he should be, Belle thought, considering the amount she was paying Jacintha to look after him.

She took another swig and thought about the ordeal of a few hours ago. The audition had been with the young, maverick hotshot running an avant-garde production of *King Lear* in a small Soho theatre. He had a vacancy; the actress playing Cordelia had had to go away for a few weeks. 'To LA, to see a director, ironically enough,' the hotshot had smiled. Belle had stared levelly back at him. It didn't sound ironic to her; it sounded homicidally infuriating.

There was an understudy for the absent actress's part, but the maverick young hotshot had naturally jumped at the chance to cast a Hollywood name like Belle, even if Belle's name was rather faded and besmirched of late. Indeed, so enthusiastic had been the director – business at the box office had been less brisk than hoped – that Belle had been assured by Mitch that she was a shoo-in for the role, and all she had to do was turn up.

The phone at her bedside rang. Belle groped clumsily about for it.

'How'd it go?' Mitch asked.

'*Gross*. That nude stuff. You never warned me.'

From the LA end, Mitch blinked. Indeed, the London director, a quick-thinker clearly wishing to maximise the opportunity, had stipulated that Belle would have to play her part clothesless; his take on *Lear* having suddenly become, Mitch learnt, an all-naked version 'for artistic reasons. We're pushing this one to the edge'.

165

Mitch hadn't mentioned this to Belle for the simple reason that it had never seemed important. Nudity was Belle's middle name. She stripped off at the drop of a hat; never blinked an eyelid at it. Nudity was her calling card, how she had got where she had got – or where she had been, rather. The fact that this production combined nudity with Shakespeare had seemed, far from being an impediment, a stroke of sublime luck to Mitch. A divine helping hand.

'You never mind being nude normally,' he bewilderedly pointed out.

'*I* don't, no,' Belle snapped back. 'It wasn't *me* I was worried about.'

'What then?' None of this was making any sense to Mitch.

'*Him*,' Belle ranted. It seemed to Mitch she was almost retching at the memory. 'He was so saggy and old. Swinging everywhere. You should have seen him on the trapeze. *Ew.*'

'The director?' Mitch demanded. He'd thought he was a young guy. He'd sounded like one on the phone.

'The guy playing Lear. I had to do a scene with him. For the audition. He has his dick out all through the performance. Can you imagine? *Gross.*'

Mitch, from his end, sighed. None of this was working out the way it should. First there had been the disappointment about the baby; admittedly, the timing seemed to have been slightly out there. And now London was going tits up too. Belle had sounded drunk just then and possibly, Mitch suspected, he had overestimated her ability to cope without a vast quantity of help. He had advised that the usual Hollywood entourage of bodyguards, a personal assistant and press officer would adversely affect any efforts to give her image the realistic, authentic, down-to-earth edge the studio clearly felt it needed. He had reminded her that you never saw Dame Judi Dench mob-handed with stylists, security, personal trainers and spokes-people.

But Belle had insisted on the Portchester, London's best and grandest hotel, and the penthouse suite to boot. She had also insisted on bringing Morning's nanny; it seemed she couldn't even pick her new adopted son up without help. Well, given the amount she seemed to be drinking, that was probably true, Mitch reflected gloomily.

I'm all alone, Belle snivelled to herself now, wincing at the horrid memory of the audition and still shaken from her ghastly dream. She lay, miserable and naked, her face still smeared in last night's make-up, in the crumpled linen sheets of the penthouse kingsize bed. She was, for once, oblivious to the comfort around her.

'Has anyone ever been so lonely?' Belle wailed. Had anyone ever suffered like her? Jacintha, of course, was always busy with the baby, and when she wasn't, she radiated disapproval of everything Belle did. Or at least, that was how it felt. So what if she drank in bed, Belle thought rebelliously as she took another swig. So what if she watched cable until her eyes glazed over? So what if she was so hungover she didn't get up until lunchtime?

Jacintha had no idea, Belle knew, of just how terrible her life had become. That there were times when she just couldn't go on, when her situation overwhelmed her. Really, she almost envied Jacintha. The nanny's life was so wonderfully simple compared to her own, Belle thought. Had Jacintha ever suffered like her? Had she ever been abandoned by her lover and her profession at more or less the same time? Admittedly, it was hard to imagine the rather chilly, angular nanny in the throes of passion. Had it been so, Belle thought, she might even have tried it with her. It wouldn't be the first time and, given the absence of suitable men, bicuriosity was better than nothing. It could actually be pretty good. But Jacintha was so flat and chilly it would be like sex with an ice tray.

She reached for the bottle of warm champagne and took another swig. She closed her eyes. Behind her eyelids, the carousel spun past her, whirling above her fallen body, music playing, lights glittering, glinting with gold and mirrors, full of shiny happy people having the time of their lives. But she had spun off and what was worse, had not the faintest idea how to get back on.

Chapter 17

For Darcy, the pampering of the plane proceeded seamlessly into the pampering of a limousine sent by Mitch to meet her at LAX. Whisked, with the rest of First Class, off the aircraft before everybody else, Darcy whirled through Immigration and out of the baggage reclaim at a speed far faster than she imagined possible.

She spotted her driver in the arrivals hall. He was a peak-capped diminutive Puerto Rican holding a sign with 'Mr Darcy' written on it.

'It had *what* on it?' Mitch, calling her on the mobile once the limo was underway, did not see the joke.

'It doesn't matter,' Darcy said, blinking with tired eyes through the tinted windows at LA. Her first impression was that it was bright and hot and busy; shiny, unfamiliar-shaped cars, sunlit roads, low, magnolia-coloured buildings, dusty palm trees, cloudless blue sky. Seeing it through glass gave it a distance, as if she was watching it on the television. Actually, it looked like it always did on the television. Perhaps she actually *was* watching it on the television and this was all a dream.

'I thought it was funny, actually,' she added about the

chauffeur. She wanted to comfort Mitch, who seemed upset about it for some reason.

She thought it was *funny?* The hell it was funny, Mitch fumed to himself. A bad start was what it was. That limo company with its caps cost a freaking fortune. It was supposed to impress clients, not make them – and him, more to the point – look stupid. 'Don't worry,' he assured Darcy in a voice of grim determination. 'Pretty soon you'll be so famous that no one could even think about making a mistake like that.'

'I'm *not* worrying,' Darcy assured him back. She wanted to add that she neither particularly believed the bit about being famous nor wanted it all that much. But she desisted; it seemed impolite, given how excited about the Jack Saint meeting Mitch was.

'How about dinner tonight?' Mitch asked. 'Go to your hotel, have a siesta and I'll come by and pick you up at about seven thirty.'

Darcy slumped against the slippery leather limousine seats with relief. She had been half fearful Mitch might suggest lunch or a meeting or something else she would be duty-bound to go to, but the fact was that, for all she had slept on the plane, her head ached and her eyes throbbed and she longed to sleep some more.

Darcy's hotel was a cream-painted palace whose staff all looked like supermodels and whose entrance was flanked with lawns as smooth and glossy as bright green velvet. There were ornate fountains, palm trees and beds of almost painfully colourful flowers whose every petal seemed hand-tweaked into position. It occurred to Darcy, as she looked about, that the extra brightness could be due to the fact that everyone seemed to wear sunglasses; you had to overcompensate on the colour front as nothing was ever viewed with the naked eye. Or was it because any colour out there had to compete with the California sky, a powerful swimming-pool blue?

Inside the hotel, by contrast, all was muted and calm. Her room, which faced front over the zinging gardens, was vast and cream, with cream-coloured furniture. It was, she thought, a bit like being inside a meringue. The only non-cream aspects were striped white and yellow – the awnings on the enormous windows and the parasol and cushions of the chairs outside on the balcony. And of course, when you combined white and yellow, cream was what you got.

'Can I get you a glass of champagne, madam?' the chipper bellboy who had shown her up asked on leaving. Darcy shook her head. She didn't want to even think about champagne now. She felt that she had drunk her own weight in the stuff on the flight; her head throbbed and her mouth was dry. Apart from water, something comforting and sweet was what she wanted; something that would send her into an afternoon doze. Suddenly, she could see it, in a tall glass in a silver cradle, foamy, light, warm, wonderfully thick and sweet.

'Got any . . . um . . . hot chocolate?' she asked.

The bellboy looked thunderstruck, then collected himself and nodded. 'Certainly, madam.'

When the hot chocolate came it exceeded all expectations. It was in the tall glass she had imagined, complete with the silver cradle, topped with cream and chocolate shavings, studded with marshmallows and with two chocolate chip cookies on the side.

Afterwards, Darcy lay down on the big bed, sinking immediately into the airy, cool, linen-scented embrace of the duvet and padded mattress. It was still hard to imagine she was really here.

Mitch, ramping up her excitement levels on the mobile at the prospect of meeting Jack Saint on the morrow, had effectively swept away the last of her reservations. She, an obscure British actress, was here in LA to have a meeting with a big director about a big film. Whatever Niall said, whatever her mother said, it was definitely exciting. Partly because of what they said, Darcy could now admit to herself. Away from their influence, their disapproval, she felt a rush of freedom that was all the more delicious for having a guilty edge to it.

She burrowed into the billowing cream bedlinen, feeling that her grandmother was smiling down on her. Alone of all her family, Darcy knew, Anna would have encouraged the LA visit – she was no stranger to the town herself, after all. She would, Darcy knew, also have appreciated the meringue décor. And she would certainly have appreciated all the champagne.

When Mitch turned up at seven thirty, Darcy's first impression was that he was most unlike her idea of a Hollywood agent. His voice on the phone had been urgent and persuasive, and she had pictured someone smooth, slim and snappy, some handsome, hawk-eyed Hollywood machine. But Mitch was large – enormous, in fact, billowing and bulging in all directions – and had an apprehensive, chaotic air to him that, contrary to such airs in England, was obviously not something he was cultivating. Rather, it seemed to be something he was desperately trying to hide. As for hawkish, she sensed that he was much kinder than he wanted people to suspect. She liked him.

He looked at her, also approvingly. Darcy wore a vintage Dior sleeveless sheath dress she had been delighted to find in a charity shop the day before she had flown out to LA. She had spotted it, gleaming darkly on the rail, and swooped with a gasp of delight. Knightsbridge, Darcy felt, had its drawbacks, but the second-hand shops – crowded with the cast-offs of various local countesses – were not among them.

It was, Darcy had thought as she examined the dress, almost as if it had been waiting for her. It was in excellent condition. She knew instinctively that it would fit her perfectly; knew too that its rich, inky-blue satin would give a velvety depth to her dark hair and a creaminess to her pale skin. Immediately after buying it she had, in an uncharacteristic seizure of extravagance, splashed out on a pair of Prada heels to match it, which cost far more than the budget she had mentally earmarked for her entire LA wardrobe. She had not told Niall about these; although, admittedly, he was so angry about the LA trip in general that a pair of shoes was hardly likely to make a difference.

'You look great, baby,' Mitch assured her. His enthusiasm was genuine, mixed with excitement and not a little relief. He had no real idea of what to expect; there had been no pictures of Darcy on any websites apart from the one run by those mad old trouts in London who called themselves her theatrical agents. On that, Darcy appeared in the usual hideously unflattering monochrome headshot that British thespians for some reason preferred. It was incredible any of them ever got work.

The headshot gave no indication of how very pretty Darcy was in real life. Her skin was a pure, milky white; so white it almost glowed; only as he looked at it did Mitch realise how boring the uniform roast-chicken tans of LA could be. Her face was a pale oval with a touch of pink in the cheeks. Her thick, shiny black hair was unhighlighted, so far as he could tell; thanks to his profession rather than any personal interest, he was now able to spot the subtlest efforts in this direction. Mitch stared at it in awe as it slid about her white shoulders, probably the only undyed young female hair in the whole of the city.

She was taller than expected, and not as thin as he had imagined. Slim, certainly, but no twig. No typically LA lollipop lady, with a big head and a stick-like body. She had breasts *and* a bottom. She filled that stunning dress beautifully, Mitch thought. People were staring at her as they left the hotel lobby – and no wonder.

The third surprise was that she seemed both pleased and excited to be here. A long way, Mitch thought, from that first conversation, when she had turned down his overtures and declared herself loftily uninterested in Hollywood.

That Brit reserve, all that hoity-toity stuff about the theatre she'd laid on him during that first phone call, seemed to have melted away like snow in June now she was here. As she greeted him in the hotel foyer she was beaming – those teeth looked natural too, although, being white and straight, entirely unlike the snaggly yellow ones the British were famous for. She seemed positively bubbling with the excitement of it all.

It was hard to believe she had just that morning stepped off an eleven-hour flight, but this, Darcy told him, giggling, was due to the restorative properties of a huge hot chocolate she had ordered from room service.

Mitch had almost fallen over at this. 'You're kidding.' *A hot chocolate! With cream and cookies on the side?* 'Hey! Young actress in Hollywood orders calories shock,' he grinned.

Her face flashed with surprise. Then she smiled. 'Oh. Now I get it.'

'Get what?'

'Why the waiter was amazed. Oh!' Darcy covered her mouth with her hand. 'And I ordered a hamburger when I woke up as well. He must think I'm such a pig!'

'Good for you,' said Mitch approvingly, leading her to the limo waiting outside.

'Actually, can you believe it, but I'm hungry again,' Darcy admitted, looking excitedly about her as they emerged from the hotel entrance into the scented summer evening. 'Where are we going to eat?'

'Puccini's,' Mitch announced, and confidently awaited the exclamations of surprise and delight.

Darcy smiled politely. 'Great.'

Mitch gave her a sideways look. 'You heard of Puccini's, right?' Surely even some ingénue from deepest, darkest, obscurest theatrical London . . .

'Er . . .' She bit her lip and looked worried.

'LA's hottest Italian restaurant,' Mitch supplied, his chins rolling as he nodded. 'You have to book a month ahead even for Siberia.'

Her brow furrowed. 'Is that another restaurant?'

'Its worst table,' Mitch sighed. Jeez, didn't this woman know anything? It didn't annoy him, however; rather, filled him with a sort of fatherly exasperation that wasn't unpleasant. There was something so infectiously open and unpretentious about this girl, her big black eyes everywhere, missing nothing, so obviously interested and amused. She was like a breeze blowing through the open window of a hot, noisy room, Mitch thought, as the limo drew up outside the hot and noisy room that was Puccini's.

Darcy, crouched in the limo, nose pressed to the window, watched as they swept up to the front of a long, low building swathed in vines, and with tables outside with cream shades. It took some time for Darcy's eyesight to return to normal after the blaze of paparazzi at the door – not for her, she realised with relief, but for Jennifer Aniston just behind. Darcy had been amazed both by the way the lights exploded; fast, furious, noisy, frightening; and the way the actress – far smaller and thinner even than she appeared in magazines – just smiled her way through it and walked to her table with her companion, seemingly undisturbed by the fuss.

'That'll be happening for *you*, soon,' Mitch assured Darcy quickly. She looked, he noticed, less delighted than expected by this promise.

Darcy's eyes were darting excitedly round Puccini's. Her first impression was that it was crammed and claustrophobic. Breathy, ambient music pulsed behind a background of shrieking voices, bouncing off chrome walls, which also doubled as mirrors. A waiter shot eagerly over, looking at Mitch intently, obviously recognising him.

This did not surprise the agent. It was the usual way in restaurants like this, where every member of staff was a star in the making. Even someone, like himself, at the bottom of the Talent Incorporated pecking order could be good for a bit part in something. Feeling a rare frisson of power, Mitch grandly gave the order for two champagnes and the waiter sashayed off.

'Like this place?' Mitch reached for a breadstick. The table they had been given was one of the worst; restaurants of this sort, he suspected, had a Fame Board like his agency's in the back somewhere too. He would be somewhere way down the bottom of it. Darcy, on the other hand, wasn't yet on it at all. But she would be, Mitch was certain. She had to be.

Darcy nodded, eager to be polite. Actually, now she was getting more used to it, Puccini's seemed rather delightfully silly. Menus as vast as billboards rose from the tiny metal tables.

'But you have great restaurants in London, right? Sheekey, The Wolseley, Gordon Ramsay and all that stuff?'

Darcy shrugged. She had never been to any of them. Possibly she might have liked to, but she was determined to live on her earnings and anyway Niall scorned such places, preferring to eat either at a tiny, cheap Chinatown Chinese where plastic washing-up bowls of dirty plates stood in the doorways or a bargain-basement Italian in Soho where the old lady patrons slopped around in ground-down shoe-heels with teatowels over their shoulders. Eating out with her parents was even less sybaritic: vegetarian Indians near Euston station being their favourites. These, admittedly, were better than the places Niall preferred, but still some considerable distance from glamorous.

The champagne arrived. Darcy picked hers up gingerly; her head still felt slightly tight and thick from the wine on the plane.

'To you!' Mitch declared, in a voice so loud that she cringed. She chinked back, reddening, desperate for people not to stare. Mitch, on the other hand, had the opposite intention. He was pleased at how his protégée was going down. Darcy had yet to notice the subtle signs that her presence was being noted; shifty glances from surrounding tables, the odd head straining over another to see.

The champagne having helped suffuse her embarrassment, Darcy started to look about her again. Her wandering eye caught a well-known face. She leant over to Mitch. 'Is that . . . ?'

'Drew Barrymore, yes.'

'And that . . . ?'

'Is Cameron Diaz.' Mitch grinned delightedly. This was fun.

A waiter glided to the table. The same one as before, Mitch saw. Looking more disdainful than ever. 'May I take your order?'

'Oh, yes. Sorry.' Darcy beamed. 'I've been too busy staring to look round.' She applied herself conscientiously to the vast menu, then raised her head. 'Did you say this was an Italian restaurant?'

Mitch and the waiter affirmed that this was indeed the case.

'But there isn't any pasta on the menu.'

The waiter's eyebrow arched upwards. The agent put a fat paw on Darcy's small, slim hand.

'This is Hollywood,' he reminded her. 'No one eats pasta here. Carbs are a no-no.'

Darcy's brows drew together in bewilderment. 'But . . . but . . .' The Italian restaurant Niall had favoured in London immediately seemed less dire a memory. Scruffy it may have been, but at least it had spaghetti.

'Perhaps madam would like the steamed fish with lemon?' put in the waiter acidly.

Darcy smiled at him. 'I'd rather not. What about . . . ?' She scanned the menu again. Her face lit up suddenly. 'Hey. I've found some pasta. Nude ravioli. What's that?' she asked, her voice dropping slightly. 'What's, erm, nude about it?'

'It doesn't have any pasta,' said the waiter, with a touch of triumph. 'It's just the stuffing.'

'Which is?' Darcy asked hopefully, her hungry imagination conjuring up rich patties of red wine ragu. Or something deliciously cheesy and herby . . .

'Steamed spinach balls.'

'Oh.' She struggled to moderate the disappointment in her voice. 'I'll have that, please,' she added politely.

The waiter pressed his lips thinly together and made a scribble on his pad.

'I'll have the shark consommé,' Mitch said. It was the standard power order. Shark – for sharks. The nearest Hollywood restaurants got to a joke.

He handed the vast bill of fare over, and Darcy watched, amused, as the waiter struggled to incorporate it about his person. There was nowhere to put it apart from under his arm.

'An Italian restaurant without pasta!' she exclaimed as the waiter disappeared.

'You don't get it.' Mitch grinned at her. Her directness was a blast, it really was. He had never met anyone like her before. 'Restaurants in Hollywood aren't for eating in. They're to avoid eating.'

The black eyes staring into his widened in amazement. 'But *you* eat.'

'Yeah, but not in restaurants.' Mitch thought guiltily of the jelly doughnuts and the doctor's advice he routinely ignored. He resolved to change the subject. 'This meeting with Jack Saint,' he began, deciding to get straight on to the important business, rather than waiting.

Darcy nodded, tilting her head slightly and attentively. Her eyes slid slightly to the right of Mitch's face. It was then that it happened.

The chat and buzz of the restaurant disappeared. Mitch's voice faded to nothing. The remains of her hangover vanished. Darcy was aware of nothing but a singing sensation in her every nerve-ending – and the eyes she was looking into. In which she felt caught, unable to move, almost unable to breathe.

They were a ridiculous blue even from this distance, drilling into hers. He was, she managed to absorb, almost stupidly handsome, all cheekbones and lips and glossy, ruffled black hair. He looked like something from a perfume advert, one of those bulging crotches in white underwear that women crashed their cars into walls straining to look at. He ought to have made her laugh.

But Darcy had never felt less like laughing. Her heart thumped painfully. Several times, she swallowed. His lips curved as he looked at her, his gaze intent but lazy, almost insolent, full of erotic promise. Springing, perfectly formed, into Darcy's mind came the thought of him naked, kissing her, doing all sorts of delicious things to her. She caught her breath. She had never seen anyone whose raw sexuality was so evident. He was someone it was impossible to look at and not instantly imagine yourself in bed with.

Her heart leapt in mixed terror and excitement as he rose to his feet; her scrambled senses realising a few seconds later that he was leaving. The two people he was with led the way: a man and a woman; the woman thin and fiftysomething, not lover material, Darcy quickly noted. His agent, maybe? The man looked businesslike too: tanned, grey-haired, trim, sharp-eyed; the Hollywood player type she had imagined Mitch being. Her eyes followed the younger man; his remained locked to hers. For all she was focused on his face, she could sense the power of his body; broad shoulders, a graceful animal muscularity, like some jungle big cat.

'Hey, are you listening to me?' Mitch interrupted. This girl was charming, but crazy. Was this situation possible? Here she was, sitting in one of Tinseltown's prime power spots, being briefed by her agent about a dream meeting with the director who could change her life – a meeting three quarters of this very restaurant would kill for – and what was she doing? Staring into space.

His gaze followed Darcy's; he breathed a sharp inward breath. His small eyes narrowed in dislike. Oh, no. Not *that guy*. Anyone but *him*.

'Um, yes, um, sorry . . .' Darcy's distracted black eyes swivelled back to Mitch's. Their expression, he noted, was one that seemed to be coming back from a long way away. They flexed in surprise as they registered the thundercloud that had descended on his formerly genial brow. 'Yes, of course I'm listening. Go on, please.' Seized by an uncontrollable impulse, she grabbed his hand, leant over and hissed, 'But before you do, tell me who that man is.'

Mitch's heart sank at the urgency in her voice. He had heard it before. He did not need to look up to confirm who she was talking about. He spoke stonily into the wooden table. 'Christian Harlow.'

'And who's he?' Darcy asked, her eyes following Christian through the restaurant, her heart steadily sinking because any moment now he would disappear through the door. Then, to her delight, he stopped, paused at the entrance and, eyes still on her, raised two fingers to his lips and kissed them. Then he disappeared into a hail of flashbulbs.

Darcy whirled back to Mitch, her eyes blazing. 'He's *famous*?'

'Famous for being an asshole,' Mitch growled, his good mood severely dissipated. Famous too, he added to himself, for being the man who had caused all Belle Murphy's problems. Ruined her career, pretty much. And, to endear him to Mitch ever further, Christian had just this week joined Greg Cucaracha at Talent Incorporated, Greg having prised Christian away from the agent he had been with since the beginning. Although given Christian's loyalty record, that was, Mitch imagined, probably as difficult as prising apart two halves of a cheese sandwich.

The sight of Harlow reminded him of everything he was hoping, for a couple of hours at least, to forget. Of Greg, whom he hated. Of Belle, who remained the biggest thorn in his admittedly large sides. Thank God he was leaving the restaurant.

Darcy was still gawping at the door through which Harlow had just departed. Then something clicked in her head. She blinked and felt a strange sensation, as if released from a spell. She was conscious again of sound, colour and movement about her, of smells and music and people talking and laughing.

She was conscious too of a wave of sickening guilt. Where was Niall in all this? Where was her loyalty? She felt hot with self-disgust. How could one glimpse of a stranger wipe out so completely all thoughts of the man she loved?

She had called him repeatedly on landing but he had not answered. He had an audition today, she knew – yet another. She desperately hoped it would go well. Or, at least, not as badly as the others. Sitting in the LA restaurant, sickened and ashamed, Darcy concentrated all her love and thoughts on her boyfriend and, from over six thousand miles away, wished him luck from the bottom of her anguished heart.

Chapter 18

Belle lay on the bed in the Portchester Hotel penthouse, clutching the half-empty bottle of champagne to her like a teddy bear, wreathed in creased linen and gloomy thoughts. The bedside telephone rang. Alarmed, Belle jerked the neck of the bottle in her mouth and the warm, fizzing contents ran out of the side of her mouth and into the deep clavicles below her chin. She wriggled; it tickled, although not pleasantly.

'I'm ringing to remind you you've got an audition this morning,' Mitch said with a firmness that masked the worry he increasingly felt.

He had hoped that, in the absence of a PA for Belle, the Portchester Hotel, prompted by him, could organise alarm calls, limos and so forth.

As indeed it could, in theory. And, according to the manager, actually had. The problem was, the hotel couldn't physically make Belle go to the auditions. From the sound of her voice during some of their phone conversations, Mitch suspected the limos just took Belle straight to the nearest bar.

And it wasn't just the directors she wasn't showing up for. The journalists were complaining too. The various newspapers that, hearing of her presence, had demanded to interview Belle, had found themselves sitting alone in various pre-agreed restaurants, staring into the bottoms of cooling cappuccino cups. While Belle, Mitch suspected, was alone in a bar somewhere else altogether, staring into the bottom of a wine glass.

'You haven't forgotten about this audition?' he added suspiciously, into the silence.

'No,' Belle said in a tiny, sheepish voice that Mitch hardly recognised from the thundering complaints of old. 'What is it?'

'*Titus Andronicus.*'

'Tight-ass *who?*'

'*Titus Andronicus.*'

Mitch wanted to scream. She *had* forgotten, damn her. Meaning she wouldn't have learnt any of the lines. She'd have to get through the audition on star power alone, and her wattage was dimmer than it had been.

'What's the part?' Belle said sullenly. She sounded utterly unrepentant, Mitch thought. Not to mention ungrateful. He'd had to pull some serious strings to get the director to agree to see her. Word about Belle and auditions had clearly been getting around. Didn't she want to save her career?

'A queen,' he replied carefully. At least, he thought it was a queen. Some society dame, anyway. He had only had time to absorb the vaguest outline of the plot, which hadn't sounded too good. The high point of the part Belle was auditioning for was the character realising she has just eaten two of her children in a pie. He decided not to draw this to his client's attention just now.

'There's a limo for you downstairs,' Mitch urged, his wheedling tones spiked with impatience. 'And the paps too. Make sure you look good, yeah?'

Belle reached for the bottle of warm champagne and took a final, resolve-stiffening swig, which went straight to her empty stomach. She could not remember the last time she had eaten – a proper meal, that was, instead of the skinny lattes and crackers that she normally got by on – any more than she could remember not having a hangover. Her head ached with one now. Low level but persistent, like someone slowly levering her brain apart. She had a feeling they had become constant around the time that Christian left. But she could not be sure. She hadn't been sure of anything since then.

Belle took another final swig and set to work. But a full face of re-done make-up was more effort than she was prepared to make. She wiped off the worst smudges from yesterday's mascara, pressed a powder puff to the shiniest bits of her cheeks and forehead and reapplied her lipstick.

She pulled unsteadily at the door of the walk-in wardrobe next to the vast and mirrored bathroom, staggered back as it flew unexpectedly open and grabbed at the first thing that came to hand, a Diane von Furstenberg leopard-print wrap. Rummaging in the bottom among the shoeboxes, she pulled out a pair of gold Manolos and gazed critically at her toenails as she pushed them in. She needed another pedicure – but what was the point? She took off the sandals and found some long brown suede Chanel boots with a medium heel instead.

She pulled her unwashed, unbrushed blond mane into a ponytail with a black silk Chanel scarf and considered the effect in the dressing-room mirror. Bed hair wasn't very Californian, but it *was* quite London, where everyone seemed pretty scruffy. Or 'edgy', as they apparently thought of it. Edgy was about the size of it, thought Belle. She'd felt edgy ever since she'd been in this goddamn city. She peered into the further, gloomier recesses of the cupboard, looking for a bag big enough to hide the three-quarters-finished bottle of champagne in. She needed something to help her through the audition.

Her eye fell on the very thing. The new, shiny, orange leather Birkin she'd bought yesterday during her blitzkrieg of Bond Street. Various other purchases she had made stood elsewhere in the cupboard, still in their bags. Belle stared at them for a second or two, vainly trying to recall what any of them were.

With a blast of strong perfume to disguise any smell of alcohol, she was ready. Swinging her bag defiantly, she walked out of the bedroom into the penthouse sitting room where Jacintha sat with Morning. Jacintha wore her usual disapproving expression. Seeing her, Sugar leapt to his feet and started yapping frenziedly; Jacintha's frown deepened. There was, Belle knew, no love lost between Morning's nanny and her pet. Possibly even less than between Morning's nanny and herself.

She bent, picked up Sugar and, crooning softly to him, stuffed him in the Birkin along with the champagne bottle. Then she hurried out of the door, into the private penthouse lift and down to the limo.

Ken sat on the wall opposite the Portchester Hotel, his camera idle in his lap. It was a cold morning, although it was June, and it was an unpleasant feeling, the chill from the concrete entering his buttocks.

Madonna had just jogged by, in the park across the road. He hadn't bothered snapping her. As she was wearing the same black tracksuit and shades as always, there was no point. Madonna was no fool; she knew the name of the game. Or the clothes of the game, at least, which was why, when she was out and about, she'd had on the same outfit for the last three years. To make the pictures look the same as they had for the last three years and render the image unsellable. It was a clever trick, and one all these celebrities who moaned about invasion of privacy would use if they really didn't want to be photographed.

Invasion of privacy! Ken shook his pinkish head with its thinning gingerish hair and snorted. It was ludicrous, it really was. He could think of at least two young actresses, bitter rivals, both of whom moaned endlessly about having photographers follow them, but both of whom kept small pet dogs entirely so that they would have a reason to go out several times a day. The photographers knew that they could be counted on to be in certain places at certain times, straight from the attentions of their personal stylists. One of them had special outfits just for going to Starbucks in. And yet they complained constantly that the press never left them alone.

If they really wanted privacy, Ken thought, they'd stay in, like Liz Hurley and Charlotte Church did until they'd lost the weight after the baby. Or they'd disguise themselves. Properly, like David Bowie always did, travelling on the tube wearing a pair of cheap sunglasses and reading a Turkish newspaper.

At least Belle Murphy, whatever else one may think about her, made no bones about the fact she wanted the publicity. She gave good pose too. No one who had never seen a celebrity in full facing-the-paps mode, Ken knew, had any idea how the pictures that appeared in the newspapers were achieved. They imagined they were just shots that were snatched in a second, and of course some were. But the ones like Belle, the ones who really wanted it, left nothing to chance. Belle would stand there, absolutely still, for minutes on end. Then she would change position very carefully, very slowly, the dazzling smile held for an infinity, even as the flashes went off. And she never blinked when the lights flashed. She had inbuilt sunglasses in her eyes, that girl, Ken thought.

Actually, she probably had. From the look of her, she had inbuilt everything else. Although not inbuilt famousness, as it turned out; hers was on the wane, and although it had received a spike upwards from the adoption of the baby – always a good trick, that one – she was hardly big-time any more. Still, she was bigger time than most of the celebs about in London at the moment, which was why Ken was here.

'Come on, Belle,' he groaned now, shifting his buttocks on the cold wall. 'Come outside and give us all a break. Preferably with the kid.'

He glanced in desultory fashion around him, at the other eight or so photographers present that morning. He knew most of them; they were freelancers like him. Some lounged on the wall as he did, flicking through YouTube on their laptops. Others muttered into mobiles, their eyes slicing about like switchblades, ever alert. Some bantered and joked with the hotel doormen, their eyes on every passing limo, scanning number plates for registrations they recognised. The Portchester was one of London's top hotels; a favourite of the particularly flashy type of celebrity that tended to beat all other comers in the column inches stakes. Celebrities like Belle, in other words.

Ken glanced at the cadaverous features of the man next to him. Keith, a long-time colleague and competitor, worked for rival agency Top Pictures. Keith's skin was flaky and grey – as, Ken knew, was his own – with the constant pap diet of crisps and coffee.

Keith looked preoccupied and was rustling through one of the London freesheets. As he stopped and sucked loudly through his teeth, Ken leant over to see at what. A large photograph of Tom Hanks shopping in Covent Garden dominated the page.

'Spent all day waitin' outside 'is 'otel yesterday,' Keith complained. "E never came out, the bastard. 'Is limo was outside all day, though.' He tapped the picture irritably. 'So what these jokers are doing running this picture sayin' 'e were out shopping is anyone's guess. It's obviously a stock shot, could be years old.

That's what they do, drag an old one out, stick any old caption on. Yeah.' He tapped the paper again, lips pursed authoritatively. 'That's what it'll be.'

Ken bent over and peered at the caption. 'No, mate. It says 'ere it was taken yesterday.'

'It can't!' Keith grabbed the newspaper in panic and pressed it close to his face. Then he lowered it. Ken clapped him on his leather-jacketed back, sensing his comrade had sustained a bitter blow.

'Bloody 'ell.' Keith shook his head resentfully. 'That's *great*, that is. *Bloody* great. You spend all day sitting outside some hotel in Knightsbridge and he's there in bloody Covent Garden. What kind of a job is this, eh?' He drove a fist into his forehead.

Ken nodded absently. His eye was on the double yellow line on which his car was parked. It was at least twenty minutes since the traffic warden had last appeared and he would be back any moment. Ken tensed himself, ready for the dash across the road, the throwing open of the door, the roaring away and the driving round the block until the danger was passed – at least, for another half an hour.

His eye lingered on his car. It was dirty and battered, and piled high with yellowing newspapers, scrunched crisp bags and torn chocolate wrappers. A number of other cars in similar stages of decrepitude were parked nearby, belonging to the other paps. It wasn't the line to be in, Ken thought morosely, if you wanted a decent car. It wasn't the line to be in if you wanted a decent anything. Flat, life, relationship – you name it.

The hotel doors revolved and a *frisson* swept the line of photographers, but only a couple of grey-suited businessmen had come out; tanned, smooth-skinned, bouffant-haired, who regarded the line of snappers with supercilious amusement. The photographers stared back with loathing. Wankers. Bankers. Hedge-funders, most likely. All very well for them with their million-pound bonuses.

'I meant morals,' Keith moaned on. 'There used to be a sort of etiquette to it. Now everyone just storms in. I blame digitalisation. Mobile phone cameras. People think all they have to do is wait outside some celebrity's house and they'll make a fortune.'

Ken looked at him. 'Well, that *is* all they have to do. So long as the celeb turns up.'

He stared at his feet again. He was a short and thickset man whose feet looked even smaller and stubbier in the dirty white trainers. He knew what Keith meant. He himself had entered the business peachy-keen and fired up, lens primed, all agog, convinced he was about to hit the big time, or at least photograph it. Now he knew better. The paparazzi life was a grindingly dull one. The last thing it was was glamorous.

It was also, he was increasingly beginning to feel, worthless. Pointless, intrusive, prurient, even damaging sometimes. The editors of the magazines that ran his photographs were always defending themselves; banging on about them supplying a public need, an information service, the images that defined the times and the rest of it. But it sounded more like bollocks to Ken all the time. How could waiting outside a hotel for some semi-washed-up American celebrity – or whoever else chose to rock up in the meantime – be anything else?

But on the other hand, what else could he do? This, so far as Ken was concerned, was the most depressing aspect of all.

There was a *frisson* again as the hotel revolving doors spun and Belle stepped out, blinking in the daylight, her half-tied dress rippling like a leopard-skin flag in the breeze and flying up to expose thin legs in long brown boots. She carried an orange bag in which the head of her small dog could just be seen; its malicious black eyes swivelling about.

An electric ripple of excitement shot through the crowd of snappers. Ken, zooming and shooting away with the rest, noticed that Belle looked less groomed than usual; she had a hurried, thrown-together, rather sluttish appearance that rather suited her, he thought. Of course, it would be deliberate down to the last misplaced hair; a new, rumpled look, more Bardot than her usual varnished Barbie one. Yes, thought Ken with a leap of spirit in which excitement was mixed with relief. From Barbie to Bardot. It was a picture story. Everyone would buy it. So long as he got there first.

His fingers frantically switched the calibrations on his lenses, moving the infinitesimal distances back and forth with the pulsing muscles in his fingers, playing them with the practised skill of a clarinettist. 'Look over here, Belle. That's right, down the lens,' he shouted. The difference between a face staring straight into camera and off to the left could be hundreds of pounds. Thousands, sometimes.

'Belle, over here!'

'Over *here*!' insisted Ken.

He noticed, as he always did, how unreal celebrities looked compared to the people who shot them. Compared to Belle, albeit a less polished Belle than usual, the row of jumping, gesticulating paparazzi looked like creatures from another world: stunted, dusty, grey and flaky, like something nasty you might find under a stone.

'Marry me, Belle,' yelled another in the line of cameramen. Ken, as his finger pulsed the camera button, registered the tactic. Anything to stand out. A comic approach might get the celeb's attention and a better picture.

'Hey, Belle,' called someone else. 'Got a new man yet?'

She laughed theatrically at this and shook her rumpled head. Her mussed hair flew around her like an aureole. Very fetching, thought the massed paps, snapping away. 'I'm giving them up!' she shouted.

'Don't do that,' one of the paps shouted back. 'Get another one. Give us something to shoot.'

'I'll do my best,' Belle yelled, slipping her emaciated body into the car. You could hardly see her sideways on, Ken saw. As her limo slid away, he packed away his lenses. That was a story, the new Bardot look. Enough for today. He walked towards his battered car just in time; the traffic warden was coming round the corner, face grim, a fixed penalty notice-dispensing machine poised.

But he'd be back tonight, Ken knew as he started up his knackered engine and drove away. Jennifer Lopez was supposed to be checking in, straight off the plane from LA. He felt weary at the very thought of it.

The theatre corridor, with its sunken spotlight, and hard black plastic chairs ranged along the exposed brickwork, struck Belle as horribly intimidating. Cold too. And those purple carpet tiles were gross; far too bright for her aching eyeballs.

The other auditionees swept her a surprised glance when she entered and trilled a champagne-fuelled 'Hi!' at them. They were sitting slumped against the brickwork in their loose black clothes, staring at experienced-looking copies of *Titus Andronicus* and mouthing the words to themselves.

It was difficult, Belle thought, to make out which of them, if any, was female; all had that rather Gothic, waxen-faced, consumptive, crinkly-haired look she had come to associate with British thespians. Also as usual, they were dressed in loose black clothes with black hairy jumpers over the top. It did nothing for their pallor, Belle thought. They didn't look edgy, just ill. Nor did they look particularly friendly. If they recognised her, which surely they did, they seemed determined not to show it.

'ITV's in the next building,' one of them remarked in lofty tones.

Belle stared. She had no idea what ITV was. 'Isn't this the National Theatre?'

'Yeah. You're in the wrong place. Chat shows are next door.' A pair of cold, dark eyes flicked over Belle.

'Actually, I've come to audition for *Tight-Ass Andronicus*,' Belle assured him brightly, thankful for the champagne she had swigged in the taxi and the swirling, light-headed courage it gave her.

This caused a sensation among the seated. 'As who?' one of them asked.

Belle giggled. 'The Queen,' she said airily. She had tried to learn some lines in the car but the print had just fuzzed and swum about before her eyes. She was vaguely thinking of doing a tap dance for the director. It had helped Catherine Zeta Jones interest Michael Douglas, after all.

The thespians looked at each other, rather sneeringly, it seemed to Belle.

'You mean as Tamora?' one of them asked. 'The one who eats her children in a pie?'

Belle blanched. 'Are you kidding?' She shook her tousled blond head in astonishment. 'This Shakespeare guy was wasted being Shakespeare. He'd have been dynamite in horror movies.'

Niall had almost not bothered coming to this audition, only there was sod all else on offer. His agent had begged him to try out for the Scottish serial killer part currently on offer in *The*

Bill, but Niall had refused it on the grounds that he didn't do cheap sensational murders. Although it had occurred to him on the way here that as cheap sensational murders went, you would have to go a long way to beat *Titus Andronicus*.

He'd entered the theatre with the usual lack of expectation. Things were bad at the moment. Worse than he had imagined they could ever be. He had been turned down recently for Shakespeare parts he had not realised existed. At the moment, Niall knew, his self-confidence was taking the downward lift to the basement. As it had been ever since Darcy left for LA. Travelling in First Class into the bargain, as if her stupendous success needed to be any further underlined.

He'd begged her not to go. In vain he had pointed out the artistic and moral consequences of her getting on the plane and going to meet the big, famous director. Had she no self-respect? Respect for her art? Respect for him? She had wailed and clung to him, her big black eyes filled with fetching tears, her slim body pressed to his in supplication, her arms lovingly about him. But she had gone, all the same.

He felt betrayed. Emasculated, even. Not jealous, of course. His current resentful feelings were nothing to do with the money, the fame, the first-class flights, the celebrity friends, the fun, the glamour, the money, the fame. The money, the fame. No, it was because he and Darcy had dreamt the same dream. Believed in the same things. Or so he had imagined.

It was with boiling, resentful thoughts such as these that Niall had given his name to the box office and been waved to the corridor to await the director's pleasure.

Belle had been poised to flee. After everyone had laughed – nastily – at her horror movies remark, she had been about to turn on her medium-height Chanel heel and leave. Athough whether back to the hotel or simply to the nearest bar, she had not yet decided. Then the black-painted door at the end of the corridor had opened and someone had come in. It was at this point that Belle decided things were not quite so bad after all.

Chapter 19

There was such a thing as a sexy British actor after all, Belle decided, as the newcomer came through the door into the corridor.

He was about the same build as Christian. Thick-necked, broad-chested and powerfully muscular, if rather paler. Very pale indeed, entirely different from the universal mahogany of Hollywood. This struck Belle as somehow refreshing.

He was also handsome, but in a non-Christian way. This man, Belle saw, lacked her former swain's rolling shuffle, which drew attention to his pelvis. This man walked with a long stride, as if he were accustomed to walk the streets, whereas Christian, for all the recentness of his fame, had already perfected that hotel-lobby-to-the-limo hop.

His blue eyes – much paler than Christian's, but just as striking – looked assessingly about as he moved. There was even a touch of anger about him – a resentful flash to that blue glance – that struck her as very exciting. Belle felt a catch in her throat.

Niall, too, was finding it hard to believe what he saw. Among the drab and dreary drips in black, whom one found for some reason at every Shakespeare audition, was a woman in her early

Wendy Holden

twenties in boots and a clingy leopard-print dress. She had big
blond hair, big red lips, big black eyelashes, and tits which
were rammed up so high and hard they almost touched her
chin.

Touching her chin in actuality was the head of a small and
nasty-looking brown dog with twitchy triangular ears and big
black protruberant eyes. It poked from the neck of an expensive-
looking handbag; the sort that, Niall imagined, cost more than
he had earned during the whole of the last month. He struggled
to place this apparition, more suited to the pages of celebrity
magazines than to this dingy theatre corridor where everyone
waited to be put through their paces in one of the more obscure
and stomach-churning of the Bard's prodigious output.

'Hey,' she said, in a husky voice directed straight at him, as if
no one in the room existed for her. Which, actually, they didn't.
'Come and sit by me.'

Niall's legs moved independently of his will. Almost before
he realised what he was doing he had shot across the purple floor
tiles and done as she asked.

Belle's entire body surged with excitement as the large,
long, strong, jeaned thigh brushed hers. She swallowed and
forcibly resisted the urge to run her long, manicured fingernails
along it.

Her nostrils filled with an unfamiliar scent. It was, she
realised, the unadulterated smell of a man's body. Christian, and
most of her lovers before him, had doused themselves with so
much cologne you could almost smell them coming as their car
turned the corner of the street. They had had more facial
products in the bathroom than she had. But this – this was
natural allure. Musky, sweaty, salty, darkly intimate. She was
almost shuddering with desire now. This was what she had been
waiting for. One hundred per cent solid, muscled, masculine,

red-headed, mouthwatering, nipple-stiffening, gasp-making, rootin' tootin' prime beefcake.

Meanwhile, with a paparazzi-type flash of memory, Niall had recognised her. He realised that a celebrity magazine cover was exactly where he had last seen her. Even if you didn't buy them, as he didn't, avoiding her was impossible as she was a fixture on every newsstand. This was Belle Murphy, the American film star. The ultimate Hollywood bimbette.

'Hi,' she smiled at him. Between the forests of thickly mascara'd lashes, her pupils appeared a deep, unnatural green that reminded him of washing-up liquid, 'I'm Belle. Great to meet you.'

His initial flattered daze was now replaced by disapproval. Well, it wasn't great to meet her. This woman represented everything he loathed most about the acting profession. If you could call what she did acting. From the odd clips he had seen – and try as you might you couldn't avoid it, so omnipresent was the Hollywood culture – it looked more like lapdancing in period costume.

'Hello,' he said shortly. 'How's it going?'

The washing-up eyes dilated with surprise. She flashed him a nervous, blazing smile. 'I didn't realise you were French,' she said.

It was hard not to burst out laughing at this, and Niall did not resist the urge to do so as contemptuously as possible. 'I'm Scottish.'

Her eyes widened further. Her smile increased in wattage. An emaciated hand, the thinnest Niall had ever seen, and with the longest nails, tiptoed across his thigh. 'Wow. That's so cool. Scottish, huh? Like Mel Gibson.'

'He's Australian, actually,' Niall said damningly, casting a swift glance about. But if the others were listening, they didn't seem to be. On the other hand, they were actors. Had they seen, from under their hair, the hand playfully going up and down his thigh? Just what was going on here?

'Isn't that near Australia?'

'No.' This, crushingly. And, he hoped, finally.

'Where in Scotland do you come from?' Belle asked next, brightly. Her little-girl huskiness was intensely irritating, as if she'd watched *Some Like It Hot* too many times. 'I think I've got some ancestors in Scotland. The Murphys?' she added, looking at him hopefully. 'Do you know them?'

'Glasgow,' growled Niall, ignoring the last half of the question. Murphy, as everyone knew, was about as Irish a name as you could get. 'I grew up on a council estate – a housing project to *you*,' he added forcefully. 'My father's a butcher and my mother's a cleaner.'

He gave Belle a cold look, but she simply beamed back, batting the thick black lashes. She was, he thought, infuriatingly irrepressible, like one of those seventies toys that wobbled but didn't lie down. Weebles.

'Wow. A butcher. A cleaner,' she said in admiring tones. 'That's so, like, authentic. Really real, huh?'

Niall ignored her. He unrolled his copy of *Titus* and stared at it hard, hoping she would take the hint and go away.

'Auditioning for *Titus*, huh?' she asked brightly.

'Isn't everyone?' he grunted, his eyes still trained, unseeingly, on the title page. She too, of course. He knew her game, Niall thought furiously. It was all too common, this sort of thing: Hollywood stars of trash commercial movies coming to London to try to get industry cred points by acting on stage, or in Shakespeare. It was almost as stupid as Shakespearean actresses like Darcy going to LA and trying out for rubbish commercial films. Niall felt a burning contempt for both of them; Belle especially, as she was the nearer.

Belle Murphy, queen of the schlock-flicks, attempting to project words to a serious theatre audience! Niall had remembered more about her now; recalled vaguely seeing Belle in various newspapers he found lying about – never buying – falling drunk out of taxis with no knickers on and her breasts tumbling from her dress. She'd been compared to Lindsay Lohan and Britney Spears at their hell-raising worst. No wonder she needed some gravitas. But – Belle Murphy, in *Titus Andronicus*! It was ridiculous. The Bard would turn in his grave.

Except that, Niall knew, the Bard probably wouldn't. Far from it. If ever there was a bums-on-seats man, an utter tart to ticket sales, it was William Shakespeare. He pushed the inconvenient thought away.

Belle was jiggling up and down next to him. Did she want to go to the loo, he wondered irritably. 'I'm cold,' she added, snuggling up to his sheepskin-lined leather flying jacket. 'Nice coat,' she added.

'Thanks,' Niall bit out. The jacket really was nice, actually. It was vintage, possibly even a Second World War original. Darcy had bought it for him from one of the Knightsbridge charity shops she haunted. He had thought resentfully at the time that even second-hand clothes were more privileged in Knightsbridge; all the same, he had accepted the jacket.

'What part are you going for?' Belle persisted.

Niall tore his eyes from the page and raised them heavenwards. He wished she would shut up. He wished he hadn't sat down by this ridiculous woman. He wished she would be called in next to see the director. The plump, potato-faced assistant director with her shock of red frizzy hair had been in a couple of times since he had arrived, but only the black-clad wraiths had loped out and Belle remained seated beside him.

'Lavinia,' he said ironically.

Belle looked at him. 'Isn't that a female . . . ?' She searched, in vain, for the proper term.

'Role?' Niall snapped. 'Yes it is. I'm extending my range. Besides, all Shakespeare's female characters were originally played by men,' he added piously.

'Is that right?' Belle's eyes were wide with surprise. 'He was into cross-dressing too?'

Niall ignored this. It was unworthy of a response. 'What part are you going for?' he asked, his tone unrepentantly sneering.

Belle was staring into her cleavage, adjusting something. One of her implants, Niall supposed. Then she tossed back her uncombed hair, clasped her knees with both hands and announced breathily that she had no idea.

'No idea?' Niall echoed.

The hair swished about in a negative. 'I've forgotten. Someone who eats her children, I think,' Belle sighed. 'Gross.' Her face seemed to slip. She looked suddenly doleful.

Up close, her make-up looked less immaculate, Niall registered. The mascara was crusty and the lashes bent. Her eyeliner was wobbly, like Amy Winehouse's, and there was, now, a car crash air to her that reminded him of the troubled chanteuse too.

'I wish I wasn't here,' Belle said passionately and, Niall saw, with obvious truth. The effects of the champagne were wearing off and now she felt cold and depressed. The familiar boom of pain was beginning in her head. If only she could get out her champagne bottle. Her glance darted towards the Birkin, which she had now put on the floor. Sugar was scratching about inside it; ruining it, no doubt. Or possibly relieving himself in it; this occasionally happened and, Belle knew, accounted for the enormous number of large and expensive bags women like herself got through.

'So why are you here?' Niall was asking. 'If it's so awful,' he added.

Belle felt suddenly reckless. All the careful speeches Mitch had prepared with her for the benefit of whatever directors and journalists she might encounter, speeches about loving Shakespeare, his genius at illustrating motives and basic human truths, and loving England and its theatre audiences and wanting to go back to the basics of her craft, suddenly vanished from her mind. She could hardly remember them anyway. She felt bored and frustrated. She wanted champagne. To get out of here. She turned to Niall.

'Listen. I don't give a rat's ass about Shakespeare,' she told him. 'I don't even care about acting. But I need to look like a serious actor if I'm gonna be a star again in Hollywood.'

The speech had a seismic effect on Niall, far more so than if Belle had declaimed Lady Macbeth word-perfect from start to finish. First there was the honesty, which was disarming. Then, more powerful still, the reminder that this woman had once had Hollywood at her feet. Whereas he, Niall was suddenly horribly aware, with a clarity he had never allowed himself before, hadn't got anything at his, apart from his shoes. What right did he have to despise her?

'You don't like acting?' he repeated.

The blond hair whooshed about in an adamant negative. 'Hate it. Far too much like hard work. But,' Belle added, her head stopping and the green eyes revealed suddenly filling with tears, 'I really *liked* being famous. Being a celebrity was *great*.' Her face lit up, then the flame died down again. 'And not being as famous is . . . horrible,' she added, in a tragic whisper that had a sob at the end of it.

She was underselling herself, Niall found himself thinking. She was good at acting. She was incredibly expressive.

'But I'm not giving up.' Another expression, in which resolution mixed with resentment, had now appeared on Belle's fragile features. 'I'm willing to do anything it takes to get it back, even act in this shit.' She waved her copy of *Titus* at him.

Niall looked around him, at who else might be witnessing this heresy. There was no one but themselves now remaining in the corridor. Apart from the dog in her bag, whose hostile stare was fixed unblinkingly on him. Since Belle had started to cry, it seemed to be quivering with aggression, poised to attack at any moment. He tried not to look at it.

He tried, too, to recall his principles. He reminded himself that this woman was loathsome, the industry she worked for was loathsome, the whole reason she was here was loathsome – to make herself appear, of all things, a serious actress by taking Shakespeare parts away from those, like him, who really needed them.

'I mean, I know it's pretty disgusting,' Belle was sniffing. 'Trying to make myself look good by taking parts away from people who really need them. But, baby, *I* really need them. Things have kinda gone into freefall for me in LA. I need them bad.' There was, Niall recognised, real anguish in her face as she looked at him.

He felt, to his amazement, sympathy for her. Or, more precisely, recognition. Their situations were not so dissimilar after all. He needed a part badly as well, and he too was willing to do anything it took. He looked at Belle speculatively. Here was a famous actress. Not as famous as she had been, admittedly, but still a million times more so than he, or Darcy – at the moment – for that matter. Could she help him?

Belle's blast of honesty felt to Niall as if it had dislodged something fundamental in him. Something that had been blocking his progress. Tacitly, carefully, he now felt around the hideous possibility that what had lain behind the determination to stop Darcy going to LA was jealousy. That he was savagely envious of her stroke of good fortune and that, when push came to shove, he was as desperate to experience the glittery high life as she was; possibly a good deal more so. That he, like Belle, wanted to be famous. And as frank about what he wanted as she was.

'You must think I'm such a flake.' Belle was weeping now. 'Pretending to be a real actress when I'm not.'

He leapt to reassure her. Something was now telling him it would pay dividends to be nice to her. 'Of course you're a real actress. You're very successful. You were in that huge hit movie, the one everyone saw . . . *Marie.*'

'*Marie* wasn't acting,' Belle wailed. 'It was lapdancing in period costume.'

Niall stared at her in amazement, stunned again by her frankness. His thoughts entirely. As he searched for a reply to this, he felt his mouth twitching. His lips spreading and parting. A laugh welling up in his throat.

At the sound of his chuckle, Belle lifted her head. Two wet eyes regarded him from a tangle of messy blond hair. Niall felt a clutch of concern. His charm offensive was ruined. She was furious. He waited for her to rise to her feet in fury, rive him with her talons, perhaps even smash him in the face with that bag, dog and all. But instead, a long-nailed hand crept to her mouth and Belle's entire skinny frame began shuddering. She was laughing too.

'Just listen to me.' She pushed her hair back, sniffed and gave him a rueful smile. 'What a wreck. My career's in ruins, my boyfriend's left me . . .'

The last four words, sharp with possibility, pierced Niall's inner ear. He remembered Belle looking at him when he had come in; staring at him as if she could eat him up on the spot. He remembered the emaciated hand on his thigh. Yes. This woman – this famous, rich, successful and almost certainly useful woman – had definitely been coming on to him.

'My girlfriend's left me,' he volunteered immediately, before he could stop himself, or wonder why he had come out so unexpectedly with such an outrageous lie.

Then other questions beset him. Did he want to stop himself? Was it such a lie? What relationship did he and Darcy have anyway? With a stark, unrelenting clarity that was entirely new to him, Niall could see he had lusted after her at first; had been excited by her lofty and famous connections. But had he ever felt love for her? Sympathy, even? It seemed to him there had always been resentment on his part. Jealousy, even. Had his love for Darcy ever been more than love for what her family represented? For what being with her could do for him? Only it hadn't.

So if something or someone better or more useful came along, he was available. He sensed now that in Belle someone had, and that it was a chance that might not come again.

He blinked for a moment, rather stunned at what he was uncovering about himself. It wasn't comfortable, but it felt strangely liberating. For one thing, for the first time in as long as he could remember, ever since arriving in London, certainly, he didn't feel angry. His constant sense of rage had left him.

There was a movement beside him. Belle was diving to the orange bag that sat on the floor. For a horrible moment Niall thought she was getting out the dog for him to cuddle, as a sort of bonding exercise, but then he realised she was pulling out something big, green and glassy. Something with a gold foil neck and a label. A bottle of champagne. With the cork out. He watched as she took a deep swig, her eyes closed in apparent rapture.

'Have a drink?' Belle wiped her fizzing lips and proffered the bottle.

'Er, fine . . . thanks.' As he grasped it, Niall registered that the bottle was room temperature. She carried around warm bottles of open champagne in her handbag? Jesus. This woman was a serious mess. Which, so far as he was concerned, might be a seriously good thing.

'You must think I'm such a worm.' Belle was watching him drink with eager eyes. 'Being so shallow, when you're really deep and authentic. A proper actor, huh?'

Perhaps it was the champagne, which always went straight to his head, but there was something about her absolute, unexpected honesty and his own recent self-revelations that made Niall now want to unburden too. 'I'm not really that authentic,' he confessed.

Belle giggled. 'Sure you are. You're from a housing project in Glasgow, aren't you? Your daddy's a butcher?' Her green eyes stared questioningly into his.

Niall swallowed and took a deep breath. He had not even told Darcy what he was about to admit now. 'Well, I am from Glasgow, yes. But my dad's not a butcher. Well, only in a manner of speaking. He owns a chain of meat-processing plants.'

There was a burst of laughter from Belle. 'You don't say.' Her expression was radiant with delight. She began to laugh. 'Hey. I really believed you, you know. You were very convincing.'

Niall felt mirth rising unstoppably up his throat. 'Well, I *am* an actor. In theory, anyway.'

Belle exploded again. 'Me too. I'm an actor *in theory*.' And off she went into peals again. 'Here, have another drink,' she gurgled, passing him the bottle. 'Oh,' she added, shaking it, 'it's empty. Never mind. I got another.' She dived into the orange bag again, emerged with another gold-foil-topped bottle, uncorked it with expert speed and thrust it at Niall.

Niall took a long swig, wiped his mouth and handed the bottle back.

'I'm not even called Niall. My name's actually Graham.'

'Graham!' yelped Belle.

Niall could hardly get the words out now for laughing. 'My mother's a ps . . . psy . . . psycho . . .'

'Psycho?' shrieked Belle, face suddenly blank with alarm.

This struck Niall as funnier still. '*Psychologist.* I grew up in a detached house in one of Glasgow's smartest suburbs. We had gardeners, a nanny and a weekend cottage on Loch Lomond.'

'Hee hee . . .' She was shaking her messy blond head in delight. 'You'll be telling me next that you don't even like Shakespeare and, um, his genius for exposing motives and basic human truths.'

'I don't!' Niall shouted. 'I don't! I don't! I don't!' The sense of lightness was almost as intoxicating as the drink. He felt crazy and reckless; fabulously irresponsible. No serious actor could afford to admit what he now realised he had always felt; crushed and uncomprehending when it came to many of the plays and bored at having to learn the lines. No wonder he never got cast in anything.

He pulled a comically doleful face. 'To be or not to be,' he declaimed in hollow tones, his eyes turned up and hands crossed, corpse-like, on his breast.

'Lend me your ears,' Belle intoned, looking similarly po-faced. She frowned. 'Is that the same speech?'

'That is the question,' Niall continued in a mournful bass. For some reason, his failures to land leading roles at Stratford now seemed hilariously funny. He remembered the faces of some of the directors auditioning him – floppy-haired shorthouses to a man – and wanted to double up with laughter.

Then he stopped. He remembered that he and Belle were here in this theatre for a reason. She had to get a part to save her career, while his own career might, Niall now acknowledged to himself, depend on a rather more physical part he had in his possession.

'I can help you,' he told her suddenly.

Belle, in mid-swig, flashed him a lecherous grin. 'Sure you can, honey.' The alcohol was reinflating her libido. In a sudden, lightning move she was on one of his knees, facing him, pushing her breasts – naked and exposed in her suddenly open dress – into his face and gasping.

He was surprised at how erotic he found her. She was so obvious-looking. But, quite suddenly, he was coursing with lust. 'Not that sort of help,' he protested, pushing her away.

'Aw! Spoilsport!' Belle pouted through her hair. Her hand was on his penis. 'Someone here wants to,' she smirked, stroking her nails in a practised fashion up and down his ramrod-straight organ.

'Just ignore that, will you? I meant I could help you with your audition,' Niall growled. He had to take control of this situation. The director could come at any moment. Any of them could.

'I can hear your lines, now,' he groaned. 'You'll be called in a minute. It's been ages since the last one went.'

It really was ages, Niall thought. He felt as if the world had revolved completely on its axis since the assistant director last appeared. That he was a different person now, with a different outlook. He felt a surge of guilty gratitude towards the maligned Bard. Shakespeare might not be his thing, but so far as exposing his own motives and basic human truths, Niall felt, the Swan of Avon had been right on the money this morning.

Belle was still gasping, however. Her fingers were still kneading his penis.

'You're here to get a part, aren't you?' Niall yelped. 'You've learnt a speech?'

Then, as suddenly as if he had poured water on her, Belle deflated again. She drooped her head and looked miserably through her hair at him. 'I haven't learnt any lines,' she confessed.

The old Niall would have stared at her in frustration and contempt. The new Niall, however, thought quickly. 'I could teach you a few of mine,' he suggested. 'It's a male role but it could catch the director's imagination if you were to attempt it.' Then, as Belle began to tie her dress back up, he added, 'Don't tie that too tightly.'

Belle's speech, after all, might not be the only thing about her to catch the director's imagination.

Chapter 20

From his usual position on the wall opposite the hotel, Ken looked up at the white clifflike façade of the Portchester, with its ornate balconies and striped awnings fluttering agitatedly in the unseasonal breeze. He'd had a tip-off from Ignatio, one of the doormen, that Lanelle and Dizzi, newly minted reality TV stars, were about to storm out in a huff. There'd been some misunderstanding over a cocktail, apparently. Ken had briefly wondered how you could misunderstand a cocktail. Unless they had misunderstood they had to pay for it, which wasn't impossible.

Keith was on the phone. He snapped it away. 'One of my tippers. He says Jordan's in the Wolseley. Interested?'

Ken shook his head. 'Nah. I'll wait for Lanelle and Dizzi.'

It wasn't the most exciting of prospects, but it hadn't been the most exciting of evenings. It was half-past nine and very little had happened. The rumour that Kate Moss was about to swing by for Peking duck in the hotel's basement restaurant had proved to be as lacking in substance as the supermodel herself. Lionel Blair had been in for dinner, but that was hardly going to make the front page of the *Sun*. The one possibility was Belle Murphy;

211

she had not yet returned from wherever she had gone with her hair all over the place. And that had been ages ago.

Although even Belle was obviously fading fast on the picture desk popularity index, the Barbie-to-Bardot pictures, which Ken had imagined were good for a couple of grand in *Heat* or *Hello!*, had in the end not come out as well as he had expected and only fetched fifty pounds from *Woman's Weekly*. All the picture editors – apart from *Woman's Weekly* – had said the same thing, that the only pictures of Belle they would pay any serious money for were ones of her with a new man on her arm.

Twelve floors above them, in the penthouse of the Portchester hotel, Jacintha the nanny was reaching the end of her tether. It wasn't just that Belle Murphy had no interest whatsoever in her adopted son. This was entirely to be expected. Plenty of people she worked for had no interest in their children; this was usually why they employed her.

Occasionally, admittedly, after too much champagne, Belle would be overcome by sentimentality, pluck Morning from his cradle when he was sleeping and waltz theatrically round the room with him. Morning, however, rarely appreciated being yanked from his warm slumbers. Then, affronted by his crying, Belle would shove him bad-temperedly back at Jacintha.

The nanny was not concerned about the obvious fact Belle had adopted the baby only to generate positive publicity for herself, to appear a caring person. It was hardly unusual behaviour among celebrities, after all. Non-celebrities too, come to that. Plenty of people she knew of had had children for the murkiest of motives. To snare a husband here, an inheritance there, usually.

No, it was in other ways that Jacintha was finding Belle Murphy impossible. 'Mind if I call you Jackie?' Belle had asked breathily when they first met. It was a suggestion that made Jacintha – the twentieth generation of her family to bear the name – cringe and squirm. But with – as she had imagined – all Hollywood before her, she had been unable to refuse Belle anything.

Hollywood had not, however, materialised, still less the *Celebrity Supernanny*-style programme she had, in her wildest dreams, imagined herself fronting. Instead, she had found that working for a film star could be extremely boring. There had been a confidentiality contract to sign, which had been thrilling. However, its promise that there was something to be confidential about proved groundless.

Where were all the parties, Jacintha would wonder. The weekends with celebrity friends? The jetsetting? Far from flying round the world from one glamorous location to another, they never even left London. And far from glittering at the centre of a sparkling circle of friends, her life a non-stop whirl of fabulous events, all Belle ever did was lie around and drink, occasionally rousing herself to stumble off to an audition. Or a bar, as Jacintha was beginning to suspect. And, as neither Jacintha nor Morning was required at auditions, still less in bars, Jacintha had only, since the moment she had arrived in it, ever left the Portchester penthouse in order to go push Morning around the park opposite.

Not that this hadn't been exciting at first. It had been thrilling to run the gauntlet of the paparazzi, who had rushed up close to the buggy. As the flashes had gone off, Morning began to scream.

'Can't help but feel sorry for it, can yer?' one of the photographers had remarked to Jacintha. 'Sweet little thing. I hate to 'ear babies cry,' he had gone on, 'especially if I'm the one who's made 'em.'

Jacintha had stared blankly back at him. Whether babies cried or not made no difference to her. She had heard it so often for so long, she was immune.

But before long the prospect of snapping the same woman pushing the same buggy to the same park palled among the photographers and it had now been some days since Jacintha had faced a lens wielded in anger. What happened now was that the paparazzi descended on the buggy as she passed them – as close as she possibly could – in order to coo at and pet him. An unphotographed Jacintha would then move off to push her charge endlessly round the crisscrossing paths among the tree-shaded, statue-studded green of the park.

Belle, in the back of the limo, was feeling on top of the world. The audition had gone better than she had ever imagined it could; the director had actually looked impressed as she had parroted the few lines Niall had taught her. Then she had whipped off her dress for a grand finale. The director had looked even more impressed. He had hired her on the spot. She had yet to hear as what, exactly, but what did it matter? She'd play a dormouse if she had to. The point was she had a part in a proper play in London. Her career was saved.

Niall, too, had made an impression.

'The director was really taken with your joyous and loose interpretation of the part,' Niall's agent now called to say.

'Jesus,' said Niall. 'I should go into auditions pissed more often. That's where I've been going wrong.'

'What?'

'Oh, nothing. Thanks for letting me know,' Niall yelped. 'Ooof,' he gasped.

'What's the matter? You sound as if you've hurt yourself.'

Hardly, thought Niall, looking down at Belle, on her knees

in the limo's footwell, busy about his fly zip with her wonderfully flexible tongue.

After the afternoon drinking session in the back of the limo, which constituted their celebrations, Belle started to feel more warmly towards the city that had finally delivered on its promises. It was possible she had been a bit hard on London. Sure, it rained a lot, but you got to like the grey sky after a while. It looked like it did in paintings, or the few paintings Belle had ever seen.

And, say what you like about the place – and Belle had said most of it – it kinda had atmosphere; the city lights as the sun went down glowed in an almost magical way and as they crossed the Thames for the umpteenth time, Belle was struck on the one hand by the great dome of St Paul's, its surmounting gold cross shooting rays back at the sinking sun, and the fairy towers of Westminster on the other. The Houses of Parliament in particular looked romantic, she thought. King Arthur and his handsome knights should live in it, not those puddingy-looking people who ran things round here.

'I mean, it's not as if there's any money in taking pictures any more,' Keith, alongside Ken on the wall, was moaning. They stared at the façade of the Portchester and sighed.

'Everyone with a mobile phone camera thinks they're Arthur bleedin' Edwards these days. An' I bet 'e's finding it a struggle as well,' Keith added of the legendary *Sun* photographer.

'Hasn't he retired?' asked Ken. He thought he might even be dead, but didn't like to say so in case he wasn't.

But Keith was not listening anyway. He was lamenting the golden days that had passed. 'I mean, it used to be good fun. A bit like hide and seek. But now there are too many muppets hanging around.'

'Clampers!' someone yelled.

Ken, Keith and the eight or so other photographers idling along the wall outside the hotel entrance suddenly snapped to attention.

'That's all I need,' groaned Keith. 'I've already been bleedin' ticketed today.'

'You're joking!' yelped another pap into his mobile. He flipped it back together, shoved it into his pocket and shared with the rest of the group the unwelcome news that Leonardo DiCaprio had been spotted going into one of the hotel's side entrances while they all monitored the front. There was a groan of disbelief.

'What a life, eh?' said Keith to Ken.

Ken nodded. 'Wouldn't it be nice,' he said, rather dreamily, as the thought occurred to him, 'to do something more useful? Take some pictures that mattered, for once? That were useful in some way. That meant something?'

'*Meant* something?' Keith stared at his colleague. 'You feelin' all right, mate?'

A few minutes later, Belle's limo pulled up. They all recognised its registration. Despite hers being a steadily sinking star there still was, Ken noticed, as he always did with someone famous, that unmistakable change in the temperature.

But it wasn't until she got out that the mercury really soared. Belle was not alone. She was with a man. A young, handsome man. With red hair and jeans. There was no mistaking their relationship. Belle's dress was hanging open, exposing almost the whole of one breast, and the man's face was covered in red lipstick.

The pack, so passive and lethargic even a mere few seconds ago, were now leaping about, electrified, frenzied. 'Belle, Belle. This way, Belle. Who's your friend?'

Not that it mattered that they didn't know. The papers found out all that sort of thing.

Her friend, Ken saw through his lens, looked ruffled and startled, staring at the cameras like a rabbit at headlights. Then his face disappeared as Belle swallowed him in a huge, prolonged kiss. When he emerged, he was looking at the cameras quite happily, even smiling. He even looked as if he were enjoying himself.

The photographers were loving it too, their interest more intense than it had been for days. Ken snapped away with the rest. Finally, some shots he could actually sell.

Jacintha had been sitting with the usual tray from room service, facing the prospect of yet another evening in front of the penthouse widescreen television watching yet another hospital drama as Morning snored in his cot, when Belle burst in, shrieking with laughter, with a man.

Which would, Jacintha thought, have been just fine had the man been Russell Crowe, only it was someone with ginger hair she had never seen before. They had obviously just practically devoured each other in the lift. Belle's dress was undone, leaving nothing to the imagination, Jacintha observed scornfully, apart from to wonder what she might look like with more flesh and fewer implants. The ginger man, meanwhile, was fumbling with his fly zip; whether upwards or downwards Jacintha had no interest. It was disgusting, whichever it was.

Both he and Belle were extremely drunk. 'More champagne!' Belle yelled into the telephone.

It arrived and Belle whipped the napkin off the bottle. Her face contracted with fury.

'This is the wrong sort,' she barked at the waiter, who looked terrified. 'This is Krug.'

The waiter nodded, puzzled. 'Yes, madam. It comes with the manager's compliments.'

Belle put one sticklike arm on either of her partially leopard-print-dress-covered hips and glared at the unfortunate hotel servant.

'Well, it's a fucking insult. What's he trying to do to me? I can't drink *Krug*, for Christ's sake!' she snarled, as the waiter gathered up the bucket and glasses and fled.

'Krug! Can you believe it?' Belle stormed, pacing about the penthouse. She was in her element. It had been months since she had felt happy and self-confident enough to throw a tantrum on this scale. Things really were returning to normal.

The red-headed man shook his red head.

'The hotel should *know* that the only champagne I drink is Ultra Brut. Sixty-five calories a glass, yeah?' Belle yelled.

The waiter receded and Belle and the redheaded man threw themselves on the sitting-room floor. They seemed, Jacintha thought, still waiting for a single acknowledgement from her mistress, oblivious to her presence.

The penthouse doorbell rang and, apparently as apology for the champagne mix-up, a tower of seafood was now carried into the room by two tall, soft-footed waiters with professionally blank faces.

The lovers, writhing and panting on the floor, took no notice. Jacintha, still sitting, her tray of croque monsieur on her knee, was the sole audience. She watched with reluctant admiration as a fantastical jagged tower of lobsters, oysters, langoustines and prawns was constructed by the blank-faced waiters, skilfully built up on a framework of silver dishes on the central coffee table. She inhaled the salty whiff of the sea, which immediately conjured up pictures of all the glamorous resorts she had imagined flying to in Belle's private jet, and which had never materialised.

The waiters glided soundlessly out. The penthouse door closed loudly behind them – perhaps on purpose – and at this crackshot sound the lovers stopped writhing on the floor and noticed the seafood tower.

The man's pale blue eyes lit up greedily. He pulled Belle to her feet and together the two staggered to the tower where they immediately, in every sense, fell on the oysters. The construction, which had taken such skill and care to build, now crashed to the floor. Shellfish of all descriptions flew everywhere. Clams shot under the television and the oysters fell shells down into the deep-pile carpet. Belle and Niall scrabbled, giggling, to save what they could: Niall cursing as he knelt on a langoustine.

Jacintha stood up once Belle started to run her tongue suggestively up and down a razor clam.

'What's the matter?' Belle paused mid-slurp, her eyes fixed on the nanny's face with what looked like genuine surprise.

'I'm leaving.' Jacintha's hands were folded calmly over the silver buckle of her uniform belt.

'Don't go!' Belle exclaimed. 'It's too early to go to bed yet.'

'Have a mussel!' chipped in Niall, waving a bivalve invitingly.

Jacintha turned on her heel and exited the room. As she packed her bags and wrote her letter of resignation, she was able to hear the cracking of shells and smacking of lips from two rooms away. She reflected that, while seafood was allegedly an aphrodisiac, any romantic associations it might have for her in the future would always be ruined by her memories of this evening.

Chapter 21

'*Cow!*'

'*Pig!*'

The children's angry-sounding shouts were the first thing James heard as he opened the front door. He closed his eyes briefly. A wave of misery swept through him, followed by the reflection that perhaps it was only to be expected. The honeymoon period with the new nanny was over.

Hero and Cosmo were arguing. Chaos had come again. He'd known Emma was too good to be true and now here was the proof – she'd lost control of the children, just like every other nanny before her. From now on it would be the familiar downward spiral to her inevitable sacking. If she didn't walk first, that was. He'd seen it many times before.

Only this time, he wasn't going to.

Soaring into James's mood of glum acceptance now came a thunderbolt of determination. Usually he just watched the collapse of their childcare regimes from the sidelines, but this time he couldn't. The other nannies hadn't been much of a loss anyway, but Emma was different. The fact that she cared about the children, loved the job and was brilliant at it meant that on no account was she to be let go.

He would talk to Vanessa about it as soon as she got back. This resolve was followed by a sense of sunken despair. But would Vanessa care? The fact that his wife, for all she paid lip service to Emma's wonders, seemed inexplicably irritated by her had not escaped James. Vanessa had a particular bee in her bonnet about Emma being northern; all Hero and Cosmo's friends' nannies were, or so she asserted, the daughters of the gentry.

Not that they looked it. Whenever James had been exposed to them – and exposure was the word – they seemed to be barely half dressed. Emma's usual uniform, by contrast, was a practical polo top and jeans, which struck James as much more appropriate than the leopardskin high-heeled boots and red leather skin-tight jeans he had seen other people's nannies wearing, in particular that very tall blonde one with the risible name – Totty.

Her eyelashes alone looked long and sharp enough to slash things, and her nails, James had observed with distaste, were painted claws. Her unnaturally blond hair was obviously jam-packed with chemicals and she always reeked strongly of perfume. Emma's hair, by contrast, had a soft, natural shine, she smelt cleanly of soap and she wore minimal make-up – with that face she didn't have to, as he had observed once to Vanessa. Vanessa had given him an odd look. It had flitted briefly across James's mind then that his wife suspected him of more than strictly professional interest in the new nanny, but he had dismissed it instantly. How could Vanessa imagine anything of the sort? He was, admittedly, scared of her, but he was also devoted to her and always would be.

It was with a clear conscience and pure motives therefore that had James consistently shore up Emma's position within the household, praising her to Vanessa whenever he could, and in the strongest terms.

Why could she not see it, James wondered. Was it not obvious? Having Emma in their house had improved so many things, not least their relationship. Emma's social calendar, unlike that of many of her predecessors, did not require every single night off. She did not seem attached – James had no idea about her romantic history; had never enquired and had no plans to. The point was that she was happy to babysit whenever they wanted, so he and Vanessa could go out together. And they had been, lots, since his return from Equatorial Guinea. They had been out for dinner, to the theatre, for drinks.

An early evening cocktail on the terrace of the Oxo Tower, leaning over the rail together and watching the sun set on the Thames, was one of the most romantic evenings they had spent together for years. Sex – a strict and grudging once a week during the nanny troubles – had lately become more frequent, and Vanessa was even turning to face him these days, instead of grunting 'Don't wake me up' over her shoulder.

'*Pig!*' Cosmo now screamed, derailing his father's train of thought.

'*Cow!*' yelled back Hero.

The situation was clearly deteriorating. James set a determined foot on the bottommost stair.

'*Dog!*'

He couldn't hear Emma's voice at all, James realised. Panic seized him at the thought that she had gone already. But surely not, without telling anyone? Nannies in the past may have walked out on the spot, but not Emma. Surely, even in the highest of dudgeons – and he found it hard to imagine her in one of those – she would not leave the children alone when he

223

was not yet back from work and Vanessa was out at one of her committee meetings. A Children's Society one, if he remembered rightly, which seemed rather ironic.

'*Elephant!*' screamed Cosmo.

James had gained the landing now. A great sense of relief flooded through him as he saw, on the sisal floor of the upstairs hall, his children in clean pyjamas – pink gingham for Hero, blue gingham for Cosmo – hair neatly brushed and no doubt teeth too, sitting opposite each other with great grins on their faces and their legs stretched out. Between those legs a pile of cards with animals printed on the back.

At a movement behind him, James turned. Emma, drying her hands on a floral teatowel, was hurrying up the stairs behind him. She smiled apologetically. 'Sorry, didn't hear you come in. I was in the kitchen.' She looked happily at the children. 'I've just taught them to play Snap and they're having a quick game before bed. They love it. I didn't realise they didn't know how . . .' She faltered, then stopped, clearly worried she was sounding critical.

James sighed. There was, despite the private childcare they had enjoyed – if that was the word – since birth, so much the children didn't know how. Emma's methods, her constant engagement with the children, showed in sharp relief the extent to which the other nannies had not bothered at all, unless it was to dump them both in front of a DVD or to shove Cosmo in the direction of his PlayStation.

Since Emma had come, the DVDs had largely been phased out, access to computer games rigidly controlled and the children taught Snakes and Ladders and Tiddlywinks, both of which they had quickly taken to. In addition, besides teaching Hero and Cosmo the beginnings of reading and some rudimentary arithmetic, Emma had taken them out into the world and showed them how buses worked, the tube, post offices and shops.

It was, James said admiringly to Vanessa, nothing short of a miracle. She had sharply pointed out that Emma was not the first of their carers to take the children shopping. James remembered that the nanny three nannies ago had indeed taken Hero and Cosmo to the Oxford Street Topshop almost every other day. Only not, he suspected, for their benefit.

'Mouse!' shrieked Hero, slamming her card on the pile, on top of which Cosmo had just put down a mouse. 'Sna-a-ap!'

As Cosmo groaned with the agony of losing, Emma bent down, gathered up the cards – 'Yes, children, *you* help. We tidy up our playthings' – and shooed them off to bed.

'Come on, Hero,' Emma urged the little girl as she lingered over a card with a cat on. Of all animals, cats were Hero's absolute favourite. 'You need your sleep. It's a big day for you tomorrow. What day is it?' she enquired gently, dropping to her knees before the child and taking both white, chubby hands in her own.

Hero's big blue eyes looked shyly into Emma's pretty, ruddy, beaming face. 'Birfday,' she whispered, before collapsing with an excited squeal on Emma's white-cottoned chest.

A surge of horror possessed James. While he had not forgotten it was Hero's fourth birthday, he now remembered he had heard nothing about the arrangements for it. Usually, when the children's birthdays loomed, Vanessa was storming about the house in a blue funk as she and whatever nanny was resident at the time tried to secure Madonna's favourite children's entertainer, a personal appearance from the real-life Charlie and Lola, or whatever that year's must-have happened to be.

But there had been no such scenes recently. That Vanessa had forgotten was surely impossible, but James resolved to talk to Emma after bedtime. If Hero's birthday party had somehow slipped through the net, perhaps they could come up with something together. Emma was a resourceful woman and he had absolute faith in her.

'Bed!' Emma was commanding the children, in amused tones which none the less held a hint of steel. There was a flurry of movement and laughter, a blur of blue and pink gingham, and almost before James realised, his children had pressed warm, flannel-covered, bath-scented little bodies to his, deposited hard wet kisses on his cheek and tumbled into their room, whence the comforting sound of Emma singing nursery rhymes now issued.

As he went back downstairs, James felt a clench of envy. He would like to be in that bedroom himself now, all snuggled up in the warmth and the dim light, hearing Emma's soft northern tones relate a reassuring traditional favourite. But there was a fair chance she might consider that odd.

Lost in these thoughts, he only half registered the fact that, halfway down the stairs, an unfamiliar smell surged round his nostrils. Making his way along the threadbare sisal of the passage into the kitchen, James now discovered the source of the mysterious, but by no means unpleasant, scent.

It was baking. The sweet, warm, rich smell of cakes cooking. He hadn't recognised it because cakes were so rarely cooked in their house. Whenever needed, they were bought in from whatever fashionable delicatessen enjoyed Vanessa's favour at the time. Cakes which, while they were always delicious, lacked the buttery, springy freshness of something home-made.

James's stomach gave a mighty rumble. He loved home-made cakes, and the sight that greeted him now was not only a fantasy made reality, but as if someone had, in one fell swoop, sought to make up for the baking deficit of years in their particular kitchen.

Every available surface – the table, the units, the cooker itself, the top of the fridge – was covered in cupcakes in paper cases. Sixty at least, James swiftly calculated. All decorated, and all in different ways. Some had the squodge of buttercream icing – a generous squodge too, James noted approvingly – and twin sponge wings of the traditional butterfly cake. Others were jam and cream splits. Some were covered in hundreds and thousands, others with chocolate, still others with silver balls on top of icing that had a pinkish iridescent sparkle. James stared at the shining, glittering, glowing mass of sweet-scented cakes in childish wonder. It looked like heaven as a five year old might imagine it.

The cakes on the table, James now saw with a more adult appreciation, had been particularly beautifully iced. They had that thick, flat, smooth professional look, some the pale pink of sugar almonds, some white. And with something iced on top of that – cats' faces, James recognised with a stab of delight. The pink ones had an outline in white, lovingly hand-done, of a cat's face with silver sugar balls for eyes. The white ones had the same outline in pink.

A tremor of pure joy now seized him as he noticed, at the back of the kitchen table, a large white cake in the shape of a cat's face, with eyes, nose and whiskers in pink icing. Other details of fur and eyelashes had been added in the same iridescent pink sparkle – edible paint, James realised – he had spotted on top of the silver-ball cupcakes. Around the cake's edge was tied a fat pale-pink satin ribbon to which was attached a small silver bell. Four silver candles stood, two each side, among the whiskers.

James felt his mouth split in a huge grin. Of course. These were for Hero. For her birthday. Had to be. The grin took on a slightly incredulous aspect. Is this what Emma had been doing? Had she really made all these?

Certainly, the activity bore all her hallmarks of maximum achievement and minimum mess. Emma had quickly established herself as the least sloppy nanny they had ever had. Despite encouraging the children to produce a constant stream of paintings, she made less mess than the nannies who had never gone near the paints. Hadn't known what paints were, or so it had seemed.

He looked carefully about, but James could see none of the splatters, scatterings of flour and sugar or piles of dirty bowls everywhere one might have expected, and which would indeed seem perfectly understandable given the scale of production. All there was in that regard was a discreet pile of bowls in the sink, into which a couple of whisks and spatulas had been inserted.

He shook his head in wonder, smiling as his eye caught the cat cake again. Hero was going to erupt with excitement. Her father felt almost tearful at the prospect.

Hungry too. Everything looked so delicious. He hadn't had a home-made cake like this for years and it seemed years, too, since the canteen bacon sandwich that had constituted today's scrappy office lunch. He reached for the nearest cake, which happened to be one of the butterfly ones, and quickly, furtively peeled off the wrapper.

When Emma entered the kitchen, seconds later, the cake had just entered James's mouth. She saw what he was doing and grinned. He saw her and crimsoned with embarrassment.

'Sorry,' floundered James, his mouth full of crumbs. It was worth the shame, however. The cupcake was delicious; every bit as sweet, fresh and buttery as it looked. Substantial too, not like those cakes you bit into to find your teeth instantly meeting, that seemed to contain nothing but gritty, sugary air.

'Don't worry,' Emma assured him. 'There's plenty to go round. I'm expecting ten children tomorrow . . .'

She moved to the sink.

'Ten?'

'Yes. For Hero's birthday. We're having a tea party.' Emma looked up from stacking the dirty bowls on a small tray in order to transfer it to the dishwasher in the utility room. It wasn't the most convenient of washing-up arrangements, James knew, but alone of all the nannies he could remember, Emma hadn't complained about it. The opposite in fact; dishwashers were, she had explained, non-existent in the house of her parents, with whom she had lived before coming as nanny to Hero and Cosmo. Vanessa had been astonished by this; that people existed who didn't have dishwashers had stunned her.

'A tea party?' James was aware that all he was doing was repeating everything Emma said, but found he could not help it.

As she looked up, nodded and smiled, a hank of reddish brown hair dislodged from the rest and fell fetchingly across her face. 'It seemed the easiest thing,' Emma said, rather breathlessly. 'From what I gather from Vanessa, birthdays had become a sort of torture for her.'

James raised an eyebrow. Many things were a sort of torture for his wife. Opening credit card bills, owning up to having run up said credit card bills, filing the weekly column she was employed to write by a national newspaper, seeing any friend succeed, researching any articles of any sort, and even sometimes – at least this is how she made it seem – having sex with her husband. Although, thankfully, this was less the case of late.

'And she hadn't got very far with organising Hero's – obviously she's busy and everything,' Emma added hastily. 'But of course she was thinking about one of those expensive party places,' the nanny continued, her eyes wide and enthusiastic. 'And I suggested that, really, that wasn't necessary. That she could save a fortune and Hero would have a much nicer time if

– well,' she shrugged, 'we just had an afternoon birthday tea party at home for Hero's friends. With a few games. Old-fashioned, I know, but nice. Back to basics.'

James's eye flicked towards the glowing, glittering, pink-and-white display of cakes. There was nothing remotely basic about those. Or if there was, it was his sort of basic.

'Vanessa seemed quite keen,' Emma added with a tinge of pride, which James guessed related to the fact that, for all her skill, Emma rarely received approbation from her difficult boss.

'As indeed she should be,' James assured her hastily. Of course Vanessa would be keen. She would save money – only to spend on something else, obviously – and score a social coup by providing the kind of picturesque, old-fashioned children's gathering one only ever saw these days in Boden catalogue photoshoots. The kind no one else could possibly lay on because no one else's nanny would be capable of it, let alone volunteer.

Emma lifted the tray. As he rushed to the kitchen door to hold it open for her, a hideous thought struck him.

'Who'll do the games?' James's heart was pounding as he pictured himself standing, vainly shouting about Musical Chairs, in the middle of a pack of rioting children. He pulled himself together quickly. He'd be at work, for one thing, and for another, if Emma asked him, he *would* do it. She'd done everything else, after all.

Emma was looking at him in surprise. 'Well, me of course. Musical Chairs, Pass the Parcel, that sort of thing. All quite straightforward.'

James stared at her. She was going up in his estimation all the time. Not only was she professionally super-competent and a marvellous cook, she was possessed of astounding courage into the bargain.

'It sounds,' he said, rummaging for a superlative sufficient to encapsulate all the bursting gratitude he felt, 'just fantastic.' It wasn't the word he wanted, but the fervour with which he said it seemed to have got his message across.

Emma shrugged. He noticed the creamy, slightly freckled skin of her face redden. 'I like making cakes,' she muttered. 'And Hero's such a sweet little girl.'

At this last, on top of everything else, James felt about to burst. 'You're *wonderful*,' he exploded passionately, ears thumping too hard with excitement to hear the rattle of the front door. Just in time to hear him say this, Vanessa walked in.

Chapter 22

Vanessa said nothing to James about what she had heard pass between him and Emma in the kitchen. He, meanwhile, made no apologies or explanations.

These did not seem necessary to James. He had nothing to explain or apologise about. Emma *was* a wonderful nanny and she was making sure Hero had a wonderful birthday party. That there could possibly be anything wrong with this, or, rather, that his wife saw it differently simply did not occur to him. The extent of Vanessa's insecurity and his own occasional tactlessness was something James both misunderstood and underestimated.

That coursing not very far beneath Vanessa's confident exterior was another, vulnerable, Vanessa – one uncertain of her talents, social position, fitness to be a mother and how to be happy – was something of which her husband had no idea. That Emma, instead of being a miracle in human form, was a constant reminder to her of her shortcomings, the comparatively straightforward, simple James could not imagine.

But even Vanessa had to admit that the party looked wonderful. On the afternoon following the James and Emma love-in, as she waspishly thought of it, she came back at teatime after a long lunch with the editor of her column to find the house transformed. The sitting room was full of paper flowers and cardboard trees. The carpet was completely covered in a thick green mat of fake grass, the sort one sometimes saw in greengrocers'. Dotted around the edge of it were a large variety of cats; some fluffy toy cats from Hero's own collection, some cut-out large pictures of cats mounted on cardboard, some hand-drawn or painted in bright colours and mounted the same way.

'It's a surprise for Hero. She hasn't seen it yet. A pussycat's picnic,' Emma, in the middle of the room, positioning the last of the animals, explained. 'Like a teddy bear's picnic, but because Hero so loves cats I thought—'

'Yes, yes,' snapped Vanessa, irritated at the suggestion that she was incapable of making the imaginative leap from teddies to pussies. It occurred to her to wonder when Emma had had the time to make all these cats. Surely she could not have stayed up late for nights on end to make them all? They must have, Vanessa persuaded herself, been manufactured during time with the children, when Emma ought to have been looking after them.

'It must have taken ages to make those cats,' she remarked. Emma, catching the spiky note in her employer's voice, realised at once she had done something wrong, but could not imagine what. Should she have made the cats faster, or something?

'Not really. I've been doing them in the evenings, after the children were in bed and I'd finished my coursework.'

While this answered Vanessa's question regarding the time, it provoked unflattering reflections on the nature of Emma's social life. Unlike her former nannies, she never stumbled in late from smart nightclubs like Boujis or Mahiki or anywhere else Vanessa might read about in the *Daily Mail*. Instead, Emma seemed to lead an almost monastic existence, devoted to the children during the day and doing coursework – Vanessa knew not what and cared less – at night.

'That green grass thing looks expensive,' Vanessa remarked next, starting to prowl around the room. Emma could think again if she imagined landing her with an expenses bill for it.

'It didn't cost anything,' Emma assured her. 'The greengrocer on the high street let me have it. You know, the one I take the children to sometimes . . .' She stopped short of adding '. . . because I was so shocked when I realised Cosmo had no idea what a courgette was, Hero had never seen an aubergine and neither of them were entirely sure about tomatoes.'

Vanessa was hardly listening. Her attention now was on the expected guests. Each cat, she saw, had a plate before it and a ribbon round its neck on which a bell and a label was attached. The ribbons were blue and pink; blue for the boy guests, pink for the girls.

'Each guest has their own cat,' Emma started to tell her. 'They use the plate for their cakes—'

'Very nice,' Vanessa interrupted her icily. Those bloody cakes. She pictured the glittering, shimmering, sugar-scented array of confectionery in the kitchen.

She had long since moved from the position of regarding Emma's home-made tea party as a social triumph – something no rival nanny or household could have replicated – to feeling the rivalry was in her own home.

Even if she hadn't heard what James had said, the sight of such perfection, done with such skill and attention to detail, above all with such obvious love, would have made her want to self-destruct with guilt and self-disgust. Not that Vanessa particularly realised that this was what it was. She knew only that it made her feel intensely angry, and for reasons that, if only to herself, she had to justify.

Now, justification had presented itself. The fact she had heard James tell Emma she was wonderful only intensified Vanessa's former feeling, now her conviction, that Emma had to be got rid of. Before, Emma's main sin was to make Vanessa feel inadequate; now she had more or less concrete proof that the nanny would be content with nothing less than her husband.

What made the discovery especially dangerous was that the family was about to go on holiday. To Italy. Where, among the wine, the delicious food, the mellow villages and the sunshine, romance could only thrive.

Emma, of course, could not be further from any such intention, although she was keenly looking forward to the Italian visit, having never been there before. She would have been staggered had she guessed what Vanessa suspected about her and James. Emma was as fond of him as any conscientious and dedicated nanny would be to the kindly and supportive father of her charges. And if she had ever wondered why such a nice man had married such a termagant as Vanessa, she kept it to herself. Besides, she could see when the couple were together that, in their own way, they were very fond of each other. Which was all to the good, Emma felt, as it meant security for the children.

It had never occurred to her to desire him, however. While she liked him, she did not find him physically attractive; James was ancient – in his mid-forties at least – and looked like a slipshod professor. As for the material benefits of snaring him, Emma intended to make her own money her own way. She would not consider doing otherwise.

'Hengist Westonbirt?' Vanessa was tweaking a blue ribbon. 'As in Lord and Lady Westonbirt?'

Encouraged by the leap of interest, even approval in her employer's voice, Emma nodded eagerly. It puzzled her why, for all the efforts she made with the children, Vanessa only seemed to get crosser. It was almost as if the more effort she made, the crosser Vanessa got. But of course that could not possibly be the case. That would be ludicrous. So Emma did her best not to let Vanessa's moods affect her and concentrated on what was important: the children. And today, anticipating Hero's great delight at what had been prepared for her, even the worst Vanessa could do would have no impact on Emma.

Vanessa seemed pleased about Hengist Westonbirt, so she had done something right there by inviting him, Emma reflected. Not that she had wanted to; Hengist was a peevish boy, much inclined to sulks and tantrums, and pathologically disinclined to share. At his own birthday party, while the other children sang the time-honoured song round the cake, Hengist had put his fingers in his ears and cried. But perhaps that was not entirely his fault, Emma reminded herself, trying to be fair. Hengist did, after all, have to suffer having the appalling Totty Ponsonby-Pratt as his nanny.

Remembering the tall, sneering, superior blonde with the tigerish yellow eyes, who always wore unfeasibly tight trousers, breast-revealing tops and too much make-up, Emma hoped with all her heart that Totty, who would no doubt be delivering Hengist to the party, would not stay. Hopefully none of them would stay.

In theory, of course, the presence of each child's nanny would greatly decrease Emma's workload as they all pitched cheerily in and assisted with food, games, discipline and the rest of it. But in practice, she knew from her experience at other birthday parties, the nannies all sat or stood at the back, forming their own little party and ignoring their charges altogether. Emma had been appalled to discover that she herself was the only one who ever troubled to help with anything.

'I do hope Hengist's nanny stays,' Vanessa observed. 'I rather like that girl – Totty, is it? Great fun, I always think. Great style. And of course very grand. Her father's a duke, isn't that right?'

'I'm not sure,' hedged Emma, who didn't know, and cared less.

Vanessa gave a snort of frustration. Fancy not being sure about something so crucial. Ridiculous. She moved along the row of cats, and swooped down on another name. 'Augusta St Lennards!' she exclaimed appreciatively.

Emma repressed a groan. Augusta St Lennards was even worse than Hengist Westonbirt. While he cried and sulked, her party piece was to take her clothes off at any opportunity and forcibly resist anyone who tried to put them back on. Her nanny, while not quite as ghastly as Totty – such depths were not easy to replicate – was similarly snooty and lazy and, for the purposes of the party, just as useless.

Emma, as she positioned the last of the cats, felt the fun had rather gone out of things.

Yet Hero's face, when, at the prearranged time, she came into the sitting room and discovered her cat picnic, soon put it back. The little girl's porcelain skin flushed with delight; her squeal of pure joy reverberated in Emma's ears for many months afterwards and comforted her in many an hour of dark need.

'Oh, for fuck's sake, Hengist, just get out of the car, can't you?' The blonde in the tight white jeans tugged hard at the little boy in the back of the car. Hengist had rammed himself down in the rear passenger seat footwell and was hunting about for something.

'I've lost my King Arthur,' he wailed, raising the flat, pale, rather hopeless-looking face that always so irritated his nanny.

'Sod your King Arthur,' Totty snapped viciously. Now that she was about to be sacked by the Westonbirts, there seemed no reason to hold back the dislike she had always felt for their son. Hengist was unbelievably boring, and his penchant for small plastic figures of knights, which constantly slipped down the back of the seats and threatened her manicures in extracting them, more boring still.

'I've lost the sheep he was riding on as well,' bleated Hengist, his voice muffled under the seats.

Totty wrinkled her short forehead. Sheep? She had picked up little at school, admittedly, despite her parents sending her to the best ones in the country. But surely King Arthur had ridden on a horse?

'I couldn't find a horse to fit him,' Hengist explained. 'So I used a sheep from my toy farm.'

'Oh, for God's sake,' muttered Totty under her breath. How bloody boring Hengist was.

Not that her dislike of him was exclusive. Totty disliked all children. She had only come into nannying because, after the police raid on a party she had held in her flat, during which cocaine with a street value of thousands had been discovered, her father, a duke, had threatened to cut her off from her inheritance unless she got a proper job. Nannying, which was just driving kids about, after all, had struck Totty as the easiest possible work. She had had no idea how dull children could be.

But getting sacked was especially boring. Lady Westonbirt, who had been so nice at first and so delighted to have someone of Totty's aristocratic descent looking after darling Hengist, had turned considerably less nice after Totty failed to report for morning duty three days in a row. That the cocktails at Boujis were to blame had not been accepted as a defence. Nor would it be by her father, Totty knew, which was why it was essential to land a new job as quickly as possible, before he found out and the prospect of lifelong penury became a reality.

Lady Westonbirt had refused to give her a reference, which was also boring, as it ruled out nanny agencies such as Theodora Connelly-Carew's, who could always be relied on to favour girls with 'background', as she called it. It had been Mrs C-C who had got her the job with the Westonbirts, despite her lack of formal – or indeed any – training in nannying. But even an arrant snob like Mrs C-C couldn't do anything without a reference. And now she had to go to this bloody party in Peckham, of all places. It really was, Totty thought, incredibly boring. They were late, too, but that was probably no bad thing.

Dragging Hengist violently out of the car, she pushed the shocked boy, clutching his plastic king, up the steps and banged on the door. As she waited for it to open she looked with dislike at the hand-drawn cat's face stuck on it, with a speech balloon coming out saying 'Happy Birthday Hero'.

The door was opened by a medium-height blonde wearing what Totty, eyes everywhere behind her Chanel sunglasses, guessed was head-to-toe Boden. Or perhaps that skirt was MaxMara. And at a pinch those shoes could be Emma Hope but were more probably L. K. Bennett. Either way, none of it was the couture Lady Westonbirt preferred and which Totty often amused herself trying on in her ladyship's bedroom when Hengist's parents were out. No more, however. Damn it. Where was she going to get another job from?

'Totty, isn't it?' The woman was smiling at her. Totty recognised that smile. Lady Westonbirt had worn it at first. It was a smile of acknowledgement of her lineage as much as it was of herself personally. With the native cunning often gifted to those with no other intelligence to speak of, Totty sensed possibility. She pushed her enormous sunglasses up on top of her head, swung her shining hair about and beamed.

'Hi, there,' she barked in her grandest, most gravelly tones.

'We were wondering where you'd got to,' the woman added. The sense of possibility strengthened. This woman, Totty recognised, gratified, was almost deferential. Also, it was rare for a mother to be present at a children's party. Most could not be seen for dust at the first mention of a party bag. Did this woman not have a nanny? Was there an opportunity here?

'I'm Vanessa Bradstock, Hero's mother. You probably know me from my columns.' Vanessa flashed her an expectant smile.

'Absolutely,' Totty assured her, although she had no idea whether the columns referred to were of the newspaper sort or the sort that stood, eight-strong, supporting the portico of the family stately home.

Vanessa nodded, gratified. 'And you must be Hengist,' she mewed, bending over the snivelling boy Totty had been shoving roughly before her but whom she now made a great display of stroking comfortingly on the shoulder.

No, there must be a nanny, Totty deduced. This woman had none of the easy rapport with infants she associated with those smiley, cake-baking, laid-back losers who looked after their own children all the time. She also wore much more make-up and her recently highlighted locks showed evidence of hair straighteners.

As she followed Vanessa down the narrow hall, along whose walls more cats had been stuck, Totty remembered who the nanny was.

'Jacintha!' she exclaimed. 'Isn't Lady Jacintha Toffington your nanny?'

Vanessa skidded to a halt in front of her, her kitten heels almost slicing through the sisal. Hengist froze too. Lady Jacintha

Toffington had been his nanny before Totty. It was a moot point as to who was worse.

'Jacintha *was* our nanny,' Vanessa sniffed. She had determinedly dropped the 'Lady'; had even contemplated calling her 'Jackie', but lost her nerve at the last minute. 'Unfortunately we had to let her go.'

'Oh, yah,' Totty loudly interrupted. 'It's coming back to me now. She went off to work for that film star – what's her name? – Belle Murphy. Who was in *Marie*.'

After a few moments' agitation, Vanessa regained control. She hadn't realised Jacintha had left the famous – *more* famous – author already. If ever there was a more unprincipled snob than that nanny, Vanessa thought hotly, she had yet to meet one. 'She was much more suited to that sort of person,' she sniffed. 'Americans have no idea what real class is, of course.'

'Yah. Absolutely,' agreed Totty.

They had reached the sitting-room door now. The sound of singing and laughter could be heard from behind it. Vanessa pushed open the door, whose white paint was rather battered, Totty noticed.

She stared in astonishment at the cat-decorated sitting room, which even she recognised as rather adorable. While the sight of twelve or so of London's most difficult, spoilt children all clapping and singing a nursery rhyme with plates of delicious-looking cupcakes before them seemed to push credulity too far. Who was in charge here? Mary bloody Poppins? 'Who did all this?' she breathed. It really was rather amazing. In Totty's entire nannying career – which, admittedly, had been short – she had never seen anything like it before.

Vanessa, who was still beside her, leant close. 'My nanny,' she murmured, pointing Emma out as she welcomed Hengist into the room and admired his King Arthur figure.

'I love King Arthur too,' Totty heard her tell Hengist. 'We love playing the Round Table here. In fact, Hero and Cosmo and I have just made a great Camelot out of cardboard boxes. We painted it and everything. It was really easy and great fun.'

I bet it bloody was, Totty thought sourly.

Hengist's eyes were shining. He followed Emma adoringly as she led him to the cat with his name on. Then, to cheers from the children, she picked up an enormous Pass the Parcel parcel and handed it to a sweetly ecstatic Hero.

Totty realised she recognised Emma now. Of course, it was that fat northern one. The one she'd been so rude to when she'd first met her. Bloody funny, though. She sniggered at the memory.

Vanessa pounced on the snigger. 'What's so funny?'

Totty's cunning ear caught encouragement, rather than annoyance, in the other woman's voice. She guessed that, strange as it seemed, criticism of this apparently perfect nanny would not be unwelcome. 'Oh, just that when I first met her I asked her what part of Eastern Europe she was from,' she tittered in an undertone.

'Ha ha,' guffawed Vanessa, unnecessarily loudly. Emma, hearing the laugh, looked up and saw her employer and Totty Ponsonby-Pratt both looking at her with smirks on their faces. She felt a pang in which dislike, annoyance and panic combined, but then Augusta St Lennards started to take her clothes off again and she was distracted. By the time Emma looked up once more, both women had left the room. With luck the ghastly Totty had gone home.

She returned to Pass the Parcel with a burning feeling of resentment, however. It was so unjust. What did one have to do to please Vanessa? The children were the most important aspect of the job, of course, but there was no reason to tolerate such sustained rudeness and discouragement from their mother. Not when there were lots of other jobs out there that she could apply for, especially now she had a base in London and a month's notice either side. As she comforted a hysterical Hengist Westonbirt, who had missed by one place the unwrapping of the prize in the parcel, Emma decided that a warning shot to Vanessa that she could look elsewhere might be salutary.

The ghastly Totty had not gone home, however. She was in the kitchen with Vanessa. She had lost no time in driving her advantage home. The possibilities proved to be far more extensive than she had ever dreamt.

'You can't be serious,' she was exclaiming in a low voice, her eyes wide over the rim of the champagne glass Vanessa was refilling. It wasn't often she had a duke's daughter in her kitchen. 'She's really after your husband?'

Vanessa nodded. Her own eyes, with their fixed-bayonet lashes, were bulging with all the indignation she could summon, as well as with alcohol, which always loosened her tongue. Somewhere within herself she rather wished it hadn't, but the cat was out of the bag now and she had the satisfaction of holding an aristocrat in thrall with her conversation. Totty's unusual yellow eyes were staring into hers with unadulterated fascination.

Totty was gasping, exclaiming, slapping the table and generally responding as dramatically as she could. She could see clearly now what the issue was. And what the opportunity was too.

'I caught them in the kitchen,' Vanessa confided. 'He was telling her she was wonderful.'

'Wonderful!' exclaimed Totty in a voice of gravelly outrage. It didn't seem to her that there was much evidence for this woman's suspicions. Frankly, one look at that party more than proved that Emma was pretty bloody good at her job and deserved all the praise she got. Wonderful was the least of it. But Totty was not in the business of praising others, not when there might be something in it for her.

'God, that's unbelievable,' she cried. 'Slept with her yet, has he?'

'Not so loud!' Vanessa waved her hands frantically. It was the content as much as the noise she wished to suppress. That her devoted, gentle, long-suffering James could ever be unfaithful was a possibility so ghastly she could barely even frame the thought, let alone discuss it in such a matter-of-fact way.

'Well? Has he?' The yellow eyes were holding hers.

'I – I don't think so.' Something within Vanessa struck a vague note of warning, that the waters she was about to enter were deeper and more dangerous than any she had ever encountered before. But she ignored it.

'Well, it's only a matter of time, obviously,' Totty opined. She looked at the table, counted two beats and then looked up, her yellow eyes glinting. 'I've got it!' she hissed. 'The answer.'

'What is it?' Vanessa hissed back, her heart thumping.

Totty's eyes narrowed. 'Get rid of her,' she growled.

She had judged her right, Totty saw as Vanessa absorbed this, nodding. If ever a woman had wanted to be told what to do, it was this one.

'I'd need another nanny, though,' Vanessa sighed. Totty watched her, triumph twitching at her lips. This woman was such a bad actress. Unbelievable. Fortunately, Totty knew her own lines.

'Well,' she said casually, even hesitantly, 'there's always me, of course.'

Across the kitchen table, Vanessa gasped. 'You!'

'Me.'

'But you work for Lady Westonbirt!' Awe and excitement brimmed in Vanessa's voice. Totty Ponsonby-Pratt, the smartest nanny in London, the daughter of a duke, no less, was offering to work for her!

'That could, um, change. With, ah, immediate effect, actually.' Totty beamed at Vanessa and drummed her fingers on the table. Take it or leave it, they seemed to be saying.

'Aren't you on a month's notice?' Vanessa's words were galloping over each other.

Totty pursed her glossy pink-painted lips. 'Yah. In theory. But . . .' her voice dropped and her face approached Vanessa's confidingly across the table, 'to be really honest with you, I'm not very happy there at the moment. Actually, I might leave. There've been a few problems . . .'

'Problems?' Vanessa's eyes were wider than ever.

Totty looked carefully down at the table. 'Drugs . . . that sort of thing. Parties.'

'Drugs!' Vanessa almost shrieked. 'Parties! *Lady Westonbirt?*'

It was hard to imagine, from her hair downwards, anyone more upright than Lady Westonbirt. She sat on all the grandest charity committees, ones Vanessa could only aspire to join. It just showed, Vanessa thought, tutting and shaking her head in wonder.

It never occurred to her to doubt what she was hearing. Or what she thought she was hearing; Totty was careful to do no more than insinuate.

'Yah. Cocaine and parties . . . yup.' Totty shrugged and pulled a face.

One read about such things all the time in the *Daily Mail*, Vanessa excitedly reflected. There was a case only the other week, some billionairess smuggling wraps into an embassy party.

'Cocaine,' Vanessa said ruefully. 'What's that they say about it?'

Touch it again and you're no daughter of mine, Totty thought. That was what her father had said, anyway.

Vanessa had now located the rest of the quote. 'God's way of telling you you've got too much money,' she finished.

Totty's eyes held hers, giving no hint of what an idiotic thing to say she thought that was. Was it ever possible to have too much money?

'It's top secret, though. About Lady Westonbirt. Don't tell anyone. But, you know . . .' She shook her hair. 'I'm not sure it's an environment I want to be in, you know what I mean, yah?'

'Oh, absolutely. *Absolutely.*' Vanessa blinked, still absorbing the stunning news. Then she shook herself. 'And of course I'd love to have you, Totty,' she ardently assured the girl across from the table.

'Great. Perfecto. Start Monday, yah?'

Vanessa now remembered something. 'Well . . . the thing is, I've got Emma on a month's notice.' If she felt a certain relief that this was the case, Vanessa tried to ignore it. 'I can't get rid of her before that. Actually,' she added, 'we're about to go on holiday. To Italy, to a rather smart villa,' she added with a proud sniff. Then, as Totty remained apparently unimpressed by this, she added, 'We could talk about it when we get back.'

But Totty, with her goal in sight, had no intention of letting an obstacle as paltry as a notice period block her path. 'You can sack someone on the spot,' she insisted. 'There are certain situations when dismissal on the spot is entirely justified,' she stated with the confidence that came with her intimate knowledge of the subject. Lady Westonbirt had only not dismissed her on the spot because she wanted a week to find a replacement. But other nannies of Totty's acquaintance, one whose room had been found by her employers to contain drugs, for example, *had* been

247

fired on the spot. Totty thought of the wrap of cocaine in her handbag at this minute and her yellow eyes gleamed.

She folded a pair of slender brown arms rattling with thick gold bracelets and an expensive-looking watch and looked directly at Vanessa. 'Which of the upstairs rooms is your nanny's?' she asked sweetly.

Chapter 23

'Jack Saint's a pretty tricky character,' Mitch remarked to Darcy as they drove towards her meeting with the director. 'The one thing you musn't do is talk about the film. He hates that. He—'

'*Not* talk about *Galaxia*?' Darcy interrupted, her straight black brows drawn in even more of a frown than the one they wore anyway against the blindingly bright LA sunshine. Even through the car's tinted windows, the blaze and glare of the passing traffic drove like needles into her brain. She had overindulged on the champagne again.

'That's right. Talk about anything but that. He likes to get a feel for your personality. "Holistic casting", he calls it. Let him ask the questions. He likes to be in charge.'

Darcy nodded, trying to conceal the fact only a third of her was concentrating on the meeting, which, as Mitch kept hammering into her, could change her life. As well as battling with her hangover, she was wondering about Niall, which was equally painful. She had called him many times now, both on his mobile and at the flat in Kensington, but he had not answered. Mixed with the sense of sickening worry she felt was an equally sickening sense of guilt, almost as if he had been there in the restaurant last night and seen her gawping at Christian Harlow. She crimsoned at the memory. Her face, neck and chest burned with shame. What had she been thinking of?

Mitch was rattling on happily. 'Yeah, holistic casting, kinda unusual I know, but, honey, a man with his track record can do what he damned well likes . . .'

Mitch hummed as he drove along. He felt unprecedentedly confident. The whole Darcy thing was going as well as he had hoped, possibly better. They had a great platform to build on. The showcase dinner with her at Puccini's had been a success – people had stared and one or two of the paps had snapped her as they had left – a really good sign.

There had, of course, been the Christian Harlow incident, but perhaps, Mitch now acknowledged, he had overreacted to that, been a bit too protective. Darcy had a boyfriend in London after all – that grumpy-sounding guy that always answered the phone and said she wasn't there, even when Mitch could hear her quite plainly in the background. Mitch had a feeling he hadn't been too pleased about her coming out here.

Frowning, he thought about Harlow again. Then the frown straightened out. There probably really wasn't any danger for Darcy from that department. Harlow was far too self-serving to try to land some obscure British actress, whatever the future for her might hold. And there was no reason to think Harlow knew anything about Darcy and *Galaxia*. Saint, in line with his controlling reputation, preferred to keep things under wraps until everyone was cast.

Besides, Harlow was, as everyone in town knew, currently squiring – as the euphemism went – a big A-list actress, slightly long in the tooth perhaps, but powerful and well connected. Not someone whose bed he was likely to leave in a hurry.

No, there was nothing to worry about there, Mitch assured himself happily. Worry, at the moment, seemed a thing of the past in general. Take that incredible business with Belle. Given her descent into alcoholism and self-pity in London he had begun, not to lose hope she would be cast in some production – he had lost that long ago – but to lose even a glimpse of a snatch of a hope that she would get back on her rickety, high-heeled feet ever again.

And then, out of the blue, had come the incredible news that not only had she succeeded in landing a part in a Shakespeare play but had found a new man, a rising young British actor too, not some drugged-up loser. Some of the wrecks Belle had been pictured with during her various lost weekends – lost entire weeks, in fact – after Harlow had dumped her didn't bear thinking about. Although Mitch had had to think about them, rather a lot.

There were photos of Belle and the actor in the American tabloids this morning; he had skimmed them at his desk but planned to take a better look at them while Darcy had her audition. They lay beside him on the passenger seat and from time to time, as he drove, he darted a glance of anticipation at them. It was a whole new feeling for Mitch to see a newspaper and actually look forward to reading about Belle in it.

It was a dazzlingly sunny day – not that it was ever anything else here – and it seemed to Mitch, as he drove off the freeway and headed up into the Hollywood Hills, that there seemed as much optimism in the air as exhaust pollution.

He was aware that, in the back of the car, Darcy's mood was less buoyant. Perhaps she was nervous. She hadn't remarked at any of the famous blue and white road signs, as he had expected. She seemed absorbed, quiet; no doubt because of the momentousness of the meeting about to take place.

But the meeting was far from Darcy's mind. She was fretting about Niall. Why didn't he answer her calls? Had he hurt himself? She visualised his body sprawled in the flat, or knocked off the emphatically rusty old bicycle he made a point of keeping in the glamorous entrance hall of the building, to the annoyance of many of its residents.

She wished with all her heart that she was back in London. LA's glitter and glamour had conclusively faded. She'd been there, seen it, got the idea, been briefly seduced by it. Now she wanted to go home.

And to add to her other woes, she was hungry. She longed with all her heart for the sort of bacon sandwich, in thick white bread that the grease soaked into, that she and Niall enjoyed from time to time in London. As the son of a butcher, he naturally approved of bacon sandwiches, and bacon in general. Darcy felt guilty now about the annoyance she sometimes felt about his talking about butchers – his father's business in particular – all the time. She missed him so much that if he mentioned butchers on the hour every hour for the rest of his life, Darcy felt she wouldn't mind in the least.

'Hungry? Here. Have this.' Mitch handed her a half-eaten jelly doughnut from the driver's door, the grease seeping through the white paper bag.

It was disgusting, Darcy thought, taking a bite. Bland and claggy and filled with jam whose relationship with fruit was distant, if non-existent. It wasn't real food. It was the least authentic thing she had ever tasted, seeming to sum up everything about the place she was now in. A pang of homesickness, of Niall-sickness, butcher-sickness, even, mixed with the pangs of guilt and nausea Darcy already felt.

'Here we are,' Mitch announced. 'The beginning of the rest of your life!' he added gleefully.

Darcy, bobbing and craning in the back seat to get a better look at the place, had never seen a house quite like Jack Saint's. Her favourite type of building tended to be old, romantic and mellow, with plenty of flowers and a garden. The house whose drive they were now entering was a futuristic nightmare, painted silver, a series of low, broad, round concrete pods linked together with huge circular windows fronting every link. It spread across the front of the hill it was built on like some fat cartoon caterpillar, throwing a ferocious silver blaze back at the fierce LA sun. Darcy felt that even if she hadn't already decided California held no charms for her now, this place would have caused her to think so.

As they got out of the car Darcy saw there was no garden; nothing green at all apart from a few dusty cacti and aloe vera plants on the pale, dry, dusty slopes at the side of the house. It all felt very exposed and dry and somehow unfinished.

Mitch, leading her up a concrete path from the parking area, turned and grinned. 'How LA is this?'

'Very,' answered Darcy, not at all in the sense that Mitch meant.

She looked good, he thought. He'd advised her to wear another dress and this one was fitted and yellow, which went well with the rather bleached landscape. She looked vivid and radiant against it, her black hair richly shining, her pale face now showing the faintest hint of rose.

They arrived at the front door, or the aperture that seemed most likely to answer the description. It was a flat, open rectangle leading into a round room. Darcy, following Mitch inside, saw white, marble-floored emptiness with a domed roof curving overhead.

'Totally *Star Wars*,' Mitch whispered. 'Totally *Galaxia*,' he corrected himself immediately. 'Hey, maybe Saint will show up in some crazy Jedi-style outfit, or maybe as one of those space councillors with trailing robes.' Seeing Darcy's tense face, he shut up. Excitement, Mitch knew, always made him slightly silly.

When, without warning, the famous director appeared from behind hitherto unsuspected sliding doors in the wall, he was actually wearing jeans and a checked shirt. To Darcy's surprise, her first impressions of him were positive. He was handsome, with a neat, wiry figure that seemed to radiate suppressed energy, shiny white hair brushed jauntily up from his tanned brow, a trim moustache and a small, pointed beard. His eyes were dark and lively beneath white brows still threaded with determined black.

Mitch billowed forward to salute the great man. 'Mr Saint!' he gasped as he narrowly avoided falling over his own ankles. 'May I say what an absolute, unbelievable honour it is to meet you? I've been a fan of yours for many years, you're quite simply . . .'

Saint nodded briefly at him as he strode quickly across the marble floor, his boot heels clacking on the hard surface. It was clear that Mitch was not the one he was interested in. He seized Darcy in a firm handshake, looked closely into her face, ignored Mitch's continued genuflections completely and swept her away with him to the lift.

Mitch, his heart rate pounding, returned to his Town Car to wait, gasping slightly as he left the cool interior of the house – caterpillar, whatever it was – for the dry, blazing heat pouring from above and bouncing back off the concrete parking area.

He started up the Town Car's aircon and sat at the wheel gazing excitedly out through the tinted windscreen into the heat and dust outside. Slowly, he came back down to earth like one of the hot-air balloons he so resembled. A feeling of tremend-ousness strained him that had nothing to do with the way his stomach pressed against his belt, especially when, as now, he was sitting down. He was on the belt's last notch now. The doctor had warned him again.

Mitch pulled the papers on the passenger seat towards him, opened them to the articles about Belle and her new man and prepared to enjoy himself. This was a great day for him and he was going to savour every minute.

The room in which Darcy sat with Jack Saint was a big light one in the basement of the house. He had taken her down in the lift and out they had stepped into this spacious, airy rectangle whose exterior walls were glass sliding doors leading out on to a patio with a wide view down over LA. There it was, this mythic city, its hills studded with houses, crisscrossed by streets, rising and falling all the way to the sea. The view was misty in the morning smog and looked, Darcy thought, rather ethereal. Had she not wanted to leave it so desperately she might have been enchanted.

The room was dominated by a pair of big drawing desks spread with highly detailed, fantastical-looking illustrations. Large tables were covered in what looked like toys; little scenes with futuristic, sheer-sided, vaguely medieval buildings, or desert-like sandy landscapes, on which small human-looking figures were dwarfed by bizarre dinosaur-like monster shapes, or contraptions that seemed to combine helicopters with ballistic missiles. Darcy guessed she was looking at prototype sets and characters for *Galaxia*, but, remembering Mitch's warning, resisted making any remark about them. She wasn't sure what she would say about them anyway. They looked, she thought, rather ridiculous.

Jack Saint was opposite her in a director's chair, which was turned back to front so she could see his name on the back, white letters on black canvas. He seemed friendly and smiling, one hand dangled over the back of the chair in relaxed fashion – he wore a wedding ring, she saw. His legs lounged apart around the chair frame, his beige tooled boots occasionally drumming on the wooden floor to give emphasis to what he said.

For all Mitch had said about him – his importance, his influence, his power, his steely control of everything and everyone to do with his projects – there seemed nothing frightening at all about Jack Saint, Darcy thought. He seemed very understated. There was something almost relaxing about the rhythmic way his hand kept stroking his beard. His eyes, black and intent, never left hers.

But all the same, she no longer wanted to be here, if indeed she ever had. God knows why she had come. She didn't want any of this, not any more. She had been briefly seduced by first-class flights, by five-star hotels, by celebrity restaurants. But now she was filled with a great, tearing urge to be home, to leap from her chair, to get Mitch to drive her to the airport and get the first plane back to Heathrow. To be with Niall again. To be grounded again, amongst her true priorities and ideals, the ones they shared together. To be away from this ludicrous Hollywood circus.

The sooner this stupid interview – audition, holistic casting, whatever – was over, the better. She could imagine what Niall would think of it. How he would despise it.

Saint leant forward. 'What's your earliest memory?' he asked in his low, quiet voice.

Darcy supposed she should not be surprised. Mitch had warned her not to expect anything ordinary. Holistic casting sounded rather psychobabbly, after all.

She knitted her brows and thought. To her surprise, the

memory came thundering back, fresh as a daisy despite the years. She lifted her chin and looked at him.

'Yes?' prompted Jack Saint.

'When I was at primary school – you know, the beginner's level of school in England . . .' she added, with an uncertain glance at the director.

'I know what primary school is. Go on.'

'Well, the teacher asked the children to sing a song. One child sang "Sing a Song of Sixpence" and another sang "Three Blind Mice" – you now, nursery rhymes.' She looked at him uncertainly again. He nodded.

'And then it was my turn. And . . .' Darcy felt a plunge of embarrassment at the memory. 'I sang "The People's flag is deepest red, it glorifies our something dead." You know, the "Internationiale".'

Darcy could not tell what Saint thought of this. His expression gave nothing away. She rushed to explain. 'My parents were committed – fanatical, in fact – socialists, you see. But the teacher thought it was quite strange and so did the other children.' She crimsoned. 'It was quite funny, I suppose,' she added lamely.

'Very funny,' Saint confirmed, without laughing. He still looked pleasant, however. 'You like LA?' he enquired next.

Darcy looked at him despairingly. Her earliest memory had obviously misfired in some way. On the other hand, did she care, with all she had on her mind? As for this new question, she was too agitated to make anything up. The truth was all she could think of. 'No,' she said.

Saint laughed at this – a Santa-like ho, she noticed, accompanied by a flash of white enamel. 'Where do you like to be, then?' he asked her.

'London,' Darcy said, finding it difficult to get the name out without a sob, she wanted to be there so badly.

Saint nodded. 'We'd be shooting a lot of *Galaxia* in Italy. Not here in LA. There are palace scenes we've scheduled that can be shot only in Florence. The Kingdom of the Anoos is particularly magnificent.'

She absorbed less the geographical location than the fact he spoke about the outlandishly named kingdom as if it was real. She avoided taking up his mention of the film. Mitch had told her not to and she intended to stick to the script to that extent at least. It wasn't as if she was likely to be in it, given her performance so far. And that was fine with her.

'Like acting?' Saint asked next, in his light, low voice.

Darcy hesitated. Acting was in her blood, in the sense that both her mother and father had done it. She had been expected to do it. And do it she had, and defended it, and respected it, and cherished it, and believed it was important. But it had never occurred to her before to wonder whether she actually liked it. 'I don't really know,' she answered, frowning. 'Sometimes I think I'm only doing it because of my parents. So they will approve of me.'

Saint did not seem overly surprised about this. His pleasant expression gave no hint of what he might be thinking. He carried on in measured tones with his questions. 'You don't want to be famous? Rich? A celebrity?'

Darcy shook her head vehemently. 'Can't think of anything I want less.'

'OK. What *do* you want? To do? With your life?' he asked her next. 'Apart from to go home, that is,' he added with a smile and a tug of his beard.

Darcy sighed. She felt tired, confused, lost. She had a vague idea that many people at this point would make speeches about using their art to change lives, easing the suffering of humanity and reversing climate change. But in her own heart of hearts, she had no idea what she wanted to do, she now realised. She had thought it was acting, but now she was not so sure.

'What do you like?' Saint pressed.

Quite unexpectedly, the vision of the bacon sandwich she had longed for now came rushing back to her. 'I like eating,' she blurted, flushing the next second with red-hot, heart-beating shame. Of all the stupid answers.

Saint raised a black and white eyebrow and pulled his beard. 'That's all,' he said, rising to his feet.

Jesus, thought Mitch, examining the newspapers closely. Belle wasn't holding back in any of these pictures. She was pretty much sucking this guy's face off. He was obviously enjoying it, though. And he was good looking, which helped, and looked pretty clean, which helped even more.

. . . the lucky man is Graham MacDonald, 24, actor son of top Glasgow psychologist Professor Eleanor MacDonald and processed foods tycoon Sir Humphrey MacDonald. He is to act alongside Murphy – star of last year's mega-blockbuster *Marie* and who recently showed her compassionate side by adopting an African orphan – as she makes her much-anticipated stage debut in the experimental Upside Down Theatre's new production of *Titus Andronicus* in London . . .

'Star of last year's blockbuster *Marie* . . . showed her compassionate side by adopting an African orphan . . .' Hey, that was good, Mitch thought. None of the usual spiky, snide asides. Anyone reading about Belle for the first time might actually think she was both successful and had a conscience. Had the press tanker turned round already? He had a feeling it might have. 'Much-anticipated stage debut.' It sounded as if people were actually expecting her to be good at it. The PR plan was working – a bit late, but working after all.

As a flash of yellow caught Mitch's eye, a ripple of surprise ran through him. Darcy was out already? Here she came, down the path, the fat silver caterpillar house shining behind her.

He glanced at the watch on his broad, hairy wrist, trying to suppress his panic. She'd been in there barely fifteen minutes. Was that a good thing or a bad thing? He screwed up his eyes to see her face, but could not make out her expression.

Darcy opened the car door, shoved aside the papers and plonked herself down on the passenger seat. 'Take me back to the airport,' she said in a low voice, looking straight ahead at the tinted windscreen.

'*Whaaa-aat?*' Mitch gasped. For a moment, time, movement and sound all stopped. Then he started to gabble. 'What's the matter? What happened? Didn't he like you?'

'No. I don't think he did,' Darcy answered quietly.

It seemed to Mitch that there was a singing silence in the car, and then something inside him started to scream. Something outside him was screaming too. He realised it was him. *He* was screaming.

He saw that Darcy had stopped staring out of the windscreen and was looking at him in horror. He stopped and took a deep breath. 'What happened?' he said, wrestling to regain control of himself. His eyes were watering. Hot flushes were rushing up and down his back and chest. 'Tell me,' he said, breathing heavily between words. 'Tell me what happened in there. What *he* said. What *you* said. *Tell me.*' Mitch was trying with great difficulty to stop himself screaming again.

Darcy met the small eyes blazing maniacally from behind the agent's thick glasses, and felt a clutch of fear. 'I told him,' she began reluctantly, 'that my parents were fanatical socialists, that I didn't like LA or acting, that I didn't want to be rich and famous but that I liked eating.'

Mitch frowned. He couldn't be hearing right. Nothing about this seemed to be making any sense. It didn't fit together. Every word she spoke went into his brain like a triangular-shaped object trying to fit a round hole.

'Let me get a few things straight. You said your parents were committed socialists?' He spoke in a monotone.

'Fanatical,' she corrected. Darcy was nothing if not truthful. 'Yes. And that I sang the "Internationale" at primary school.'

He passed over that. 'You said you didn't like LA?'

She nodded.

'Or acting?'

'Yes.'

'And that you didn't want to be rich or famous?' His voice was a whisper now, scraping, or so it felt, along the side of his throat as he spoke.

'But that you liked eating?'

'Mmm.'

'Oh. My. God.'

For a second, everything blurred, then went black. When Mitch's vertical hold returned, he gazed at Darcy forlornly. There was, in the midst of his horror, a hint of admiration. As answers went, they were perhaps the worst things one could say to anyone in LA. It was stupendous. Spectacular. He'd never heard anyone mess things up as royally as this girl obviously just had.

She was speaking to him. He sensed from her expression – black eyes big and pleading – that it was something apologetic. But his ears were so thundering with blood he could not hear the words.

'Look,' Darcy was saying, slightly defensively. 'I'm sorry, OK? But I don't want to be a film star. I want to go home to Niall.'

The boyfriend, Mitch realised, his heart sinking. He shook his head. He felt his bottom lip start to quiver. His dream was shattered, his career was shattered, everything was shattered. He sighed a sigh that could have been dredged up from the other side of the world.

Darcy watched him, guilty but determined. 'I'm really worried about him, Mitch. I need to see my boyf—'

She stopped, suddenly. She was, Mitch realised, staring at the newspapers on the car floor. He heard her gasp sharply and watched as, with terrible deliberation, she picked one of them up and stared at the picture of Belle and her new boyfriend.

'I don't believe it,' Darcy said in a cold, slow voice Mitch had never heard before, not even when she was being her chilliest and most disdainful on the telephone from London.

It was dramatic enough to distract him from his own grief. There was something deathly about this voice. He did not answer her; he sensed there was nothing he could say. Then she seemed to pull herself up, to snatch at some brief hope. 'It can't be,' she muttered. 'It says here he's called Graham and his mother's a psychologist, but *no*, it's definitely him . . . that red hair . . . he was going for *Titus* . . . oh my God.'

Once again, Mitch had a sense of everything stopping as he watched her read the short report and look again at the picture. Slowly she put the paper back down and picked up another. She read this once faster; her breath coming short and sharp now. She threw it down, picked up another, growled. Faster and faster she tore through the pages, panting now, roaring almost. There was the sound of tearing, of snarling, then suddenly she was hurling screwed-up balls of newspaper at the windscreen and screaming every bit as loudly as he had been earlier.

'The fucking bastard!' Darcy yelled. The tendons on her neck were standing out like rope cords, Mitch observed in wonder. Her face was redder than the lobsters in Spago's restaurant. He wondered if he had ever seen anyone so angry. Or do a mad scene so well. What a loss to acting in LA she was going to be.

Chapter 24

Once she had got over the shock of being sacked, Emma had wasted no time crying over spilt milk. To do so would be self-indulgent with so many urgent practical matters to think of. In order to stay in London, she had to earn money. Vanessa, prompted by James, had at least agreed to supply a reference, and so she was able to apply for jobs.

Emma was sure that James believed her when she protested – in the ghastly aftermath of Hero's party – that she had been set up. That the cocaine in her handbag had been planted there by someone. But when Vanessa – with vicious scorn – had demanded who in the world would want to frame some obscure nanny from the north, she had been completely unable to provide an answer. Did she have any enemies? Not that she knew of. There seemed no explanation whatever, and in the absence of one, she had had to accept that the only thing it was possible to do with a nanny caught with Class A narcotics in her handbag was to fire her.

'But you must give me a reference,' Emma had, with a great deal of effort, summoned the courage to ask.

Vanessa had practically exploded at this. 'Are you joking? You've just been caught with drugs in your handbag.'

Emma had held her gaze levelly. She had spoken with as steady a voice as she could manage. 'Yes. The drugs were in my handbag. I didn't put them there, though. And one day I'll find out who did. But until then, I need a job and I'll need a reference to get one. I've been a good nanny and you owe me that at least.'

'Owe you? *Owe you?*' Vanessa's face had flushed bright red, her bayonet eyelashes had stuck out more indignantly than ever, and she was, Emma saw, about to give vent to insults, accusations and refusals, when James had stepped in.

'I think we should do as she suggests, darling,' he had murmured to his wife.

Vanessa had rounded on him then, more savagely than ever. 'What? You believe *her*?' Her eyes, as she looked at Emma, were no longer wide with outrage and accusation. They were narrowed with a rat-like hatred, almost a fear, that, it seemed to the nanny, had nothing to do with the discovery of the drugs.

James had sighed and pushed up the glasses that were forever slipping down his nose. 'I'm not sure what I believe,' he had said quietly. 'But the law, after all, is that people are innocent until proven guilty.'

His wife's eyes were wide with terror. 'You're not thinking of . . . court . . . again?'

Emma had been almost in favour of reporting the whole business at first, as the police might be able to help find the real culprit. But for some reason Vanessa had been adamantly, almost hysterically, opposed to such a course of action. And Emma quickly realised that making the matter public would not only endanger her own future, but increase the risk of her parents finding out. She felt she would do anything to spare them the shock, shame and disgrace they, having never transgressed in their lives, would certainly feel.

James shook his head. 'I just mean that it all seems very strange and very out of character. Emma's been a wonderful nanny. She's never put a foot wrong.'

'Until she was caught with drugs in her handbag,' Vanessa cut in savagely. She was almost snorting with fury now, Emma observed. And there seemed to be a panic about her which, for all the genuine drama of the situation, seemed disproportionate. It was as if she wanted the whole business concluded as quickly as possible.

'Or so it would appear,' James corrected. He turned his bewildered, bespectacled, above all, disappointed glance on Emma. 'Personally, I would like to believe that she was innocent.'

'Innocent!' screeched his wife. Her chest was heaving violently up and down. A flame of hope, meanwhile, leapt in Emma's. Might James actually persuade his wife to let her stay?

'Yes,' James said firmly. 'And if Emma believes she can clear her name, I'd be delighted.' His face fell then, however, and the flame within Emma died proportionately down. 'But until such a time, I agree, in the absence of evidence that she isn't responsible, she has to go.'

The day Emma had left had been the worst of her life – or the second worst; the discovery of the drugs having been the absolute nadir of her existence. She felt she would remember the scene as long as she lived: entering her room on a summons from Vanessa to find her employer standing there with burning eyes, a small fold of white paper on her violently outstretched hand with a scattering of white powder on it. James stood uncomfortably behind her, shifting from foot to foot, his face red and his expression a mixture of tragedy and disbelief.

'And what,' Vanessa hissed, pointing at the outstretched hand with her other finger, 'is this doing here?'

Emma had stared at it. 'I don't know.' She guessed it was drugs immediately, of course; she had never seen them in real life but one could hardly avoid them on the television. But what they were doing in her room she could not imagine. Her eyes flicked to James, speculation leaping suddenly within her. Was it his? Did he have a secret habit? It was a crazy thought, but what other explanation was there?

Of course, she did not believe that for more than a second. She did not believe it now. Where the drugs had come from, who put them there, was still a mystery, a horrible mystery. Could it have been someone at the children's party? It was possible, but again, who and why? One thing was certainly true about the party for which she had worked so hard, however. It should have been an unadulterated triumph. It had proved to be a drug-laced disaster.

Pushing at the back of Emma's mind was the possibility that Vanessa herself had put the piece of paper with its explosive contents in her handbag. She could almost imagine it, Emma thought. It was clear, for all her competence and success with the children, that there was something about her Vanessa resented. Especially recently, she had been so poisonous it seemed she was capable of anything. But something – Emma hardly knew what it was – made her hesitate to blame her boss. Nasty and cruel Vanessa could certainly be, but once or twice Emma felt she had glimpsed something beneath the surface: something rather lost, helpless and vulnerable, something touching, almost, that made her doubt, at the last minute, that it was her.

So there was no answer, and perhaps there never would be. Emma tried instead to focus on what future she might still have here in this city, where she wished to remain in spite of everything.

Returning to the provinces would not only mean the end of her career ambitions, but the end of the possibility of redeeming herself. Whoever had done this to her was, after all, in London.

And so she tried not to think about the injustice of it all, about Vanessa's poisonousness, about James, whom she could not help feeling slightly let down by whilst recognising there was little else he could have done. She regretted the holiday to Italy, somewhere she had always longed to go, but which would now never happen. It had sounded such fun. Venice and Rome. Pasta and ice cream and song. They liked children there too, she had heard. Cosmo and Hero were going to love it. She hoped they still would . . . but without her.

Especially she tried not to think about Hero and Cosmo, who she had loved so much and yet who, from the moment the drugs had been discovered, she had not been allowed to see. But whose eyes, round with horror and red with weeping, she had seen briefly through their bedroom windows and felt following her down the street as she walked away from the house for the last time.

As she turned the corner, the sob pressing in her throat finally broke out. When she had first come to London the world had seemed her oyster. Now it was just an empty shell.

It was like a house collapsing, Darcy felt. Everything that had seemed solid and dependable now lay in shards around her. Her profession. Her philosophy. Everything she had believed in. It was all different.

Niall had left her for the type of Hollywood bimbo he most affected to despise. He was a lying hypocrite of the first order. He had tried to prevent her going to LA, but only because, it appeared, he wanted to go there himself. His high principles had been jealousy, nothing more.

After driving back with Mitch following the meeting with Jack Saint, Darcy had headed straight to her meringue burrow of a hotel bedroom and stayed there. Having completely lost her appetite – the mere thought of food made her feel queasy – she had ordered nothing from room service. When she was thirsty – if she noticed she was thirsty – she simply put her mouth under one of the gold taps in the vast marble-lined bathroom. Otherwise, she merely cried and raged.

She had believed in Niall, his principles and his art even more than her own. Far more than her own. But he had left her for Belle Murphy, a woman whose only interest in art, given her veneered teeth and obviously artificial breasts, was that of the plastic surgeon and cosmetic dentist.

Whenever she closed her eyes and tried to sleep, she saw the pictures in the newspapers. Niall, his tongue so far down Belle Murphy's throat it was almost coming out of the other end. He had never kissed her like that, Darcy thought. Nor had he ever turned to her with that rampant desire in his eyes; unless he was talking to her about parts he desperately wanted. She had never suspected, never ever dreamt, that what he wanted was a woman like Belle.

On the other hand . . . why not?

Darcy ran her mind's eye over the pictures of Belle again. Blonde, big-breasted, slender; a blow-up doll in human form. She was probably every man's fantasy. Every ambitious actor's fantasy, in particular. What couldn't a woman like Belle give Niall? (Darcy still couldn't bring herself to think of him as Graham.) Hollywood contacts. Film success. Fame and fortune. Was that what he had wanted, all along? Oh, come off it, Darcy told herself angrily. Wasn't it what every actor wanted? Didn't bears shit in the woods? Who was she kidding?

How could she not have realised? Have believed him when he

talked of principles? Because she had wanted to, of course. She had always been too trusting, too eager to believe the best of people. Take Belle herself. Darcy remembered with contempt the interview she had read in the celebrity magazine on the plane. The adopted African baby. What had Belle said? Something about how she had never felt such love? How she felt she was a member of a whole tribe of mothers? And yet I almost wanted to believe it at the time, Darcy thought. She wondered darkly how Niall would fare with the baby. He had never been remotely interested in them. Which, no doubt, gave him another thing in common with his new paramour.

I was so easily taken in, Darcy berated herself. For all her university-educated intelligence, she had been ripe for the picking, or the tricking. And now, with an unprecedented clarity, she felt she could see why. Secretly uncertain about the choice of career she had made, yet buffeted by the mighty winds of her parents' certainties and keen as any child for their approval, she had been no match for someone like Niall, with serious ambitions he thought contact with her would further. An actor, to boot, who could don a persona like a coat. In particular, the persona of a grittily working-class butcher's son from Scotland, whom the Hampstead-reared daughter of a socialist acting dynasty felt ticked all hers – and her parents' – boxes.

She remembered with particular fury his descriptions of the flat meat patties that were apparently his father's speciality. While Darcy had always thought they sounded hideous, she had never doubted their existence. And perhaps they did exist, only not in any butcher's Niall's father had ever owned. Niall's father, it now emerged, was the multimillionaire, knighted owner of a chain of plants specialising in the mechanical recovery of meat. Making hot dogs out of chicken skin and pulverised beak and feet. The kind of food people like her mother campaigned to have banned. There was an irony in that.

And yet another in the way Niall had had no luck getting cast in any plays. Although the only casting he deserved now was in concrete, it was difficult not to admit that he was a much better actor than she had ever suspected. His interpretation of the angry Glaswegian butcher's boy had been practically Method. Perhaps that was the problem – he had put so much of his acting energy into the part he played for her every day, there was nothing left for anyone else.

Had he ever really loved her? It was hard to remember times when Niall wasn't cross with her for some reason. But she had loved him. Hadn't she? As well as being good looking he had been the image of everything she wanted to believe in most.

Believe in then, that was. Darcy had no idea what she believed in now. And yet, even so, everything seemed clearer. And colder. Like stark trees in winter that had been previously clothed in pretty summer green.

This new clarity raised uncomfortable questions. Were she and Niall, after all, both as bad as each other? Flitting across Darcy's mind now came the possibility that she too might have loved what Niall stood for more than the man himself. Otherwise, might she have not looked closer beneath the surface?

Only – and it was a big only – she had not two-timed him with some screen bimbo while he was away. Well, not *exactly*. With a surge of acid guilt, she remembered seeing Christian Harlow in the restaurant.

But that had been a moment's lapse; she had been drunk, tired, jet lagged. And the moment Christian had gone she had come to her senses, which, to judge from the pictures in the papers, it didn't look as if Niall was ever likely to do.

Anger rose within her again. Authenticity, art – he could stuff it. Although of course he had stuffed it. More so than his father had ever stuffed a chicken, or rolled up a loin of lamb. She'd quite like to roll up Niall's loins, come to that, butcher-style, with very tight string. It seemed to Darcy that if she saw another sausage ever again, let alone a square one, she would not be responsible for the consequences. It would be like Proust and his madeleine, only more bloody and violent.

Darcy rather regretted the fact her own Hollywood career was over before it had begun. She felt differently about the whole Hollywood question now. It was no longer so simple, so cut and dried. Not least because, now that her artistically committed, high-principled, anti-commercial boyfriend had turned out to be a fame slag, she could have taken him on at his own game. Why not? She would have enjoyed trumping Niall and Belle at every turn. *Galaxia* sounded ridiculous, admittedly, and looked even worse, to judge from those sets in Saint's studio. But it would certainly be big. There was no doubt about that.

Revenge may be a dish best eaten cold, but dressed up like the Grand Duchess of the Galaxy in the kind of rubber collar you found in the hairdresser's, in some international smash-hit film, wasn't a bad way of eating it either. But of course, now, it was not to be.

Chapter 25

Emma's savings meant that a long-term stay in the bed and breakfast she found near King's Cross Station was out of the question, even if she had wanted to, which she didn't. The place had the pall of failure over it; all the residents, mostly young, seemed to be there all day, half dressed, unbrushed and up to nothing in particular. Or things Emma would rather not think about too closely.

Her room, all the same, was small and clean, with a wardrobe in which to hang her one good suit. The hotel owner, Mrs Cupper, was a hardbitten Cockney but generally cheerful. The nearby façade of St Pancras, with its turrets, machicolations, carvings and fantastical towers, still lifted Emma's heart when she saw it, although she felt differently now from the day when first she had set eyes on it, the day of her arrival. The nearby library, although considerably less of an architectural treasure, being sixties, concrete and brutalist, was none the less a warm place to write applications. It might be full of smelly tramps reading the papers, but it had a computer she could use if she booked times with the front desk.

Emma used her sessions well, writing down details of nanny

agencies all over London and applying to the smartest-sounding ones. Her confidence was badly knocked, her sense of justice and fairness rocked, but her aspiration was undimmed. She was an excellent nanny; she would apply to the best agencies.

Off went letters to You Rang, Madam?, Servants' Hall, Mrs Poppins and Domestic Bliss. Emma felt both relieved and vindicated when, some ten days later, a reply arrived – first class – in a thick cream envelope.

'Looks posh, that,' commented Mrs Cupper as she handed it over. 'Most o' the letters we get for folks 'ere are in brown window envelopes from the DSS. Or else white from the police,' she added darkly.

The letter, on thick cream paper, contained the longed-for news that Mrs Theodora Connelly-Carew of Domestic Bliss, office address 24 Sloane Mews, SW1, would like to see her for interview the following day.

The phone at Darcy's bedside warbled. Sighing, she reached for the receiver.

'Hey there!' It was Mitch. Sounding upbeat. She hadn't heard from him since he had dropped her off at the hotel two days ago. From time to time, in the midst of her own grieving, it occurred to her to wonder how he was. He had seemed almost as suicidal as she following the meeting with Saint. Not now, however.

'You sound pleased,' Darcy said, rather crossly. A new thought struck her: was Mitch to blame for what had happened? After all, had it not been for him she would never have left London and perhaps the Belle incident might never have . . . Well, *perhaps*.

Mitch was bubbling. He bounced around on his high-backed, black-padded office chair in delight; under his weight, it squealed and groaned in protest. 'Pleased. You bet I am, baby.'

He was more than pleased. Thunderstruck was the word.

Five minutes ago Mitch had been seated, as usual, chewing mournfully on a jelly doughnut and reflecting on the depth his career had reached. He'd just taken a call from his absolute least favourite client – and that was a hotly contested distinction – a British rock singer whose pushiness was in inverse proportion to his success. He blamed this, naturally enough, on Mitch. 'When I signed up with you you were going to help me crack America, man,' the singer had whined. 'You haven't helped me crack the top of a bloody crème brûlée.'

What had made him agree to represent this guy, Mitch had wondered. It had been a moment of madness. But then, his entire career seemed to consist of moments of madness, all linked together.

Perhaps the maddest moment of all had been believing Darcy could land the part with Jack Saint. Although it hadn't seemed mad at the time; the whole thing, in fact, had seemed as near to a certainty as anything he had ever been certain about. Perhaps that should have told him something, Mitch sighed. Nothing was certain in LA. Apart from sunshine, plastic surgery and cosmetic dentistry. And things not working out, particularly for him. Mitch stared at the grey carpet tiles and wondered if he was sitting on some particularly inauspicious ley line. It was incredible, the bad luck he had.

Whilst he had been thinking these thoughts, his eyes had been trained gloomily through the slatted blinds of his office window on a street cleaner working below. As the man toiled gently in the sunshine, pushing his barrow along and picking up papers with the aid of a long pincer, it had seemed to Mitch that he was deriving more satisfaction from his job than Mitch ever had from his own. He too worked mostly with rubbish. But it rarely made him feel as serene as that old guy down there looked.

And then everything had changed. His phone had rung and Jack Saint had been on the end of it. When, finally, he had put the phone down, Mitch had wondered whether he had dreamt it all, or whether he was dying and it was one of those wish-fulfilment scenarios people apparently sometimes experienced on the point of expiring. Then he had pinched himself, rotated a few times on his long-suffering office chair and stabbed out Darcy's number on his phone.

'I'll cut to the chase, baby,' Mitch said now. 'I just got a call from Jack Saint. He liked you. He liked your answers. He thinks you're honest. Original. Authentic.' Mitch paused for effect. Then he announced, 'Congratulations, baby. He wants you in his picture.'

Then, as Darcy did not react, he added, 'Are you listening to me? You're the Grand Duchess of the Galaxy in *Galaxia*, honey. Shooting starts in Florence, two weeks from now.' The sentence ended in a squeal. Unable, from sheer excitement, to prevent itself, his bottom slammed up and down on the soft and saggy seat of his chair.

'You're joking.' Darcy sat up. All the weariness she had been feeling fell away from her. She felt numb, then excited, then numb again, then excited again. Into the vacuum that had been her life shot a large object, not unlike the missile-cum-helicopter objects she had seen on Saint's model table. Whether or not she actually wanted to do it seemed less important than the fact that she now had a distraction and a direction in life. Moreover, one that would probably really annoy Niall. Or Graham, as she was trying hard to think of him.

'That's incredible,' she managed to say to Mitch. 'Amazing.'

Miraculous, more like, Mitch thought. He'd never heard of anyone saying what she had apparently said to Jack Saint and been cast. Cast out, more like. And yet Saint had seemed to dig it. 'Makes a change not to have a bimbo,' he had remarked to Mitch. 'Got plenty of them already in this film, believe me.'

Mitch wondered who. Due to the huge scale and fantastical nature of his productions, Saint generally started filming before the movie was entirely cast. The end was sometimes shot before the beginning and any number of intermediate scenes were filmed as the sets were completed. Much was done at the editing stage and there would be the computer graphics sequences, for which the director was famous, to put in too. To an outsider, and to many of the insiders, it was all incredibly confusing. The only person who ever knew exactly what was going on was Saint; it was part of his legend that he and he alone had the whole apparently rambling edifice organised down to the last tiny detail in his head. For all their apparent complexity, his schedules ran like clockwork and the end results were always spectacular. The reasons, Mitch knew, why he was so sought after as a director.

'Saint's people will be in touch about Florence. Sounds pretty nice,' Mitch added enthusiastically. 'All those canals.'

'That's Venice.'

'Oh . . . yeah. Right. Well, frankly, baby, if Saint wants canals in this film, Florence might well get 'em too.'

He put the phone down on Darcy, glowing with pleasure. Below him, through the slatted blinds, the street sweeper continued to pick up litter with his pincers. Mitch no longer envied him, however. He had the rare feeling of wanting to be no one apart from himself.

As joy seized him again, he swung round on his office chair. When, shuddering, lurching and creaking, the chair completed the circle and faced front again, Mitch found himself staring at the long, sly face of his least favourite colleague. Greg Cucarachi was staring at him with an expression of cool superiority on his long, sly face. Or more cool superiority even than usual, Mitch corrected himself.

'Lot of excitement in here,' Cucarachi remarked in a voice as smooth as his black hair. He was wearing well-cut, obviously expensive grey trousers. His pink checked shirt and pink silk tie looked, Mitch thought, not without a hint of jealousy, like a doll's picnic party. He envied his colleague his trim frame, although not the work he did to maintain it. Cucarachi honed his body hard. He jogged at lunchtimes, he worked out, he did marathons. While, Mitch knew, the only part of him that raced was his heart.

He folded his plump arms and fixed Cucarachi's eye with his own. 'Yeah. It's kind of an exciting morning. My client Darcy Prince has just landed the female lead in *Galaxia*.'

Take that, asshole, he wanted to add, but didn't. There was no need. It was a body blow.

Relishing the moment, Mitch happily anticipated Cucarachi's response, confidently expecting that thin, handsome-if-that-was-your-idea-of-it face to spasm and contort with jealousy.

But instead Mitch's most loathed co-worker simply smiled. His hand, with its gold-signet-ringed little finger – a European affectation that Mitch especially despised – stroked his smoothly shaved chin in a relaxed fashion. 'Hey, I'm glad for you, buddy,' Cucarachi said.

Mitch wobbled on his chair. *Glad?* What was the guy talking about? No agent was ever pleased about another. Unless they were failing.

'Because, let's face it,' Cucarachi added lightly, 'you've hardly been doing well lately. You've been doing pretty bad, actually.'

Mitch's folded arms folded tighter. He resisted the urge to throw his telephone at his colleague. Thrown telephones were never a good idea in Hollywood. Look what had happened to Russell Crowe. He would not be provoked. This was his finest hour. No one was going to spoil it.

He maintained a fixed beam at Cucarachi. *Say what you like,* this beam invited. *My client's got a big part in the film of the year. You can't take that away from me.*

Cucarachi lounged elegantly against the door frame. 'Yeah, the CEO was thinking of firing you. Did you know that? Thought not.' He smiled as Mitch visibly lurched at this. 'You needed something pretty big to keep you in the job. So, hey, congratulations.'

'Thank you,' Mitch said through gritted teeth. His arms were now folded so tightly they threatened to cut off his circulation altogether. His heart was thundering. *The CEO was thinking of firing him?*

'You look flabbergasted,' Cucarachi said. His eyes, amused, sardonic, rolled over Mitch. 'But then, I guess there's a lot of flab to gast.'

The memory of Saint's phone call, glorious though it was, was fast retreating in the face of this determined battery. Mitch tried at once to call it back and to hang on to what composure he had left. He was aware that his face was radiant with indignation. Aware, too, that two great patches of sweat had crept from beneath his armpits and were spreading across his shirt at such a rate that they threatened to meet both before and behind. He watched Greg's merciless eyes notice the sweat patches.

'Yeah, congratulations,' Greg repeated. 'I'm so happy for you and Darcy. And I know you're going to be just as happy for me when I tell you that I had a conversation with Jack Saint this morning as well. That I, too, have a client with a starring role in *Galaxia.*'

'You do?' Mitch gasped, now giving up all semblance of self-control. His finest hour, and he had to share it with the person he hated most in the office. In the entire world, at this moment, at least.

'My client Christian Harlow has been contracted to play the Duke of Lilo.' The words exploded like bombs in Mitch's disbelieving, red-hot ears.

'Christian . . . *Harlow*?' The world's number-one actress-disaster zone? The Bermuda Triangle for female film stars – they went into him – or rather he went into them – and they were never heard of again? Tell me it's not true, Mitch silently begged a higher power. The higher power failed to respond.

'That's right,' Greg beamed, showing his strong, square white teeth. 'The Duke of Lilo. The Grand Duchess of the Galaxy's number-one enemy. At first, that is. They're lovers by the end.' He winked at Mitch, smirked and withdrew.

Mitch, filled with a sudden rage, screwed up the paper bag that had held his last jelly doughnut and hurled it furiously at the open doorway. But, as usual with his poor aim, it missed.

Chapter 26

Sloane Mews had gateposts with balls on either end, after which, Emma thought, the actual houses were rather a disappointment. It was a small, quiet, cobbled road with a row of low, white-painted buildings on either side. The cobbles struck Emma as rather picturesque, but the houses were tiny and rather plain-looking, with big wooden doors across their fronts into which smaller doors had been inserted. They reminded her of garages, albeit very old-fashioned ones. Number 24, where Domestic Bliss was, looked just like all the others. Emma rang the bell.

The white-painted door opened to reveal a middle-aged, careworn Filipina wearing a white cap and apron over a black dress.

'Is this Domestic Bliss?' Emma asked with a friendly smile.

The woman raised miserable eyes to Emma and gave a brief, unhappy nod.

'I've got an interview with Mrs Connelly-Carew.'

The maid nodded again and made a gesture inviting Emma to come in. Emma followed her over the threshold and into a large garage-like area that seemed full of odds and ends. The door to the actual house was at the far end of this. Emma followed the maid into a tiny kitchen, which she was surprised to find already inhabited. A polished brunette with long brown legs, which began in a denim miniskirt and ended in a pair of black ballerina flats, was propping up the sink and talking into a mobile. Emma was reminded, immediately and irresistibly, of Totty Ponsonby-Pratt.

The maid gestured at Emma to wait, and disappeared through a door. Emma arranged herself carefully against the cooker, which did not look entirely clean. The brunette, whose only acknowledgement of her presence was to roll uninterested brown eyes over her, continued with her conversation amid much flicking of hair and inspection of perfect nails with the mobile-free hand.

'New job going well is it, Totty? Must be if you've got all this time to talk on the mobile . . .'

Emma, staring at the kitchen's rather grubby floor tiles, blinked. Totty? *That* Totty? She had a new job? Emma felt relieved for poor Hengist Westonbirt, who had obviously not liked her; the antipathy, in fact, had seemed mutual. But she pitied from the bottom of her heart whatever children Totty was now looking after – in the loosest sense of the word.

'The kids are a nightmare? Poor you, Totty. God, you always get the difficult ones, don't you? The mother's mad? The house is horrible? Oh, Totster. But they're taking you to Italy? Well, that's good, isn't it? Pantelleria? Costa Smeralda? Oh . . . *Tuscany.*' This in a tone of the utmost disgust. '*Yawnorama.* God, how *boring*. Poor you, Totty.'

Emma felt awash with contempt. These spoilt, ridiculous people. Personally, she'd be happy to go anywhere in Italy. Then a thought struck her. If Hengist Westonbirt was no longer enduring Totty, might he not need someone else? Her, for example? It was a thought. Definitely a thought.

'Where am I?' the brunette barked in a gravelly, well-bred voice. She looked scornfully around the kitchen. 'Waiting to be interviewed. Daddy's threatened to cut me off if— yeah. I know. You've had that too. Where am I? Theodora's, of course. She sorts us all out, doesn't she? Didn't you get a job here once? What did you say?' The brunette screwed up her face. 'Signal's a bit weak . . . you didn't realise I had childcare training?' She let out a goose-like honk of laughter, so loud it made Emma jump. 'Course I don't. Did you? Thought not. Oh, you gotta go? Yeah. OK. Bye, Totty.'

The maid appeared. 'Isabella Gough-Chumley-Fylingdales?' she asked, with obvious and understandable difficulty.

The brunette gave a curt nod.

'This way,' said the maid.

Emma watched them leave. Her mind was churning with what she had just heard. Isabella Gough-Chumley-Fylingdales had not only seemed to be saying that she had no childcare training herself, but Totty hadn't either. Not that that was hard to believe, but what was was the additional inference that Totty had been given a job by Mrs Connelly-Carew. Surely that couldn't be true.

By the time the brunette reappeared, shuffled past with a smirk and was shown out by the maid, Emma had convinced herself she had somehow misheard.

Now it was Emma's turn. She straightened her spine, cleared her throat, pulled down her jacket and followed the maid through the kitchen door into Mrs Connelly-Carew's inner sanctum.

This was a small dining room whose walls were crowded with paintings that seemed rather too big for them, and the furniture, while grand, seemed oversized as well. Emma edged past an oval dining-room table that almost pressed against the walls.

And yet this room was evidently Mrs Connelly-Carew's office; the headquarters of the Domestic Bliss empire. The table was piled with papers from whose midst a pair of silver candelabra rose incongruously. The tops of a silver salt and pepper pot could be seen elsewhere among the mass of letters, files and office stationery. Emma recognised the cream corporate paper of Domestic Bliss piled haphazardly on top of a typewriter.

A thin woman of about fifty-five was sitting at one end of the desk, looking keenly at Emma over a pair of gold-rimmed half-moon glasses on chains. Emma's main impression of Mrs Theodora Connelly-Carew was that she was very brown and she wore layers of expensive-looking beige knits. Her hands were thin and brown and her hair was brown too, rising in a perfectly styled wave from her uncreased forehead. It was obviously heavily hairsprayed and looked neat, if iron hard.

There was also something hard about Mrs Connelly-Carew's caramel-frosted lips as she looked Emma critically up and down.

'Come in,' she commanded, as Emma edged past the table, trying not to get tangled in the furniture legs. Mrs Connelly-Carew was rather more duchess-like than Emma had anticipated. She had expected a more comfortable, altogether less imperious sort of person to be running a nanny agency.

'Sit down,' Mrs Connelly-Carew ordered, pointing to an elegant dining chair. With difficulty, Emma pulled it out as far as it could go and inserted herself as best she could between the wall and the edge of the table. Wedged thus, she felt at a disadvantage. The expression in Mrs Connelly-Carew's eyes, staring at her keenly from the glasses with chains on them, did nothing to raise her spirits.

'I'm Theodora Connelly-Carew,' said Mrs Connelly-Carew in distant patrician tones. 'And you must be Emma.'

Emma forced herself to rally. What was she worried about? Unlike the last person, her experience and qualifications were excellent.

Theodora Connelly-Carew was rummaging in a plastic file. Emma watched as she drew from it her own letter. Theodora Connelly-Carew glanced down at it and cleared her throat. 'Emma, er . . .'

'Sidebottom,' supplied Emma, wondering why Mrs Connelly-Carew was asking when the name was printed there on the paper right in front of her.

'Sidebottom, yes. Mmm.' The frosted lips pursed. She raised her head and looked at Emma piercingly with grey and glittering eyes. She was, Emma thought, a good-looking woman; thin, with classic bone-structure. But, with her sharp nose and thin fingers, not to mention those eyes, there was something of the bird of prey about her.

'Your qualifications are impeccable,' said Mrs Connelly-Carew, her fingernails sweeping Emma's letter.

Emma nodded. A surge of confidence swirled through her.

'However, that is not the issue.'

Emma frowned. 'It's not?'

'Not entirely.' Mrs Connelly-Crew took off her glasses, stood up and strode the five paces or so to the small window where she stood with her hand in the small of her back looking thoughtful. Emma took in the elegant brown suede trousers and brown leather ankle boots, and Mrs Connelly-Carew's sharp profile against her busily patterned pink and white curtains.

She jumped as Mrs Connelly-Carew turned round suddenly, her beige layers whirling. 'What would you say,' Mrs Connelly-Carew asked, 'if I told you most of the nannies we employ are Hons?'

'Ons?' echoed Emma, completely at a loss. On what?

Mrs Connelly-Carew sighed. 'Hons. *Honourables*. Daughters of the gentry. For example, I've just placed the girl before you, whose father is a marquis, with Lord and Lady Westonbirt.'

Emma felt her heart sink. Bang went the job with Hengist then. But hadn't she heard Isabella say with her own ears that she had no qualifications?

'Well-connected girls are our speciality,' Mrs Connelly-Carew trilled on in her imperious voice. 'It's what people come to us for. Our USP, if you like. If you know what that means.'

'I know what a USP is,' Emma said levelly. She would never have imagined she could have borne being extensively insulted by a snob of the proportions Mrs Connelly-Carew evidently was. She was like Vanessa all over again, only older and in different clothes.

Of course, it would be nice to stand up and stalk out of the room. But that would mean going back home and admitting she had failed. Which, frankly, was a much bigger humiliation than staying in this room and fighting her corner, with whatever tools came to hand. 'My USP is that I'm a good nanny,' she said determinedly, wanting to get down to business, or the only business that mattered.

Still standing, and looming very tall above Emma, Theodora drummed her café-au-lait-tipped fingers on what could be seen, beneath the papers, of the polished surface of her dining table. 'Mmm,' she said. She inhaled. And exhaled again testily. The action made her nostrils flare so wide that Emma, watching them, expected them to turn inside out. Then Mrs Connelly-Carew passed a hand across her tanned brow as if all this was the most fearful bother. 'OK,' she said eventually, with the air of one conferring a great favour. 'Let's get on with it. I need to ask you some questions.'

'Of course.'

'About how you would deal with, um, certain situations,' Mrs Connelly-Carew was looking at her almost slyly.

Emma waited. She could ask what she liked. There could be no situations in the nought-to-five category that, over the years, she had not either learnt about or personally dealt with. The discovery of cocaine wraps in her handbag, not least. She swallowed and pushed the thought away. She could not afford to be distracted just now.

'Imagine the scenario,' Mrs Connelly-Carew said, fixing Emma with an intense stare, 'if, at a children's birthday party, the son of an earl went to the food table before the son of a duke. What would you do?'

Emma considered. It was not a situation that had ever arisen at Wee Cuties. Not even at Vanessa's.

'Well?' demanded the head of the nanny agency. 'What would you do?'

'Make sure they'd both washed their hands,' Emma said triumphantly as inspiration struck.

Mrs Connelly-Carew stared back crossly at Emma. 'It's a question of precedence,' she said haughtily. 'Dukes come before earls in the social order. So the earl's son should go in after the duke's.' She leant forward. 'Have you never read *Debrett's*?'

Emma paused before answering. She had a feeling that the work alluded to was not in the category of *The Gruffalo, Goodnight Moon* or *The Duck in the Truck*.

'Well?' Mrs Connelly-Carew snapped.

'Not recently,' Emma admitted.

'Not at all?' enquired the other, smiling tersely, her aquiline head on one side. Mrs Connelly-Carew took off her glasses and stood up again. 'Thank you so much for coming,' she said in syrupy tones as she wafted to the entrance door in a caramel flow of woollens. 'We'll be in touch.'

Seconds later, Emma found herself outside in the cobbled mews, Mrs Connelly-Carew's dry scent in her nostrils and a feeling of ashes in her mouth.

Chapter 27

Picking her way carefully across the cobbles of Sloane Mews in her heels, Emma passed the stone balls at the entrance. She briefly imagined wrenching one from its position and hurling it through Theodora Connelly-Carew's window.

The sun was now high and hot but the sky's dazzling blue seemed a mockery. It would have suited her mood better if a gale had been howling and cold fingers of rain were feeling her collar.

She suddenly realised how hungry she was. And thirsty. For all her emphasis on class, Theodora Connelly-Carew hadn't had the manners to offer so much as a glass of water.

What now? The obvious thing was to return to the bed and breakfast and the library and apply for more posts. But would she meet with the same fate at every one? Just for once, Emma allowed herself to entertain the prospect of returning home. She pulled into her lungs the city air, in which, even now, possibility seemed to teem as much as pollution. She thought about changing it for the air at home which, though fresher, had no possibilities at all; at least, not any she was interested in.

As she turned from the mews into the street, something shot between her legs. Emma swayed and clutched at a stretch of stuccoed wall. She looked around for what had tripped her up. A small animal of some sort. Yes, there it was. A brown dog, the smallest she had ever seen, was cringing against the front of one of the mews houses on the other side of the road. It was staring at her with enormous black eyes and making whimpering noises.

Something about its evidently wretched condition tugged at Emma's heart. Her love of small things in general had found its main outlet in children, but there was plenty left over to be kind to little animals like this one.

'Come here, boy,' she cooed, clacking gingerly across the cobbles towards it.

The dog let her come close. It was trembling, and the expression in its huge black eyes was one of petrified fear.

'Hey, I won't hurt you,' Emma crooned.

But something else might, she now realised. There was a bloodcurdling snarl, a deep bark, a slide of claws and suddenly, round the corner, skidded an enormous Alsatian. It was evidently in pursuit, ears erect and eyes blazing with the obvious intent to murder the creature Emma intended to help. Without stopping to think about what she was doing, she snatched up the small dog, kicked out at the Alsatian, which stopped in surprise, and staggered away as quickly as her heels would permit her.

She looked back to see the Alsatian standing at the entrance to the mews, its brown eyes full of apology, its tail wagging amiably.

Emma put the dog she had rescued down to examine its collar. The collar was, she noticed, very ornate – covered in diamonds, which had to be fake. But there was no address on it, as she had hoped, merely the word 'Sugar', which was presumably the dog's name, and a small silver disc with what looked like a mobile phone number engraved on it.

Emma, of course, no longer had her own mobile. She looked about her in vain for somewhere to ring from.

In her arms, the dog wriggled and whimpered.

Emma comforted it. 'Shh, Sugar. I'll get you home as soon as I can . . . boy,' she added, after a confirming glance at its rear end.

'*Oi! You!*' An almighty bellow now filled the quiet road.

At first Emma could not make out where the voice was coming from. Or whom it was addressing. Then, turning, she saw a ginger-haired man in jeans making his unsteady way towards her down the mews.

'Hey! You!' the man repeated.

'Me?' gasped Emma, still clutching the dog.

'Yeah. You. What the fuck do you think you're doing with that dog?' His accent was Scottish and aggressive. He was quite big, Emma saw too. Broad and powerful; strong arms, big chest.

In her arms she felt the dog growling; a low-level rumble that resounded menacingly through her body. She sympathised; she felt like growling herself. Or else running away.

He really was in a very bad mood, she thought as the man came closer. He was handsome, with sensuous lips and brooding brows, but apparently far from well. His face was grey and his eyes, which were screwed up, looked almost as red as his hair. He was also unshaven; a haze of red fuzz haloed his determinedly square chin, and he looked as if he had thrown on his clothes in two minutes flat. The laces on his trainers flapped in his wake, his grey pullover had been pulled over back to front and the fly zip was down on the baggy, apparently beltless jeans, which he held up with one hand as he approached.

'You stealing that dog or something?' He was squinting at her; the bright light seemed to be causing him some discomfort.

'Actually, I rescued him,' Emma said haughtily. 'He was

about to be murdered by an Alsatian. I was just looking for somewhere to phone his owner from.'

'Dinnae bother,' the man snapped, hoisting his jeans up. 'I'm his owner. Well, my girlfriend is. He's lost. I've been looking for him for the last hour.' He looked at the dog with dislike. Emma sensed there was little love lost between man and beast. But that was not the only matter to claim her attention.

The newcomer looked, she thought, vaguely familiar. She was sure she had seen him recently, as recently as the last couple of days. But surely that was impossible. Unless he was staying at the bed and breakfast or was a regular user of Camden Library.

'Let me put him down,' she suggested, lowering Sugar gently to the ground.

'Be my guest,' growled the other. 'I'd like to put him down permanently,' he added grimly.

This observation did not help his case. As his claimant approached, Sugar immediately let out a terrified yelp and leapt back up into Emma's arms again, digging his claws into her skin.

Wincing, she stepped forward, holding the dog out. 'Here you are.' Immediately Sugar let out a bloodcurdling growl, accompanied by the no-less-bloodcurdling flash of a line of razor-sharp fangs.

Emma looked down at the dog crossly. Why had it taken such a shine to her? 'Go on, boy,' she urged through gritted teeth, placing Sugar down again. He howled and ground his bottom against her legs. It was not a pleasant feeling.

'He won't go with you,' she concluded flatly.

From his sanctuary against Emma's legs, Sugar sat and licked his nether regions complacently.

The red-haired man, one hand on his descending trousers, came forward again and held out his other hand gingerly. The dog thrust forward its pointed nose and snapped viciously at his fingers.

'Ow!' He leapt backwards, wagging an injured digit.

'I thought you said you knew him,' Emma said suspiciously. 'You said he was your girlfriend's dog.'

She wondered now if she believed in the girlfriend story. She glanced again at the dog's diamond collar. It was almost painfully dazzling to look at in the sunshine. Perhaps, incredible though it seemed, it was real, after all, and this man was trying to steal it.

'I do,' grumbled the other. 'But I guess we haven't been together that long. Sugar man! Sugar baby!' He thrust his other hand in the dog's direction, unwisely in Emma's view, and with predictable results.

Her suspicions grew. Did she really recognise him? Or did she just recognise the type? Perhaps he just reminded her of someone in the bed and breakfast. Like the young men there, he looked a bit down on his luck – his clothes were creased and his overall air, not to mention hair, was of one who had just got out of bed.

Emma suddenly resolved not to part with Sugar until she had returned him to his rightful owner. It was not an especially convenient decision for her; it could lead to any number of difficulties, not least persuading Mrs Cupper, who had a No Dogs rule, to let it into the bed and breakfast. Nor was Emma herself particularly fond of the animal. She disliked his bony brown head, which felt horribly fragile, and found his big, round, prominent eyes very strange; entirely black and apparently consisting entirely of pupil.

Any other charm Sugar may have possessed, meanwhile, had decreased steeply in proportion to the number of times he ground his bottom into her legs. And he quivered in her arms in a manner she found most unpleasant. She had realised by now that he did not do this out of fear, but because he was the sort of dog who quivered. It did not add to her regard for him. Nevertheless, she felt that to surrender a small dog to someone whose designs on it might be nefarious was irresponsible at the least, and might even be cruel. She held Sugar and looked challengingly at his claimant.

The red-headed man seemed to read the message in her eyes. He shrugged his shoulders theatrically. 'Fucking nightmare this is,' he complained in his thick Scottish accent. 'I just don't need this. I really, really don't. I've got the mother of all hangovers.' He clutched his head.

And whose fault is that? Emma felt like pointing out. 'Well, it's not exactly convenient for me either,' she settled for saying.

As an apparently final effort, the man made another lunge at the animal. 'Sugar! Come on, Shug, baby,' he wheedled. Endearments which, Emma thought, sounded especially peculiar in a Scottish accent.

Scottish accent or not, the endearments had no effect. Sugar tensed to an iron hardness and growled so terrifyingly that Emma wondered why he had not tried this approach on the Alsatian. It had obviously been a good-natured coward at heart and would have fled without a second thought.

His would-be captor now abandoned all attempts at charm. 'You . . . you . . . *arsehole!*' he hurled at Sugar in frustration.

While feeling it was wrong to shout at an animal, Emma could see the claim was not inaccurate. The specified part of Sugar's anatomy, quivering upwards towards her beneath its tail, was indeed very prominent. She could also see the situation had reached stalemate. And that, while she had not created the difficulty, it was up to her to provide the solution. No one else was going to.

'Look,' Emma offered, all other options now appearing to her exhausted, 'what if I come with you and bring Sugar back?'

The man shrugged his shoulders. 'OK then,' he said grudgingly.

'Ever heard of please and thank you?' Emma asked sternly, as if addressing one of her nursery charges.

The man's red eyes flashed open with surprise. In the split second before they screwed up again Emma could see they were an amazingly pale blue.

'You sound like a nanny,' he grumbled, scratching his red hair.

Emma drew herself up. 'Actually, I *am* a nanny.'

She had not expected the admission to have any particular effect, and certainly not the one it had now. The red-headed man's face changed completely. All trace of greyness and resentment were washed away in what looked like a wave of the profoundest imaginable relief. His eyes burned blue with excitement and he beamed. Suddenly he looked both healthy and handsome.

'Excuse me,' he said, his Scottish voice losing its roar and graveliness and sounding both polite and charming. 'I've been very rude. I haven't introduced myself. I'm Niall.'

'I'm Emma.' Her mind chugged. *Niall . . . Niall . . .* Yes, it was coming back to her. *Something* was coming back to her. But not enough of it, sadly, to work out exactly what. Her suspicion that Niall wanted to steal the diamond collar – which Emma, despite her complete lack of familiarity with precious stones, grew more certain with every passing minute was real – dwindled from this point, however. Something was telling her that he was somehow connected with wealth and fame, although exactly how remained unclear.

'So you're a nanny, Emma?' His tone was conversational now. He was rolling gently from foot to foot and grimacing at her horribly. She realised this was meant to be a smile, but the sunshine was making it difficult.

'Yes. I'm a nanny.' She waited to see what this had to do with anything.

'Working round here, are you?'

Emma shrugged. 'Actually, I'm, um, between jobs at the moment.' She regretted the confession immediately. What business was it of his?

He looked, if anything, even more enraptured by the revelation, however. '*What?* Oh, wow, I mean, that's *fantastic. Incredible.* God, I mean . . .' He pushed the hand not holding his jeans up through his hair again, rubbed his eyes and stared at her as if she were a miracle.

'Why's it so fantastic?' Emma asked stiffly.

'I mean, it's unbelievable,' he gushed on. 'Like, *we* need a nanny. Me and the girlfriend. Like, *now*. This minute.' He shrugged and grimaced at her again. His blue eyes seemed a mixture of pleading and desperation. 'Please, Emma. You come along with me, Emma. Meet my girlfriend and the baby.'

He took her arm and ushered her down the mews to where, at the bottom, a big silver car was slowly drawing up.

'Er . . .' Emma's eyes darted wildly between the car and Niall. Was this all some sort of a trick?

'Look, *please*. You said you'd bring the dog back with me, yeah?' Niall wheedled.

'Well, yes, but . . .' She looked at the car. It was smart and new and a Mercedes. It shone in the sun almost as brilliantly as Sugar's collar.

'Well, get in then,' urged Niall. His hand was firm on her arm.

'Where are we going?' Emma bleated as she found herself propelled inside the pale leather interior.

'The Portchester Hotel.'

Emma frowned. Even she had heard of the Portchester. One of London's grandest. The one all the celebrities stayed at. The something she was trying to remember revealed itself a bit more. Not enough to know what exactly it was, but to sense that he spoke the truth and that she wasn't in danger. She got in the car, which shot away with a screech of tyres. Emma gasped, panic at once shooting up her throat. She looked apprehensively at Niall, watching his hands, especially for any twitch that might precede the pulling of a knife or gun.

His hands, big, white and with red hairs on the back, stayed folded composedly in his lap, however. She noticed he wore a row of rings of complex Celtic design on one of them, which looked rather like a knuckleduster. Far from threatening, however, Niall seemed both relaxed and relieved, a long way from the gruff and threatening figure he had been at first.

'Incredible bit of luck, you being a nanny,' he nodded at her, beaming. He seemed to have recovered entirely from his hangover. The greyness in his face had gone and from beneath his heavy brows his pale blue eyes positively shone.

'Not to mention finding the dog,' Emma said, wincing. Sugar, sitting on her knee, was digging his sharp claws hard through the thin suit into her flesh.

Niall's beam wavered. 'That's not such great luck, actually,' he said rather bitterly. 'I was rather hoping I'd never see the horrible animal again, to be honest with you. I hate him, but my girlfriend worships him. God knows why.' He directed a contemptuous, pale blue glare at Sugar, who growled and dug his claws even deeper into Emma.

'What happened to your last nanny?' Emma asked, when she had forcibly moved the dog to a more comfortable position. She eyed Niall narrowly as she waited for an answer.

He looked shifty for a minute. 'Jackie?' he said, rather too brightly, Emma felt. 'Not sure, to be honest with you,' he hedged. 'I think she and Belle – that's my girlfriend – had kinda different ideas about things.'

Belle. *Belle*, thought Emma. That name rang a . . . Belle.

She tried to remember what, and get a general grasp on things. But the only one with a firm grasp on anything seemed to be Sugar, who had now shifted position again and was sticking his needle-like claws in yet another part of her thigh. It was difficult, distracted as she was by pain and uncertainty, to think straight.

She stared out of the window. Streets of white-painted, porticoed houses framing bushy green gardens streamed past outside. The heavy tinting of the vehicle's windows made the blue sky appear pink.

'We're here,' said Niall.

The car had drawn up in front of an imposing hotel, an enormous building of golden stone with striped awnings and trees in pots. Two white-gloved doormen in green tailcoats with red facings and top hats scurried towards them. 'The Portchester', read Emma above a glass revolving door behind which golden lights glittered.

The Mercedes' doors opened with perfect sychronicity. A white-gloved hand appeared and Emma found herself assisted out with the type of deference she imagined more usually accorded to royals.

The doorman smiled at Sugar and held out a white-gloved hand to pat his head. He withdrew it hurriedly as the dog gave a vicious growl. 'Nice doggy,' he said, in an Italian accent. Sugar gave an earsplitting bark.

'Actually, he's not a nice doggy,' Emma confided in an undertone. 'He's horrible. But he's not mine so it doesn't matter.'

The doorman grinned and ushered her through the shiny brass-and-polished-wood revolving doors after Niall. She emerged into a high lobby, gilded and glittering, and hung with chandeliers so huge and heavy it seemed extraordinary they could stay up there. And how did they clean them, the practical Emma found herself wondering.

Beyond the marble-floored entrance stretched an area the size of a football field; plushly carpeted, softly lit and scattered with gilded chairs and tables. Each held its own group of smiling, smartly dressed people with piles of shining carrier bags heaped beside them. Emma glimpsed champagne glasses, heard the sound of a piano, caught an atmosphere that was hard to define, slightly elegant, slightly bored, slightly seedy, entirely expensive. She had heard about hotels like this but had never yet been in one.

Niall, still holding up his jeans, his laces still trailing, walked jauntily across the marble floor as if he owned the place. Unsure of her high heels on the marble's polished surface, Emma stumbled after as best she could. She fared worse still on the thick-piled oyster carpet in the corridor he now turned into. Struggling for balance, still holding the dog, she glimpsed carved and gilded showcases full of enormous diamond necklaces before almost falling into an ornate lift.

The gold doors slid together. 'Here we go!' Niall grinned. There was a brief whooshing sensation and within seconds the doors opened again into another marbled lobby, smaller than the one downstairs but no less grand. The walls were painted cream, picked out with gold and had small scenes and figures painted on them. It reminded Emma of the backdrop of a theatre. The two vast beige urns mounted on pedestals either side of the lift door were filled with lilies, from which a wonderful smell wafted. The place seemed to breathe luxury and decadence.

'Belle!' shouted Niall. 'Hey, Belle. Come here. I've got a surprise for you. Two surprises.'

Belle. The hotel. The red-headed man. It was all coming together, but before Emma could put the final piece of the jigsaw into place, it arrived in person.

She heard the approaching cry of an infant. A woman holding a baby wrapped in white entered the lobby. Sugar immediately erupted into crazed barking. Not to be outdone, the baby doubled its yells.

Emma gasped, partly from the shattering noise and because the woman before her was so radiantly beautiful. She was tiny, seemed about twenty-five and thin to the point of emaciation. Her face, which seemed heavily made-up, was almost completely hidden behind enormous sunglasses. This of course was odd, as they were indoors, but Emma reminded herself that new mothers frequently went without sleep and that light intolerance was possibly an issue.

There were, Emma thought, few other signs of new motherhood. This woman's hair was white-blond, long and glossy and tumbled over her slender shoulders as far as her elbows. On her thin brown arms she wore a great many large and ornate bracelets, which seemed impractical for one nursing a small baby, and dark denim jeans of a tightness beyond what Emma had imagined bearable, especially if one was bending to pick up a child. Her look was finished with a flimsy leopardskin short-sleeved blouse and high-heeled red sandals.

'Sugar!' the blonde gasped. 'My little baby-waby,' she crooned into the dog's bony head with its bulging black eyes and disproportionately huge black-tipped ears. Emma's heart contracted in concern as these actions thrust the head of the yelling baby, dangling loosely in the woman's arms, close to the dog's dangerous and malevolent jaws. 'Where have you been, my naughty waughty little doggy-woggy?' the blonde cooed.

She spoke in a breathy, girlish American accent that Emma felt she recognised.

The baby, in her arms, roared on. The blonde looked at it impatiently. 'I just can't shut him up,' she complained. 'He's been going crazy for hours.'

Hunger, Emma knew. Those sharp, pulsing yells were unmistakable. She was surprised that the mother did not know this herself.

'Well, our problems are over!' Niall announced. 'As well as rescuing Sugar, I've found Emma. She's a nanny.' He threw out a hand towards Emma in a *ta-da* fashion. 'To replace Jackie.'

'Hey, great!' grinned the blonde, with a huge flash of sunglasses, as well as white teeth and red lips. Immediately, she thrust the baby into Emma's arms. 'You know what to do with it. You're a nanny. So go on. Nanny.'

Emma felt a mixture of indignation and uncertainty. *Niall* had rescued Sugar? *He'd* found her, a new nanny, as well? And on top of that, what made these people so sure she wanted to work for them? But no. All this could wait.

In her arms, the baby, which felt incredibly light and frail, bawled its pulsing, relentless, desperate bawl. It was clearly starving. Meanwhile, at the level of the parquet floor, the dog barked on. The din was so deafening that Emma felt she might scream too. Or else bark.

'Look,' she said in concern. 'He really needs food.'

'Sugar gets fed later,' the blonde declared breathily. 'Room service bring up his fillet steak at six on the dot.'

Emma hoisted her dropping jaw determinedly back up. 'I didn't mean the dog,' she said curtly. 'I meant the baby.'

She noticed that the blonde's tight leopardskin top revealed disproportionately big breasts for one of her small frame. And the baby, whose face remained obscured by its blanket, was very small and light, obviously a mere few weeks old.

'Are you breast-feeding?' Emma demanded over the noise.

Unexpectedly, the woman burst out laughing. 'With these?' She gestured at her bosoms. 'They're one hundred per cent silicon, sweetie.'

Emma swallowed. But there was no time to absorb this. 'Got any formula?' she shouted above the din.

The woman shook her blond hair. 'Hey, whaddya think I am? Einstein?'

Emma narrowed her eyes. Was this woman joking? It was unbelievable.

'*Milk* formula.'

'Oh. Right. There's some, like, powdery stuff in the kitchen, if that's what you mean.' The blonde wafted her hand vaguely behind in what Emma assumed was the direction of the kitchen.

It was. The suite kitchen was small, white, functional and modern; decorated in a completely different style from the opulent gilded apartment, with its ornate mirrors, great glittering chandeliers and painted scenes on the walls. It contained a fridge, a cooker, several working surfaces and a number of cupboards.

Wrenching open cupboards and doors with one hand, Emma soon found powdered baby milk and a number of bottles and teats. To her great relief, the fridge was well stocked with still mineral water, as well as, she could not help noticing, a great many bottles of champagne. Hastily, Emma prepared the formula.

The bottle ready, she removed the material mostly draping the baby's face. She had not until now looked at it closely; the earsplitting sound it made had been the focus of her attention.

But now she noticed something so unexpected it made her almost drop the bottle with surprise.

The baby was black. *Very* black, with liquid Malteser eyes that looked desperately up into hers. While Niall and the woman – Belle, he had called her – were white.

It was the clue she needed. With a thrumming in her ears Emma finally remembered what she had been straining to recall. The reason she recognised the man was because only yesterday he had been on the front of every tabloid newspaper with Belle Murphy eating his face off. The article accompanying it had mentioned that Belle Murphy had recently adopted an African orphan.

Emma gazed down at the child now sucking happily away on the bottle with huge, strong draws on the teat. 'Compassionate' the article had called Belle. Emma frowned, trying to square this description with the woman she had met in the lobby, who had seemed more interested in her dog; who hadn't seemed to realise the baby was hungry.

Suddenly, Belle burst into the suite's kitchen, Sugar under one braceleted arm. Despite her doubts, Emma now experienced the piercing, pleasurable shock of having someone famous close by.

Belle headed for the fridge, her platinum hair swishing. She had now taken her sunglasses off, revealing intensely green eyes, which reminded Emma of the Go signal at traffic lights. She put Sugar on the floor, where his sharp claws skittered unpleasantly on the tiles, and got out one of the bottles of champagne. Emma watched Belle tear the foil off and start worrying at the cage covering the cork with clearly practised fingers.

The cork went with a violent explosion. Emma jerked in shock, as did the baby in her arms. Its tiny arms and legs flew out in the classic panic position, its eyes snapped open and it began to roar, its mouth a horror-struck pink hole in its black face. 'Oh, darling. Shush! Sh!' Emma clutched it to her, stroking it, murmuring comfort. Belle took no notice.

Sugar, also alarmed by the cork, was barking hysterically. Belle had dropped immediately to her knees and was comforting the dog. 'Sugar! Shug-shug-shug!' she crooned extravagantly. 'My baby! My precious pet. Mommy's so sorry her naughty wine made her baby jump. Let Mommy hug you, there you are . . .'

Emma, meanwhile, jiggled the baby. Restored to its teat, with a few comforting words whispered, it soon stopped crying.

Belle looked up from where she cradled the dog on the floor. 'Thank God he's shut up,' she remarked ruefully.

'He's a pretty noisy dog,' Emma remarked, looking down to where Sugar lay on his back, legs out wide, exposing himself in the crudest fashion to Belle's caresses.

Belle raised her lovely, if rather plastic face, regally tossed back her shimmering hair and regarded Emma with annoyed green eyes. 'Not Sugar. I mean thank God *Morning's* shut up.'

'Morning? That's his name? I was going to ask—'

'Morning, yeah,' Belle butted in as she took out two champagne flutes from a cupboard. 'He's actually called something unpronounceable and African, but I can't even say it, let alone spell it. So I thought Morning would be just fine. It's such a beautiful time of day – or so I'm told,' she tittered.

'He's an orphan, is that right?' Emma tried to remember what the paper had said.

'Sure as hell is,' Belle said matter-of-factly as she slopped the foaming wine into the two glasses. 'You should have seen the orphanage. Like, gross.'

'It must have been very difficult to go there,' Emma said carefully.

Belle put the bottle on the counter and tossed back her

shimmering mane of hair. 'Yeah, it was, so I didn't. I got the orphanage people to send my people some shots of the kids they had available on JPEGs and chose one that way.'

'You never went to Africa at all?' Emma exclaimed.

The strange green eyes pierced hers. It seemed to Emma they held a hint of warning. 'Hey. Don't get me wrong. I'm gonna go there. Some time. Keep him in touch with his heritage.'

Emma judged it expedient not to reply to this. She cradled the child, now finishing the bottle, infinitesimally tighter.

'Hey! Look at that! He's going to sleep,' Belle breezed, picking up the two brimful champagne glasses. 'You've obviously got a way with babies.'

Yes, I feed them, Emma thought. She studied the child's contented face, tiny and dark brown against the white cotton wrap. He was snuggled up so trustingly in her elbow. She felt a powerful surge of affection for him.

'We'll talk contracts in the morning,' Belle announced over her shoulder as she left the kitchen.

Emma stared after her. It was obviously taken for granted that she would be looking after the baby from now on. But did she want to? Neither Niall nor Belle seemed particularly . . . what was the word. Pleasant?

On the other hand, Vanessa had hardly been without her problems. With an effort Emma forced herself not to think about Hero and Cosmo, although the very act of not thinking about them brought the realisation that, throughout the whole day, subconsciously, she had done nothing else. How were they? Who were they with? Who was looking after them now?

And, of course, if she didn't work for Belle and Niall, back on the train home and obscurity was the alternative. Possibly to no job, either. Once she went back there, the gates of Life would clang shut behind her, never to reopen.

Working for Belle would certainly be an experience. She was a film star, a celebrity with a glamorous, exciting life. Emma reminded herself that the reason she had come to London was to gain experience, to learn things, to see another and more exciting side of life.

It might not always be pleasant, but did she really have a choice?

And then there was Morning. Emma looked down at him snuggling in her arms. He slept happily, drawing the air greedily, slurpily in through his nostrils, snoring vigorously. She smiled at the sound, reminiscent as it was of old men sixty or more times the age of this tiny creature.

She held the slumbering child close, as close as she dared, given his fragile-feeling bones, sensing him warm yet frail and vulnerable beneath the white towelling babysuit that was possibly not as clean as it could be. She sniffed. How long was it, she wondered, since he last had his nappy changed?

She would do the job. But really, it was nothing to do with fame and glamour, and everything to do with the fact that, during the few moments she had cared for him, the baby had won her heart.

Chapter 28

Sam Sherman, head of the Wild Modelling Agency, London, sat tapping her desk impatiently in her glass-walled office. Her round hazel eyes, ringed firmly with kohl as usual, blazed through her curtains of russet hair. She was giving an interview, which she never enjoyed. Especially since all the stupid fuss about size zero, journalists were apt to ask difficult questions.

But modelling was a competitive business. The Wild Agency might be one of London's most important – and important internationally – but it still needed good publicity. New agencies – not to mention established ones – were always snapping at Sam's heels, competing for the best girls and boys, and so Wild needed to be constantly in the public eye, to be able to remind everyone, especially anyone who might be about to be the face of the moment, that where Sam led, everyone else followed. That Wild was a big and enduring success, representing some of the most sought-after models on the planet.

It was for this reason that Sam assembled her own slightly heavy but still handsome features in as obliging an expression as she could manage and answered each query with smiling acquiescence and the phrases 'I'm glad you asked me that', and

'Good question!', in rotation. Flattering the journalist, Sam had learnt over the years, led to better copy. It also made it harder for writers to be nasty and ask difficult questions.

Eye contact was also important – it made you look sincere – though Sam could not help the occasional glance away from the beady scrutiny of the woman opposite and through the transparent walls of her goldfish-bowl office, where twenty-seven lissom twentysomethings, all dressed in skinny hipster jeans and clinging T-shirts in the agency's signature black, buzzed about the business of beauty. Something loud and fast boomed from the stereo as showcards were shoved in envelopes, tickets were booked, visas arranged and details finalised on any number of contracts. Some of her staff gazed at computer screens; others chatted into telephone headsets; still others yelled to each other across the big, black desks, or greeted the long-legged, long-necked, long-haired young women who glided in and out in a steady stream.

'Er . . . could you repeat that?' Sam smiled apologetically at the writer, having completely missed the last question.

The journalist – crop-haired, red-lipsticked and wearing a figure-hugging plum polo-neck, rearranged her long, bare legs beneath her grey pleated miniskirt. They were good legs, Sam had noted, smooth, lightly tanned and with no sign of thread veins or bruises. She guessed they were being displayed for her benefit.

Most young female journalists who came to see her were not, Sam knew, after a career-making scoop about the modelling industry at all. What they were longing to hear was something completely different: those six words that could tip them out from in front of a computer and into a glittering, perfumed world of heady fame and untold riches. 'Have you ever thought of modelling?'

The question she had missed, now repeated, confirmed Sam's hunch that this girl was as eager as the rest to make the jump from grind to glamour. 'What are you looking for when you spot a new model?' the journalist asked.

Sam had by now decided that the legs being displayed for her benefit had no commercial value. They were slightly too thick at the ankle. The girl was also too old. But frankly, anyone much over fourteen was old these days. Unless they were famous, of course.

'What makes the difference between a pretty girl and an exceptional model?' the journalist pressed, her large eyes wide with hope.

Sam played with her tanned fingers, her lips pursed as she pretended to be considering her answer deeply. 'That's a good question,' she remarked as she prepared to trot out her stock response. 'The difference is a lot of things. But mainly, it's what I like to call . . .' she took a deep breath and paused importantly.

The girl was rapt. Her eyes urged Sam on. 'Skinniness?' she suggested, with a provocative smile.

Sam disguised the fact she wanted to hit her by giving a deep stage laugh at this, as if nothing could be further from, rather than nearer, the truth. Although of course thinness wasn't the only issue. Girls were successful for other reasons too: a rock star father never hurt; a film star mother; any other kind of celebrity or billionaire, come to that, and of course aristocratic backgrounds in particular seemed to breed a certain sort of strangely elongated waif. But, of course, what they all had in common was thinness. Extreme thinness in many cases.

How did they achieve it? Officially, it was high metabolisms and genetics. Unofficially, of course, was a different and rather murky matter, and one Sam had no intention of discussing with this woman.

'The difference is what I like to call atmosphere,' finished the agency head.

'*Atmosphere?*' The journalist sounded puzzled, but fascinated.

Sam nodded, her hair swishing around her slightly leathery tanned face. Not for the first time she thanked the day she had come up with this one. The idea of atmosphere intrigued people, injected an air of mystery and individuality into a business that frequently lacked both. 'Yeah, atmosphere. The sort of feeling that surrounds a girl. All my most successful girls have had atmosphere. And boys.'

Across Sam's mind scampered, as it often did, the ever-irritating thought of the beautiful boy who had escaped her in Covent Garden. That had been weeks ago now. Boy, had *he* had atmosphere. Just for once, when she thought of him, Sam found herself believing her own line. That atmosphere really existed.

But she had never seen him again and, despite her urging them to keep their eyes extra peeled, none of her scouts had either. The only compensation was that, so far as she was aware, none of Sam's rival agencies had snapped him up either. But she was prepared any minute for some new campaign to be announced by Gucci, Armani or some such, featuring the Hunk Who Had Got Away.

The writer seemed to be making packing-up movements. Sam, wrenching her thoughts away from the long-lost god, cheered herself up by reflecting on the skill with which she had avoided the size zero quicksand.

Then the writer looked up. 'One more thing,' she smiled.

'Sure,' muttered Sam, glancing at the BlackBerry at her elbow on which was displayed her schedule, updated every morning by one of her two assistants. A meeting with a Spanish photographer was slated next. Carlos Cojones had a hook nose, wild curls and the usual bad-boy photographer reputation. As well as the usual hatred of waiting. He would, Sam knew, expect to sweep into her office the moment he arrived. Better get this wittering woman out as soon as possible.

But the writer remained. She changed the position of her legs and regarded Sam earnestly. 'I'd just like to ask you, by way of winding up the interview, what you think about the size zero debate.'

Sam, who had lifted a glass of water to her lips, stopped herself with difficulty from spluttering. She shook her hair over her face as she composed her features. 'Good question,' she muttered. 'I'm glad you asked me that.'

Sam parried the thrust with her usual dexterity – genetics, metabolism, acknowledging the pressure but emphasising Wild kept a strict eye on the dangers – and eventually saw the journalist off without having conceded ground. She felt exhausted, but relieved.

With a mixture of satisfaction and dismay she saw Carlos Cojones had arrived at reception. She couldn't possibly see him without a caffeine shot. Her hand hovered over the buzzer, to alert her new assistant, Xanthe, who had replaced the uppity Nia, to her urgent need for a fat-free cappuccino.

Xanthe, however, albeit in an entirely different way, was proving just as unsatisfactory as Nia. While Nia had been uppity and overconfident, Xanthe was timid to a degree amazing in one who had apparently lived in London for most of her life. As Sam's private telephone rang, she stretched a rigid, skeletal hand to answer it, her face a picture of fear. 'Call for you, Miss Sherman,' Xanthe's light whisper came through some seconds later.

'I can't take a call now,' Sam thunderered, her eyes rolling towards the photographer waiting in the foyer. Carlos Cojones had been here less than a minute and was already stamping from foot to foot like a flamenco dancer, his skin flushed dark with annoyance. 'Who is it?' Sam snarled, irritated and intimidated in equal measure.

'Someone called Brooke Reed. She says it's important, but I can tell her to go away,' Xanthe pleaded in her almost inaudible voice.

Sam snorted. Brooke Reed was the extremely forceful head of public relations for NBS Studios, Hollywood. The idea of Xanthe telling her anything other than what she wanted to hear would have been laughable had it not been so inconvenient. Sam herself was scared of very few people; Brooke Reed, however, was one of them.

Iron-haired, iron-willed, iron-clad, Brooke was the original – and, many maintained, the best – Hollywood PR. She knew everyone and everything. When she called, even Sam had to answer – or face the consequences.

Her fingers worrying at the turquoise beads around her throat, Sam looked nervously over at Cojones, who was now circling the reception desk like a matador coming in for the kill. From time to time, over his black, padded-leather shoulder, he threw in Sam's direction a glance as hot and black as burning tar. But even Cojones, Sam knew, would have to wait if Brooke Reed was calling.

'Shall I tell Mr Co-Jones to wait?' Xanthe fretted. She saw herself, Sam could tell, as being very much between a rock and a hard place. Nor was she wrong. Apart from the pronunciation of his name, that was.

'Brooke. So nice to hear—'

'I'll cut to the chase.' Brooke's rasping tones came over the line from California. 'I'm calling about *Galaxia*.'

'OK,' said Sam, expectant beneath her businesslike manner. She knew about the impending Saint film. Everyone in the

fashion and media industries did. *Galaxia* would be the
cinematic event of the year; the fashion, publishing and retail
event too, once all the clothes, toy and book spin-offs – everything from T-shirts to luggage tags – that generally accompanied
a Saint release got going.

'I want R and P on some talent,' Brooke informed her
shortly.

Sam's thick lips curved in a satisfied smile. She understood
this code. R and P stood, in Brookespeak, for Repackaging and
Polishing. Talent meant an actor; presumably the female star of
a new film. It was standard NBS procedure. Part of the studio's
preparations for any big movie would be Brooke contacting the
Wild Agency to help launch the female star by arranging high-
profile shoots with top photographers and leading glossy
magazines.

Brooke might be pushing sixty – although, with her skeletal
figure, iron hair, immobile face and Jackie O suits, she could
pass in a kind light for mid-forties – but she knew better than
anyone – it was her job, after all, to know these things – that the
line between being a model and being an actress was, these days,
so fine as to be non-existent. No young actress wanting to make
the big time had a hope unless she could pass as a model as well
– as thin, as perfect, as stylish.

Which was, of course, where Wild came in; in particular its
contacts with fashion editors, designers, make-up artists,
hairstylists; everyone who was anyone in fashion, in other words.
Everything one needed to repackage and polish the talent the
studio had invested in. Everything to make it appear as glossy
and glamorous as possible.

Sam watched Cojones still pacing the reception area.
Whereas before he had looked like the matador, now, with his
powerful leather-covered shoulders and the horn-like twists of

his unruly black hair, he resembled the bull; pawing the ground threateningly. She could almost see the steam coming out of his nostrils. But he could wait.

It was much more important that Brooke Reed contracted out to Wild the business of making this new, unknown girl as much of a fashion and style phenomenon as she would be an acting one. And it might just be, Sam mused, deftly diving her eyeball downwards as Cojones tried once more to catch it, that the Spanish photographer could play his part in this transformation.

'Who's the girl?' Sam asked.

'Completely unknown. British.'

'British?' Sam was surprised. It was rare a home-grown actress starred in a great American blockbuster such as *Galaxia* promised to be.

'You got it,' said Brooke in her throaty rasp. 'British. And with the usual British sense of fashion. Second-hand clothes, no idea about make-up, hair like a friggin' rat's nest . . .' Brooke, for all her elegant appearance, could be very earthy.

'You mean vintage and unstructured,' Sam corrected. She owned a model agency; she had to keep her end up. 'Very now.'

'I mean what I said,' snapped Brooke. 'She looks a friggin' mess.'

'Right,' said Sam hurriedly. There weren't many people who could talk to her like this, but Brooke was definitely one of them.

'Get Lagerfeld,' the studio PR instructed. 'That should do it.'

Sam's round eyes widened in surprise. *Karl* Lagerfeld? The all-powerful veteran German designer/photographer and head of the house of Dior who had been at the top of the fashion tree for three decades? Brooke, as usual, wasn't asking much.

'Er . . . I know Karl's pretty busy right now,' Sam hedged.

She knew this because four desperate glossy magazine editors in the last week alone had called and pleaded with her to use her influence with him on their behalf. Unfortunately her influence, while considerable, was not of the mountain-moving variety.

'What about Carlos Cojones?' Sam suggested, as inspiration struck. Talk about killing two birds with one stone. Cojones, certainly, looked about to kill something. Catching his dark, burning eye, Sam felt sufficiently heartened to flash him a grin.

'*Popinjay*,' snapped Brooke.

'He's very hot,' Sam defended.

'Hot *now*, sure. He'll have icicles dangling off his ass by tomorrow.'

Sam thought fast. 'I could try Rumtopf,' she said doubtfully.

There was a considering pause from the other end. 'Mmm,' said Brooke. 'Rumtopf's definitely a thought.'

'Yes.' Although also a legend, the Swiss designer/photographer wasn't, Sam knew, quite Lagerfeld, despite his pretensions in this direction. But Rumtopf was a definite name and – Brooke, as ever, was right about this – definitely better than Cojones.

'OK. I'll try Rumtopf,' Sam said.

Brooke inhaled sharply. 'Better do more than that, baby.'

'Sure. But I heard somewhere that he was booked up until 2020.'

'He'll be *dead* by 2020,' Brooke snapped. Then she cackled. 'But I guess you could call that the ultimate booking.'

Sam sighed. Brooke drove a hard bargain. 'OK. I'll *really* try. What's this girl's name by the way?'

She had to have heard of her. This actress couldn't be completely obscure. Surely she had been in *The Bill; Midsomer Murders*, even. Sam was a fan of both – indeed of anything involving homicide.

'Darcy Prince,' rasped Brooke. 'You heard it here first.'

Sam blinked. The name rang no bells whatsoever.

She put her phone down and it buzzed immediately. 'Mr Co-Jones has left the building,' Xanthe whispered dolefully.

Chapter 29

Emma put Morning in his cot. Happy after his evening bath, clean clothes and nappy and a rapturously received bottle, he snuggled into his mattress and dropped off instantly to sleep.

Emma studied him enviously. She was extremely tired, having spent a third restless night in one of the suite's many spare bedrooms, a box next to the kitchen which, being windowless, made her feel rather as if she were in a submarine. It was always a surprise to enter the enormous sitting room and see daylight through the French windows and, far below, the great green carpet of the park.

In striking contrast to her tiny quarters, Belle and Niall's room was enormous, occupying half the entire penthouse. You could tell, Emma thought, that it was supposed to be lovely; everything mint green, white pink or gold. There was a rose-patterned, silk-draped canopy over the vast, silk-draped bed, and a graceful suite of silk-upholstered furniture facing a carved marble fireplace. The effect was, however, routinely ruined by the piles of screwed-up sheets, untidy room-service trays, clothes all over the floor, food and champagne bottles in the bed and newspapers absolutely everywhere, which Belle and Niall left behind them whenever they went out.

Nor was Emma alone in her room. Morning's cot had been placed in there too. He required service several times in the night. Now he had found a reliable source of food and attention, Emma sensed, the baby needed to reassure himself she was still there, that he hadn't imagined it all. She didn't blame Morning for this in the least. Rather, each time she had soothed him, cuddled him, attended to his blankets, his nappy, his bottle or any of his other concerns, he had looked back at her with liquid brown eyes so full of delight that she felt a warm glow of affection for him. There was no doubt that he appreciated her. She was making someone happy, that was certain.

Personally, Emma was grimly aware, she had never been less so herself. Since the cocaine had been found in her handbag, her nerves had been on edge, especially at night, when she would revisit the scene of the apparent discovery. The same sequence, still hideously clear in every particular, would play in her head; the shout summoning her upstairs to find her small, cheap, utterly unremarkable brown bag turned upside down on the bedroom carpet and Vanessa there with the wrap in her hand, eyes burning. Then the accusations would start. Vanessa, shouting. James, shocked and puzzled. And when the sequence had played itself out, Emma would be left asking the same question. *Who* had done it? *Why?*

While this apparent unanswerable remained the same, a different aspect of the situation struck Emma during her nightly reconstructions. This time it was to wonder how Vanessa seriously thought that, given the wages she paid, her nanny could afford drugs at all. Emma's financial situation was such that she conducted a relative cost survey of all personal requisites and could barely afford Nurofen, let alone cocaine.

Nor, for all the obvious glamour and wealth of her new employer, did it show much hope of improving. Belle was utterly unpindownable about terms and conditions.

'Later!' the actress would snap whenever Emma attempted to present her case. 'I'm busy learning my lines, OK?'

'Learning my lines', Emma soon realised, was a euphemism for disappearing into the bedroom with Niall and having prolonged and very noisy sex, after which Belle in particular was given to parading about the penthouse naked.

While Emma never failed to look away quickly, it was always with shock at the sheer perfection of Belle's figure. For all her apparently unlovely soul, her body was that of a graceful statue: long legs, delicately moulded arms, narrow hips dipping in to a tiny waist. Even the thinness of her ribcage, which, from what could be glimpsed of it between the streaming, elbow-length platinum hair, looked breakably brittle and delicate, and contrasted strangely with the full, projecting breasts above it. Compared to her, Emma always felt big and awkward in her jeans and white polo shirt. She felt her unmade-up face fairly blazing its bareness, and her ponytailed hair's plainness and lack of highlights.

Of Niall's naked state, Emma was thankfully less certain. He at least had the restraint not to advertise it in her presence. For this, at least, she was grateful.

A buzz at the door interrupted her cogitations. Emma went to open it to find a dark-haired waiter in a buttermilk jacket standing behind a white-draped table on wheels. As he pushed it in, past her, Emma's eyes followed a number of silver domes reposing alongside plates, smoothly ironed white napkins and shining glassware. There was a pink rose in a vase.

Emma, assuming this was her dinner arriving, was delighted. She was hungry, and just about to order the usual cheese and ham panini from room service, accompanied by a cup of tea. The arrival of the table was the first evidence that her new employers realised she was a being like other beings, and needed feeding properly.

'Smells good,' she smiled encouragingly at the waiter, hurrying in after him, lifting the shining domes and perusing the contents.

The smells, savoury and delicious, issuing from among the glass and silver, made her feel light-headed. 'Chocolate mousse,' the waiter elucidated in his Baltic accent as her eye lingered hungrily on a glass dish filled with light brown foam and bristling with golden twisted sugar biscuits. 'Poached salmon,' he added, as she looked at the plate of firm-fleshed pink fish with new potatoes and a deliciously fresh-looking dressed salad. 'Foie gras,' he explained, as she inspected something yellow and shiny.

Emma raised grateful eyes to his. 'How delicious. I'm so hungry. Thank you so much for bringing it for me.'

The waiter's smile switched suddenly off. Concern and even fear swept his thin face. 'Ees not for you, madam,' he explained. 'Ees for the dog.'

'What?'

There was a skittering of nails on parquet and Sugar now arrived from the lobby. He bounded through the thick carpet and, with one leap, launched himself into the midst of the silver and glass on the trolley. For a second there was nothing but the sickening sound of Sugar's tongue licking the hotel porcelain. The waiter hurriedly departed.

When he had gone, Emma had attempted to help herself to the salmon at least. Sugar had not yet touched it and surely dogs didn't eat fish? But, as her hand had approached, Sugar had looked up and growled nastily, baring his sharp little teeth.

Emma had held his eye with hers. 'You owe me one, baby,' she warned the dog. 'I rescued you from that Alsatian, remember.' But Sugar, it seemed, did not remember. After a few more seconds' snarling, Sugar gave her a filthy look and began to apply himself to the chocolate mousse.

Emma was beginning to despair of gaining an audience with Belle outside actually going to the one in the theatre when, one afternoon after the matinée, the actress returned, most unusually, alone. Realising there would be no sexual activity until Niall returned, Emma seized her chance.

Belle looked at her, her strangely coloured green eyes filled with irritation. 'You want to talk? About your job? *Now?*'

'Now,' said Emma, gently but firmly.

Tutting and tossing her head, conveying with every fibre of her body just how inconvenient this was, Belle led the way into the suite's drawing room. Emma followed, through a pink and green carpet as thick as a field of corn. Summer sunshine streamed through the windows, reflecting off the chandeliers and candlesticks, and throwing an intense spotlight on the otherwise dim frisking cupids and goddesses painted on the panelling. It was a cheerful scene and Emma found her spirits rising. Perhaps everything would be all right after all.

Belle, perched on a striped sofa and directing at her a narrow-eyed smile, clasped small bejewelled hands round knees in tight white jeans.

'OK, so you want to talk terms,' she said ungraciously. 'And here's the first one. You sign a confidentiality agreement, OK?'

Emma nodded. Hollywood stars routinely made staff sign confidentiality agreements. She felt a flicker of excitement; this, at least, sounded glamorous.

'The agreement is as follows,' Belle announced, holding

Emma in her cold green gaze. 'You work for Mr and Mrs Smith.'

'Oh. I thought I worked for you.'

Belle exclaimed angrily, 'You *do* work for us! *We're* Mr and Mrs Smith.'

'Oh, I *see*.'

'You *never* talk about us to anyone.'

Emma nodded. It was obvious that *that* would be a clause in a confidentiality contract.

'You call me Miss Murphy at all times.'

'Not Mrs Smith?'

'No! *Not* Mrs Smith!' There was a crack as Belle drove her fist impatiently into her palm. 'Mr and Mrs Smith is what you call us if you talk about us to anyone else.'

'But . . . but . . . I thought I wasn't supposed to talk about you to anyone else.'

They were interrupted by a buzz at the penthouse door. 'Niall,' Belle said, rather testily, to Emma's ear. Had they had a row, she wondered.

It seemed so. 'Great,' said Belle as a handsome waiter entered. 'So much less of a drag.' She winked at the waiter, who was carrying in the three fresh bottles of champagne that routinely arrived at this time of day. The champagne stocks of London, Emma estimated, must have suffered a considerable blow since Belle had arrived. The actress got through so much of the stuff she probably peed it.

Certainly, she ingested little else to get in its way. Belle's capacity for champagne was as impressive as her lack of capacity for food was inexplicable. Her lack of interest in it seemed genuine and Emma had started to wonder if it had been removed as part of a surgical process. Many other things apparently had, after all.

The waiter bowed as he approached with the shining,

condensation-beaded champagne chiller swathed in its white napkin from which the gold top of a champagne bottle peered. With infinite care he polished the glasses with a snowy linen cloth.

'Just the one glass,' Belle said in her best breathy voice, as the handsome waiter placed a flute before Emma. 'In front of *me*,' she barked, as he failed to remove it. Emma looked down to hide a smile.

As the waiter, with a shaking hand, filled her flute and then made his escape, Belle continued setting out the terms of the agreement. 'There will, of course, be no salary.'

Emma stared at Belle in shock. 'Sorry—'

'It's an education, working for me,' Belle cut in, obviously intending to win the argument through sheer force of decibels. 'I'm a celebrity, remember?'

Emma eyed her putative employer steadily. 'But, Miss Murphy, presumably I'll still be in charge of Morning.'

'Yes, of course,' Belle snapped. 'But you'll be working for someone *famous*. You should be paying *me*, by rights. For broadening your horizons.'

Emma took a deep, stiffening breath. 'I can't accept not being paid.' She took another deep breath and willed her knees not to shake. 'And if you insist on not paying me I'm afraid I really can't take the job.' She met Belle's angry gaze with a flintiness belying her nerves. There was deadlock.

The suite telephone now rang. Exclaiming crossly about Niall again, Belle reached for the nearest receiver. Just as she did so, Morning started wailing from the bedroom.

Her heart thumping, Emma walked swiftly to her bedroom to attend to what was, for the moment at least, her charge. She bent over the side of the cot and looked down into Morning's black pupils in pure, glowing whites. He made a gurgling noise and smiled up at her.

She stood transfixed, her eyes locked on to his. She felt a surge of tremendous love as she picked him up. He snuggled contentedly in her arms, a small smile puckering his pink little mouth, a smell of warm, washed baby wafting up from him. Emma tightened her arms round the baby's little body and planted a kiss on his forehead.

She reached for the ready-prepared bottle of milk. Morning sucked rhythmically, steadily draining it with long, powerful draws.

Could she really leave this baby with Belle? On the other hand, could she really stay without a salary? Of course not. It was impossible. Belle was impossible . . .

Emma's ruminations were interrupted by a loud and persistent shrieking from the next room. Such sounds, of course, routinely emitted from the bedroom, but there was a less orgiastic quality than usual to what Emma was hearing now. Seizing Morning, she leapt to her feet and ran to see what the matter was. It sounded as if Belle was being murdered.

In his Los Angeles office, Mitch was feeling slightly stunned. There he'd been, asleep after that rare thing in Hollywood – a colossally indulgent lunch – and deep in a wonderful dream in which all four of the Oscars Best Actress nominees were clients of his.

His dream had then promised to turn to reality as he was woken by a call from Jack Saint saying he'd heard good things about Belle's current turn in London as an evil child-eating manipulator and would she be interested in being the Countess of Tyfoo; *Galaxia*'s evil, man-eating manipulator?

'Guess it's what you might call a natural progression,' Mitch had said, as casually as he could manage above his hammering heart. His every nerve end thrummed with the news that

Belle was back in business. Back in the movies. Back in Hollywood.

He still could not quite believe what had happened in London. Although Mitch would never have predicted it and could imagine it had happened only through the most extraordinary fluke, the production of *Titus Andronicus* in which Belle appeared – naked for much of one scene, admittedly – had proved an unexpected triumph. Belle had even been singled out by one critic 'for adding undisputed buoyancy to the production'.

When the call was at an end – never long with Saint – Mitch spun himself round in his seat so hard the chair shot across the room and fell over with him in it. The resulting shattering noise was enough to draw Greg Cucarachi to the doorway – but then, the merest sneeze was enough to do that. Especially lately. Mitch was sure Cucarachi spent hours of every day with his ear glued to the partition and made sure he banged it hard at regular intervals to discourage him.

'Celebrating, are we?' Cucarachi enquired snidely.

'Sorta,' Mitch said, defiant from beneath the avalanche of papers he had knocked from his desk. 'My client Belle Murphy's got a part in *Galaxia*,' he added, replacing his glasses with a flourish.

'Congratulations,' Greg said smoothly, without missing a beat. 'My client Christian Harlow's gonna be very interested to hear that.'

Mitch stared back at the trim figure lounging elegantly in the doorway. An alarm bell was shrilling in his heart. Amidst all the excitement of finding Belle back on the Hollywood bandwagon, he had completely forgotten that this particular bandwagon had Harlow on it already. He glared at Cucarachi, who was obviously cock-a-hoop at having holed him below the waterline yet again.

Mitch had not thought it possible until that moment to loathe his most loathed colleague any more than he did already. Then inspiration struck. Belle had a new man, after all.

'Your client can be as interested as he likes,' Mitch said steadily, 'but my client no longer is. Things between her and Niall MacDonald are both steady and serious,' he extemporised, watching with satisfaction Cucarachi try and fail to reply to this. As his hated co-worker departed, Mitch picked up the phone to call Belle in London. Her scream of triumph at the news was louder than any he had ever heard; admittedly that was not many.

Chapter 30

The camera flashed and whirred.

Darcy, her knees raised in their tattered fishnet tights, her naked back against the cold marble floor and her head thrust into one of the none-too-clean corners of the ornate fireplace, wondered, not for the first time that morning, afternoon or whatever time of day it had got to by now, what the hell she was doing here.

She reminded herself hurriedly that this was high fashion photography of the most esoteric and artistic kind, under the direction of the style legend Rumtopf. And that she, an actress about to make the breakthrough into the big time, ought to be grateful for the opportunity.

Darcy knew this because her newly acquired model agency, Wild, had told her so. Sam, its rather fearsome head, had banged on endlessly about how difficult it had been to get Rumtopf, and how practically impossible in addition to get him to fly to Florence for the shoot. In the end, a special private jet had been chartered.

The Rumtopf shoot was, Sam had explained, the first in a series of photographic sessions and features aimed at launching

Darcy into the stratosphere ahead of *Galaxia*'s release. The fact that the film had not yet been made was immaterial; interest had to be created right from the start. Whether Darcy actually wanted to be in the stratosphere was, she gathered, immaterial too. The studio making *Galaxia* wanted it and fashion shoots were part of her contract.

Darcy had never seen anything like her contract. It was the size of a telephone directory – possibly two – and bristled with little yellow plastic stickers denoting where she was to sign. There were so many of these that it had taken most of a morning in Mitch's office to scrawl her name on all the dotted lines. Her arm had been aching by the end. The amount of money she was to be paid was simply unreal. She had difficulty picturing such a huge sum, let alone what she would do with it; Mitch, on the other hand, to gather from the yelps and whimpers of joy that occasionally escaped him as he watched her sign, was suffering from no such difficulties.

Darcy squirmed on the hard studio floor, feeling her ribs press painfully against it. It was just as well she had lost so much weight following her break with Niall. Rumtopf, however, didn't seem to think she was thin enough. He had stood glowering in the back of the changing room as Darcy was tugged, rammed and generally shoehorned into a basque so full of rips it looked as if a lion had attacked it. This was, she discovered, one of Rumtopf's own designs. It did not make her warm to him, in any sense. The studio was ice cold, and the floor she sprawled on felt gritty, as if it could have done with a good sweep.

Rumtopf now crashed the silver-topped ebony cane he habitually carried against the floorboards. '*Nein, nein!*' he stormed in his miaowing German accent. 'Spread ze legs more. Push out ze chest more. *Ja!*'

It probably wasn't Rumtopf's fault, Darcy reflected. He was clearly surrounded by people whose sole function was to convince him he was the most important being on the planet. His arrival, three hours after the scheduled time, had been a case in point. Darcy's endless waiting in the white silence of the appointed studio – she'd have got on with the cleaning had she known – was suddenly interrupted by the arrival through the double doors of a slender, balletic, white-blond man dressed in a clinging white polo neck and white trousers.

'Get ready to welcome the Master!' he had instructed excitedly, gesturing her to rise from the chair on which she was apprehensively perched. And in Rumtopf had swept, a scattering of white-clad, pale-faced acolytes scuttling in his wake and murmuring in adoration. Against the background of the white-walled studio, Darcy had found it quite hard to see any of them.

Rumtopf himself wore white; white jeans, white cowboy boots, a white leather jacket and white circular spectacles that did not appear to have lenses in them. His hair was white and cut short apart from a fringe which flopped over his glasses. He turned glittering, strangely slitted eyes on Darcy through the lenseless frames and regarded her unsmilingly and at inordinate length.

Then he clapped his hands. 'Rumtopf is ready to create!' he announced.

The various white-clad acolytes, in sepulchral silence, now started to perform various ritualistic tasks. One produced a large aluminium case from which a number of scented candles were taken, dotted about the studio and lit. During a break in the shoot, another handperson tremblingly delivered the Master a plate of peeled kumquats, only to be sent away because they were not all of a perfectly uniform and predetermined size.

'Wrong! Wrong! Wrong for Rumtopf!' the Master screamed, after trying to force the offending fruit through a hole in a square silver panel designed – a handperson explained in low tones to Darcy – by Rumtopf himself especially for this purpose.

'It forms the basis of his homewares collection,' the acolyte added.

There was no champagne, to Darcy's disappointment. She had imagined that Moët and loud music were a feature of all fashion shoots. But the closest thing to alcohol was the water cocktail Rumtopf was served with the kumquats and which had been found wanting too.

'Was it four parts Badoit to one part Evian?' Darcy heard another handperson hiss at the hapless water cocktail bearer as he returned, rejected, from The Presence.

'I think so,' the second acolyte sighed. 'Though I might have put two parts Evian in, come to think of it.'

The first assistant slapped his forehead. 'Oh. My. God. You didn't! He can always tell.'

Now, as she arched her back away from the chill of the marble and the minutes dragged by in the stillness, Darcy found herself depressed by the silence. As for the candles, which were still very much in evidence, their combined powerful effect was to make Darcy feel sick rather than awed at the knowledge she was in the presence of genius. Tuberose had never been her favourite. And she had recently read somewhere that a liking for very strong perfume signalled depression or madness.

The scenario Rumtopf had cast her in seemed strongly to support this theory. 'The Master's vision,' one of the acolytes had explained in awed tones, 'is The Murder House.' Darcy listened with disbelief. Every shot – or 'tableau' – was to feature a different room, a different murder, with herself as all the victims.

The first 'tableau' had been the bathroom; she had lain in the freestanding, claw-footed, candlelit tub in a satin ballgown in whose design Rumtopf's trademark rips and tears were generously represented. It was ripped particularly around the area of her breasts where a bloody fake stab-wound appeared. The apparent culprit had stood some distance away, a male model in his early twenties with thick, short, blond, side-parted hair. He wore tartan boxer shorts and held a toy dagger of bright pink neon plastic. Darcy had tried but failed to get him to say anything; even react much. She was starting to wonder if he was a robot.

She tried hard to remember what Sam had said, that this shoot was crucial for her career, it would 'position' her. 'Position' was a word Sam used a lot. And that this man was the great Rumtopf; one of the most influential designers, stylists and fashion innovators of the last thirty years. Most models, Sam had emphasised, would kill for the honour. And delight in being killed, as she was being now, many times over.

As the next 'tableau', to feature her strangled in the bed-room, got under way, Darcy's uncomfortable feeling that the shoot crossed the line from the artistic to the downright psychopathic increased. Perhaps, she now tried to convince herself, it was just as well that Rumtopf, an obvious homicidal misogynist, had an outlet for his fantasies. It may be humiliating and unpleasant for her as the model, but she was probably doing humankind a favour. What might have happened had the Master been obliged to bottle this sort of thing up hardly bore thinking about.

It was obvious that women weren't Rumtopf's thing. The white-blond, powerfully muscled figure in black who sat on the sidelines behind the snaking cables of the lights was, Darcy had gathered, the Master's current muse, Stefan. He wore a black baseball cap on his head, which was turned back to front and the piece of material attached to its reverse to shield the wearer's neck from the sun hung in front of his face. And these, Darcy thought despairingly, are the people telling everyone else what to wear.

One of Rumtopf's acolytes now came over to position her toes in the exact manner the Master desired. 'Such an honour to be working with Rumtopf!' he breathed reverently as he pushed her big toe out and brought the toe next to it slightly in. 'Especially at such a time, when his curiosity and creativity are at their peak. And he looks so incredibly young! We all think he's got a portrait of himself in the attic. You know, like Donald Gray.'

'Dorian,' Darcy corrected. Rumtopf, *young*? He was on the wrong side of fifty by some considerable distance, yet evidently anxious to disguise the fact. Few of his features seemed the original ones. His eyes, she had by now realised, had that strange Asiatic look because they were lifted. In addition, he had a mouth like a bouncy castle and his nose looked as if it belonged to someone else. Perhaps it had.

The next 'tableau' was The Grand Salon, and so she was lying under a table, her make-up smoothly immaculate apart from the fake bullet wound in her temple. The side-parted and pouting male model in boxer shorts was back; he stood beside her, holding a toy pistol of green neon plastic. Darcy had noticed that, while his chest was waxed, the legs protruding from beneath the houndstooth checked boxer shorts he had changed into were extremely hairy. As the Master prodded her again, Darcy felt a giggle rising irresistibly in her throat.

'*Nein! Nein!*' shrieked Rumtopf, the spurs on his cowboy boots ringing as he stamped his feet. 'Think murder! Think

Sweeney Todd! Think Jack the Ripper! Think Dr Crippen! Think—'

'Yeah, OK,' Darcy interjected hurriedly, anxious to be spared more of the grisly roll-call that had evidently provided inspiration. What she was really thinking about was lunch, however. Her stomach was a storm-tossed sea of hunger. She had been rushed to the Rumtopf shoot directly the plane from Los Angeles had touched down in Rome and had seen hardly anything of Italy. Least of all the leisurely-lunch-in-shady-vine-draped-taverna type of Italy she would so appreciate now. She swallowed as the saliva rose.

'A silent scream, you know? Zat is the effect Rumtopf is looking for,' the Master interrupted, poking her prone body with the end of his cane.

Finally, the end came. Darcy, hurriedly gathering her small number of things together – her luggage, such as it was, waited outside in the car that had brought her from the airport – looked up to see Rumtopf's strangely diagonal eyes gazing assessingly at her through his lenseless white frames.

Darcy's heart sank. She had been so close to escape, so close to the car outside and being driven out to the villa the film company had booked. Darcy had imagined it longingly all the flight back: the pool, the cypress trees, the red-tiled roof, the undulating green and brown of the countryside under the famous Tuscan sun, the olive-wood table spread with all manner of delicious food. After her recent trials, it was everything she wished for.

There was mute appeal in her eyes as she looked at Rumtopf. Surely he wasn't going to announce some last-minute extra ideas, although it was hard to imagine what they could be. It seemed to Darcy she had embodied every possible type of murder in every available room. Or perhaps there were some gaps. Raped on the roof? Chopped to pieces in the coal hole?

'Have you met Stefan?' Rumtopf asked.

Stefan rose from his chair and walked over with the stiff, turkey gait of those with over-muscled thighs. Darcy winced slightly. She disliked obvious muscles on men and hated gyms or any form of strenuous exercise. As he approached, Darcy absorbed with some surprise that Stefan's tight-fitting black suit was made entirely of nylon. But she smiled and held out her hand. As Stefan gripped it in his own, a searing pain tore through her fingers.

'Apologies,' Stefan muttered as Darcy blinked the tears of agony away and swallowed hard, several times. 'Ze static. From my suit.'

Rumtopf seemed not to have noticed any of this. His slit eyes remained riveted on Darcy. He twitched his full lips. He inhaled and made a sweeping gesture with his hands. 'Rumtopf,' he declared suddenly, in thrilling tones.

Darcy eyed him uncertainly, wondering what was coming next. Perhaps nothing was. Perhaps the mere iteration of his identity was meant to be sufficient, reminding the lesser mortals in the room like herself that one was in The Presence of Genius.

'Rumtopf,' the Master declaimed again. 'Rumtopf will now make you a wonderful offer.'

The acolytes gasped. They turned awestruck eyes on Darcy. Stefan, meanwhile, looked more suspicious than ever. He folded his powerful forearms with menacing slowness.

'The most wonderful thing a woman in your position could wish for,' Rumtopf continued in his Germanic monotone.

Darcy could not help a swift, hopeful glance in the direction of the camera. Frankly, the most wonderful thing a woman in her position could wish for was the destruction of the images just taken.

'Rumtopf has decided a matter of great importance.'

Fearfully, Darcy raised her eyes to Rumtopf's. She could not imagine what he was about to say. The silence rang loudly in her ears. Rumtopf still held her in his gaze.

'Rumtopf will make your dress for the Oscars.'

Chapter 31

It was a hot day in London; the sun glared off the streets, the shop windows and the bonnets of the passing cars. Inside the limo, all was cool, shaded and comfortable. Apart from in Niall's brain, where thoughts as hot and crowded as the people on the pavements outside teemed in their angry millions.

His red brows knotted, his pale blue eyes narrowed and cold, he sat glumly in the back of the Mercedes conveying himself and Belle to the airport. But of the two of them, only Belle would be boarding the first-class flight to Florence. Only Belle would be taking a lead role in a guaranteed blockbuster movie.

As the car ground slowly through the London traffic, Niall raked a resentful hand through his dark red hair. It was *so bloody unfair*. Just what was it about him? Why was it that every woman he went out with automatically got a part in *Galaxia*, tipped to be the biggest thing since Everest, while he remained treading the boards, a mere bit-part player?

Granted, he was a bit-part player in one of London's current hits, but now Belle's own particular bit parts were leaving it seemed unlikely the success would continue. Not even the most ardent Shakespeare loyalist in the cast was deluded enough to imagine that the audience came to hear the Bard's words alone. The chance to see a Hollywood celebrity bare all had had more than a little to do with it too.

The director, certainly, had been devastated to hear Belle had been struck down with a mystery bug and would be unable to continue with the run. Niall had been even more devastated to discover that the mystery bug was Jack Saint and that Belle was leaving for Italy to resume her career as a leading film star.

Granted, her behaviour had been imperious and difficult of late. There was now no trace of the blackly humorous, irreverent car crash he had met at the audition. Belle had then been at rock bottom, but now success in *Titus* had reinflated an ego whose titanic proportions Niall had not suspected but which had terrifyingly combined with the voracious sex drive of which he was all too aware. Performing for Belle twice a day, in addition to performing at the theatre, made for an exhausting ride in every sense of the word. In a nutshell – and shells were what they felt like these days – Niall felt used.

While he sat angrily upright, resentment emanating from every stiffened muscle, Belle lounged against the beige leather seat next to him in an exaggeratedly relaxed fashion. Her long white legs, dangling one over the other, were exposed – from the top of her cowboy boots at least – almost to the pubis in tiny denim shorts with frayed edges. From time to time she swung her legs the other way; Niall, at her side, only narrowly missing – thanks to a well-judged dodge – being hit by the boot-heels each time.

He threw several hurt and offended looks in her direction, but it was impossible to see whether they had hit their target. Belle's green eyes were hidden behind black sunglasses so huge they made her look like a fly, while her attention was completely focused on the silver mobile mostly hidden in her cascading platinum hair. Her inflated lips, slicked a glossy pink, chewed gum energetically, breaking off from their efforts occasionally to allow a loud and theatrical laugh to escape.

'Tom Cruise said *that*? You're kidding me!'

Niall was sick of hearing how all her celebrity friends were taking Belle's calls once more. Or, rather, he was sick of hearing, in every word Belle said, how completely and utterly she discounted how much she owed to him, Niall, or rather Graham, MacDonald. It had been he, had it not, who helped her with her lines at the audition, which in turn had got her a part in *Titus*, which had led to all this.

'Harvey Weinstein did *what*? No-ooooo!'

But had she breathed one word of gratitude to him, let alone one word into the ear of the director that might get him a part too? Had she hell. He had been right, all along, to loathe the commercial film industry, Niall brooded.

'Well, everyone knows Nicole can't stand her . . .' Belle cackled delightedly, swinging her legs about again. It was, Niall thought furiously, as if he simply didn't exist any more. She hadn't even been especially keen that he see her off at the airport.

'But we're . . . together,' Niall had reminded her, in hurt, indignant tones.

'Sure,' Belle had said vaguely, looking up from her texting.

Suddenly realising she had finished the Tom Cruise/Harvey Weinstein/Nicole Kidman call, he leant forward to say something loving, something to rekindle her passion or, failing that, her conscience. But he received only a blank flash from Belle's sunglasses before her silver nails hit the speed-dial and he found himself listening to her brief her agent about her accommodation requirements in Italy. 'My sheets have gotta be Frette. Linen, yeah. And I want the room sterilised on arrival and daily the whole time I'm there . . . you got that, Mitch?'

She was relishing every moment, Niall realised with a hot, burning feeling. While he – what did he have? Once she was gone, not only would his link with the big time have gone, but the very roof over his head as well. The manager of the Portchester was hardly likely to let him stay in the penthouse by himself; not for anything less than five grand a night.

'And a bathroom fridge for all my products. Oh, and all the champagne's gotta be Ultra Brut. Sugar's gotta have Evian, filtered at least three times . . .'

Niall watched jealously as Belle's jewelled hand dandled fondly on the brown, bony head of the animal that was, of all beasts in the world, his least favourite. Sugar was, as usual, under Belle's armpit, staring evilly at him out of the corner of a red Marc Jacobs tote. There was, Niall saw, a hint of smugness in the evil, as if Sugar saw the future and it pleased him. It made Niall, despite himself, feel nervous.

Now they were on the motorway going out to the airport, the car had picked up speed. The increase in velocity increased Niall's insecurity, as if events were moving more quickly than he was. He had an uncomfortable impression of things moving beyond his grasp. He drummed his big, red-downed hands on his denim-covered knees, racking his brains for the right thing to say to her.

'Plasma screen. WiFi. Horizon pool . . .' Belle drawled from behind her sunglasses.

Niall stared out of the window, swallowing hard. She was ignoring him, and she owed him so much. More than she owed that greedy bastard of an agent of hers, sitting over there in LA, raking in the money. What was so difficult about that, Niall fulminated silently, his eyes pale slits of resentment as he watched the traffic flash past. Whereas he . . . *he* . . .

You just had to take the last few days. Having saved

her career by getting her a part in *Titus*, he had gone on to save her reputation when, having got the nod from Saint, Belle was all for heading straight to the film set and dropping everything. Including the baby and the nanny, whom she was refusing to pay. It had taken him, Niall reminded himself, to point out that flouncing off to Italy leaving an abandoned African orphan in a London hotel room might not play the press all that well. Especially when she was taking her goddamn dog with her.

'Well, the press didn't care when I adopted him,' Belle sulked. 'No one took any notice.'

'They'll care a lot when you unadopt him,' Niall assured her. 'They'll take plenty of notice if you just leave him by himself in London.'

'Who says I was going to leave him by himself in London?' Belle swung her mass of brittle, perfumed, white hair back over her shoulder.

'Who else were you going to leave him w—' Niall did not finish the sentence. There was a purposeful glint in those green eyes. His heart hammered. She could not mean, surely . . . ?

'You, of course,' Belle said breezily.

'Me? *Me?*' Niall's head spun. 'But,' he gibbered, 'I'm no good with babies . . . I drop them . . . I can't change a nappy . . .'

He'd managed to persuade her not to sack the nanny only by adopting the lowest of tactics. He had despised himself for such oleaginous insincerity, but desperate times had demanded desperate measures. 'If you fire her, Emma will go to the papers,' he had warned. 'Remember how, um, *hugely* famous you are now, Belle.'

'Famous *again*, you mean,' corrected Belle, curling her pneumatic lips like the cat who got the cream. The tactic had worked, however. Belle had, with the utmost reluctance, agreed to pay Emma a minimal salary and she and the baby had left for Italy earlier that morning. Much earlier; their bargain flight had been scheduled to leave before six.

The Mercedes, Niall saw from the signs above the motorway, was now nearing Gatwick. As usual, the place was heaving with cars moving in all directions and people dragging luggage about. Seeing the crowd of photographers outside the glass doors at the terminal entrance, Belle gave a theatrical sigh. 'Oh. My. God. Just *look* at those goddamn paps,' she drawled, as if, Niall thought, these were not the very same men whose attentions, a mere few days ago, she would have tap-danced round a toilet seat to attract.

'I'll come with you,' he offered eagerly. 'See you onto the plane. I'm strong. I can shove my way through.'

Belle held up a hand. 'No.'

Niall stared. 'But why not? I mean, I've come with you all this way . . .'

'I didn't ask you to,' Belle said with a curl of her pink glossy lip.

As, beside her, he caught the glint of Sugar's teeth, a sickening feeling now spread through Niall. The despicable animal was *grinning*. Ignoring it as best he could, Niall fought for a passage through his swirling emotions. 'I came,' he assured the dog's mistress with all the passion he could muster, 'because I love you, Belle. We haven't been long together but you've come to mean so much.'

Belle was texting. She wasn't, Niall saw despairingly, even looking at him.

'It's over,' she said, frowning over the keys. 'I was gonna text you when I got to Florence, but I guess I may as well tell you now. Eyeball to eyeball,' she added, from the other side of her enormous sunglasses.

'Over?' Niall croaked. His mind whirled. Oh God. Where was he going to sleep tonight?

'Over,' Belle confirmed, pressing the send button on her text. She looked up and flashed him a megawatt smile. 'I've gotta move on,' she explained.

'*Move on?*' Niall exclaimed in a tragic croak. He was determined to give this one the works. The YMCA was beckoning otherwise. 'Move on from *me*? But *why*? I thought you loved me.' His voice broke on a sob.

'*Loved* you?' Belle's tone was astounded. 'Baby, this is Hollywood.'

Hollywood this, Hollywood that. Niall was getting fed up with hearing the wretched word. 'It's not Hollywood,' he pointed out, irritated. 'It's the back of a Mercedes in West Sussex.'

'Whatever.' Belle shrugged. 'It's just the way things are, baby.'

As the chauffeur opened the door, she slid out. He watched her stalk past the paparazzi, sunglasses flashing disdainfully, and disappear inside the terminal. She didn't even look back.

What now? He could hardly go back to Darcy's Kensington flat, not now that he had left her for someone else. Any hope that Darcy, from the distance of America, was unaware of the liaison had been shattered by the widespread publicity it had received. Any hope that she might forgive him, moreover, had been similarly removed by a couple of uncharacteristically venomous texts he had received from her on the subject. That their relationship was over was in no doubt.

He'd left his bicycle at her flat, Niall recalled gloomily. It would have been useful now that the days of limos and chauffeurs had come to an emergency stop.

Chapter 32

Orlando Fitzmaurice sat in the airport, his legs, in their cut-off jeans, stuck out in front of him, his large, trainered feet subtly drumming the ground along to the iPod whose earphones were entirely hidden under his tangled, dark-gold hair.

The place seemed full of leggy teenage girls with long blond hair, which they swished about while looking coyly at him through it. Well-heeled Jasmines and Elizas, he could tell, heading for Daddy's villa in Tuscany. As he was himself, even though Daddy, in his case, had rented it – shuddering at the price – and his mother twitteringly referred to it as the *aubergo*. And they were, of course, sharing it with the Faughs.

Although it had been some weeks since the invitation was issued, and he should probably be used to it by now, Orlando still found it hard to believe that his mother, for reasons he could not imagine, really had invited the world champions of freeloading on their summer holidays with them, and that they would be present when his A levels came through.

He turned up the volume on his iPod, hoping to drown his troubles in music, and slid a glance across the riotous geometric carpet at his parents. They sat on the opposite row of fixed-to-the-floor airport seats; his mother next to his father, or the pair of chinoed legs emerging from beneath the *Daily Telegraph* that were standing in for his father this morning. Richard, Orlando knew, was dreading the holiday as much as he was and, like him, was pursuing the well-trodden but ultimately futile line of pretending it was not happening.

Georgie was largely hidden behind a copy of *Hello!*; all that was visible was a pair of expensive sunglasses pushed atop some frazzled hair, ten coral-coloured nails holding the magazine, two thin legs in pressed white jeans neatly crossed over each other and a pair of Tiffany-blue Tod's driving shoes revealing thin ankles and the veiny tops of salon-tanned feet.

Orlando now stared fixedly at the floor as a gaggle of giggling Elizas passed by, all eyeliner and exposed legs. They were nudging each other and looking at him. Why were they so interested? He did his best to disguise what everyone found so fascinating; pulled his hair over his face to hide his features, bit his lips and pressed them together so they wouldn't look so big. He scowled at the girls, who seemed to be lingering; they giggled more but eventually passed on.

Orlando shot an apprehensive look across at his mother, but she was, thankfully, still lost in showbusiness and hadn't noticed his fan club. If she had, Orlando knew, she would be up on her feet and shrilly introducing them to her son, in the hope that one of them would be related to Mick Jagger or a peer of the realm. Given this time of year and their destination, Orlando knew, the chances of meeting well-connected people were strong, although thankfully he had not seen anyone from Heneage's yet. Or, even more thankfully, the Faughs.

There was a rustle from the seats opposite. His mother had lowered her magazine and was looking at him. Her mouth was moving up and down but he heard nothing through the thunder from his earphones. She was making turn-it-down gestures. Orlando turned it down.

'Darling?' Georgie shrilled.

'I've turned it down, Mum,' Orlando mumbled, shooting a self-conscious look at the people passing about them.

'Honestly, darling,' Georgie said in a more normal voice, 'you're supposed to be looking out for Laura and Hugh and you're just staring at the floor, from what I can see.' Her thin face creased with exasperation.

'Sorry, Mum,' Orlando grunted in the resonant baritone he had recently acquired. His voice had become deep and gruff in a way that seemed to catch even more female attention. Unwillingly, he raised his chin and cautiously, beneath his cliffs of brow, began to scan the airport for the Faughs.

'Look! Look! Over there!' Georgie yelped, her face ablaze with excitement. He stared in the same direction. Was it the Faughs she had spotted? Surely not. His mother definitely had an exaggerated view of their charm and interest, but this was going too far.

His father, Orlando saw, had lowered his newspaper. The same thoughts were evidently going through his head; through his lopsided glasses his eyes were cagey and his long, thin mouth closed in an expression of apprehension.

'Look!' Georgie exclaimed again, pointing.

On the wide carpeted gangway that led through this departure hall into the next, a blonde woman was walking quickly, gesturing angrily, surrounded by photographers. They were all yelling and letting off their flashes.

Orlando was interested. He had never seen a full-on celebrity paparazzi attack before, although he didn't recognise the woman. Was it Pamela Anderson?

'Isn't that Belle Murphy?' Georgie gasped.

'*Who?*' asked Orlando. He had no interest in celebrities, apart from the distraction from himself that they afforded his mother.

There was a sharp, irritated intake of breath from Georgie. '*Honestly*, darling. Don't you know who *anyone* is?'

'I'll go and see if I can find the Faughs,' Orlando mumbled, untangling his legs to stand up to the whole of his six-foot-plus height. He had every intention of avoiding their guests if he saw them, but it got him out of the maternal firing line.

'Ow!' yelled Emma, as a colossal training shoe crushed down on her foot.

It had not been a good day. She had arrived at the airport and checked in what seemed like weeks ago, only to discover that the bargain flight she and Morning had been booked on had been delayed by up to four hours. In the interests of calming the baby, who seemed to hate airports with a passion, she had walked around the heaving terminal more or less constantly since, and now knew every single item in every single shop.

And now some clumsy oaf had walked slap-bang into her and crushed her foot. As well as, Emma saw, annoyed, made a dirty smudge with his sole over her white plimsoll.

'Sorry,' Orlando blurted. Wandering around, lost in a pleasant daydream in which the Faughs were not, after all, coming with them, he had not seen this woman until it was too late and he had practically knocked her over. He felt horror clamp his insides as he saw she had a baby strapped to her front. Facing out, too. Fortunately it did not seem to have woken up. 'I'm really sorry,' he grunted, in the new deep voice he still didn't feel entirely comfortable with.

Her assailant was very tall, Emma saw. About her age; maybe younger. He wore a pair of cut-off denim jeans and a sagging white T-shirt. His face was hidden beneath lots of blond hair and there were iPod earphones curling around his neck. So far so bog standard, Emma thought.

'I'm a clumsy idiot,' Orlando added, rather pleadingly.

He pushed his hair back to expose his face and instead of the spotty and misshapen bunch of bog-standard teenage features she had been expecting, Emma now found herself looking at a face of celestial beauty. He had the most extraordinary eyes; a brackish green ringed with yellow. She was immediately conscious of her pre-dawn lack of make-up and the way her hair was scraped back in an early morning ponytail from which it was constantly escaping. Her exposed ears seemed to double tenfold in size, turn purple and pulsate.

Of course, she thought he was an idiot, Orlando realised. You could tell by the way she was looking at him. She had a very direct gaze. Most girls he knew sort of squinted, giggled and whooshed their hair about. They looked to make sure you were looking at them, rather than to notice anything about you. This girl's cool and interested appraisal was something entirely different.

For a moment, the world around Emma had simply melted away. But now, against her front, Morning stirred, propelling her back into the heat, noise and movement of the busy terminal and her own tiredness. Panic swept through her lest Morning scream now; *please don't let him, not after all the effort over the past hours preventing him.*

But the only sound from directly south of her was a happy gurgle; looking down, Emma saw that the baby was smiling at the boy. The boy, in turn, was smiling back. Seeing those astounding, beautiful eyes crinkled in delight as he extended a big, long hand towards the baby, Emma felt a sensation inside her like the ringing of bells.

'Nice baby,' said Orlando appreciatively. He liked babies and children. He didn't come across many, but when he saw them running about Hampstead Heath or charging about some school playground, screaming, he was always struck by how much they were enjoying themselves. With utter abandon and every fibre of their being. He couldn't remember what that felt like. But then Georgie had no doubt had him networking in his cot. Or power-playdating in his baby bouncer.

'What's his name?' Orlando asked. He had not failed to notice, of course, that the baby was black. Very black, in fact, more so than one might expect if this girl was, as seemed likely, his mother.

'He's called Morning.'

Orlando nodded. 'Pretty,' he said. '*Name*,' he added swiftly, colouring up and feeling his heart charge suddenly. 'Um, why did you call him that?'

'Oh, he's not my baby.' Emma, catching his blush and blushing too, smiled in swift correction. 'I'm his nanny.'

But she was, even so, the nearest to a mother Morning had. Especially now that Belle, grudgingly agreeing to pay her after all, had made it abundantly clear that she wished to see as little of the baby as possible.

She had seen Belle go through the airport just now, heading for the VIP lounge and followed by the paparazzi. Emma had kept her own head down, reluctant to be drawn into the circus surrounding the star and knowing – not least because the star had told her so – that Belle didn't want them there anyway.

Where this situation was ultimately leading to, Emma could not guess. But if current form was anything to go by she would be spending the next twenty years following Belle, flying bucket class and on slave wages, until Morning was old enough to look after himself. Obviously this could not go on, but at the moment she had no option with which to stop it. She must keep this job if she were to apply for any others.

'His nanny,' repeated Orlando, interested in her northern accent. To his ears, it had a novel ring. Hardly anyone ever spoke to him in anything other than an English upper-class accent, or what they imagined was one.

Emma was getting more used to the boy's extraordinary appearance now, but looking directly at him was still a bit like looking directly into the sun. Especially when he smiled. He reminded her of someone, she thought. But perhaps it was just that universal beautiful look, familiar from advertisements and magazines.

'I'm Orlando, by the way,' Orlando began.

She looked amused at that.

'What's so funny?' he asked, mildly indignant.

'You look like an Orlando.'

Immediately her face was hot with regret. *Why* had she said that? It was hardly his fault, after all, and she knew enough silly names herself. Hengist, for one, who had that ghastly nanny, Totty Ponsonby-Pratt. Cosmo – but no. There was nothing silly about Cosmo. He was adorable, as was Hero. She missed them terribly. Emma took a stiffening breath and, fighting tears, ran her hands caressingly over Morning's shoulders. She was tired, that was all.

Orlando had seen the concern pass over her face and now rushed to reassure her he was not in the least offended. 'If you think that's a silly name, you should hear some of the people I'm at school with,' he grinned. Then he remembered that he wasn't actually at school with them after all. He had left school and this was the summer his A level results were due out. He felt a nasty surge in his stomach at the thought.

He was very easy-going, Emma thought, relieved. And much less conceited than she would have expected someone of his looks and apparent background to be.

'And you're . . . ?' Orlando asked her.

'Emma.'

He nodded. 'Yeah, you look like an Emma.'

She raised her eyebrows and smiled. *Touché*.

She *did* look like an Emma, he thought. The simple grace of the name suited her. There was something very fresh and English about her face, which was open and clear, with smooth, close skin – not a single spot, he noticed – and large, brown, shining eyes. There were touches of pink in her cheeks that reminded him of roses. He liked her brown hair too, which was falling out of its ponytail more and more all the time. Released, it looked glossy and weighty and incredibly healthy, and was shot through with rich red threads. She had nice little ears, too, tinged with pink.

She wore either none or very little make-up, which was also good. Girls with too much make-up on always looked dirty. But this girl looked so clean she might squeak. The more he looked at her, the more he liked her. It wasn't just that she was pretty; it was something rarer that he could sense; something solid and real and reassuring. She was not thin, but not fat either. She looked as unlike as it was possible to look from the rickety, kohl-eyed, blonde Elizas and Jasmines he knew from school and, horrors, those endless pages on Facebook. One could not easily imagine any of them holding a baby with the confidence Emma was doing now, nor gaining such obvious pleasure from it. She was, Orlando sensed, very kind.

Morning, who had been playing all this while with the ends of a leather bracelet tied around Orlando's wrist, now began to mew. 'He's hungry,' Emma said. 'I need to go and feed him.

Give him his bottle,' she added hurriedly, crimsoning and shoo-
ing hurriedly away the sudden, startling connection between
Orlando and her breasts that the mention of feeding had
brought flooding to her brain. 'Well, bye then . . .' she began.

A force beyond his usual diffident self now impelled
Orlando. 'How about a coffee?' he blurted, surprising himself
and sending a violent charge through Emma's knees. 'I've got an
hour until my flight,' he added, more apologetically, as
awareness of what he had done filtered through. It was the first
time he had invited a girl to do anything, apart from go away or
perhaps lend him a pen that worked. He stared at the floor,
amazed at his temerity and expecting refusal.

They walked slowly along, Emma slightly in front to hide the
blush which, annoyingly, would not go away, and trying not to
think about what her bottom might look like from behind.

In the terminal Costa Coffee, Orlando flicked some torn
sugar papers from the table. They had established in the coffee
queue that they were both going to Italy, although on different
flights.

'I'm not sure my plane really exists,' Emma sighed as they sat
at the table, looking up, as she did every few minutes, to the
announcements screen. Certainly, it was not up there yet.

'You're lucky to be working,' Orlando remarked, his green
eyes narrowed beneath his brows. From the moment she had
mentioned it, it had struck him as the answer to his problems.
At a loose end? No money? Young and healthy? Then why not
get a job? It was so simple.

Lucky! The rejecting twist of her lips with which Emma
greeted his remark she concealed by glancing down at Morning,
who was sucking contentedly at his bottle. Lucky was not the
way she would have described it. But she had signed a confidentiality agreement and so was not at liberty to describe anything.

Fortunately, Orlando was pursuing his own train of thought. There was, he thought, something really rather distractingly pretty about the way her hair kept falling out of its ponytail. And the shine of her lips and eyes when she looked at him.

'I wish I was working,' he said, resuming his theme. 'I'm about to go on holiday, but it's going to be a nightmare. And I'm expecting my A level results and they're going to be the worst ever recorded.'

Emma raised her eyebrows at this outburst. It was not what she had expected such a gilded youth to say.

'Why are they going to be so bad? Was your school bad?'

He shook his blond hair. 'No, the school was fine.' More than fine, he knew. Heneage's was one of the best in London, meaning it must be one of the best anywhere. Shame and defiance washed over him like hot and cold water.

'What school was it?' Emma was curious.

'Heneage's,' he confessed. His eyes scanned hers. 'Heard of it?'

Emma vaguely remembered Vanessa bandying the name about. 'Sounds like a department store,' she said, which was what she had thought at the time.

He laughed at this. 'Well, it is, sort of. It sells education. And contacts,' he said ruefully.

'But you didn't do any work, anyway?' Emma probed. She felt disapproving, but not as disapproving as she would have liked to be. There was something about Orlando that prevented censure.

He grinned guiltily. 'Not much. No.' He considered mentioning the borderline dyslexia he had been diagnosed with – an excuse Georgie had made much of over the years – but he feared Emma might not believe him. He had never been entirely sure he believed it himself.

'Didn't revise?' Emma pressed, her eyebrows arched as she

shifted the feeding baby in her arms. To her satisfaction, Morning had put on a considerable amount of weight since she had first met him.

Orlando shook his head. Of all his weak academic aspects, revision was his weakest. Until an exam was actually upon him he could never believe it would actually happen. And then, of course, it was too late.

'Shame to miss the opportunity,' Emma said tacitly. 'After going through all those years at school.'

Orlando considered this. He had trained himself to be deaf to anything his mother ever said about wasting his privileges. Coming from this girl, however, failing exams sounded like something other than failing to get on the next level of social achievement, as Georgie so obviously saw it. It just sounded like a waste of effort, which, he supposed, it was.

'I suppose you got lots of As,' he said wistfully to Emma. 'You look the clever sort.'

For all her censure, Emma blushed with pleasure at the compliment. 'I never took A levels, actually. I decided to leave and start work.'

'Lucky you,' Orlando said again. 'The only way my mum would've let me leave is if I'd passed all my exams and a degree freakishly early and become the youngest brain surgeon ever employed at University College Hospital.'

Emma laughed. 'Are you saying your mum's a bit pushy?'

He pulled a face. 'I mean, she's nice. She means well. But . . .' He stopped. Where did he start, with the buts?

In the obvious place. He started with the Faughs. Out it all came, as fast as a lanced boil, the fact they were coming to Italy with him; everything they had said and done to him, everything he felt about them. Strangely, describing their horrors made him feel strangely lighter of heart. He realised this was because she sympathised. At home, of course, Richard sympathised but dared not say so. As for Georgie . . .

But Emma jogged Morning in her arms, the expression in her shining brown eyes one of mixed outrage and amusement. 'Poor you! They sound *horrendous*. And you've got to go on holiday with them!'

'I know!' As Orlando spoke, he forgot his awkwardness about his voice. He felt a new confidence blossom; he had not realised he was possessed of such eloquence, particularly before a girl. Or that anything he might have to be eloquent about would interest a girl.

As Emma listened, the urge rose to tell Orlando about the almost equally peculiar conditions of her own Italian trip. It felt a long time since she had had a ready and sympathetic ear; someone her own age, not an employer or other adversary, but someone who would understand. She felt for the first time how lonely she had been in London.

She stopped herself, however. Emma was unsure to what extent the confidentiality agreement was watertight, but was certain that whatever water it held Belle would squeeze to the last drop if she breached it.

She listened to Orlando instead. It certainly made colourful hearing. 'How awful.' She shook her head. 'They obviously think they can do what they like just because their father's an MP.'

'And he thinks he can do what he likes as well,' Orlando added. He had not yet told Emma about Hugh Faugh's views concerning hanging or single mothers in the lower social classes. But there seemed no reason to hold back now.

Emma was speechless for some minutes. She opened and shut her mouth. Her expression was absolute amazement, Orlando saw, satisfied.

'But . . . this man. He represents people. In Parliament.'

'Yes.'

'People voted for him.'

Orlando confirmed that, incredibly, this was so.

'He's supposed to be all about . . . what did you say? . . . family values. Family values!' Emma exclaimed.

She had, Orlando thought, accurately put her finger on the most unbelievable aspect of all.

'He has constituents.' Emma's voice was low with anger now. He sensed she would have shouted, were it not for Morning in her arms. 'He has power and influence. And *that's* what he thinks?' Her nostrils flared. 'People *trust* him.'

Orlando regarded her with blazing eyes, his heart surging with the joy of, at last, finding someone who really understood. 'I know. It's unbelievable. If only his constituents *knew*.' He tore a sugar paper open and began layering the top of his cooling cappuccino.

'Do you realise,' Emma interrupted him, 'that you're putting salt on your coffee?'

'What? Noooooo!' Orlando wailed. Despair flooded him. Could he not do even the simplest thing? She was looking at him gravely. Pityingly, even. Then he saw the corner of her mouth – that mouth that reminded him of strawberries – start to twitch. She was laughing. Enormously relieved, Orlando laughed too. Then he saw her look away and her expression switch abruptly from amusement to panic.

'I don't believe it,' Emma exclaimed suddenly, scrambling to her feet as quickly as Morning and his bottle made possible. 'My flight's actually up there! Boarding now!'

Orlando leapt up too. The table rattled. He raised his hands in an instinctive gesture of prevention. *Don't go*, they said. 'Er . . .' Orlando stammered, rather helplessly. 'Um, thanks for the coffee.'

'You bought it,' Emma pointed out as she strapped Morning into his baby carrier with the dexterous speed of a professional. The brown eyes ricocheted between Orlando's and the baby. 'Look, it's been nice meeting you . . . Hope it's not as bad as you think in Italy. Um . . . good luck!'

She had gone, disappeared into the crowds, before he could even ask her where she was staying. Before he could get her mobile. If she was near him they could have met. Had another coffee. He could have told her about the Faughs and she could have helped him to bear it; he, in turn, could have asked her about her job. He realised now, with a crushing sense of inadequacy, that he had hardly asked her a single question. What a self-obsessed bore she must think him, Orlando berated himself, watching her diminishing figure weave across the concourse.

As Emma handed over the tickets, and hers and Morning's passports, her hands were shaking. Her entire body seemed awash with sensation: heat, cold, surges of dread and elation in her stomach. All of which seemed to intensify whenever she thought of Orlando. Probably it was just as well she would not be seeing him again.

Chapter 33

Two men were walking despondently through Gatwick's main departure zone. One was tall and thin with a lugubrious grey face, a long nose and greyish, thinning, long hair. His companion was short and pink, with reddish, thinning short hair. Otherwise, they were more or less identical in jeans, trainers and black leather jackets, the front of which bristled with black camera equipment; huge lenses, flashes and various other black cylindrical objects, all suspended from their necks by broad black straps. In their hands they held takeaway cappuccinos and croissants.

'Bleedin' 'ell,' said Keith. 'Hardly got a single shot there. Agency's gonna bang me nuts between two bricks.'

The photographers sat down and stared moodily at their cappuccino cups. 'Always the bloody same, ain't it?' Keith added. 'These stars, they're desperate for us when they're struggling, but the minute they're back up there it's—' he mimed someone throwing out a hand – 'oooh! No photographs! They get all bloody grand again. And there we were, taking pictures of Belle Murphy when she couldn't get bloody arrested in London, let alone a part in a big film.'

Even though he had heard it all before, Ken gave a slight, despairing, disbelieving shake of his head in support.

'No bloody gratitude, that's the problem,' Keith went on.

'No. Yes.' Not that Ken cared. He had long since stopped expecting gratitude. Why should the celebs be grateful? The paps made money out of them; they, in a less direct but probably more profitable way, made money out of the paps. It was a straightforward business arrangement. Gratitude – and the moral values associated with it – didn't come into it.

'Never thought Belle Murphy would be back up the greasy pole, though. If anyone looked down and out, it was her.'

'Yeah.' Ken stuffed the rest of the croissant into his mouth and, chewing vigorously, screwed up the paper bag it had come in and lobbed it at a distant bin, which it missed.

'But then she gets a part in this new film and she's off like a greyhound at Walthamstow.'

Ken said nothing. He had nothing to say. What was there to say anyway?

The two men sighed in unison and surveyed the scene around them.

Ken heard Keith grunt as a tall, lissom blonde in very tight white jeans undulated slowly past, her high red heels clacking sharply on the shiny floor, her rather close-together eyes, which had a yellow tinge, fixed on the two photographers all the while. She had obviously realised they were paparazzi. 'Poor man's Paris Hilton,' Keith, leaning over, rasped in a stage whisper to Ken.

The blonde, who had two young children in tow – and tow was the word; they dragged at the ends of her arms unwillingly – narrowed her yellow eyes. 'Poor man's Mario Testino!' she spat viciously at Keith, before pulling the children after her so hard Ken feared their arms coming out of their sockets.

He looked after her in concern; the little party had stopped a few yards away and the blonde was shouting. Ken gathered, with his quick ear, that the little boy, who was straining desperately to break free, had dropped something, which had rolled away; a little red toy train. 'Oh, for Christ's sake, Cosmo,' the poor man's Paris was yelling in a harsh patrician voice. 'Just *stop* messing about. If you've lost it, you've lost it. That'll teach you. If you must take those bloody trains everywhere, you've got to keep hold of them. No. *No!*' she shouted, dragging the child back as he made a break for freedom. 'We've got a plane to catch, OK?'

'Please, Totty,' the boy begged. '*Please*. It's over there. I can *see* it.' His white-haired sister pleaded in his support, pulling hard on the arms determined to drag them away.

'Totty,' she cried. 'I can see the twain. It's just there . . .' She stabbed the air urgently with her other hand, which was holding a small, pink-striped toy cat.

It was true. Ken could see the little red twain. It was just there. It had sped across the hard, shiny walkway and come to an abrupt stop against a white-painted plant pot housing a weeping fig. He could see it. The children, all too agonisingly obviously, could see it. The blonde could see it too, Ken knew. It was sheer sadism that was preventing her from allowing him to go the few steps to pick it up.

'Mummy would let me. *Daddy* would,' the boy pleaded, obviously intent on using every weapon in his arsenal.

'Well, Daddy's not here; he's had to go abroad again,' the blonde retorted with what seemed to Ken an inappropriate sneer. 'And Mummy's working. It's not her holidays yet; she's coming out next week. *We're* going ahead,' she added savagely, 'we're going to have a *lovely* time in Italy by ourselves. Lots of your friends are out there already, like Hengist. He's in his villa . . .'

The boy was desperate now, Ken saw. He was sobbing and straining towards the plant pot with every muscle in his little body. 'Please, Totty. I *can't* lose it. Emma gave it to me.'

'*Emma!*' exclaimed the blonde, swishing her hair about her like a whip. 'If I hear that name *one more time* . . .' Her face contorted with angry contempt, she pulled him roughly away down the hall. The boy's desolate howls echoed after him and twisted Ken's soft heart. With terrifying suddenness he leapt to his feet and ran to the weeping fig so fast he almost skidded into it. Swiping down, he seized the train and pelted off down the departures hall after the boy. He was just in time, he saw. The blonde and her two charges had reached the passport control.

The boy, mewing in despair, was still resisting every inch of the way and casting longing looks over his shoulder. As Ken dashed up, as fast as his short legs could carry him, wheezing and holding the small red object out in front of him, the boy's eyes widened in an expression of unadulterated joy. He gave a shout of delight. All of a sudden, quite unexpectedly, Ken had a powerful feeling of wanting to cry too. He wondered if he had ever brought such joy to anyone before.

'This yours, sonny?' he asked in a gruff voice, disguising his emotion. The boy grabbed the train and clasped it passionately to his breast. He nodded and his eyes filled with tears again. Ken dropped to his hunkers and patted him on his dark blond head.

'Hooway!' cheered his sister, jumping up and down. 'Thank you, Mr Man.'

'No problem, little miss. What's your name then?'

'Hewo,' she lisped. 'And that's my bwother, Cosmo,' the child added, after a quick glance at her sibling confirmed that he was, as she apparently had anticipated, too overcome to speak.

'Well, nice to meet you, Hero.' Ken tweaked the girl's pink cheek, straightened and eyed the blonde, who was intensely occupied with the passports. She did not meet his gaze.

'Bit rough with them kids, aren't you?' he observed. 'Reckon you ought to be more careful.'

The yellow eyes narrowed and glittered as they met his. 'Reckon you ought to eff off,' she snarled, her accent mimicking his.

Ken shrugged and walked away. He'd done his best. He'd have told the parents, but they obviously weren't around. He shook his head. What was the point of having kids – especially nice kids like that – and handing them over to that blonde monster? Parents these days.

Nannies these days, come to that. The one Belle Murphy had had looking after Morning; the snotty skinny one with the hat and badge. She had been dreadful; Old Lemon Lips, he and Keith had dubbed her. Although the new one had been better, had been quite friendly in fact the few times he had seen her.

Ken wondered where Morning was at the moment – nice little baby, he was – and concluded that he too had probably gone off to Italy in advance of his mother. Did any child travel with its parents these days?

He returned to Keith, who was still grumbling. Ken paid no attention. He felt strangely light after the encounter with the boy. It was as if, for the first time in his life, he had done something worthwhile. The child's face had been dazzling in its teary happiness; wish I'd taken a photo of it, thought Ken.

Keith fiddled with his focus. 'You goin' to wait around for Angelina?' he asked conversationally. 'Hear she's comin' through later.'

'Ballerina or Jolie?' Ken asked facetiously. Dancing cartoon mouse or pillow-lipped, multi-fostering celebrity; suddenly, he didn't care.

Keith stared at him. 'Jolie, of course. The mouse ain't real. 'Ere,' he said, pushing his lugubrious grey features closer to Ken, 'you feelin' all right?'

Ken did not answer. Actually, he wasn't feeling remotely all right. A strange sensation had possessed him. Quite suddenly he felt, not mildly bored at the prospect of famous people – this was not unusual – but almost violently antagonistic. He felt as if he didn't want to see another celebrity in the whole of his life. It was no mere skittering thought, either; rather, a powerful, burning, almost acid antipathy that began in the depths of his stomach and radiated in every direction to the end of his every nerve.

'You all right?' Keith repeated. 'You look a bit funny, like.'

'Might have been a dodgy curry last night,' Ken murmured, rather alarmed by the powerful feelings now gripping him. He knew, even so, that the local Taj Mahal was in no way to blame for the sensations currently besieging him. His scrappy, stressful, badly nourished, low-job-satisfaction, pointless, unhappy and most of all lonely life now seemed to appear before Ken with a hideous and uncompromising starkness. He had one life – only one life. And what was he doing with it?

Keith was looking away now. He lifted his camera and squinted through it. 'That's the woman from *Dragons' Den*, ain't it?' he was asking himself. 'Nah . . .' he added, lowering his equipment. 'Too thin. Looked like her, though.'

Ken hardly heard. He was in the grip now of a strong urge to escape; the airport, the people, the cameras round his neck, his job most of all. He wanted to go somewhere where no celebrity would ever go, where paparazzi were unknown, where he could unwind a little and perhaps take stock.

Was it a mid-life crisis? Ken had waved forty goodbye some years ago, after all. Or did it come from watching all these people going past, happily bound on holidays, or making other interesting, glamorous journeys? But he had done the airport beat many times and never been seized with such a sensation before.

Keith, beside him, had raised his camera again. 'Chantelle from *Big Brother?*' he was murmuring now.

Ken stared down at the lenses protruding from his chest and felt, with a heavy, weary certainty, that if someone pressed a gun to his head and asked him to use the camera, he wouldn't be able to. As if he had come, with a dead stop, to the end of his professional road. He felt as if he never wanted to take another picture in his life.

'I think I need a holiday,' he said uncertainly. He could hardly remember the last one he had taken. With no one to go with, there had never seemed much point. A holiday. That would sort him out.

Keith nodded. 'Don't we all, mate?' he said briskly. 'I've got me eye on the Maldives, meself. Where you thinking then?'

Ken glanced up at the departures screen above them. The one at the top was a flight to Florence. 'Italy,' he found himself saying. Suddenly he had a vision of hot, sunny hills rolling away to a purple horizon and narrow, shadowy streets winding up through peaceful, ancient towns. He pictured himself, at some rustic taverna, at a rough-hewn olive-wood table drinking rich red wine from a thick, greenish glass and winding basil-scented spaghetti round his fork. Yes. Italy.

'Oh, yeah?' Keith's high-pitched Cockney voice drew him back to the unwelcome realities of Gatwick. 'Nice, Italy,' his colleague nodded. 'Ain't never bin there, but it always looks nice.

When you thinking of, then? I was wondering about August for the Maldives, meself.'

'Now,' said Ken, looking up at the departures screen again. There was another flight for Florence in two hours. Why not? He always carried his passport with him – you had to, in his job – and he had credit cards. Anything else, he could buy.

'Blimey,' said Keith, shaking his grey locks in amazement.

Chapter 34

The chaotic-looking chef with the big sunken eyes stood outside his establishment in his creased whites, frowning in the bright sunshine. He was trying to look at the front of his restaurant dispassionately. As someone who didn't live, breathe, sleep and, most of all, eat it might.

He was wondering whether he had done the right thing by painting the two large restaurant doors, curving together at the top beneath the entrance arch, sage green. Perhaps it had been too much to have all the outside chairs and tables painted the same shade.

Rodolfo, his old schoolfriend, now a decorator, had certainly been doubtful about the colour he was being asked to use. But I was right, Marco decided now. The sage did work. It was a cool, pretty colour, gave the place a contemporary lift and made the heat feel less oppressive on an intensely warm day like this one. Anyway, sage was one of his favourite herbs. The only herb Marco loved more than sage was basil, but basil green was not right for the restaurant; too dark. He had, however, planted basil in the two large terracotta pots that flanked the restaurant entrance.

His mind drifted back to sage. It perfumed and gave character to one of his favourite dishes, the *saltimbocca* of Rome, that combination of veal, prosciutto and sage that, with a squeeze of lemon, jumped in the mouth, which was what the name meant.

Marco swallowed, just thinking about it. Was there anything better than a really good *saltimbocca*? Well, there was plenty that was just as good, he thought, an image of the perfect San Daniele ham leaping effortlessly to mind; the waxy, near-transparent light red slices edged with white fat rippling over a heap of fresh rocket dressed with oil and shaved Parmigiano. Parmesan cheese, now there was another thing, and a thing he often ate for supper, late at night after the restaurant closed. Just a lump of Parmesan; rocky, saltily pungent, pale yellow and dressed with a little balsamic vinegar, nothing more. Except for a handful of peppery rocket, perhaps, the real stuff that blasted back down your nostrils. Sensational flavours. What more could anyone want?

Although, actually, when first he had become interested in cooking, Parmesan had not interested him in the slightest. Why should it? He had grown up with it; a large lump of it had sat on the big wooden family dining table for almost every meal, including breakfast. It had been another member of the family, almost, and more active than some, like Uncle Piero, who fell asleep as soon as he sat down.

The fact that his grandmother, mother and aunt all cooked had been nothing unusual; everyone else in the village did, after all. Delicious smells were as much a part of the décor of homes in Rocolo as the large, loud television, big table and tiled floor. In all the houses he knew, those of his family and schoolfriends, pots bubbled eternally on the stove; no oven was without something baking or slowly roasting. In the older people's houses, the ones with open fires, they still continued the ancient Tuscan custom of putting some beans in a glass flask with the end of the Chianti in it and leaving it in the embers to cook slowly overnight. There was nothing like the taste of *that*, Marco remembered. Soft beans in a winy, smoky sauce. He had never forgotten it.

Which was why, after chef school, after honing his trade in some of the great kitchens of Europe, he had come back to focus on the country cuisine of his homeland and youth. The memories of the simple food he had eaten as a child, food that had its roots in necessity, resourcefulness and whatever ingredients were to hand at the time, came to dominate his thinking and his cooking.

Respect for both customers and staff, as much as good food, was the other cornerstone of Marco's philosophy. Having experienced himself the miserable life of those employed in the great kitchens of the world, he had vowed that he would never replicate it in his own establishment. No one would shout. No one would lash out. No one would be, as Marco had been in London, forced to eat cornflakes in the kitchen while, outside in the restaurant people dined on luxury dishes he had helped to prepare but never tasted. Everyone would work reasonable shifts and would be paid properly, even the people who did the dishes.

Everyone he knew in the trade had warned Marco he was making life ridiculously hard for himself. But he had the courage of his convictions, and his counterintuitive attitude, together with his food, had paid off. Marco and his food was something the magazines were getting increasingly excited about. *Cucina povera*, as the magazines liked to call it. Simple flavours that spoke for themselves.

Marco, while grateful for the praise, was always embarrassed by the descriptions of himself. 'Shy', 'charming' and 'rangy' were the words most often used. But he was amused by the way the write-ups made it sound as if his décor was the result of months of agonising with a team of interior designers.

'Artfully simple' was a frequent phrase. But there had been nothing artful about it; simple had been the no-choice option. When he opened, money had been tight. He had not been able to afford carpets, or even particularly nice tiles, so the oak floors that had been there for centuries had been sanded and polished – he had done the sanding himself and now had those scars to add to various cut and burn injuries. The place had been filled with utilitarian wooden chairs and tables, bought second-hand and stained to look like the local olive wood, which he would have bought had he been able to afford it.

Marco pushed back some of his rumpled dark hair from his forehead and ground his big, clumsy-looking hands into his violet-circled eye sockets. The effect as he rubbed his closed lids produced, he noticed, a light red similar to that of a new Chianti.

He looked at his watch. Time to put the oxtail on. In six hours' time it would be a thick, dark, silky sauce rich with meaty, winy, bone-marrow flavour. After that he'd peel the peas. No other chef would bother, he knew, but getting the purée completely smooth was a point of pride.

He remembered how Rodolfo had laughed about his pea purée. 'You've got it wrong,' the decorator had declared.

'Have I?' Marco's heart had quickened. While he had never thought of Rodolfo as much of a cook, he had learnt over time that tips come from the most unexpected places. One must be receptive, that was the main thing.

Rodolfo grinned. 'You're missing something.'

'Yes? Yes?'

'It's obvious.'

'What is it? What am I missing?' Marco felt his eyes about to pop from his head with desperate eagerness. What did Rodolfo know about pea purée that he didn't?

'A life, *amico mio.*' And with that, Rodolfo had plunged his brush into his pot and cheerfully carried on.

Rodolfo didn't understand, Marco mused, how much food meant to him; how much pleasure he got from the simplest of things. The simpler, the more pleasurable, in fact; just-picked fennel and dewy lettuce were the most exquisite luxuries imaginable and the taste of a fresh carrot could bring tears to the eyes. He had said this to Rodolfo, who had laughed and said that, personally, onions were the only vegetables that made him cry.

He looked at his restaurant again, and felt a hot wave of love and pride. It was a former wine cellar, whose cave-like mouth stretched across the entire front of the building in a shallow arch. This formed the restaurant entrance. Inside was a long, wide space with a plain wooden floor and a brick barrelled ceiling painted white. It was simple and intimate, as well as wonderfully cool on hot days, especially given the elderly but vigorous vine that trailed around the doorway.

It held twelve small tables and chairs, and a wood-topped bar and serving area down one side, from the back of which a flight of ancient spiral stone stairs led up to the kitchen. Above that was another room, large, beamed and dusty, which Marco intended at some stage to convert into another dining room, and above that, in the roof, were the tiny pair of low-ceilinged, whitewashed rooms – bathroom and bedsitting room – in which Marco slept the few hours he was not in his restaurant.

All this was contained in a higgledy-piggledy yellow stone building with a scattering of different-sized windows, each flanked with dark-wood louvred shutters, across the front. It was one of a row – or rather a curve – of similarly ancient, mellow and slightly crumbling structures, which followed a winding, cobbled street rising from the bottom of the hill on which the village was built, up to the main square at the top where the church and the shops were.

Marco's stood on the steepest bend, almost at the top, and one of the advantages of this was that everyone in Rocolo passed it regularly – on foot, mainly, too, as the ancient, golden-stoned village, perched on its hill, had been classified an Ancient Monument and cars were not allowed. Although scooters and bicycles were, thank goodness; dragging supplies up the steep hill on foot – as his forebears no doubt had had to – would, Marco felt, be taking his enthusiasm for authenticity rather too far. He would not be without his little red Vespa, his companion since the age of seventeen, for anything.

Most Rocolo residents tended to keep their cars in the purpose-built car park at the bottom of the hill and walk about the village otherwise. This meant that, happily for Marco's business, there were few locals who didn't partake of a morning cappuccino, daytime espresso or Prosecco at lunchtime or in the evening there. At dinner and lunch moreover, especially on Sundays, the place was heaving with Rocolo families; the large-hipped mothers, the smiling fathers, the wise-looking grannies and the children with eyes like dark pools among whom Marco had grown up. All crowded round tables piled with bread, wine, pasta and whatever big-flavoured delicacy the popular local chef had produced that morning.

The second advantage of the bend was that the long-ago builders who had erected the buildings round it had set Marco's particular one, which was right in the middle of the curve, at a slightly different angle from its neighbours, creating a small courtyard before it. This, covered in cobbles, was picturesque in its own right, but looked positively festive covered in the tables under the large cream shades Marco put out during the summer months. Its position on the bend, in addition, was the perfect vantage point to watch anything and anyone coming or going.

'*Ciao!*' Some coffee-drinkers were leaving and he waved them off.

He watched approvingly as Daria, the waitress, came out and cleared away the coffee cups from some earlier breakfasters. Daria was pretty, certainly, with her doe-like face with its creamy skin and the shiny black ponytail, which flopped down her back. But what Marco admired most about her was the speed with which she could chop a carrot and her neatness at table-setting. Order and cleanliness was at the base of everything, Marco reflected, pushing a big hand through his disorderly mop of dark hair.

The hair was clean, though. He washed it every night in the flat above the restaurant that had been just a temporary place to sleep at first, but had now become his home. Would he stay there alone into old age? Maybe.

He was hardly most women's idea of good looking, after all, he knew. First there was his hair, dangling in curly clumps, chopped at with the kitchen scissors whenever it got too long. His face, with its great, wide eyes, long cheeks and squashed nose, looked, even to him, as if someone had trodden on it. His towering height, with long arms and big hands, which seemed to wave about awkwardly and redundantly whenever – and admittedly these occasions were rare – they found themselves without a knife or ingredient of some kind. His long legs, forever becoming tangled in things; his large feet forever stumbling over things. Outside the kitchen, he was clumsy and ill at ease. Only within it were his movements sure, fluid and graceful.

Only in the kitchen did he miraculously not bang into anything, not even the other chefs at the scurrying, hurrying height of the lunch or evening rush hour. Only in the kitchen was his every move as assured, perfect, beautiful and full of intent as a ballet dancer's. In his kitchen, he was an artist. And to his kitchen he would now return.

He looked over the courtyard once more before disappearing inside. And it was then that he saw her.

She was walking up the steep cobbled street towards him; flushed as even the fittest usually were by this point. She was about twenty-five and the hair that swished about her shoulders was as thick and shining as squid ink. Her wide, creamy face made him think instantly of pannacotta and her pale arms and legs, the beautiful sheeny white of freshest leeks, were set off by a dress the bright yellow of saffron rice.

As she got closer, he saw her pretty, full mouth was a rich, strawberry-semifreddo pink. A hot wave of excitement washed suddenly over Marco. Rocolo, being one of the jewels of the Chianti tourist trail, attracted its fair share of beautiful women. Some of them even famous. But he had never looked at any of them the way he was looking at this woman now. She was enchanting. In an understated sort of way. But understated was good, Marco thought. You could have too much of that painted-up, tight-skirted, high-heeled Italian look. After a while, it could all seem a little obvious, a bit intimidating, even.

Darcy was starving. All the way up the narrow, winding street of the village she had been assaulted on all sides by tantalising smells of cooking issuing from the houses on either side. Powerful whiffs of garlic and onions, snatches of tomato, deep base notes of wine and beef and sharp, grassy jabs of herb. She had not eaten since leaving the hotel in Florence that morning, where there had been only time to snatch a roll and a quick cappuccino.

Admittedly, until now she had hardly noticed the state of her stomach. She had spent the entire time she was being driven down the motorway on the mobile. First there had been a long call from Mitch about the delay in starting the principal photography – 'They always are, and it's only to be expected, baby, on something so goddamn big and complicated as this one' – and then another from Sam at Wild about another forthcoming fashion shoot, this time for shoes. The prospect, after what she had endured at Rumtopf's hands, made Darcy's heart sink.

As Sam finally rang off, Darcy unlocked her eyes from the beige back of the driver's seat at which she had been staring to notice, with a jolt of joy, that they were off the motorway and driving through some of the loveliest countryside she had ever seen.

She pressed her nose against the tinted glass, open-mouthed with admiration. So this was the famous Chianti. Darcy wasn't sure what she had been expecting – dust and heat, perhaps – but, looking at the land outside the window, her first thought was that it was like the most beautiful garden. The countryside they were passing through, on winding grey roads that dived up and down, was full of gentle green hills packed with verdant, decorative detail: some fluffy with pines, others ridged neatly with vines, still others topped with the dark green flames of cypresses. Here and there, a glimpse of sun-warmed, golden stone, a hint of red-tiled roof, the occasional exciting turret, even, denoted some dwelling.

It was so extraordinarily neat and ordered, Darcy thought, framing the tranquil scene in her fingers and thumbs. It glowed richly in the afternoon sun, below the hot purple-blue of the sky.

She felt a warmth inside; a sense almost of recognition. For all the fact that the place was new to her, she felt immediately at home.

It was all so peaceful. Nothing moved, though every field and hill showed signs of labour – the vines, after all, had not planted themselves in those orderly rows; the cypresses had been spaced thus neatly and carefully by human hands; the rich, chocolate-brown powder of the tilled fields been achieved by no other means than applied effort. Yet no one was labouring at any of this now the sun was high and white and burning. No doubt they were all at lunch. Which was, Darcy suddenly felt, where every sensible person should be. She slid the window down and a gust of hot, herby air sprang into the car.

A wave of energy and excitement seemed to spring in with it. For all the disappointment, exhaustion and bewilderment caused by recent events and travels, Darcy felt suddenly refreshed. She had a vision of vine-shaded trattorias in ancient hilltop villages where dark, cool streets wound up to sunny main squares presided over by barn-like churches with marble fronts. She thought of brilliant sunshine and cool shadows, of resonant flavours; thick-crusted breads, golden slicks of oil, and red wine that was almost black. As her stomach gave a mighty roar, Darcy also thought that lunch could be delayed no longer.

She leant forward and asked the driver, whose name was Marcello, if there was anywhere good to eat in the area. She watched the back of his neatly trimmed black head nod enthusiastically. '*Sì, signorina.* Very good restaurant in Rocolo.'

'Rocolo? That's a village?'

'*Sì.* Ees over there.' He stabbed a tanned digit to the other side from where she had been looking.

Darcy looked out, and gasped. Some distance back from the main highway along which they drove rose a good-sized hill reached by a winding road. Its lower reaches were studded with scrub, trees and flashes of rock, but nothing beyond halfway up could be seen of the original promontory, covered as it was with a sunny hilltop village of exactly the type she had imagined.

While no doubt in the place itself there were streets and spaces and order, the effect from a distance was chaotic: houses in all shapes and sizes and all shades of the spectrum from cinnamon to apricot were seemingly crammed and piled one on top of the other, like a fantastical and ornate stone hat. On the very top, the towers of what was presumably the church protruded like two yellow stone fingers. All the other roofs – universally red tiled, but of all ages – bristled with TV aerials, which made Darcy think immediately of fish bones. Her stomach roared again, demanding to be fed.

'There's a good restaurant there?' Darcy asked Marcello, swallowing at the thought.

'The best. Ees at the top. You cannot miss it.'

'Let's go!' Darcy exclaimed.

The driver explained that no cars were allowed in the village. 'But ees all right. I wait for you here. Villa, she ees not far from here. We go there afterwards.'

Try as Darcy might to persuade Marcello to come with her, he refused. He seemed amazed by the offer. 'My wife, she pack me lunch,' he smiled, producing a wicker hamper from the footwell of the passenger seat. 'I sit here. I read the paper. I fine.'

Darcy walked happily into the village, glad to be out of the car and under this deep blue sky, relishing the heat. The climb up the cobbled street pulled enjoyably on her muscles as the gradient steepened and twisted. The clearly ancient buildings on each side rose sheer as cliffs, albeit cliffs covered in flaking plaster and romantically rioting creeper and vine and, via deep-silled windows, emitting delicious smells from their shadowy depths.

As she walked, Darcy, getting steadily hungrier, looked about her for the restaurant Marcello had mentioned. Ah yes, that must be it. On the bend, with cream sunshades, and pretty pale-green chairs and tables. And that strange-looking wild-haired man outside, who was staring at her for some reason.

Chapter 35

Just as Darcy was arriving at the restaurant at the top of Rocolo, Emma, with Morning, was arriving at the bottom in a bus from the airport.

Armed with nothing more than the vaguest of directions from Belle as to where the villa actually was, she had decided to make her way to what seemed the nearest town and make further enquiries from there. Morning was too small and the terrain too unfamiliar to permit any other course of action. She needed, Emma knew, to be near shade and a source of mineral water for mixing the baby's formula.

Catching the bus had, in the end, been a much simpler matter than expected. The clerk at a travel enquiries desk had been pleased to identify the bus she needed – to a village called Rocolo – and advise where to get it from. A smart brown air-conditioned coach had arrived at the advertised time and a couple of businessmen had got on with her; much smarter than British businessmen, it seemed to Emma, with neat, short hair, woven, greenish jackets, charcoal trousers and squashy leather briefcases. They also smelt deliciously of very strong aftershave.

With Morning his usual peaceful self in her arms, Emma sat

happily by a window halfway down the aftershave-scented bus. The comfortable coolness, the thrum of the bus and possibly the aftershave too combined to relax the state of constant vigilance she had been in since leaving London. Emma drifted gratefully into a light sleep. She awoke to find that the coach had stopped.

'Rocolo!' the driver was shouting, leaning out from his cab and looking back down the bus through his mirror shades.

Emma, confused with sleep, scrambled hurriedly to her feet. As she grabbed the bag of her and Morning's things, which she had placed on the seat next to her, the baby woke with a start and began to wail. Trying to strap him into his carrier whilst hurrying down the bus with a bag was no easy business, but Emma managed it and stumbled out into a small car park. The intense heat bouncing up off the tarmac hit her almost with the power of a fist.

Squinting upward in the brilliant sunshine, Emma saw the hilltop town above her. It was, she thought, an extraordinary sight, wonderfully romantic and ancient, with its red-tiled eaves and the higgledy-piggledy windows looking down on her like hundreds of little eyes. As Morning gave a sudden mew and another, much nearer, pair of little eyes flew open, Emma recollected herself and set forth purposefully. She couldn't stand gawping while a hungry baby clamoured to be fed.

The businessmen from the bus were, she saw, heading for the end of the car park. Hurrying after them, jiggling the fretful baby, Emma saw a narrow cobbled lane, which disappeared beneath an ancient arch. This, presumably the entrance to the village, was reached via a small, pretty bridge over a stream. Immediately before this old, gracious bridge, redolent of a more peaceful age, was something modern, ungracious and anything but peaceful: the young, sunglassed driver of a shining red sports car, who was addressing a policeman in a cap and blue short sleeves in a less than respectful tone.

The drama, Emma saw, was drawing quite a crowd; the businessmen had stopped, as had several people coming down from the village. They seemed as interested in the car as in its driver. Low, flat and wide, all gleaming red metal, curved tinted windows and enormous silver twin exhausts, it was, Emma thought, an arrogant-looking vehicle and its driver, wide of shoulder, chiselled of face and evidently aggressive, an arrogant-looking man.

He was very tanned and strikingly handsome, with rippling cheekbones, big mouth and strong white teeth. The women who had stopped – from a willowy young mother to a thickset granny – were staring at him in admiration. But Emma, whose idea of extreme male good looks were turned entirely on a certain tall, awkward blond boy she had met in the airport, viewed the man – now gesticulating rudely at the policeman – more critically.

He looked, she thought, expensive but vain in a tight white T-shirt on whose front, beneath the mass of gold chains, crosses and pendants he wore, the glittering name 'Gucci' flowed over undulating pectorals. His bare, brown and powerfully muscled arms bristled with bracelets and an expensive-looking watch, and he wore a black and white knitted hat covered in interlinked Chanel Cs.

'Whaddya mean, I can't get my car up there?' he was demanding in an American accent, stabbing one of many beringed fingers at the small cobbled lane leading under the arch. 'I'm starving. I need a burger, like, now, man. Look, man,' he complained to the ever-more-obdurate traffic policeman, 'you don't know who you're dealing with here, yeah? Don't you know who I am?'

Christian Harlow was not having a good day. This bone-headed Italian cop's refusal to let him drive at top speed up the village street was merely the latest example of how events at the moment seemed to be conspiring against him. Why the hell shouldn't he, anyway? The crumbling old heap of a village needed something fast and new in it. The place was a mess, you could see that from here.

But hey, Christian told himself, the cop was jealous. Sure he was – the Ferrari he'd had the film company hire for his entertainment while in Italy was a great car. He'd had a blast roaring up and down the country lanes in it this morning – Jesus, they made them small round here – but now he was hungry and this shitty little village was the nearest place to where he was staying. He'd zoom in and stop at the burger bar.

'*Walk?*' he shouted angrily as the policeman mimed ambulatory movements. 'Are you kidding? I'm a star, baby, OK? Stars don't walk. *Losers* walk.'

It was on the tip of Christian's foot, expensively shod in Versace sandals, to put the pedal to the metal and roar away. But where the hell would he get his burger then? Besides, he wanted to check out the scene – and the chicks. He could do with some company, Christian thought. There was bound to be someone willing to have a little fun with a Hollywood superstar.

Until, that was, the opportunity arose for the other fun he was planning. With his co-star Darcy Prince, whose picture Greg Cucarachi had shown him. She was cute, Christian thought, although slightly fuller of figure than the ladder-chested waifs he was used to. What was most important, of course, was that she had a big part in the film. But the fact she had nice tits was a bonus. English too, with that kind of dewy look. Darcy would, Christian thought, make a nice change from all those Fake Bake blondes he'd had in Hollywood so far. Of course, she'd be unable to resist him. No woman could when Christian Harlow really switched on the charm.

And he'd already switched it on Darcy when he'd smouldered at her in Puccini's. She'd been there with that loser Mitch Masterson, who Christian knew hated him because of the mess he had made of Belle. He'd meant nothing by the look at the time, apart from to tease Mitch and amuse himself by mentally undressing his companion. She had given him a pretty hot look back, however. And the promise in her eyes – and the rest of her – was one Christian fully intended to take advantage of now.

What was this freak of a cop saying to him? Christian frowned and tried to understand, not a process that came to him easily. *Vespa?* What in hell's name did *that* mean?

Christian was now aware of someone stepping forward. 'I think,' that someone said in English, in an English accent Christian didn't recognise, 'that the policeman means you can ride a Vespa up into the village.'

It was, Christian saw, a young girl with a baby that had spoken. He stared at her, his big lips twitching assessingly. No, not his sort. No make-up. There was something about her look that he didn't like either. Kind of stern. Gay, probably. No straight woman ever looked at him like that. Although she had a baby, but he didn't do babies, especially black ones.

What she had said now filtered through to him. 'Vespa?' He frowned in disbelief. One of those stupid little scooters? There was no way he was getting on one of those. A Harley, maybe. But something that sounded like a pissed-off wasp . . . ?

The policeman now started to bend his legs in a circular fashion, one after the other, whilst holding his arms out in front. 'Or you could ride a bicycle,' the girl translated now, as the policeman, now evidently enjoying himself, made his movements more exaggerated and comic and the watching crowd, growing all the time, tittered. Thunder gathered in Christian's heart. He threw his arm across the low, black leather back of the driver's seat, flung the Ferrari violently into reverse and screeched away. Grudgingly, he parked the car and, once the crowd had dispersed, trudged across to the bridge to begin the ascent to the village on foot.

The cobbles dug into the thin undersides of his sandals as he climbed up the steep slope. The sun beat down on his perspiring forehead. Bloody Italy, thought Christian. He'd never wanted to come here in the first place; had no interest in Europe whatsoever. Who did? As markets went, it was a million miles behind the only one that really mattered, his own native US of A.

And now, of course, he was stuck here for weeks on end. One of the other reasons that this morning had been such an ass-pain was the call he had got from his agent, Greg Cucarachi. Cucarachi had informed him that principal photography on the film had been set back by a week or so while locations were finalised.

'Jesus,' Christian had shouted. 'Nothing on this goddamn film is finalised. Locations, actors, whatever. What is it with this guy Saint?'

'The fee he's paying you and the fact the film will be huge,' Greg had replied immediately. 'And as it happens, another actor *has* been finalised.'

Christian then learnt that Belle Murphy had been given a part in *Galaxia*. 'You're kidding me!' he screeched.

He felt sick at the prospect. He had moved on from Belle; she had been a stepping stone and he had well and truly stepped on her. The nearest Christian ever got to guilt stirred weakly within him whenever he thought of how he had treated her. He never wanted to see Belle again and had never expected to. He was on the fast track up; she was on an equally speedy plunge down, they had met on the way, he had used her, that was all. So why had Jack Saint cast her in the biggest film of the year?

'Don't you read the papers?' Greg asked.

Christian, who was capable of extreme sensitivity but only in relation to himself, bristled at the mild exasperation in the agent's tone. 'No, I fucking don't,' he yelled. 'I pay people like you to read them for me.'

'In which case,' Greg rejoined smoothly, 'let me explain. Belle had a hit with some Shakespeare play in London. She's hot again – well, pretty warm.'

'You say this movie's gonna take eight weeks to shoot once principal photography actually starts? Eight weeks with *her*?'

'Eight weeks in Italy, yes,' Greg said. 'But that's only the ceremonial space city bits – Saint wanted real palazzo interiors for them. There's about three months of shooting elsewhere, plus post-production—'

'I don't wanna see her!' Christian interrupted violently. 'Saint's gotta drop her from the film!' Not least because his chances of bedding Darcy Prince would be badly scuppered by having his banshee of an ex around.

'Not much chance of getting her dropped,' Greg remarked, in a strangled voice that Christian suspected might be suppressing a laugh. He felt a surge of fury. How dare that asshole Cucarachi laugh at him? Him, the hottest actor in Hollywood right at this moment. He was about to explode again, but Greg, sensing this, got in first. 'Hey, but don't worry,' he soothed. 'There's a way round this. You don't have to see her. Or, rather, she doesn't have to see you.'

'How d'ya figure that out?' Christian demanded hysterically. 'We'll be on set together.'

'Sure, but whenever you're on set you're in disguise. You're the evil lord Jolyon Wooloo, half lizard and half man,' Greg reminded his client gingerly, unable quite to believe that Christian was unaware of this central fact.

'That's the main part, yeah?' Christian said aggressively.

Greg confirmed that it was. 'It's a great part. Your costume's gonna be incredible. You'll wear a lizard mask made of latex. It takes four hours of make-up every day . . .'

'*What?*'

'Hey, all this is in your contract. Didn't you read it?'

Christian fired hot air impatiently out of his nostrils. Of all the stupid questions. He hadn't read anything in the contract apart from how much he was getting paid. 'I've got a latex mask on my head? In the middle of an Italian summer?' he demanded, returning to what he considered the main point. 'I'm gonna cook, man.'

'You get cooled between takes by air pumped through a tube.'

'Big fucking deal,' growled Christian. His big film break was looking less sexy all the time. Eight weeks in Italy with Belle Murphy, dressed as a lizard in a latex mask. Great.

'Remember, it's a big part,' Greg reminded him. 'It's gonna make you huge.'

It had better, Christian thought as he stomped up the cobbles into Rocolo.

Chapter 36

Rocolo seemed to Emma the most romantic place she had ever seen. And certainly one of the oldest. Following the cobbled street as it snaked up the hill, between the ancient houses, made her feel she was a character in a storybook.

She climbed past a tempting-looking restaurant, where cream parasols stood about a cobbled courtyard and a pretty woman in a yellow dress was sliding a spoon meditatively into her mouth. Beyond this, the street gave another twist before flattening out into a small arcaded square.

There was a church at one end with an elaborate frontage of white stone scrolls and pillars against a background of soft raspberry pink. In the recesses of the arcade arches, which framed the other three sides of the square, were intriguing, old-fashioned-looking shops. They were cheerful and brightly lit with glass doors and, inside, shopworkers in white jackets stood behind big display counters.

The shops seemed, on the whole, to specialise in one item, or one type. 'Salumeria' announced the first one. Emma stared down into a window heaped with dried sausages, of all shapes and sizes and different colours, neatly piled, arranged in rows, bristling with tickets explaining types and prices. From the ceiling hung a chorus line of bronzed pig haunches, again distinguished by various ribbons and labels. Some even had rosettes, as at a horse show. Whenever the door opened, which was frequently – the shop seemed extremely popular – a gust of tangy, briny, savoury air swirled round Emma's nostrils.

Further along the ancient, shadowy arcade with its broad, ancient vaulting, between touristy shops selling pottery and postcards, was a baker with big, unfamiliar-shaped loaves in his window, and a cheesemonger with great wheels of Parmesan in his. The combination would make a giant's picnic, Emma thought. Behind the heaps of parsley and lemons in the fishmonger's front window, a piratical-looking character was gutting silver fish at incredible speed, the fish and his knife flashing as he worked. There was a greengrocer with boxes of fruit outside and a general store with pasta and bottles of olive oil in the window. Emma went in and was delighted to find an enormous supply of mineral water.

Women and small children milled about the square and under the arcades, carrying baskets and bags and pushing little carts. The morning shop was obviously in full swing, and not one person, Emma observed, seemed to be lacking something to carry. It was a cheerful and lively scene and looked infinitely more fun than going to Tesco.

As she passed near the church the sound of children laughing drew Emma, and she found, round the back, to her immense delight, a sizeable, safe-looking and obviously new children's playground, all ropewalks, foam-padded ground and colourful metal climbing frames. There were benches under shady trees, and even a water fountain, which the children were making enthusiastic use of, both to drink and to splash each other.

Definitely somewhere to bring Morning, Emma thought,

kissing the dark head of her charge, who, after a quickly admini-stered bottle, was now looking about contentedly. Of course, he was too little for the equipment, but just seeing other children at play would be good for him and help start to develop and expand his sense of the world. Children loved other children, and at the moment Morning was unaware that any apart from himself actually existed. Although he seemed to be making up for it now, his head swivelling excitedly as he watched the others running about.

Emma remembered the man in the red sports car. He too was self-evidently the centre of a universe in which no one else mattered. That people might wish to preserve their ancient and beautiful village from being turned into a racetrack had not seemed to cross his mind. Or what passed for a mind under that stupid hat. He was handsome, yes, but there had been something big-boned, brutal and elementary about his broad forehead and wide face and cheekbones. His was not a delicate type of beauty, like the boy in the airport. Like . . . Orlando.

She suppressed a sigh. Of course she wasn't going to see him again; there was no point thinking about it. She could not help wondering, all the same, how Orlando was managing with his parents, his approaching A level results and his truly hideous-sounding houseguests.

'It's *your* restaurant?' Darcy was asking the crumpled man in whites in surprised tones. He really was very tall for an Italian – over six feet, she estimated. But you obviously got tall Italians. There seemed no reason why not.

'Every inch,' Marco declared proudly. 'I am chef-patron.'

And there she had been, thinking he was some sort of idle vegetable chopper. Washer-up even. He looked too earthy, somehow, to be a chef.

'My name is Marco,' the chef added. 'I grew up in Rocolo, and even though I've worked in restaurants all over the world, it was always here, back in Italy, that I wanted to open my own.'

She nodded. 'I'm Darcy.'

Darcy. Pretty name, he thought dreamily. Unusual.

'That sounds great. What sort of food do you do?' Her eyes, he noticed, were febrile with interest.

He sighed happily. He was tongue-tied with women, but this was the one subject in the world on which he could hold forth with the utmost confidence to anyone. 'Country food, you know. Of the region. Traditional dishes, with perhaps a little modern twist here and there.'

'Is that what I can smell?' Darcy was sniffing hard. The scent was strong, herby and delicious.

'*Sì.* Today we are doing a minestrone with beans and pesto. We make it with rice too, so much rice you can stand your spoon up in it and watch it fall slowly back down. Oh, and with a big glug of peppery, golden olive oil to finish . . . What is that noise?' Marco asked suddenly, inclining his big shaggy head the better to listen.

Darcy did not answer. She had no intention of admitting it was her stomach.

Lunch started with an *aperitivo* of crisp Prosecco with salami and olives, along with a dish of bright green beans; a speciality of the region, Marco explained. Then followed some sausage and pea risotto and afterwards lemon ice cream. A succession of wonders, Darcy thought.

Never before had she tasted such food. Everything was so fresh, so colourful, so obviously full of goodness and flavour. It seemed to Darcy, as she ate, that of all the things she regretted about her past, she regretted its utter lack of flavour the most. Food had never been a priority, or even an interest among the people with whom she had so far spent her time. And how much better things would have been if it had. Even Niall's deception would have felt better from the other side of a really good meal.

Funny, too, how eating on her own, far from being a self-conscious and uncomfortable exercise, was actually a treat, as the lack of someone else to distract her meant she could really concentrate on the flavours. It seemed to Darcy, as she absorbedly ate this lunch, that she had only ever fuelled herself at tables before. Only now, here under the cool shade outside this little but excellent restaurant, was she really eating for the first time.

From the upstairs window, Marco watched her. He, too, was struck with wonder. Her face was so beautiful; the long sweep of lashes like the tiny tentacles on the most delicious of sea urchins. The perfect ears that actually really were shell-like, reminding him of the tiny, tasty clams he liked to use for *spaghetti alle vongole*. The cheek whose flushed, delicate pink reminded him of the creamiest peach pannacotta. Her lips, meanwhile, were not, as he had first imagined, the colour of the most perfect raspberry sorbet. No, they were redder, more like the tomato ice he had recently been experimenting with and which had actually turned out rather well.

He watched, swallowing, as, again and again, she passed the shining fork, piled with risotto, between the pink pillows of her lips into the warm red cave beyond. He felt a rush of excitement as her mouth eagerly closed round the fork, pursed and flexed outward in a suck. At the exact moment, he knew the nutty, creamy flavour of the rice was combining with the fresh sweetness of the peas. As she ate the final forkful he saw her chin jerk upwards in ecstasy, her throat and long, beautiful jawbones tilt backwards as she swallowed. With a satisfied sigh she opened her eyes.

This, thought Marco, was a woman who, for all her slight build, really appreciated food. He had sensed this was so from the start, which was why he had arranged a handful of his prized green fava beans, the early, baby broad beans he so loved to eat raw, in a dish for her; a privilege he accorded normally to only his very favourite customers.

His hands now shook with excitement as he assembled the dessert course she had ordered. What was the matter with him? Beautiful women came to the restaurant all the time. Most of them left him cold. The arrival of a really beautiful woman was something he had grown to dread. Pretty women usually didn't eat at all, just poked salads about and crumbled the breadsticks, which Marco hated to see. They were taking up a place at his table a food-lover could have had.

Darcy, lost in contemplation of how absolutely delicious that pea risotto had been, almost jumped when the white plate bearing two creamy scoops over which strips of candied lemon peel had been laid descended to the table in front of her. She looked up, startled, to find herself staring into the distracted eyes of the chaotic-looking chef, who seemed so ill at ease. But why, Darcy wondered. He was obviously spectacularly talented.

'Lemon pannacotta ice cream,' Marco murmured in a low voice that made Darcy immediately think of rich chocolate. The big brown hands – they were scarred, she noticed, yet had long and sensitive fingers – moved in explication. 'Made with Sicilian lemons. The best.'

He watched her dark eyes glow at this; they had the burnish, he felt, of candlelight on a perfect chocolate-covered coffee bean. Then, out of the corner of his eye, Marco saw something move behind him.

He turned, and his heart sank. An arrestingly handsome man, dressed from head to foot in obviously expensive designer clothes as well as a great deal of jewellery, was making his way up the slope. He had the muscle-bound swagger Marco associated most readily with the gym and was obviously heading straight for his restaurant. Marco sighed. The few minutes alone with the beautiful food-lover had been delicious, but they were all too obviously over. Not least because the muscle-bound swaggerer seemed to recognise her.

Does that restaurant do burgers? Christian had been wondering as he panted up the slope. There were no familiar American megacorporation logos plastered all over its sunshades, as he would have preferred. But that chick in the yellow dress sitting underneath one of them, there was something familiar about her. Christian's thick-cut, sensuous lip curved in triumph as he got closer. That dark hair, that pale skin, those very nice baps under that yellow dress.

'Darcy?' he called. 'Darcy Prince?'

Darcy, whose tastebuds were exploding like a firework display with intense lemonness, looked up, disconcerted. She did not immediately recognise the man standing at the edge of the parasol-shaded tables. But then he strode forward, positioned himself in front of her and tore off his sunglasses. With a lift of her heart and a swoop in her stomach Darcy found herself staring up into the same pair of eyes that had hypnotised her in LA. Christian Harlow. She never forgot a name, and his face was unforgettable anyway.

'Darcy,' Christian repeated, pleased at the effect he had had. She would be putty in his hands, he could see that immediately. He fixed his eyes on her breasts. Jesus, they even looked real. That was an unexpected bonus. Especially considering she had no bra on.

Marco, pretending to push chairs in a few tables away, glowered from behind the sunshades. This muscle-bound beast of a man, all cheekbones and cock. He was staring at her breasts without even attempting to hide it. And I, thought Marco, I stood before her for five minutes studiously trying not to notice how her nipples were like small cherries, deliciously round.

'Christian,' Darcy breathed, all confusion. Soaring to the top of the muddle in her brain came the memory of Mitch calling this man an asshole in the LA restaurant, but this faded immediately, and after that Darcy found herself unable to frame a single coherent thought. Her ability to appear normal deserted her. She blushed hot, went cold and felt shaky and oddly light, as if she might float or fall off the chair. 'What are you . . . I mean . . . what are *you* doing here?'

'Same as you,' Christian returned triumphantly.

'You're in *Galaxia*?' Her eyes were wide with surprise and excitement.

'Yeah!' he growled.

'I had no idea!' Darcy exclaimed.

He *loved* her voice. That prissy, high-end English, all repressed fire. Sexeee! He smiled at her with lazy confidence. Man, was he gonna enjoy himself. You could just tell by looking at her that she'd never had a really good bang.

'You alone?' he asked her, pulling out a chair and sitting down. He placed his elbows on the table, sank his chin on to them and looked up at her with his biggest, softest eyes as she nodded. Great. So that loser of an agent, who hated him anyway, wasn't with her, nor some geek of a boyfriend or other. These British actresses always had geeky boyfriends. Greasy and pale, with thick glasses. That was how they made the guys over there, Christian assumed.

'No boyfriend?' he pushed. Unsubtle, sure, as they'd only just met, but best to find out where you stood from the start.

Christian didn't like to waste time and had discovered, moreover, that women didn't mind him asking them about their boyfriends. Darcy Prince, he realised with satisfaction, was no exception. Better still, a spasm of anger shot across her face as she shook her hair in a negative. The bust-up had been messy, Christian triumphantly deduced.

'You weren't both on the same page, huh?' he hazarded, his voice and eyes melting.

Darcy blinked. She disliked American phrases like this normally. They were lazy and implied the whole of life to be some over-generalised mush of unremarkable experience that took no account of individuals and circumstances. But in Christian's mouth – with that expression in his eyes – it sounded profound and sympathetic and, besides, it wasn't inappropriate.

'In a bad place?' Christian probed.

Darcy shrugged. 'Not really. In a luxury flat in London, as it happens.'

Christian didn't do irony. He looked puzzled. What had London got to do with it? He knew the place: Harrods, hotels and a pub run by Madonna. Or something like that.

'But if you mean, were we happy, then I suppose we weren't,' Darcy illuminated. She raised her eyebrows and shot him a rueful grin.

Christian returned this with a more predatory one of his own. He was perceptive in the extreme, but only when it came to his own wants, and he knew a woman on the rebound when he saw one. This girl was, he guessed, ripe for the picking. And anything else he chose to do to her.

'Yeah,' he said, pulling a sympathetic face. 'I guess I know where you're coming from. I've been in a bad place too.' In his case, the bad place was the discovery that the powerful actress whose companion he had recently been had slipped a little in the

Hollywood hierarchy. A part she had wanted had gone to someone else. Christian had already decided that, as a result, he would go to someone else too. The only question had been who, but now the answer was obvious. This up-and-coming British actress, his latest co-star.

'He deceived me,' Darcy remarked, her tongue loosened by wine, tiredness, the good lunch she had just eaten and, most powerfully of all, loneliness. There was, she felt, real enquiry in the eyes of the handsome man opposite. He seemed genuinely to want to know; to *care*, even. As she outlined some of the circumstances, Christian, as he always did at this point in his conquests, started to switch off. Then a name dragged him unexpectedly back.

'It was when I saw him on the front page of all the papers with *Belle Murphy* . . .' Darcy was saying.

Christian fought to conceal his horror. He was an actor, after all. The coincidence was appalling. *His* ex . . . *her* ex . . . *together?* He vaguely remembered the pictures she was talking about.

'I mean, of all the stupid, plastic, artificial idiots . . .' Darcy's face was flushed with annoyance now. Her eyes flashed and her nostrils flared. It wasn't, Christian realised, going to help his campaign if he now admitted he had been with Belle himself. Perhaps, later, he could gently slip it in. But – *Jesus* – that woman. She got everywhere. Still, he could control the situation; there had been plenty of similar ones before.

'What do you think I should have for lunch?' he asked, changing the subject abruptly.

The mention of food, he saw, had a miraculous effect. All trace of annoyance vanished from her face and was replaced by an expression of excited delight. She picked up the little, handwritten menu on the table – couldn't this place afford printing, Christian thought with scorn. She flashed him a bright look.

'Well, everything's great. I almost had the lamb with aubergine myself . . .'

He switched off again, his only interest in what she was saying being the way her full lips pouted and parted in speech. They were very kissable. He caught a tantalising glimpse of pink tongue.

Would it be tonight or tomorrow, Christian wondered complacently. Tomorrow might be better; anticipation was half the pleasure. On the other hand, she looked like a lot of pleasure to him and it had been some time – days in fact – since he had last . . .

His eyes licked her nipples once again. Forget tonight, even. Make it this afternoon. Belle Murphy was due to descend any minute; possibly ruining everything. Best to make hay while the sun shone, Christian calculated. Or, better still, make Darcy.

She watched him admiring himself in the shiny bowl of a spoon. 'You're pretty vain, aren't you,' she teased, eyeing him carefully to see how he would react.

Christian agreed readily. 'Yeah, I guess I am quite vain,' he admitted. 'I asked for more powerful hairdryers in my health club. Is that vain?' He put his head on one side and smiled and instead of feeling contemptuous she found herself melting, amused, charmed even. As Christian chatted on Darcy noticed he talked about his willy quite a lot, but perhaps that was refreshingly honest. The sort of British men she had been wont to spend time with – sensitive actors mostly, probably didn't talk about their willies enough. Perhaps bottling up all that angry sexuality had led Niall disastrously to Belle. And who knew, it may even have had something to do with the swinging giblets she had been forced to spend each night on stage with in *Lear*.

'You're very flirty,' she commented.

Christian flashed her a grin. 'I know. I can't help it. Believe me, if I wasn't flirting with you I'd be flirting with that fork over there.' His grin broadened and Darcy found herself smiling back. There was something irresistible about his candour, not to mention the rest of him.

As the man and the woman laughed – the man's laugh containing the unmistakable triumphant rumble of *de facto* sexual possession – Marco felt something burning his insides and realised it was jealousy. He had never felt jealous of a woman before. Of a restaurant, of a recipe, perhaps. But never, before, a woman. He told himself to forget it. It wasn't as if he was going to see this one again.

The muscle-bound oaf was waving at him, Marco noticed now. Shouting, too. 'Hey! You!'

The woman looked uncomfortable at this, Marco saw, allowing his eyes to roll infinitesimally in her direction as he approached. '*Signor?*'

'Get me a burger and fries with relish, pickles and cheese.' The oaf lolled lazily in his chair; he was handsome, Marco saw, but with the type of pretty-boy looks that time and overindulgence ruined more quickly than most. He was wearing ridiculous clothes, like a magazine advertisement. So much jewellery. And that hat, thought Marco. Worn by someone less spectacularly – albeit obviously – handsome than Christian, it would look like something his aunt might wear in the shower.

'We don't do burgers,' he said pleasantly. 'We are an Italian restaurant here.'

'And a delicious one,' Darcy chipped in encouragingly. Marco flashed her a look of appreciation, which Christian intercepted.

'Hey, you don't say,' he remarked to Darcy, trying to conceal his annoyance with a teasing tone. 'OK then. You tell me. What should I eat?'

There was something brutish about this man, Marco sensed. Something viscerally dislikeable. Why couldn't this woman see it? There was the small matter of his blinding good looks, of course. Marco felt disappointed. The woman had displayed such impeccable taste up until now.

'I'll come back for the order,' he muttered, gliding away, a soul in torment.

Chapter 37

Oh, the joy of being in Italy, in the sunny south of Europe, with the wind in her hair and the sunshine on her face! Although the sunshine should probably not be on her face, Darcy knew. Or on the arms left bare by her yellow dress. She could imagine what Sam would say about exposing her newly valuable features to the full force of midday Italian glare in an open-topped Ferrari. 'Factor fifty sunblock at all times,' the model agency head had warned. 'And hats from eleven to three.'

She shouldn't be in this car, even, or with this man. But she had been powerless to resist, especially when he ordered yet another bottle of Prosecco, Christian's suggestion of taking her for a drive after lunch. The limo in the car park had been sent away with her luggage. 'They're expecting me at the villa,' Darcy had gasped. There was a housekeeper there, Mitch had told her. Someone to cook and clean. The prospect was thrillingly luxurious.

'So what, baby?' Christian had shrugged as he took a slug of sparkling wine. He had not been impressed by the fact Marco's did not stock champagne; only the Italian equivalent. 'You're a star, you do what you like. What the hell does it matter about anybody else?'

'But they'll be waiting . . .'

'Baby, they're paid to wait. They expect to wait. So let 'em wait.'

'It's a bit rude . . .'

Christian plonked his glass down hard and burst into incredulous laughter at this. 'You're too nice to people, baby. You're a star, remember?'

Darcy let herself be persuaded. She felt a rush of recklessness and confidence. Of course, she was not a star yet; and until now hadn't been sure she wanted to be. But Christian, with his designer clothes, his flashing gold, his cheekbones and, most of all, his swaggering self-confidence, made fame look like such fun. The fact he wasn't famous, not yet, was immaterial; Christian was certain to his polished fingertips that the part in *Galaxia* would make him a global celebrity. He'd talked about it endlessly throughout lunchtime, hardly noticing the food, it seemed to Darcy, as he outlined just how seismic the effect of the film would be on both their careers.

'There'll be dolls,' he said eagerly, sticking his fork into a pile of pesto and pasta; the one item on the menu he had recognised.

'Dolls?'

'Yeah, you know, like Barbies. For your character, that is. It'll be action figures for mine, obviously. There'll be kids' lunch-boxes.'

Darcy giggled. The idea of being on a child's lunchbox was for some reason hilarious. Christian's wide smile faded. 'What's so funny?'

Darcy toyed with the base of her Prosecco glass. 'Just – you know. Merchandising. It seems a long way from . . .' Her words trailed away on the pesto-scented air. She was about to add the word 'acting', or even 'art', but realised how pretentious that would sound. Did she even care any more about the art of

404

acting, she wondered. There was an art to blockbuster movies, anyway; and a difficult one, to judge by the number of flops. Her eye caught the green slick of pesto sauce on Christian's golden hanks of steaming pasta. That seemed the only real art round here. So why worry about the rest?

'Just enjoy yourself, baby!' Christian shouted, grinning, as they raced along in the Ferrari. 'You English chicks, you're so uptight!' His white teeth flashed in the sunshine almost as brightly as the Ferrari's chrome fittings.

Darcy pretended to frown – ignoring what Sam had said about that too. Sam had even advised her to go to bed with Sellotape on her head, to prevent her getting wrinkles in her sleep. But Christian was right. She needed to relax, Darcy told herself. To abandon herself to the moment. She was in a glamorous car, in a glamorous place, with a glamorous man. Why worry?

The thought made her feel fast and reckless, almost as fast and reckless as Christian's driving. Glancing over the thick, deeply suggestive gearstick, she admired his handsome profile and felt a deep swirl of excitement. The air rushing at her was exhilarating; she felt like a plane taking off. The speed was such that she felt they might. The whine of the engine grew even higher and even more urgent. The trees, whose leaves and trunks she had been able to see before, flashed past in a green and white blur. It occurred to Darcy – briefly – to wonder how much Christian had drunk too.

If fear clutched at her bowels as, now, they went even faster, it was soon immolated in the brilliant smiles Christian kept shooting at her; paparazzi-like flashes of white in his handsome tanned face.

'Where are we going?' she shouted excitedly, not really caring.

'My place,' he yelled back over the air screaming past them. The look he now sent her was more of a smoulder than a smile, all suggestion. Darcy felt her mouth dry and looked straight ahead to conceal the turmoil in her stomach. She realised that, despite hardly knowing this man, she would soon be making passionate love with him and the knowledge was both alarming and delicious.

If it didn't feel quite her, Darcy pushed the sensation aside. She didn't want to feel like her. She wanted some fun, after what seemed, in retrospect, years of deprivation. She had an alter ego now, a reckless, pleasure-seeking, beautiful young film star. And going to bed with your co-stars – especially if they looked like Christian – was the sort of thing film stars did.

'Up there!' he pointed.

There was a hill to their left, sharper and higher than the rolling countryside round it; a hill rather like a jagged tooth, with clumps of pine and exposed rock; the slightly unlikely sort, Darcy thought, one saw in the background of Old Master paintings.

Enticing glimpses of a glamorous building could be seen between the trees at the top. Darcy caught a flash of carved edging to the roof and the top of some elaborate-looking windows. It was impossible to see more, as a tall, deep stone wall concealed the rest. Yet the wall was an attractive one: glowing yellow in the rich afternoon sun, flat and bright against the hot purple-blue of the sky above and the cool dark green of the surrounding pines.

The car began to roar up the hill, eating up the corners as the road bent and twisted under the trees. Darcy continued craning her neck at the glimpses of the building afforded as they mounted. The honey-coloured stone, she thought, had the exact shade and texture of something she could not quite remember.

Then it struck her. Yes! Coarse peanut butter! The comparison surprised her; really, she was beginning to think of nothing else but food.

'Watch out!' she yelped, as he narrowly missed a tree.

On top of the hill, groups of pines and cypresses provided a dark green parasol over a small, neat gravelled area, surrounded by a low wall and clearly meant for car parking. Darcy could hardly wait for the car to stop.

Herby scents tugged at her nostrils as she swung her legs out of the passenger seat. She crunched across the gravel in the cool shadows of the pine trees to where the countryside tipped away beneath them.

'My God,' she breathed. 'The view!'

Around and below the little promontory, swelling and dipping beneath the brilliant blue sky, were the soft hills of Chianti once more. The ones visible from here were heavily cultivated, their earth the colour of chocolate powder, ridged on top by green stripes of vine.

'What are you looking at?' Christian was behind her suddenly. As he lifted her hair and kissed the tender, warm, secret back of her neck, Darcy felt she would explode with pleasure.

He led her to a pair of lichened stone gateposts topped with white marble lions holding intricately carved shields. The tall, ornate iron gates stood open and a wide, gravelled path led through the middle of a garden to a large villa whose central door was surrounded by a great deal of grandiose carving. There was a wide terrace in front, edged by a balustrade topped with weathered statuary: gods, goddesses, fauns with cloven feet. How very, very, *very* Italian, Darcy thought in delight.

As Christian, holding her hand and sending volts of ecstasy up her arms to her breasts, led her up the steps to the roomy terrace, Darcy imagined long, delicious suppers watching the sunset and the first stars come out. It was the perfect setting for food. She pictured herself sitting there, glass of chilled white wine in hand, nibbling on salami. Or olives, or the tiny green fava beans Marco had served, the early broad beans he had told her that the Florentines ate raw and regarded as a great delicacy.

Her picture was interrupted as Christian now led her towards the massive front door, dark wood in its ornate stone setting. Despite looking as if it could withstand an army, it opened to his touch with ease. Inside was a vast, white-toned entrance hall, marble-floored and with a ceiling the full height of the enormous house. A huge staircase of wide, shallow marble treads zigzagged upwards, taking in two sets of landings on the way. There must, Darcy thought, be *hundreds* of bedrooms.

'You're staying *here*?' she asked Christian, in awe. 'On your own? It's incredible.'

Christian shrugged. Incredible was one way of describing it. Huge and creepy was another, and he didn't like the way the place was so old. Second-hand was bad enough; this place was probably hundredth hand. Not for the first time Christian rather regretted his insistence that the film company book him the biggest villa in the area, all for himself. 'There are a couple of servants around the place,' he said airily. 'They cook, but I don't really like their stuff. Their chicken-fried steak . . . Jesus . . .'

Darcy was hardly listening. 'Can I look at the kitchen?' she asked Christian eagerly.

Quite suddenly she had imagined something whitewashed and stone-floored, with a roasting hearth and a big central wooden table of oak or olive wood on which, very probably, stood some fat ripe tomatoes in a blue and white bowl. Perhaps a golden bottle of olive oil too, and a thick-crusted wheel of country-style bread. On the walls would hang onions and pink ropes of garlic; there would be bunches of drying herbs and dried vegetables soaking in oil in huge jars. There would be hams, sausages, yellow crags of cheese . . .

Christian stared, affronted. 'The *kitchen?*'

Darcy grinned at him. 'Don't worry,' she said matter-of-factly. 'I want to have sex with you. I was just interested. But the kitchen can wait.'

'Oh. Right.' Surprise ricocheted through Christian. Such straightforwardness was a novelty. He smiled back at her. But, hey, it was the kind of straightforwardness he liked. 'You're so beautiful,' he murmured, folding her into his arms.

Darcy felt her whole body thrum with anticipation. She traced his face, her eyes hungrily devouring his features. They had been together a mere few hours, but really, Darcy felt, her mind all excited, alcohol-fused, pleasure-hungry whirl, they had known each other for ages. Ever since their eyes had met across a crowded, neck-craning restaurant in LA; a defining moment. Maybe even the turning point of her life.

'We're gonna set that screen alight,' he whispered to her, his eyes wide with excitement. 'You an' me, we're gonna be the new Burton and Taylor.'

Darcy gasped. 'You think so?' There was something about Christian that made anything seem possible. They were meant to be together in a way she and Niall had never been. Niall, Darcy was sure, had never looked at her with the whole of his soul in his eyes, the way Christian was looking at her now.

She pressed herself against him, her nipples burning, her lips aching to be kissed. As he dipped his mouth to hers, she felt a stab of joy between her legs.

'The bedroom's up here,' he muttered thickly, pulling her gently but firmly up the stairs. Darcy, floating upwards, looking downwards, watched the stairs pass beneath her feet in their black sequined flipflops. The pink-painted toes – a legacy of the Rumtopf shoot; the Master had been appalled at the state of her feet – now passed along a grand landing passage with a beige runner and then a door opened. Darcy looked up to find herself in a big, high-ceilinged room with huge shuttered windows that went down to the floor. In the muted light a tall bed with white curtains rose like a magical ship in full sail.

On the bed, in the cool shadows cast by the canopy, he pushed her gently back, his mouth locking hers down. Pushing up her dress to reveal her breasts, he kissed them reverently, flicking the tips with his tongue. She shuddered with delight, arching instinctively towards him.

He looked up, his eyes soft with surprise. 'Hey. They're *real!*'

'What did you expect them to be?' Darcy asked, laughing. But of course, he came from Hollywood, the land of plastic women.

'Oh. You know. The usual silicon valleys,' Christian grinned. 'But – real tits!' He nuzzled them again in delight. 'It's like having real . . .' He frowned. Christian's mental stock of authentic experiences was low. 'Oh, I dunno. Real something.'

'Caviar? Foie gras? Champagne?' suggested Darcy, giggling and gasping in equal part as he sent shivers of delight all over her body.

Afterwards, she rose from the bed, flung open the shuttered windows so that the dazzling light poured in and looked out over the sunny garden. It lay still in the singing heat. As she stood there, a gentle breeze sprang up and hurled soft balls of scent from the earth against her bare skin; rosemary, sage, pine. Darcy closed her eyes and breathed slowly, luxuriously, in.

He rose in a rustle of linen and came to stand behind her, his hands either side of her, moving up and down, caressing her waist and thighs. She could feel from the hot hardness pressing into her that he was ready again. Slowly, she turned to him.

It was perfection, Darcy suddenly felt, as she melted once again under his touch. The perfect man, the perfect place. Was it possible to be more perfectly happy?

Chapter 38

Emma stood at the gate. The name chiselled in gold on the neat white marble nameplate – 'Villa Rosa' – was the address Belle had given her.

She felt relieved, but exhausted. It was dazzlingly hot and Morning, whose weight seemed to be doubling daily – he'd soon be out of the baby carrier altogether – hung like lead around her neck. Fortunately, he was quiet and content under his little white sunhat; looking about him with interest as he had throughout the journey.

While Rocolo had been a useful stopping-off point and watering hole, finding the Villa Rosa from it was a difficult business, not least because the villagers she asked were so busy exclaiming at Morning that mere dull directions were hard to extract. Still, she was here now. There had been a bus – Italian buses were so useful – almost to the turning of the main road that the villa was reached from. It stood back from the road on a gentle hill, behind a screen of cypresses.

Would Belle be here, Emma wondered as she pressed the buzzer on the thick stone gatepost. She had not seen her employer since Belle disappeared into the VIP area at Gatwick.

And while travelling alone with the baby had had its hair-raising moments, being in charge had been enjoyable. Emma realised, with a clutch of regret that her feeling of autonomy was about to end.

'*Benvenuto!*' someone called from the other side of the gate. To Emma's surprise, it sounded both cheerful and Italian; neither of which, particularly the former, suggested Belle.

Emma peered through the wrought iron to see a middle-aged, beaming woman of wiry build and wiry cropped black hair, which was tinged with grey. She wore a black skirt and white blouse. 'I'm Mara,' the woman smiled as she punched a code into somewhere unseen the other side of the gatepost and swung open the wrought-iron screen. 'The housekeeper. I do housework, laundry, cooking . . . ah. *Bello bambino!*' She tickled Morning under the chin and beamed at Emma. 'You have had a good journey, Signora Murphy?'

'Actually, I'm not Signora Murphy.' It was amazing anyone could ever think she was. How could they, Emma wondered, with her make-upless face, ponytail, jeans and polo shirt, both journey-creased and stained to some considerable extent by a hiccup attack Morning had suffered on the bus.

'*Not* Signora Murphy?' For a moment, the housekeeper looked suspicious. Then she smiled again. 'Ah. You Signora Prince then.'

Emma lifted her chin, puzzled. Prince? The name meant nothing to her.

Below Mara's neat white short shirtsleeves were a pair of wiry brown arms. The housekeeper folded them now and trained a close look on Emma. 'You not actress? You not in thees film?'

Emma shook her head. So that was it, Signora Prince, whoever she was, must be one of Belle's co-stars. If such people were allowed to exist, which seemed unlikely. But just as she had begun to frame the thought of what it might actually be like, sharing a house with Belle sharing a house with some other actress, Mara spoke again.

'I am told,' the housekeeper said, rather crossly, 'that Signora Prince and Signora Murphy, they both arrive at lunchtime. I cook my special beeg lasagne.' She flung an arm out in a gesture presumably in the direction of the kitchen. 'But they no here.' She shook her head disapprovingly.

At the thought of Mara's special big lasagne, Emma's stomach growled. She was here. She was hungry too. But being fed seemed at present a remote eventuality. She realised now that Mara was regarding her with something akin to suspicion. The housekeeper was obviously considering throwing herself and Morning back out of the gate.

Hurriedly, Emma waved the piece of paper Belle had written the address on and hastened to explain. 'I'm Signora Murphy's nanny. Signora Murphy's *son's* nanny, rather.' Could it possibly be true that Belle had not given any advance warning?

The housekeeper looked satisfied with this explanation, however. 'Ah. *Sì.* I see.' There was a flash of black eyes, a smile and friendliness was restored.

'I carry the baby?' Her voice was as much command as it was suggestion. Gratefully, Emma unbuckled the heavy child and handed him over. Morning's reaction was to open one eye and survey Mara sleepily before closing it again.

'*Bello!*' Mara deposited a loud and smacking kiss on the top of his head. 'I ham frustrated grandmother!' she explained, shaking her head and grinning ruefully. 'I have no children, only nephew. And he never find right girl!'

'Oh dear,' Emma muttered. She wasn't sure she was terribly interested. The full weight of the afternoon sun seemed to be pressing hard on her head. Even though she had only walked from the bus stop she longed to be somewhere cool.

The villa before her looked, she noted, very cool. It was an attractive, mellow building, a long oblong of pale yellow stone with a red-tiled roof. It had all the dignity and simplicity of a place built long ago for a specific and uncomplicated purpose. At one end, a flight of stone steps rose to a low doorway, a clue that that end of the building was once a haybarn and the space below for animals. The rest of the place had been a farmhouse, Emma guessed; guessing in addition that there would be little of the simply rustic within it now.

The glare of its exterior, of the omnipresent local golden stone, which blazed in the sun, was punctured at intervals by shuttered windows hinting at comfortably shadowy apartments within. There were windows everywhere, at all heights, of all periods and of all sizes. It looked, Emma thought, as if someone had picked them up in a fistful and just thrown them at the wall. The whole effect was delicious.

Mara's thoughts, meanwhile, were obviously still with her nephew, of whom she was evidently very fond. Her face was rueful but loving as she continued to exclaim about him. 'He very nice. Very funny, Very 'ardworking. He chef.' Then she shook her head regretfully. 'But Marco, he work too 'ard. No time to meet right girls.'

She looked Emma up and down. Her lips pursed and one black eyebrow raised speculatively.

Emma looked away, embarrassed. Mara seemed very nice, but she'd only met the woman five minutes ago. What made her think she would be interested in her nephew? Besides . . .

An image of a handsome blond boy rose and fell in her mind's eye. Briefly, Emma let herself dream, while knowing there was no point. Orlando was in Italy, certainly, but it was a big place.

She recovered to find Mara now led her down the middle of a sunny green lawn with a leaping, foaming, scented, gloriously colourful border of roses.

'What beautiful roses,' Emma said in delight. 'Do you do the garden?'

'No. *Gino.*'

'Gino?' Emma repeated. The way Mara said it, it sounded as if the whole world should have heard of him. But then, she thought, her eyes skimming the exuberant riot of coloured petals again, perhaps the world should.

'Gino! Yes! He has been gardener here for long time. More than thirty years. He love just roses. He say they are the queen of the flowers. He no want to plant anything else.'

Emma felt she could see Gino's point. There were brilliant roses of all colours, of pink, yellow, white, apricot and red, and endless variations, rippling pink through purple, yellow through red. Some were classic Valentine's blooms, huge, dark and velvety, each curl-edged petal distinct. Others were tumbling, old-fashioned, pink floribunda, petals tightly squished and gathered like the skirt of a ballgown. Still others, smaller and more businesslike, scurried along the ground. Others clambered the weathered stone walls, wrestling with honeysuckle. The scent, even in this hot part of the day, was powerful. Emma could imagine, in the cool of the evening, that it would be almost overwhelming.

The rose garden gave way to a big, flat, sunny terrace in which an enormous oblong of water sat like a bright blue jewel. There were chocolate-brown recliners beside the pool, trimmed with white, each with its own matching shade. It was, Emma thought, disbelievingly, like something from a magazine.

'Fun for the baby, no?' Mara twinkled, kissing Morning on the head again. He had woken up now, and gazed about him

417

with big, brown, interested eyes. Looking up at Mara, he gave her a big beam. 'Aaaah,' said the housekeeper, sniffing and wiping her eyes.

Emma shook her head. Morning might be less than six months old, but he already had a sound grasp of how to play the world. No doubt, she reflected soberly, he had had to. It would have been a matter of survival.

Mara was leading her into the villa through an open French window that gave into a large sitting room. It was cool, shadowy, stone-floored and white-walled and had a lot of white sofas in it, was Emma's first impression, as Mara quickly led her out through an archway in the back and up a stone staircase.

'Your room,' she beamed. 'I leave you for a few minutes, get your bearings, no?'

Before Emma could say anything, she hurried away with Morning. Emma could hear them both chuckling as they went down the stairs.

Feeling oddly light and free, she looked about in delight. She was standing in a small, pretty bedroom, mostly white, as the room downstairs had been. A delicate silver chandelier dangled from the bleached wood beamed ceiling; there were two deep and squashy armchairs and a small sofa at the foot of the wide and very comfortable-looking bed with its carved, silvery-wood headboard. Everything was either painted or upholstered in white. A tiny carved canopied fireplace, and the four small, deeply recessed windows through which the light streamed, gave the air of a romantic tower.

There was, Emma observed as she strode to the window, nowhere for Morning to sleep, but no doubt Mara had a cot somewhere.

A small, arched door at the back led into a bathroom; white again, with another beamed ceiling where a freestanding, old-fashioned bath stood on an oak platform reached by two small wooden steps. Emma regarded it with awe. How long did it take to fill that tub? Not long, she realised the moment after turning on the high-pressure taps. There were two large, white, old-fashioned basins with mirrors above, between which stood a host of smartly labelled bottles and jars. Emma picked one up, unscrewed the top and sniffed the rich, fruity perfume. It smelt expensive.

The delicious scent still lingering in her nostrils, she crossed the polished wooden floor and knelt on the windowseat to look out. The view stretched for miles over the green hills behind the villa. The famous Tuscany. Emma felt, despite her tiredness, a leap of the spirit as she took in the groups of dark green trees, the lime-green ridges of vineyards, the low, golden farm buildings that here and there caught the sun.

She now noticed, as she pulled her gaze back from the far distance, that the Villa Rosa was not entirely alone. There was another house a couple of fields away. Similar to this one, but not as big, and lower down the slope too. Emma examined it with interest. She could see the azure oblong of a pool, and a terrace with green parasols. She wondered who lived there.

A couple of fields away from the Villa Rosa, Richard Fitzmaurice was trying to settle into his holiday. Granted, they had just arrived at the *aubergo*, which might account for his feelings of displacement and anxiety. But there were plenty of other reasons too.

He sat beneath the big green parasol, his spare frame, in its white short-sleeved shirt and old blue gardening trousers, hunched over the dining table, a bottle of Nastro Azzuro next to him, ostensibly buried in the *Daily Telegraph*.

His surroundings were gracious; out in front of him spread

the golden stone of the patio, clean and brilliant in the sun. At its far end had been sunk a large, round-ended swimming pool whose blue water, enlivened by gushing pumps, danced and sparkled and sent spiky reflections over the white recliners at its edge. Around the patio was a garden which went as far as the wall bordering the main road. The intense green of the lawn had surprised Richard at first until he had spotted the twisting sprinkler, which jerked back and forth like a whirling dervish.

Behind Richard was the farmhouse, the *aubergo*, although Richard doubted that any of the building's former residents would recognise the glamorous succession of double bedrooms decorated in the best contemporary 'rustic-luxe' manner and with adjoining power-shower-featuring bathrooms. Nor the impressive lounge with denim-blue suede furniture, satellite telly and bright contemporary paintings. Although the huge, canopied golden-stone fireplace, big enough for a man to stand in, probably hadn't changed much.

The kitchen, with its lifestyle-statement six-ring cooker, butcher's block-cum-champagne bar and huge Smeg fridge would probably be even more alien to its origins. As would the recommendations of local eateries listed in the leatherbound Visitor's Handbook.

They sounded good, he had to say. One of the places, Marco's, apparently had a national reputation and was heading to its first Michelin star. Its speciality, it seemed, was local rustic cuisine; presumably the cleaned-up, pared-down, white-plated version of whatever used to be cooked in the *aubergo* kitchen. But delicious-sounding, if the sample menu enclosed with the Handbook – which seemed to anticipate their every whim – was anything to go by. Which no doubt it was.

Yes, Richard reminded himself. He was in a beautiful house, in a beautiful country, with his wife and son, whom he loved.

Even if Orlando had disappeared into his room immediately on arrival and had not emerged even for lunch. And even if, moreover, any hope of saving him some from the big spaghetti carbonara that Georgie, with her usual resourcefulness, had whisked up, had been soon dashed by the combined efforts of the Faugh males, who had made short work of it. But he must not dwell on such matters, Richard told himself. It was only a packet of pasta. There were many reasons not to give in to the sense of bitterness that swept him whenever he thought about how Hugh and Laura Faugh had hijacked his holiday.

If Richard raised his head a fraction and looked over to the pool he could see a darkly sunglassed Hugh, big hair glossy in the sun, stretched out in a pair of well-packed electric-blue trunks on a recliner. His sons lay next to him, one reading, Richard saw, a glossy called *FHM* and the other one called *Nuts*.

They had lost no time in making themselves comfortable; they had only been in the damned place, Richard estimated, an hour.

Hugh's big, long, trunk-like legs were slightly apart and, like his huge, fleshy chest, covered with sun oil and black hair. There was, Richard thought, something horribly virile about him.

He watched the shadow of Hugh's big long arm, raised slightly in the air, juddering over the patio stone as he keyed into his BlackBerry. He was obsessed with the thing. He claimed it was full of messages from constituents, as well as – of course – those from the centre of Shadow power.

This Richard found puzzling. Hugh's constituency was quite similar to his own. His own comprised the tenants of an impoverished Hertfordshire housing estate as well as their near neighbours in one of the country's wealthiest villages. Only very few of either group – uneducated and poor on the one hand, elderly and conservative on the other – had the faintest idea how to send an email. Certainly not enough to keep him as busy as Hugh seemed to be, his thumbs and forefingers in a blur of almost constant movement. He seemed very cheerful about it too, as if he didn't mind in the least being interrupted; rather welcomed it, in fact.

But perhaps such keenness had got Hugh where he was. If his constituents wanted to get in touch with Richard, they rang him on the telephone. Or on the mobile, as he was on holiday, but only in dire emergency would he expect any such calls now. In twenty-five years of representing his constituency, Richard could count on the fingers of one hand the number of times he had been disturbed by a constituency emergency on summer holiday. It was one of the benefits of being a backbencher, as was freedom from the necessity of having to network with people such as Hugh. Only Georgie had put paid to all that. They were stuck with the Faughs for the duration.

Hugh grunted, sat up, looked around and waved at Richard. He ambled over to where he sat, stared at his Nastro Azzuro and boomed, 'Any chance of one of those beers you've got there, old boy?'

Richard's reply was drowned in the sudden *chug-a-chug-a* of a helicopter overhead. This was just as well.

Chugachugachugachuga . . .

Emma had just put Morning to sleep in her own bed. Mara, not having expected a baby, did not have a cot, not even a travel cot, although she had explained to Emma that Florence, the nearest big city, was her best chance of getting one. But that of course wouldn't be until the morning. In the meantime, she had to do her best with pillows and duvets and hope Morning was too tired by the journey to roll about much.

Having seen her charge off to sleep, Emma had herself been

sent to the rose garden by Mara while the housekeeper prepared supper.

The scent was as heady as a boudoir and the colours of the flowers blazed in the rich evening light beneath the still-azure sky. It was a beautiful blue and gold end to what had been a beautiful blue and gold day. The air rang with competing birdsong – some of it surprisingly loud.

Very loud indeed. There was a thudding noise – a helicopter, Emma now realised as, suddenly and without warning, everything was plunged into shadow and the black underside of some huge airborne beast suddenly appeared above her.

Emma dived out of the rose garden on to the pool patio and peered up at the menace roaring above, dark and heavy, slashing violently at the air. Surely – surely – it wasn't trying to land in the *garden*?

Mara appeared, her ovengloved hands holding a covered dish. She stared up at the approaching aircraft with an expression of utter incomprehension.

The helicopter was lower now; it filled the sky. Emma could no longer see the sun for it. Where there had been birdsong and an expanse of warm blue, there was now earsplitting noise and blackness.

Who was this idiot who'd so spectacularly lost his way? She must stop this enormous, destructive, noisy *thing* landing. She ran back on to the lawn of the rose garden, her arms waving wildly.

'It's not a helipad!' Emma screamed, leaping up and down, trying to spot a pilot, a passenger, *someone* behind the expanse of impassive black plastic covering the front of the helicopter. She couldn't see anyone; could they see her? Could they see *anything*?

'The rose garden!' Mara screamed, as the scented air was

smashed and sliced by the deadly whipping blades. Emma ducked and ran towards the villa, not just her ears but her entire body full of the hideous screaming of the engine.

It was incredible, but it actually was happening, the helicopter really was landing in the rose garden. Right in the middle of the path. The heads of the blooms were being pulled into the air, sucked into the blades, mashed by slashing lengths of metal. And now the blades were slowing down, the scream of the engine was subsiding – and not a single rose head remained.

The silence that now flooded Emma's ears was as violent and absolute as the noise had been. Not a bird could be heard; all had fled in terror, Emma imagined. Probably they'd never come back.

As for the garden, that beautiful rose garden, full of colour and scent and movement. Gone.

Shattered petals plastered the front of the helicopter. The grass beneath it was gouged and black, churned, torn and crushed as the beast had juddered in landing. All that love, Emma thought, all that care and time, all the planting, weeding, spraying, watering, all the pride, joy and knowledge that the unknown Gino had put into creating this beautiful garden. All destroyed in an instant.

Instinctively she went to stand beside Mara. The housekeeper did not react, but the hands that held the covered dish in the ovengloves were, Emma saw, trembling. She put an arm about Mara as the two of them waited numbly for the perpetrator of all this destruction to emerge from the helicopter.

Emma rarely got angry, but a terrible rage filled her now. Whoever was in that helicopter, whoever it was who had done this horrible thing, they were going to hear exactly what she thought of them.

The helicopter door now slid back. A woman emerged.

Emma started forward, her anger hot on her lips, but then she fell back.

The woman was blonde and held a small dog. Her platinum mane blazed white in the sun as she shook it out. Shadowy caves shifted beneath her cheekbones. She wore a tight, short black dress, bright red lipstick and huge black glasses.

'Well, don't just stand there,' Belle exclaimed angrily to Emma. 'I've got a cockpit full of luggage here.'

Belle obviously had no intention of unloading any of it herself. Not in those shoes, Emma realised. They were about eight inches high, black patent and festooned in buckles. The heels ended with a sharp spike which even now was sinking into the mud.

'You've ruined the rose garden,' was all Emma could say. Belle might be her employer, but some things – the destruction of great art – went beyond such petty considerations.

'Oh, did I?' Belle looked about her and surveyed the devastation. Not a muscle of her face moved. She looked back at Emma. 'You're *sure* that was me?'

'Quite sure.'

'Never mind,' Belle beamed. 'It'll grow back.'

Chapter 39

The Italian landscape, in which Darcy had so delighted before, now seemed to flash past her as in a dream. All she was conscious of was Christian. His watch, which was thick and large and had tiny diamonds round the face, flashed in the sun as his muscled arms changed position on the Ferrari's padded leather steering wheel.

They were driving to the villa where Darcy would be staying for the duration of the filming. A quick call to Mitch had pinpointed the location.

'You haven't checked in there yet?' The agent had sounded concerned.

'Not yet, no,' Darcy confirmed gaily. 'But we're on our way,' she added.

'We?'

'Me and, um, Christian.' Her voice had fallen to a defensive mutter. From what Mitch had said in the restaurant he was hardly likely to be pleased. *Asshole.* How *could* he have said that?

'Christian!' Mitch yelped in horror. Then, mindful of Greg Cucarachi just the other side of the flimsy wall, he lowered his voice to a growl. 'Not . . . Christian Harlow?'

'Uh-huh,' Darcy said in a breezy tone designed to defy Mitch and at the same time scotch any suspicions Christian might have – he was listening as carefully to the conversation as was possible, given the wind noise. 'I'd better go. Talk to you—'

'Not so fast,' Mitch shouted in panic. 'Your model agency's been after you. Sam Sherman.'

'Oh?' Darcy's heart sank.

'She called me; she couldn't get you on the phone. You had it switched off?'

'Um, yes.'

Mitch caught the shifty, guilty note in her voice. His final shred of hope melted away. No prizes for guessing why it had been switched off, he thought heavily. Harlow had had her already. Not for nothing did he have a reputation as a fast worker. In bed, at any rate.

He'd been right to fear the worst in Puccini's. The slimiest, most calculating asshole in Hollywood – and a hard-fought title *that* was – had struck again. Of course he had.

Mitch could have kicked himself. If only he was more of a calculating asshole himself. He'd been insane, hopelessly optimistic or just plain wrong to think that his latest protégée, dewy-eyed, new to Tinseltown, unaware of its ways, could in any way withstand Christian Harlow on a full-scale charm offensive. He'd been even more insane to have hoped, as he had, that once Belle discovered Christian was in *Galaxia* too, they could somehow pick up where they had left off. Or vice versa; Belle, brought back from the career dead by her Shakespeare stint, was a more enticing prospect for Christian now, after all. But not as enticing as Darcy, obviously.

Mitch clenched his fists with frustration. Darcy and Christian together was the worst possible scenario.

Complicating it was the fact that his client still had no idea that Belle, the woman who had publically stolen her boyfriend, was in the film. Mitch had been keeping the news from her in the hope that he would think of a way to break it acceptably. He was aided in this by the standard Jack Saint practice of keeping the cast of his films a mystery until the very last minute. Of course, there were rumours, but Darcy did not appear to have heard any. By the time she did, hopefully, she would be too far committed to *Galaxia* to withdraw.

Mitch moaned and clutched his head. Because this, messy though it was, was not all, of course. Not by a long way. The final piece of unexploded ordnance was the prospect of Belle's reaction on discovering Christian and Darcy together on set. Mitch winced; he could almost hear now the shrieks of both his clients shouting about each other down the phone.

'Well, you've got a shoot tomorrow, in Florence,' he managed to grind out to Darcy from between clenched teeth. 'Some kinda shoe thing.'

At least that would keep her out of Harlow's way for a day, Mitch thought. The delay in principal photography, in Darcy's case, wasn't only irritating, it was downright dangerous. He could imagine Harlow oiling himself up and parading about by the swimming pool, flashing those persuasive teeth at his giggling client. Or his other client, Belle, pushing Darcy right in that pool and holding her under, or perhaps the other way round . . .

'Yeah,' Darcy said. There was, Mitch thought as he ended the call, a vagueness in her voice that worried him. Along with everything else that worried him. He took a big bite of jelly doughnut and swung his chair round to his window. Between the blinds his eye caught the streetsweeper again, shuffling happily down the sunlit sidewalk. Mitch experienced a surge of heartfelt envy. Who'd be a Hollywood agent?

*

Irritated in Italy, Darcy slipped her mobile back into her pocket. What right did Mitch have to spoil things? If, at the very back of Darcy's mind was the niggling thought that she had given in too soon, slept with someone she hardly knew and that such behaviour was not to her credit, Darcy forced it away. She deserved some fun, after all that had happened with Niall. She must grasp the moment, gather the rosebuds, enjoy herself. Live a little – or even a lot. She was a big star, after all, as Christian kept saying. Or about to be one.

'Everything OK, doll?' Christian beamed at her, knowing perfectly well that it wasn't. He could well imagine what that fat creep Mitch Masterson had said.

'Fine,' Darcy beamed back, immediately deciding that it was. How could it not be? The sun was shining, she was in a glamorous country, in a glamorous car. Being driven by the most glamorous man ever born, who had, during the last few hours, assured her many times, in a low, testosterone-fuelled growl that had thrilled her to her very nerve ends, that she was the most beautiful woman he had ever seen.

She gazed at Christian from her ringside seat in the sports car's long, low passenger seat and felt that she, in turn, had never seen anyone so handsome. His handsome profile confidently raised, his strong teeth bared in a white grin, his brown limbs shining like metal in the blazing sun, he looked, Darcy thought, like a young god. She felt a rush of sudden desire, even after all the desire she had just felt and which had been sated, over and over again. He had made love to her in positions she had not realised possible; raised her to heights of pleasure so intense they had almost been pain. As starburst followed starbust behind her eyes, she had become lost in sensation. Time, space and even identity had melted away.

He was looking at her appreciatively; his thick dark lashes were lowered suggestively over his eyes. Was he thinking the same as she was, Darcy wondered.

'Hey!' Christian shouted, taking a hand off the wheel. 'Italy really suits you. Your hair looks great against that blue sky.'

Delighted, Darcy shook the black mane that was whipping her rather painfully across the face. She found herself arching her back and pouting; wishing he would stop the car, pull her out and take her all over again, on the warm and scented grass at the roadside. He would start, she knew, by kissing her gently. All over. Luxuriating in the always-sure touch of his tongue, her nostrils full of his expensive aftershave, warm skin and hot sun, she would surrender, shuddering with anticipated delight.

'And the dark green of those trees really goes with your eyes,' Christian yelled, trotting out his second most useful endearment. You just changed the name of the place – Italy, New York, California, wherever. It worked every time; as it had here.

Perhaps too well. You could see in her eyes she wanted more. Christian was worn out, however. Darcy might look composed, but she had been a fireball in bed. It wasn't only her breasts that were real. Every other bit was too, and it had all needed attention.

Clearly she had been making up for lost time. 'Are we anywhere near?' he called above the wind. He needed to deposit her at this villa, go home and recover.

Darcy looked confused for a moment, then remembered the instructions. The turn-off to the villa should be coming up soon. Yes, here it was.

'There!' she pointed frantically, yelling over the scream of the wind. But Christian was still hurtling forward, certain, it seemed, to overshoot it. He flashed her a grin and with a twist of his biceps, a jerk of the wheel, a mighty screech from the tyres, the car pivoted at full tilt on two wheels and hurtled up a lane along which a wall ran as far as a pair of gateposts.

'Villa Rosa,' Darcy read. 'Here we are,' she yelled to Christian, as they shot past.

A mighty pull of the brakes, again a screech of tyres and then silence. A flood of birdsong entered the space where before there had been only the roar of an engine. Darcy, heart racing and head thumping from where it had just smashed back against the seat as they stopped dead, took a deep, relieved breath. Of course, Christian was in control. But in any other hands, that speed, that turn . . . well . . .

The powerful, sweet scent of roses drove out the reek of petrol fumes in her nose. Surprised, Darcy realised it must be coming from the villa garden. How absolutely perfect. The Villa Rosa smelt of roses.

She unbuckled her seat, heaved herself out and hurried to the gate, which was of graceful black wrought iron. Through it, in the distance, could be seen what was presumably the villa; a long farmhouse-like building with a patio with parasols and a pool before it. But the beautiful garden, whose scent filled Darcy's nose and which suggested ordered rose-beds, fountains and manicured lawns, was nowhere to be seen. Instead, immediately before the gate was what looked like horticultural carnage; a cut-up mess of flowers and leaves and a stretch of churned-up grass. Churned-up grass, mud, devastated bushes and roseheads everywhere.

Darcy turned to Christian who, unrestricted by any seatbelt, had leapt out immediately to follow her. 'What on earth do you think has happened? It looks as if someone's landed a helicopter on it.'

Christian, about to reply indignantly that he didn't care what had happened; the idea of this place housing a future superstar like Darcy was not only ridiculous but downright goddamn insulting, now felt the words dry in his mouth.

'But that's impossible, surely . . .' Darcy was continuing.

The hell it was. Christian had spotted the patio now. Standing there was a creature he recognised. And who recognised him, moreover. A tiny brown dog with big pointy ears began to run back and forth agitatedly, emitting a series of shattering barks. Its protruberant black eyes were trained directly on him. The slightest element of doubt was removed by the fact it wore a collar so full of diamonds you could see them glittering from the gate.

'No one would land a helicopter in a rose garden . . .' mused Darcy.

Oh, no? Christian could think of someone with a dog like that, who was more than capable of landing a helicopter in a rose garden. Belle had never had green fingers. Gold fingers, more like.

'I, um, gotta go,' Christian muttered, pushing hastily past her in his way back to the car.

She turned, her eyes wide with alarm. 'You're not coming in?'

'Sorry. Gotta go home, look at the script again.'

Christian had opened the trunk of the Ferrari and was almost throwing Darcy's few bags – still bearing their BA First Class tags – on to the road. He dived back into the driver's seat. There was a burst of thunder as the ignition struck up. 'I'll call you,' he yelled, reversing with a screech and hurtling down the road. Within a few seconds he had turned the corner and was gone, leaving only a blue cloud of exhaust fumes hanging over the sunny road.

Darcy, blinking after him, realised the yapping noise she had been faintly aware of was growing louder. She looked round to see that a small, brown, big-eared dog with a glittering collar and a loud, irritating yap was racing over the mangled rose garden towards the gate, a murderous expression in its horribly protruberant black eyes.

'Sugar! Baby!' A thin woman in a short black dress, with long blond hair, red lipstick and enormous sunglasses was picking her way in high black heels over the shattered bushes after it. 'There, there,' she was calling, exclaiming in annoyance as her sharp spike heels sank in the mud. 'Come back to Mommy! What's the problem, sweetie . . . ?'

Darcy was transfixed by Mommy's shoes. Incredible. At least eight inches high, of black patent leather, which blazed in the sun, and covered in silver studs and buckles, which blazed even more. It was, Darcy thought, amazing she could move.

'Is it a nasty man? Let Mommy see.'

Mommy spoke, Darcy registered, in a babyish voice with an American accent. Presumably she was another of the actors in *Galaxia*. The dog really was a horror, Darcy saw. Small and nasty looking. It stared at her malevolently.

Oh!

Suddenly, all Darcy's scattered thoughts and senses came rushing together.

She *knew* this woman. She had seen this hair, these sunglasses before. She might even have seen this dog. Pored over them for hours, in fact. On the front page of several newspapers.

Darcy felt her whole body burning in a way which had nothing to do with the sun. Shame, fury and hurt thundered in her heart and stomach.

This was Belle Murphy. In the flesh – or what flesh there was. Apart from her breasts, which were considerable and every bit as fake-looking as expected, the rest of her body looked strangely emaciated. Against her highly visible ribcage, her tits, Darcy thought, looked like two upturned bowls placed an inch apart against a ladder.

Belle Murphy. The plastic doll. The personification of everything Darcy most despised, as an actress and as a person. The woman who had stolen Niall while she had been away in LA. The woman who had trampled heedlessly over her life in those hideous spike heels. Who had precipitated a personal and professional crisis.

For a second, Darcy pictured herself either punching Belle in the face or turning on her own, flat, flipflop-shod heel and striding away in a magnificent gesture of contempt and rejection.

A pointless gesture, however, in both cases. Belle's face looked so thin and sharp she might cut herself in the first instance, and in the second she had no transport; the main road at the bottom was long, hot and dusty and, moreover, she had nowhere else to stay. This was the villa that had been booked for her by the film company.

But she had not realised she was sharing it with Belle Murphy; that Belle Murphy was in *Galaxia* too. Mitch had not mentioned it. On purpose? Darcy wondered darkly, now. Particularly after what he had said about Christian, she was beginning to wonder if Mitch really did have her best interests at heart. Perhaps, like Christian, she should change agents annually. 'Keeps 'em on their evil, grasping toes,' he had laughed.

For a second, Darcy teetered on the edge of abandoning Mitch, the film, Jack Saint and incipient stardom, and returning to London. Only the knowledge that this inevitably meant abandoning Christian too drew her back. She then reflected that there was nothing to return home for anyway. Largely thanks to the woman in front of her.

*

Belle had gained the gate by now and retrieved her pet. It was of course annoying and uncomfortable to have to walk this far in heels only ever intended for the few steps between limo and lobby. But Sugar would obviously respond to no one else. And now she had got this far in pursuit of him she would have to answer the gate, too.

Of course, strictly speaking, that miserable old bat of a housekeeper was there to perform any menial tasks, but she'd disappeared in a sulk some time ago. OK, Belle admitted to herself, so she'd messed up a few plants, but the garden would grow again – what was the problem? That's what gardens did. Some people, Belle considered, had no sense of proportion.

A cross-looking, dark-haired girl was staring through the ironwork, right at her. Did she not know who she was? She was having the gate answered by a film star, for Chrissakes. To drive home her point, Belle gave her a dazzling Hollywood smile.

The girl's face did not change; on the contrary it looked more hostile. Belle met the hostile look with an equally hostile one of her own and looked her up and down, unimpressed. Ordinary looking, tall with black hair that lacked a single highlight and wore a yellow dress of no recognisable designer, unless it was a some years-ago Roland Mouret number. She was also very pale and not particularly thin. And that, of course, was the telling detail. Not thin, so not someone important. Very obviously none of the people rumoured to be acting with her in *Galaxia*. Not Cate Blanchett or Nicole Kidman.

There had been so many rumours about her co-stars – Jack Black, Brad Pitt, George Clooney, Russells Brand or Crowe – none of which had been confirmed. Mitch had been particularly pathetic on this score, pleading endlessly the iron control Jack

Saint exercised over every aspect of his films. 'No one really knows. They won't until he wants to tell them.'

'But you're a goddamn agent, you're supposed to be on the inside track,' Belle had stormed. Really, now she was on her way again she ought to get rid of Mitch. It was obvious that the only inside he knew anything about was that of his refrigerator.

'Is it true that Christian's in *Galaxia*?' she had demanded next.

'I really have no idea,' Mitch had replied carefully. Well, it wasn't a lie, he reasoned to himself. There were many things he had no idea about. How to cure the common cold, for instance. Women. Self-control in the face of jelly doughnuts. Whether there was a God. Agenting.

Frustrated, Belle had finally, conclusively lost her temper. 'You're fired.'

As Belle's end went dead in his ear, Mitch stared up at the artificial ceiling, feeling relieved for the first time in days. He'd been wrong to have no idea, about one thing at least. There was a God, that was for sure.

'Can I help you?' Belle asked Darcy disdainfully now. 'Are you a housemaid or something?'

She was taken aback when the other snapped. 'I'm not a housemaid, thank you very much. I'm an actress.'

'An actress?' Belle repeated. The woman spoke in an English accent. But she wasn't Keira Knightley or Helen Mirren. And what other English actresses were there?

'My name's Darcy Prince.'

Belle recognised there was something expectant about the silence that followed. She fixed a disdainful stare on the girl the other side of the gate. Was she supposed to have heard of her or something?

'If my name doesn't ring a bell,' the other said steadily, 'then my boyfriend's might. Niall MacDonald?'

Belle stared for a moment, then gave a peal of laughter. 'Oh, Niall. I'm so glad to hear he's moved on. Got over me.' She tossed her hair. 'Hey, I hope you'll be very happy together.'

Darcy's mouth dropped open. She had expected blustering denial, smirking acknowledgement, embarrassment, even. A whole rang of possible responses. Apart from this one. 'You mean . . . you're not with him any more?'

'No, sweetie,' trilled Belle. 'It was never gonna work. We just weren't on the same page.' She flipped her blond mane to one side and made as if to consider. 'You see, it's kind of like this. I'm on the successful page and he's in more of a failures type of scene. That's showbiz, honey.'

Sheer surprise had stolen away much of Darcy's outrage. She frowned at this strange-looking blonde with a body like a thin stick on which two brown balloons were hanging. She tried to think of some shattering rejoinder, but nothing came to mind.

'I've never been crazy about redheads anyway,' Belle now remarked with an airy trill. 'But, you know, like I say, I'm just so glad to hear he's moved on. I hope you'll be very happy together.'

'We're not together,' Darcy managed to grind out furiously. 'Thanks to *you.*'

'Me?' Belle blinked, all innocence, and put a birdlike hand to the soaring curves of her breasts. 'You're not together, thanks to *me?*'

'You slept with him in London. While I was in LA,' Darcy hurled at her in a shaking, uncertain voice. 'You broke us up.'

'I so did not,' Belle exclaimed indignantly. 'He said he was single.'

Anger flashed through Darcy, followed by a crushing sense of resignation. Of course Niall had said he was single. 'I bet,' she said heavily, 'that he told you his father was a butcher as well.'

Belle looked back at her with eyes of a curiously artificial green and shook her white-blond hair. 'Yeah. He did.'

'He was lying,' Darcy said, with hot satisfaction. 'His father owns a chain of meat processing plants.'

Belle's forehead puckered in a faint frown. 'Yeah. He told me that too.'

This made no sense to Darcy. 'He told you that too? And you didn't mind? That he wasn't telling the truth about the butcher?'

Belle grinned. 'Baby, why should I care about the truth? It wasn't the truth I was trying to sleep with.'

As Darcy looked hotly back at her, churning with embarrassment and resentment, Belle shrugged her skeletal brown shoulders. 'Hey. I did you a favour, honey. What's the point of being with Niall? That guy's going nowhere, baby.'

None of the mud Darcy was flinging was sticking. She folded her arms and gave the woman on the other side of the gate a hot, resentful stare. 'You don't get it, do you?'

Anger flashed across the thin face of the other. '*You* don't get it, you mean. You're an actress, did you say? In *Galaxia*?'

'Yes.'

'Well, you're at the wrong place, OK? I guess there'll be a hostel in town for all you crowd scene guys. This villa's for those with major roles. I,' announced Belle, drawing herself up proudly, 'am the Countess of Tyfoo.'

'And I'm the Grand Duchess of the fucking Galaxy,' Darcy snapped. 'Let me in, will you?'

Chapter 40

Marco, settling some diners into their courtyard table, looked up at a loud, agitated, female voice. He smiled politely at the girl who passed by with a subdued blond toddler attached to each of her hands. She wore, it seemed to Marco, high-heeled shoes inadvisable for the scaling of Rocolo's hill, as well as a pair of extremely tight white jeans even less suited to the purpose.

The blonde stared haughtily back at him and continued talking in a loud and honking voice into the mobile phone to which she was attached by earphones. 'Nightmare, honestly,' she was complaining. 'Bloody kids running riot. Just ghastly. *Cosmo!*' she screeched, as if to underline the point, even though the blond little boy she was addressing didn't seem to Marco to be doing anything particularly offensive. Apart from looking unhappy, that was. Both he and the silver-haired girl, presumably his sister, looked much glummer than children their age should, as well as tired – shouldn't they be in bed at this hour? What were the parents thinking? It was obvious this woman was not their mother.

Marco guessed the tight-trousered blonde was British and a nanny, no doubt to that type of wealthy, pushy British couple that flocked to Tuscany in droves in the summer. Many of them ate in his restaurant. That was the only problem with running a successful restaurant: you attracted successful people, who seemed to think that being successful was all about treating other people badly.

Marco took the order from the just-settled table – Daria and the other waitress were busy elsewhere – and was about to go into the kitchen when another group loomed up.

The dominant figure in it was a tall, solid man with red cheeks, thick black hair and an air of staggering self-satisfaction. He wore the standard-issue middle-class-Brit-male-on-holiday uniform, Marco saw. Pale blue shirt, beige chinos, white Panama trimmed with dark band.

The rest of the group comprised a frazzled, skinny, fifty-something woman in a yellow and cerise clinging scrap of dress, a couple of smug-looking teen boys with big hair and bigger bottoms, and another downbeat man, presumably the thin woman's husband. The well-preserved, rather sly-looking brunette was unquestionably the wife of the big dark-haired man.

'Table for seven,' he boomed in one of those loud, fruity, bullying English accents Marco knew from experience meant trouble.

'I'm sorry,' he said apologetically, 'we're completely full tonight.' Two, he might have managed. Three at a pinch. But seven? In a restaurant the size of his? Wasn't it obvious that would have to be booked?

The frazzled woman stepped forward. 'What do you mean, you don't have a table?' she demanded hysterically, clacking her matching pink shoes on the cobbles in agitation. 'We have two members of parliament in our party.'

She was interrupted by the big, broad-shouldered man whose

eyes blazed in annoyance below thick black brows. 'I want to speak to the owner,' he boomed.

Marco sensed a stir at the tables about him at this. Many were filled with regular customers. He could feel them all waiting for the trump card to be played.

'Actually,' Marco said gently, 'I am the owner.'

The man's red face flushed redder. He stared at Marco in disbelieving fury. 'You? But you're taking the orders . . .'

'Yes.' Marco regarded him levelly. He would not trouble to point out to this man that, besides the best food possible, his restaurant was all about treating people fairly, with respect. There were no tantrums in his kitchen. No one was more important than anyone else, only, in some cases, more experienced. Marco sensed this would mean little to a man like this.

'But I'm in the Shadow Cabinet,' the big man bleated, clearly unable to believe his large, red-tipped ears.

Marco raised his hands in a gesture of helpless defiance. He was determinedly avoiding the amused gaze of the large table nearest to him, which was filled with Rodolfo the painter and his family.

The black eyebrows snapped together. 'You say we need to book?'

'That's right. Yes.'

'Even if we were God Almighty, presumably.'

Marco smiled tightly. 'I could possibly make an exception for Him. But He would be the only one.'

Hearing Rodolfo chuckle softly at this, Marco flashed him an irritated look. He saw Rodolfo now rise to his feet, his eyes bright with laughter, passing a napkin over his mouth in a gesture of finality.

Marco watched apprehensively. Oh no. Rodolfo liked to

tease, but this was going too far. Surely Rodolfo wasn't going to . . .

But he was. '*Finito!*' Rodolfo announced, clattering his espresso cup back into its saucer. The rest of the table was rising in a muddle of chatter, laughter, reaching for bags and wiping the mouths of children. Turning to the Honourable Member of Parliament, Rodolfo added, 'We have finished. You can have our table.'

'*Grazie, amico mio,*' Marco bent and hissed furiously into Rodolfo's ear on the pretext of picking up a napkin that had fallen on to the cobbles.

'*Prego,*' Rodolfo beamed.

The MP now made some appreciative grunts, punctured by squeals of appreciation from the frazzled woman. The group, in that British way, rushed to sit themselves down in the seats before the vacating party had finished its manouevres. It was now that Marco noticed the boy, the last to sit down, at the back of the group and plainly wishing he was anywhere but here. A tall boy with a transportingly beautiful face which he seemed to be trying to hide under his hair. Marco shook his head faintly in wonder. He looked like a saint from a Raphael fresco.

The beautiful boy looked up as he slid into his place. He seemed to slide him a glance of mute apology. Marco gave him a sympathetic smile with more than a hint of conspiracy about it.

At the Villa Rosa, a brilliant disc of sun, bright as a beaten penny, was slipping down from a sky entirely saffron yellow. Thin scraps of gold cloud reflected the vanishing furnace. Below, the darkened hills rose and fell like waves. The air was sweet and still and warm.

Upstairs, Emma was putting Morning to bed. Tomorrow she

would go to Florence and buy the travel cot. Until then she had to hope that the pillows she was hemming him in with would prevent the baby, a lively sleeper, who could turn completely upside down in the course of the night, from falling out or suffering some other mischief.

When eventually Morning drifted into sleep, smiling happily to himself, Emma got up and crossed to the window, where she could see, on the patio below, that the table had been set for dinner by Mara.

It looked beautiful and very inviting. The parasol had been dismantled and the silver of the cutlery gleamed in the rich, but much milder, evening sun. The wine glasses flashed and the snow-white napkins glowed. The late glow also made luminous the petals of the white roses – salvaged from the wrecked garden and placed there in silent rebuke, Emma guessed – which were arranged in a simple white jug in the centre. A crisp green salad, almost leaping out of the wooden bowl with vitality and fresh-ness, sat next to a golden phial of oil and a burgundy one of vinegar. Beyond this enticing scene, the blue rectangle of the swimming pool winked and flashed; a sheet of rippling blue silk in the dying light.

A wonderful warm, savoury smell was wafting out across the terrace from the kitchen. Emma sniffed. Whatever Mara thought about Belle – and it obviously wasn't much – she was clearly not taking her dislike into the kitchen. The smell was rich, tomatoey and winy, heavy with garlic and herbs.

Emma's stomach seemed to leap within her. She longed for dinner. She was gratified to note there were three places; one for her too, presumably. The move to Italy had meant a rise in status; she had never eaten with Belle before. Partly, admittedly, because Belle never really ate; only drank.

Darcy now appeared on the patio below her. She was

frowning over her mobile phone, as if she expected a text from someone. Then the scent of food seemed to hit her; she sniffed the air appreciatively and went immediately to the table, which she proceeded to inspect with relish. From the vantage point of her room, Emma smiled as, first checking to see that no one was looking, Darcy tugged the thick and crispy end off a piece of bread, took the oil phial and poured some of the bright yellow contents on it. As she chewed, her face assumed an expression of ecstasy.

Darcy had, Emma thought, turned out to be something of a surprise. As she was also an actress, and in the same film as Belle, Emma had expected another tantrum-prone diva, but Darcy seemed good-natured and to have no airs at all. She had cooed over Morning and had been especially polite to Mara. Most endearingly of all, she seemed anything but fond of Belle. Her expression when Belle had airily explained what the helicopter had done to the garden had been one of mixed disgust and horror.

Emma watched Darcy chewing. She had finished the whole of her first piece of bread by now and was launched on the second. The level in the oil phial was dropping drastically. Emma reflected that Darcy had eaten more in the last few minutes than she had ever seen Belle eat the whole time she had known her.

She felt herself warm further to the dark-haired actress. She had a certain distance and dignity – especially with that cut-glass voice – but was the complete opposite of Belle; while Emma readily acknowledged her employer was beautiful, it was a hard, artificial kind of beauty. But there was something altogether lovely about Darcy; she had a pretty, fresh face with what looked like the original features. Her body, compared to Belle's, looked almost normal. She was slim, certainly. Much thinner than me,

Emma thought. But at the same time nothing on the emaciated, artificially inflated scale of Belle.

There was a clattering sound now and Belle herself clacked on to the patio in an even higher pair of heels than the ones she had worn earlier; from this distance they seemed to be pink with a black lace covering. Several feet of tanned leg above was the bottom of a very short, figure-hugging dress of some stretchy black glittery material. Her white hair streamed over her shoulders and her red mouth glistened from beneath the black sunglasses.

In her skinny brown arms Sugar looked about him with his habitual ill-natured stare. In the candlelight, the diamonds on his collar flashed brilliantly, almost rivalling those on Belle's fingers and wrists. She had, Emma thought, made a considerable effort for dinner at home with the nanny.

Or perhaps she wanted to outshine Darcy; a competition Darcy, simply dressed in jeans, a white shirt and black glittery flipflops, seemed uninterested in taking part in.

Emma began to back away from the window. It was time she went down herself now. Dinner was evidently about to start.

There came the sharp clacking sound of spike heels on ancient stone as Belle went to the table and sloshed some wine into a glass. 'Hey,' she exclaimed. 'She's set the table for dinner.'

'Yes!' Darcy agreed delightedly. 'Isn't that great?'

Belle swirled her hair in what Emma knew from experience to be a contradictory gesture. Below the sunglasses, the glossy red lips were turned down sulkily. 'No it freaking isn't. Who asked her to do that? I've asked the driver to come at eight. I wanna check out the local scene, see what's going down.'

'Er . . .' Darcy began.

Just at this minute, Mara appeared with a large plate of what looked like sliced meat. Sugar, in Belle's arms, immediately started to strain and snap.

'Oooh!' Darcy exclaimed. 'That looks amazing, Mara!'

Mara smiled. 'Is antipasto. Local specialities,' she said proudly.

Emma, pausing upstairs, remembered the *salumeria* in the village square. Curious as she was about tasting its wares, especially now she was so hungry, something was telling her not to join the three on the patio. She sensed that things might be about to get nasty.

'Salamis, prosciutto, air-dried ham, sliced smoked sausage and chorizo,' Mara elucidated for Darcy's benefit.

Using one of the forks on the side of the plate, Darcy peeled off a dark red layer of ham. 'Wow!'

'No, thanks,' Belle snapped as Mara offered her the plate. 'I never eat anything with a face.' Sugar, who most definitely did, snapped at a row of salami at the edge.

Mara tugged the plate away in disgust. 'You are vegetarian?' she asked Belle. 'OK, fine. I bring some grilled vegetables.'

Belle allowed Sugar back at the plate of meat. 'Like I said,' she retorted rudely as he dragged off a pile of ham, 'I don't eat anything with a face.'

Darcy, who had been hovering anxiously on the edge of this exchange, now jumped in. 'Vegetables don't have faces.'

In a whirl of white hair, Belle turned on her. Sugar, torn from licking at some sausage, yelped angrily.

'Sure they do,' Belle snapped. 'Have you ever looked really closely – I mean *really* closely – at an onion?'

There was no immediate answer to this, the watching Emma thought. From Darcy's face, it seemed that she felt the same.

Mara's lips had tightened angrily. 'I go get *secondo piatti*,' she muttered, stomping off with the dog-licked antipasto, which she now held at arm's length.

Belle frowned. 'What's that? Pasta, did she say? I can't eat that. I'm wheat intolerant.'

Food intolerant, more like, Emma thought from above.

'*Secondo piatti*,' Darcy replied, her patience evidently wearing out. 'It means main course.'

'But I don't want to eat here,' Belle stormed, stamping her high-heeled foot.

'Ah,' said Darcy. 'That could be tricky,' she added.

From above, Emma now saw the housekeeper emerging from the villa bearing a huge plate on which what looked like a leg of lamb reclined on a bed of roast tomatoes and aubergines. The smell, as it floated up, could have wakened the dead, Emma thought.

'That looks delicious!' Darcy gasped to the housekeeper, her eyes lingering greedily on the lamb.

'Is delicious,' Mara confirmed, taking care to keep the platter at a safe distance from Sugar, who was straining in Belle's arms, evidently desperate to savage it. 'Is old family recipe.'

'Well, enjoy,' Belle cut in rudely. 'We're going out.'

Darcy looked alarmed at this, as if she had not expected to be roped into the plan. Sugar let out an incredulous yap. Mara, meanwhile, looked stony and her fingers twitched around the edge of the plate, as if she was considering hurling it at someone.

Then came the loud bleep of a text message being delivered. Darcy whipped out her phone and flicked it open. Emma saw, instantly, her entire demeanour change.

'I'm terribly sorry,' she gasped apologetically to Mara. 'But actually, I have to go out myself. Can't the lamb keep?' she added pleadingly.

'Or feed it to my nanny,' Belle suggested in a sneering tone. 'She needs to keep her weight up.' As the listening Emma gasped with fury, Belle grabbed Darcy's arm. 'Let's go.'

*

At the table occupied by the seven Britons at the Italian restaurant, a discussion about corporal punishment was in, as it were, full swing.

'I don't believe in hanging,' Hugh declared, to Orlando's amazement. Given some of the views he had already expressed at dinner, a more likely champion of the gallows was impossible to imagine.

'I don't believe in hanging either,' Richard agreed.

'Quite right,' Hugh said heartily. 'Hanging's too good for them. Bring back drawing and quartering, that's what I say.' He dug his fork into his spaghetti with relish.

Orlando and his father stared at each other in amazement. As ever, following one of Hugh's particularly outrageous statements, Richard found himself irritatingly slow to think of a reply.

The twins, Ivo and Jago, now leapt into the vacuum and began to amuse themselves in trying to prise from Orlando what he intended to do during the ritual year off before university. 'If, that is, you're actually *going* to university, Orlando,' Ivo taunted.

'He is,' confirmed Georgie grimly from where she picked over lobster linguine at the end of the table.

Orlando drained his glass of lager crossly. Did he have no say in the matter? Were his opinions irrelevant? Actually, he wanted to go on a gap year even less than he wanted to go to university. He had no desire to save pygmy elephants in Borneo or teach English to villagers on the slopes of Kilimanjaro. He didn't want to do film-making in Paris or surf skills in South Africa.

Far from it. God, he hated all that surf-head stuff. Blokes with bulging muscles, shaved legs and red swimming trunks at St Ives getting all the yummy mummies drooling. Eye candy for the Boden catalogue brigade. Orlando couldn't surf anyway. Frankly, he could only just swim.

Listening to his mother and the Faughs wittering on about teaching theatre skills in the Gaza Strip, Orlando realised that what he really wanted to do was get a job, any job and actually have some money of his own. Like that nanny, Emma, he had met in the airport. He bitterly regretted not getting her address, or, what would have been easier, her mobile phone number. She kept slipping into his head, and whenever she did he had a sensation like a fresh breeze on a close and humid day. Her unaffected smile, her scrubbed and shining cleanliness, her keen and searching gaze, her air of independence and of being absolutely frank. It would, he thought, be good to see her again. More than good. Her breasts, in their white polo shirt, tended to flash frequently through his memory too, and whenever they did he felt a sensation entirely different from that of the breeze.

'You'd never last a gap year anyway,' Ivo was scoffing as pudding arrived on the table.

'Better bugger off and do Surf Science at Mousehole University or something,' mocked Jago, tucking into a large portion of tiramisu.

Seeing Orlando's miserable face, Richard was about to come to his son's defence when he realised his leg was trembling in a disconcerting manner. It took some time to work out that, unexpectedly, he was receiving a call on his mobile phone.

He cleared his throat. 'Excuse me,' he said softly as he stood up. 'I seem to be required by one of my constituents.'

'Good man!' roared Hugh from the other end of the table, unsteadily holding aloft at least half a bottle of Chianti in an extremely large glass.

'I know what Orlando should do in his year off.' It was Laura who had spoken, lounging at the other end of the table from Georgie, eyes glittering in the candles that had now been lit, one hand playing with her long black-red hair which, combined with her white face, reminded Orlando of evil queens in Disney films.

'What?' asked Georgie eagerly, while Orlando met Laura's teasing gaze apprehensively from under his brows. He had no idea what was coming but had every idea that he wasn't going to like it.

'Ensnaring,' Laura said, in tones of nasal triumph, 'some plain and dumpy heiress with his looks.'

Everyone turned to look at Laura. Orlando felt sick. What was she talking about? What sort of hideous, Victorian fantasy was this? 'Why not? He's *marvellous* breeding stock,' Laura drawled, looking Orlando up and down in a way that made him blush and burn.

Hugh, who prided himself on intimate acquaintanceship with the ways of the gentry, now joined in. 'Absolutely,' he boomed, his sharp, wet teeth flashing in the candlelight. 'A thoroughbred stallion that any landowning family with a suitable mare would be thrilled to get into stud. Could make you millions. Eh, Orlando?'

Orlando pressed back into his chair and stared stonily at the table, but his heart hammered beneath, his guts twisting with embarrassment that he had been spoken about, in public, in such sexual terms. Beneath the hair he tried to shake protectively over his face, his cheeks burned. He looked helplessly at his father, but Richard obviously had other things on his mind. He was walking up and down the stretch of steep hill just beyond the restaurant courtyard talking agitatedly into his mobile.

'Mr Fitzmaurice!'

Richard, his mobile pressed to his ear, supposed it was odd and possibly rather pathetic that he could recognise one voice instantly out of so many thousands of the constituents he had. But Honora Greatorex had no ordinary voice. Besides being loud, it had an operatic vibrato, as if about to burst into 'Land of Hope and Glory', which, the blue-rinsed, tweed-chested, Parish Council Chair of the village of Wellover, Hertfordshire, had once confided to Richard, was her favourite song. But Mrs Greatorex did not seem to be in a singing mood now.

'Mrs Greatorex, what can I do for you?' Richard forced a pleasant tone into his voice. If one of his constituents chose to call him on holiday, then so be it. Representation of the people was a noble calling – or so he persisted in trying to believe, despite the contradicting presence of Hugh Faugh.

'Mr Fitzmaurice, I'll cut to the chase.'

'Be my guest, Mrs Greatorex,' Richard said generously. He had never known her do anything else in any case.

'Have you any idea what, ahem,' Mrs Greatorex, in Wellover, took a deep, dramatic breath, '*doggering* is?'

On the steepest part of this particularly stiff incline, Richard started so fiercely he almost fell over. 'Doggering?' he exclaimed, in a loud voice that instantly became a soft one as a passing man in clerical dress gave him a quizzical look.

'You don't mean,' Richard hissed, bending slightly and heading instinctively for the shadows cast by the houses, '*dogging*, do you, Mrs Greatorex? The practice of, *ahem*, how exactly shall I put this . . .'

'Casual sex with strangers in the open air? I most certainly do, Mr Fitzmaurice,' thundered his interlocutor from her former chantry in Hertfordshire as Richard, hundreds of miles away in Italy, reeled across the village street. 'We all do in Wellover, let me assure you. Every Friday night, without fail.'

Richard's jaw fell slackly open. Was he hearing properly? Had the heat done something to his head? *Wellover?* Mrs *Greatorex?*

It could not be possible. Dogging was something footballers did in pub car parks in Essex. Wellover was as far from such a scenario as could be imagined. It was the archetypal English village. Its doorways rioted with roses, its gardens nodded with gladioli, its windows were mullioned and its inn, a muzak-free zone, was full of polished brass and quiet bonhomie. Its church was well attended and adhered to the King James Version, its village green was clean and kempt, its inhabitants, all white and mostly fifty plus, subscribed to the *Telegraph* en masse and had stockbrokers.

Wellover was in the Domesday Book, and regularly and effortlessly saw off all comers in Best-Kept Village competitions. Period dramas were regularly filmed there. Keira Knightley had been in the village shop and Colin Firth in the post office. The only dogging Richard had ever associated with Wellover were ladies in tweed briskly striding the local leafy lanes in the company of brushed and glossy spaniels.

'I didn't realise,' he said faintly, wondering why he was being selected for this extraordinary confession. Was Mrs Greatorex suggesting he joined them?

'No, neither did we,' Mrs Greatorex replied, with a heaviness in her voice that belied the possibility she was extolling the virtues of a thrilling new sexual hobby. Richard felt the mist in his brain clear a little. He waited for Mrs Greatorex to speak again. He had to be sure of what was being discussed here, whether the practice was being condoned or condemned. Fools not only rushed in where angels feared to tread, but ran the risk of losing their seats.

Mrs Greatorex spoke. 'It appears,' she said in stately tones, 'it appears . . .' the stately tones shook a little, 'it seems . . .' she added, with an audible sniff, 'that Wellover, our beautiful Wellover, is . . .' there was a shuddering sound as Mrs Greatorex seemed to fight for self-control, 'the dogging capital of Europe!'

'Oh dear,' said Richard, staring hard at the tarmac.

'Russell's Leap – you know Russell's Leap, of course?'

Richard confirmed that he did. The landmark referred to was a well-known beauty spot in the woods not far from Wellover.

'Well, it's there they go. Every Friday night.' Mrs Greatorex's voice was shaking again.

It was the 'they' that clinched it. Mrs Greatorex *was* ringing to complain then. Richard felt oddly relieved. The thought of the Parish Council Chair bent backwards over a car bonnet, tweed culottes round her ankles, had been a disturbing one.

'Oh dear,' he said again.

There was a hissing sound from the other end, as of someone drawing a large amount of air into a pair of powerful lungs. '*Yes!*' boomed Mrs Greatorex, sounding quite her terrifying old self. '*Oh dear.* And what I'm ringing to ask, Mr Fitzmaurice, is . . .'

'Yes?' Richard whispered shakily.

'. . . what exactly *you're* going to do about it.'

Richard suppressed a sigh. What the hell did she think he was going to do about it? He was in Italy, on holiday. Hundreds of miles from Russell's Leap and its promiscuous habituees.

Chapter 41

'Whaddya mean we gotta walk?' Belle screeched as the car drew up in the car park at the foot of the village.

'It's a historic site,' Darcy explained agitatedly, anxious to get Belle out of the car as soon as possible. Her heart was pumping double speed; her very nerve-ends were tingling at the thought of seeing Christian. She was relieved and excited to have received the message for which she had waited ever since they had parted, which seemed an age ago now.

Of course, it would have been better if he had texted earlier to suggest they met in Rocolo, then she could have given poor Mara more notice. Darcy felt clammy with guilt when she remembered the delicious roast lamb, burnished and juicy, arranged so beautifully on its bed of roasted vegetables, all offered up by Mara with such evident pride.

But when, finally, Christian's call had come it had been unignorable. Darcy's main regret, as they bowled along in the limo, was that she had not had more time to prepare herself. Anticipating an evening at the villa she had got out of the bath and just pulled on jeans and a simple white shirt. Her hair was twisted back into a rough ponytail and her face was free of make-up. She reminded herself as the car sped along that none of this would matter to Christian. She was, he had assured her, the most beautiful woman he had ever seen.

'I don't do walking,' Belle snarled as the driver opened the rear door.

Hardly surprising, in those. Darcy glanced at Belle's shoes. Seven inches and counting, and with soles that looked as thin as ballet slippers. She would feel every cigarette butt on Rocolo's cobbled main street.

Nine o'clock at Marco's, Christian had said. Darcy stole a glance at the heavily jewelled timepiece on the thin arm clutching the dog. Five minutes to. Darcy's heart skipped. Get Belle up the hill in those shoes in five minutes?

'I'm sure Sugar will enjoy stretching his legs,' Darcy gasped, desperate to get the show on the road. Surprisingly, for once, Sugar seemed to be on her side. The dog slipped out of his mistress's grasp, jumped out of the car, cocked his leg against the tyre and directed a powerful stream of urine at it. The acrid hot scent from this, borne on the warm air, drifted into Darcy's nostrils.

'Hey!' objected the driver. 'Ees my car. I clean heem thees morning.'

Belle did not trouble to reply. She cast him a withering look and allowed Darcy to lever her to her feet. Slowly, swayingly, they set off.

At the restaurant, Richard had returned to the table. He sensed an air of conflict and resentment, particularly from Orlando, but could not attend to it now. 'Sorry,' he muttered in his wife's ear. 'Can you excuse me again just a sec? I've just got to make a phone call. It's rather important.'

Excitement flashed across Georgie's face. 'Ooh. The Leader, is it?'

Richard shook his head. Georgie, for some reason, persisted in believing he was only ever one phone call away from the promotion of a lifetime. He had long since stopped trying to persuade her otherwise. The real state of his political career was irrelevant to her, as it was increasingly becoming to him, albeit in a different way. Close exposure to Hugh Faugh, and the unintentionally unflattering light that, in the course of boasting about his own nearness to The Leader, he shone on the inner workings of the Party, was hardly deepening his commitment. But here was Mrs Greatorex, and a whole village that needed his help. Finally, an issue of public concern he could really get his teeth into. But first he had to speak to Guy, his constituency agent; the man on the spot in Wellover. Find out what the real story was.

Richard walked away, trying to find Guy's number in the mobile phone's address book. Some keen-as-mustard researcher had offered to input all his numbers some years ago and Richard had gladly handed over the battered exercise book that had held all his contacts up to that point. The researcher, having completed the task, had handed the phone back with an air of tangible disappointment; he had, Richard guessed, been hoping for more impressive power phone numbers in the collection of such a long-serving MP. Just as Georgie did.

Ah. Here it was. As Richard finally hit on his constituency agent's number, he felt something of his old campaigning spirit stir. But Guy, with whom he planned to campaign, did not answer.

Richard dejectedly returned to the table. To his surprise, the mood of conflict had disappeared. They all seemed now, with the possible exception of Orlando, to be gripped by a febrile excitement.

'Look!' Georgie hissed as he came up, her expression strained and feverish. 'Look over there!'

Richard looked. Everyone in the restaurant seemed to be looking. Some were even holding up their mobile phones to take pictures. There was nudging and gasping and exclamations. The subject of all the excitement seemed to be a blonde woman in huge sunglasses, a very tiny dress and huge heels, holding a small and ridiculous dog.

'Who is it?' Richard asked Georgie blankly.

'Belle Murphy!' Georgie gasped. 'The film star. You know. She was in *Marie*, that film about . . .' She cast him an exasperated look. 'Surely you remember! It was our wedding anniversary!'

After some effort, Richard did remember. In particular he remembered feeling short-changed. He had expected a historical film but it had been more like lapdancing in period costume. He looked at the blonde woman, and the woman standing behind her at a slight distance, considerably less flashily dressed and looking anxiously at her mobile phone.

It was like a bad dream, Darcy thought. First there had been the ascent of the hill – she'd actually had to push Belle up the steeper bits. Moreover, the actress had not been remotely grateful for her help, seeming to Darcy, anxious to move forward as fast as possible, to be as slow and awkward as she was capable of being. Which was very slow and awkward indeed.

The bells announcing nine o'clock had rung out when they were still no more than a quarter of the way up. In any other circumstances Darcy felt sure she would have been charmed by the unsteady, clearly ancient chime from the bell tower at the top. But now it only announced the fact that Belle was making her late for Christian. She felt almost sick with mixed anxiety, excitement and resentment.

As, finally, they arrived at Marco's – which looked even

prettier at night than during the day, with white fairy lights twisted round the vine at the entrance and candles on all the tables – the bells chimed the quarter-hour. The panic this plunged Darcy into was deepened when she looked searchingly round the crowded tables full of moving, eating, laughing, talking faces. But nowhere among them was the face that, above all other faces, she longed to see. Christian had not yet arrived. Or, worse, he had arrived and, seeing she was not there, had left again.

As it happened, Christian had not yet arrived. He had got lost in the darkening lanes in the Ferrari. The ancient peasant he had asked for directions – almost giving the old guy a heart attack as he roared up unexpectedly beside him in the sports car – had for some dumb reason given him the wrong ones.

A glance at the jewelled watch on his tanned and muscled arm revealed that it was nine fifteen by the time he nosed the gleaming red roadster into the car park at the foot of the village. He was late. Christian, however, had no fear that Darcy would not be there when he got to the restaurant. Of course she would be. Women always waited for Christian Harlow.

He locked the car from the inside and swung himself out of the open top in one fluid, athletic movement. He walked away from the powerful vehicle, pinging in the heat of its recent exertions, deliberately not looking back at it as he strode with unhurried confidence through the car park.

A knot of loitering Italian youth watched him enviously. Christian paused before them, thrusting his fists in the pockets of his white linen trousers, and rocked on his feet, tanned and unsocked in their black leather Gucci loafers. 'You wanna have a Ferrari?' he asked them.

The boys, slouching against the bonnet of a beat-up beige

Fiat, regarded him sullenly. '*Sì, signor,*' one of them said eventually, flashing a set of impressively snaggly teeth.

Christian masked his contempt by giving them his best blitz grin, the one he saved for magazine covers and women he particularly wanted to screw. 'You wanna be rich and famous like me? Huh?' Christian spoke no Italian, but guessed that 'rich and famous' and 'Ferrari' were words that transcended language boundaries.

This brought more of a response. Excitement rippled through the little gang. '*Sì, signor! Sì, signor!*' gabbled the boys. 'Rich *e* famous! American star!'

Christian pushed a hand through his oiled black hair, quiffed up for the evening, and scrutinised them from behind his wraparound shades. A skinny lot, he thought scornfully. Runty, gangling, with terrible curly hair and faces like baskets of fruit.

He folded his gym-honed arms across the black designer waistcoat which was all he wore on his oiled torso apart from a hip-hop thick layer of silver crosses, diamond initials, shark's teeth on leather thongs and gold medallions. Most of them had been given by women over the years; the shark's tooth by his first conquest, the diamond initial by his most recent. Belle had provided one of the silver crosses. Christian thought of them as his trophies. His war medals, gained on the campaign route to stardom.

'All you gotta do, guys,' he told the boys in a patronising voice, 'all it takes is . . .' He paused for effect, flashing another grin.

'*Signor?*' The boys against the beige Fiat were breathless. All ears, Christian saw with amusement. Jeez. Did he know how to grab an audience or did he know how to grab an audience?

'Just . . . you know . . . believe in yourselves. That's all it takes, guys.' Christian paused, amazed as ever at his own acting abilities. He was so convincing, he almost believed himself. Believed that really was all it took and that self-belief, conceit, egomania, call it what you will, was sufficient in itself and had in no way to be supplemented with hustling, bed-hopping, backstabbing, cosmetic surgery and membership of half the gyms in LA so he was never more than five minutes from a PowerPlate. 'You know, you gotta have a dream. Then *believe* that dream. *Live* that dream. Yeah? You know what I'm saying?'

Christian strode off, delighted with himself. Really, if he hadn't been such a shit-hot actor, he could have been a mentor. Giving young people the tools to sort out their problems, make a success of themselves. He was an inspiration, that was what he was. He had touched the lives of those kids; dazzled them. They would never be the same again.

The boys looked after him, bemused at first. Then something happened that was like a release from a spell. Their dark brows drew, a murmuring of disquiet rumbled among them. After that, the storm broke. '*Vaffanculo!*' one of them shouted as Christian crossed the bridge. 'Go fuck yourself, signor.'

Belle's arrival in the restaurant caused a sensation. It came as a shock to Darcy. Having been at close quarters with her for some hours now, and finding her anything but impressive, Darcy had almost forgotten Belle was famous.

She was reminded in dramatic fashion when a woman in a pink and yellow dress exclaimed loudly, 'Look! It's Belle Murphy!' People looked, nudged, whispered, held up their mobile phones. A current of wild excitement ran through the whole place.

Even though she was not the focus of the attention, it alarmed Darcy none the less. Having everyone suddenly turn and stare was both novel and unpleasant. It was like having a spotlight turned on one without warning when one had been sitting comfortably in the dark. Even though it was only an audience of, on the whole, harmless-looking diners, a far cry from a mob of screaming red-carpet-gazers, she still felt naked and vulnerable.

Belle, on the other hand, seemed to be milking every minute. She preened and posed, tossing her hair about, soaking up the attention. Darcy could hardly believe how excited people seemed to be about Belle, not least because after just one minute of her company it was hard to imagine why anyone could possibly admire her.

It was with relief that Darcy saw Marco, the chef, now appear from his kitchen. She could ask him if he had seen the actor; hopefully he would remember Christian from earlier.

This possibility was scotched by Sugar's immediately exploding into barks. The dog was straining in Belle's arms, trying to snap at Marco. He backed away, annoyed.

'You've upset him,' Belle accused. 'Upset my little baby-waby!' Swaying slightly on her heels she clutched the dog closer and smothered him with kisses.

'I'm very sorry to hear that,' rejoined Marco pleasantly.

Behind Belle, Darcy tried to catch his eye. Perhaps, she thought with a leap of hope, Christian might even have left a message for her.

'We need a table for three,' Belle barked.

Marco suppressed a sigh. Not again. Did he have a table for three? No, he did not. Did this shouty, American, plastic-looking woman not realise that booking was essential on busy nights like this? Weeks in advance, in the summer months. No matter who you were – and this pushy, large-breasted blonde, one of that idiotic tribe who wore sunglasses at night, obviously was someone. A Hollywood actress, he had gathered. But so what?

'I'm sorry, signoras,' he started to say, intending to include her companion in the apology. He glanced at the dark-haired, white-shirted woman who seemed to be with the blonde, albeit some distance behind her.

Her. His nerves jangled, his palms moistened, his breath felt suddenly constricted. *It was . . . her.*

She looked less coiffed than before, more casual in her jeans, her black hair was damp and twisted as if she had just jumped out of the bath. The bath. Her in it. Marco paused, fleetingly, at the thought. She looked more beautiful than ever. For all her dishevelment, much prettier than her trussed-up and contrived-looking companion.

There was a question in her eyes, he saw now. She seemed about to speak and ask him something. He narrowed his eyes and cocked his ear, anxious to help. But the blonde barged in.

'Whaddya mean, you're sorry?' Belle blustered. 'You've got no tables? Don't you know who I am?'

She was looking at him so intensely, the beautiful girl with dark hair. Marco felt suddenly light and unanchored and giddy. He looked wildly around. There *had* to be a space somewhere. If not, he would make one. Out of thin air, with his bare hands.

As it happened, a table for two had just become free. And Daria, wonderful Daria, with her usual efficiency, was already clearing it.

'No problem,' Marco assured Belle, leading them through the gaping diners. He was so delighted about the presence of the lovely brunette he no longer cared about the imperious blonde. 'I can add another chair.'

'Should think so too,' Belle huffed over her shoulder to Darcy. There was a satisfied note to her huff, however. Darcy ignored her. Every fibre of her being was trained on asking Marco about Christian at the first possibility. She seized her opportunity as they reached the table. 'Have you seen my friend?' she murmured to Marco as he fussed over chairs. 'My friend from lunchtime,' she added, in a voice too low for Belle to hear.

He looked at her, forcing down the disappointment that rose like a lump in his throat, and shook his head. So that was the third guest. He wouldn't have bothered had he known. The muscle-bound swaggerer. The one who had asked for ketchup with his spaghetti. What did this woman – who obviously so appreciated food; who had a genius for it in fact – see in such a bonehead? Evidently something, Marco realised. Her face had fallen to her flipflops on hearing the swaggerer had not called in.

'He likes his steak rare,' the blonde interrupted. She proffered Sugar, who stuck his nose in Marco's face and growled viciously. The chef leapt back in alarm, almost losing his footing on an awkwardly placed cobble. 'And he'll have foie gras to start with. OK?'

The fact that there was no foie gras – French delicacies not figuring largely in the peasant cuisine of Italy in which he specialised – now impressed itself less on Marco than the sudden, incredible realisation that the dog, not the bonehead – or at least a different type of bonehead – was intended as the third diner at the table.

'I'm sorry.' The chef collected himself and spoke decisively. 'Animals are not allowed in the restaurant.'

'Not allowed?' Belle's platinum mane sliced the air like helicopter blades as she turned on him in shrill fury. 'You're saying that my dog – my dog – is *not allowed*? I'm a VIP, OK?'

Marco felt, behind and around him, the ringing silence from the rest of the diners, all of whom were following the drama with bated breath. Even the ones eating inside, in the brick-vaulted room, had crowded out round the entrance, below the vine with its fairy lights.

'Animals are not allowed, as I say. It's the rules, signora. Even for VIPs.'

Belle drew herself up to her full height, which was impressive, given the extra seven inches. Her back was arched and it seemed to the watching Darcy that her very breasts were bristling. 'Sugar,' Belle said icily, 'is not an *animal*.'

Marco looked at the skinny scrap of brown fur in her arms. '*That* isn't an animal?' It looked like a dog to him. A nasty sort of dog, too, with its over-big ears, protruberant eyes and violent nature.

Belle shoved her sunglasses close to Marco's face and hissed, 'Sugar isn't an animal, he's a VID. A Very Very Important Dog.' The creature in her arms gave a rolling, affirmative growl.

There was a faint gasp from the listeners at this. More whirring, snapping sounds, as people recorded the scene on their mobiles.

Darcy, beetroot-faced behind her co-star, wished the cobbles would open up beneath her. Poor Marco. The only upside to this toe-curling scene was that Christian, at least, was not present to witness it.

Did Darcy but know it, this was not the case. Christian was, at that very moment, climbing the steep village street, fists thrust in his white linen pockets, returning with interest the admiring glances the promenading female youth of Rocolo were bestowing on him. But as he approached the lights and bustle signalling the restaurant, some instinct within urged him to slow down. Something was happening. A crowd had gathered. Softly, quietly, stealthily, Christian approached the outer ring of spectators and inserted himself into the crowd.

The centre of the attention seemed to be a woman in jet-black sunglasses and a very short black dress; white-blond hair spilling over her shoulders. Christian narrowed his eyes behind his wraparound shades and scrutinised her appreciatively. Not bad. Good legs. And her tits were impressive, if so obviously fake you could park a Harley between them. She was holding a small, nasty-looking brown dog whose diamond collar picked up the candlelight and threw it back with ten times the force.

That dog. He'd seen that dog before, Christian thought. Most recently a mere few hours ago. It was Belle's dog, Sugar. Which must mean . . .

He looked at the blonde again. That . . . was Belle? It couldn't be. She looked so different. So confident, so polished, so utterly unlike the crushed wreck who had begged him not to leave her back in LA, whose career was as broken as her spirit. That woman, Christian saw, had disappeared completely. The Belle he now saw before him, buoyed up by her new starring role in a big film, and her success in Shakespeare in London, was a total glamazon. She stood proud and tall – very tall in those heels – radiating attitude.

She was gesticulating, shaking her hair about, in the apparent middle of an argument with that great shambling loser of a restaurant owner who'd given him all those snooty looks earlier in the day. Well, go girl, Christian found himself thinking. He liked that red lipstick. He liked the way everyone in the restaurant was staring. Belle was the centre of attention, and he liked that in a woman.

Christian's scrutiny travelled approvingly again over her erect breasts – more erect than he remembered them – tiny hips and long brown legs. He felt a stir of lust in his white linen trousers.

Christian was about to step forward, attract her attention, when he spotted, in the shadows behind his former girlfriend, the woman he was auditioning for the role of the present one. Darcy Prince. Actually, Christian thought, his eyes behind his wraparounds sweeping critically over the creased white shirt and battered jeans she wore, Darcy wasn't looking so great tonight. Her hair was a mess, she looked as if she'd just got out of the bath. She wasn't even wearing shades, for Chrissakes; no Hollywood star went out without them, especially if they weren't wearing make-up. Didn't she know anything, Christian wondered, irritated. And the way she was hiding in the shadows looking like a scared rabbit; you hardly noticed her. It was as if she was desperate to avoid being associated with Belle, not trying her damnedest to get some of the reflected glory, as any sane person would.

He returned his gaze to Belle. She was looking good, there was no doubt about it. So good that Christian was starting to wonder if he'd thrown her over too soon. Now she was going to be a big star again, it was kind of beginning to look like a mistake.

But what could he do about it? What passed for his brain wrestled fruitlessly with the problem. One fact alone emerged. If he stepped out now he ran the risk of being claimed by Darcy, which would ruin his chances with Belle. Belle might even be mad at him; she was pretty pissed at him when he'd left her and that hadn't been so long ago. Or she might still be with that British guy, the one who had left Darcy for her. He frowned and shook his head. Jeez, it was confusing.

Either way, it was now clear to Christian, making himself known to these two actresses was a high-risk strategy. Too bad if Darcy was expecting him, and he could tell she was from the way she stared around from time to time, a desperate expression in her eyes. He'd have to go away and think about this. After all, he'd be seeing them both on set in the next couple of days, when principal photography started. Which might have its tricky moments. He needed a strategy, Christian realised.

Stepping softly out of the crowd in the courtyard, he gained the street and melted swiftly away, a flash of diamond and white linen in the shadows.

'Sugar is a Very Important Dog,' Belle repeated, to a Marco who was having difficulty accepting this really was what had been said.

For some seconds, there was deadlock. Marco's eyes held Belle's – or the area where he imagined Belle's were. It was difficult to tell behind the sunglasses.

Belle shook her hair, signalling the end of the stalemate. 'OK. Here's what we do,' she announced briskly. 'I'm willing to compromise with you.'

'*Signora?*' He couldn't wait to hear this. Neither, he sensed, could the crowd.

Belle tossed her hair again. 'It's a public place, right? So get rid of the public. Empty the restaurant. We'll eat on our own.'

Chapter 42

His guidebook had been spot-on about this place, Ken thought. Rocolo was a peach, no question. Crumbling houses, narrow passages, ancient church, tiny main square at the top with funny little shops full of ham and cheese and suchlike. Straight out of Italian village central casting, it was.

Not much space in his room, but he was pleased with it none the less. Above a bar right at the very top of the village, behind the barn-like church in the square. Took five flights of stairs to get to it, but worth it: white-walled, simply furnished, with the bathroom in the room, behind a little wall. Loo, shower and basin, but what else did you need? At the other end of the room, the other side of the slightly saggy but otherwise perfectly comfortable double bed, were a pair of French windows. Ken had discovered, with an almost childlike delight, that these led out on to a little balcony with a spectacular view of the village below, the roofs spinning out below him, the ridged dips in the tiles making it look like a flamenco skirt made of terracotta instead of frills.

Great skyline it was, Ken thought, that skirt effect, those TV masts bristling against the sunset. Make a good photo. But he had to stop thinking like this. Educate himself out of it. Learn to live life, not merely frame it in a viewfinder. Things were more enjoyable when you just stood and looked, rather than assessed any given image before you in terms of what you could sell it for.

He stood on his little balcony, clad in the clean, pressed, new shirt and jeans he'd bought at the airport, freshly washed and shaved for once, enjoying the scent of aftershave, not just his own but that drifting up from the narrow cobbled street below him as couples on their evening walk strolled by beneath. The contrast with what he would have routinely been doing in London – what Keith was no doubt doing that minute – struck him forcefully. Sitting on the wall opposite the Portchester, most likely, waiting for some self-regarding celebrity to emerge.

But instead of locking his eyes and lens to that revolving mahogany door, with its cut-glass and its brass fittings, that wheel of fortune which might produce anyone from Carla Bruni-Sarkozy to the latest reality TV droid – usually the latter – he was here. Enjoying the peace and the sunset, watching the sky turn from deep blue to yellow opal, and watching the swifts swooping; crossing and recrossing the sky in search of insects. The swifts, Ken reflected, were the only ones with an eye to the main chance in Rocolo.

Directly below his balcony was the children's playground by the church. It had been a bit noisy when Ken arrived: tea-time and the kiddies had been having their last runabout. Probably some people might have objected, their Italian village idyll ruined by screaming brats and all that, but Ken didn't mind it at all. Who could possibly mind the sound of children playing? He liked kiddies. Had always imagined at some stage that he'd have a few of the little blighters himself. Hadn't happened though, but that was another story.

Dinnertime, Ken told himself, patting his stomach. There'd been a restaurant he'd spotted on the winding hill up through the village: nice little place on a corner, set on a courtyard with cream parasols. It had been crowded even then, but hopefully they'd have room for a little one.

Ken proceeded down the winding main street towards where he remembered seeing it. There were plenty of other people besides him taking an evening stroll, he saw, many looking like holidaymakers too. Rocolo was a bit touristy perhaps. Probably inevitably when the place looked as cute as this. But you could sense it still had some authenticity, some original features. Very original features, Ken chuckled to himself as an ancient, brown-faced, toothless crone with centre-parted white hair under a black headscarf poked past with her walking stick. There was a photo op round every corner.

But so what? Ken reminded himself that he wasn't taking any photographs this holiday, that was the point of it. He was having a break from photographs, maybe even a permanent one. Since his moment of apotheosis in the airport, his urge to abandon the paparazzi life had not weakened; on the contrary, it had grown stronger. He had not realised how sick to the heart, the back teeth, the very soles of his much-scuffed trainers he was of the way he had been living. Without the long lenses permanently slung round his neck he felt lighter in more ways than one.

His practised eye had not shut down, however, and Ken found a certain pleasure in spotting all the shots that, normally, it would have been second nature to take and sell to the photo libraries. Make a little money on the side; subsidise his stay. But his stay, Ken realised, was the whole point. It did not need subsidising. He'd been subsidising it for years, at the expense of his own sanity, it seemed now.

473

There were subjects aplenty. At the turn of every street, and particularly the winding main street, which twisted up like a snake from the bottom of Rocolo to the top, there was something picturesque: a faded icon in a niche, an ornate fountain, an ancient, sunny windowsill ablaze with geraniums, the dark glint of red wine bottles in the depths of a cool shop, a child large-eyed under a mop of dark curls.

But he had not photographed any of them and as a result felt more content than he could ever remember. The gathering darkness soothed his tired spirit. The mellow walls of the houses, he found, trailing his fingers lightly over them as he passed, were slowly exuding, like breathing, the heat of the day. The warmth was enveloping, like a hug.

And the smells! Winding with the warmth and aftershave in the evening air was the scent of a hundred individual cooking dinners from the houses he was passing: the sharp spike of garlic, the mouthwatering surge of tomato, the dry burst of herbs, the nose-nipping rush of onion. He was starving now, Ken realised. And for proper food. After all those years of crisps and nasty coffee, ready meals and dodgy takeaways, he longed with his soul as much as his stomach for something real to eat.

He had been right to come here, Ken felt, spotting gratefully, as the road bent round, the lights of the restaurant on the next corner. For a refugee, like him, a casualty from the front line of a world obsessed with fame, what better place than somewhere so old, so peaceful, a place that must have seen it all in its time and that cared nothing for the vicissitudes of stardom; was barely aware of it, in fact.

The church clock chimed; a thin, foreign sound most unlike the more full-throated bells of home. London seemed so far away. Lurking for hours outside hotels waiting for celebrities, even further.

' 'Scuse me,' Ken exclaimed, skipping deftly aside to avoid banging into someone.

'Hey, watch it, willya?' snapped the other in an American accent, irritably shaking a shiny black shoe that Ken had not been entirely able to avoid all contact with. He shook it, Ken noticed, as if it had been in contact with dogshit or something. What an arsehole. But, Ken reminded himself, he had been in the wrong. He had not been looking where he was going.

'Sorry.' Ken repeated his apology to the disdainful youth, who was, he noted, flashily dressed in wraparound shades and with a great many necklaces draped about him. He had jet-black hair, wore nothing but a waistcoat on his top half, was muscularly built and rather reminded him, Ken thought, of an actor called Christian Harlow.

The reminder was not pleasant. Harlow's dogged and seemingly unstoppable ascent up the Hollywood greasy pole had been greeted with dismay by every paparazzi Ken knew, all of whom loathed the actor to his fingertips. Even in a world where paps were in general immune to the diva strops thrown by stars, where egos were rampant and brattish behaviour expected and even encouraged, Harlow had distinguished himself.

Ken paused and turned as the Harlow-look-alike continued on his way downhill, his muscular legs in their white linen trousers flashing in and out. The engine of recognition that had started up within him was urging him to look again. The Rolodex in his mind whirred. Ken had not spent years as a successful paparazzi for nothing. Hard-wired into his memory were millions of images of well-known people. He knew most famous faces so well that he could identify a celebrity from the tiniest of clues; a pair of lips, a nose, a way of walking, even. And all these clues, as he stared after the man in white trousers, was telling him that this, incredible as it seemed, wasn't just someone who looked like Christian Harlow. It actually *was* Christian Harlow.

Ken reeled to the side of the road and stood against the warm wall for support, as well as comfort. Christian Harlow! The worst and nastiest of the lot. If he'd had to identify in one person, Ken thought, everything he wanted most to leave behind him, Christian Harlow would have been that person.

Ken shook his head in slow incredulity. Disappointment mingled with his disbelief. His refuge had been violated. He'd thought he'd got away from it all, only to find it had followed him. Or perhaps had beaten him to it. Christian Harlow was in Rocolo. But what was Christian Harlow doing here? Did he have a villa nearby or something?

Ken felt that all the magic had been drained from the evening. With a heavy heart he continued descending the hill towards the restaurant.

His spirits rallied a bit as he neared Marco's. It was a nice little place, bright, optimistic and stylish, with all those small tables set out on the courtyard, all those candles and fairy lights twinkling in the vine behind. It was obviously very popular, every table crammed with people laughing and talking; it seemed very vivacious. Excited, almost. And the food looked and smelt just the ticket, Ken thought, watching strands of spaghetti winding round forks and remembering how hungry he was.

Just as he was about to step into the courtyard, someone knocked him out of their way. 'Don't they know who I freaking well am?' a woman, apparently exiting, was complaining in an American accent to her companion.

Ken froze. His Rolodex whirred again, but for a split second only. He knew who she freaking well was. There was no doubting the identity of the sunglassed blonde hobbling out of the restaurant in shoes so high they were, strictly speaking, stilts.

Just as there was no doubting the identity of that nasty-looking dog she clutched in her skinny arms. Belle Murphy. Two minutes ago he'd seen his least favourite Hollywood actor. And now here was his female equivalent.

A plump, bespectacled, mild-looking man in his sixties was hurrying after Belle in high-waisted white trousers and broad-soled shoes. 'If I might just interrupt, Miss Murphy . . .' Ken heard him ask in a respectful voice.

Belle heaved a testy sigh. 'Whaddya want?' she snapped.

'Just to let you know what a great fan I am of yours, Miss Murphy,' said the man humbly. 'My kids organised this trip to Italy for my wife and me as my sixtieth birthday present, and I never thought . . . what I meant to say is,' he shook his big grey head in wonder, 'that if my kids only knew. They'd be so excited. If they could see me now, here, talking to *you* . . .'

The sunglasses were turned on him witheringly. 'I can't believe,' spat Belle, 'that they let you reproduce children.' She turned on her heel and tottered out.

'I didn't want to eat in that shithole anyway,' Ken heard her snarling. 'What's so great about Italy anyway – apart from shoes and Bobby De Niro, one of my best friends, incidentally.'

Ken shut his eyes and opened them again. He scratched his thinning, reddish pate. Was he dreaming? Or, rather, was this a nightmare?

He watched Belle Murphy swaying off down the street on the arm of some woman in flipflops and a white shirt. Was there no escape from these people? Was he doomed to encounter celebrities for the rest of his days? He exhaled a sigh that seemed to have dredged itself up from the bottom of his boot-soles and prepared to step forward into the restaurant.

His appetite, however, seemed to have gone.

*

'Did you hear that!' Georgie squealed, as Belle Murphy, with the help of her – frankly scruffy – companion wobbled out of the restaurant on her vertiginous heels and Marco, having delivered himself of a resounding negative, his hands working agitatedly through his hair, returned through the excited tables to the kitchen. 'She told him to empty the restaurant!' Georgie gasped to Richard.

Richard nodded distractedly. His mobile phone was ringing again. Apprehensively he dragged it out. Please God, not Mrs Greatorex again. He still hadn't got hold of his constituency agent to find out exactly what was going on. Except that Richard now saw that the number on his display panel was that of Guy, after all.

He got up from his chair and hurried hastily out to the relative privacy of the street.

'Guy! At last!'

'Oh. Richard. Hello,' came Guy's light and vaguely sardonic tone. 'To what do I owe this pleasure? I thought you were on holiday.'

'Yes, I am. But I've been called.'

Guy's voice jumped slightly. 'Called? By,' he took a deep breath, 'The Leader?'

Richard rolled his eyes. 'By Mrs Greatorex.'

'Oh.' Guy sounded disappointed.

'About the, um, dogging in Wellover. Is it really happening like she says?'

Guy snorted. 'They're calling it Legover now, apparently.' He snorted again.

Richard felt Guy's attitude lacked something. But then again, Guy's attitude always had. He affected a lofty, patrician amusement with the world and its doings, which sat oddly on a supposed servant of democracy.

'Well, it's a bit shocking, isn't it?' Richard demanded. 'Mrs Greatorex says Russell's Leap is heaving with people at it every Friday night. At it like rabbits.' Richard stopped himself, faintly alarmed at the relish with which he had exaggerated. Mrs Greatorex had said no such thing.

'So I hear,' Guy confirmed with a snigger.

Richard assumed his best Battle of Britain tones. 'Well, shouldn't we be doing something about it? It sounds one hell of a mess, Guy.'

Guy sniffed. 'Yes, well, now it's all out in the open, they rather seem to expect us to sort it out at the double. To bend over backwards as it were, ha ha.'

'Ha ha,' said Richard mirthlessly. 'But – has anything been done? Have the police been informed, even?'

'Yes, but from what I can gather some of them are worse than the punters.'

'You don't sound very worried,' Richard remarked heatedly, raising his voice only to lower it again immediately as Hugh looked up from the table and peered in his direction. As Georgie called a waiter over, waving an empty bottle in explanation, Richard saw Hugh's sneerily curious expression become one of melting sycophancy. Georgie had, of course, volunteered in advance that the dinner would be their treat. Richard felt the knife of dislike twist tighter in his guts.

'This beautiful village is being defaced,' he thundered to his agent.

'From Domesday Book to dogging websites, you mean?' Guy chuckled.

Richard ignored him. No wonder Guy had never made it as a candidate and was reduced to running the constituency office. 'There are all these confused old people – outraged, disgusted and possibly even frightened by these lewd acts being committed on their own doorsteps.' His voice rose as his conviction mounted. 'They're our constituents, Guy. They're turning to us for help. They need our protection.'

He was interrupted by a guffaw from the agent. 'Need our protection? Mrs Greatorex? Come off it, Richard. She could tear a burglar's head off with her bare hands.'

'But she sounded *very* disturbed, Guy,' Richard protested.

'By a load of saddoes going down on each other over the gearstick? I don't think so. What's worrying her is that that's not the only thing going down.'

Richard was alarmed. 'You don't mean . . . animals?'

'House prices, my dear fellow. All that's scaring Greatorex is that the value of her house will be affected. She wants us to protect the price of her property. That's the only reason any of them care, believe me.'

Richard felt rather punctured.

'It's true, Richard.'

'But . . .'

'Believe me. Morality's got nothing to do with it.'

Richard subsided. He suspected, miserably, that Guy was right. He had worked himself up into a righteous and defensive lather only to be told he was being used as an adjunct to the local estate agent. Was this all democracy now meant? The sense of disillusionment growing within him was almost physical, like a tumour.

'We have to do something about it, none the less,' he maintained stoutly. 'Though God knows what I can do from here.'

'Well, you need evidence of what's going on, for a start,' Guy advised, his manner changing, to Richard's relief, from the satirical to the more-or-less sensible.

'Yes. Yes. But how?' Richard asked sharply. 'I'm not breaking off my holiday to go sneaking through the woods to watch . . . well . . . whatever there is to watch.'

'No. You just need to look at the websites. Wellover's mentioned on all of them. There are pictures too . . .'

Richard swallowed. He wasn't sure he wanted to look. His image of Wellover at the moment was all roses and sun through trees. Mooning through trees would put a completely different aspect on things. 'There isn't a computer here,' he said, with relief.

Guy batted this excuse away immediately. 'Well, are you near any big towns?'

'Florence.'

'Bob's your uncle then,' Guy said comfortably. 'An internet café's what you need. I'll give you the website addresses. Got a pen? Actually,' he added, as Richard started slapping his pockets, 'on second thoughts, ring me up when you're sitting in front of a screen. You're hopeless on the internet and finding these dogging websites can be complicated. Knowing you, you'd Google "dogging" and end up sitting in front of the Crufts site all afternoon.'

Chapter 43

Emma looked out of the bus window and felt a surge of optimism. It was a beautiful, bright, blue and gold day. The vehicle, with its throaty roar of engine, moved briskly along the near-empty roads through the sunny countryside. The brown hills, with their neat, thin, green stripes of vineyard, looked, Emma thought, exactly like neatly combed green hair.

She was going to Florence in search of a travel cot. Or rather, she and Morning both were. It would have been useful, of course, to have left the baby with his mother, but by the time she had left for the bus, Belle had not even got out of bed. She had had hopes of Mara, who loved to play with Morning, but she had been going to the market.

Darcy had been about, although she seemed very pre-occupied. She had spent breakfast time frowning into her mobile, texting frantically between grabbing at the rolls and biscuits Mara brought to the table. 'I shouldn't be eating this, I'm doing some modelling today,' Darcy announced with a rueful grin as she helped herself to another of Mara's delicious home-made *bice*; crumbly chocolate biscuits sandwiched together with mascarpone cream.

They were passing the Rocolo car park now. Emma looked up, enjoying the fantastical sight of the old village hanging on the top of the hill, shining bright in the morning sun. The buildings crowded together, no shape the same, all shades from terracotta to apricot, bristling with towers, gables, aerials and satellite dishes.

In the car park below, some children were being unloaded from a car; the boy, only visible from the back, was Cosmo's age, while the little girl had white hair. Just like Hero.

Emma's happy mood disintegrated instantly. A sick, anxious feeling possessed her and she wondered miserably, as she often did in tired or weak moments, where the children were now, what they were doing, whether they were happy, whether they ever thought of her.

Her anxiety was followed by the usual burning sense of injustice. Who had put those drugs in her bag? And why? Would she ever find out? It seemed increasingly unlikely.

'Whatever did you dream about?' Georgie exclaimed when Richard woke from a troubled sleep. Her eyes were wide with concern over the Tuscan-patterned duvet. Richard muttered something about eating too much. How could he tell her his night had been haunted by visions of Mrs Greatorex enjoying ecstatic congress over a steering wheel with various men in policeman's helmets? Even less than he could tell her that now, after breakfast, he had to go into Florence, and look, not at the Duomo or Piazza della Signoria, but at websites of people having casual sex in the woods? As he pulled on his T-shirt and his battered summer chinos, Richard reflected that none of it, exactly, was what he had entered Parliament for.

He had decided that the best thing would be to take Orlando to the internet café with him. Orlando was a teenager and therefore *au fait* with computers, as well as internet cafés, whose appearance and possible whereabouts were something Richard could not easily picture. He could explain the reason for their trip in the car on the way.

In as far as it could be explained.

He arrived at the breakfast table feeling he wanted to get the café visit and the website over with, only to find that his son was not present. Richard wrinkled his brow. Orlando was fond of his bed, sure enough, but he also had the ravenous appetite of the lanky teenager. It was unusual for him to prefer the first to the second.

The Faughs, of course, were there in force. Hugh was on his BlackBerry, as usual, rolling and clicking with one hand while with the other he fed cereal into his great cruel jaws. Ivo and Jago were slathering butter on a pile of croissants. Laura, meanwhile, regarded him coolly from beneath a straw sunhat, sipping her coffee with her usual distant, disdainful and faintly amused air.

Richard sat down under the green parasol and reached for a piece of the strange, hard, square toast people seemed to prefer round here. 'I've, um, got to go into Florence,' he announced. 'I've got to, um, visit the . . .'

Dogging websites of Europe? 'Mayoral office,' he finished, relieved at the sudden inspiration. 'There's a possibility of some twinning.'

Hugh looked at him. 'Wellover?' he boomed, disbelievingly. 'Twinning with *Florence*? Bit ambitious, isn't it?'

'I think it's a lovely idea,' Georgie trilled loyally. 'You know, I'd rather like to come too. Not to see the silly old mayor, obviously. But some sightseeing might be nice.'

Richard buttered his toast in horror. He had counted on no one but Orlando for company. He had imagined Georgie, as was her usual habit, staying by the pool all day, reading Martina

Cole. He'd have liked to do the same himself, although substitute P. G. Wodehouse.

'Yeah, we're on for that,' said the twins.

Richard's heart sank. He cursed himself for mentioning the trip at all. He should have just melted away, as the butter round the twins' croissants was doing.

As Georgie passed him some coffee, his thumb closed over the saucer and then jerked violently, threatening to throw the whole lot in the air, as Laura, most uncharacteristically, uttered a sharp yell.

'Orlando! We're out here!'

His son was just visible in the shadows of the house, Richard noticed now. He was lurking about as if trying to avoid someone. Upon Laura's greeting, he came slowly outside, his eyes glued to the trailing laces of his trainers, his expression hunted. Richard noticed this but was not entirely surprised. After what Georgie had told him about Laura's remarks at dinner last night, it was a wonder Orlando could face her at all. Even if, as Laura had apparently insisted afterwards, she had been joking.

Georgie patted the chair beside her. 'Do have some breakfast, darling,' she said absently.

'Bugger,' exclaimed Hugh suddenly. He was stabbing at the fascia of his BlackBerry. 'Bloody thing's broken. Bugger, bugger, *bugger.*'

'Fancy coming into Florence with me, son?' Richard asked quickly and in a voice loud enough to drown what he considered were Hugh's appalling bad manners. Swearing in front of ladies. Swearing at breakfast. Swearing in front of ladies having breakfast.

Orlando, whose face looked puffy and tired, seemed uncertain. 'Er . . .' He darted a glance at Laura.

'I'm going too,' Laura smiled tightly.

Orlando's green eyes flashed with alarm beneath his heavy brows. 'Er, actually, Dad, I was thinking of, um, staying here.' He swallowed and looked at the pool, which sparkled invitingly at the end of the terrace. 'Might, um, do a bit of swimming.'

Richard stared back at him, his eyes a silent plea. But as he could hardly spell out to his son why his company was so urgently desired, there was nothing more to say. He was on his own, apart from four unwanted fellow-travellers. And Guy, of course, waiting by his telephone to help him through the cybersexual minefield.

'You're not going?' Georgie regarded her son. 'But Ivo and Jago are,' she added brightly, as if that was an incentive and not the exact opposite.

'No thanks, Mum,' Orlando muttered. 'I think I could do with a rest.'

There was an explosion from the Faugh boys. 'Yes,' sniggered Jago. 'You're probably *exhausted* after all that work you put in on your A levels.'

'Worn out!' chimed in Ivo.

Orlando looked steadily back at him. Richard noted his son's expression. He clearly could not understand why the twins were so nasty to him. It had not occurred to Orlando what was so abundantly obvious to his father – that the Faugh boys were jealous of his beauty. Orlando, his father guessed in a moment of insight, was still registering and being alarmed by his effect on women; that men were affected too had not yet even occurred to him.

Beneath her straight-brimmed straw sunhat, Laura smiled a lazy smile. 'You know,' she drawled lightly, 'I've changed my mind. I think Orlando's right. A rest is a good idea. I think I'll

487

stay at home as well. It's going to be hot.' She purred slightly on the hot, Richard vaguely noticed.

What she said was true: the sun was high in the sky already; the shadows from the parasols black and crisp against the pale stone of the patio. On the breakfast plates, the left-over butter next to the Faughs' croissant crumbs were yellow liquid pools.

Ivo and Jago, Richard saw, had not yet finished baiting his son. 'Are you sure you don't want to come to Florence?' Ivo asked Orlando in sneering tones. 'Several of the wonders of the world are there.'

'Well, they'll all be there once you get there,' Orlando riposted hotly. His father stifled a snigger.

'You're very keen on history, aren't you, Orlando?' Jago hit back immediately. 'I understand it's one of the, ahem, *two* A levels you took.'

'Oh yes,' drawled Ivo. 'When are the results coming, again?' The brothers looked expectantly at their victim.

But, to his father's amazement, Orlando beamed at Ivo. 'Hey, you know, you're right, Ivo. Florence sounds pretty cool. Maybe I will come after all.'

'You know,' Laura added without missing a beat. 'I think I'll come as well.'

'Actually,' Richard interjected, deciding enough was enough and it was time to take firm action, 'I'm not sure all of us can fit in one car. It's a business trip anyway. We'll be there and back in a jiffy. I really think,' he said, assertive as he rarely was, 'that it's best if just Orlando and myself go.'

A tough-looking redhead in ginger suede trousers sat in the foyer of Florence's best hotel waiting for her taxi. It was late.

Sam tapped her manicured fingers – blood red, like her mood – impatiently on the marbled top of the coffee table in front of her. She glared at the foyer's various pieces of tasteful furniture on which stood various tasteful things. A pebble or two. An ammonite. A small dark vase. But no bloody taxi. Where the hell was it? Didn't they realise how important it was, how important she was?

It was Brooke from the studio who had got her here. Sam had taken a call from her yesterday. 'That Rumtopf shoot with Darcy Prince? I've just been sent the images on JPEG.'

'Great, wasn't it?' Sam purred complacently.

'No,' said Brooke uncompromisingly, cutting straight to the chase as usual. 'I'll be straight with you, Samantha.'

At the other end, Sam twisted her full, plum-painted lips in disapproval. If there was one thing she disliked more than being called Samantha, it was people being straight with her. It always meant that they were about to say something unpleasant. She knew this because she herself was often straight with people.

'Well, what's wrong with it?' she blustered. 'Getting Rumtopf was a serious coup. He was booked up till 2020.'

'Yeah, yeah, yeah,' Brooke interrupted. 'Thing is, she looks fat.'

'*Fat?*' Sam gasped. The idea was impossible. What was possible was that Darcy, while a long way from fat, was less thin than most of her girls. But even if that were true, Rumtopf routinely airbrushed his pictures – slimming here, youthening there, lengthening, glossing, bronzing, so the finished images bore practically no resemblance to the real person who had posed for them. It was the entire reason he was so sought after. 'Fat on a Rumtopf picture? Hell, he could make Beth Ditto look like Kate Moss.'

'Well, he hasn't here,' Brooke snapped. 'She's bursting out all over. This is not the image we wanted.'

Sam fought to retain her self-control. She was slightly

hungover as it was and rattled by Brooke's lack of appreciation. She'd got Rumtopf for the studio, for Pete's sake. And the pictures had been fine. Darcy had looked a little rounded in some of them, but so what?

'Darcy's a woman,' she began. 'She's got a few curves, sure. Curves are where it's at, you know,' she added, gaining confidence as she hit on a theme. 'You know, after size zero and all that trouble about being too skinny—'

'Screw that,' Brooke thundered. 'And let me tell you something. You can't be too skinny in Hollywood. Jesus, Samantha, I thought you knew that.'

'Yeah,' Sam had muttered, her other hand playing worriedly with her outsize amber necklace. Of course she knew that.

'And, let me tell you, Darcy's a long way off being even slightly skinny, let alone too skinny. She's seriously huge.'

'Huge?' Sam exclaimed. 'Let's be clear, here. Darcy's about an English size ten. Twelve, tops.'

'Sure, and most of our stars are American double zero,' Brooke riposted. 'I mean, Belle Murphy's in this picture. She's a zero. Next to her, Darcy's gonna look like Nellie the goddamn elephant.'

'Now just hang on. Just wait a minute . . .'

'Baby, ain't no time for that. Jack's going crazy. Saw the pictures and went shouty crackers.' Brooke, Sam remembered, liked to lace her conversation with what she imagined were upmarket English expressions. 'We can't have a fat star in this picture. You gotta do something.'

'Like what?' Sam snapped. 'Go and trim some flesh off her or something?'

'Whatever. Anything. Just do something. Now. Or Jack's gonna start principal photography without her.'

Sam had put down the phone with a hand so shaking that it

rattled all her bracelets. Then she had raised her beringed fingers to her throbbing temples and thought hard. Darcy, she knew, was scheduled for another magazine shoot tomorrow, in Florence, with Carlos Cojones. It should have been the triumphant second salvo in the campaign; the publicity that conclusively launched the actress as the hottest and most beautiful new star around.

She needed to be at it, Sam realised. If she was there herself, supervising, suggesting, styling – whatever Carlos said – she might be able to prevent complete disaster. Because it wasn't only Darcy's career on the line here. If this next shoot went wrong, Sam knew, Brooke was unlikely to be picking up the telephone to her again.

If only that wretched taxi would show up. Sam, keyed-up to explosion point with tension, glanced angrily around again. Still no manager, although a number of taupe-uniformed hotel flunkeys had appeared in the taupe foyer. There was too much taupe in this place, Sam thought irritably. It might be Florence's foremost fashion hotel, but it was like swimming around a pan of pea soup.

Scowling, she clomped over to the desk. 'I'm waiting for a taxi,' she snarled at the blonde, red-lipsticked, taupe-jacketed receptionist.

The receptionist turned on her a bright, attentive look, which held in it a hint of assessment.

'Allow me to make a phone call, madam.' The blonde lifted the grey receiver and whispered into it in rapid Italian. Within a few moments, the manager swept into the foyer with a clack of heels and a swirl of powerful aftershave. He, too, was dressed in taupe. The colour was beginning to make Sam feel queasy.

The manager's manicured hands were outstretched in expansive concern. 'I am chasing your taxi, signora.'

The taupe flunkeys, Sam now noticed, were trotting backwards and forwards to the hotel entrance, returning each time with big shiny boxes and smart carriers bearing the logos of designer shops. These were gradually being assimilated into a small and obviously very expensive mountain by the reception desk. 'Can you take it up to Suite Six?' Sam heard the blonde concierge instruct a colleague with a melting, red-lipsticked smile. 'It's Sir Evelyn and Lady de Rothschild's shopping.'

An idea, born of desperation, now hit Sam. 'Did it come in a taxi?' she exclaimed. 'Now mine's obviously not coming, can I have Lord and Lady de Rothschild's shopping's taxi instead?'

Chapter 44

Amazingly, within half an hour of arriving, a travel cot was hers. Florence, Emma gratefully realised, might look all towers and flags and winding cobbled streets between canyons of ancient brown buildings, but it was no slouch when it came to twenty-first-century tourism and the needs of twenty-first-century tourists like Morning. Two minutes after entering the tourist information office she was outside again clutching a map on which a helpful and extremely efficient Italian tourist official had ringed not one possible cot shop, but three. Ten minutes after that she had ordered a cot and arranged for it to be delivered to the villa; that very afternoon, the salesman had promised. '*Bello bambino!*' he had added, tickling Morning's cheek. 'You sleep well now, you hear?'

And now, Emma decided, for some fun. She had checked the bus return times. She and Morning had, she calculated, an hour free to explore the ancient city.

Florence spread about her, bright in the brilliant sunshine. Everywhere she looked held interest: the cafés on the pavements, the unfamiliar signs across the grand fronts of the buildings, the jagged snatches of Italian she caught as the speakers passed; the crowds of elderly tourists, necks stretched upwards as they gaped at some tower, in matching baseball caps that made them look like children.

Emma jiggled Morning up and down in his carrier in happy anticipation. 'Where first?' she beamed at him. 'You choose.'

In the hire car next to his father, Orlando looked out, unseeing, at the passing landscape. He rubbed his eyes, heavy after a sleepless night of worry. It was hot by the window, with the morning sun pouring through, but the only burning Orlando was aware of was the shame that would not go away.

He pushed his long fingers through his corn-coloured locks, squeezing his eyelids to try to excise the memory. But the inside of his own head, Orlando was finding, was not somewhere he could escape from easily.

It had happened last night, after the trip to the restaurant. And now Orlando was in shock. He had no idea she had thought of him that way. Even after what she had said about him servicing plain women for a living. At that thought too, Orlando's insides knotted further and the temperature of his cheeks soared.

Laura was a friend of his parents, for God's sake. The wife of a Member of Parliament. And unbelievably ancient – over forty at least.

The irony was, he had been relieved when the restaurant visit was over, imagining it to be the end of the day's trials. When they got back to the villa, he'd made himself scarce at the first opportunity, planning to listen to his iPod for a while, and maybe watch something incomprehensible and Italian on the tiny TV. From what he could see, Italian telly was even worse than that at home, but Orlando was a connoisseur of poor-quality television. The more terrible it was, the more he liked it.

Yet in the event he had not gone immediately to his bedroom. He had stopped in the kitchen to get a beer from the fridge. The others had been milling about in the sitting room. No one had seen him and he had reached his room safely. Or so he had thought.

It had been dark when he opened the door. But when he had felt for the light switch and pressed it, nothing had happened. Orlando had shuffled forward, waving his hands about in the black void so as not to bump into anything, trying to see in the darkness. But this wasn't London, with its permanently orange-tinged gloom; it was the middle of the Italian countryside, and therefore as black as ink.

Then, to his surprise, the lamp by his bed was switched on. To reveal, lying on the bed, his parents' friend Laura Faugh.

'Oh. Sorry,' Orlando muttered, turning away in horrified embarrassment. He had strayed into the wrong room. Into Laura's room. His was at the end of the corridor by the sitting room; there weren't any others near. Somehow, he had gone completely the wrong way.

Then his eyes dropped to the floor and he frowned. Hang on a minute, those were *his* trainers down there. His CDs and screwed-up T-shirt. This was his room.

'Don't be sorry.' Her deep, gravelly voice came from just behind his shoulder. A hand with red fingernails crept round his front and placed itself over his crotch. Paralysed, he stared down at where it clenched over his balls like a large white spider with red shoes on. The hand began gently to rub.

'Very nice,' said Laura huskily.

Orlando sprang to escape, got his feet tangled in sheets and fell backwards on to the bed. 'Mrs Faugh!' he squeaked, terrified.

She had unbuttoned her fitted, herringbone-patterned blouse. Beneath her demure double rope of pearls he glimpsed a neat black bra with small white polka dots on it, trimmed with a small white ribbon. 'Call me Laura,' she smiled as she shrugged off the shirt. Her eyes under their hoods glittered blackly as they travelled him slowly up and down. The dry red lips twisted in amusement.

'You're married,' Orlando, still tangled in the sheets, reminded her desperately.

She gave a gravelly chuckle. 'Yes, but Hugh and I have a very open marriage.'

He watched transfixed, as she peeled her bra off. Her breasts, larger than Orlando had expected, sprang out. They looked hard and pointy, with jabby little nipples on the end. Rather like a pair of missiles, he thought, none the less feeling a jolt of desire, which horrified him. He wrenched his gaze away, his face suddenly burning.

She was unzipping her black skirt now. Frozen to the spot, he watched her step out of it. Bells clanged chaotically in his head. Laura wore no knickers and her pubic hair was neatly trimmed and demure, black against her milk-white flesh, as the straps of the suspenders were black. Orlando had never seen the full rigout in real life before, had never believed anyone, besides Jordan and possibly Russell Brand, actually wore it. He felt the betraying surge again. Oh God.

'You're a virgin, aren't you?' Laura purred, sitting down at the edge of the bed and reaching for his hand. He felt horribly powerless as she took it, pulling him towards her. Slowly, one by one, she pulled his fingers into her mouth and sucked them, her mocking, hooded eyes never leaving his face.

'What's the matter?' she asked huskily, kneeling up so her breasts pushed into his face and a nipple touched the edge of his lips.

The bells in Orlando's head were now blaring traffic horns in an angry midsummer car jam. He surged and shook. While his face was hot other parts of him were in a cold sweat, apart from one part, which seemed to be acting independently of him. He felt it surge, spread, burn insistently behind his fly zip.

'Don't you like girls?' murmured Laura, pushing her hand behind his T-shirt into his clammy chest, where his heart banged.

Orlando swallowed heavily, the newly arrived equipment in his throat ratcheting noisily as he did so. He had no idea whether he liked girls. They had changed from rejecting him to wanting him virtually overnight and he was completely confused about them. And in any case no way could Laura Faugh be described as a girl. The friend of his parents, just feet away down the corridor. The wife of her husband, also feet away. The mother of her children, who were there as well. All this Orlando knew, and yet the insistence in his trousers was swelling, pressing, throbbing. He felt as if he might explode if he did not give way to it.

'Come on, Orlando. You know you want to.' Laura was sitting on the edge of the bed, naked apart from her suspender belt. Her smile was sly, mocking.

As she opened her long white legs in their black suspenders, Orlando saw the hoods over her eyes flick upwards to reveal a glittering, predatory expression. He knew he should resist and yet felt pulled helplessly towards her by the magnet in his crotch.

He stared about him in panic.

On the bed, Laura cupped her missile breasts in her hands and caressed the nipples with her thumbs. 'Like them?' she grinned. 'I've just had them done. They cost the equivalent of a year's school fees.'

The mention of school fees – the bane of his life – brought Orlando to his senses. His more practical senses, that was. He realised that, contrary to what his examiners always said about him, he *could* think ahead. He *did* have an idea of consequences after all. He leapt to his feet. He opened the bedroom door and fled out into the dark corridor.

He had hidden in one of the loos until, some considerable time later, he heard the door of his room unlock and bare feet slap along the tiled corridor. The feet paused for a heartstopping moment outside the bathroom door behind which he hid, and then, to his huge relief, moved on.

Once he had recovered from the shock and the fear of Laura returning, he lay sleepless and pondering two pressing subjects. One was the question of whether to tell his parents. Laura and Hugh's longstanding friends. He had concluded that probably he should, but he couldn't. He was physically incapable of telling it and Georgie in particular, highly strung as she was, was probably incapable of being told it.

As for Richard . . . Orlando slid a sidelong glance at his father, who was driving along towards Florence, his forehead creased in thought, breaking out of his ruminations only to curse occasionally as someone overtook him at speed. After that his face would settle again into preoccupied frown lines. Richard was never exactly chatty, Orlando reflected, but the only thing he had said on this trip so far was to ask him whether he knew what an internet café was. It seemed a strange question. His father had something on his mind himself, Orlando sensed. Perhaps now was not the time. He must bear his burden alone.

And burden was what it was. Orlando had a pressing sense of shame about what had occurred with Laura, as well as a nagging worry that it was somehow his fault. But why was it his fault? He had not encouraged her. And she, all too obviously, felt no embarrassment about it. This morning, far from avoiding his company as he had expected, she had tried to arrange to be alone at the villa with him. His heart had hammered with horror. He had felt wrongfooted, checkmated, helpless, a fly in the web of an utterly shameless spider.

He wished the whole thing would just go away. He wished he could erase it from both their memories. Murder followed by suicide was the obvious solution, but he didn't have a gun and it seemed a bit extreme. So how exactly was he to get through the rest of the fortnight after what had just happened with Laura Faugh, wife of Hugh, mother of Ivo and Jago and one of his parents' oldest friends? How was he to get through the rest of the day?

In Florence's famous Piazza della Signoria, Emma felt awed at the great brown medieval Palazzo Vecchio rearing up before her, the row of bright red, blue and gold-painted shields along its front shining in the sun, its long thin central tower pointing into the bright blue sky.

And just over there, looking rather smaller than she had imagined, but instantly recognisable, was Michelangelo's statue of David. She crossed the wide, paved square towards David, weaving between knots of tourists. Contemplation of the marble youth was, however, compromised by an anxious-looking elderly woman in a dusty-pink anorak, who was standing just beneath it while a man, presumably her husband, in jade nylon slacks and grey slip-on shoes, attempted to focus his camera with shaking hands.

A couple of children now shot excitedly up to David.

'It's Daddy!' announced the smaller of the children, an adorable pink-cheeked moppet with dark curls who Emma guessed to be Hero's age. The parents, harassed and obviously English, came panting up and swooped on their brood.

'Look, Daddy, it's you,' repeated the smaller child, pointing at the naked statue.

Daddy, who Emma guessed walked around the house naked a lot, flushed a deep red.

She smiled as she turned away from Michelangelo's masterpiece. She had anticipated being moved and impressed by the celebrated work of art. 'But I didn't realise it could be funny!' she chuckled to Morning, who chuckled in reply.

'There you are, Dad.' Orlando stood before the silver, purple and red logo'd door of the first internet café his father had ever visited.

Finding it had been a much simpler matter than Richard had ever imagined. He hadn't really needed his son at all, as it turned out. The ladies in the tourist information were wonderfully helpful and intelligent. They spoke English – better than he did in the circumstances – and didn't seem to find anything strange about his request. Nor did they seem to notice his red face and shaking hands. Within minutes of reeling out of their office, Richard, clutching the map they had passed to him on which several possible establishments were circled, had arrived with Orlando at the door where they presently stood.

'Come on then, Dad.' Orlando was on the step, squinting against the brilliant sun, which penetrated even the cave of his hair.

'Er, Orlando . . .' Richard cleared his throat and searched for an excuse. 'Thanks for your help. But I, um, I'll be fine now. I can manage. In there.' He stabbed a finger through the hot air at the shop doorway.

Orlando pushed back his locks in surprise. 'Manage? You? In an internet café?' One of the many reasons he loved his father, Orlando thought, was that at times, for all his intelligence,

Richard made even him look competent. These times were almost always related to technology in some way.

'I'll be fine. Really.' Richard grinned a rictus grin. He would be. He would have to be. There was no question of Orlando coming with him and seeing what he had come to see. It would be embarrassing beyond belief. He could not be responsible for exposing his impressionable, cocooned son to such horrors. He would keep his secret, burdensome though it was. 'You go and do some sightseeing,' he urged Orlando.

'Sightseeing?' Orlando repeated, puzzled. 'On my own? Without you?'

'Yes,' said Richard firmly. 'Go and look at the Duomo. The Uffizi. The Piazza della Signoria . . .'

Seeing his son looking back at him blankly, he rummaged in his pocket for his wallet. 'Here. Buy yourself a drink.'

Orlando brightened considerably at this. 'Oh. OK. Thanks.'

'I'll give you a ring on your mobile when I've, um, finished.' And with that, Richard disappeared into the internet café.

Chapter 45

'Something *so* appalling happened to me last week,' the make-up artist painting Darcy's lips metallic blue told her in tones of horror.

'What?' Darcy asked as best she could without moving the lips that were being painted. Like dentists, make-up people always chatted as if one could respond quite normally.

The make-up artist, whose name was Skye, did not inspire confidence. She had frizzy yellow hair and wore layers of smocks: a billowing white cheesecloth lace-trimmed one on top of a nylon clinging one patterned in swirling yellow and purple Pucci print. She wore black leggings and clumpy Mary Jane shoes in bright red patent.

'I drank a can of Diet Coke,' Skye gasped. 'But guess what, it was *fat* Coke and I *never realised*. Can you *imagine?*'

Skye's assistant, who huddled on the floor rubbing baby oil into Darcy's bare legs to produce a suitably gleaming look for the camera, exclaimed at the make-up artist in horror. 'Omigod! What did you do?'

'Rang my personal trainer *in hysterics*, of course.' Skye shuddered at the memory. 'He told me to calm down and get on the treadmill for two hours . . .'

'*Two* hours!'

'Yeah, which wasn't bad, considering.'

'No, I'd have expected three at least . . . now, did Genevieve say the tweed bikini top and the ostrich feather evening skirt for the second shot,' the assistant mused. 'And maybe the chainmail waistcoat too, or is that a bit much?'

'Darling, this is fashion,' observed a passing man with pale pink dreadlocks carrying a wind machine. '*Nothing's* a bit much.'

Darcy's thoughts drifted away, pulled like iron filings to the great magnet that was Christian. Since his no-show yesterday evening he had texted her only once, despite the avalanche she had sent him. 'Got held up' had been his explanation for last night, while her suggestion that they should meet later that day had not yet drawn a response. It was difficult not to avoid the conclusion that he had, in some way, lost interest.

Tears pricked the back of the eyes now being made up by Skye in a shade the yellow-green of fluorescent coats.

What had she done wrong, Darcy wailed inside. Been too keen? Or inadequate in some other way? Had the sex been no good? He'd made every effort to disguise his disappointment if so, she thought waspishly. She could barely remember the number of times he had tensed, shuddered and groaned inside her – after she had insisted on him wearing a condom, that was. In that respect if no other she had been responsible.

Between the troughs of her uncertainty came high peaks of hope. Christian was a film star, after all. He was a busy man. No doubt he was occupied with *Galaxia* in some way; it was a huge and complex film and principal photography, after all, started the next day. Meaning that she would be on set with him then, she would see him then, which was probably what Christian was counting on too. Of course that was what he was thinking. There was no need to arrange meetings beforehand. Darcy cheered up.

Genevieve, fashion director for the shoot, now arrived. She had rioting, snaky black ringlets, vast black sunglasses, which glittered in the shop lights, skintight jeans and a little fitted jacket. She paraded around in her high-heeled snakeskin boots as if, Darcy thought, she owned the place, mobiles in each ring-festooned hand. Slung around her child-sized waist was a huge buckled belt on which a pair of BlackBerries sat in holsters like revolvers ready to fire.

The shoot, which was a shoe feature for a leading glossy magazine, was taking part in a smart Florence shoeshop. The shop, Darcy thought, was a typical over-styled luxury emporium: shiny, glossy, sparkly, all zebra-print carpet, ribbon-wrapped mirrors and snakeskin-covered pouffes. The shoes seemed almost incidental to the décor; indeed, part of the décor. There were no display racks, nothing so conventional as shelves. Instead, cubbyholes in the red velvet walls held variations on the stiletto-heeled, sparkling, skinny-strapped look that had made this particular designer a household name.

His latest creation was what Darcy was to wear in the shoot; shoes of brilliant black patent with a peep toe and two-inch-thick black platform. The heel behind was sharp, silver and six inches long. The look fell, Darcy thought, somewhere between the porn star and the vaguely orthopaedic, and was horribly similar to what Belle had been wearing last night when Darcy had pushed her up the hill.

The shoes were being fitted on the end of Darcy's feet by one of Genevieve's assistants, a skinny, tongue-tied English boy whose hairstyle – a blue-black-dyed diagonal long fringe – was considerably less shy than he was. His hands were trembling with fear. The fact that Genevieve was standing over him, shouting, was clearly not helping.

'Walk!' Genevieve commanded Darcy.

Darcy obeyed, standing up in the shortie black leather belted mackintosh, which comprised the rest of her wardrobe for the shoot. The shoes were, if anything, even more hideously uncomfortable than they looked.

Genevieve surveyed them critically. 'Hmm. How tall are they? I think I need about six inches.'

'Don't we all, dear,' drawled Kenneth, the shoot's Director of Hair.

Genevieve was now grabbing shoes out of the alcoves left, right and centre. 'Could you redo those in black for us?' she demanded, shoving a pair of gold heels at the shop's PR, a diminutive Italian woman called Lucia de Torquemada. Lucia went pale beneath her tan.

'I'm sorry, Genevieve, they're not available in black. Just gold. Of course, we have other black shoes. Lots of them . . .' Lucia, obviously anguished, waved a shaking hand at some examples. 'But *this*, this has been designed as a *gold* shoe . . .'

Genevieve turned on Lucia, her black hair whirling irefully through the air. 'I want them in black, OK?' she screeched. 'Do you want to be in this feature or don't you?'

Darcy cringed at the rudeness. It was like Rumtopf all over again. Why did fashion people have to behave like this? What made them think they could?

'OK,' whispered Lucia, her eyes large with tears, making a note with thin and trembling hands.

The photographer for the shoot had introduced himself as Carlos. He was a piratical, wild-haired Spaniard, black-leather-jacketed and full of attitude, Darcy hadn't terribly liked the way he looked at her: insolently, assessingly, with more than a touch of droit de seigneur. But perhaps photographers always looked at models that way.

'O-kaaaayyyy!' Carlos called now, tossing his mane of uncombed black hair. 'You look red 'ot, baby,' he told Darcy.

Probably because I am, Darcy thought. Carlos's Japanese assistant was positioning her, wobbling in her perilous heels, before five brilliant spotlights. She was sweating in her leather coat but stretching her smile wider even so.

The in-store stereo started to boom out Sister Sledge. Darcy tried hard to give Carlos what he wanted. 'Chin down!' he yelled, throwing his hair about behind the camera. 'Bottom out! Pout!'

Darcy had learnt from the assistant on the Rumtopf shoot about the alert-but-at-rest look essential for a good photograph. Looking as if you have just exhaled was the trick of it. 'Aaaaah,' she breathed. 'Aaaaah.'

'Relax!' shrieked Carlos.

Darcy could not relax, however. Perhaps it was the shoes. Perhaps it was the heat.

'Ees 'ot,' pronounced Carlos, to her relief.

Five wind machines were now produced, grinding noisily in front of her and blowing so violently Darcy feared falling over in the shoes. It was like being on deck during a gale. Carlos was frowning and waving his arms at the Japanese assistant. 'No, no, no. Lose the wind,' he barked.

Sister Sledge resumed. 'Aaaaah,' went Darcy, again. She had also heard that saying 'Sex' produced a great smile, but she didn't want to encourage Carlos, who obviously felt entitled enough as it was.

She stretched her smile yet wider. She tossed her head to bring some of her black hair tumbling over her face and stretched her lips in another huge smile. Her jaw was trembling with the effort.

But Carlos had once again raised his head from the camera. 'Where's Kenneth?' he demanded. 'Gimme 'air, Kenneth.'

Kenneth shot over and began to toss and twiddle, exclaiming under his breath all the while.

''Air behind ze ears, I theenk, Kenneth. Yeah. OK. 'Ere we go.'

'Aaaah,' pouted Darcy.

Sister Sledge started up yet again. And then stopped yet again.

Carlos was looking up from his camera, frowning from beneath his heavy black brows. ''Old eet. *'Old eet!* I'm *not* loving ze 'air behind ze ears.'

'I'd better mousse those tufts,' Kenneth exclaimed, bouncing over.

'Okayyyyyy!' Carlos roared at last. 'Eyes, *go*.' Darcy widened her eyes obediently. 'Teeth, *go*.' She forced her aching lips yet further apart. 'Hair, *go*.' She tossed it wildly. 'Aaaaah.'

Afterwards, they broke for lunch. Darcy lined up in her leather coat and agonising heels at the crew buffet, which had been set up on a white-draped trestle table in front of the ribbon-wrapped mirrors.

Eagerly, Darcy dived in. Her haul comprised one large slice of juicy quiche and a great square of pizza sprawling with mozzarella, tomato and herbs.

'God, are you *sure*?' someone said in surprise. Turning, Darcy saw Genevieve eyeing her plate. 'You're really going to eat all that?' asked the shoot's fashion director.

Genevieve was sipping mineral water through a straw so as not to smear her lipstick. 'I thought all you Hollywood types were on the baby food diet at the moment,' Genevieve remarked. 'Those of you that are eating anything at all, that is.'

Darcy almost choked on her pizza. '*Baby* food?' And what, exactly, was a Hollywood type? Not her, that was for sure.

'Yeah. You have a baby jar of tomato pasta for supper followed by a baby can of baby chocolate mousse. It's the latest thing in portion-control. I know someone who lost four inches.'

'I'd lose my mind,' Darcy said, cheerfully taking another bite of pizza.

Skye came up. 'Wow, you must be so excited about *Galaxia*,' she breathed, toying with the tiny amount of sliced raw fennel on to her plate. 'I once went on Jack Saint's yacht at Cannes. It's *massive*. There are entire *trees* in pots on the deck and a real open fire in the main sitting room. There are so many servants in white gloves about, it's like bloody Cinderella.'

Darcy nodded. Yachts had never really done it for her; all that blazing white plastic. She disliked sailing too, but sensed it was better not to say so.

Skye's rather prominent eyes were rolling. 'Seriously, his boat is so huge that when I accidentally dropped my mobile off the side, it took about *ten whole minutes* before it hit the water!'

Darcy nodded, biting into the pizza again just as a short, middle-aged woman with thick beige hair, heavily eyelined eyes, tight ginger trousers and a lot of jewellery burst into the room.

Orlando wandered through Florence. He had been following for some time the line of a winding and obviously ancient street, which now opened into a huge and sunlit square.

The square was full of colour and movement. People in T-shirts and trainers sat everywhere, on walls, on the bases of the numerous statues, at the bars, with their colourful sunshades and scurrying waiters. This square was obviously a major hanging-out place, of the sort you didn't get in London. Apart from Leicester Square and Trafalgar Square, of course, both of which were pretty grotty. It would be nice to have somewhere like this, Orlando thought. He looked up at the sky stretched hot and blue above him. And you didn't really get this weather much in London.

Florence was pretty impressive, Orlando decided. He stuck his hands in his pockets and strode off. Might as well see what else there was to look at. Spotting a sign saying 'Duomo' and remembering that his father had said something about it, Orlando followed the direction the arrow was pointing. He supposed he should know what it was, but general knowledge had never been his thing at school. Nor had art. Or geography. As for Italian, forget it. His thing at school had been – nothing. It was something that, as he walked away, Orlando realised he rather regretted.

Emma was looking at the Duomo. Morning had, most thoughtfully, dozed off under his sunhat and she was able to concentrate fully on the magnificent structure. She gazed, quite lost in admiration, at the massive and complex white marble mountain, alive with arches and pointy bits and round windows and all sorts of other architectural devices she wished she knew the name of.

The extraordinary thing about the building was that the more you looked at it, the more you saw. And it was so incredibly old too, she thought, straining upwards, her neck beginning to ache almost as much as her arms did from carrying the baby. It had crouched massively on this spot for century upon century. There was something about those deep round windows in the front, with their carved tracery, that made her think of very ornate plugholes . . .

'Um, Emma?'

At the voice, she froze. Despite having heard it only once before, she knew the thick, deep, hesitant sound instantly.

Slowly she turned, and found herself looking up into a pair of smiling green eyes with a ring of yellow at the centre. A large hand went up uncertainly to push back tumbling blond hair in which gleamed strands of pure gold. A violent flash of electric excitement passed through her knees and stomach. 'Orlando!'

'Hi,' he muttered, in a voice husky with awkwardness. His entire inside had leapt with excitement to see her, but now he felt awkward. She might be here for any number of reasons – meeting someone else, for one.

'Hi,' Emma muttered back, aware of his broad shoulders and brown arms beneath his T-shirt sleeves. Instantly, helplessly, she pictured them clasped about her. She found herself gazing at his lips and tried to rein in her excitement. No doubt he would say in a moment that he had come to meet somebody else. Some beautiful, lissom Italian girl, any number of which were sashaying past all the time.

'What an . . . amazing coincidence,' Emma stuttered.

Orlando nodded energetically. 'I, um, recognised you from behind,' he blurted.

Emma felt her face drain of colour, then flush violently. *What* had he recognised from behind? Her bottom?

She jiggled the sleeping baby gently. 'Had to come and get a travel cot for Morning. The villa we're staying in doesn't have one. What about you?'

'Here with my dad. He's gone to an internet café.'

She smiled at this. 'Trendy dad.'

Orlando snorted. It wasn't a word he had heard in association with his father before. 'It's his first visit. Something to do with his work, I think. He didn't want me around, anyway.'

She nodded.

'I was such an idiot not to get your address in the airport.'

Orlando rushed the words out, coursing hot and cold with embarrassment. 'I've been kicking myself ever since.'

It was a big admission, and he instantly regretted making it. She's never given me a thought, he said to himself. She didn't even seem particularly pleased to see him. On the contrary, she seemed oddly choked up and stilted, not open and easy as she had been before. He felt miserable with disappointment and lapsed into silence. Her turn to speak next.

Emma looked down, breathing quickly, busy gathering her scattered composure. 'So what have you been up to?' she asked.

The memory of Laura Faugh came stabbing back like a javelin. 'I . . . er . . .' He shrugged.

She looked at him – searchingly, it seemed. He braced himself for a brisk goodbye.

'Let's go and have a cup of coffee,' she said.

'OK.'

Emma looked challengingly at Orlando. Was there a note of reluctance there? She moved to cover herself. 'Sure you haven't got better things to do?'

He shook his tousled, dark-golden head. 'Not really,' he said disarmingly. 'This is the most fun I've had all holiday, to be honest.'

It was all very straightforward in the internet cafe, Richard had found to his relief. A clutch of mainly young-looking people in jeans and T-shirts, evidently travelling, their rucksacks rammed down by the rows of benches with computers on. There was a large, hissing coffee machine at the front with a small, smiling woman operating it behind a counter full of delicious-looking cakes and biscuits. From her, Richard haltingly acquired a cappuccino and then, cup and saucer clattering with nerves, shuffled along to what appeared the heart of the operation. A man with wild greying hair, a rather tight blue V-neck jumper and glasses on a chain sat frowning at a newspaper under a sign full of prices.

Richard stared at the prices. He had passionately opposed Britain joining the Euro but now wondered if he had not, after all, been too hasty. It was wonderfully useful and easy, especially when one was in situations such as this.

The man got up from the table, gestured towards a machine that was, to Richard's enormous relief, at the back and therefore discreet, and, without ever really looking away from the football pages, stabbed at various buttons on the keyboard. He grunted and shuffled back, leaving Richard against the wooden wall, staring at the blank screen. Sipping his coffee with a nervous hand, Richard fished out his mobile, dialled his agent and prepared to go on a journey of discovery the like of which he had never imagined himself making.

'Guy? I'm ready.'

As Richard keyed in the address, he looked furtively around him. No one was looking. No one had the least interest in what he was doing. Everyone was busy with their own worlds. On the screen immediately before him one crazed-looking youth with a black beard, whom Richard had on entry thought a dead ringer for some terrorist of the smoking shoes variety, was typing in a message that read: 'Darling Mumsy, having a simply ripping time in Florence. It's a marvellous city and I've met some awfully nice young people. I hope you're looking after my guinea pigs, lots of love, Bobsy.'

'You've got there?' Guy asked a few minutes later.

'I think so,' Richard whispered in horror, unable to tear his eyes away from the image on his screen.

'You've got a big hairy bottom, right?' Guy asked, matter-of-factly. 'Well, not you personally, of course, ha ha, but—'

'*Yes!*' Richard hissed shakily. He was in no mood for Guy's sallies.

'Well, click right in the middle of it, where the buttock cheeks—'

'Yes, yes,' snapped Richard, louder than he had intended to.

He was aware of a movement in front of him, of someone very big suddenly rising up and looming over him. In vain and too late did Richard spread his skinny arms over the screen.

'Well, well, well,' said the voice of Hugh Faugh.

Richard felt the colour drain from his face. There was an unpleasant sensation around his groin area, as if he very much needed to relieve himself. He gulped drily at his Parliamentary colleague, his head empty of all words, and in particular any that might explain and excuse him now.

'Twinning, eh? I didn't realise you called it that. I thought it was called dogging.'

Hugh, one large, signet-ringed hand spread out to support him as he leant heavily on Richard's desk, smiled at his victim. It was not a nice smile; sideways, cunning and delivered with a cocked black eyebrow. It was, Richard recognised, a smile that said 'Aha! Got you!'

'Rather spotty, isn't it?' the MP remarked, scrutinising the screen bottom.

Richard had finally located his vocabulary and hauled it out from where it was hiding.

'Hugh,' he gasped. 'I can explain. It's not what you think.'

Hugh regarded him pityingly with his large, bright black eyes. 'Of course it isn't,' he purred in tones of such oleaginous sympathy that Richard felt he would have preferred outraged condemnation. 'Don't worry. I can keep your little secret.'

'It's not a secret!' Richard shouted in anguish, dropping his voice instantly as some of those seated nearest twisted round.

He looked miserably back at Hugh, whose expression was wolfishly conspiratorial. 'Don't worry, old chap. I'm only in here myself because my BlackBerry is bust and I need to e-mail Fanny.'

'Fanny?' stammered Richard. 'Who's Fanny?'

'Well, it's not so much who, as what.' Hugh grinned. 'I call them all Fanny. But I have to say that this one definitely puts the tit in constituency.'

'Oh I see,' said Richard, understanding and feeling disgusted. A mistress. The latest of many. He felt he disliked Hugh more than ever. He gestured at the bottom on the screen. 'But *this* isn't that sort of thing. I'm looking at it on behalf of one of my constituents.'

Hugh gave him an 'they all say that' grin. 'Don't worry, I won't tell Georgie. Not if you don't tell Laura.'

'There's nothing not to tell,' Richard repeated plaintively as Hugh, winking with one of his fleshy, sheeny, thickly lashed eyelids, went back to his seat.

Richard felt horribly compromised. Previously, all his dealings with Hugh had made him feel to be on the moral high ground. That, at least, had been some comfort. But now he felt smeared; down in the slime too. At the bottom, in every sense of the word.

He stared at the hairy white buttocks on the screen. They struck him as a succinct representation, not only of what was going on in Wellover, but of his political career in general.

Chapter 46

Orlando was looking broodingly at Morning, dozing in Emma's arms. He was thinking that it must be wonderful to be a baby, so warm, cosy, looked after, all that was required of one being to sleep and smile, no responsibilities or expectations beyond that. And to be looked after by Emma, not least. To be cuddled up against her breast. He swallowed and felt a sudden glow sting his cheeks.

'Done anything good lately?' Emma asked, sprinkling sugar over the foam of her cappuccino. They were sitting at a café table with a large square spread before them, full of sunshine and people. She felt ridiculously happy.

A chill shadow fell on Orlando's sunny content. Recent events were not something he wished to discuss. He kept his eyes fixed on the floor lest the experience with Laura somehow showed in them. 'Um, we went to an olive oil factory yesterday,' he muttered.

'That sounds good.' Emma was beginning to appreciate the virtues of olive oil, which had never featured in her diet before, to Mara's amazement. Mara, it was obvious, could no more imagine life without olive oil than she could imagine it without breathing. To her it was a semi-divine elixir that cured all ills. She had even recommended Emma rub Morning with it after his night-time bath; it was, the housekeeper insisted, better than any commercial baby oil. Emma had taken her advice and, once the feeling that she was preparing Morning for the roast had been got over, she had been impressed with the results.

Orlando listened to her explaining all this. It was interesting to hear there was a point to the stuff. At the time he had been unable to summon up any enthusiasm for the oil factory, except to fantasise about pushing Ivo and Jago into the vats of smooth, thick, surprisingly bright green fluid and holding them under for however long it took.

He watched as Emma bit into one of the small, sweet biscuits that came with the coffees. They were delicious, but so crunchy that the noise when you munched one was deafening. He liked the fact that Emma ate them. None of the girls he knew in London would even have looked at them.

She was, he thought, as pretty as he remembered, if not more so. So many times since their airport encounter he had recalled the soft shine of her brown hair, the sparkle in her eyes, the white of her teeth, the red of her lips against her creamy skin.

'Got your exam results?' Emma asked next. She had been trying to avoid the question but could think of absolutely nothing else to say. 'You have got them?' she gasped, as her companion's face went into freefall.

'No.' Orlando shook his golden head unhappily. 'I don't know which is worse,' he groaned, addressing his huge feet, 'not having them and *thinking* they'll be bad or having them and *knowing* that they are.'

Emma looked up. A provocatively dressed woman was slinking past with swishing dark hair and a long neck. Her lips,

Emma noticed with awe, were even bigger than Belle's, and possibly even more natural. She had been aware for some time that sidling girls with short skirts revealing long brown thighs were stepping closer to where they sat than was strictly necessary.

The obvious centre of their attention was, Emma saw, clearly doing his level best to ignore it. His big hands uncertainly raked his unbrushed golden hair and his long brown legs stretched defensively out in front of him.

Emma felt she could not blame the women, even if some of them were giving her less than friendly looks. Orlando's brooding, discouraging stare – eyes narrowed under level brows, full mouth set in a line – made him look more intensely handsome than ever. His haphazard clothes – battered beige shorts, raggy red T-shirt and huge, scruffy trainers with no socks – contributed even more to his air of casual, even reluctant beauty.

He smiled at her and again she felt that electric flash. She looked away hurriedly.

After the Cojones shoot, Sam was exhausted but triumphant. The fiery Spaniard had been reluctant at first, but once Sam had explained that if this shoot went wrong, they all went wrong, Cojones had suddenly seen reason. He had used a lot of shadow on Darcy to slim her down as much as possible. The Polaroid test shots had looked good. Sam was fairly confident that Brooke, who had demanded to see the shoot results immediately, would be satisfied.

Darcy had been less keen. 'I look pretty skinny,' she had said, squinting critically at the test shots. 'Sort of thin and ill.'

Sam had stared at her. 'That's the point.'

'Is it?' Darcy had said slowly. 'I'm not sure I want to look as if I haven't eaten for a month. It sends out the wrong message, and it's not what I look like anyway—'

'Oh, get real,' Sam had cut in, frustrated. 'Times are thin, OK? Thin, thin, *thin*. There's a racehorse vibe, a legs-spilling-everywhere thing, kind of newborn colt, y'know?'

Darcy had giggled. 'You make modelling sound like a farmyard.'

'Yeah, well, that isn't so far from the truth,' Sam snapped. 'It's full of shit. You deal with a lot of pigs and a helluva lot of cows. And the figure on the bottom line,' the agent added, as inspiration struck her, 'is usually zero. Or double zero.'

'Well, I'm a long way from that,' Darcy returned, comfortably.

Sam shot her an exasperated look. You said it, baby.

Darcy had now gone to an art gallery and Sam needed to return to London. She decided to walk back to the hotel. After her earlier experience, she had no intention of waiting around for a taxi and besides, her London habit of spotting talent on the hoof could just as easily apply here. As she walked along, she looked closely at the people passing her. Returning to her agency with a new face in the bag would more than make up for the trouble she was having with one of her most recent.

Orlando was holding Morning now. It made a touching sight, Emma thought; the gangling, broad-shouldered, god-like youth cradling the small dark child. 'Lovely baby!' Orlando crooned now, peering down at the infant, who chose that moment to stir, open his big eyes with their liquid chocolate pupils and give Orlando a huge pink smile. Emma watched him lift Morning up above his head. The baby giggled delightedly and waved his hands.

'You've got a way with babies,' Emma observed. 'You must have held lots of them before.'

Orlando, who had in fact never held a baby before Morning,

was secretly staggered that he wasn't crying. He had thought all babies did that as soon as you picked them up. He had seen people handed new babies hold them rather as one might hold a bomb: fearfully, as if expecting it to go off any moment with terrible consequences. And usually it did. But holding one was far easier than he had imagined; they snuggled into you, their warm little heads tucked against your chest. He was surprised at how enjoyable it felt.

He jiggled Morning, treasuring the moment and savouring the unexpected sensation of peace and contentment. It was wonderful, after feeling so constantly under attack oneself, to extend protection and security to someone else vulnerable. Holding the baby felt that most unusual and rare thing for Orlando – worthwhile.

'You know,' Emma said, as the thought crossed her mind. 'You say you've no idea about a career. So why not be a nanny? You're obviously in your element with children.'

There was a whirl of unbrushed golden locks as he looked at her in astonishment. 'A *nanny*?'

'Yes.' She raised a wry eyebrow. 'Try not to sound so disgusted. It's what I do, after all.'

'Yes, I'm sorry, I didn't mean . . .' he gasped hurriedly.

'So what did you mean then?' Emma teased.

'I meant, you know, that . . . men don't . . . I mean they aren't . . .'

'Yes they are,' Emma said firmly. 'Male nannies are trendy. They're called mannies.'

'Mannies!' He gave a shout of laughter. Then the amusement died from his expression. 'But I can't . . . I mean, who would give me a job?'

'I would, like a shot,' Emma assured him.

'But you haven't got a nursery.'

521

'Not yet.' She was thinking aloud again. 'But I might one day. I just *might*.'

He looked at her admiringly. For Orlando, there was no might about it. He was quite sure that whatever Emma set her quietly determined heart on, she would get.

They sat, the three of them, companionably in the sun, enjoying the pretty sunlit square with its rim of decorative, imposing buildings. One had an outside covered in paintings; another was a marble-fronted church. Orlando stared at them unseeingly. For all he had initially dismissed it as a joke, he found he was now seriously thinking about Emma's suggestion.

He could tell by the happy flicker it produced inside him that it was a good one. Because it was true he loved children. He had found, in Emma's company and that of Morning, relief not only from the miseries of his present and the uncertainties of his future, but a degree of self-respect he had never experienced before.

He knew he had a talent for amusing children, for understanding them, for gaining their trust and sympathy. He was gratified by the fact they behaved so well when they were with him. He couldn't think of anything he would rather do than work with them.

But, of course, there was no point being good with children. No point even thinking about working with them. Georgie was determined he would be something impressive, preferably famous and definitely rich. A university lecturer – but only at certain universities – a successful lawyer, a Cabinet Minister – perish the ghastly thought. To Georgie, people who worked with children were society's footsoldiers, unworthy of note. Which was both ridiculous and ironic, Orlando thought, given that becoming a primary school teacher, say, was way, way above his capabilities. He was unlikely to get a single A level, after all.

He sighed heavily, raised his eyebrows and looked up at the sunny blue sky.

'It's just so nice here,' he said happily. 'It's so . . . damn it, can't think of the word . . .'

His eyes, as she met them, held a wistful sincerity that twisted her heart. 'Relaxing?' offered Emma, smiling.

'Yes, that's it.' He rubbed his forehead ruefully. 'God, I'm so thick. I think Morning has a bigger vocabulary than I have.'

'You're not thick,' Emma said warmly. 'You're very clever, I think.'

He looked up, eyes narrowed, long lips flinching, unsure whether she was joking. 'Clever?' he repeated. 'Me?'

She nodded. 'Absolutely. You know exactly how to amuse Morning. In my book, that's not just clever, it's brilliant.'

Orlando snorted but felt inwardly ecstatic. No one had ever said he was clever before, had intimated in any way he had anything to offer the world, apart from Laura Faugh's disgusting suggestion he inseminate ugly rich women. He pushed the thought of Laura violently away. This had nothing to do with her.

'Oops,' said Emma now, as Morning's bottle rolled off the table and fell to the cobbled floor.

'I'll get it,' Orlando offered, holding Morning carefully as he reached downwards. His hand crossed Emma's. He felt her begin to jerk it away, and caught it.

Her lips, Orlando saw, were very close. His heart began to thunder and his mouth felt as if a very strong magnet were pulling it forward. Before he knew it he was kissing her. As Emma's lips parted, he felt a flicker of surprise. Gently, he touched her soft, warm tongue with his. A judder went through his entire body, followed by a spreading sense of wonder. So this was what it felt like.

*

In the depths of her Luella tote, Sam's mobile phone was ringing. She dragged it out.

'Brooke Reed,' came the piercing nasal voice of the NBS studio PR.

'Hey there,' Sam said brightly, trying to gauge from the other woman's voice what was to come. It was early in LA, about eight a.m. Could she have got the pictures and looked through them already?

'These pictures,' Brooke said. 'I got 'em.'

Sam was entering a large, sunny square, she saw. She pointed herself towards the nearest bar. This would probably require sitting down for. For positive reasons, hopefully. 'And?' She waited to hear confirmation that, after the Cojones shoot, Darcy was once again on the straight and narrow. The *very* straight and *very* narrow.

'She looks like a sumo wrestler.'

'Sumo wrestler!' Sam exclaimed, once the blockage in her throat had disappeared. She sat down so heavily on the nearest available chair that she almost tipped it over.

'You heard me,' Brooke replied crisply. 'It's a bad angle to start with – who *is* this photographer guy?'

'Carlos Cojones. He's very well known,' Sam said tightly, feeling her professional integrity was being called seriously into question. 'Up and coming.'

'Not any more he ain't. He's down and gone. He's obviously photoshopped these shots a bit, but Darcy's still got a double chin. Not to mention pork roast.'

Sam groaned. Pork roast was not good news.

'Those tight strappy sandals, with flesh bulging out between the straps?'

'I know what pork roast is,' Sam grumbled.

'Well, it looks like Sunday lunch here. Looks bad on the red carpet, more to the point. I haven't even shown 'em to Jack. I daren't. And I can't begin to imagine what Arlington will say.'

Arlington Shorthouse, Sam knew. The studio head. This was big-time stuff, for him to get involved.

'She's gotta start a diet and exercise regime now,' Brooke ordered. 'Otherwise she's out of the picture. We can't afford anyone papping her and getting a bad shot. She's gotta be perfect or she'll get caught. Cameras can be hidden in buttonholes, rings, you name it. Some of our other talent got caught by one hidden in a room service meal. She's the first person ever to get papped by a French fry.'

'Right,' muttered Sam, feeling rather stunned by the machine-gun rattle of words from LA.

'Jack can hold her scenes for a week or so after the start of principal photography. Luckily, we'd already talked about this.'

'You had?' There didn't seem anything too lucky about it to Sam. Although she was getting the distinct feeling that the studio PR was enjoying the crisis.

'It was the worst-case scenario,' Brooke drawled. 'We had to plan for it. Hit emergency mode. You know, I was seriously thinking about sending her off to a hard-core juicing camp in Thailand that I know. But I guess a thinstructor would be better.'

'A thinstructor,' repeated Sam. Hollywoodese, she knew, for a personal trainer. She would have liked to object, put some ideas forward, at any rate; Darcy was her client, after all. But there was no stopping Brooke in full, determined, emergency-mode flow.

'There's one guy,' the LA end rasped, 'he's actually known as the Hero of Zero. I've used him before. He gets people down from size six into something you can barely see side-on in time for the awards season.'

525

'Right.' A waiter had come up to her. Sam flashed him a jumpy, irritated look. He backed away.

'Saw him at an industry awards ceremony just the other night,' Brooke was saying. 'He's pretty busy, though. Said he had four lots of A-list batwings and some Golden Globe-nominated cellulite to deal with, plus some thunder thighs in Pacific Palisades that might be up for Best Actor. But I can call in some favours. Get him out to you.'

'Great,' Sam said heavily. She snapped her phone shut, pushed up her sunglasses and rubbed her eyes.

'*Signora?*' The waiter was at her side again. Sam skimmed him with a jaundiced, professional eye. Too old. Too thin – on top as well as everywhere else. No good for modelling. But he had other, better uses.

'Get me a double Jameson,' she snapped.

A diet and exercise regime. How the hell was she going to get this one past Darcy? She loved food – had been stuffing her face with pizza at the shoot when Sam had arrived, in fact. And Sam had a feeling that she wasn't big on exercise.

She pulled out her mobile and dialled Mitch Masterson. 'Houston? We got a problem.'

'Tell me about it,' Mitch groaned. 'I've just had Arlington Shorthouse on to me. If Darcy doesn't drop two dress sizes by the end of next week she's out of the picture. Brooke's sending in some crack personal trainer.' Mitch shook his head sorrowfully and reached for a jelly doughnut.

'That's right. So when are you going to tell her?'

'Me tell her?' exclaimed Mitch. 'I thought you—'

'You're her agent,' Sam said firmly.

'Yeah, and you're her model agent. It falls within your remit.'

'No it doesn't.'

'Yes it does.'

'Doesn't.'

'Does.'

'OK,' Mitch sighed. 'Let's toss for it.'

'Over the phone?' gasped Sam. 'Where I can't see it?'

'Don't you trust me?' Mitch's tone was indignant.

'No. You're an agent.'

'So are you.'

'Exactly.'

'OK. I'll tell her.' He'd known he would have to, all along. Domineering women always got their way with him. It was, he supposed, a sort of fetish.

Sam's drink now arrived. She took a great swig; the fiery liquid blazed a trail to her stomach and she felt immediately better.

Now more in control, she started to look around her, assessing the clientele. There were some pretty good-looking people in this bar. Take that boy over there . . .

Sam narrowed her eyes. He really was handsome. She watched the hollows beneath his cheekbones catch the sun as he pushed back his gold-flecked hair. He was laughing, his full lips parted, his long eyes sparkling beneath his brows.

Excitement gripped Sam, as it rarely did. As it only did, in fact, when she received vast cheques or came across someone truly exceptional who could result in vast cheques. And this boy was exceptional. Every nerve in her body was shrieking the fact. She was panting. She felt hot. She hadn't felt this excited since she had spotted The Hunk That Got Away in Covent Garden.

Suddenly, Sam gasped, a tearing gasp that felt more like a choke. Could it be? Hurriedly, she scrambled in her bag, fishing for her mobile again. She grabbed it – it fell from her frantic, fumbling grip – then pinged it open. Within seconds she had found the picture of the boy she had taken. Her eyes ricocheted back and forth, from the fuzzy image to the living young man some tables away, gathering the evidence. She felt almost sick with excitement. My God. It *really* looked like . . . it really *could* be . . .

It was. It *was* him. She had no doubt at all. Sam shook her head in wonder. She'd hoped for a new face, but had never expected *that* face. The face that had, to her eternal regret, got away.

And now one thought and one thought only possessed her. The boy that had got away could not be allowed to get away again. Stealthily, as one stalking a butterfly might, Sam drained her whiskey glass and raised her ginger-suede bottom from her chair.

'I have to go,' Emma said to Orlando. Ten minutes until the bus went. She had left it until the last possible minute. She would have left it altogether had not Morning's nap time beckoned.

'What? Already?' He looked devastated.

'You'd be better off without me.' Especially after the kiss, she felt confident enough to tease him. It had removed any last element of doubt; all mutual distrust or shyness had evaporated the moment their lips met. Now things between them felt easy, relaxed, full of delicious promise. 'Every woman in town wants me out of the way. Like that one.' She nodded at a stunning brunette casting Orlando glances from beneath her improbably long eyelashes. 'She's awfully pretty.'

'Not as pretty as you,' Orlando countered immediately. Obeying a shy, yet joyful impulse, he bent over and kissed her nose. As his lips moved down her face to her mouth again, a great plunge of desire swept through Emma.

'Give me your mobile number,' Orlando detached his lips to

528

mumble. She felt them move against her cheek; felt his breath. 'I'll text you.'

She felt she was drowning in the green of his eyes. 'I don't have a mobile,' she managed to mutter through a constricted throat.

'Don't have a mobile?' Orlando's lowered lashes now jerked upwards in surprise. He looked at her with smiling, puzzled amazement. In his world this was tantamount to not having a head. Everyone he knew had mobiles. You couldn't live without them. Everyone texted, about everything. His form master – ex-form master, thank God – was going to text his A level results. Even his mother texted, although he wished she wouldn't. Her attempts at slang made his toes curl. 'U R L8' and so on.

Emma shrugged defiantly. 'Well, to be honest I can't afford one and I don't really need one, not in London, anyway. If I get into trouble I can always use a phone box.'

'A phone box?' He had never used a phone box in his life. He wasn't sure he would know how to. He looked at her in awe. He had never heard someone admit they couldn't afford anything, either. In the circles in which he had been accustomed to move, people were at pains to imply the opposite. His admiration for Emma doubled. Tripled. Quadrupled. It flashed through his mind that not only had she probably never been on Facebook, but she probably didn't care either. Incredible. No wonder he was in love with her.

Emma's eye had now caught those of a middle-aged woman a few tables away. She had a long, thick, striped black and red fringe through which she peered like some sort of dog; and some sort of dog very interested in Orlando. She was staring at him with terrifying intensity.

Orlando caught the puzzled look in Emma's eyes. He glanced

over. When his gaze met that of Sam, he stiffened in horror. He recognised her instantly. That awful pushy model agent woman from Covent Garden.

She was getting up; heaving herself out of her seat in some tight ginger trousers. There was, Orlando recognised, terrifying purpose in her stare. She was obviously about to come over and ask him to model again, in front of Emma. He couldn't bear it. She already thought it was funny that women stared at him. This extra embarrassment would be excruciating.

Orlando leapt to his feet. He looked at Emma in anguish. 'Look, I've got to go . . . I'll be back . . .'

'Go!' exclaimed Emma. She had to go too.

'I'll be back . . . wait for me . . .'

Sam was hurrying along the front of the tables towards him, bracelets jangling, flicking her hair out of her eyes as she ran.

'I can't!' Emma cried. Her hand clasped Morning. 'We can't . . .'

'I'll be in touch,' Orlando shouted, backing away, his eyes glued yearningly to hers.

She watched helplessly as the tall, blond figure rushed off across the square and disappeared into the crowd.

Chapter 47

So violently had Darcy opposed the idea of a personal trainer from America that her agents had eventually given in. Running alone was no fun, but preferable at least to the prospect of sprinting through Rocolo accompanied by someone calling himself the Hero of Zero.

Her victory was not absolute, however. Within days, a pair of DVDs addressed to Darcy arrived from LA via a courier. Apprehensively, she took them into the villa's large, light, stone-walled sitting room and slipped them into the gleaming, state-of-the-art player. Immediately the enormous, gleaming, state-of-the-art plasma screen was filled with some gleaming, white, obviously state-of-the-art teeth. The camera panned back to reveal a manically grinning man with big hair, a pink mesh vest and a glistening caramel tan.

'Hello, Darcy!' he exclaimed with showbizzy emphasis. 'I'm Rupert. Otherwise known as the Hero of Zero.'

Darcy looked at the shining black swept-back hair, unlined forehead and superhero jaw. He was extremely thin. His legs reminded her of pipecleaners; very brown ones.

'Otherwise known,' the dazzling teeth on the screen

continued, 'as the Captain of Thindustry and the Queen of Lean. The guy the stylists to the stars all have on speed dial.' He made a little exuberant, skipping movement. 'And why? Because, dear, I can make you thin. I'll give you a derrière you can bounce dimes off. I'm the man the model agencies call in times of crisis. And you're one lucky lady to have me make an exclusive and tailor-made programme just for you!' He rubbed his hands together gleefully.

As Darcy stared at the screen, dumb with surprise, there was a tinny, ringing sound. Rupert rolled his eyes. 'Hold on, dear. My Thighphone. It's going crazy.'

He lifted his bright pink mesh vest to reveal a row of slender mobiles slipped into holders strapped along a belt. 'All on vibrate, for emergency use only. It's a service I offer ultra-triple-A-list clients – people like *you*, Darcy,' he added triumphantly, 'when they have a problem. All part of my very special service,' he explained to the camera with a smile like a flashgun.

'Each of these phones relates to a different part of the body,' the Captain of Thindustry now revealed. 'Clients ring the number relating to their particular body issue zone. This,' he pointed to the first pocket, 'is the Batphone. That's for batwings and bingo wings. This,' the second pocket, 'is the Buttphone – self-explanatory, obviously. Then the Bellyphone – my little joke, dear, rhymes with telephone. And, last, but by no means least, the Thighphone and the Pork Roast Hotline,' he added, indicating the others. 'Hold on, hold on, I'm coming,' he exclaimed, pulling out the Thighphone and frowning at the number. 'Yes, Nicole?'

He listened for a few minutes, his face grave. 'OK, Nicole. Not a problem.'

He put the phone away, flashed another grin and proceeded to bound about the screen like a young gazelle. 'We'll do some cardiovascular every day, of course,' he told Darcy brightly. 'Tricep dips to streamline those upper arms. My special Butt Blaster lunges – you'll enjoy those, dear. Everyone does. And running, of course. A good brisk jog with some uphill for an hour a day at least.'

Running! Pure aversion seized Darcy. She hated running. Anything but that. It was painful, hot and boring. Whenever, in the past, she had done it – usually in pursuit of an about-to-depart train – her chest had heaved violently, painful cramps had stabbed her sides and her lungs had gulped agonisingly for air. She had always felt amazement that anyone could run for fun – could run at all – without a gun being pointed to their head. Running for her life was the only sort she could envisage.

'. . . the quickest and most effective way to shed those naughty unwanted pounds . . .'

Darcy lunged for the DVD player and switched him off.

She slipped the other disc in. This one was about food, and featured the Hero of Zero in a bright, white kitchen with a white apron over his pink mesh vest. The horror that had gripped Darcy during the first disc started to subside. If it was about food, it could not be all bad, surely.

'Pasta's *off*,' Rupert beamed. 'Ditto bread. It's all about low carb, low cholesterol, low fat . . .'

Low fun, thought Darcy in dismay. She strained to listen. Had he really just said egg white omelette, poached chicken fillet, steamed broccoli and as much undressed salad as she wanted to eat? How much undressed salad did *anyone* want to eat?

'Seaweed protein shakes and tree syrup are an option,' Rupert was beaming. 'And if you've got any food allergies, now's the time to really let them rip. Or else develop some. Food allergies can be very useful.'

Crouched on the cool stone floor, Darcy felt hot with the horror of it all. The light, pretty sitting room suddenly seemed a dark and fearful place. It was bad enough from her point of view, but what the proud cook Mara was going to make of it hardly bore thinking about.

The voice from the plasma screen trilled blithely on. 'Finally, let me tell you something about diet *food*. Which is that nothing, absolutely *nothing*, tastes as good as . . .'

He paused. Darcy, eyes riveted on the screen, held her breath. Was some stomach-filling, acceptably tasty low-fat wonderfood about to be mentioned?

Rupert's televisual black eyes gleamed. 'Thin.'

Thin what? Thin mints, Darcy wondered hopefully.

'Nothing tastes as good as thin *feels*,' Rupert finished, his mouth huge in a messianic grin.

Darcy switched him off and sat gazing, unseeing, into the sitting room's great empty fireplace with its carved canopy.

Never had the ridiculousness of Hollywood seemed quite so ridiculous. Not that the Hero of Zero was the only example of it; Darcy had now read the script and discovered that bidding other equally unlikely-sounding characters to 'Come forth, loyal servant of my late father' seemed to be the main function of her role as the Grand Duchess of the Galaxy. It was not a part to get excited about in any artistic sense; in any sense, it was increasingly beginning to seem.

'Lose the weight or lose the part,' Mitch had warned her. He could talk, Darcy had thought hotly.

The situation was simple enough. The sooner she reached the requisite point on the scales, the sooner she would be allowed to go on set in Florence and film her scenes. And while the scenes and the filming did not in the least excite her, something else about the part certainly did.

Christian.

She missed him. Not spiritually or companionably, but physically. They had met only briefly, but searingly. Christian had lit her blue touchpaper and now she wanted more. He was passionate and skilled. Was there a better lover in the world? No. Did she believe in love at first sight? Well, she hadn't, not before. But now everything seemed different.

Up until the point Orlando's lips actually touched hers, Emma, staring fixedly at that great, red mouth, had not been able to believe that it was actually going to happen. And when it did, and she had melted into it, the kiss had been altogether deeper, more protracted, more tender than she had imagined possible.

But then he had run away.

It had taken Emma some minutes to work out, amid the confusion, that the bossy redhead in the tight ginger suede trousers was a model agent. She had, apparently, spotted Orlando in London and he had run away then as well.

Emma, while aghast at his sudden departure, could see why he might. She had assumed he would come back. But when, after the agent finally stomped off, Orlando failed to return before she had to leave for her bus, Emma's sympathy turned to despair. She had no address and no phone number for him – a fact the exasperated agent clearly had not believed.

The night that subsequently passed was one of the most miserable and joyous Emma had ever known, as alternately she recalled the kiss, and the probability the kisser was lost to her for ever.

As she tossed and turned, Emma put her mind to the possibility of returning to the square again. But Florence was a long way away; a hot journey for Morning. Besides, would it be worth it?

The miserable possibility that Orlando had run from her as much as the agent stabbed at Emma as the night wore on. Perhaps he wasn't really interested at all. But the kiss, that kiss, had been as intense and sweet as the ripest berry. As the memory of it rushed over her like a warm sea, Emma buried herself in her pillows and groaned.

'You're in love,' Mara teased in the kitchen the next morning.

Emma was aghast. How did she know? How had she guessed? Was she teasing? The housekeeper's dark eyes in her creased and sunburnt face were very lively, certainly. But they didn't look mocking.

'Of course I'm not,' she riposted. 'Don't be silly.'

'So if you not in love, why you leave the milk to boil over all the time,' Mara chided, snatching the pan off the stove. 'Why you put Morning's clothes on back to front and walk around in a daze?'

'I don't!'

'And your face!' Mara teased. 'You are glowing!'

'I'm just hot,' Emma exclaimed, embarrassed.

'And you are not eating!' the housekeeper accused. 'Last night, I serve you some of my cannelloni, you not eat a thing.'

Emma reddened further at the memory. It had been particularly embarrassing as poor Darcy, who had been condemned to some sort of diet and was eating broccoli, had stared at the steaming dish of pasta with eyes like saucers.

'And why should you not be in love?' Mara had returned to the main theme. 'You deserve love. So kind, so sensible, so *wonderful* with the baby!' Mara clapped her wrinkled brown hands. 'And so pretty now you have lost a bit of the weight!'

'Have I?' Emma said in surprise. So much had happened recently that the question of her own weight had scarcely crossed her mind. She ran a finger round the waistband of her jeans. They felt looser, certainly.

Mara raised her emphatic dark eyebrows. '*Sì*. Olive oil, pasta, is good diet.' She nodded her dark head in which, despite her age, there was not yet a fleck of grey.

Emma shrugged the compliment off. But the next time she went to the bathroom she gazed at her face in the mirror. Perhaps it did look different; thinner. You could almost see cheekbones if you turned it to the right light. And the sunshine of Italy had touched her hair with blonde highlights; added a mild tan and a few more freckles for good measure. Her teeth, when she smiled, looked whiter than ever. Remembering the kiss, Emma beamed at herself; remembering Orlando's flight, the smile faded and a sad expression crept into her reflected eyes.

Chapter 48

Darcy looked behind her. There was no one about. Mara had just gone back into the kitchen after having carefully put down a dish of pork fillet with cannellini beans at the table under the parasol. It was the same dish whose sumptuous sweet-savoury scent had been drifting around the villa all afternoon and driving Darcy mad as she performed her star jumps.

All throughout her squat thrusts Darcy had been aware of this dish being prepared in the kitchen. The same savoury smell that had set her stomach rumbling then, sent it positively roaring now.

Her own scheduled dinner was poached chicken and steamed broccoli, prepared by a Mara still tight-lipped after the experience of having to watch the Queen of Lean's dietary instructions on the DVD. Her face, when she had emerged from the sitting room, had been twisted with contempt and she had marched into the kitchen in disgust.

Darcy looked dumbly after her. How could she explain? It was difficult enough explaining it to herself. Only the thought of Christian made it worthwhile.

It was intensely frustrating, communicating only by text. But as Darcy found herself effectively banned from the set, Christian seemed more or less permanently on it, and as texts were the only form of mobile communication Saint apparently allowed, it was the only way. Until she was thin enough, that was.

It was ridiculous. She, who adored food, was in an Italian palace equipped with a wondrous cook. And yet she was on a diet of steamed broccoli and undressed salad.

'Nothing tastes as good as thin feels.' She tried to recall Rupert's words. But it wasn't true. Just about anything tasted better. She'd only been on the diet a day and already, with the right sauce and seasoning, she felt she could eat the tablecloth.

No one had yet emerged from the villa for dinner. Meaning, thought Darcy, tiptoeing towards the food, the mice could play. Or at least taste what everyone else was having for supper.

As a great stab of hunger pierced her stomach, Darcy picked up a shining silver fork from where it lay on a crisply folded white linen napkin. She reached over towards the pork and bean dish. Her mouth watered as she anticipated the taste of bean, crunchy on the outside, giving in the middle, soaked in all the juices of the sage-infused meat.

'Hoo, hoo, hoo, hey hey *hey*! *Whoa*, there!'

There was a flash of pink. Something whooshed across the terrace and grabbed her fork.

'Thank God,' panted Belle, with the air of James Bond having saved the world. 'Darcy, you should be thanking me. I've just saved your career.'

'Thanks,' muttered Darcy heavily, trying not to notice how Belle's rake-thin body looked thinner than ever in the hot-pink wrap dress. Was she dressing skinnier on purpose? To make the point?

Belle shook her shining hair mock-sorrowfully. 'I sympathise, Darcy, I really do,' she breathed.

'You're very kind,' Darcy said shortly.

'I mean, it's just *so* hard to stay thin,' Belle added in syrupy tones. 'For people like you, that is.'

'*Sorry?*'

Belle smiled. 'Personally, I don't know my BMI and I have no idea what I weigh. I'm just made like this, I guess.' She smoothed her tiny hands over the hipbones jutting through her pink wraparound dress and gave another of her tinkling laughs. 'Hey, cheer up. Life's full of ups and downs. I've been there too, baby. The hard times. Like when my ex-boyfriend was in rehab?' Her eyes, behind the sunglasses, drilled into Darcy's. 'Imagine what *that* was like. Huh?'

Pushing determinedly away what she knew of Belle's last known boyfriend – she now accepted Belle didn't realise Niall had been attached – Darcy tried to summon some sympathy.

'It was hard,' Belle declared. 'I could *never* decide what to wear for the paparazzi. Oh, c'mon, Darcy, cheer up,' she urged. 'At least you're eating off a whole side-plate. Some actresses I know had to eat from a saucer for months. Or a teacup,' she added with a tinkling laugh.

Marco sighed happily as he finished off the pieces of chocolate that had, along with a croissant fresh from the restaurant oven, made up his late breakfast. As the last bitter-sweet grains melted from his tongue, the chef's dark brow creased in thought. It was splendid chocolate, the best he had ever tasted, and from a new supplier, someone who dealt with the oldest, most traditional chocolate houses in Italy. Just an old man and his brother had made this; they made very little, apparently. But what they made was good. Excellent.

*

The run so far had passed in a blur of pain. Darcy remembered the opening moments, when it had seemed almost bearable; downhill from the villa through the shady, dewy, morning pine trees, inhaling the fresh sharp scent. Then, along the flat, it had got harder, and harder still when the first incline had started.

The only way she could bear it, Darcy was finding, was visualising food. The reality of the hard road beneath her melted in the dream of buttery pesto stirred through freshly made spaghetti. Linguine with clams. Chargrilled lamb with aubergine. Calves' liver and polenta.

The roadsides she ran along sent up warm snatches of herbs – sun-warmed rosemary, the tang of thyme, sweet drifts of basil – which Darcy eagerly added to the dishes in her imagination. Great pots of slowly-cooking sauces, exuding succulent scents as the ingredients melted together. Wonderful wines; big velvety reds, crisp, chilled whites; foaming Prosecco.

Langoustine risotto, which Mara had promised to make. The housekeeper had demonstrated her special method for risotto; toasting the rice grains in the bottom of a pan and adding a glassful of wine. Only when the wine was completely absorbed should the rest of the stock be added, she had instructed. And then only a little at a time. Although of course she wouldn't be making it now, or at least if she did Darcy wouldn't be eating it.

She was entering the village now, Darcy saw. The thought of the steep hill sent a sick wave through her stomach. Only by thinking about chocolate could she bear it. Dark, rich, powerfully flavoured, melting on the tongue. Forbidden, fatal, but all the more delicious for it.

*

Marco picked up another piece of chocolate and slipped it into his mouth. It really was the best. He knew because of the way, like all wonderful ingredients, it fired his brain with ideas.

He closed his eyes and savoured. Real, pure chocolate, using genuine Venezuelan criollo, the Ferrari or Lamborghini of cocoa beans, complex and sophisticated like no other and producing a rich, fruity flavour of amazing power. Virtuoso chocolate you could do anything you liked with. Nougatine, parfait, mousse . . . the only question was which.

On the other hand, Marco asked himself, why choose at all? You could do all those things – mousse, nougatine, parfait – but on the same plate. A tasting plate, with little pieces of everything. What fun that would be for the customers as well as the chefs; they could show off their skills and the many ways in which such a perfect ingredient could be used.

Marco stretched. His mind was, suddenly, full of chocolate tart. A small slice, with the nougatine and parfait, on the tasting plate. What could be better?

Something moving rapidly up the cobbled hill now caught his eye. Marco looked; speed of motion was not something usually associated with Rocolo's main street. People tended to struggle up it, panting and straining, red-faced and pop-eyed with the effort.

As the figure came nearer, Marco saw that it was a woman. She really was a beauty, he thought, admiring the long pale thighs, the high bottom, the pert and deliciously unanchored breasts, the black hair flashing in the sun.

Before his rational brain could register it, something deeper and more visceral within him had produced a swell of excitement, a racing of the heart, a certain breathlessness.

It was her. The food-loving brunette who had come to lunch the other day. The one with the ridiculous swaggering boyfriend in the tight white trousers. Who had appeared in his restaurant later that day with that ridiculous blonde and her ridiculous dog.

Excitement gripped Marco. His new chocolate. This woman would love it. She had a boyfriend, she had no interest in him, but what Marco now wanted to offer went beyond flirtation, beyond romance, into the blessed realm where one food lover reached out to another.

'Hey,' Marco called, as she staggered past. He raised his plate of chocolate. 'Come and try this!'

He was unprepared for her response. Darcy looked at him in horror and sped off.

'Mr Saint is ten minutes from the set.' The information boomed through the Tannoy. The great marble hall of the palazzo was a swarm of activity. Great wheel-borne cameras rolled along lines of tape on the floor, cables snaked, lights rose, fell and were twisted into position amid shouts and arm-waving from the assistants. There were people everywhere, some dressed as aliens, some as space mercenaries and some, the technicians, in black T-shirts and baseball caps with the *Galaxia* logo on.

Belle, sitting in a director's chair, the script on her knee, felt a thrill of triumph. She was back. Back among her people. Even if most of them were wearing helmets and white plastic armour and some of them had three eyes. Her own costume looked like some kind of satellite, all great silver cylinders and intersecting tinfoil ruffs. You could probably pick up Sky on it; maybe even NASA. She had a silver face too – looked like the goddamn Tin Man, frankly. Still, she should complain, Belle told herself. Look at that guy over there, with a lizard's head. A red, black and white lizard's head.

The guy with the lizard's head kept looking at her. But he could forget it. Belle shot the lizard a disdainful look. Reptiles weren't her thing.

Speaking of reptiles, Christian was supposed to be in this film too. Belle was insufficiently familiar with the script to be sure in what scenes he appeared – in what scenes she herself appeared, come to that. But she was curious about seeing him again, for the first time since he had walked out on her in LA. How would he react, she wondered. Defiant? Ashamed? Ashamed, had to be, especially after the way he had treated her.

Never had she imagined, then, that her star would rise in so unexpected a fashion and they would find themselves on the same cast list. It was pretty obvious Christian hadn't imagined it either. But Belle's sense of triumph, of relief, was such that she almost felt warmth towards him. When you were successful, you could forgive people almost anything. Especially people as good looking as Christian.

'Mr Saint is five minutes from the set,' announced the Tannoy.

Belle's gaze returned to the lizard. He was closer to her now and was walking up and down, flicking through his script in a concentrated fashion that she, who had no concentration whatever, found rather sexy. He had a pretty good figure too, which his black rubber-effect costume was hugging tightly. Broad shoulders. Neat, tight tush. Strong thighs. And it was abundantly obvious he was well hung. Looked like he had a salami down there.

Belle shifted in her director's chair and parted her thighs slightly under her cumbersome dress. There was a familiar ache there, an ache that demanded satisfaction. She was burningly aware of her nakedness beneath the costume; behind the hot plastic bodice her sweaty breasts, artificial though they mostly were, yearned to be touched. What was it about that lizard? Who was it, come to that?

Beneath his reptile mask, Christian smiled. He could feel from afar that she was hot for him again. Just as he had hoped. Had she been able to see his face, there could have been trouble. She might have wanted to settle a few scores. But now all he had to do was give her the ride of her life and reveal himself afterwards. She could hardly argue then.

Everything was going his way, Christian reflected as he walked slowly, purposefully towards a Belle squirming and preening in her chair. The set had been alive with the news that Darcy Prince had been banned until she dropped a few pounds. If Christian thought about it at all, it was vaguely to regret the condemnation of those splendid curves, which hadn't been all that big, for Chrissakes. But if Hollywood dictated otherwise, so be it. Just as well he'd decided to move on from her. Once again, his instincts had been unerring. He wished she would stop texting him though. It was embarrassing.

'Mr Saint is now on the set,' announced the Tannoy. Christian turned to see the spry director with his check shirt, jeans and neat white beard walking energetically into the midst of the cameras and cables, followed by a retinue bristling with clipboards and clapperboards.

Belle had bobbed up to her feet hearing the director was now among them. Christian rushed to her side. 'You're not needed yet,' he growled at her. 'Not by Jack Saint, anyway.'

Belle peered into the lizard's face. It was completely covered in latex and red, black and white paint. There was something about it that reminded her of someone – the guy out of Kiss, maybe.

She smiled. 'Hey. You're cute. For a lizard.'

She thrust her hands seductively upwards, expecting to push

them through her hair, remembering too late that her hair had been plaited, gel-sprayed and now stuck up out of her head as if she had suffered an electric shock.

The lizard seized her round the waist and, in a deft, bold movement, pulled her into the darkness under a nearby flight of balustraded marble stairs. Belle found herself being devoured in an urgent kiss; kissing him passionately back she felt herself being slowly pushed down to the marble floor of the terrace. Above the rustling of her plastic dress, as, gasping, she pulled it up, Belle was aware of a squeaking and snapping of poppers as he eased himself out of his rubber suit. 'Oh God,' gasped Belle, from somewhere deep in her throat, deep within herself, as he entered her. '*Oh God*,' she repeated, rolling her head from side to side, stretching her arms above her head as he began to slowly thrust in and out. 'I've never been screwed by a lizard before,' she squealed. 'I didn't realise what I was missing. You're incredible. *Oh!* Do that again! *Ohhhh!* The last fuck I had that was this good was Christian Harlow . . . oh . . . oh . . . ohhhhh!'

'Funny you should say that,' Christian breathed into her convulsing, silver-painted neck. 'Because . . .'

Chapter 49

Darcy groaned as she pulled on her trainers. She had not thought it possible to be so hungry. She thought about food all day and had even started dreaming about it; a recurring dream about a castle made of chocolate cake.

Still, better get the hated run over with. She summoned all her willpower, pulled her baseball cap down hard and made a move across the patio. Then, at the prospect of the torture ahead, she emitted a loud wail and retreated to the shade of the parasol.

Emma, by the pool and dangling Morning's legs in the water, could not help noticing this little show. She made no remark but sensed that Darcy, having staged her little tableau of resentment, was looking for sympathy.

She vowed to proceed with caution, however. The dark-haired actress with the cut-glass voice and intelligent face seemed both grand and very grown-up, and not inclined to suffer fools.

Darcy had sunk into a chair by now. 'Apparently even after I've been running for half an hour I've only worked off the equivalent of two slices of toast,' she said with a sort of despairing restlessness. 'And you know what?'

'Er . . . what?'

'I'd *so* much rather have had the toast!' Darcy buried her head in her arms on the table. She looked up again, the picture of despair. 'You know, *dripping* with butter. Like that pile Toad eats in *The Wind in the Willows*.' The image glowed in her imagination and her head pounded with longing.

'Oh yes!' Emma exclaimed. *The Wind in the Willows* was one of her favourites. 'When poor old Toad's in prison . . .' She stopped, remembering with a pang how Hero and Cosmo had loved it too.

'What's the matter?' Darcy asked, seeing the nanny's expression fall.

'Nothing.' But as the actress's dark, rather piercing eyes remained on her, Emma found herself continuing. 'Some children I used to look after. They loved that book as well.'

Darcy waited, half sensing a story, but as nothing more was forthcoming, she embarked on her warm-up, bending and stretching. Her muscles resisted and protested. 'Ouch.' She stopped and groaned. 'God, I don't want to be doing this. I want to be sitting in the shade with a drink.'

Emma gave her an apologetic, sympathetic smile, uncertain what she was supposed to do about this. Apart from listen, that was.

'But alcohol's off. Ouch. *Ouch!*' Darcy jerked energetically up and down, trying to ignore the pain. 'One glass would be two hundred sit-ups.'

'Really?' This statistic was astonishing enough to jerk Emma out of her caution.

Darcy stopped. 'A minute in the glass, a month on the arse,' she grinned. 'This DVD I've been sent from LA, it's got these useful little tips all over it. "A couple of sips, hey presto, big hips . . ." Oh God. Can you believe it?'

Laughing, Darcy looked up. Beyond the edge of the sunshade, the blue air was full of birdsong and that cricket rasp that is the sound of still, hot weather. Beyond, the green and brown hills baked under the summer sky. Did she want to go running? No she did not. What she wanted to do more than anything was to sit there, or perhaps lie by the pool, flicking through some of Mara's recipe books until lunch was ready.

She had seen Mara making the lunch as she had walked through the kitchen. She had been preparing aubergines; cutting slits in them, pushing bay leaves into the slits, wrapping them in foil and putting them in the oven to bake. Banana and chocolate beignets were, Darcy knew, to follow. Not that she would be having those.

'Still, it'll all be worth it,' Emma said, wanting to sound encouraging. 'You'll be massive after this film – in the star sense, I mean,' she added hurriedly.

But, too late, she saw Darcy's level dark brows had snapped together. 'I'm not doing it to become famous,' she said impatiently.

'Of course not,' Emma said hurriedly, dabbing at a posset that Morning had thoughtfully deposited on her polo shirt. She had read enough celebrity interviews to know that it never was about the money or the fame.

'God, no,' Darcy added. 'Who'd want to be famous? I mean, I thought I did for about five minutes, but I can see now that it's a bloody nightmare. Look at Belle. Who'd want to be like that? Oh, sorry,' she added, seeing Emma looked uncomfortable. 'I shouldn't be nasty about her. You work for her, after all.'

But why? Darcy wondered. Emma did not seem a particularly Belle-like person. She did not say much – had an admirable reticence, in fact – but you could tell from the set of her jaw, her intelligent eyes, her kind and sympathetic smile, that she had strength and character.

Pretty, too, Darcy thought, with her thick, glossy hair, shining eyes, rosy cheeks. And, for all her clothes were not figure-hugging – she wore simple jeans and a white polo shirt; serviceable rather than sexy – she looked extremely clean, glowingly well scrubbed. There was something about her, Darcy felt, that was both comforting and utterly trustworthy. How Belle had landed herself a gem like this, had persuaded this obviously good person to come and work for her, seemed hard to explain.

'And I'm not doing it for the art, either,' she remarked. 'Just in case you're wondering.' As Emma looked blank, she added, 'Those celebrity interviews. People in them always say they aren't doing it for fame and money, it's all for the art and their first love is fringe theatre.' She snorted.

Emma smiled uncertainly. After some weeks with Belle, she neither understood nor expected such honesty from someone with a starring role in the same film. Nor was she sure she trusted it.

'Art!' Darcy was chuckling. 'There's not a lot of art to *Galaxia*, I can tell you. Well, there may be in the special effects, the fight sequences and the rest of it. But the acting's just a case of standing around in silly costumes saying, "Welcome, my trusted counsellor," and things like that.'

Emma blinked. Darcy was a puzzle. These views were, she sensed, not typical of a young actress on the verge of big-time stardom. 'But won't you get better parts after this? More serious ones?' she ventured.

Darcy shot her a look. 'I've done serious. Before this I was doing Shakespeare in London.'

Emma assumed her most impressed face.

'Don't be too impressed,' Darcy smiled. 'I mean, of course that was better, but if I ask myself whether I really loved it, whether I really wanted to do it, well, I really don't know.' She looked sadly at Emma. 'I mean, I bet you always wanted to be a nanny, didn't you?'

Emma nodded. 'I always knew I wanted to work with children.' She suppressed the sigh that might have told Darcy what she wanted to add: that she wasn't quite so certain about working for their parents.

Darcy held her in a long, cool gaze that, Emma sensed, might have detected it anyway. Then she began to speak. 'My parents are actors. Quite famous ones . . .'

'Ooh,' said Emma politely, feeling it was somehow expected.

Darcy snorted. 'Honestly, don't be impressed. The theatre is sort of the family business. I was expected to go into it and I did.'

'It sounds very glamorous, though,' Emma remarked.

'Not really. Either my parents were away acting or they were at home obsessing over their causes. We had a big house,' Darcy said.

Emma nodded, unsurprised. Darcy's assured voice, her elegant face and figure, her confident sense of humour; all had marked her out as the big-house type. Emma imagined somewhere huge with bow windows, a vast kitchen, a great green garden with mature trees, and felt a clutch of envy.

'But we never had it to ourselves,' Darcy added sadly. 'It was always full of my parents' protégés: monks from Tibet; freedom fighters from Chechnya; refugees from – I don't know, outer space. Or anywhere you care to name.' Darcy pulled a mock-comic face. 'I used to come home from school never quite knowing which particular variety of Communist defector I'd find occupying my bedroom.'

'How awful.' Emma's eyes were wide. She wasn't entirely certain what a Communist defector was, but it sounded alarming. She thought of her own tiny bedroom at home; so small there was room only for the bed and a wardrobe tucked in beside it, with a sudden, searing affection.

'Family meals were always shared with hundreds of people – an entire Indian village once. My mother is a dreadful cook – I think that's why I so love food myself,' Darcy was saying, a dreamy, wondering note in her voice. 'Perhaps it represents everything I never had at home. Mummy can only make spag bol. And often she didn't even bother doing that. It'd be fish and chips all round from the local chippy. The Indian village really loved that,' Darcy added, a grin momentarily illuminating her face.

Emma smiled. She sensed she was not required to comment.

'But look where liking food's got me!' Darcy grimaced. 'I'm too fat to save the galaxy at the moment.' She began running on the spot. 'And frankly, if it wasn't for the sex I don't think I'd bother trying.'

'Sex!' Emma was startled into an exclamation. She coloured immediately.

Darcy was grinning at her, Emma saw miserably. Of course, growing up in bohemian splendour with famous actors probably meant you talked about sex all the time.

'There's someone on the film set,' Darcy revealed. 'He's called Christian. Christian Harlow.'

Christian Harlow. Emma remembered the name. She could even see the face; it was a staple of celebrity magazines. Christian Harlow. Undeniably handsome but rather arrogant looking; cavernous cheekbones, thick black hair and a flashgun-bright smile. 'I've seen him,' she said. 'He's very handsome.'

'Gorgeous,' Darcy agreed.

Orlando, in all his unkempt, golden beauty flashed before

Emma. She could almost feel his face close to hers. She pushed the images away. No point thinking about that now.

'Yeah, Christian's gorgeous,' Darcy was saying in besotted tones. 'But I can't see him unless I get on set.'

Emma said nothing, least of all what she was thinking, which was that not even Christian Harlow could be worth the hell Darcy was putting herself through. Surely no one was that fantastic in bed?

'But enough of me, what about you?' Darcy gave Emma a broad smile. 'Any romantic attachments?'

Emma shook her head. But the picture, never far away, rushed back: a tall, blond boy with long green eyes and a deep, nervous voice that made her stomach turn over. A lingering, passionate kiss.

But what was the point? She had now entirely given up the idea of returning to the square in Florence. That lightning had struck twice – and lightning was what it felt like – had been unlikely enough. It was impossible that it would strike a third.

'Ah!' Darcy saw the shadow cross Emma's face. 'There *is* someone.' Her voice was teasing.

Emma heaved Morning up into her arms and hugged him. 'There's this one. I'm in love with Morning.'

'Don't change the subject,' giggled Darcy. 'I've told you about mine. So tell me about yours.'

'He isn't mine,' Emma insisted.

'*Who* isn't yours?'

Emma sighed. There was no way out. 'Well, there *is* this boy . . .'

'Such excitement!' Georgie greeted Orlando as he shuffled into the kitchen. It was just before lunch; she was uncorking some wine – to pour down the ever-ready maw of Hugh, Orlando guessed – and her habitually anxious eyes were shining. 'Ivo and Jago have made a *marvellous* new friend in the village,' she twittered, frowning as she struggled with the corkscrew. 'Very stiff,' she muttered,

Stiff was the word. Was anyone stiffer than Ivo and Jago, Orlando wondered. As the days had dragged past, one of the few enlivening moments had been the appearance of the brothers in their holidaywear. They had a particular penchant for Hawaiian shirts, whose bright colours made them look even spottier and pastier and their unpleasantly red lips even more unpleasantly red. With every day that passed, Orlando felt, he hated everything about them more, from their big curly black hair and horsy teeth to their horrible, sniggery laughs. The churning, burning feeling that rose in his throat whenever he saw them was as violent as his self-loathing over Emma.

It made eating dinner in their company impossible. Their physical presence was bad enough, but their conversation was almost as objectionable. Last night's had centred on some shooting the Faughs were apparently planning to enjoy in the autumn in Scotland. Sponging off some more unfortunate acquaintances, Orlando guessed.

'I'm having some new bespoke tweeds made,' Ivo told the table, to gasps of admiration from Georgie.

Orlando could imagine that ample figure in plus fours. Plus Faughs. He thought of the ghastly brothers striding about, slaughtering innocent wildlife. If only it were the other way round.

Georgie was still struggling with the cork.

'Let me help you with that,' Orlando said, taking the bottle from his mother.

'Terribly grand, a wonderful contact.' He realised she was still talking about whatever unfortunate it was who had fallen into the twins' clutches.

Orlando concentrated on liberating the Pinot Grigio. He was not interested in Ivo and Jago's contacts. He was not, come to that, interested in anything any more. He no longer cared, even, that his A level results were surely about to arrive at any moment. He'd met Emma again, and straight away he'd run away from her. Had been given another chance, and ruined it. Or, rather, that fearsome hag from the model agency had ruined it for him.

But even that no longer seemed an excuse. What had he been running away from anyway; he could have just turned her down and got on with his day. Emma would have thought it amusing, even interesting. It was all so obvious now. His intense frustration with himself went beyond anything he had ever experienced before.

'Yes,' gushed Georgie as she shook some crackers on a rustic plate. 'She's called Totty Ponsonby-Pratt.'

'What a stupid name,' Orlando remarked.

'Her father's a *lord*!' Georgie exclaimed, as if this explained or excused it. Orlando looked up to see his mother's eyes glowing nuclear with excitement. 'According to the twins, Totty's very attractive. *Hot,* they said.' Georgie giggled, savouring this piece of contemporary slang that, as always with his mother, Orlando recognised, was a bit less contemporary than she believed it to be. 'They're out somewhere with her now,' Georgie added.

Orlando shrugged and returned to his room. Here he would sip cold beer and stare at the ceiling; otherwise stare at Italian television. None of this got him any closer to seeing Emma again, although it did have the advantage of keeping him out of the way of Laura who, like the Mounties, never gave up.

Frustrated by the chair and chest of drawers he now rammed nightly against his bedroom door, her strategy was attempting to fondle him anywhere she found him alone. He never dared venture by the pool these days as it was shielded from the house by some large lavender clumps and anything could happen there. Even the garage, where he had discovered a battered orange neon foam football he sometimes liked to kick around, was haunted by the possibility of Laura suddenly apprehending him.

Of course, he could not speak to his mother about it. And what hopes he had harboured about talking to his father were now fading, as Richard seemed so distant. Orlando had no idea, could not imagine, what had happened during the trip to Florence. But something evidently had. Richard had set off on the trip as a man of few words and had returned as a man of no words at all.

As it happened, Richard would have told Georgie, Orlando, Laura and anyone else who insisted on knowing, the whats and whys of his visit to the internet café. But to do so inevitably brought up the question of what Hugh was doing there too. And even though Freebie Faugh was the holiday guest from hell, it struck Richard as unhostlike in the extreme to expose the adultery of someone staying under his roof. To that extent at least he clung to the libertarian principles that had propelled him into parliament in the first place. But, as with Mrs Greatorex, he was left feeling that his principles were being exploited.

He also had to bear constant innuendo. Since the internet café incident, Hugh, having evidently decided Richard was a sexual adventurer like himself, never passed up an opportunity to act lewdly. Hugh Faugh, Richard thought, would be more accurately called Hugh Phwoarrr.

Last night he had pranced around with a large salami stuck down his trousers during pre-dinner drinks. This had not only been criminally unfunny, but a criminal waste of a good sausage. And then there was the way he routinely treated women.

'Phwoaarr! Look at the boobs on that,' the MP would leer whenever any female under forty hoved round the curve of a village corner. 'Talk about a well-stacked bird. What do you reckon to those, eh, Richard? Orlando?'

The only redeeming feature of such interludes, Richard felt, was the way women thus singled out by Hugh reacted. Without exception they gave him curl-lipped looks of magnificent contempt. It was so absolutely the look he wanted to give Hugh himself that Richard almost wished he was well stacked too. The idea that he was colluding with such a reptile was sickening, and yet it was not his own activities Richard wished to conceal.

To add to his woes, matters in his constituency were getting worse daily. Wellover property prices were plunging, thanks to the dogging, reported Guy. Conversions and restoration projects were being abruptly terminated. 'People are pulling out all over,' the agent reported. 'So to speak, ha ha.'

'That's not funny,' Richard snapped. Guy could be so bloody inappropriate at times. Did he take nothing seriously? 'I suppose that architectural salvage guy who's restoring the old station's going as well,' he said gloomily. The station project was a flagship one for which Richard had personally helped arrange grant funding; the possibility of the old steam railway being restored hung on it.

'Actually,' said Guy, 'there's good news on that front. He's staying.'

'Great!' Richard was surprised and relieved.

'Well, perhaps great's not exactly the word. He's one of the keenest doggers of them all, it turns out. But there is some good news,' Guy added quickly.

'What?' Richard hissed, gripping the mobile.

'The website.'

'It's gone?' Richard's voice leapt with hope. He tried not to think of the big hairy bottom, but it was difficult. He had found to his horror that such was the power of association that the mere sight of a computer made him think of it; the mere mention of the word, in fact. It was all very unpleasant, and he felt polluted.

'It is gone in a sense. The antis have set up their own website. Called DogGone. The resistance starts here,' Guy added.

Richard clicked him into the ether. Resistance, it seemed to him, was useless. Everywhere he turned.

The fact that his father was obviously, if for reasons he could not quite guess, having almost as bad a time as himself with the Faughs was comfort of a sort, Orlando supposed. Another reason to be cheerful was that his loathing of the twins seemed to have penetrated even the ten-foot-thick social hide of Georgie, who had finally stopped suggesting brightly every morning that 'you boys probably want to do something together'. But otherwise, all was black, black, black. He had no idea how to get in touch with Emma. And his A level results could arrive at any moment.

Chapter 50

Darcy strained and panted up the hill into Rocolo. She was struggling for breath. The boiling sun pressed heavily down on her like a giant, invisible hand. She clutched the bottle of water hard, as if this would somehow transfer intravenously the liquid she had not stopped to drink. She had felt that if she stopped she would never start again.

Her heart was thudding in her chest and she felt as if she were about to die. The Hero of Zero had waxed lyrical about the ketosis stage of exercising, the sought-after nirvana when the body stops burning fat and starts burning muscle. Perhaps this was what was happening now. The emptiness in her stomach had spread. Even her arms felt empty; the very tips of her fingers felt hollow.

As she heaved up the hill, snatched smells of savoury lunches hit her on the nose and in the stomach with the force of a punch. The merest hint of garlic or tomato brought a surge of saliva into her mouth and the sight of bread – especially the thick-crusted country bread that seemed a speciality of the area – made her want to weep. Running past Marco's brought the most delicious smells of all wafting into her nostrils, which was usually why she tried to get past it as swiftly as possible. Today, however, her lungs bursting with effort, her whole body wilting beneath the sun, she felt herself slow down as she approached it.

Marco sat outside the restaurant, enjoying a mid-morning snack. He had forgotten to have breakfast, as he often did if particularly excited about something. He was very excited this morning. His mind was full of fish. A magnificent consignment of trout had just been delivered, with eyes so fresh and bright they looked, for all they were dead, more vital and alive than many of the people who would eventually eat them. The rainbow glimmer of the scales had sent Marco into raptures. Such beauty. Such nobility. He had almost wanted to weep.

A case of magnificent lobsters had also arrived, also absolutely perfect. The question was how to serve them the absolute best way. His own approach, which applied to everything from the humblest courgette to the most sublime, expensive truffle, was to listen to the ingredient. Eccentric, he knew, crazy, possibly, and people had certainly laughed at him in the past about it – fellow cooks had gone about kitchens with carrots held to their ears and intent expressions.

But no one was laughing now, with his slew of rave reviews, his growing reputation and his restaurant packed lunchtime and evening. And Marco believed more than ever that if you really looked at something properly it would suggest to you the best way to cook it.

And, obviously, what those lobsters were clamouring for – apart from being returned to the sea, of course, but he couldn't help them with that, although he'd kill them as humanely as anyone could, stun them in the freezer and slip a knife behind their eyes – was to be grilled. Yes, grilled, so their sweet, fresh meat could be savoured with as little adulteration as possible. Apart from, of course, a spot of butter and a touch of lemon.

Marco heaved a happy, absorbed sigh. Or he could serve them with tomato sauce and linguine, of course, that magnificent dish where the pasta seemed to spill out of the majestic red shellfish and stream round it like some stylised sea in a Japanese drawing. Some restaurants liked to split lobsters open, smother them in cheese for lobster thermidor. He'd done it himself in the past – had been obliged to at some of the big Paris restaurants – but he'd never dream of doing that now. It would be as much of a crime as that restaurant where seabass, shimmeringly fresh and alert of eye, the kind of fish that cried out to be grilled whole and served with a simple slice of lemon, were filleted and drowned in buttery yellow sauce.

Marco rolled his eyes at the memory. Outrageous. Tragic.

He shook his shaggy hair, which felt hot. It was indeed a hot day, hotter even than usual; the sky above was brilliantly blue and had no clouds whatsoever. It would get even hotter this afternoon.

It was, Marco knew, time he returned to the kitchen. But before he did that, he thought, stretching his long legs under the table, he'd just sit out here a second longer, under this deep blue sky, enjoying the sunshine, the feeling of being, as he always was, tired but generally happy, and admiring the familiar, yet to his eyes, ever-beautiful village with its different-height roofs, deep and shadowy arcades, windows at all levels and of all styles, rioting creeper and vine, busy with people and dogs and children.

He lit another cigarette, took another bite of bread and tomato, and waved his hand at a passing mother and child. *'Ciao, Marco!'* they chirped in unison. He smiled happily, wrinkling his nose in the sun and feeling, as he so often did, a wave of profound gratitude for all that had been achieved.

His heart gave a sudden, violent leap. It was her. Darcy. Struggling up the road towards him. She did not look happy at all; her big dark eyes glaring, that rosebud mouth of hers in a flat, cross line. It was obvious she was hating every minute of her run. She was almost bent double with the effort. It could not, Marco thought, rising hurriedly, be good for her to run in this heat.

'Hey! Hello!' he called to her. 'Come and have a rest. You look as if you need one.' He waved his big hands at the table he sat at.

Darcy paused at the entrance to his courtyard. 'I can't,' she gasped, hands on hips, bent double as she drew in great lungfuls of hot, garlic-and-herb scented air.

'Why not?' Marco walked towards her. She was shaking, he saw. 'You really have to sit down,' he said, concerned. 'Have some water . . . some coffee . . .'

Darcy felt her every nerve end agree with him. At that moment, nothing else on earth seemed more attractive than a rest in that pretty courtyard. Apart from Christian, that was. He had not been in touch for a whole day now. She was beginning to feel panicky. 'I can't,' Darcy growled.

Marco shook his head, perplexed. He was glad to see her. She had been in his thoughts, after the swaggering idiot had turned up at the restaurant last night with the ridiculous blonde and some other, equally silly people. They were making a film in Florence, he gathered. The blonde and the idiot were now together, Marco saw; certainly, they had spent more time eating each other than any of his food. And while this was offensive, the fact that the idiot was obviously no longer with the brunette was good news. Very good news, Marco felt.

'Come on,' he urged her. 'Just for a minute. I can run you back to wherever you're staying on my Vespa,' he added naughtily, pointing to the battered little red scooter just inside the courtyard entrance.

Darcy looked at the Vespa and then back to the chef. The expression of outrage that was gathering on her face gave way to a grin. She caught sight of the table behind him and what was on it. A great hunk of crusty bread, a jar of green oil, some tomatoes as plump, red and audacious as Carmen's smile . . .

She swallowed. Her stomach erupted in a thunderclap of hunger. Marco heard it, and scented victory.

'Come on,' he urged her. 'It's only tomatoes. It won't make you fat.'

Seconds later she was sitting down, in the shade, with, in her hand, a hunk of the freshest, chewiest bread she had ever eaten, with a fresh, sweet tomato pushed into it, slicked with green olive oil and ground over with salt and pepper.

'The simplest sandwich in the world,' Marco grinned. 'The tomatoes came in this morning. They are perfect. From the south of Italy and full of flavour. You have never had a tomato like this one before.'

Darcy nodded, her mouth full. She found herself cramming it in, savouring the sweet explosion of tomato, the bite of crust, the chewy pulp of bread, the pungently scented oil. Nothing had ever tasted so delicious.

'When did you last eat?' Marco asked gently.

'Breakfast time,' Darcy muttered, aware her intestines were gurgling like faulty plumbing.

Marco nodded. She'd had breakfast. That was something, at least. 'What did you have for breakfast?'

'Can't remember,' Darcy muttered. She had absolutely no

intention of admitting it was an egg-white omelette, which had tasted of precisely nothing.

Marco sighed. He could never understand how people forgot what they ate. Personally, he could remember almost every meal he had ever had in his life. The way he recalled events, people, important business meetings even, was to think about what he had eaten that day and work his way back from there.

Darcy bit into the tomatoey, oily bread. It rocketed her back to the land of taste after what seemed years of deprivation in the steamed-broccoli wilderness. The flavours exploded in her mouth with an eye-watering intensity. She felt as if she were coming back to life. Her legs and arms had stopped shaking, the dizziness had faded, her heart had stopped rattling and resumed its usual smooth beat.

Marco had stretched back in his chair again and was looking at the sky. The call of the trout and lobster, which had been so loud, was now fainter. Daria could take care of them. She was good with fish.

'You know what I think?' Marco said softly. 'That the very best things in life are the simplest. Take that tomato. Could there be anything more perfect and luxurious? It tastes of itself, of having ripened in the sun slowly and lazily over the weeks and months. You know?'

Her jaws crashing over the crust, Darcy could only nod. She was taking another bite, which really would be the last. Oil and bread. She wasn't allowed either of them, especially in this quantity. He must have handed her half a loaf.

Marco stared up at the blue sky. 'True luxury's nothing to do with spending, you see. It's not about showing the world you've got the flashiest car or whatever . . .'

Christian's car flashed into Darcy's mind. She bridled,

slightly. Had he seen the Ferrari? She shot a sharp, defensive look at Marco but he was still staring into space, musing.

'Real luxury's about,' Marco inhaled dreamily, 'salad leaves with the dew still on them, a day like today, a walk in the woods, the singing birds, the light on the new leaves, the smell of the earth. You know?'

Darcy nodded. The bread and tomato was finished. She had eaten every mouthful.

'Well, you're a really great eater,' Marco said appreciatively. 'A true gastronome.'

'You mean a great guzzling pig,' Darcy wailed, thinking of the weighing scales.

He rushed to reassure her. 'No, I mean the opposite.' He spoke very precisely, she noticed. His English was perfect. 'Great guzzling pigs don't appreciate their food. I was watching you and it was obvious you appreciated every mouthful. You've got a great palate.'

Darcy giggled. She'd been admired for many things in her career. But this was the first time her palate had got a mention.

She settled back in her chair and closed her eyes, sniffing the warm air swirling with delicious scents from the kitchen. She was exhausted after the run and the feeling of her limbs relaxing utterly, her stomach full for the first time in what seemed months, was delicious.

'I expect you always wanted to be a chef,' she remarked lazily.

Marco looked at her. 'Not at all,' he said. He saw her eyes jolt in surprise. 'I never thought about being one, not for a very long time. It was all complete chance.'

Marco hesitated before continuing. What he was about to say wasn't something he told everyone. None of his staff; few in the village, even, knew the whole story. It was not something he even thought about very much; the pain remained, even after all these years. It always would, he knew. It was part of him.

Now he explained to Darcy that, while he had always eaten it with relish, the ingenuity and tradition of the cooking of his region, of his family, had for years just passed him by. He had not noticed or been interested in how his mother and grandmother could coax rich flavour and sumptuousness out of a few scrag ends, how the fact that nothing was wasted became a culinary art form in itself. The risotto that had not been eaten at dinner was formed into small balls in the palm, stuffed with ragu and fried as a snack which, eaten after school, tasted even more delicious than the original dish.

All this, however, Marco had taken for granted. His main interest in life, after football, had been natural history; he loved nothing more than to pack up a satchel with a lump of cheese and some rough-crusted, home-made bread and set off into the rough, hot, stony, herb-scented summer hills with his binoculars and magnifying glass to spy on the insects and bird life.

And then, as a boy of eight, he had gone to Paris on a trip with his mother and aunt. And after that, his attitude to food was never the same. And all because of a biscuit.

'A biscuit!' Darcy smiled.

'Yes, a biscuit! And also because of . . .'

She saw his chest swell in a sigh.

'. . . my mother,' he added.

His mother, Marco explained, had been ill for some time and had been sent to visit a special doctor in Paris. Woven in with the experience of visiting the beautiful city had been the suspicion – for the facts of her cancer had not then been explained to Marco – that something was terribly wrong.

'Cancer,' Darcy groaned. Her eyes shut harder, remembering the loss of Anna, her beloved grandmother.

'Yes. Cancer.' His voice was softer now. 'I knew something was wrong in Paris, but I didn't know what it was then.'

Nor did he know later, he told her, during that terrible time when they had returned and his mother was ill upstairs at home, when doctors with concerned faces and hushed footsteps padded softly up and down to see her. And afterwards when she went to hospital and never came back, those few happy days in the domed, gilded, triumphal-arched and wide-boulevarded city would seem to Marco almost a dream.

'Oh Marco!' Darcy whispered through the lump in her throat. With her eyes closed she could see it all so clearly; the intense, curly-haired little boy, his dark eyes wide and puzzled, understanding nothing but the one central fact, the one thing that mattered, that his mother wasn't there any more.

He said nothing for a few minutes, looking away so she could not quite see his expression. But then he seemed to shake himself and began talking about Paris again. For the days there, he said, had been happy; his mother, despite the reason for her visit, and very possibly because of it, was determined to enjoy herself in the city where, Marco now learnt for the first time, she had spent part of her youth. His grandmother, who had since died, had had ambitions in fashion and had worked for a time at one of the Parisian couture houses, meeting his Italian grandfather in a café in the city. They had returned to his native Tuscany when his mother was quite small, Marco now learnt, but not without planting in her the sweetest of memories.

Marco's voice was lifting now, as he explained excitedly how his mother had taken him and her sister Mara, Marco's aunt, to the Rue Royale, where stood, she smilingly explained, one of her favourite shops in the world. Ladurée, the home of the most wonderful macaroons. Marco had stared entranced at the polished plate-glass window and the tiny pastel-coloured, cream-filled biscuits which seemed to fill the space behind it in a riot of pale yellow, rose pink, soft orange, pale coffee brown, darker chocolate brown and delicate green.

Darcy's eyes snapped open in shocked delight. She sat up abruptly and stared at him with shining eyes. 'Ladurée! My grandmother was obsessed with their macaroons!' The coincidence was astounding. She felt quite winded with astonishment. 'She decorated her whole apartment in macaroon colours.'

'Great idea!' Marco laughed. 'I'd love to have seen it.'

'You will,' Darcy assured him passionately. 'It still looks like that. It's my flat now and I haven't changed a thing.'

'I'll hold you to that,' Marco grinned. 'Next time I'm in London.'

'You will be,' Darcy stated with an odd, but absolute certainty. 'Now carry on your story. Please.'

'You're sure?' Marco raised a heavy eyebrow. 'I'm not boring you?'

She shook her head with more energy than she had realised she had. 'I've never heard anything less boring.'

He looked at her for a moment, then went on to describe how he had stared and stared at the shop. He had never seen anything like these graceful fairy biscuits with their stripe of filling the exact same colour as their shells. The equivalent at home, the strongly flavoured *amaretti* with their scattering of sugar, were either hard and crunchy or soft and dry. They were delicious, but had none of the delicacy of this pretty pastel riot of patisserie. The macaroons seemed to him to be the essence of femininity; small wonder that he connected them, immediately and for ever, with his beloved mother. The rose pink one, anyway, was the exact colour of his mother's blouse that day – his mother always had very pretty clothes, no doubt the influence of her own mother – while the pistachio green reminded him of a favourite dress of hers. The chocolate brown, meanwhile, was like her hair.

'She sounds lovely,' Darcy sighed.

'She was,' he replied shortly.

He had, Marco explained, watched his mother through the shop's plate-glass window, smiling and gesticulating at the assistants. Then she had come out, obviously delighted, with a large be-ribboned box of the precious macaroons. Giggling naughtily, the three of them went straightaway to sit on a bench and eat the whole lot at one wonderful, greedy sitting. Listening to his mother and aunt excitedly exclaiming, watching them close their eyes with rapture as they bit into the biscuits, Marco felt something surge within him that was nothing to do with the almighty hit of sugar rioting round his system. He was seeing, as if for the first time, the intense and unrivalled pleasure that food can give. 'These,' his mother had smiled at him, holding a pink biscuit, 'are about the most difficult things that a chef can make. They're almost impossible to do properly.'

'That's what my grandmother always said,' Darcy told him, wondering again at the coincidence.

Marco went on. For his mother, a consummate cook, to say such a thing made an impression on the eight-year-old boy. He liked the biscuits and he liked a challenge. He also wanted to help his mother. Might the macaroons make her better?

And so the obsession began. Marco, now sitting in the sun over thirty years later, smiled ruefully as he described his eight-year-old self to Darcy, sieving and mixing with fierce concentration and then piping, breath held, on to a baking sheet. He could see himself, as clearly as if it were yesterday, bent over, bottom aloft, peering into the oven to see if the shells were rising. Try as he might to follow the recipes – as many different ones as he could get his hands on, none seemed quite right, somehow – his macaroons were always too flat, too soggy, or stiff and dry like meringues. They cracked, they stuck, they failed to rise and merged with the ones next to them in a flat, hard pool. Never once did they appear round and perfect with the shiny, shell-like dome on the top and the yielding softness beneath.

Darcy listened, touched beyond measure. Her eyes were closed even harder than before, so he shouldn't see the warm, unstoppable wetness there.

But Marco's voice was warm with laughter now. His family, he told Darcy, were amazed at his efforts. He had never shown the smallest interest in cooking before. Why now, all of a sudden, try to make the most difficult thing of all? But Marco took no notice. He was a boy on a mission. A child with a challenge. The battle with the biscuits had begun to seize him; he was determined to get the better of them. It became an epic struggle made possible only by the fact that the family had hens laying plenty of eggs for him to endlessly separate and weigh, and almonds, which grew in the area, were also readily available and cheap, as was mascarpone for the filling. But for months all Marco's pocket money, earned from paper rounds and odd jobs, went on food colouring and icing sugar.

Slowly but irretrievably, he became sucked into an obsession with cooking. He learnt the joy of combining the best ingredients. He learnt the value of precision, the importance of getting every last detail right. He learnt patience. He learnt that things go wrong, sometimes inexplicably, that effort is necessary for any achievement. As his schoolfriends on weekends perfected their sliding tackles and their goalkeeping, Marco hit on the right temperature, the right amount of egg white, the right amount of elasticity and stiffness in the mixture. His friends had mocked him, but reservedly – risible though it was for a boy of fourteen to prefer patisserie to soccer practice, Marco was big and tough and strong. And so, as they kicked balls about the park, working out their team formation, he worked out how to beat the eggs to perfection, how to sieve the almonds to fairy dust, how to make sure no air remained in the piping bag so a steady stream of glossy gloop emerged on to the baking tray.

'Good for you!' Darcy smiled, risking opening her eyes at last. She was just in time to see the remembered triumph in Marco's fade, to be replaced by a terrible sadness.

'Good for me,' he said in a whisper. 'But not good for Mama. Macaroons, however perfect, do not save lives.' He paused.

Darcy looked down, feeling choked. Her fingers twisted around each other, hard.

But what a legacy she had left him, Marco explained, his voice strengthening. Nothing less than his restaurant. From experimenting with macaroons he had gone on to develop an interest in cooking generally, and ultimately a pungent, earthy, full-tasting branch of his national cuisine that could not have been further removed from the insubstantial pastel confections in Ladurée's window. 'I don't know what Mama would think,' Marco confessed, grinning.

Darcy did not care now that her eyes, as she looked at him, were red and full of tears. 'I'm sure she would be enormously proud,' she told him through the ball of emotion blocking her throat.

She looked up. Marco was smiling at her gently, a beautiful, kind, generous smile, Darcy noticed. Not crooked at all. She felt herself held in his gaze. His face was not regular, not textbook handsome, not by a long way.

But how much more special were the black, chaotic swirls of hair, the warm brown eyes lit with excitement, the enthusiasm and passion evident in every fibre of his being. A warm glow spread through her, to her very finger ends. It felt, Darcy thought, oddly like relief.

'Come by the restaurant again some time. Come by tomorrow. I've got some great new cheese I'd be interested to hear what you think about.'

Interest blazed in her eyes. She paused. Then she walked away, down the hill. He watched her slight figure retreating until it passed round the next bend.

For the next few hours, after she had gone, Marco tasted, advised, planned, even tolerated the good-natured ribbing of his brigade – had had no idea he was doing any of it. His cooking senses were all present and correct but every other part of his mind somewhere else altogether. He replayed, up close, Darcy's passionate face – such a pretty name too – the way she had closed her eyes when tasting, her brows contracting as if it almost hurt.

That skin; soft and pink-flushed, with its dusting of faint freckles, like strawberry-infused cream with a scattering of chocolate powder. Those coffee-bean-dark eyes. That hair, as black as liquorice from a few paces away, but up close, tumbled from its ponytail, not just black but with threads of brown and even gold and orange. Hints of carrot, cinnamon, Parmesan, saffron and, glinting here and there, the sheet of gold leaf that one of the restaurants he'd worked in had, rather ridiculously in his view, always laid on top of truffle risotto. Literally gilding the lily. It doubled the price, that was the main point. That had been in the eighties, of course . . .

Was it all too quick? Did he believe in love at first sight? Of course he did. Why not? He was an expert judge of whether a dish was right; knew in an instant whether it looked right, was composed of the right things, had been made properly, whether its heart was right. So why should a woman not be the same?

Chapter 51

Ken had enjoyed a late breakfast on his terrace and was now taking a gentle constitutional round the environs of Rocolo's church. The building amazed him; the ancient, round-arched door opening to a flight of descending steps as wide as the building, leading down into the body of the church. There was a notice as you went in: a camera with a line through it. No photographs. Not a ban that bothered him any more.

All was cool, dark and quiet. The rows of chairs – no pews here – stretched away towards the gloomy, gaudy altar. Along the side aisles and by the immensely thick pillars a few candles picked out the gilt of the icons and on the paintings that, otherwise indistinguishable subjectwise, hung massive and dark on the walls. The place smelt heavy, sweet, cold and unmistakably foreign. You got the sense, Ken thought, of something very old, of people having worshipped here for century upon century. People must have married here knowing that they would have their funeral services here, had their children baptised here knowing that they, in turn, would have their weddings here. The certainty of it all astounded him.

He emerged like a mole, blinking in the light and warmth,

and a surge of deep joy for the beauty of the day assailed him, as perhaps the designers of the church had meant it to. The sensation was powerful enough to drive away Ken's small, everyday worries such as the sighting of two particularly unpleasant and ridiculous celebrities in the one place he had imagined he was safe from them.

Not that spotting Christian Harlow and Belle Murphy had been the end of it. Halfway through his starter, which had been a particularly peppery rocket salad topped with delicious, oil-slicked Parma ham, Ken had realised who the big, dark-haired man with the booming voice at the table opposite was, and why he had looked familiar.

Politicians weren't Ken's usual beat, but Hugh Faugh was colourful, high-profile and self-publicising enough to stray into his patch from time to time. Ken's eye dwelt with interest on the party with him; two startlingly unpleasant-looking boys with big hair and huge teeth who just had to be twins. Cripes, bad enough to get one like that, Ken thought, but two, well, unfortunate was probably the word.

And that vampire-like woman was Faugh's wife; presumably the boys' mother. Ken did not recognise the other man and woman, who looked harmless enough, if slightly crushed, or the other boy, who was quite amazingly good looking. Ken stared for a good few minutes. Tall, rangy, with that swollen-mouth, half-closed-eyes look the agencies were clamouring for. Was he a model? Ought to be, if he wasn't. Film star, even. Oh, listen to me, Ken thought, half indulgent. You can take the boy away from the paparazzi, but you couldn't take the paparazzo out of the boy.

You could tell the Faugh boys hated the handsome one, Ken saw, savouring the unfamiliar sensation of salad crunching against his teeth. They kept giving him the filthiest looks. Quite funny, really. Almost made him wish he had his camera with him, but it was locked in the hotel room and he intended to keep it there.

It was not with him now, as he walked outside in the warm square, swerving slightly to avoid the children, dogs, low-slung grannies with their straw baskets full of the morning's marketing. He wandered around again and found himself opposite the entrance to the children's playground over which the balcony of his room looked.

Nice playground, Ken thought, with those cypresses all around it stretching up into the pure blue sky, a soft breeze ruffling the leaves and making them glitter in the light. He stood at the edge, outside the gate, watching for a while.

He had already gathered, from his balcony, that the play-ground was a rallying point for nannies in charge of holidaying British infants from miles around. While he hadn't stood there watching the playground – you had to be careful these days about that sort of thing, especially as a middle-aged man travelling alone – Ken had been vaguely aware of various British voices, most of them pretty posh, shouting at various children.

Now, between the plants and bushes that the playground was plentifully supplied with, he could see glimpses of the children. Yes, definitely British, definitely upmarket; he knew the look, he saw it several times a day with its wealthy parents disappearing through the revolving door of various five-star hotels. The kids were dressed like miniature versions of trendy adults with, especially among the boys, over-long hair. Yeah, and the nannies were true to form too.

They looked more or less alike, with long glossy hair all shades from blond to black, vast sunglasses and miniskirts exposing long thin brown legs and feet in glittery flipflops. They were, Ken noticed, all standing together, smoking, talking, gesturing, shrieking with laughter, answering their mobiles. The children they were nominally in charge of seemed more or less forgotten, although from time to time one of them would turn round to yell at their charges in throaty upmarket voices. 'Don't do that, Cosmo!' and 'No, Hero! No!'

He recognised that voice, Ken thought as he turned away. The Rolodex in his head rotated. Where had he heard it before? Those names, too. Hero and Cosmo. Somewhere very recently.

He turned back round, frowning. His eye caught a small blond boy and a white-blonde girl, about four and three respectively, charging about after each other. Of course. That boy from the airport. The one with the train. And, Ken remembered, the horrid nanny.

The tender, protective feelings the boy had evoked now gave way to dislike. Yes, there she was. In the midst of the chattering nannies, laughing her scornful laugh, that long-legged, heavily highlighted, thoroughly unpleasant blonde. What had the kids called her? Titty? Totty?

Ken lingered protectively, watching the children for some minutes. He felt strangely reluctant to leave them with her. Totty, Ken now noticed, seemed to be looking for someone. Not the kids, though. They were walking up one of the slides now, a strategy certain to end in an accident of some sort. Totty was oblivious, however. She kept casting glances towards the gate, where he stood himself, as if someone was expected there. Not wishing to be seen by her, Ken slowly, reluctantly, moved away.

In doing so he narrowly avoided bumping into two grubby-looking men in baseball caps and leather jackets who seemed to be heading for the playground. Fathers going for their children, Ken supposed. As they passed him, Ken felt the strong, hard pull of a scent he recognised tugging at his nose. Strong tobacco. A few minutes later, back in the square, he realised it was cannabis.

*

Darcy, heading towards the gate for her run, walked past Emma and Morning on the terrace.

'I'll see you later,' Darcy called gaily. 'I'll keep an eye out for that man of yours, as well.'

She was rewarded with a blush and a frown from an Emma now fervently wishing she had never mentioned Orlando. The whole story sounded so ridiculous.

'You're in a good mood,' she riposted. 'Has Christian been in touch?'

Darcy nodded. There had been a text late last night, a mere two sentences in which the actor explained that he was involved in a complicated scene at the moment. He knew she would understand. Another reason for her improved outlook, Darcy knew, was that she had gone to bed last night, for the first time in days, without her stomach feeling as void as a robbed bank. The bread and tomato at Marco's, topped up with the grilled chicken fillet and broccoli reluctantly served by Mara, had kept her going all day.

Now, the next morning, she was starving again. The egg-white omelette Mara had banged down before her for breakfast had not even taken the edge off it. But of course, they could not continue, these little gastronomic stop-offs at Marco's. He had mentioned cheese, which would be death to her diet. She would have to scurry past and hope he didn't see her.

Darcy reached over to chuck Morning under the chin. He really was sweet. She had not, until now, realised babies could be such fun, so well behaved and so responsive. Morning was also so appreciative of her every effort to entertain, from waggling her fingers over his face to tickling him. He always smelt delicious, powdery, warm and with a slight milky undertone. Emma kept him wonderfully clean and happy.

Nonetheless, it had started to occur to Darcy to wonder what Emma thought of her employer. The nanny obviously loved her charge, but it seemed strange that someone so no-nonsense, obviously intelligent and so good at her job was prepared to put up with the imperious, ridiculous Belle. Of course, some people were blinded by showbiz, so dazzled by celebrity that they were prepared to bear any humiliation at the hands of a star. But Emma did not seem one of these, on the contrary.

And, even if she was, Darcy argued to herself, surely Belle's utter lack of interest in the baby would undermine any possible respect? Belle's version of herself as devoted mother, as read in the interview on the plane, was clearly the thinnest of acts. Belle hadn't been back to the villa for days, nor had she even been in touch. Hopefully she'd been blasted off into the stratosphere in one of the film's space bombers.

Clearly, so far as the baby was concerned, she might as well be. The circumstances of Morning's adoption, and the reasons, were something Darcy could only make dark and cynical guesses about – good manners forbade questioning Emma on the subject. Sometimes, Darcy thought, it would be nice not to have scruples about these things. Perhaps there was a way of probing subtly.

'You know,' she remarked now, watching Emma using the sugar lumps on the table to play a counting game with Morning, 'you're really good. You could get a much better job. Why bother with the Evil One?'

Emma looked at her in alarm. 'Evil One?' It was fine for Darcy to insult Belle, obviously, but for her, the employee, it was a dangerous matter.

'Belle's name in the film,' Darcy assured her, smiling. 'What all the good characters, like mine, call her. Belle's character is a beautiful but evil man-eating female monster who wants to destroy the universe. Typecasting or what?' She raised her eyebrows and snorted.

Emma glanced down to hide a grin.

'You can't *like* working for her,' Darcy pressed, as the smile had not been quite hidden after all.

For all she liked Darcy, for all she appreciated their growing closeness, Emma had decided she could not possibly tell the actress all that had happened with Vanessa and the drugs. Once made, such a confession could not be retracted and, if it got out, could be disastrous. Ending up penniless and unemployed in Italy was not something she could allow to happen, even to contemplate.

Pitted against her caution was, however, her pride. For the sake of her own self-respect, Emma longed to unburden herself. She could imagine how she must seem in Darcy's eyes: Belle's slave and vassal, tolerating the routine contempt with which the actress treated almost everyone, when she bothered to notice them at all.

'But aren't you bored?' Darcy persevered. 'Isn't it a bit – well – dull?'

'It's not so bad,' Emma insisted, wishing Darcy would stop this uncomfortable line of questioning. She looked over to the Villa Rosa's long, mellow, golden front, topped with its sunbaked red tiles, glowing in the morning sunshine. Her eyes dropped to the dancing pool in front of it, the parasol-shaded table, the sunloungers. None of it compared with the nursery in Heckmondwike. Or even the bedroom at Vanessa's house, with its peeling walls and lethal-looking light fitting.

'I've been in worse places,' Emma said, in what she hoped was a final tone.

'Yes, but wouldn't you rather do something else? Like – I don't know – run your own place? Your own nursery. Be your own boss.' She had plucked the idea from thin air, having never thought about it before, but now Darcy saw an answering flash of excitement in Emma's eyes.

She had, since, buried the idea that had first, so airily, so unexpectedly, seen the light of day in the Florence square. It had been laid to rest along with everything else to do with Orlando. But now Emma felt it come rushing back, with redoubled impetus. Her own nursery. Her own business. The bliss and freedom of working for oneself. 'It *is* a good idea,' Emma admitted cautiously, over the excited thundering of her heart. She had, after all, lots of experience. Plus all the necessary qualifications, plus administration experience from Wee Cuties.

'Former nanny to the stars,' Darcy teased. 'You could put that on your sign as well. Might as well get something out of your time slaving for the Evil One. You'll be turning people away.'

Emma giggled.

'You could even have a Mediterranean menu,' Darcy suggested now, excitedly. 'Loads of pasta and olive oil. That'd get the aspirational parents beating down your door!'

Emma agreed that it would, indeed.

'So what's stopping you?' Darcy urged. 'Nothing!'

Well, there was Morning, Emma reflected, holding her small charge close. He looked up at her and beamed from under his little white sunhat. So adorable, she thought, always chuckling when you tickled his cheek and grasping your finger with his own tiny ones. And yet, not even six months old, he had been abandoned by not one but two mothers already, albeit for wildly varying reasons. She couldn't be the third. But perhaps there might be some way, when the nursery was open, if it ever did open, that Morning could actually come to it.

And, of course, there was money. 'I'd need startup funds, but I might be able to get a grant . . . yes, I'm sure . . .'

'No need for that!' Darcy leapt in. 'I've got some money,' she added impulsively. 'You set up a business, I'll invest in it!'

Emma clutched Morning so tightly in excitement he squawked in protest. 'What! Really? You mean it?'

'Absolutely. You wouldn't believe what they gave me just for signing the contract for *Galaxia*. It would be great to put it into something worthwhile.'

Emma's mouth opened and shut. She felt lost for words. Ten minutes ago her career had seemed a dead end. But now, a famous actress – or about-to-be-famous actress – was offering a dream escape route. Offering to invest in her business. Suddenly, anything seemed possible. It was all too good to be true.

'Er . . .' Emma shook her head, helpless, excited.

'I really think you ought to look into it, you know, like *now*,' Darcy enthused. 'Strike while the iron's hot, find out what you need to do, what certificates you need and all that.'

Certificates. The thought hit Emma like a slap in the face. Official checks. Of course. She felt her excitement subsiding, leaking air like a pierced balloon. It was all too good to be true. It was, in short, impossible. There was one crucial thing she lacked completely. A clear name. Should Vanessa ever find out about her plans, there was no doubt that the relevant authorities would be informed in short order about the cocaine in the handbag. And that would be that.

She had a sense like falling from a great height. It was a brick wall, slap bang in the middle of her plans. She had no idea how to get round it, what to do.

Darcy watched Emma's expression change from delighted to disappointed. 'What's the matter?'

The nanny looked at her with panicked eyes. 'Nothing. It's fine.'

Getting advice seemed the first step. Legal advice. In the face of the obvious impossibility of finding the person who had put the drugs there, especially if that person had been Vanessa herself, the law was her only hope. But the law was expensive, and the wages Belle paid were meagre. Emma wanted to wail and scream. The idea had been such a wonderful one. She could not bear to let it go.

'Something I can help with?' Darcy asked. Emma could hear the sympathy in her voice. Again, she wanted to unload some of her troubles. But again the inner voice warned what a mistake this could be.

Darcy looked at her for some moments then, realising nothing else would be forthcoming, set out finally on her run.

Chapter 52

Orlando was dawdling through Rocolo. He had no particular reason for going there, apart from the wish to get away from the *aubergo*, where the atmosphere was unbearable. The Faughs had gone up another level on the smug-o-meter, his father had descended even further into depression, while his mother, distracted at having lost her precious pink Gucci wallet, was turning the villa upside down in search of it. It had, apparently, vanished without trace. The imminent arrival into this volatile situation of his A level results would be, Orlando felt, like tossing a match into a barrel of petrol.

It was a sunny day and, despite his circumstances, the picturesque Italian village, its golden stone shining in the sun, lifted his spirits. He had walked up past the restaurant and was entering the arcaded square at the top when something made him stop. Right in front of him, on the cobbled surface of the square, a small, blond boy of about five years of age lay on the ground, unmoving.

Orlando looked about him. Various people were passing; some glancing over, but on their various faces – young, old, male, female – there leapt no spark of recognition; no exasperated, relieved, claiming cry. Orlando squinted towards the arcades that ran around the square's edge, but no one was emerging, laden with bags, from the shadows of the arches, bearing a bag from one of the shops. No mother, no nanny. There seemed no one around who was in charge of this child at all.

Orlando approached the boy cautiously. He recognised a scion of the middle classes; blond-striped pageboy hair and dressed in navy shorts and navy and white striped Breton top. It didn't seem long since he was wearing such outfits himself, Orlando thought. The boy's little denim shoes, stretched out behind him, were scuffed, but looked almost new.

Orlando bent over. The boy was breathing – a relief – but very still. Had he fainted? Fallen and broken something? 'Are you all right?' Orlando asked. 'What are you doing?' He felt instinctively that the boy was British.

To Orlando's great relief the child lifted his tousled, sandy-blond head and looked round with unconcerned blue eyes. 'Looking at a caterpillar,' he said in a matter-of-fact treble, sticking a small plump digit out in front of him to where a small, plump grub slowly progressed up and over one of the cobblestones.

'That's quite a nice one.' Orlando squatted on his hunkers. 'Fat and furry.' He grinned at the child. 'What's his name?'

Still lying on the ground, the boy propped himself up on his elbows. He frowned at Orlando. 'Don't be silly. He's a caterpillar. Caterpillars don't have names.'

'Oh.' Orlando straightened up, feeling he had rather been put in his place.

'Who are you?'

At the imperious little voice behind him, Orlando turned to

find a pair of solemn blue eyes beneath a fringe of perfect white blondness. A girl of about four, dressed identically to the boy, had materialised apparently from nowhere and was looking at him with an unnerving stare. Orlando looked about the square again, fully expecting, now, some man or woman to be striding towards them, panic on their face. But, among the chatting shoppers, ground-sniffing dogs, skipping children and dawdling tourists, no one of that description could be seen. Orlando glanced back to the children, perplexed.

They, on the other hand, seemed perfectly calm. Even pleased, Orlando saw. The girl was smiling at him. She was, he thought, an enchanting little thing, silver fair, with white skin and naughty, dancing blue eyes. Her brother, who had now scrambled to his feet, red impressions on his small knees from the cobblestones, looked altogether more serious.

'Teletubbies,' the girl remarked.

Orlando nodded. 'Tinky Winky, Dipsy, Laa Laa, Po,' he sang to the show's theme tune, jerking his head comically. The little girl giggled.

'You know the Teletubbies?' the boy piped up. He sounded pleasantly surprised.

'Oh, I know about the Teletubbies,' Orlando assured them with a certain ruefulness. He knew more about them than either of his A level subjects because he had spent more time watching them on television than he had revising. The same applied to *Postman Pat* and *Thomas the Tank Engine*.

'Eh Oh,' the little girl said now, the traditional Teletubbies greeting. 'I'm Hewo.'

'Eh Oh, Hewo,' Orlando replied gamely, and was gratified by the huge smile he received in return. She flung both her arms around one of his tanned legs in their baggy beige shorts and looked up, awed, at the tree-like height of him.

'And I'm Cosmo.' The blond boy, obviously her brother, was staring at him with challenging pale blue eyes. 'Do you know Thomas?' he asked.

'Thomas who?'

'The Tank Engine,' expostulated the boy, as if the question were ridiculous, which, Orlando realised, it probably was when you were five.

He folded his arms and put a finger to his lips. 'Now let me see,' Orlando said, in comic-pompous tones that had their origins in Hugh. 'That's the one with Percy in, isn't it?'

'And Harvey the Breakdown Train,' Cosmo returned eagerly.

'Harvey the Breakdown Train?' Orlando raised his eyebrows. 'I see you like the most obscure ones.'

'Cranky, Mavis, Troublesome Trucks, Sir Handel,' chanted Cosmo, in a tone Orlando realised was a challenge.

He picked up the gauntlet unhesitatingly. 'Rheneas, Skarloey, Lady, Neville . . .'

'Salty, Bulstrode, Culdee . . .' hit back Cosmo.

'Catherine the Mountain Coach,' Orlando continued with ease. He hadn't watched *Thomas the Tank Engine* every morning on Nickelodeon for nothing. He could go on for ever if Cosmo wanted.

Looking down, he saw Cosmo's small, serious face was flushed with pleasure. 'You know a lot about Thomas,' he admitted.

'Doesn't everyone?' Orlando sounded mock-shocked.

'Totty doesn't,' the children chorused.

'Who's Totty?'

'Our nanny.'

Orlando was so relieved to hear there was a nanny, the tone of gloom in their voices almost passed him by. 'Where is she then?' he asked. Totty. *Totty.* It sounded familiar.

The children looked blankly at him from their large blue eyes. 'We don't know. She left us here. She sometimes does.'

'Your nanny leaves you by . . . *yourselves?*' Orlando repeated. Surely that wasn't what nannies were supposed to do? He thought of Emma. She would, he was quite certain, be horrified. Orlando sighed. Emma. Where was she now? He'd had her so close, in his arms. The kiss haunted his nights.

'Yes, she does. Always.' Hero's chiming voice interrupted.

'You mean . . .' Orlando frowned, 'you mean, she's just gone into a shop or something?'

They looked blankly back at him. 'Totty didn't say,' Cosmo said eventually. 'She just,' he shook his head and shrugged, 'went off.'

Totty. Where had he heard that name before? Orlando furrowed his brow in thought; to no avail, however. He had no memory for names; admittedly, as his A level results were abundantly about to illustrate, he had no memory for anything.

'I'm hungwy,' Hero announced now, suddenly. 'Can you take us for somefing to eat?'

Eleven o'clock, Orlando saw from his watch. Some way from lunchtime, but, having been unable to face the communal breakfast – the great Faugh jaws and the twins' tumble-dryer mouths – he now felt rather peckish himself. A panini and a beer at that restaurant on the hill would be spot on. And he'd be happy to take Hero and Cosmo too, but one couldn't just take children one had only just met. What if their nanny, this mysterious, obviously stupid and incompetent Totty, returned? He could be accused of abduction, anything. Arrested, thrown into gaol.

He looked at them, helplessly. 'Please,' said the little girl, her eyes round and appealing. 'I'm weally, *weally* hungwy.'

'So am I,' added the little boy plaintively.

591

'Totty gave us hardly any bweakfast,' Hero said, sighing tragically.

'She never does,' agreed her brother.

'She's awful . . .'

'Horrid . . .'

'But what about your parents?' Orlando broke in. 'Can't they give you some more breakfast? Can't you talk to them?'

Two pairs of eyes now fixed themselves on his. 'Mummy's always busy,' Hero stated baldly.

'And Daddy's always away,' Cosmo assured him eagerly.

'Yes, but aren't they here now? You're on holiday, aren't you?' It was a guess, but it seemed likely.

Hero nodded. 'But Mummy and Daddy aren't,' she solemnly informed him. 'They're coming soon, though.'

'It might be today,' Cosmo added hopefully.

Orlando regarded them. A wave of sympathy broke over him. It all sounded so miserably familiar. Mother too busy, father away. Holidaying with the nanny. Fourteen, fifteen years ago, this could have been him. Except that, of the many nannies who had cared for him, none was exactly criminally negligent, unlike the absent Totty.

'Well, can we get in touch with your parents? I mean, where do they live?' The hope that it was some tiny hamlet with only two houses that was easily traceable flared wildly within him.

'London.'

'Oh.' That was that then.

'There's a nice restaurant just round the corner,' Cosmo remarked longingly, returning to the food theme.

'But what about Totty?' Orlando objected.

'She won't care,' the children chorused in unison.

Orlando had no idea what to do. He could hardly leave them, and although it seemed impossible that the nanny would not materialise soon, there was no sign of her yet. He felt that there were a few things he would like to tell her when she did.

Perhaps he could leave a note somewhere. Or perhaps, if he took them to the restaurant, he could keep returning, every ten minutes, say, to see if Totty had materialised. But was it a good idea, Orlando asked himself worriedly. Weren't there laws against this kind of thing?

The decision was out of his hands, however. He looked up now to see the children skipping away to the edge of the square, to where the road down the hill began.

'Hey!' Orlando shouted, running after them.

Marco walked among his tables, repositioning a chair here, brushing off a crumb there, taking deep breaths of satisfaction as he surveyed his kingdom. It was almost lunchtime and all these tables would be completely full. The bookings diary said so, and there were regulars who just turned up, scorning bookings diaries. But as they came every day he put them in the bookings diary anyway; not that they knew.

He glanced at his watch, the watch he had been given for his eighteenth birthday and whose glass was split after a bullying chef in a top London restaurant had hurled a pan at him in fury. He had deflected the heavy object with his wrist and the watch had taken the brunt, but he had not had it repaired. It would remain as a reminder never to abuse staff; a reminder, too, of the boiling hatred underlings such as himself had felt for their oppressors. He never wanted any of his staff to feel that way about him.

And how did he want people to feel about him? One person, in particular?

He looked at his watch again. Where was she? He had

estimated she would arrive here around this time, but his calculations had all gone wrong. It was annoying; he was skilled at time estimates; his job and his dishes depended on split-second timing. But women, of course, were not soufflés or even stock reductions.

She was later than he expected and he couldn't hang around outside much longer. Scallops were on the lunchtime menu – magnificent ones with pearly flesh and brilliant corals – to be served chargrilled, meaning that only the sauce had been prepared in advance. Marco thought briefly about the scallops, how sweet they would taste, how much the customers would enjoy them, what a noble calling it was to work in a profession where one could give so much deep pleasure, so regularly, to so many people . . .

'An espresso, Chef?' Daria was at his elbow. Marco looked gloomily at her through the tangles of his hair. He felt guilty and rather silly. Here he was, poncing about outside, when they had full covers for lunchtime, both early and late sittings.

'*Grazie*, Daria, but I'm coming in now.'

Daria dimpled. Her almond-shaped brown eyes shone naughtily. 'Are you sure, Chef? Your friend is here.'

'What?' Marco gasped, his head and hair flying up. Excitedly he saw that Daria was right, there she was, finally, a small figure among all the other milling shoppers, tourists or mere loiterers, but a figure he had come to recognise in an instant.

'You might want to stay outside a little longer, possibly?' the waitress smiled. 'I can take care of the scallops,' she added.

She glided off, leaving Marco staring after her, confounded. How on earth did Daria *know*? He had said nothing about the girl to his staff. They must have watched him, have worked it out for themselves. Honestly, Marco thought, they were irrepressible. All happily ensconced in partnerships themselves, his staff were always trying to set him up with some woman or other.

It was annoying – well, no, actually, it wasn't, really. As, happily, he watched Darcy approach, Marco smiled. That his staff cared was wonderful. It showed concern for his happiness and wellbeing, which in itself showed he was achieving at least some of his goals as a restaurant owner. The only person he could imagine wanting to set any of his own former bosses up with was Cruella de Vil.

She hadn't meant to. But Darcy couldn't resist. She had set out for the run that morning determined to pass the restaurant by. But she had slowed down, almost immediately, when out of eyeshot of the villa, as if the Hero of Zero could somehow see her from inside the DVD.

The lovely countryside looked much better when you weren't belting through it at full tilt feeling that at any second your heart might give out. You had the chance to appreciate it. In the woodland outside the village, Darcy slowed down still further, admiring the sun-dappled shade on the stippled, slender trunks of the trees. The morning was hot and still, the air sharp with pine scent, the woods apparently empty. But appearances deceived, Darcy guessed. The air rang with competing birdsong – some of it surprisingly loud – and the earth was full of rattles, scuffles, shakes, snapping twigs. Small animals and birds were busy, although at what and where, could not be seen.

When she struggled up the hill into the village Marco was waiting for her, as he had said he would be, with a large piece of pale, crumbly cheese. 'It's made for us by one very small-scale producer in Italy. I'd like to know what you think of it.' He placed the plate before her with a flourish, and watched her expectantly.

The scent of the cheese, borne upwards by the fresh morning air, tugged at her nostrils and the words of absolute, categoric refusal died on Darcy's lips. It would, she sensed, be an insult to Marco. He might look chaotic, but he was a serious man with obvious passion for his craft. And with a certain *savoir-faire*; there was no denying that. And certainly a *savoir-manger*.

Before she could stop herself she had chiselled out a small lump from the cheese's golden crumbly side and put it in her mouth. The result was a terrific explosion of creamy, nutty saltiness that left her senses in freefall. She listened to Marco explain where it came from, by whom and how it was made and that one of the best ways of enjoying it was with a ripe sliced pear with some good olive oil drizzled over. She should try it; he would go and get it.

As he headed back into the restaurant she looked round happily at the pretty, pale-green tables with their creamy shades with, here and there, a few coffee drinkers under them. She felt warm and alive. That tight, scraping feeling of hunger had gone. It was like a car alarm that had shrieked for days being suddenly turned off.

Marco returned with a sky-blue plate on which a peeled, fresh, opalescent pear lay arranged in beautiful concentric circles, scattered with pepper and drizzled with golden oil. It seemed impossible he had done it in the time. Had he prepared it in advance, especially for her? Savouring the perfumed flavour of the fruit combined with the sharp cheese, she flicked a glance at Marco, who grinned, squinting in the bright morning sun that lit up the brown depths of his eyes. They were, she suddenly thought, rather beautiful.

'Good?' He cocked an eyebrow in her direction.

'Very good.'

'Oh, and try these olives, too.' He produced some, seemingly from nowhere.

'You're a magician,' she laughed delightedly.

He shook his head; that crazy hair, she thought with affection. 'Not me. Nature is the magician. Take these olives . . .' Off he goes again, she thought happily. Marco's generosity and high spirits were irresistible. He had a glow, a confidence, an energy that excited and touched her. He was a man on a mission; a chef on fire; he genuinely believed in the power of food to spread happiness. And who would want to prove him wrong? Who could?

'No, no, you can't just pick them from the branches and eat them.' Olives had, Marco explained now, to be pickled for weeks in brine. Her respect for the squat, gnarled olive trees she saw everywhere around with their drily rasping and subtly silver-green leaves had increased after Marco had told her they lived for hundreds of years. Some in Lebanon apparently went back almost to Biblical times. 'A beautiful olive, it looks like a simple thing, but it is a great luxury,' Marco said.

She smiled at him. 'You talk a lot about luxury. What's the greatest one of all?'

'Love. Of course.' He spoke lightly, pulled a face and shrugged as if it were a remark of absolutely no consequence. But Darcy felt hit between the eyes as if by lightning. She'd walked right into that one. Her heart bounced disconcertingly around inside her, crazed and jerky, like a pingpong ball.

'Love is the greatest luxury of all,' Marco added, more musingly now, his voice low and his eyes narrowed. She noticed his intense and faraway expression. Was he thinking about someone in particular? Who? she wondered, suddenly interested.

'Beauty and love, they are both very simple,' Marco expanded suddenly.

'Are they?' Neither seemed particularly so to her. Beauty – the Hollywood variety at least – could only be attained after starvation and painful marathons. And love? Christian hadn't been in touch, not even a text, for days.

'Very simple,' Marco asserted gently. He was careful to keep his gaze trained on the two old ladies talking animatedly in the middle of the square. If Darcy saw his expression now, she would guess.

A pair of small children suddenly wheeled off the main street and came clattering into the restaurant.

'Excuse me,' Marco said, smiling, to Darcy, 'I seem to have some customers.'

The small girl ran up to him. Marco found himself looking into a pair of grave blue eyes beneath a silver-fair fringe.

'Have you,' Hero asked him earnestly, 'got any spaghetti?'

Marco chuckled. 'Plenty,' he assured her, as Darcy, nearby, giggled.

Cosmo, catching up, folded his small white arms. 'Tinned spaghetti?' he pressed.

The gasp of horror from the coffee drinkers could, Darcy thought, be heard all round Rocolo.

By the time Orlando arrived, it was a *fait accompli*. Cosmo and Hero stood in the doorway of the restaurant, their faces split in huge beams. When they saw him, they ran towards him, waving little fists clutching tall, pale breadsticks.

The chef now emerged. Orlando regarded him cagily. He was so big and chaotic-looking; that wild dark hair and big sunken eyes gave him an air of drama and unpredictability. He stood before Orlando in his creased chef's whites, frowning in the bright sunshine, his stubbly chin bunched in disapproval.

And no wonder, Orlando had to accept. His mother and the Faughs had not exactly distinguished themselves the night they had all dined here; it seemed likely Marco would remember. Orlando clung to the possibility that, cowering at the back of the party, he might not have been noticed.

'These children are yours?' The chef seemed very agitated.

'No,' said Orlando, horrified. 'I'm looking after them . . . for now,' he added hurriedly.

'They asked me for tinned spaghetti,' Marco told him levelly.

'I'm so sorry,' Orlando exclaimed, imagining what an insult this must be in Italy. Probably the sort that lost you your kneecaps – at best – in some places. The chef seemed a reasonable kind of bloke but, all the same, the image of himself hanging, lifeless, in the shadowy underside of a bridge, now rose irrepressibly in Orlando's imagination.

The chef rolled his brown eyes hugely at Cosmo and Hero. 'You don't like real pasta, huh?'

Hero screwed her face up. 'No.'

Orlando blushed – for the children and himself. Clearly, the absent Totty didn't unduly exert herself when it came to feeding her charges. Finding the tin opener seemed about the extent of it.

'Woo woo!'

Cosmo, Orlando now saw, was busily lining up, one after the other, about ten chairs from all the surrounding tables and was sitting at the head of the line, revolving his arms at the sides.

'Choo choo!'

'Cosmo!' exclaimed Orlando. 'Sorry,' he added to Marco, plunging to restore the chairs to their rightful homes.

'Is all right. It's fine,' the chef reassured him. He strode over to the little boy, dropped to his muscular hunkers and tickled Cosmo under the chin. 'You like trains, huh?'

599

Cosmo nodded.

'Well, what you say I cook you train wheels pasta?'

'Train wheels?' Cosmo's blue eyes glowed.

'Come with me.' Marco crooked his finger.

Darcy, nibbling the last of the cheese, watched and felt rather choked. The big, awkward chef was so gentle with children. As was the blond boy, who seemed to handle the toddlers extremely well. He was, Darcy noticed – indeed, it was impossible not to notice – extraordinarily good looking. And yet she sensed, from the way his long green eyes shrank from contact, that this boy was extremely self-conscious; shy, even. He had a directionless air about him too; despite his looks a certain shrugging, rueful hopelessness seemed to cling to him. Darcy thought involuntarily of Emma; her description of her lost Orlando could almost fit this boy.

She was distracted in her musings by a small explosion from the restaurant. 'Train wheels, Orlando!' Cosmo yelped.

Orlando! Darcy stared, electrified, at the blond boy. Could it be? She reached for a napkin and dabbed her mouth as, hurriedly, she stood up. She needed to get back to Emma at once.

Cosmo rushed towards Orlando, unclenching his hand and spilling about fifteen small, round, spoked pieces of dry pasta out on to the small, square, sage-painted table.

Marco appeared from the doorway. '*Rotolline.* That's Italian for wheels. I keep this pasta in the restaurant for when families come. Children usually like my menu but sometimes we have –' he rolled his brown eyes hugely at Cosmo and Hero – 'Picky Eaters. Can you imagine that?'

Round-eyed, they shook their heads.

'But even picky eaters like train wheels with home-made tomato sauce,' Marco said indulgently.

'*I'd* like them!' Cosmo gasped.

But Hero shook her silver-fair head. Her pale brow was knotted and there was a steely glint in her narrowed blue eyes. 'Not me,' she insisted. 'I want *tinned* spaghetti.'

There was a silence. Orlando, Darcy saw, looked tense. She felt tense herself. Her eyes slid to Marco. How would the impassioned chef, the champion of all things authentically Italian, take this philistine attack, albeit from a child who looked some distance under five?

Marco's face, she saw, was expressionless. Then, as he continued to regard the indomitable, fair little figure, it became thoughtful. 'Maybe I can do something,' he said at last in a quiet voice. 'Maybe, at the back of a cupboard in my kitchen, I have a tin of spaghetti . . . *just maybe*,' he warned, raising a scarred finger as Hero began to exclaim and jump about in excitement.

The pretty dark-haired waitress who was clearing some nearby tables smiled at this, Darcy suddenly noticed. Personally, she felt admiration rather than amusement. Some chefs, she imagined, would have hit the roof at such a request. Harsh words, pans even, would have been hurled as culinary reputation and national identity was defended. It seemed so typical of Marco, the gentle giant, the most modest of men, to make such a concession to an ignorant child, ignoring the personal pain such a request must cause him, both as an Italian and as a chef.

She savoured the glow this reflection gave her for a second, then rose from the table. 'Marco. I've got to go.' There were other matters afoot than tinned pasta, after all. The excitement of being able to give Emma the good news about Orlando was enough to obliterate completely the thought of the painful run back to the villa. She moved off across the courtyard.

The chef, with the little blonde girl hard on his heels, paused on his tinned-spaghetti-hunting mission. He was smiling broadly now, which seemed to Darcy yet further proof of his humanity, his genius for his job. To be so consummate a host, so determined for those who came to his restaurant to enjoy themselves that he was prepared to go to almost any lengths – even these – to make them happy. That he could even tolerate tinned pasta on the premises was in itself extraordinary, she thought. No doubt he had been given it as a sample. Or, more likely, a joke.

'Come back tomorrow,' Marco called to Darcy. 'I'm expecting some truffles.'

'Truffles.' Now that was more like it. 'Not in a tin, I hope!' she called over her shoulder.

'Pah!' Grinning, he shook his shaggy head. 'How could you suggest such a thing?'

'I'll see you tomorrow.'

Darcy did not move homewards fast. It was obviously unwise on a full stomach. She floated, rather than walked down the steep hill. Rocolo had never seemed so beautiful, with its sunlit buildings all shades, from shortbread to peanut brittle, and its dark chocolate shadows. No wonder Marco was proud of it. He had said at one point that his family had lived here for hundreds of years. An old family from an old country. With serious roots here, deep in this hot and ancient earth. It must be a wonderful feeling.

Her mobile beeped. Another text? From Christian? She dragged it out of her shorts pocket, feeling the cheese she had just eaten rising up her throat in sick excitement.

'R U horny? Wish I cd be scrwng U now. Tmorrow night?'

Darcy raised her eyebrows. It wasn't exactly Romeo. But it had something of his sentiments regarding Juliet, as well as a certain visceral directness that gave her a charge. Why bother with anything more elaborate? What good had that ever done her in the past?

Her eyebrows lowered, her eyes narrowed knowingly and a warm, lazy smile released itself over her face. Besides, her interest in Christian wasn't in his abilities at literary composition anyway. It was much less complicated than that.

Darcy inhaled a deep, warm breath of air. She dawdled downwards over the cobbles, joyful and relieved. She had known he would be in touch. *Touch.* She swallowed, closing her eyes for a moment. His touch, how she longed for it.

You shouldn't, Ken knew, judge a book by its cover. Still, he found it hard to shake from his memory the sighting of the two men near the playground. He had had enough experience of undesirables to recognise them when he saw them and he felt increasingly strongly that the proximity of such people to small children was worrying. Drugs – albeit soft ones like cannabis – and kiddies were never a good combination.

Particularly if, as had seemed likely, the men were going to the playground to meet one of the nannies. And not just any of the nannies either, but the nasty blonde who was in charge of the two children who had made such a strong impression on Ken at the airport. Who were, in fact – and the boy especially – the entire reason he was here.

But what could he do about it, Ken asked himself. It was all very well having his suspicions, but he could hardly hang around the playground himself and order the men to stay away. Nor did there seem much point alerting the local police – wherever they were – as there was no evidence of any wrongdoing. But Ken's hunch that something was wrong continued to preoccupy him.

Eventually, in a flash of inspiration, he realised that the

answer lay in a combination of the balcony in his room, which overlooked the playground, and also in his own baggage. To be precise, in the black padded zip case under a heap of creased clothes in the corner of the room. This contained the Leica and long lenses he had hoped never again to use, but which, as they were actually around his neck when he made the spur-of-the-moment decision to fly to Italy, he had been unable to avoid bringing with him.

And thank God he had, Ken thought now. He could use them to survey the playground from his balcony. Because, while his roster of skills numbered neither cooking nor dancing nor playing the piano, nor even – he dolefully suspected – being a particularly nice or useful person, one thing Ken was supremely good at was watching – sometimes for hours or even days – other people's movements through the end of a long-lensed camera.

Surviving as a paparazzo had demanded that he was and while Ken, in turning his back on his former business, now regretted the years he had spent hiding in people's bushes or crouching down by their cars, he could now see a way to turn those questionable abilities to good use. Possibly even atone for the sins of the past.

Stealthily, swiftly, he set up his camera in the corner of the balcony where it would least likely be noticed by those from below. He pulled the rickety chair from the bedroom outside and positioned it behind the lens. He sat down, twisted the lens, and got the playground gate in focus. He was immediately filled with a sense of satisfaction. Whatever happened now, if those men turned up, if they met one of the nannies and nefarious business was afoot, he would capture it all on film.

Ken was, in accordance with general paparazzi law, expecting to have to wait some time before anything occurred. There was also the possibility that it never would; that the men he had seen had been a one-off. His instincts, however, which were rarely wrong, told him otherwise.

He armed himself with some bottles of ice-cold lager from one of the shops in the square, a salami sandwich the length and breadth of his forearm, settled down and prepared to wait.

Chapter 53

Mitch Masterson, in his LA office, was chewing anxiously on his third jelly doughnut of the morning. But the sweet, chewy pastry, while it plugged the ever-present hole in his stomach, could do nothing about the gap in his soul. That his spirits were lower than they had been when he was the least successful agent on the company's books seemed ironic as now, along with Greg Cucarachi, he was almost at the top of the pecking order with two of his actresses in the new Jack Saint movie.

As Mitch finished his doughnut he saw, out of the corner of his eye, Cucarachi trying the door of his office. He had started to close it; even contemplated locking it, to avoid the daily torture from his co-worker that he knew was coming now.

Greg rattled the door open with a flourish. 'Good morning, Mitchell!' he exclaimed. 'And how are you today on this bright and beautiful Hollywood morning?'

Actually, this bright and beautiful Hollywood sun, coming straight between the slats of the Venetian blinds, was at a height that caught Mitch right in the eyes. Being obliged, as he was, to duck to avoid it he knew made him look deferential.

To claw back some dignity, he pretended to be busy with a pile of papers on his desk, which was the usual slew of confused, tottering, about-to-slide heaps.

'I'm fine,' Mitch grunted, staring hard at what he hoped Greg would assume was some important missive and not just the menu from the newly opened macrobiotic café on the corner. The bill of fare – mung beans, what the hell were they? – made Mitch feel worse.

'Hey! Fantastic!' Greg trilled. 'I take it then that Darcy's lost it . . . the weight, ha ha. Not the part.'

Mitch eyed his fellow agent with loathing, feeling stress-related perspiration break out on his brow. He did not know the answer to this question; had hoped to find it out first thing, but when he had called the villa Belle's nanny had told him Darcy was out for a run. Which had to be good news; you could hardly run and put weight on, could you?

'Belle learnt her lines yet?' Cucarachi added, his head on one side in mock-concern. 'I do hope so. I hear Jack's getting pretty pissed at her. Some of the cast are asking whether she can actually read . . .'

'She can read all right,' Mitch snapped. No one who had seen Belle grab her contract and devour it with her eyes could doubt that. That she hadn't shown the same alacrity in learning her part for the film was, Mitch knew from Saint's frequent irate phone calls, becoming almost as much of an on-set issue as Belle's unpunctuality. 'Gonna have to start looking for someone else if she doesn't shape up,' had been the last, and most terrifying, threat.

He rummaged in his mind for some well-turned, stinging phrase that would send his hated colleague away with a flea in his ear, but as usual he rummaged in vain. One of the things he most hated about Greg, Mitch thought now, was the way, with his lean, marathon-fit body, he always seemed like some skinny, swift-moving attack dog, and Mitch himself, sweaty in his crumpled suit and creased shirt, a great, lumbering, slow-of-wit, heavily bespectacled bear.

'Arlington Shorthouse isn't very happy,' Greg added gleefully, landing a fearsome bite just where it hurt most.

'Yeah.' Mitch had had Arlington on to him all the previous afternoon. It had not been a pleasant conversation and, together with those from Jack Saint, had made Mitch almost long for the days when the only phone calls he received were from producers' assistants on obscure Latino soap operas. 'You know,' Mitch said now, as inspiration struck him, 'I'm kinda wondering if Belle's, um, issues haven't got something to do with your client Christian Harlow. Whether the influence he's exerting on my client Belle Murphy is, shall we say –' Mitch put his head mock-questioningly on one side and drummed his fat fingers lightly on his desk – 'entirely a good one.'

Ha! Take that, Cucarachi.

Greg, however, was ready. 'Interesting,' he mused, stroking his long nose. 'An interesting thought.' He looked up and smiled. 'Perhaps you'd prefer it if my client Christian Harlow – who, incidentally, knows all his lines backwards – transferred his interest back to your client Darcy Prince?'

A pang of murderous fury went through Mitch. The bastard. The horror of Christian Harlow and Belle Murphy being back together again had had a silver lining only in the fact that Darcy was now free of that slimy actor creep. That she'd seen sense at last. Mitch had, however, soon worked out that the only person unaware she was free of him was Darcy herself. The fact she'd find out as soon as she got on set was yet another sword of whoever-the-hell-that-Greek-guy-was hanging over Mitch's desk at the moment.

'Catch you later!' Greg sang, swinging Mitch's door shut with a bang that made the walls rattle.

'I mean, Jack's, like, just so unreasonable,' Belle stormed as they climbed into the Ferrari at Christian's villa. 'He's bullying me,' she pouted, settling herself and the dog in the passenger seat. 'You know something?' Her voice had climbed several decibels. 'I should sue him. Yeah. For deliberate cruelty. Misanthropy – that's hatred of women, isn't it?'

'I wouldn't know,' Christian said wearily, fumbling for the ignition. But while he did not know the word Belle was searching for, he knew the sentiment behind it. Getting back with this particular woman had been one big mistake.

Jesus, had he got it wrong. He'd jumped back into bed with Belle, believing her star to be once more on the rise. Only to find her addled by self-importance and, Christian suspected, whatever drink she could get hold of. He felt he almost preferred her on the skids; she'd been clinging, sure, but at least she hadn't imagined she was Nicole Kidman, Cate Blanchett and Elizabeth Taylor all rolled into one.

'Penelope Cruz . . .' Belle would say airily.

'Yes?' Christian was all ears. Belle was, after all, a veteran compared to him; in her *Marie* days she had met almost everyone. He anticipated a juicy titbit, perhaps one he could use to his own advantage. Diarists on the Hollywood gossip columns were always willing to run positive stories about you in exchange for a spicy anecdote about a major star.

'. . . is sooooo jealous of my tiny waist.'

'Oh.'

'Let me tell you something about Kate Winslet.'

'Yes?'

'She's always been crazy about my hair.'

'Oh.'

'People think that Tom Cruise is strange . . .'

This really did sound promising. 'Yes?'

'. . . But he's actually a really lovely, caring guy,' Belle had sighed. 'He and Katie are the most down-to-earth celebrities I've ever met.'

Which was more than one could say of Belle, Christian fumed to himself. She'd also lost more weight since last time he'd screwed her; doing it now was like slamming yourself against a ladder. The fact she couldn't be bothered to learn her lines was the most dangerous aspect, however; the entire set knew she and he were together and Christian found himself obliged to mount a charm offensive of spectacular proportions on the director to avoid becoming tarred with the same brush.

He'd even bought Saint a present the other day; one of those little red Vespa scooters. There'd been a discussion about Italian scooters during a break in filming; Saint had described them as design classics. Christian, whose idea of a design classic was a yacht with two helicopters and a submarine, and felt scooters were for losers, none the less wasted no time moving heaven and earth to get one for Saint – or obliging his agent, from the distance of America, to move heaven and earth to save him the trouble.

Belle lifted her huge, black sunglasses to turn a pair of artificially green eyes on him. There was nothing counterfeit about the anger in them, however. 'Thanks for your support,' she blazed. 'That bastard's making my life a misery. He's victimising me. He hates women.'

'No he doesn't,' Christian snapped. 'He just doesn't like people who turn up six hours late on set without knowing their part. It costs money, that sort of thing. The schedule's pretty tight.'

Belle's clinging top was even tighter than usual. The swirling pattern made her breasts look bigger than ever. Whereas her shorts were so tiny they looked like denim panties. Had he known what an imagination was, Christian might well have reflected that Belle left little to it.

A vision of Darcy in her floaty yellow dress swam before him. He'd texted her before they left and now felt a warm rush of anticipation in his groin. From her reply she was more than on for it. And screwing Darcy was much more fun than Belle. Less painful, in every sense.

It might be a little complicated, but Belle probably wouldn't be around much longer. He'd heard Saint was calling agents left, right and centre to get a replacement for her, although he still seemed to be holding out hope that Darcy would return to the set. 'A rare talent,' was how he had described her, in Christian's hearing. He'd felt a little sick at that. Darcy had been the better horse to back, all along,

Whereas Belle was a sinking ship; or as sinking as a ship could be with assets as inflated as hers. Maybe he'd dump her after this lunch.

Slamming the pedal as far to the metal as he could manage meant thrilling speed, certainly, but also the fact that Belle's hideous dog had to crouch out of sight inside her handbag in order to avoid being blown right out of the car. The noise of the screaming wind also meant that Belle's constant, infuriating whine, as she kept up her litany of complaint, could not be heard.

He started the Ferrari with a roar that, as had been intended, sent Sugar diving for the depths of Belle's handbag.

'Shit!' she exclaimed, peering in after him.

'He's died?' Christian asked hopefully.

'No. He's shat all over the script.'

*

It was twelve o'clock now; the sun was high and hot in the sky. The shouts of the children in the playground were borne upwards to Ken on the lunch-scented breeze. It was very warm on the balcony; he had followed the shadow round, lugging his chairs and camera to the shade, but now it threatened to disappear altogether. Neither Totty nor the suspicious men had yet materialised, and if they didn't soon Ken knew he faced the prospect of having to await them under the full heat of the blazing sun.

He was beginning to lose heart. Perhaps they were all having lunch. Perhaps he ought to follow their example and have some too.

Ken stood up and stretched. And, as soon as he took his eye from the camera, he saw Totty. She was rounding the corner from the church end of the square.

Her long hair swung and her long brown legs undulated as she walked. She was, Ken saw with distaste, wearing a staggeringly short skirt, which exposed a gap between her thighs large enough to drive a bus through. Was it, he wondered, suitable wear for looking after children? No, it was not, he thought. Come to that, though, where were the children?

Totty's mouth was screwed up and her face preoccupied under her customary huge sunglasses. She seemed to be in a rush. Ken drew a swift breath in and sat hurriedly back down again at his chair, knocking the carefully set-up camera as he did so. His hands shook as he fumbled to refocus the lens.

Totty slowed down as she approached the entrance to the playground. Ken watched her pass it, and walk down the encircling pathway directly below his balcony. Apprehension began to clutch him – was she headed somewhere else altogether? – and then relaxed its grip as she stopped just beneath where he sat.

Right next to where she had paused was a bench, half-hidden from the pathway by bushes. As Ken followed her movements down his lens, Totty, after looking about her for a few seconds, slipped behind the bushes and sat down in the concealed area behind. She took out her mobile and began to talk agitatedly into it. Ken strained his ears but, for all she was directly underneath him and the air was still, it was impossible to make out what she was saying.

Almost immediately, the two men he had seen before appeared. They walked with heads bent and hands shoved into their pockets; quickly, purposefully. And looking, Ken thought, lining up the first shot, if anything, more undesirable than before; loping along in battered jeans, tanned in a dry, dirty sort of way, their features mostly hidden in the shadows under their baseball caps. One held a mobile in a scarred and tattooed hand. Ken guessed he was talking to Totty.

Taking shot after shot, he now watched, excitement and amazement bunching in his throat as the two men slid behind the bushes where Totty waited.

The encounter was businesslike. Little seemed to be said. Action was all: quick as a flash dirty hands went into grubby pockets; a slew of small white plastic bags containing white powder suddenly appeared on the bench beside the nanny. Ken zoomed in and fired again and again, his brow dark and furrowed with disgust. Cocaine. Even worse than he thought. And she a nanny. In charge of children! Unbloodybelievable.

He kept the lens unwaveringly on her. Snap! Snap! Totty, taking the packets. Snap! Snap! Totty, slipping them into her handbag. Snap! Snap! Totty, getting out a crocodile-skin wallet, opening it, handing over a wad of notes. Snap! Snap! The two men, taking them. Snap! Snap! The two men, getting up and leaving, loping away as swiftly as they had come, down the shadowy pathway until they turned the corner into the sunlit square.

Carefully, Ken detached his face from the camera. He had pressed his eye and forehead to it so hard in excitement that it was now almost stuck. He rubbed his sweating forehead and blinked, feeling rather drained with the drama of it all. Still, he'd got them now.

Glancing below, he saw that Totty had not yet moved. He guessed immediately that she was waiting. There was another act of this unsavoury drama to come. Someone else was expected. And, to judge by the shadowy, furtive location in which she remained, they were coming for what she had in her bag. Why else stay there, behind the bushes, out of the sunlight? She had her mobile out again, Ken saw; reporting that the coast was clear? That the goods were here?

He put his eye to his camera again. It could be quick; he had to be ready. Ken recognised, but could not at first place the two young men with big hair and teeth who now hurried up the path by the playground. He got them in focus, fired away, his mental Rolodex spinning all the while. He'd seen them recently . . .

Oh, yes! He'd got it now. The restaurant. They'd been part of a group, with that good-looking boy. And, more to the point, with a certain big, booming, colourful, well-known and, Ken had always felt, particularly unpleasant Member of Parliament. Striding up the path now, looking inordinately pleased with themselves with their striped shirts, pressed jeans and snaffled loafers, were the sons of Hugh Faugh.

As the boys slipped behind the bushes, Ken's camera whirred away. Snap! Snap!

Kissing Totty on both cheeks as if they were meeting at a drinks party. Snap! Snap! One of them reaching into his pocket and producing an oddly feminine pink wallet that looked as if it might belong to their mother. Snap! Snap! Drawing out a handful of notes and being given a handful of plastic packets in return. Snap! Snap! Totty laughing. Snap! The boys laughing. Snap! Snap! The three of them getting up and leaving together, arm in arm. This was, Ken realised, his insides tight with excitement, shaping up to be quite a story.

Chapter 54

With a boom like thunder, the red Ferrari roared into the Rocolo car park. Christian scanned wildly about him for a parking space, threw the car into one and wrenched up the handbrake.

Belle's annoyance about Saint had, somewhere along the way, metamorphosed into raging lust. She had kept reaching over and stroking his penis as he drove, and with such a practised hand that, despite himself, he had found himself stiffening.

Christian looked up. Was the tree hanging over the space enough to hide them? It was lunchtime and the car park was sizzling in the heat, empty of people. He could probably get away with a quick one; it would be the last one, after all. She was clawing at his fly zip now. Grunting, Christian unbuckled his belt.

Full of excitement at having spotted the lost Orlando, Darcy pelted down the cobbled hill out of Rocolo. Slowing down to avoid some people crossing the bridge over the stream, she flicked a glance into the car park and saw the red Ferrari under the tree.

A great surge of excitement possessed her. Christian! Had to be. She even thought she recognised the registration. Skipping between the shining bonnets of the red-hot parked cars, Darcy dashed across.

As she approached, she recognised the dark, oily quiff of Christian's head, his tanned and handsome brow; facing downwards, bobbing up and down. She could hear a grunt. Were there problems with the car? Was he fixing something?

'Christian!'

The word hung in the air, in the bright, hot sunshine. Darcy could now see that he was indeed fixing something. He was fixing a woman, who lay beneath him, moaning in ecstasy. Christian, a climactic cry breaking from his own throat, looked up and met Darcy's horrified eyes.

For a second, she was stunned. Then her eyes rolled from his face to the woman writhing below him; her breasts jutting upwards, her bare thighs wound round his muscular buttocks like the tentacles of a tanned octopus, snakes of platinum hair shaking across the car seat like Medusa's own.

Belle! It was Belle!

'Darcy!' Belle's tousled blonde head now emerged. 'Fancy running into you! It seems like ages!' She flashed a brilliant smile through extravagantly smeared lipstick. 'Hope you don't mind me saying, sweetie. But I'm not sure it's working.'

The woolly feeling was still enveloping Darcy. She moved her tongue, but it felt as dry and heavy as a block of wood. Her eyes rolled over Christian, who seemed similarly lost for words, stuttering in his sunglasses above his lipstick-smeared torso.

'Of course,' Belle added smugly, 'some people just have to face the fact that exercise doesn't work for them. I'm so lucky, of course, not having to do anything to keep my shape. But – and I'm saying this as a friend,' she added, batting her somewhat bent eyelashes – 'I gotta say, Darcy, that you've actually gotten *bigger* since you started running.'

Christian, meanwhile, was following his instincts. Self-preservation, which dictated his every move, was dictating now that he started the engine and got the hell out. There was nothing to be gained from hanging around and trying to explain himself to both of the women at the same time. Even if he could have done.

'Hey, c'mon,' Belle was calling to Darcy. 'Don't get mad. You win some, you lose some. Although, to be honest, sweetie, you haven't lost any.'

Christian screeched the car into reverse and roared around the car park to the exit, heedless of anything or anyone that might have been in his way. Belle's hair streamed out like a white flag. 'But don't take it personally,' she was shouting. 'It's not you, it's your metabolism.'

As the cloud of blue smoke from the Ferrari's exhaust enveloped her, Darcy felt light-headed and nauseous. There was a buzzing sensation around the edge of her vision. The trees looked blurred; the shining vehicles in the car park wobbled violently. She took a step back and stumbled. Oh God, Darcy thought, I'm going to faint.

Christian roared off down the road. Belle's shrieks in his ear and the scream of the wind merged into one. She was clutching at her clothes and her hair whipped around her face like a lash.

Rounding a bend, Christian saw too late the scooter coming towards him. He slammed on the brake, clung to the steering wheel, battling for control as the heavy, blood-red car screamed, skidded and convulsed into a great sliding side arc, which crashed violently into the verge, taking the scooter and its rider with it.

*

A couple were walking up through Rocolo village. The man was tall, thin and pale, with sparse sandy hair and wonky glasses that slipped down his nose no matter how often he pushed them up. He looked worried and cross, and was striding some distance ahead of the woman, a trim blonde in a red flowered dress and with red-rimmed blue eyes.

Vanessa had cried all the way from the airport. She had never thought it was possible for James to be so angry. He had been stonily furious throughout the flight, but it was only when they were alone in the hire car that he had really let rip. 'You let the children go by themselves to Italy? I just can't believe it.' His knuckles, clenching the steering wheel in fury, were bone-white. His neck was thrust forward and his eyes strained through the windscreen.

'They're not on their own. They're with Totty,' Vanessa bleated, for what seemed the hundredth time.

'Totty!' James snorted, with a depth of loathing Vanessa had never heard before. 'Totty! You know, I never liked her. Never trusted her. But you let her take the children. The most precious things we have. And now we can't get hold of her, we don't know what's going on . . .' His voice rose to a desperate wail, a cry of fearful misery that Vanessa found more terrifying than his anger. 'What possessed you?' he hurled at her, his usually mild blue eyes now turned to balls of aquamarine fire as he glared through his spectacles.

'I've told you,' Vanessa wailed, her fingers on her lap tearing at each other in terror. 'It was a last-minute work thing. A feature I couldn't turn down . . .'

'You mean a free couple of days at a luxury spa run by some duchess,' James screamed. 'You've lost our children – all for the sake of a free backrub and a complimentary pedicure and tea with some fucking aristo.'

'I thought it would be OK,' Vanessa wept, trying weakly to defend herself even though she felt like a mouse in the claws of a huge and pitiless eagle. 'I thought Hengist's parents were there, in their villa, to keep an eye on things. I didn't realise it would only be Hengist's nanny. I thought Lord and Lady Westonbirt were there.'

'Lord and Lady Westonbirt,' James spat. And he really did spit, Vanessa noticed miserably. The windscreen in front of him was quite bobbly with spittle. 'That's you all over,' he snarled, hurling the blue fireballs at her again. 'You'll believe anything, accept anything, give anyone anything, even our children, if you think they're upmarket. And now you've ruined both our lives with your fucking pointless, ridiculous, contemptible snobbery.'

'Don't!' cried Vanessa. As the car hurtled along she stared at the blurred verges, pressing away the realisation that any of this was really happening. That she had called Totty several times now and there was no reply. That the children had been in Italy for several days without her and she had no idea where they were. That she was the worst mother who had ever lived, the worst wife, the worst person.

Chapter 55

Emma was sitting at the table on the terrace lost in gloomy contemplation. As she had sat since Darcy had left for her run. The especially sunny morning seemed to place her future, or lack of one, in particularly stark relief. Her job, her love life. Briefly, each had shone like a diamond. Now there was nothing to see at all.

She gazed without enthusiasm at the polished-crystal surface of the swimming pool, barely touched by a ripple of breeze. The sunloungers were, as usual, all arranged perfectly by Mara; the sunshades up, the cushions attached. The house beyond spread serene and golden in the sunlight. It was, of course, all beautiful.

But Darcy was right. It was dull. It was dull because she was dull herself; hopeless, weighed down by a sense of failure and the unfairness of life.

Nor did there seem any end to the dullness, until the filming ended, and who knew what would happen then? Emma guessed that Belle would return to America, and she and Morning would be obliged to go too, to start a new life in a strange land among strange people. Very strange people, if Belle was anything to go by.

'Why you sit here sulking?' Mara demanded.

Emma started in surprise. She had not heard the housekeeper come out on to the terrace. Morning, playing with some pasta shapes on a blanket at her feet, looked up and smiled at Mara. She bent and tickled him under the chin. '*Bello bambino!*' she grunted indulgently.

The indulgence had faded from her eye by the time she straightened up to look at Emma. 'Pretty girl like you,' Mara chided. 'You waste your time just sitting here. You should go out. You meet nice man that way.'

After the disappointments of the last few days, this was more than Emma could bear. She looked hotly at the housekeeper. 'I don't want to meet a nice man.' The only nice man she wanted to meet had a tendency to melt away whenever she saw him.

Mara shrugged. 'So something has happened with your boy, huh? So what?' She raised her hands. 'Plenty more fish in the sea. You go out. It will do you good.'

Hero nudged Orlando again. Realising she wanted his chocolate-sprinkled cappuccino foam, he obediently began to dispense spoonfuls with his huge brown hands.

Hero and Cosmo had eaten their lunch now – in two seconds flat – it had seemed. His own planned beer and panini had transmogrified into a bowl of the most delicious minestrone he had ever eaten, with a glass of light red wine. He had been reluctant to order this at first; wine, in his mind, being strongly associated with the horrible Hugh Faugh. But Marco had insisted and the combination was, Orlando had had to admit, perfect.

The benefits of the lunch had gone beyond mere flavour, it seemed to him. Perhaps, he thought ruefully, a bowlful of minestrone before each exam might have considerably improved his A level results. Certainly, it had affected his brain for the better.

The evidence of this was that Orlando had had a good idea. A feasible way forward had finally suggested itself with regard to the children. He was still certain that Totty could not be far away, but in her continued absence the most obvious thing to do was return to the playground. If Totty was not there, surely one of the other so-called nannies would know where the children were staying. And if that route failed, then the police were the obvious next stage.

The bus came and Emma got on. Looking out of the window at the passing sunny countryside, cuddling the baby, she felt her drooping spirits rally and her thoughts drift towards the other subject that currently preoccupied her. The idea of her own nursery, as suggested by Darcy, had now taken firm hold. Of course, for the moment at least, with the stain on her reputation, it was impossible. But hopefully, in the future, it might happen. Hopefully, too, Darcy's offer of backing the project would still hold good then. Emma sensed it would. Darcy was not the type to make promises and not keep them.

In anticipation of this, of her dream one day becoming reality, Emma had started to compile a notebook of ideas. She had filled it with astonishing speed. The first, much underlined, being 'Pay People Properly'. So few nurseries did, risking high staff turnover and ignoring the fact that well-paid, well-treated staff would be loyal.

The actual premises Emma now had planned in her head in almost every detail. They were not lavish or luxurious, but comfortable and purpose-built. Large rooms, high ceilings, a homely feel. It would have a large garden and big, safe playing area, colourful and inviting. It would have its own kitchen, where fresh food could be prepared daily for the children. Using a lot of olive oil, as Darcy had suggested.

It would be somewhere in London, Emma had decided. There would be competition there, obviously, but also the best potential for expansion and growth. She knew, though, in her heart of hearts, this was not the only reason. Buried along with the hope that one day she would be proved innocent was the equally fervent – if admittedly almost equally far-fetched – hope that she would see Hero and Cosmo again. And maybe, somehow, Orlando, whose city it was as well.

Marco looked lovingly at the chicken stock reduction boiling away in the pan. It was almost ready now, mere minutes from reaching its perfect state of being a shallow pool of unctuous, gloopy, dark, silky flavour, almost like chocolate sauce but with a taste at the opposite end of the spectrum: savoury, deep, intense, essential. And then, what would he do with it. What wouldn't he? He could transform sauces, add depth to stews. The possibilities were endless. He sighed with joy.

Yes, just a minute or so more now. Some chefs, he knew, would have taken the stock off at this point, but he liked to take it to the brink, to risk it, to literally play with fire, reach the moment when the reduction nearly burnt, then just scooped it off in time, caramelly, thick, rich and brown.

She had had strands that colour in her hair, Marco thought rapturously, matching the brown in the pan to Darcy's remembered hair. The Italian sun must have lightened it.

He thought about the truffles he had promised her, for when she came next.

Truffles!

His heart soared at the thought of them. Was there anything like them in the world? A miracle from underground, with a voluptuous smell that rose through the nostrils to suffuse the entire body, warming the veins, priming the brain, swelling the heart with joyful thoughts. Marco began happily to contemplate truffle recipes. Generosity was the main thing; as with all luxuries, one could not be mean. He liked to give his customers a great pile of truffle on top of the egg, the pasta, the risotto or whatever other mild base had been chosen so as not to interrupt the flavour of the main event.

Truffles. He felt his mouth watering. Exciting, mysterious, expensive, pungent, powerfully earth scented; vital, sweaty and redolent of sex.

From this Marco found his thoughts leaping naturally to Darcy. He could hardly wait to introduce her to real Italian truffles. He could see her face as she tasted them, her eyes closing, her mouth falling open.

He felt his heart rate increase. He began to breathe deeply. Steam was almost coming out of his nostrils; smoke, even. But no, not out of his nostrils. The brown and billowing acrid clouds were coming from somewhere below him, in the pan.

Damn. He had burnt the reduction.

Emma struggled up the steep, cobbled incline to the village, Morning weighing heavily on her neck and shoulders, taking care to keep as close as possible to the wall and the cool shadow it cast. How Darcy managed to get up here every day was incredible.

There, ahead of her, was the restaurant, with its pretty cream shades shining in the sun over its pretty green tables. When she got that far up, she'd treat herself to a cappuccino.

It was the children who saw her first. 'Emma!'

Emma blinked. She knew those voices. She heard them every day, in her heart. She peered into the dazzlingly sunny courtyard.

The boy in his navy shorts and striped T-shirt, his blond fringe shimmering in the sun, scampered excitedly towards her. His sister, an eager, pale little face under a mop of white hair, scampered after him. Her spoon, so recently an essential accomplice in the all-important matter of eating Orlando's coffee foam, clattered, unwanted, to the cobbles.

'Hero?' Emma whispered. 'Cosmo . . . *Oof!*' The child had cannoned into her and thrown his arms tightly round her knees.

She placed a trembling hand on the familiar, small sandy head, her throat filling. As the dear, sunken, anxious blue eyes turned up to hers, she felt her own eyes suddenly liquid, hot and pricking. Through her blurry vision, she now saw someone tall come towards her. He shook his hair, awkwardly; an unmistakable gesture.

'Emma!' There was a strange sensation in Orlando's feet. A warm feeling spread within him until it glowed in his throat and in his stomach at the same time. He felt light and wobbly, as if he could sing, dance or even fly.

'Orlando?' A flock of butterflies so big that they could actually have been seagulls swerved through her stomach.

'You be Thomas, I'll be Percy and that bench is the station,' Orlando instructed. 'And Emma's the Fat Controller.'

She dragged her eyes from Orlando at that. 'Cheeky!' Emma exclaimed.

'Choo choo!' Cosmo steamed up. 'You're blocking the line,' he said sternly to Orlando.

'You never told me you were going to let her take them,' James growled, as he and Vanessa struggled up the cobbled hill into the village.

There were tears on his cheeks, she saw. Her heart twisted and tore within her. 'The last thing you told me was that you and Totty were going together. And then I come back from this trip, ring you on your mobile from the airport to find you're still in London and they're . . . they're . . . God knows where,' he added, his voice a broken whisper.

'I couldn't get hold of you,' she said weakly, more as a statement of fact than any attempt to defend herself. That was obviously impossible. 'The spa thing came up suddenly. And like I said, I thought it would be all right.'

'You knew I was going to the Congo,' James stormed, his voice rising so that passers-by stared at him in surprise. 'You knew the FO was sending me out there. All the more reason for you to take full responsibility for once, I'd have thought. But oh no. *Oh no.*'

There was such contempt, such hatred in his voice that Vanessa was frightened beyond what she had imagined possible. This was not James. This was not her mild, hardworking husband. Not the man she had routinely put down, overruled, shouted at, bullied. This was a father who had returned from a work trip to find his wife had sent their children away with someone he neither trusted nor liked. And who Vanessa, were she able to admit it to herself, increasingly neither trusted nor liked either. There had been many incidents with Totty – small, but significant. The way she never made the children wash their hands before and after meals. The way she frequently put them to bed without bathing them or insisting they cleaned their teeth. The way in which, at every opportunity, she parked them in front of the television; Hero with a dummy in her mouth. A dummy!

Vanessa reserved particular unease for the memory, which she tried hard to suppress, of the way Totty had gone upstairs at the children's party into Emma's room, then come straight back down with the dramatic news that there was something up there she must see. Vanessa could see herself now, leaping upstairs, seeing the handbag with the tiny, incriminating piece of folded white paper in, calling Emma up, sacking her on the spot . . .

Oh God. She had asked no questions at the time. Getting rid of Emma was all she had wanted. She had never admitted the true circumstances to James about her conversation in the kitchen with Totty and had vigorously beaten off all his suggestions that it could not possibly be true about Emma. Of course it was true. It had to be, because if it wasn't, then where had that wrap of cocaine come from? How had Totty, in the less than five minutes she was up there, known where to look for it?

As the ascent tugged painfully on her calf muscles and the sun beat mercilessly down, Vanessa went hot and cold, yet again, as she thought of the clues she had not so much missed as wilfully ignored.

It seemed incredible now that she had been willing to overlook all of this on the grounds that Totty's father was a member of the aristocracy. Oh God, what a fool she had been. Please, God, forgive her, let the children be all right. Please let them be *here*.

Vanessa felt a huge, desperate sob tear her chest. Her life was over. Her children were gone and her husband hated her.

She watched him striding contemptuously ahead, almost shoving people out of his way. James, gentle James, who had never shoved anyone in his life. His thought, she knew, their only hope, was to get as fast as possible to the police station, which was apparently in the square at the top. This village was the last place she had had live contact with the children. They hadn't sounded very happy. 'When are you coming, Mummy?' Cosmo had whispered, as if someone was listening to him.

James's back blurred as the tears rose. But she could still see how it radiated loathing. Loathing of her. And he had loved her so much. Devotedly and absolutely, Vanessa knew, stung by the additional knowledge that she had never really appreciated it. Had not only taken it utterly for granted but had occasionally affected to doubt it, as when she had toyed with the idea his interest in Emma went beyond the strictly professional.

As if! James's interest in Emma, Vanessa now knew – had always known, in fact – was gratitude for the effort and enthusiasm she brought to the job of looking after their children. Their children! The children he obviously adored but whom she had never really allowed him to spend any time with, so desperate was she to force him, against his will, up the greasy Foreign Office pole. And yet, even despite all this, James had never wanted another woman. He had adored her. And she had treated him like a dog.

He was a gentleman to the backbone. He had borne her tempers, her spite, her unfairness without complaint. He had never judged her, try as he might sometimes to discourage her.

Vanessa had never known pain in her heart like this. Guilt, regret, self-loathing were infinitely more agonising than anything physical she had ever suffered; the births of the children included. The children! As she crossed the bridge, the formerly proud Vanessa, broken and pathetic, all her former fire gone, contemplated throwing herself over it. Had the water below been anything more than a tricklesome stream, she would have.

If only she had listened to James about Emma. If only, Vanessa thought in silent anguish as they walked up into the village their children were last known to have been in, she had never let Emma go.

*

'Emma! Emma! Where have you been?' Hero and Cosmo were chanting as they choo-chooed round the tables.

'We've missed you.'

'We've had no one to play trains with. No one to play Snakes and Ladders with . . .'

She glanced at the children and back at Orlando, puzzled, delighted, her eyes framing the question.

'I found them in the square,' he explained. 'No one was with them.'

'No one . . . ?' Emma gasped, in such horror that Morning let out a cry of dismay. 'They had no nanny?'

'Well, there is a nanny, but—'

'We've had no one to play Uno with,' Hero was complaining. 'Totty doesn't know how to play Uno.'

'Totty?' Emma was gripped immediately by a terrible force. '*Totty?*'

It was, Emma thought afterwards, as if merely speaking the name had summoned an evil spirit. At that very moment, Totty rounded the corner and stormed through the restaurant, blonde hair streaming in her wake, legs flashing vengefully in a tiny miniskirt, scrappy breasts heaving behind a barely-there black top.

Orlando stared at the long-legged blonde. He didn't recognise her, but he knew the people with her horribly well. Swaggering between the tables, laughing hysterically, came two stunningly unattractive youths in jeans and loafers with big bouncy hair and enormous teeth. Orlando now remembered where he had heard the name Totty before.

Totty, it seemed, was in nowhere near as good a mood as her companions. She ripped off her sunglasses to reveal eyes flashing in fury. 'What are you two doing here?' she roared at the children. They backed away, frightened.

Orlando felt sick. He had absolutely no idea what to do. His instinct was to fell Totty to the ground, but obviously that was out of the question, especially with the children present. He realised miserably that his extensive and expensive education may have included balloon debates and school parliaments, but it had conclusively failed to teach him how to handle an occasion of this nature.

Emma's, however, had been more successful in this respect. 'Don't speak to the children like that!' she growled, controlling with only the greatest of difficulties the urge to clamp her hands round Totty's long, brown neck and squeeze hard. She struggled to comprehend the unbelievable yet apparent fact that Totty Ponsonby-Pratt had succeeded her as Cosmo and Hero's nanny. What had possessed Vanessa? And James, who had always seemed so kind and sensible . . .

Totty looked at Emma. There was, Emma felt, something of the hypnotising snake in the eviscerating stare. She watched Totty's face twist with contemptuous recognition. 'Just fuck off, OK?' she snarled. 'This is my job now. Not yours.'

'Not any more, damn you,' shouted the shaking voice of James as he hurtled through the tables, a shattered, weeping Vanessa stumbling behind him.

'News picturedesk, please, darlin',' said Ken. 'Tell 'em it's Ken from Mega.'

'OK,' came the disembodied, nasal tones of the receptionist.

There was a scrape and a scramble at the other end as the call was put through.

'Yeah?'

Ken recognised the graceless voice of the news picture editor. Dick 'Dastardly' Richardson was a self-important individual he had never much liked. 'Wotcha doin' comin' through to me, mate?' Dastardly demanded, irritated. 'It's Features you want, innit?'

'Not this time,' said Ken lightly, flicking through the images at the back of his digital camera. 'These pictures are news.'

'Well, wotcha got then,' Dastardly sneered. 'Jemima Khan in a new bikini, is it?'

'Nothin' as good as that, mate,' Ken said shortly. Then, remembering Dastardly didn't do irony, he snapped into action. 'Look, I'm not wasting my time with you, mate. D'you want to see these pictures or don't you?'

Chapter 56

Her face was so beautiful; the long sweep of lashes like the hairs on *oursins*, the tiny ears that actually really were shell-like, reminding him of the tiny, tasty clams he liked to use for *vongole*, the ones the French called *palourdes*. But this was no time to stand staring at her. She had fainted. She needed help.

'Fast work, Chef!' grinned Nino, the commis chef and the latest, youngest recruit, his naughty dark eyes full of laughter as Marco entered with Darcy in his arms. Rodolfo had brought her up from the car park. Marco's heart had leapt immediately into his mouth, but was assured by Rodolfo, whose mother was a nurse, that Darcy had only fainted in the intense midday heat.

'Mad dogs and Englishmen,' Rodolfo had remarked as he handed her over, shaking his head. 'But she'll be OK with a rest and some water.'

Darcy gazed, dazedly, at the face of the man in white. She felt herself being moved from one pair of strong arms to another.

'Put your arms round my neck,' Marco instructed.

In actual fact she was so light he could have carried her however her limbs were arranged. But he had no intention of missing the opportunity of making her embrace him. As, dutifully, she now draped her long white arms where he requested, he felt, not the triumph he had expected, but something rather more tender. She was so beautiful, so light, so pale, so helpless, like a child.

He walked through the restaurant, ignoring the winking brigade of chefs. He was in fact barely aware of them, or of the excitement outside in the restaurant courtyard, where something between a fight and a reunion seemed to be taking place. For him, as he took her upstairs, the only thing that mattered was the beautiful burden he held.

The wonderful dream was continuing, Darcy thought. She was lying on something yielding and squashy in a cool, shady room. His face was very close. She could feel his breath, even. She sensed the virile energy in his passionate dark eyes, in every strong line of his face, in the springy wave of his hair. She smiled.

He spoke. 'Lemon pannacotta,' he murmured in a low voice that made her think of rich chocolate. The big brown hands moved; silver glinted; a spoon. 'Made with Sicilian lemons.'

Something smooth slid between her lips and burst in her mouth in an explosion of tangy sweetness. 'Delicious,' she murmured. 'Absolutely . . . delicious . . .'

Her eyes flew open. Recognising Marco, she gasped, jerking herself up into a sitting position, glancing round the simple, white room in alarm. 'Where am I? What am I doing here?'

'Relax. You just fainted.'

'*Fainted?*'

Tumbling into her brain now came a clatter of recollections: the red car beneath the trees; Christian's muscular bottom; Belle's tousled head. She closed her eyes again, nausea churning in her throat. The dream was a nightmare after all.

'I think you've been running a bit too much,' Marco said kindly. 'It's hot out there.'

'I have to run,' Darcy snapped, savage with misery. 'My thinstructor says so.'

'Your *thinstructor?*'

His tones of absolute amazement stung Darcy further, reminding her involuntarily of her own when the Queen of Lean had first been mooted. 'The man who's helping me get thin,' she admitted grumpily.

Marco's brain was making connections at a greater speed than his logic could make sense of them. But he wasn't sure there was any sense to make anyway. 'What do you mean, *helping* you get thin? You *are* thin.'

'Not thin enough. I'm on a diet,' she snapped, clinging to the one certainty in her otherwise collapsing life. As she struggled to her feet her knees wavered and her thighs shook. She wanted to get out of here. Away from Marco, away from everyone, to somewhere where she could lick her wounds, survey the smoking ruins of her life and decide what to do next.

'Diet?'

She winced and shrank as his big, round eyes, clearly aghast, rolled, uninhibited, all over her body in its shorts and skimpy running vest.

'I thought you were running to keep fit . . . why are you dieting?' The large eyes, having completed their circuit, rolled back to hers with an expression of bewilderment.

'I'm an actress,' Darcy said shortly. 'If I want to hang on to my career, I have to lose a stone – fourteen pounds, seven or eight kilos,' she translated, remembering Continental Europe was metric.

Marco tried to imagine Darcy's lanky frame minus another seven kilos. He imagined horrible ghoulish hollows at her collarbones, her beautiful cheekbones, presently smooth curves, sucked starkly against the bone. He imagined her knees knocking together below skinny thighs; her beautiful bottom gone altogether. It was an outrage, he felt. A desecration.

Darcy winced under the force of his scrutiny. 'Er, look, I'd really better go.'

'No, no, please. One second. I am trying to understand.' He screwed up his face and rubbed his shaggy head. 'You say you are doing it to hang on to your career,' he said slowly. 'But who would want to hang on to such a career? That does not allow you to eat?'

Darcy sighed. She had no idea. Nothing seemed worth hanging on to just at this moment. 'I don't know,' she said, staring at the worn, yet clean floorboards. 'I don't know about anything any more,' she added in a whisper. 'I've made such a mess of everything.'

He did not break her silence. He sensed there was more to come. And indeed there almost was. Darcy breathed in, gathering her strength to launch into the whole sorry saga of the film, Christian, Niall and Belle. But her shoulders slumped, her eyelids drooped, the effort seemed too much, the subject too long-winded and irrelevant now. Up here, with Marco, none of it seemed to matter. Even Christian. She felt above it and strangely distant.

The pudding she had just eaten, on the other hand, glowed in her memory; she could remember every mouthful like you might remember a great book. It occurred to Darcy that the only real, lasting joy she had experienced in recent weeks, perhaps even recent months or years, were here in this very place. She had loved sitting outside Marco's, listening to him rhapsodising over perfect razor clams or the ultimate rocket, or whatever was exciting him that morning, as she sipped coffee and watched the people going by in the square. And even better than the listening was the tasting. The cheese, the olives, the bread . . .

Marco waited, but Darcy said nothing more, just gazed at the floor and shook her head now and then. After some minutes she raised it and stared at him with what he saw with a shock were wet eyes. He thought immediately of the luminescence of a perfect, just-landed tuna. 'It must,' she said softly, 'be so much easier when you know what you want to do with your life.'

His work, of course, was so creative. He made so many decisions every day, every hour. He was in complete control of what he did and had a clear view of what he wanted to achieve. Whereas it now seemed to Darcy that she had spent her life being ordered about, first by her parents, then by Niall, then by assorted directors – she recalled the half-naked Lear and winced. And then by model agencies – she recalled Rumtopf and winced further.

Oh, what had been the point of it all? She had never been in control. Chance and the desires of other people had plotted her path, never her.

She looked at Marco. He was smiling at her, so kindly. It seemed to Darcy that never had anyone looked at her with quite such understanding. She felt herself held, cradled, in his gaze. His face was not regular, not textbook handsome, not Christian handsome, not by a long way.

But oh, how infinitely she preferred Marco's crazed, rumpled swirls of hair, his eyes huge with excitement, the enthusiasm and passion which threatened any moment to burst from his large, spare, unsteady frame. A warm glow spread through her, to her very finger ends. She wiped her eyes and smiled back.

Chapter 57

Mitch looked at Greg Cucarachi sorrowfully. 'It's unfucking-believable.'

'Tell me about it,' replied the other.

Mitch squeezed his eyes together. 'Just . . .' Failing to find a word big enough to express all he felt, he put a plump, perspiring hand to his sweating forehead and let the gesture do it for him. 'Your client Christian Harlow . . .'

'And your client Belle Murphy,' put in Cucarachi quickly.

'Were driving somewhere in your client Christian Harlow's Ferrari, but your client Christian Harlow was going too fast to be able to stop when he saw . . .'

'The scooter, yeah,' Cucarachi confirmed.

'The scooter . . . the *scooter* . . .' Mitch could hardly get the words out. 'But not, like, *any* old scooter. The scooter with *Jack Saint* on it. And not any old Jack Saint. Jack Saint the famous director.'

'You got it,' Cucarachi confirmed wearily. For the first time, he was not hanging himself round the framework of Mitch's door, the better to escape if he goaded his colleague and neighbour to the level of violence. He was in Mitch's office, right opposite him, slumped despairingly in one of the chairs facing his desk. There was to be no goading today. The two agents were, for once – for the first time, in fact – united. United in a tragedy affecting both of them.

'All that promise . . .' Cucarachi shook his head.

His eyes, Mitch saw, glistened with emotion. Mitch fought back surprise, having never imagined Cucarachi to possess tearducts.

'We'll never see the rest of it now,' Greg mournfully added.

Mitch inclined his head in a puzzled fashion. 'You're talking about the money?'

'Sure I am.' Greg sat up. 'What the hell else did you think I was talking about?'

'Just checking,' Mitch said.

Greg passed a hand over his long, steep forehead. 'All we'll get is the signing-on fee,' he wailed.

'But that's a lot,' Mitch pointed out encouragingly.

Greg flicked him a look. 'Well, it is for you. You had two stars in this movie. Your clients Belle Murphy and Darcy Prince. I just had my client Christian Harlow. Oh, and any number of losers as space ghosts and moondogs and the rest of that shit.' He raked his hands violently through hair which, close up, Mitch realised reminded him of wire wool. Black wire wool.

Mitch said nothing. He knew it was best not to intrude on private grief.

'This picture was gonna make Christian a big star. It was his *big break*,' Greg wailed, suddenly impassioned.

'Yeah, and it was,' Mitch returned drily. 'He's in hospital in Florence with both his legs in plaster. And it was an even bigger break for Belle. Both arms and several ribs. She's gonna have to be entirely reconstructed.'

'Again,' pointed out Cucarachi.

'Darcy's OK, obviously,' Mitch remarked. 'Seems pretty relaxed about the whole thing. Sorry about the accident, sure,' he added hurriedly. 'But much less worried than I thought about the film being written off.'

'That's crazy,' Greg opined. 'That's gotta be an act. She's an actress, after all,' he reminded Mitch.

'Yeah, but a British one, remember. You know what they're like.'

'Crazy.'

'Really crazy,' Mitch rejoined. He frowned. 'You know, I could have sworn she was almost relieved about it.'

'You're kidding.'

'No, really. All she seemed to care about was the money.'

'That figures,' Greg said, nodding. 'Not that crazy after all, then.'

'Except that she said she wanted to put it into a nursery.'

Greg blinked. 'She said a nursery? Not "up her nose"?'

'A nursery. Like, you know, for kids.'

'Hey, I know about nurseries,' Cucarachi rejoined. 'Got two kids at one myself.'

'You've got kids?' Mitch was interested. He liked children. He had not realised Greg had any, but their conversations had never reached a personal level. Not personal in that sense, anyhow.

'Sure. David and Jonathan. They're three and five.'

'Cute age,' Mitch nodded approvingly.

A flash of affection traversed Cucarachi's features and made him look, Mitch thought, quite human. Even warm. 'Here,' said Greg, rummaging in his back pocket for his wallet. 'Wanna see a picture?'

Mitch did. Two mini Gregs looked back at him from the front of a white-painted house with a picket fence. 'That's us last fall on Long Island,' Cucarachi supplied.

'Cute kids.'

There was a silence. Greg shoved his wallet back. Mitch reached for a jelly doughnut from the bag on the desk. 'Want one?' he offered.

His lean, trim co-worker looked at the fistful of sugar-encrusted fried dough being brandished at him. He looked about to refuse, then his trim eyebrows raised themselves in resignation. He reached for it. 'Hey,' he said, chewing. 'They're not half bad.'

Mitch, eyeing his colleague, was starting to think that perhaps Greg wasn't so bad either. Perhaps he'd got him wrong all this time. Adversity could have a positive effect on people, even people who happened to be agents. And things didn't get much more adverse in the agenting world than having three stars in a sure-fire hit movie shot down because one of the stars knocked the director off his scooter with his car.

'They say Saint's got no idea about anything,' Greg mused morosely as he chewed. 'That knock from the accident's completely changed his personality. He's got no recollection he's a film maker at all. He thinks he's a cat now.' Cucarachi shook his wire wool hair. 'Like – what's that about?'

Mitch shook his head. 'What a business. Who'd be an agent?'

'You said it, buddy.'

The two agents looked at each other in sorrowful complicity.

In the *aubergo*, Hugh Faugh was slamming his meaty fists against the newspaper spread out on the table.

The picture that formed the centre spread of the newspaper was of Ivo and Jago laughing on a park bench with a blonde in a miniskirt, who was placing small sachets of white powder in their hands. 'Peer's daughter Totty Ponsonby-Pratt (right),' read the caption, 'passes the drugs to MP's sons Ivo and Jago Faugh.'

'Oh Christ. How could you? How bloody could you?' Hugh groaned to his sons, his fingers over his eyes so as not to see, yet again, the headline 'Family Values?' in massive fat black type. 'How could you be so stupid?'

Family values indeed, Orlando thought sardonically. Hugh's anger seemed directed less at what had been done than at the fact the twins had been caught doing it. He almost felt a stir of pity for Ivo and Jago. With a father like this, what chance had either of them ever had?

'You're a pair of fucking idiots!' Hugh roared at his sons. 'Not only have you been kicked out of Oxford, you've probably cost me my job.'

Ivo and Jago were white with fear; the rims of their eyes and the edges of their noses red with weeping. Although cocaine, too, was a possibility, Orlando knew; the twins, the newspaper had also discovered, had quite a reputation in the ancient university city they were apparently taking by storm. 'Or, rather, up the nostrils,' the journalist who had done this rewarding extra piece of research noted acerbically.

That the Faughs had received a collective death blow was obvious. Alerted by some party factotum in London that the pictures had appeared, Hugh had rushed straight out to the Rocolo newsagent and then spent an agonised hour waiting for the British papers to arrive. But that agony had been sweet relief compared to his anguish when he had finally seen what the papers contained. From the blizzard of phone calls he then proceeded to field, and the loud protestations and pleadings he was heard to make, it was clear that Hugh was determinedly fighting for his political life and that his political masters were equally determined to switch off his life support.

It couldn't have happened to a nicer family, Orlando tried to make himself think. He dredged up every miserable memory of their stay he could remember in order to force himself to rejoice in the Faughs' downfall. What had happened was, after all, a sweeter and more agonising revenge on his tormentors than he could ever have planned, even in his wildest flights of retaliatory fantasy. Odd then, that he felt far from exultant. If anything, he felt rather sorry for them.

The wreck was total. Orlando even felt sympathy for Hugh. Unlike his own father, who now sat in the kitchen shaking his head with Georgie by his side and holding his hand, Hugh had no such succour from Laura. His parents had been particularly shocked about the theft of Georgie's purse. 'Under our own roof,' Georgie kept repeating. 'Our guests . . .'

Laura was the only person for whom Orlando felt not an iota of pity. The memory of her attempt to seduce him, and all her lewd innuendo since, was still horribly fresh. Mrs Hugh Faugh was not, however, around to witness his lack of sympathy. She had obviously decided to escape before the hordes of paparazzi Hugh had gloomily predicted would arrive, actually did so. The story, after all, was irresistible: the Oxford student sons of a Shadow Cabinet minister, whose watchword was Family Values, taking cocaine with an aristocrat's daughter. Who, he had gathered in the confusing mêlée outside Marco's restaurant, was also responsible for losing Emma her last job. As Totty and the Faugh twins were led away by the local police, there had been tears, apologies and heartfelt hugs from the couple who had arrived so suddenly and turned out to be Cosmo and Hero's parents. He had left Emma to it in the end; it seemed to have nothing to do with him.

A sharp cry had stopped him in his tracks as he reached the edge of the courtyard. 'Hey!' cried Emma, dashing after him. 'Phone number, please. And address, and mobile, and NHS number, and . . .'

The same information had not been forthcoming from her. Emma's next port of call seemed rather up in the air, although the couple – and Hero and Cosmo – were begging her to come back with them.

It all rather put his own news in the shade.

Just after he had left the restaurant, his A level results had been texted through. He had got a D and an E, better than he had expected. Two whole passes. Enough, even, to take some sort of course.

He was no longer a failure. On the contrary, it was the gilded youth of Oxford that had fallen.

Chapter 58

Orlando pushed his mother's trolley across the smooth marble surface of the airport floor. There was so much marble around; part of being in Italy, he supposed.

Georgie's luggage was heavy. He found himself wondering vaguely how so many flimsy bits of material came to weigh so much. And how Georgie could bear to spend so much time in the airport shops, which seemed universally boring to Orlando. Still, they probably kept her mind off things.

The Faughs' departure had been an agonised affair in which all the adults involved pretended desperately that they fully intended to see each other again once what Hugh called 'this unfortunate business' had 'blown over'. It had seemed to Orlando about as likely to blow over as Chernobyl.

'Orlando! *Orlando!*'

Someone in blue and white. Jeans and a polo top. Emma, standing there, smiling at him.

'Great!' he exclaimed, wheeling Georgie's heap over at such speed he could hardly stop it. 'You made it.'

He held her close. She held her face up to his. It was fresh and glowing, like a new pink rose, he thought. He longed to kiss it but felt shy in such a public place. Then, as she continued to look at him, he decided that he didn't feel so shy after all. When he had finished her eyes were still closed. Encouraged, he bent his neck and kissed her again.

'Guess what,' he whispered into her clean-smelling hair. 'I got two A levels!'

'Orlando! You didn't!' The air was filled with her delighted shriek. 'It's especially fantastic,' Emma added into his chest, which was as far as the top of her head reached, 'because I was going to offer you a job.'

'A job!' he squawked.

She nodded. 'I'd have offered you it anyway, but now you've got the A levels you can train properly.'

He blinked. Training? What was she talking about?

'I'm opening my nursery,' Emma explained. 'Darcy's given me the start-up money. I want you to join it.'

'What – as a nanny?' He screwed up his eyes in disbelief.

'A manny,' Emma corrected him. 'A male nanny. Men make great nannies, I told you. And I'm planning to recruit a lot of them.'

A great surge of excitement possessed Orlando. Along with a great clench of fear. His beam faded. His mother had been dealt many blows of late. Could she bear what might be the bitterest of all, that her son was about to be a nursemaid?

'I'll pay you plenty, don't worry,' Emma added, chuckling. 'Enough to make your mother realise it's a proper career with proper rewards. And don't worry, there'll be rewards. It's going to be a massive success.'

Orlando felt more cheerful. If Emma said it, it would happen. That he knew beyond any doubt. 'That would be great.' He shook his head in a puzzled way. 'Fantastic. Really cool. Wow!'

'It's a deal then,' Emma exulted, hugging him again and pulling his face down towards her. Her insides were popping with joy.

'Cosmo and Hero will be there too,' she told him. 'James and Vanessa are desperate for me to look after them again.' She permitted herself a small, triumphant smile. 'Oh, and Morning will be coming too. He'll be in the baby room.'

'Morning?' Orlando looked Emma up and down, as if she had hidden the child, who so evidently was not hanging from her front, somewhere else about her person.

'I've been given temporary custody of him. Belle's in no state to look after him – not that she was when she wasn't in traction in hospital,' Emma added, rolling her eyes.

Orlando looked puzzled. He knew nothing about Belle, Emma remembered. Oh well. Perhaps she would tell him. Then again, perhaps she wouldn't. It was all water under the bridge now. 'If all goes well it'll be full adoption,' she added. 'I'm adopting him. Going through all the official channels that Belle ignored.'

'Adoption!' Orlando exclaimed. 'That's quite . . . a responsibility,' he added, as she gave him a rather defiant look.

Emma shrugged. 'So what? No change from what I've been doing for him so far, really. Just on a slightly more permanent basis. And at least at the nursery there'll be other people besides me to look after him. You, for instance,' she grinned.

Orlando nodded, a slow smile spreading across his face. Yes. That sounded like a good idea. Looking after Morning. He would like that. 'Where is he now?' he asked.

'With Mara somewhere. She's giving him his bottle.'

'Mara?'

'The housekeeper at the villa,' Emma told him, only now realising how closely she had stuck to the terms of the confidentiality agreement. There was a whole side of her life about which Orlando had no idea at all. 'She's coming to advise on the food. She wanted a change of scene and she's got family in London.'

'Wow.' Orlando nodded. 'That sounds . . . cool.' He felt rather bewildered by it all.

'Your parents recovered from the awful pictures in the paper?' Emma asked, her joyous beam giving way to an expression of concern.

Orlando looked surprised. His present happiness so filled his vision that the miseries of the very recent past seemed like years ago.

'What about your father and Parliament?' Emma probed worriedly.

Orlando brightened. 'Actually, he's decided to step down.'

'Oh, *no!*'

'It's good news,' Orlando countered. 'Some think tank specialising in the regeneration of inner cities has asked him to join. It's what Dad's always been most interested in. He's been fed up of Parliament for ages, to be honest. He doesn't do backbiting and sleaze, and I don't think the Faugh business helped, apart from convincing my mother that it's not worth herding Dad through it all any more. She's finally accepted he's never going to be Prime Minister. Funnily enough, she seems happier for it.'

It was a long speech and he felt rather exhausted at the end of it. It reminded him of how much had happened in so short a time. All for the better. He spotted Georgie, waving frantically from across a bank of seating.

'Better go and get the plane,' he grinned, taking her hand. 'I'll see you in London,' he added, giving her a final tight squeeze. 'Boss,' he added.

*

The day seemed to Darcy not quite as sunny as usual and so the road up through Rocolo seemed to wear a more sullen aspect than normal. At the restaurant, all the chairs were set out as usual, and its vine, its sage paintwork and its sunshades were as pretty as ever. Only one, crucial, element was missing.

Marco was nowhere to be seen, and a terrible fear now gripped Darcy's heart. During all the rehearsals she had held in her mind for this moment, the possibility that Marco would not be there had never occurred to her. It couldn't, it just couldn't be possible that Marco had chosen this morning of all mornings to be out somewhere, at the market, the artisan cheesemakers, the vineyard. As she approached, her knees felt weak beneath her.

The restaurant was open; she could hear the chefs chatting and singing inside. She knocked timidly on the glass of the open door. One of the sous chefs appeared and smiled in recognition.

'Is . . . ?' Darcy began. 'Is Marco here?'

'*Sì!*' As the sous chef disappeared, Darcy leant briefly against the lintel to counter the rush of relief.

Within seconds he was in the doorway, filling the frame with his body, wiping his hands on a teatowel. Immediately she felt that her lips were the biggest and most prominent thing on her face. 'Hi,' she said primly.

'How are you?' he asked, looking at her anxiously. 'Come and sit down.' As he led her to a table, seemingly careful not to touch her arm, Darcy sensed a restraint about Marco that had not been there before.

Had she but known it, Marco's reserve sprang from a desperate urge not to put a foot wrong. He had not slept from the moment their last meeting ended. There had been a closeness then that surely he had not imagined. And yet days had passed since without any sight of her. He had heard the film had been called off and the actors leaving; such a seismic event in the hospitality trade didn't take long to penetrate Rocolo. He had been full of fear that Darcy had gone too.

He had relived over and over again the moment she ate the pannacotta. Her flung-back throat and rapturously closed eyes. In his dreams she had convulsed beneath his touch many times. And yet they had never even kissed.

As he looked at her helplessly, Darcy stepped forward and smiled. 'I want to ask you something.'

His heart raced. 'Anything!' he declared, waving his hands and putting into the gesture all the feeling he could not express in words.

'You told me once that your restaurant philosophy is all about giving your staff time to have a real life. They don't work long hours, they get paid properly.'

He frowned. Why was she interviewing him about his management techniques? 'Ye-es . . .' he said cautiously. 'Yes, that's right.'

Darcy smoothed a hair behind her ear. 'Well, I was wondering,' she smiled, showing white teeth in pink gums. She looked about sixteen, with those freckles and candid coffee-bean eyes, he thought. Her heart hammered. She took a deep breath and squeezed her hands together. 'I was wondering . . . whether you might have a job for a friend of mine.'

'A friend . . . of yours?'

At the beginning of the sentence he had, with a leap of the heart, started to form the thought that she was asking for a job for herself. Apparently not.

'Yes. A homeless woman. One who's never cooked very much before.'

He shrugged.

Darcy's heart sank. 'So you don't employ homeless women who can't cook?'

'I have no problem with a homeless woman,' he replied. 'That is fine. Anyone can make a mistake, huh?'

His eyes seemed to Darcy to be boring into her with particular meaning.

'Presuming she is willing, clean, hardworking and of good character.' He looked enquiringly at Darcy. She nodded hard. 'If she is, then I am sure I can help find her somewhere to live. I know a lot of people in this town, after all.' He waved a hand expansively around. 'There are flats, rooms in people's houses. We can sort something out.'

Darcy felt jittery with joy. He had passed the test beautifully.

'However,' Marco pressed a finger to his full, wide lips, 'it is more of a problem that she can't cook.'

'Is it?' Darcy managed from a suddenly dry throat.

'Mmm. Most people applying for jobs in restaurants can cook already.' He shook his shaggy head. 'No, that is a real problem. A big, big problem.'

'But . . .' Darcy objected, 'but . . . if she is passionate about food? Really, really wants to learn?'

He shrugged his big shoulders. 'That would help. In some ways, of course, that is the most important thing.'

'So keen to learn that she would be happy to peel vegetables, sweep up, do anything. And you wouldn't have to pay her much either, not at first.'

Marco looked at her and smiled. 'Not until she became a Michelin-starred chef, eh?'

Darcy blushed. 'That's right.'

'She sounds good,' Marco said, nodding. 'Yes, I'd like to meet this homeless woman. What's her name?'

He felt a pair of slender arms round his neck. 'As if you didn't know,' giggled Darcy into his neck.

As Marco bent to kiss her, a long, lingering kiss to which Darcy responded with an ardour that meant neither of them was any longer in doubt about anything, the sun finally broke the clouds and flooded the square in dazzling sunshine.

'Oh, Marco.' Darcy, her eyes closed, murmured into the salty-soapy-warm-skin scent of his hair and neck, 'I love you.'

'And I you.' He pulled her tighter, even though it wasn't really possible.

She breathed – as best she could – a deep, happy sigh. 'I can hardly believe it,' she told him happily, his curls tickling her lips as she spoke. 'My life's been such bollocks until now. Without meaning, without direction, and now it's suddenly as if, I don't know, the clouds have parted or something, and it's all so clear.' She raised her head and beamed at him. 'There's so much I can learn from you, you can show me so much . . . you're such an artist, such a man . . .'

To her surprise, instead of looking delighted at this outburst, the round brown eyes, so melting a second ago, now fixed on her in concern. A chill feeling now swept through Darcy; had she said something wrong? 'What's the matter?' she stammered, her throat clenched with fear.

Marco's brow lowered. He stared intensely from below it at Darcy.

'What have I said?' she burst out in panic. Her last words jangled hysterically through her mind, like a runaway train. But they had been all praise and love, surely?

Marco took a deep, slow breath and gently put her from him. The air was warm but, released unwillingly from the tight, hot circle of his strong arms, Darcy felt cold. She stared at him, eyes ping-ponging frantically about his face, feeling her knees start to tremble.

'If we are to be together,' Marco now informed her in a slow, grave voice, his eyes steady and never leaving hers, 'there is something you must know about me. Something that might change your entire view of me.'

Chapter 59

Hot and cold waves of panic were coursing through her body. Was he about to reveal the existence of a wife? An entire other family? A penchant for cross-dressing? She gazed at him helplessly.

'I have a weakness,' Marco admitted, now looking at the cobbled floor.

Nausea was pushing in her throat. Her palms and forehead felt clammy. Weakness?

Her thoughts raced. Drugs? Alcohol? Was he gay? Oh, it was so unfair. She had been so happy, so excited, so hopeful; finally her life had had a direction. And now all was to be shattered.

He was walking away from her now, towards the restaurant. 'Come with me,' he called, without turning round. As if in a dream she followed, stumbling, one leg planting itself shakily before the other, her eyes fixed on the broad white back before her, topped by its ball of dark curls. The sounds around her – the passers-by in the street behind, singing birds, her own panicked breathing – swelled in her ears with cataclysmic, hyper-real volume.

She watched as he went through the door. Whatever he was

about to divulge was to be revealed in the restaurant. Bodies in the freezer? What horrors – and Darcy had no doubt now that they were horrors – was she about to be told?

Darcy, following the tall, white-clad figure through the tables, had only the vaguest impression of what was around her. Tables, chairs, white walls. She banged painfully into the corner of a table; the sharp edge bit into her thigh and would no doubt cause a bruise. Darting through the boiling sea of impressions that constituted Darcy's thoughts came the memory of Sam. Her one-time model agent had been full of instructions about avoiding leg injuries and always but always putting on mosquito lotion as careers were ruined by bites in the wrong places. How happily, Darcy remembered, she had received the news that her own career was ruined by a combination of overeating on her own part and bad driving on Christian's.

Parting company with Sam had been such an intense relief, but would she now, Darcy wondered miserably, have to pick up the acting and modelling baton again?

Marco had disappeared through a door in the side of the room now and Darcy followed him to find a small stone stairwell. At the top, she emerged, still in a dreamlike state, into a small, hot noisy room full of shiny things, noisy chatter and people in white; the kitchen, she slowly realised. The cacophonous noise now stopped as suddenly as if someone had turned it off; Darcy passed through the people, the shiny surfaces, the bowls and glinting knifes, in silence. Marco had vanished again; through a shadowy doorway at the end, Darcy now saw as she reached it. She could see his white form moving about in the gloom beyond. She stepped in after him, knowing that whatever took place here, in this small, dark room, would affect her for ever.

He was slapping about on the walls. She could make out dim

shelves, full of bags. They smelt of flour. There were savoury tangs with sweet undercurrents. It did not seem especially sinister; it looked, in fact, like the kitchen storeroom.

'I'm a member of a secret society.' His voice was muffled, embarrassed, fearful even. His head remained turned away.

'The Mafia?!' It was out before she could stop it. Shock swept her. Bodies in the freezer – she had been right after all?

'Not the Mafia!' Marco said sharply. 'Although some people think this is worse.'

He snapped on the light. Yellow brilliance flooded her eyes and she blinked, looking at bags of pasta and flour with ornate labels. Jars and bottles of olive oil gleamed like jewels; with odd detachment she admired the range of colours from yellow topaz to emerald. She shook her head slightly as she looked at him, her mind now utterly empty. All she could do was look.

He was bending now. His hand seemed to have closed over something on the bottom shelf. 'What I am about to show you,' he said softly into the wall in a tense monotone, 'might change everything. And if it does, I promise you I will understand. I must warn you now that not many women would be able to understand. Italian women especially.'

'Right,' croaked Darcy, her every nerve pulsing with tension. Her back ached suddenly, unbearably.

'But you seem to see me as some sort of hero, and I have to show you that I am just a man, and weaker than most . . .'

'Show me,' Darcy whispered, feeling that, however awful whatever he was about to show her was, it could not possibly be more awful than the suspense. She tensed herself, cringing slightly with narrowed eyes, ready to be shattered, for her fragile dream, so frail and recent of construct, to fall finally, conclusively apart.

He turned. He held something in both his hands. Her breath

caught in her throat. He opened his hands. Standing on his palm was a tin of spaghetti.

She frowned and blinked, not understanding. 'What's in there?' Crazy thoughts whirled in her brain. Was he a drug smuggler? Did he use tins as a cover?

He proffered the spaghetti. 'Spaghetti. Spaghetti's in there.' He spoke in a broken voice; his eyes, as he looked at her, were doleful and full of shame. 'Can you still love me?' he asked, his voice now a whisper.

'Love you . . . ?' She shook her head from side to side. 'I don't understand . . . what's spaghetti got to do with it?'

'I am an Italian man. A chef . . .'

Understanding burst in on her as brightly as the light had just done. Following close on its heels was a gigantic wave of relief. This was his weakness. She remembered, in a series of flashes, the small blonde girl, asking for tinned spaghetti outside the restaurant. He had been so understanding – this was why. No wonder he had met her demands with such little fuss. The laughter came from somewhere around her navel, rose, inflated, and burst hysterically out.

'. . . have always loved it,' Marco was saying sorrowfully. 'I can't help it. Sometimes, after a hard night in the kitchen, it's all I want to eat. Of course I know it's gunk, it's nothing like real, proper, Italian pasta, God knows what grade of flour it's made with and it's never *al dente*, and that slimy sauce, but somehow it works, and I love it. I know I shouldn't. And it doesn't mean that I don't love the food I cook, the real Italian food I believe in, with every nerve in my body.' A flash of pride illumined his features before the hangdog expression returned. 'If the news got out, I'd be ruined. My brigade –' he shook his curly head in the direction of the kitchen – 'they know, of course. They had to know. And there are others . . .'

'Others?' Darcy was trying to control her mirth now. It was obviously an extremely serious matter for Marco.

'There's a whole society of us. In Italy. We're called the Societa Fapirollo and we meet in secret every month. We have to. Italians are very proud of their pasta. You can imagine . . . and me a chef as well . . .' He stopped, as she was laughing again, a helpless hiccuping mirth.

'You don't mind?' There was wonder in his voice. 'You can live with that, with knowing my secret? You don't blame me? Can you love me?'

Can! Darcy, forcing away her smile, sternly held his gaze. She had considered teasing him, pretending she did care, as retaliation for the agonies he had caused her. But his worried gaze, his crumpled, puppy face melted her heart. She pressed herself into him, shaking her head and smiling. 'You know, I think I just . . . *can.*'